# BEVERLY LEWIS

## THREE NOVELS *in* ONE VOLUME

The Preacher's Daughter,
The Englisher,
& The Brethren

BETHANYHOUSE
a division of Baker Publishing Group
Minneapolis, Minnesota

© 2005, 2006 by Beverly M. Lewis, Inc.

Previously published in three separate volumes:

*The Preacher's Daughter* © 2005
*The Englisher* © 2006
*The Brethren* © 2006

Published by Bethany House Publishers
11400 Hampshire Avenue South
Bloomington, Minnesota 55438
www.bethanyhouse.com

Bethany House Publishers is a division of
Baker Publishing Group, Grand Rapids, Michigan

Printed in the United States of America

Library of Congress Cataloging-in-Publication Data is on file
at the Library of Congress, Washington, DC.

Lewis, Beverly.
    [Novels. Selections]
    Annie's people : three novels in one volume / Beverly Lewis.
        pages cm
    ISBN 978-0-7642-1288-8 (pbk.)
        1. Children of clergy—Fiction. 2. Women artists—Fiction. 3. Women—Identity—Fiction.
    4. English—Pennsylvania—Fiction. 5. Amish—Fiction. I. Lewis, Beverly, Preacher's daughter.
    II. Lewis, Beverly, Englisher. III. Lewis, Beverly, Brethren. IV. Title. V. Title: Preacher's daugh-
    ter. VI. Title: Englisher. VII. Title: Brethren
    PS3562.E9383A6 2014
    813'.54—dc23                                                                    2014029823

Unless otherwise identified, Scripture quotations are from the King James Version of the Bible.

Scripture quotations identified NIV and the Scripture quotation in Chapter 29 of *The Brethren* are from the HOLY BIBLE, NEW INTERNATIONAL VERSION®. Copyright © 1973, 1978, 1984 by International Bible Society. Used by permission of Zondervan Publishing House. All rights reserved.

This story is a work of fiction. With the exception of recognized historical figures and events, all characters and events are the product of the author's imagination. Any resemblance to any person, living or dead, is purely coincidental.

Cover design by Koechel Peterson & Associates, Inc., Minneapolis, Minnesota.

14  15  16  17  18  19  20        7  6  5  4  3  2  1

# The Preacher's Daughter

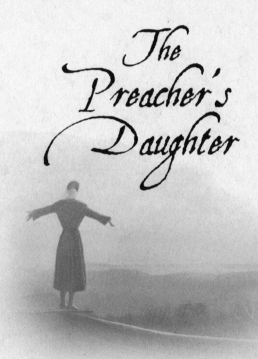

# Dedication

To
Madge S. Bowes,
a preacher's daughter times two . . .
and dear family friend.

*M*oonlight created a silken halo around two small figures as they emerged from the dark covered bridge. The younger boy dragged a shovel, while the older carried a handmade wooden box carefully so as not to tip it, having sanded the miniature coffin smooth with his own hands.

They hurried around the north side of the bridge and down the grassy slope to a grove of black locust trees. Near the creek bed, they determined the location for burial—eight long steps past the first tree, then a sharp turn and four short ones to the soil most pliable from recent autumn rains. The box laden with the beloved pup was placed on the grass, and the older boy took up the shovel and began to dig.

When the hole was deep enough, the box was laid gently inside. The little boy inched back, sobbing at the grievous sound of dirt hitting the small coffin. Big brother worked the shovel faster, and with each heave and thud, the younger boy winced, squeezing hard a peach stone in his tiny palm.

Farther he crept back, away . . . away from the shadowy grave.

Soon the hole was filled. A proper burial. The boy responsible for his small brother peered into the darkness, calling repeatedly. When there was no answer, he scurried along the creek, then out to the road, seeking but not finding.

In short order, the People began to comb the area by horse and buggy, and on foot they joined stalwart arms in an unending thread to search for the wee child who had vanished into the silvery twilight. . . .

*Ever let the fancy roam,*
*Pleasure never is at home.*

—John Keats

# Prologue

A gnawing sense of guilt defines my life, yet I am too obstinate to fess up to the sin which so easily besets me. What I want to do and what I *ought* to do get *ferhoodled* in my head and in my heart. This is especially trying when it comes to my twice-weekly visits to Cousin Julia Ranck's, where I am hired to help with her two young children and do some light housekeeping . . . *and* where I spend time working alone in the little attic room created just for me, my undisclosed haven. There, I take a measure of joy in the world of forbidden color—paint, canvas, and brushes—this secret place known only to my Mennonite kinfolk, and to the Lord God himself.

Deep on the inside, though, where it matters most, my heart is torn. I have striven to follow in the Old Ways since childhood, to match the expectations of my parents and the church, only to fail.

It annoys me no end that some Amish bishops allow for artistic expression, permitting their people to create and sell art, *while our bishop does not.*

I was just six when my preacher-father's probing brown eyes did all the reprimanding necessary to stir up shame in my soul when I was caught wistfully drawing a sleek black kitty, high in the haymow. From then on, I learned to hide my art from prying eyes, even though I wished for a way to put a stop to it altogether.

Usually *Daed* had only to read out loud the Fifty-first Psalm for me to see the folly of my ways: *Have mercy upon me, O God . . . blot out my transgressions. . . .* King David's words rang ceaselessly in my ears until the next "holy

11

scolding" for other acts of childish immaturity, though not again related to my pencil drawings . . . till I was caught again at age fourteen.

*Have mercy, indeed.*

There were times as a girl when I would sooner have welcomed a lickin' than the righteous gaze of my lanky, bearded father. It seemed he could see straight through to my heart. He had an uncanny way about him when it came to that, as well as the way his sermons stuck in my head for months on end. More times than I can count, I endured his deliberate silence, followed by his deeply drawn sigh and then a belabored reading from the Scriptures.

Unlike my six brothers—three older and already married, and three younger and looking to get hitched—I have never had the switch applied to my "seat of learning." Seeing as how some mules round these parts are less stubborn, it sure says a lot for the patience of my father, at least toward me.

Here lately, I have been urged to join the communion of earthly saints—our local Amish district. And since I marked my twentieth birthday back the end of April, I am keenly aware of concerned faces at nearly every gathering. Daed is doubly responsible under God on my behalf, *Mamm* says frequently, beseeching me to heed the warning. If I keep putting off my decision, well, that alone will become a choice, and in due time, I will have to leave the community of the People. I don't see how I could ever up and leave behind my family and all that I know and love.

But what gets my goat is the intense expectation regarding my upcoming decision. Joining church won't make me a good person. I know that. I live in this community; I know what makes most of these folk tick. Some live double lives, just as I'm living now—teen boys who take advantage of tipsy girls behind the bushes at corn-husking bees, and young women who parade around in pious cape dresses but whose hearts do not measure up to the Holy Scriptures. Most of this comes from our unbaptized youth, during *Rumschpringe*. Still there is plenty of two-facedness. We're all human after all.

Alas, another sin has embedded itself within my soul: loving Rudy Esh and leading him to think I would marry him one day. Rudy formerly held the number one spot in my heart, even ahead of the Good Lord. But now, after three solid years of courting me, he has found a new sweetheart-girl. I'm obliged to show kindness where they're concerned, the utmost tolerance, too . . . things expected of me but increasingly difficult to demonstrate with any amount of sincerity. Handsome Rudy is soon to become a baptized church member and, no doubt, husband to his new sweetheart. Although I cared deeply for him, and he for me, I never shared with him my obsession with fine art. And since

I wasn't ready to put any of that aside to join church, which is required before a wedding can take place, I am largely at fault for our breakup. He must surely be relieved, having pulled his hair out, so to speak, because of my resistance. "Heaven's sake, Annie," Rudy would say time and again, "why can't you just make the church vow and be done with it?" My answer always exasperated him: "I'm not ready." But I couldn't say why.

So I've lost my first and only love, which saddens me no end. Not that I should be bold enough to plead for his affection again, even though I was steady in my fondness for him from age seventeen till he decided he preferred Susie Yoder's company. All this adds up to three wasted years of faithfulness, to be sure . . . and now I am as lonely as ever a girl could be. A few years ago I would have shared this sorrow with my best friend, Essie, but lately my former playmate seems weighed down with her own set of grown-up problems.

Truth be told, only one other person knows about my fractured heart. My secret thoughts are safe with Louisa Stratford, an English girl who lives far away in Colorado. At twenty-two, she is engaged to be married, and for that I am most happy, seeing as how we're wonderful-good friends. Even though Louisa is fancy and I'm Plain, she's been reading my letters and writing back since she was nearly eleven years old. And if she hadn't sent that first drawing in her little letter—those delicate blossoms of forget-me-nots—so long ago, I might never have wondered if I, too, possessed any real talent.

I wish I could honor her by attending the splendid wedding she and her mother are planning. The thought of a big-city wedding in a faraway place surrounded by flowers and candles and girls in colorful dresses entices me terribly . . . things never, ever seen at an Amish wedding. Such things described in Louisa's letters have me completely intrigued, I daresay.

Naturally, I would stick out to kingdom come if I were brazen enough to go. Still I stare curiously at the pretty invitation with its raised gold lettering and wonder what it might be like.

Mamm would say it is out of the question to consider such a trip, even though I'm a grown woman. I can hear her going on and on about her fears. *You might get lost or worse in the maze of the hustle-bustle. You've never left Lancaster County, for pity's sake! You might get yourself kidnapped, Annie Zook!* Even so, I have yet to turn down my dear friend.

Honestly, my mother is wound tighter than a fiddle string when it comes to her children and grandchildren, often reminding my eldest brother, Jesse Jr., twenty-six, and his wife, Sarah Mae, to keep close watch on their two youngest, especially come dusk. *"You can never be too careful,"* she has said for the ten-thousandth time. It's not her fault, only an indication that not a soul has ever forgotten how dreadful it was for one of our own little ones to be stolen away, right here in the middle of Paradise. A heavenly-sounding sort of place, but one that's seen its share of heartache and mystery.

Here lately I've been going and standing beside Pequea Creek, staring at the well-known thicket of trees where little Isaac was snatched from the People . . . where I sometimes would swing double with him on the long tree swing. Where Isaac and I—and our brothers—often tossed twigs into the creek, watching them float away to who knows where.

Now I can't help wondering if I dare paint that setting in all its autumn beauty, as another side to the sad story. Perhaps by spreading the radiance of pastel gold on a canvas, I might somehow lessen the ominous side of the now-tranquil scene . . . even though my hand will surely tremble as I do, recalling Mamm's telling of the terrifying ordeal. When a bad thing happens to one family, it happens to us all, my mother says.

If that is true, then Rudy breaking off our courtship will also cause a wrinkle on the page of my life and everyone else's, too. For one, my future children—Daed's and Mamm's would-be grandchildren—will not have his gentle eyes and auburn hair, nor his fun-loving disposition. But even worse, I may never have babies at all. Yet if I were to abandon my paints and brushes in order to join church and marry, would I ever be truly happy? And yet . . . since I gave up the chance to wed a good Amish boy like Rudy, will I ever again know love? Oh, such a troublesome dilemma I face, and one that continually torments my soul.

# *Chapter 1*

A late October mist draped itself over fields beseeching the harvest as Annie Zook walked along the narrow road to her Ranck cousins' house. Waving at a half dozen Amish neighbors out raking leaves, she felt all wound up, hoping for at least a few minutes to slip away to Cousin Julia's attic to work on her latest painting. Once her chores were done.

A gray and dismal sort of day was quite perfect for artistic work. Something about the anticipation of eventual sunshine, its warming glow held back by the cheerless clouds, made her feel full, yet achingly empty . . . and terribly creative, all at once. Even though the desire to express oneself artistically was considered by her particular district as wrongdoing, she saw no way out whatsoever.

She was still in her Rumschpringe, the "in between" years—that murky transition between juvenile immaturity and adulthood . . . and church membership. Still, being the daughter of an ordained minister put an unwelcome clamp on her as she struggled to find her bearings. And yet, the thought of disappointing her parents went against the grain of her existence—it was the primary motivation for concealing her love of art.

Annie turned her thoughts away from her life struggle to adorable two-year-old Molly Ranck, Julia's youngest, who had been scratching herself nearly raw with chicken pox two days ago. *Dear thing.* It had been all Annie could do to keep her occupied, what with the oatmeal bath and repeated dabs with calamine lotion. So there had not been a speck of time to work on the waiting canvas last visit.

She quickened her pace, somewhat surprised to see Deacon Byler's new

15

house under roof already, and just when had *that* happened? Then, when she came upon the intersection, she became aware that the Lapps' corn was already going down and they must be filling silo, thus making it easier to see at the crossroads once again. *How'd I miss that?*

She realized she must have been walking in a fog of her own making since Rudy's parting words three months ago this coming Saturday. How had the changing landscape not registered in her brain?

*This must be grief! When you hurt this bad, you push it way down inside.* She remembered feeling this gloomy once before in her life, when, as a little girl, she'd stumbled upon Mamm in a mire of tears. But there was no sense in pondering to death *that* day.

She made a point to be more mindful of the details around her now— shapes, shadows, and depths of color. She took in the hazy morning splendor as it arched freely over muted green stalks, the burgundy-red barn of their English neighbors—the Danz family—coming into view, and the dark roof of the red-sided covered bridge not far from the old gray-stone London Vale Mill.

*I'm painting God's creation!* she thought, justifying her ongoing transgression.

She thought of her pen pal in Colorado, wanting to squeeze in a few minutes to write a letter to Louisa, who seemed to understand her best these days.

She contemplated the first time she had unintentionally embarrassed her English friend. It had happened early on in their letter writing, when brown-haired Louisa sent a small wallet-sized school photograph of herself, asking for the same from Annie. Not wanting to put Louisa on the spot, Annie had explained that the People didn't take pictures of themselves, carefully following the Ten Commandments: *Thou shalt not make unto thee any graven image.*

So she'd attempted to get around the Scripture and simply drew a colored-pencil self-portrait, showing the oval shape of her face, the single dimple, the soft blue in her eyes, and her golden-blond hair. She had also sketched the sacred symbol—the white heart-shaped head covering with its white ribbons dangling onto the bodice of her light green cape dress.

*Such a long time ago,* she thought, remembering how Louisa had written back with praise about the drawing, saying she'd immediately framed it for her bedside table. Annie wondered if Louisa still had it.

Here recently Annie had spent a rainy afternoon, counting her letters from Louisa, only to quit after reaching nearly five hundred. Smiling now at her amazing connection, not only with the outside world but with her English friend, she began to swing her arms, enjoying the pleasure of walking instead of having to hitch up the horse and carriage, as she often did to help Mamm on market days.

Yet even as she pretended to be carefree, she could not ignore the pangs of guilt.

*Good thing Daed has no idea.* She pondered the significance of her actions, or when it came to joining church, her lack thereof.

Sighing, she spied an enclosed gray buggy up ahead, pulled by a prancing steed with shiny new horseshoes. The young woman driver waved urgently. "Annie, is that you?"

*Rhoda Esh!*

Pleased as pie, Annie waved back just as enthusiastically. "Hullo, there!" she called, hoping Rudy's younger sister might stop and chat a bit.

"I'm so glad I ran into you," Rhoda said, pulling on the reins. She motioned for Annie to get in the buggy. "Come on 'n' ride with me, won't ya? We best be talkin' some."

Annie lifted her skirt and climbed into the buggy.

Right away, Rhoda spoke her mind. "I'm not s'posed to know, prob'ly, but Susie Yoder's cousin's big-mouthed sister said Rudy has been seein' Susie 'stead of you." Rhoda's brown eyes were about as big as gingersnaps.

Annie shrugged. "My lips are zipped."

"Aw, surely ya know *something* . . . after all, Rudy was your beau all them years." Rhoda eyed her curiously and slapped the reins, getting the steed moving again.

"Well, if ya must know, ask him."

"I'm askin' you!"

Annie kept her eyes forward, wishing she might've continued to walk instead of accepting the ride.

"Can't ya give me a hint . . . the least little one?" Rhoda pleaded. "Honestly, I'm in your corner. I wouldn't want Susie Yoder for my sister-in-law."

"Oh, why not? She's a right nice girl."

Rhoda paused a moment. Then she said, "Well, I'd have to say it's because she's nothin' like you."

*Ain't that the truth,* thought Annie.

"Surely Rudy didn't have a fallin' out with ya, did he?"

*Puh!* Truth was they'd fussed like two cats toward the end. One of them feistier than the other. Even so, Rudy had been the most wonderfully kind— even affectionate—boy she'd ever known during the years of their courtship. She had accepted rides home from Sunday night singing with several other fellows before him, but the minute she'd met Rudy, there was no other for her. Rhoda knew as well as anyone there was nothing bad to report about her own brother. He was not a troublemaker like some fellas. If anything, *she* had been the problem, unwilling to join church when he was ready to.

"We've parted ways, Rhoda, and that's all I'm gonna say."

Rhoda sniffled, like she might burst out crying, but Annie decided no fit of temper was going to change her mind. What had transpired between Rudy and herself was nobody's business. Least of all Rhoda's, who Annie just realized was something of a tittle-tattle.

They rode a good quarter mile in silence. Then, hesitantly, Rhoda asked, "Where're ya headed?"

"To my cousins, Irvin and Julia's, but I can get out here and walk the rest of the way." She wished Rhoda would take that as a hint to halt the horse.

"No . . . no, that's all right. Ain't so far out of my way."

In a few minutes, they arrived at the redbrick house, set back a ways from the road. Irvin Ranck owned a harness shop across the vast meadow behind the house, in a barnlike structure he'd built years ago. Daed had always spoken well of his first cousin. Irvin was a good and honest man, one Mennonite the Amish farmers didn't mind paying for their stable gear. Just maybe that was the reason her father hadn't protested her working for the Rancks, even though Irvin's family had left the Amish church many decades before.

"*Denki* for the ride," Annie said, hopping down from the carriage.

"I'll be seein' ya" was all Rhoda said with a quick wave.

Hurrying up the walkway to the prim house, Annie spied four-year-old James pushing a toy lawn mower over a pile of leaves in the side yard. "Hullo!" she called and was delighted to see his eager smile.

"Cousin Annie!" the towheaded tyke called, running toward her with open arms.

"How's your little sister?" She gave him a quick squeeze and let him go.

"Oh, Molly's got lots of bumps . . . you'll see." James hurried alongside her as they rounded the corner of the house, entered through the back door, and walked upstairs to the nursery.

James was quite right. Molly had oodles more chicken pox bumps than two days ago, wearing mittens now so she couldn't scratch. She was plumped up with several pillows, sitting in her toddler-sized bed made by her father.

"Annie's here . . ." said Molly, trying to smile.

"*Jah,* I'm here, sweet one. And we'll look at lots of books together, all right?" Her heart went out to the little blond girl with eyes blue as cornflowers.

That brought a bigger smile to Molly's face, and James promptly went to the small bookcase and picked up a stack of board books. "These are Molly's favorites," he said, placing them gently in Annie's hands.

Bright-eyed Julia sat on the edge of her daughter's small bed, looking pretty in one of her hand-sewn floral print dresses. She wore her light brown hair in a bun, similar to Annie's, only Julia's was set higher on her head. Atop her bun, she wore the formal cup-shaped Mennonite head covering.

"I need to visit one of my expectant mothers in Strasburg today," Julia said softly. "She wants me present at the birth of her baby in a few weeks. I hope you don't mind."

"Ach, no, we'll be fine," she said. "Won't we?" Annie looked at both children, who were bobbing their heads and smiling.

Cousin Julia went on to say that the word was getting out about her being a "gentle midwife, although I'm not certified at all."

"But you have such a comforting way," Annie commented. "I can see why folks depend on you."

Later, after Julia had left and Annie had read each little book twice, she pulled up the quilted coverlet and smiled down at Molly, already asleep and clinging to her favorite dolly. Annie turned and raised her pointer finger to her lips as she and James tiptoed out of the nursery. "Time now for your nap, too, young man," she whispered, and the boy willingly followed her down the hall.

When James was tucked in, Annie hurried to the attic. Instead of closing the door behind her as usual, she left it wide open, tuning an ear to the children.

Over the years, she had managed to purchase everything she needed to create her landscape paintings, as well as her few attempts at portraits: Irvin and Julia's children, either from memory or from photographs. Naturally, she didn't dare bring even James up here for a sitting. And both Irvin and Julia knew her love for creating was to be held in the closest of confidence, even though Julia had admitted to being tempted to hire a professional tutor for Annie.

Mixing paints on her palette, she dabbed some purple onto the sky, making repeated attempts to blend it to create a rich lavender streak. Next, she gave the clouds a wispy sweep with her brush.

She eyed the canvas and scrutinized the creek bed and cluster of trees. She had stood on that very spot some weeks back, studying and pondering what precisely had happened there so long ago. But now she checked off each aspect of the painting in her mind . . . the sunlight twinkling on the wide stream, the covered bridge, the density of the trees, the depth of gray and the basket-weave texture of the trunks, complete with thorns protruding from trunk and limb. And the pale autumn yellow of the leaves.

The trees could not be climbed due to the wicked thorns, yet locust wood was the toughest kind, much stronger than cedar. It made the best fence posts, too, according to her eldest brother, Jesse, soon to be considered a master carpenter.

Annie stood in the middle of the unfinished garret where the easel had been positioned so that light from the two dormer windows, especially in the afternoon, could spill around the canvas like a crown. But the grayness outdoors was hardly adequate today, so Annie turned on the recessed lighting, which Irvin had so kindly installed last year. She always felt a thrilling sensation when flicking on the light switch.

Going back now to stand before the painting, she contemplated the waft and wisp of clouds. Several bluebirds populated the painting, one in flight, two others perched on a distant branch—feathery flecks of color.

*Something's missing. . . .*

She moved closer, her brush poised. The connection of hand to brush and brush on canvas sometimes triggered something important, something subconscious pulled into awareness.

Holding her breath, she touched her brush to the first tree.

*The long swing, that's what!*

Steadying her hand, she drew a thin line down. *Jah . . . good.*

Suddenly, she heard her name being called. "Annie!" The sound came from downstairs. "Are you up there, Annie?"

Someone—*who?*—was coming up the staircase!

"I'm here," she called back, her heart in her throat.

"What the world are ya doin' up there?"

Now she recognized the voice as her sister-in-law Sarah Mae.

*No . . . no, dear Lord God, no!*

Dropping her brush, she grabbed the nearest rag and began to wipe the paint off her hands. She heard Sarah Mae's footsteps on the wide-plank hallway at the base of the stairs and her heart began pounding.

*She's going to discover my secret!*

Quickly Annie stepped out of the studio, pulled the door closed behind her, and ran down the staircase, bumping into Sarah Mae as she did. "Oh, hullo," she managed to say.

Sarah Mae's round face was flushed and her blue eyes were inquisitive. "I knocked on the front door but guessed the children were asleep, so I just let myself in."

Annie nodded, feeling nearly dizzy with fright.

"What're ya doin' clear up here?" asked Sarah Mae. Then, without waiting for a reply, she added, "Does Julia have you redd up her attic, too?"

Not wanting to lie, Annie paused, thinking what to say, stumbling over several answers in her head. She stared down at the rag and said, "Jah, I'm cleanin' up a bit."

"Well, I stopped by to see if you'd be wantin' a ride home, since it looks to be turning a bit cold . . . and I'm headed there to drop off some blueberry jam to Mamm."

"I need to stay put till Julia returns. But denki—thank you."

Sarah Mae nodded, "All right, then." She inched her way backward down the narrow staircase.

*Whew!* Annie blew out a puff of air. *I must be more careful!*

# Chapter 2

Following a supper of lamb loaf, scalloped asparagus, buttered carrots, home-made bread with Sarah Mae's blueberry jam, and topped off with Mamm's well-loved misty mint salad, Annie washed and dried the dishes, taking pleasure in redding up. Mamm put away the few leftovers in their new gas-powered refrigerator, then swept the floor.

Soon her father wandered to the corner cupboard and took down the big family Bible for evening reading and silent prayers. He went and poked his head out the back door and called for Yonie, just turned nineteen last week, Luke, seventeen, and Omar, fifteen months younger than Luke—all courting age.

Annie had heard Daed refer quite often to his "empty wallet" now that Omar was sixteen. The price of a good road horse was twenty-five hundred dollars, not to mention her father's purchase of a new open buggy for Luke, close to three thousand dollars. All this with Daed being something of a penny-pincher, too. But a new horse and buggy assured each boy attendance at the all-important Sunday night singings, as well as other necessary activities during Rumschpringe—the running-around years before a young person settled down to marry.

Later, when evening prayers were done, Annie hurried upstairs to her room and lit the gas lamp. She sat at the little maple desk Daed had made for her twelfth birthday, pulled out the narrow center drawer and found her floral stationery. She was mighty curious to know how things had turned out with Louisa's mother's idea of having dozens of white doves released from cages as the bride and groom hurried out of the church to something called a stretch

22

limousine, whatever that was. Annie had not the faintest idea about most of the things Louisa shared in her letters. Nonetheless, she began to write to her best English friend:

*Wednesday, October 26*
*Dear Louisa,*

*Hello again. How are you doing?*

*I've been thinking so much about you lately. I hope you're not as tired this week as you said you were last, what with all the places you and your mother have been rushing to. Hither and yon, goodness me! Do you ever feel like just going to bed with the chickens, the way I do?*

*Which reminds me, did you decide what to do about the doves? Or has your mother changed her mind yet again? (I'm sure you're still wishing to have your guests simply blow the little bubbles, as you described in your last letter. To be honest, I think that would be the most fun.)*

She stopped writing, trying to picture thousands of bubbles with every color of the rainbow gleaming within each tiny circumference. Smiling, she daydreamed about being present on Louisa's special day, to witness firsthand the peculiar yet fascinating way the English celebrate a wedding ceremony and reception.

"What would Daed think if I just upped and went?" she whispered to herself. *I really ought to. . . .*

But Mamm was entirely right—she had never set foot outside Lancaster County. So what made her think she could be high-minded enough to get herself a bus or train ticket all the way to the Rocky Mountains, which is nearly where Louisa's well-to-do family lived? Somewhere south of Denver, in a place called Castle Pines. Louisa had herself an apartment in the town of Castle Rock, just a hop, skip, and a jump from her parents' home.

According to Louisa, the prime location had been her father's first choice some years ago—five acres, a custom-built home set high on a ridge with sweeping views of the mountains, with three rock fireplaces, a separate library large enough for a writing desk and three overstuffed chairs, and five large bedrooms, each having its own bathroom. And although only the two of them resided there, they had four living areas, a "separate dining room big enough to entertain thirty for sit-down dinners," as Louisa described it, a butler's pantry, and a kitchen with every imaginable appliance, including electric everything—refrigerator, a regular oven, convection oven, dishwasher, garbage disposal and compactor, and the list went on and on. All this in a room the size of the entire downstairs of the hundred-year-old farmhouse where Annie lived. Most of these things Annie had never heard of before in her life.

She couldn't begin to know why Louisa's parents needed so many rooms, but it was not her place to question. *Englischers* were often frivolous, Daed had always said of outsiders. Still, in spite of that, Annie felt mighty happy all these years to have ended up with such an interesting pen pal. A true and faithful friend.

She let her mind wander back to the day the first letter from Louisa had arrived in the mailbox.

The afternoon had been unseasonably cool and rainy. Fall housecleaning was well underway, with plenty of hands making light the work. Annie kept herself busy whitewashing the picket fence that bordered the main pastureland.

When the mail truck came with a letter postmarked Denver, Colorado, but with the recipient's name and address all soiled, Annie opened it, planning only to read enough to see who the letter was meant for. The inside salutation had read simply: *Dear New Friend,* so Annie began to read the first few lines. The letter writer introduced herself as Louisa Stratford, named for her paternal grandmother. Louisa was obviously not Amish and said she was almost eleven. But she'd written that she wanted to be an artist when she grew up, "with all of my heart, I do." Declaring this in the first few lines immediately grabbed Annie's curiosity.

Reading further, Annie soon realized the letter was not intended for her. She knew she ought to check at the next farmhouse over, to see if the English farmer's daughter, Jenna Danz, had signed up for a Colorado pen pal at school, maybe. Yet eight-year-old Annie was compelled to read on, especially because some pretty drawings in the margins caught her eye. And before she knew it, she'd read the entire letter, so captivated by this faraway modern girl and the way she described herself. Most of all, her keen love of drawing.

Quickly Annie wrote down Louisa's name and her return address. Then she put on her galoshes and raincoat and promptly marched down the road stepping in all the mud puddles, taking the letter to its rightful owner. She also apologized for having opened the letter and read it all, but dared not admit why . . . that she, too, loved to draw. She left that part unsaid, hoping Jenna would forgive, and she had.

Returning to the house, she had scarcely any hope of ever getting a letter back, even if she did have the courage to write to the Colorado schoolgirl. But since she was still learning English grammar at the one-room schoolhouse, she reasoned childishly that writing to Louisa Stratford would be extra good practice for her, too.

The rest was history, as Louisa liked to say. Besides that, Annie had always felt it providential—meant to be—her getting the letter from outside the Plain community . . . the two of them so completely worlds apart, yet opening up their hearts to one another by mail. Daed had never said one word against it, though Annie was fairly sure he had no clue how often the letters flew back and forth.

But Mamm knew and was good enough to keep it to herself. Annie supposed her mother assumed there was no harm done, what with all the miles between the girls. Up until just this year, Annie never would have given a second thought to a wedding invitation such as the one she held now in her hands.

*What would it be like to see the colors of all those cut flowers . . . and the golden candelabra, and satin bows, and . . . ?*

She shook herself, knowing she must simply pick up the pen and politely reply on the RSVP card that she would not be going. Even though with all of her heart, she would be there in her mind's eye when Louisa took her father's arm and strode the lengthy walkway along the rows of church pews, the "aisle," Louisa had called it, covered with an ivory runner and sprinkled with red and pink rose petals by the five wee girls dressed as miniature brides and carrying flower baskets. All this to get Louisa on her way to her smiling and handsome husband, who was to stand with nine other men also in fine black suits, lavender shirts, and matching cummerbunds high at the chapel altar. *Formal tuxedos,* Louisa had written to describe them and had sketched them, as well.

Annie easily read the words, but without the aid of the drawings tucked into each letter, she would have been completely bewildered about the upcoming wedding ceremony of Miss Louisa Victoria Stratford to Mr. Michael Logan Berkeley at twelve o'clock noon on Saturday the nineteenth day of November. . . .

# Chapter 3

Louisa Stratford parked her silver Mercedes in the circular driveway in front of her parents' home at Crown Pointe Place. Opening the car door, she headed for the house, already missing her signature jeans and ankle boots. At her mother's urging, she had donned one of the few ultraconservative outfits hanging in her closet—a chic blue-and-gray-plaid woolen skirt and coordinating blue cashmere sweater.

"Hello, dear!" Mother called as she emerged from the front door. "Shall I drive today?"

"My car's warmed up," Louisa said. Making note of her mother's prim navy suit and pumps, she went to open the passenger door and waited for her mother to get settled in the front seat.

When they were on their way, heading north on I-25 to Denver, Louisa absentmindedly slipped in an old Sheryl Crow CD, one of her favorites. "I'm exhibiting my art students' work in two weeks, so I can't be late for class today," she said, hoping to keep their outing as brief as possible.

Suddenly, the plaintive wail of *Every Day is a Winding Road* blared into the car, and she quickly poked the eject button. "Sorry about that."

*Off to a classic start,* she thought, restless, even preoccupied. She was eager to meet with her students again, having grown weary of the wedding preparations, more than a full year of them already. Each week's schedule of events, teas, and luncheons was a reflection of her parents' tastes, but she had learned from her childhood to acquiesce to Mother's wishes to avoid making waves.

Her dream wedding—hers and Michael's—bore little resemblance to the plans being carved out for them. Both families had decided their children, their *only* offspring, deserved something of a gala *to die for*. Well, Louisa was dying all right, and it had nothing to do with the composition of the gift sachets—satin or netting?—for three hundred dinner guests, nor whether the reception china should be rimmed in gold or silver.

*Gold*, her mother had insisted, with full endorsement from Ms. Tyler, the wedding planner. The reasoning was linked to the gilded birdcages with large satin bows tied to their gleaming posts to be positioned strategically along the wedding aisle. No mere candelabra or flowers with simple bows along the aisle, no. Nothing ordinary in *this* wedding. And because the embossed invitations were also gold, it was only fitting the dinnerware be etched with the same.

On the other hand, the groom had early voiced his humorous opinion to the bride, but the notion of saying vows before a justice of the peace was out of the question. Not with his family connections. And *hers*.

In fact, Michael paid little mind to their wedding plans. If anything, his primary interest seemed to be the exotic honeymoon cruise package. She smiled to herself. *Typical guy*.

"Driving a little fast?" her mother commented as Louisa navigated the wide streets of Littleton, a suburb of Denver, to the appointed boutique.

She tapped the brake. "Sorry."

Today's quest was to select gifts for the bridesmaids and junior bridesmaids, as well as the guestbook girls—*why three?* Louisa knew the answer all too well. Everything was about Daddy's prestigious law firm. It was essential, as it had been explained to her, that the upper echelon of her father's company—their up-and-coming progeny, at least—be well represented in the Stratford/Berkeley wedding, whether Louisa and Michael had ever made their acquaintance or not.

*At least I chose my own maid-of-honor*, Louisa consoled herself, smiling at the thought of Courtney Engelman, her outspoken, even cynical, but fun-loving college friend.

The addition of bodies had begun to aggravate her, including three of the supposedly "charming" yet nameless flower girls whom Mother had lined up without her knowledge until just recently.

Sighing, Louisa parked in front of the boutique, then pulled her keys from the ignition.

"Darling." Mother turned and touched her arm lightly. "Is something the matter?"

Louisa sighed again. "I'm fine . . . maybe a little tired." Not only was she tired physically, but weary of attending to the infinitesimal details of a full-weekend wedding celebration, from calling to double-check room reservations at Denver's most exclusive hotel, the Brown Palace, for out-of-town guests to a zillion and one bridal showers in her honor—both lingerie and household—all happening in the next two weeks. Not to mention the post-wedding announcements to be sent to newspapers on the never-ending list: the *Denver Post,* for their present location, the *Chicago Tribune,* where most of Daddy's side of the family lived, the *Los Angeles Times,* where Mother's people still resided, and several more small-town papers her parents had decided were a "must send."

*Why did we hire a professional planner at all?* she wondered, wishing she and Michael might have arranged a simple but elegant wedding.

"We mustn't tire you out, darling. You tell me when you've had your fill, all right?"

Louisa forced a smile.

Growing up in opulence, Louisa was accustomed to the niceties of life. But once this wedding hoopla was past and she and Michael returned from their honeymoon—once the hundreds of thank-yous were properly addressed and stamped, with the proper return address label on the proper day—the life she now led was going to screech to a halt. She had little interest in kowtowing to the almighty dollar. Daddy's riches hadn't brought joy to Mother's heart or peace to her perfect plastered smile. Oh, they were content and at ease with their friends and societal functions, but deep down weren't they as frustrated as everyone else on the planet, well off or otherwise?

However, in the midst of this crazy and contrived world, Louisa knew someone who had long embraced a simple and unpretentious life. A young woman who knew well the meaning of genuine beauty, laughter, and love, although without a boyfriend at the present time. Annie Zook understood how to live to the fullest and on very little means monetarily, or so Louisa assumed. The Zooks supplemented the sale of cow's milk and butter by raising peacocks, and from the honest and caring letters Annie wrote so frequently, Louisa had enjoyed a front-row seat to the Plain life—the daily routine on the back roads of Paradise.

*Perfect name for a honeymoon resort,* Louisa thought, smiling.

While her mother paid for each of the two-hundred-dollar bracelets to be presented to the attendants at the bridesmaids' luncheon in a few days, Louisa wandered toward the lace-covered bay window. She looked out to the horizon, past the flurry and cacophony of traffic, and considered the Pennsylvania barn-yard where Annie often ran barefoot up until the first frost, bringing home their herd of cows twice daily and feeding the peahens and their chicks. She closed her eyes and visualized the fall plowing which was happening this week, with the help of Yonie, Luke, and Omar, the three younger Zook boys.

A "closet" artist, Annie also had a surprising knack for word pictures, even though she had only an eighth-grade education. The real-to-life descriptions in her letters helped Louisa envision the foreign world of the Old Order Amish.

Her curious connection to Annie Zook all these years had created within her a yearning for a less-complicated life, even though it was clear that broken-hearted Annie was caught in an ominous situation with her secret love of art, which was forbidden by her strict church community. *A train wreck about to happen*, she thought, wishing she could do something more than write letters to support her friend.

"She's as trapped as I am . . . in a different way," she whispered into the air, thinking how ironic it was that she had not been able to pry herself away from her parents' wishes for her own wedding. Just as Annie had not been able to please her parents by abandoning her art and joining the Amish church.

"Louisa," her mother said, tugging her back from her reverie, "let's have lunch. Somewhere wonderful."

Conscious of her mother's anticipation, she surrendered. "Sure, if you like, Mother."

Her mother waved at the thirty-something wedding planner, Katrina Tyler, who was pulling into the parking lot. "Why don't we head downtown to the Brown Palace Hotel and kill two birds with one stone?" Mother suggested. "Would you like that?"

Translation: *Why don't we sample the reception dinner entrée?*

"I'd really rather not." The words tumbled surprisingly off her lips.

"Beg your pardon, dear?"

*Pardon, indeed . . .*

Louisa shook her head. "Can't we trust the head chef, the wait staff, Ms. Tyler, and everyone else you and Daddy have shelled out tens of thousands of dollars to, to get it right? To make *my* wedding day the perfect memory. Can't we, Mother?"

Her mother's brow pinched up and her tone turned icy. "We're scheduled to meet the caterer there."

"I'd much rather grab some fast food. I'll ask Katrina to meet us at—"

"The luncheon is already set, Louisa."

*Why didn't you say so?* She glanced over her shoulder and noticed the boutique owner's face crumpling while whispering to the clerk.

Louisa turned to leave and politely held the door. She forced herself to slow her pace and wave at Ms. Tyler when she opened her car window and called a perfunctory greeting. "I can drive if you'd like," the wedding planner offered.

"I'm driving!" Louisa said. "We'll meet you there." She matched the dignified slow tempo of her mother's stride. Everything these days—*everything*—was a corresponding link to the Stratford family name and fortune. The way things were expected to be. All the years of finishing school—how to walk and not to, how to point toes, cross legs at ankles, how to present oneself perfectly in public . . . whether dressed in scanty swim attire, tea-length tailored suit, or floor-length evening gown. She knew the drill.

"I'll spring for burgers, okay?" she said, making one final attempt when they were settled in the car. "We could eat them on the way. Consider it appetizers." She snickered at her own mouthy joke.

"Far too much fat for a bride who must fit into her size two gown." Mother said, shifting into her most-determined mode.

"I'm not worried about clogged arteries or zipping up my gown. You never saw what I ate during art school."

"Well, we fed you the very best food growing up."

*The very best* . . . How often had she heard that?

At Seventeenth Street, they pulled up for valet parking at the Brown Palace Hotel, and Louisa was told they were lunching at Ellyngton's, the place to be seen and home to the "power meal." Maybe Michael might wander in for lunch with his attorney pals. She could only hope so.

*After all,* she thought wryly, *we're on the brink of marriage . . .*

When they were settled at a window overlooking Denver's lively financial district, Mother suggested the baby greens and three-tomato salad on the starter section of the menu, to which Louisa quickly agreed. In doing so, she would improve her chances of ordering what she really wanted for her main course, which was neither the spinach and wild mushroom salad nor the lemon-marinated salmon. The Angus burger would satisfy her hunger. She had enjoyed it before, several months ago when Michael had met her here during his short lunch hour, to discuss a prenuptial agreement his attorney had drawn up. She'd found it to be rather annoying at first but was informed of the "necessity" of such an agreement, as explained to her later by Michael's private attorney. And, silly her, she should have figured this might happen, with the amassed Berkeley fortune being "old money," unlike her family's more recently acquired wealth. After cooling down, which took a few days, she had signed on the dotted line, with a wink and a nod from Michael, who assured her there was "no need to worry."

Now she reached for her glass of sparkling mineral water, studying Katrina, who had taken her checklist out of her briefcase. No older than thirty-two, *this* wedding planner was earning her keep. She would not derail with an impertinent approach and had way more style than her predecessors. She also possessed the single most important ingredient of all: the ability to persevere.

*Yep, Ms. Tyler will cross the finish line.*

Later, when Mother and Katrina ordered identical desserts of apple beignets with lingonberry jam, Louisa went for broke with the black bottom pie, having chickened out on the burger and ordered a chicken entrée instead.

But it was following the meal, when the schmoozing with the caterer started, that Louisa stifled her opinion. She followed Katrina's lead, feigning interest in the reception entrée options: Filet Mignon, Roast Prime Rib of Beef, Chicken Edgar, Chicken Italia, Sesame Seared Salmon, and Herb-Crusted Haddock. Or a trio of three to please all palates.

After an hour and a half, she was no longer able to sit demurely by. She glared up at the chandelier, fidgeting idly with her smart phone and keys, wishing she dared call Michael. But his day would be demanding as always, tied up with important clients, as a busy junior partner at a competing law firm some miles from her father's.

Mother continued to deliberate the selection of ivory versus ecru linens, now kindly conferring with Katrina on the matter. Louisa let her mind drift away to the perfect daydream . . . to gorgeous Michael, who planned to drop by her apartment after work tomorrow evening. Together they would grill the steaks marinating in her fridge, but he would insist on making a walloping big Mediterranean salad while she stir-fried his favorite snow peas, oyster mushrooms, young asparagus spears, and strips of red and yellow bell peppers. Once dinner was over, she would share what was troubling her, confiding her dire frustration, asking if it was too late. *Too late for what, babe?* To make their mark on the most important day of their lives. Or, better yet, to go back to the drawing board and do it their way. He would assure her, pull her into his arms, and fervently kiss away her stress, while Muffin, her blue-gray cat, would blink his green eyes all curled up on Louisa's funky secondhand black-speckled Garbo sofa.

*A good dose of sanity . . . soon!* She could hardly wait.

# Chapter 4

Sunlight played chase with yesterday's fog, and the newly painted clapboard farmhouse beamed like a white moon against the backdrop of a considerable willow tree in the backyard. There, dozens of scarlet cardinals flocked to its branches in the early evening, as if drawn to the thousands of golden leaves.

A stand of sugar maples on the opposite side yard made a show of their dazzling red tresses, and each day more crimson blanketed the ground below.

Never in disrepair, though more than a hundred years old, the three-story house stood as a testament to hard work and constant care. Out front, just steps from the yard, a scarcely traveled ribbon of road divided the property in two—the house on one side and the barn and several outbuildings on the other.

Annie stared out her bedroom window at the radiant foliage bursting forth from nearly every tree, the array of colors reminding her of an artist's palette. She chided herself a bit. *No time for daydreaming during the harvest,* she thought, *what with everyone keeping busy—men filling silo, womenfolk making applesauce and cider, this very morning, in fact, in Mamm's big kitchen.* She headed downstairs. *I must do my part, too. For now. . . .*

Annie and her mother were soon joined by more than a dozen women, each assuming a different task. Looking around intently, she saw that one very important helper was missing. Annie held her breath, thinking of her dear friend Esther Hochstetler, hoping she might yet arrive even at this late hour.

Mamm's three older sisters, Aunts Suzanne, Emma, and Frannie were on hand with their married daughters, Mary, Katie, Suzie, Nancy, Becky, Rhoda, and Barbianne. Another half hour passed, and Esther was still not there, even though two weeks ago at Preaching service she'd told Annie she was definitely coming today.

*I hope she's feeling all right.* Esther was expecting again, and this pregnancy seemed to be the reason she gave lately for staying home.

Annie continued to help her cousins prepare the apples for cooking into sauce, cutting a neat circle in each apple to core the seeds and stem. All the while, Barbianne and Suzie chattered about the corn-husking bee tomorrow, the familiar light evident in their eyes as they talked softly of those "pairing up," unaware of Annie's hollow heart.

They continued whispering of the fun in store, hoping one of them might find the colored corn—Indian corn—for a special prize of candy or cream-filled cookies.

Then, for no particular reason, Annie happened to glance up. There was Esther coming through the back porch and mudroom area, hesitating slightly before stepping foot in the kitchen, looking awful tired and pale.

Lickety-split, Annie set down her paring knife and wiped her hands on her apron. She rushed to Esther's side. "Ach, I'm so glad you're here!" She pulled her into the kitchen. "Where have you been keepin' yourself?"

Esther blinked her pretty eyes, blue as can be. "Oh, you know me . . . 'tis easy to get caught up with the little ones."

"Well, two in diapers must be nearly like havin' twins."

Esther nodded. "Jah, seems so at times."

"Who's with them today?"

Esther paused. "Uh . . . Mamma came by, said I needed to get out a bit."

Annie agreed. "I'm glad she did!" She led Esther over to the section of the table where the cousins were still coring and peeling. "How does your big girl like first grade?"

"Laura thinks goin' to school is the next best thing to homemade ice cream." Esther gave Annie a quick smile. "But I miss her help at home . . . for sure."

They went over and began working on the first bushel basket. Then, after a bit, when the next group of women had the apples quartered and ready for the sugar, cinnamon, and water, they all took a short break while that mixture cooked.

Annie sat with Esther at the far end of the table, pouring extra sugar into her own cup of tea. "Laura's always been keen on learnin', seems to me."

Esther nodded, holding her teacup. "She's doin' all right . . . in school, jah."

"I remember I always liked spelling best." She bit her tongue and almost said *drawing,* too. But, of course, that subject was never taught in the little one-room schoolhouse over yonder. "I remember your favorite was geography. Am I right?"

Esther's lip quivered slightly and she was still.

"You all right?" Annie touched her arm. "Come, let's walk over to the outhouse right quick."

"No . . . no. I'll keep workin' here—you go on."

Annie was stumped. Esther looked to be troubled about something, so why did she clam up like that?

Hurrying out the back door, Annie headed around the side yard to the wooden outhouse. She hoped Esther was all right, really she did. Essie, as she'd called her when they were girls, had always been a most cheerful playmate. She and her family had lived a ten-minute buggy ride away, so she and Annie got to visit each other often, and Annie loved it, being the only girl in a family of boys. She also remembered that up until Essie's courting years, she'd worn a constant smile on her pretty face.

But sadly it wasn't long after Essie married Ezekiel that the infectious smile began to fade. Soon Essie was asking folk to drop her youthful nickname. "Call me Esther from now on," she insisted.

In the few months following her wedding day, Esther became sullen, even distant, and within the year, she was scarce at gatherings. When she did go to help can vegetables and fruits or put up canned meats, she didn't say much unless spoken to first. It was as if Esther had to be pried free of something each and every time.

Annie could not put her finger on the reason for the drastic change. But something sank in her like a rock in a dew pond whenever she thought about who her friend had become. What was it about getting hitched up that caused the light to go out of some girls' eyes?

Annie shook away her fretting and headed back to the house. She wished she could help, but there was a thick wall around Esther now and it seemed no one could break through.

Just then Annie spied her father and Rudy Esh's older brother, Caleb, across the road smoking cigars near the springhouse. How peculiar. In all her days she did not recall ever seeing Caleb Esh chewing the fat with Daed.

A little shiver went down her back, seeing Caleb, because he looked a lot like Rudy. *What on earth does he want with my father?*

But, alas, she'd worried enough for one morning. Taking a deep breath, she forced her attention back to applesauce-making and to dear downtrodden Esther. She opened the back door to the tantalizing aroma of tart Granny Smith applesauce.

Jesse Zook puffed on his cigar, exercising as much forbearance as possible, saying not a word as Caleb Esh gabbed away.

"My brother Rudy must have had a good reason for picking a different girl—it's just that I think your Annie's far and away a better choice of a mate, Preacher."

Jesse had not made a practice of knowing who was seeing his daughter and who wasn't. He wouldn't start speculating now . . . unlike some fathers who required a report from their sons of the scallywags who drove younger sisters home from barn singings and other church-sanctioned activities. Never had he cared to interfere that way with Annie's courting years. She was a level-headed sort and downright determined, too. *His* daughter would have no trouble attracting a fine man to marry, but only when she was good and ready to settle down.

"Rudy is makin' a big mistake, the way I see it," Caleb continued.

Sighing, Jesse removed his hat and inhaled his tobacco deeply. He contemplated the field work to be done yet, and here they were wasting time. "Well, I have to ask ya, just what's your concern in this?"

"Only that Rudy was in love with Annie. Sure as my name's Esh."

"But you say *he* broke off with her?"

"That he did."

Now Jesse was confused *and* perturbed. Seemed Caleb wasn't making much sense for a man nearly thirty-five years old, married, and the father of nine children, last count. This here Caleb had also been talked about as a possible preacher nomination back last fall after council meeting, amongst some of the brethren.

*A busybody, to be sure . . .*

"Is all your plowin' done, Caleb?" he asked right quick.

"Well . . . almost."

Jesse shook his head a bit, looked down at his straw hat, and then placed it back on his head. "Why not let nature take her course where courtin's concerned. Seems the Good Lord works all that out just right fine, given the chance."

Caleb nodded his head quick like and said, "Afternoon, Preacher Zook." Then he sauntered over to his horse and carriage, where he'd left them smack dab in the middle of the lane.

"Be seein' ya at Preaching service come Sunday," Jesse called to him, attempting to keep a grin in check.

Louisa lit each of four candles on the table, two tall tapers and two votives. She softly blew out the match and returned to the kitchen, where Michael was putting the finishing touches on his organic dressing "experiment," as he called it: extra-virgin olive oil, French sea salt, freshly-squeezed lemon juice, dry Italian basil, fresh garlic, ground black pepper, and Greek oregano—leaves only—all mixed into one dressing bottle.

"Looks exotic," she said, smiling. "And the steaks await."

He carried the wooden salad bowl, tongs, and dressing to the table. "How about some dinner music?"

"Sure. What are you in the mood for?"

He winked at her in response, and she felt her face blush.

"You pick."

She went to the sitting area of the small living room and scanned the CD tower. This was not a night for anything heavy. *Keep it mellow*, she decided, thinking ahead to the topic of conversation, which must wait until they had enjoyed the jointly made candlelight dinner.

She reached for her old favorite, legendary Stan Getz—cool tenor sax—and slipped the disk into the CD player. Smooth jazz filled up all the spaces of silence, and she sat down across from Michael.

"Hold your plate," he said and forked one of the steaks.

She watched him place the medium-rare piece of meat onto her plate. She was aware of his hands, his well-manicured nails . . . and immediately she thought of her mother's plans to do an all-day manicure, pedicure, and facial with all the bridesmaids. Then, they were all supposed to go to a glitzy tearoom Mother had booked, where Louisa was to present the gold bracelets.

But here she was having a really terrific dinner with Michael, who was making nice remarks about the steaks she'd grilled. Saying other complimentary things with his eyes, as well.

*Oh*, she groaned inwardly. *Wrong timing*.

But later, during a dessert of peach sorbet and gourmet butter cookies, it was Michael who mentioned that his mother was asking about "all those groomsmen."

"Did you tell her it was *my* mother's idea to have a million bridesmaids, which meant you *had* to scrounge up that many groomsmen?"

He shook his head. "Moi?"

"Well, it's excessive, and it seems Mother has decided this wedding is to be the most costly, the most lavish of any in Denver's recent history."

"Hmm . . ." Michael frowned. "I take it you're not happy."

"It's just that . . ." She spooned up a small amount of sorbet and stared at it. "I was hoping our wedding might reflect something of the two of *us*."

"Doesn't it? Our families aren't exactly collecting food stamps. Why not have a good time?"

This wasn't going as she had imagined. She looked at him. "It's gotten so out of hand, and Mother's calling all the shots."

He reached across the table for her hand but she stiffened. "What's *really* wrong?"

"Don't you get it, Michael? It's not a wedding anymore, it's a Las Vegas show!" She thought she might cry.

"Do your parents know how you feel?"

"It's not me they're trying to please. It's all about making impressions . . . Mother's society sisters, for one. And everyone else on the guest list."

Michael shrugged. "So? My mom's one of the society girls, too, remember? She's equally anxious to see a gala wedding for us. Everyone, both families, all of our friends, are on board."

"Except me." Her words came out like a thud, and Michael's eyebrows shot up. Until this moment, she hadn't realized how terribly disillusioned she had become. What had changed? Was it Annie Zook's friendship over the years, an Amish girl's influence from afar? No, it was more than that. Had to be.

She swallowed hard. "A quarter-of-a-million-dollar wedding won't make our day more special or meaningful, will it?" She had to hear him refute it. Instead, he pushed his chair back and reached for her salad plate, as well as his own, and carried them to the kitchen sink.

Returning, he brought along a bottle of champagne and two glasses. "Look, babe, who cares how much money our parents throw at this wedding? It's how we were raised. Our parents have more money than they know what to do with, so what's the harm?"

She shook her head. Either he hadn't heard a word she'd said or he simply didn't care. Or worse, he didn't understand.

*Wealth is all he knows . . . it's all I know. Of course he doesn't understand.*

"I'm tired of this life," she said softly.

He leaned forward, frowning. "I don't think I heard you. You said what?"

She was so frustrated, it was all she could do to measure her words, to keep from simply bursting. "I have no intention of living the way my parents—or yours—do. Look around here . . . at my apartment. This is the *real* me. I crave secondhand furniture and flea market treasures. Old stuff. Things with class but inexpensive, worn, and scuffed up . . . things that exude character." She paused. "I thought you knew."

Michael grimaced. "Isn't this merely a phase, your latest artistic flair? I didn't think you were serious." Casually he unwound the wire fastener from the bottle. "You want the look of poverty, well fine. That's cool."

She sighed. *He doesn't get it.*

"What does it matter about the wedding?" he continued. "Why not go along with the plans? You know your parents always get their way. Like they did with you and me."

His words slammed into her heart. "What are you talking about?"

He gripped the bottle and pulled up, grimacing slightly. "You know. The long-range plan." He popped the cork for effect.

She blew out a breath. "What?"

Their eyes met, and Michael flashed a smile. "Surely you remember how we met."

*A blind date.* "My dad ran into your dad. . . ." She struggled to remember. *Where?* "And they began talking, and one thing led to another, and then . . ."

He chuckled. "Well, yeah, but there's way more to it."

"More to what?"

"Oh, come on, Louisa. You can't tell me you didn't know."

She was unable to breathe. *It's so warm in here.*

He poured champagne into her glass first, then his own. He set the bottle to the side and raised his glass, proposing a toast, waiting for her. But she could only stare at him, too flustered to reach for her glass.

"Nothing changes the fact that we belong together, Louisa. Does it really matter how it happened?" He gestured toward her champagne. "I say we make a toast to the future—yours and mine, as well as to my partnership with your father's law firm . . . eventually, but certain."

She glared at him. "So that's what this is? An arrangement?"

"Louisa, don't play the drama queen."

"I thought we had something special."

"We do. Someone simply got the ball rolling, that's all."

She searched his eyes for some hint of insincerity, some indication he was teasing her. But he was incredibly earnest and more than eager to make the toast.

He winked at her, as though hoping to humor her. "To the Berkeley-Stratford merger."

Her mind whirled. *Surely we weren't merely pawns in our fathers' hands!*

He was smiling at her, attempting to charm her, still holding his glass high. "Our future is secure and rather limitless. Won't our children be perfect?"

She had not fallen for him for any of those reasons. She had been totally in the dark. "No . . . don't you see? Our beginning was a fraud," she whispered, blinking back tears.

He set down his glass. "What's the difference how it started? What matters is how it ends." His tone was one of impatience now.

*How it ends.* The words rang hollow and prophetic.

"It matters to *me*," she said.

"You're making too much of this."

She couldn't help it . . . she thought of her first boyfriend, a man a few years older whom she'd met at the start of her junior year—an art fanatic like her. Trey Douglas had loved her for who she was. But the timing was all off for them. She should have followed him to London. Instead, she'd fallen prey to her own father's misguided scheme.

She shook her head. "No, Michael! I don't want any part of this. I thought you loved *me*, no strings attached. I had no idea this was part of someone's plan to manipulate us. The whole thing is messed up." She rose and hurried down the short hall to her bedroom and closed the door.

"Louisa, baby . . . wait! Let's talk this out."

"I've heard enough." She locked the door, leaning her head against it, clutching her aching throat.

Even in spite of his repeated knocking and calling to her, she simply could not bring herself to open the door. It would break her heart even more to look into his face.

*All a charade!*

# Chapter 5

Saturday's corn-husking bee at Deacon Byler's farm was off to a grand start, even though neither the shucking of ears of corn nor the stacking of stalks had begun. Young people, and a few married chaperones, were arriving, and already dozens of buggies were lined up in a row, parked along the side yard.

Annie and her sister-in-law Sarah Mae worked together, straining their fingers to unhitch Dolly from the enclosed family carriage. Pretty soon, Obed, one of Deacon Byler's sons, walked over and helped finish the task. That done, he led the horse up to the barn, where he would water and feed each of the driving horses stabled there.

"Denki, Obie," called Annie.

Suddenly she spotted Rudy Esh and several other fellows standing near the woodshed. *Ach, he's here!* She quickly looked away. Her hands grew clammy, and a sickening lump formed in the pit of her stomach.

*I should've stayed home!*

If he happened to take Susie Yoder home in his buggy later, it would do her in but good. She'd never actually seen them sitting side-by-side in Rudy's open carriage, and she didn't want to start now.

Rejecting the urge to wallow in self-pity, she found the courage to walk with her head high. *I'm not ashamed. I've done nothing wrong.* But she knew for certain she had, for her fondness for art had come between her and Rudy. Her paintings and drawings were a result of doing what she believed the Lord God had somehow implanted in her heart. *I paint the beauty I see around me. How*

40

*can that be wrong?* Yet it was, according to the rules of their *Ordnung*, which governed much of their lives.

When she got to the house, she discovered a whole group of girls—mostly courting age—gathered in the kitchen. Some were pouring cold apple cider into paper cups; others were arranging cups on large trays.

"Hullo, Annie!" Deacon Byler's wife, Kate, called to her. "I heard tell your wailin' peacocks kept your neighbor, David Lapp, up all hours last night."

"Well, I heard nothing once I fell asleep," Annie replied.

This brought a wave of laughter.

"Must be mating season, jah?" one of the older girls said, and they fell silent, followed by a few snickers. "Them peacocks can yowl worse than an infuriated cat, I daresay."

"And they get awful lonely," Annie explained, as if the girls had never heard this about the bevy of beautiful birds she and her brothers raised. "They like bein' close to each other."

Several girls had their heads together, giggling.

"Once one of them flew off lookin' for his mate after she died. . . . I'm not kidding." Annie straightened her apron and pushed her shoulders back. "But for the most part, they stay put. They don't stray too far from home."

"Besides that, peahens are some of the best mothers ever," Kate Byler added amidst more peals of laughter. "Now, listen. What Annie's sayin' is ever so true."

More than amused by Kate's seriousness, Annie watched her dark eyes sparkle as she appointed different girls to carry the trays of drinks out to the men.

As if on cue, right then Rudy Esh appeared in the back doorway. His auburn hair shimmered clean, and he held his head at a slight angle, as if questioning her resolve even now. "It's time to team up and get to workin'," he announced.

His take-charge voice reminded Annie of all the happy yet frustrating years she'd spent as his girl. Here was a young man who knew precisely what he wanted in life, and she'd fully messed it up for him.

Turning her attention back to the girls, she refused to let on, but she missed him all to pieces.

Louisa kept to the speed limit as she headed up Highway 285 toward the town of Conifer, taking in the sweeping views of pine and evergreen. The highway was a two-lane sliver of concrete, crawling with cars filled with hikers, soon-to-be bikers, and tourists too late for peak foliage of aspen gold.

She was glad for a blue-sky day with not a threat of snow or sleet. This late in the season, a blizzard frequently enveloped the road within minutes of the first sign of snow-laden clouds moving quickly from the mountains to the eastern plains.

At Pine Junction, she made the turn south on Route 126, her ultimate destination being the cozy bedroom community called Pine a few miles from Buffalo Creek, another well-kept secret with an elevation of eighty-two-hundred feet above sea level. She knew of a secluded inn where she'd gone to work on several drawings sometime ago. The place was set back in the woods, with hiking trails that led to a spectacular overlook. She had called to reserve a room for the night, for the purpose of getting her emotional bearings. Of course, she could be reached if necessary, and she checked the time on her smart phone as the Mercedes climbed in altitude.

*"Let's talk. . . ."*

Michael's tense voice mail still ricocheted in her head. What was there to discuss? They had talked for more than an hour by phone following the superb steak dinner, only for Louisa to understand more fully how susceptible to the trappings of success Michael had become. Her fiancé's true motives had finally surfaced. *Just like Mother and Daddy,* she thought, *and all their friends.*

Excessive extravagance—the kind Michael continued to argue for, even on behalf of her own mother—had begun to slowly sicken her toward all she had grown accustomed to, although she had never known anything different. But now, enough was enough, and the way Michael had explained it, there was simply no room for compromise.

She pondered her life as Michael's wife. They were formed from the same mold, but she had come to long for something meaningful . . . the simple life, the way Annie Zook lived. At this moment such a peaceful existence strongly beckoned to her.

Most importantly, she could not marry a man who was so consumed with his career and making money that his wife—and eventually the children he wanted—would come in at second or third place. Or maybe fall right through the cracks.

She glanced at the sky now, at each tuft and curl of clouds, contemplating what she would give up by not going through with the marriage. Her father's favor and approval, for one. Possibly her eventual inheritance . . . who was to know? Anything and everything money could buy. She conjured up images of being disowned, destitute. At least she would have a say in how she lived her life.

If she were to call off the wedding, she would have to tell Michael first, then her parents. She must also be the one to tell her maid-of-honor. *Courtney will think I'm insane!* The rest could hear it from Mother.

She gripped the steering wheel as though clutching the remnants of her life. *Will my parents ever forgive me? Will Michael?*

What was she to be absolved of really? Hadn't they gotten the whole relationship started . . . that first blind date introduction?

At least she would give them an earlier heads up than most runaway brides. She would not wait until the actual wedding day, nor would she wait until the luxurious rehearsal dinner to call it off. There was still adequate time to alert guests, *immediately*. Most had not sent RSVPs yet, nor had many gifts arrived.

So much for the Fostoria crystal and the posh flatware, including two sets of silver-plated tableware. None of which reflected her taste—all chosen with Mother's plans for them in mind.

She thought back to the day Michael had accompanied her and her mother on yet another trip to register for wedding gifts; this one at Nordstrom in Park Meadows Mall, in south Denver. There had been tiny chinks in the armor again on that day. The hollow feeling she had when Mother kept insisting on the most impractical things—the one-of-a-kind placemats that had to be thrown away if ever soiled, the linen napkins, the too-delicate glassware for everyday use. Michael had seemed to approve of her mother's every selection, surprisingly.

And only the most exclusive honeymoon package would do for them. *Nothing but the best.* His mantra. And hers, as well . . . until now. Something had snapped, and there was no turning back.

Adjusting her automatic seat, she hoped Michael's parents could get a good portion of their money back. Ditto for her parents. The last thing she wanted to do was rob them blind. But even with three weeks' notice, there was an enormous risk of loss.

She thought again of her pen pal, wishing Annie had access to email. Instant messaging would be even better. She needed to talk to her, but only one telephone serviced four Amish farmhouses, and those homes were well spaced, as she understood it.

There was something quite incredible about the wisdom of the unassuming girl who'd become her truest friend, though she lived in a remote area of Lancaster County, Pennsylvania. Louisa knew precisely where, because after only two exchanges of letters, she had searched out the town of Paradise in her father's big atlas. The one most highly prized by Daddy nestled on the first shelf nearest the writing desk, in his cherry-paneled home library.

*Annie would understand. . . .*

She pulled into the inn's wide dirt driveway and found a parking spot. Turning off the ignition, she leaned on the steering wheel, looking up at the historic rock-hewn structure of Meadow Creek B&B.

The fresh, strong scent of pine hung in the air, and the trickle of the spring-fed stream bordering the property welcomed her back.

*If there's a God, He would definitely hang His hat here,* she thought, getting out of the car and pulling her backpack behind her. She had never been one for church, the result of her parents being too socially busy to bother with religion. Their god was their lifestyle, and even they would not have disputed the fact.

Suddenly a strange idea struck her, and she stopped walking. *What if I went to visit Annie . . . to see just how long I can last without the good life?*

The notion was incredible—staying with an Amish family, if they'd be agreeable to it. Actually, it was quite perfect!

But she could hear it now. Her parents cautioning her, questioning her once their anger subsided over the called-off wedding. *If they ever calmed down. You're out of your mind, dear. What are you thinking?*

Michael would sneer, *You don't think you're just like us? Well, sure, try it for a while. But you'll cave, and then you'll come crawling back, ready to accept your real life.*

Annie absolutely refused to give up, keeping an eye out for the coveted colored corn on the stalks, hoping to find it, to be a winner of a special prize. She'd heard from Rudy, who was working on the same team as she, that the prizes were not merely homemade candies and cookies this time. *Why would he tell me that?* she wondered.

She couldn't get over how nice he had been to her for all the hours they had worked to husk the corn from the stalk, but then she'd never been ditched by a beau before, so she wasn't exactly sure how she should act. And what she did know, nevertheless, was how terribly difficult it was to stand in such close proximity to him, as they tied the stalks into bundles. She caught the occasional whiff of his sweet-smelling peppermint gum, which he seemed to continually chew, no matter what he was doing.

*I must still love him,* she thought. *But I love my art even more. . . .*

Rudy had been most pleasant during their courtship. For too long, she had simply taken his keen affection for granted, just assuming it would always be there, offered to her for the taking. But here they were working shoulder-to-shoulder, yet no longer planning a future as husband and wife. Quite the contrary. They'd gone their separate ways, so to speak, all the while involved in the same church district.

She wondered, *Can it be?* Was his thoughtfulness this day a way to show he still appreciated her? No animosity between them? If so, she was grateful, Indian corn or not.

"I found some!" Cousin Barbianne called out.

"Give that girl a treat," one of Rudy's buddies hollered.

"By all means!" said Rudy himself.

Barbianne blushed, obviously a little embarrassed yet thrilled to be a winner. But her big brown eyes sparkled as she was given the large whoopie pie, its icing threatening to trickle out between two homemade slabs of chocolate cookies.

Just then Annie spotted Sarah Mae motioning to her from the cluster of workers who were taking the nicest corn from the stalk for cornmeal. "Come over here and help us," Sarah Mae said, offering a sympathetic smile.

Annie went willingly, if not quite relieved. She was sorry . . . even sad to leave Rudy and his group behind.

*How long before I don't give a care?*

Sarah Mae chattered about the delicious ham bake to follow the husking bee. She also mentioned the anticipated full evening of singing and games geared to single youth.

The sun flickered and flashed light through leaves high overhead, and an occasional breeze made the work more pleasant. At one point Annie stopped and stretched a bit when several of the other young women did the same. Stealing another glance at Rudy, she couldn't help but wonder why Susie Yoder had not shown her face here at all today.

# Chapter 6

Esther Hochstetler trembled as she made her way to the back door, glancing over her shoulder toward the barn. Time had simply flown from her, and she crept into the house, having just returned from visiting an elderly aunt.

*Past time to start supper,* she thought, pulling out the heavy black frying pan from the low cupboard. It was in her best interest to serve up a hearty platter of fried chicken this supper hour.

*I could've stayed much longer,* she thought sadly of ailing Aunt Rebecca. *If only . . .*

But she had known better than to risk it. As it was, she'd missed the imposed limit on travel time by two long minutes.

Scurrying about the kitchen, she set the table and made ready for the meal. All the while she heard her little ones upstairs, looked after by her widowed mother. Such a good thing it was to have Mamma so close by. *Maybe, just maybe I won't catch it bad this time. . . .*

Any minute now, her mother would come down, describing the cute antics of her wee grandsons, as well as saying what a big help Laura had been again this short visit. Mamma would also say, *Why on earth don't you take more time away, Esther? You rush off and rush back . . . makes no sense.* Mamma had made a point of encouraging her to get out to quilting frolics and such, frequently pressing her as to why she stayed home so much. Impossible it was to explain, so she bit her lip and never said a word, letting Mamma think she'd become a loner, content to stay put.

*She'd never understand how I feel.*

But today Esther was especially grateful for the help her mother could give with the children. While tending to her elderly aunt, she'd had the strongest urge to get out more, to pull her weight in the community. Helping Aunt Rebecca was only part of it. Actually, being in what she assumed to be a safe environment was altogether enticing to her, as well.

The potatoes came to a rolling boil, and she thought she best be calling up the steps. She leaned her head that way, getting ready to tell Mamma to bring the boys down and let them play in the corner of the kitchen on the floor for a bit.

Suddenly her heart leaped within her. *Oh no, I forgot again!* The thought of having little Zach and John play on the bare floor had triggered her memory. *What's-a-matter with me? How dare I forget this chore?*

But she knew too well. More and more, she felt angry, even defiant, having buried the resentment deep inside where it festered. Bitterness was beginning to take shape in her dreams, and sometimes she would awaken terribly frightened, being chased by a vicious animal or attempting to run to safety, only to be frozen in place. Just as she felt even now, nearly motionless with panic wondering how she could get supper on the table, the floor scrubbed well enough for an inspection, and Mamma out of the house and back home where she lived in the *Dawdi Haus* of Esther's brother and wife. All in the space of a few minutes.

*O Lord God, it is not possible. I have failed once again.*

Just then Esther heard her daughter running down the stairs. Did she dare ask happy-go-lucky Laura for help? And if so, she might be found out, having shirked her own duty.

Breathless now, she looked at the clock, calculating the time. "Laura, I need you to wash up the floor, quick as a wink. And you mustn't miss a single corner, ya hear?"

Her only daughter thus far, fair-haired Laura, tiny for six years old but quick on her feet, nodded quickly. Laura's normally bright blue eyes became suddenly dull and far too serious. "I'll help ya, Mamma . . . jah, I promise I will."

*Poor dear,* thought Esther. And her mind raced back to the day she had discovered herself expecting a baby, with her wedding day still six weeks away.

*"Show me how much you love me. . . ."* Zeke had whispered it so often she eventually believed that what he wanted from her was all right. And oh, how she'd loved him. Desperately so. But being in love at sixteen and getting hitched up soon after were two entirely different things. She had not waited till "the appointed time," like her mamma and *Grandmammi* and all the women

before her surely had, although no one ever spoke of such things. At least not that she knew of.

Laura, their precious firstborn, was said to be premature, at least that's what Zeke had told the People. But she knew the truth. They both did. And she'd never forgiven herself, let alone her husband.

Sighing aloud, she tested the potatoes with a fork—still not quite done. Then she turned over the chicken pieces, careful not to splatter the grease, wishing she didn't feel so frantic.

*Mamma . . . I need to call Mamma down this instant.*

With a fleeting look at Laura down on her hands and knees scouring the linoleum, Esther made haste and headed upstairs. There she found Mamma rubbing two-year-old John's "ouchie" on his chubby finger and watching three-year-old Zach build a tower with blocks.

Pausing in the doorway, she placed her hand on her chest, catching her breath. The last thing in the world she wanted to do was to worry her dear mamma. Nor did she wish to cause alarm in her tiny boys. *No need*, she thought.

"Time to wash up for supper," she said softly. "Mamma, can ya help with that?"

Her mother turned to look at her and her pretty gray eyes twinkled as she smiled. "Why sure. We'll be right down."

A great sigh shuddered through her and escaped unnoticed, she hoped, as she turned away from the boys' room, making her way down the hall. On the landing, she steadied herself a bit, feeling slightly dizzy as she stood at the top, looking down. *Dear Lord God in heaven, grant me added grace—*

"Mamma! I'm nearly finished." Laura was calling up to her.

*Ach, good . . . good.* She was careful not to slip as she hurried down the steps, securing her balance by holding on to the railing.

When she looked at the shining floor and saw that Laura had not only washed it but she'd also taken an old towel and dried it to a nice shine, she fought back tears. "Oh, *lieb*—dear—such a girl you are. Such a wonderful-gut help to me."

Laura ran to her, holding out her slender arms. Esther held her near, laying her hand on the top of Laura's head. "Denki, ever so much!"

"I'll help Mammi with the boys now," Laura said, and she was off.

Quickly Esther went to check on the frying chicken. She put the lid on it and removed the pan from the fire, then set about draining the potatoes for mashing.

*Saved by the skin of my teeth*, she thought, resisting the urge to go to the back door and peer out. No sense in that. Any minute now she would hear the swift sound of work boots on the walkway.

Willing herself to breathe more slowly, she took down a large mixing bowl from the shelf and began mashing the well-cooked potatoes by hand. She wished Mamma would hurry and come down as she pressed the masher deep into the bowl, the steam rising to her face.

In spite of the heat, she felt suddenly cold, recalling the last time she'd made mashed potatoes, standing here near the cookstove. A good portion of the potatoes—bowl and all—had fallen to the floor, splattering every which way, all over the floor. For the life of her, she hadn't known how the accident had even happened . . . whether she'd momentarily blacked out or just what. But she'd ended up scurrying around as she had today, heart pounding in her temples at the thought of being *schlabbich*—careless. Never before had such a thing happened, and she couldn't help but wonder if her fingers had merely slipped. Nothing more.

Fortunately for her, no one but little Laura had known of the mess. And from then till now, she had been determined to be more careful, forcing herself to pay better attention to the work at hand . . . not letting herself fall into an alluring daydream, where she had come to find a place of solace from the tempest. Where she was a young girl again, single and happy, enjoying the freedom of being as unhitched as can be.

# Chapter 7

"There's just something energizing about autumn—I feel it in the air," Mamm said as she cooked sausage early Monday morning.

*Makes me want to paint all day,* Annie thought, having just come downstairs to help with breakfast.

Mamm wore her old green choring dress and long black apron. Her face had been scrubbed clean and her silver-blond hair freshly parted and pulled back in a tight, low bun beneath a clean white *Kapp*. "I feel compelled to redd up everything in sight," she said with a bright smile.

"Happens that way every fall, jah?" Annie moseyed to the sink and washed her hands thoroughly before counting out eight place settings of dishes and utensils for *Dawdi* and *Mammi* Zook, Daed and Mamm, Yonie, Luke, Omar, and herself.

That done, she returned to the cookstove and broke twelve fresh eggs into the large frying pan, stirring the mixture ever so slowly, just as Mamm had taught her when she was a little girl. Being the only daughter had its drawbacks, she'd found out early on, especially because she cared little for domestic chores. Her head in the clouds, she couldn't help herself . . . there was a potential painting everywhere she looked: the sky both at sunup and sundown, pastureland, wheat fields, and the canvas was constantly changing with the seasons . . . even hour by hour.

"When do you want to start cleanin' for house church?" Annie asked, even though the thought of scrubbing down walls and woodwork and waxing floors made her head pound, as if she were somehow wasting brain power. She would never voice what she was thinking, because such words were considered prideful.

"Why put off till tomorrow what can be done today?" Mamm replied, a knowing smile on her round face.

50

*I should've known.* Annie began frying the bacon in a second skillet, recalling the meadowlarks she'd seen pecking away in the side yard yesterday, their bright yellow breasts adorned with a black crescent as they moved about like miniature peacocks with determined strides. *I could live to be a hundred and not run out of things to paint!*

She had no idea how long she had been daydreaming, but soon the bacon was spitting and curling sufficiently. She flopped each piece onto a doubled-up paper towel to soak up the grease.

"Jah, I'll help you clean, Mamm," she said softly. Daydreamers got lost in the shuffle of life, her father had once told her. Well, she certainly didn't care about that, because getting lost was the most fun, whether it was autumn or any season. Still, there was the pressing matter of when, or more rightly put, *how* she could ever join her parents' church. The clock was ticking on that issue, and she felt the pressure coming straight at her every time Daed and Mamm glanced her way, their eyes clearly conveying the question that weighed so heavily in their minds. *How long before I am asked to leave the People?*

She suppressed the fact that she must make a decision, pushing the urgency down into her soul, where it would resurface the next time her eyes caught her father's look of not only concern but disappointment.

*How will I live with myself?*

It was midafternoon—between relining the dresser drawers with fresh newspaper and cleaning out the cupboards—when Annie heard the mail truck stop in front of the house. Quick as a wink, she took off running down the long, sloping front yard. She slipped her hand inside the mailbox and pulled out several letters for Mamm and one for her. Not waiting a second longer, she tore open the envelope and began to read the latest news from Louisa.

*Thursday, October 27*
*Dear Annie,*

*Thanks for writing back so promptly. I hope you are well and enjoying all the beauty of autumn as we are here, although the earlier gold of our aspen trees is nothing to compare with your rainbow of colors there.*

*A lot has happened since I last wrote, so I guess I need to get you caught up. Don't freak out when you read this, because I'm not at all sorry. Well, I am for reasons other than the obvious, but I'm not devastated.*

*Things with the wedding planning had been going badly . . . in all sorts of ways. Totally out of control. And to get to the point: I won't be marrying Michael. This may sound horrendous, but I think you'll understand, because simply put, Michael is not the man for me. In so many ways, he's anything but Mr. Right. I'm so glad I discovered this before it was too late!*

*I'm really wishing for a less complicated life right now, longing to get away. I don't mean to be bold, but is there any chance I might come and visit you for a few weeks . . . even a month? I know this is sudden, and I certainly wouldn't want to put you and your family out in any way, Annie. I'd be happy to pay for my keep and help with chores, as well. I really just need to "get away from it all," as they say, and clear my head.*

*I'll eagerly await your next letter.*

> *With love,*
> *Louisa*

*P.S. I'm exhibiting my art students' work soon, and I'll take some pictures to send to you . . . or better yet, take them on my smart phone and bring them along.*

Annie was dumbfounded. "Her wedding's off and she wants to come here?" she voiced softly, feeling just awful for her friend. But she reminded herself that Louisa hadn't sounded heartbroken whatsoever, which was downright peculiar . . . especially considering how much in love she had seemed to be.

*Funny how that is,* she thought. *Head over heels in love one day and completely befuddled the next.*

But it was rather clear Louisa's situation was far different from her own. Still, Annie needed to think, to really ponder Louisa's letter, and while doing so, she headed across the road, spotting one of the peacocks strutting along, its enormous train of tail feathers spread to the full. These birds craved a peaceful setting such as their farmland here in Paradise.

Annie went and sat on the nearby fence simply observing the grand bird. *They need stretching room,* Daed had said some years back, when first he'd built the large pen and perches. With a wingspan of up to six feet, it was obvious a peacock could become stressed otherwise. Annie had seen this happen down yonder, at big brother Jesse's place, where he, too, raised the colorful birds.

*Sounds like Louisa needs some stretching room, too. . . .*

She opened the letter once again and read the part where Louisa was politely asking to come visit. Annie found it fascinating, especially because not too many days ago she'd thought of going to Denver . . . to Louisa's wedding! The whole thing struck her as odd—and to think a fancy rich girl wanted to come here. To an Amish farm, no less, where peahens sat on their nests of eggs and cows came home for milking twice a day.

*She has no idea what she's asking,* Annie thought, yet she knew of other Englischers who'd come and stayed to sort out their lives. Some had gleaned simplicity, and others had even desired to learn to speak their language. Most of the time, though, outsiders simply did not fully connect with the Plain community and didn't stay long. But Annie was quite sure that's not what Louisa had in mind. Still, she hoped her own stonewalling—not joining church—along with putting Rudy Esh off, would not go against her now. Because, with all of her heart, she wanted Louisa to come and stay for as long as she pleased.

Watching the three-year-old peacock prance toward her now, she locked her gaze on the "eye" in the center of each of the feathers. What striking violet, green, red, and gold! Where on God's earth could an artist see such striking hues all blended on the same moving, breathing canvas?

She sat very still, not wanting to distract the bird, not wanting to stress him in the least. When he seemed to stare right at her, she said softly, "Goodness' sake, you're a brave one."

The bird did not move, and she took this rare opportunity to lean forward, amazed again at the depth of color on each feather.

"If Louisa comes, you just might be one of her first paintings here," she told the peacock, feeling silly talking to an animal.

*If Daed agrees, that is. He would put his foot down if he knew Louisa was an art instructor . . . and I a disobedient daughter, hiding my sin in Julia's attic!*

She waited till the peacock turned, at last, strutting back to the pen, slowly closing his train and letting it drag behind him.

Drawing in a deep breath, she realized now what Mamm had sensed in the air earlier. Not only was it the urgency of getting work completed before the onslaught of winter, she also felt a flood of excitement. She could enjoy it for the moment, because she was not at all sure what her father would say about Louisa's request. Especially because she was considered to be on the very fringe of the church, although she still attended Preaching service regularly. And there was the knotty problem of adding a single girl to the mix of three courting-age brothers in the house.

She climbed off the fence, anxious now to talk over Louisa's letter with her parents, particularly her father.

*Won't Daed be chagrined to find out my close friend is a worldly Englischer?* She trudged back toward the house, clinging to a small ray of hope.

# Chapter 8

Finding Mamm alone in the kitchen having another tall glass of apple cider was a consolation. Neither Yonie nor Luke was in from plowing, and Omar wasn't in from the barn snitching the usual chocolate chip cookies, his favorite afternoon snack.

Annie had slipped into the room unnoticed and sat down at the table, observing her mother's purposeful movements—back and forth between the counter where she was chopping vegetables, then to the big kettle on her left, scarcely moving her feet, only her upper body, the graceful rhythm of an experienced cook. Mamm chanted the necessary ingredients, depositing diced potatoes, chopped carrots, small onions, and, last of all, the cubed stew meat, already browned in butter, into the kettle. A bit of paprika, two small bay leaves, some flour, and a dash of allspice, along with the sugar, lemon juice, a clove of garlic, boiling water, and plenty of ground black pepper, and the stew was ready for more simmering.

Mamm turned unexpectedly. "Oh, goodness me. I didn't see ya there!"

Annie hoped now was the best time to bring up Louisa's letter.

Mamm tilted her head. "What's got ya lookin' like that?"

"I was just wonderin' . . ." She stopped.

"Aw, just spit it out, Annie-girl."

"All right. Louisa, my pen pal, wants to come for a visit." When Mamm seemed not the least bit flustered by the notion of having an Englischer around, Annie added, "She wrote that she needed some time away."

"Well, sure, tell her to come."

"But . . . she might need to stay longer than just a few nights."

Mamm nodded, still smiling. "How long would that be?"

"I don't know, a few weeks . . . maybe a month."

"She's not runnin' away from home, I hope."

"Nothin' like that." *Running from her beau maybe.*

"Well, it might be a gut idea to talk this over with your father, 'specially since there are three young men still living in the house."

She wasn't surprised at her mother's sensible response, but with all of her heart, she wanted to see Louisa face-to-face for the first time ever. She had daydreamed plenty of times about it. Now her chance was here at last, and she longed to stay up late talking with Louisa in person, to see her artwork, and to show her around the farm. And just maybe to get some pointers from a real art instructor who was a wonderful-good friend! These thoughts made her giddy with anticipation.

Annie made her way through the screened-in porch, where boots and shoes were lined up along the wall nearest the door. She hurried around the side of the house and down to the road, going to check for Daed first in the barn. Not finding him there, she climbed the hayloft ladder and walked the expanse of the barn's uppermost level to the wide outside door.

Pushing hard to swing the door open, she stood at the top of the grassy barn bridge, an earthen ramp where they moved the various farm equipment in and out. Looking out at the vast field to the south, she could see Daed and Luke and two teams of mules pulling the handheld plows.

*I'll have to wait till later*, she thought, feeling discouraged again as she stood there.

One of more than a dozen barn kitties skittered across the wood floor and rubbed against her ankle. "Aw, you cute thing. Where's your mamma?"

Going to the far corner of the loft, Annie raised her long skirt to climb onto one of the square bales stacked there. The kitten followed her. Annie sat down and picked up the black kitty. "My friend Louisa has a gray cat," she whispered. "If she brings Muffin here for a visit, won't that be fun?" Annie stared at the barn rafters, watching for the bats she knew were up there sleeping the day away. And she held the wee kitten in her arms, feeling its rumbly purring.

*How can I convince my father?*

She contemplated how her friend might be feeling now, getting so close to her wedding day and then changing her mind. But Annie knew she had done nearly the same thing to Rudy, though she hadn't waited till the last minute.

Just then, she heard shuffling below in the stable area. Silently she slipped down off the baled hay and crept to one of the hay holes, where they dropped bales down to the cattle. She peeked through the opening to see if Yonie was nearby.

Sure enough. Smiling to herself, she called to him. "Yonie Zook!" Then she darted back so he couldn't see where she was, teasing him.

"Who's there?"

She could see his wheat-colored hair through the opening in the floor. Annie's favorite of her six brothers, Yonie was only eighteen months younger, part of the reason they were so close. And there was something uncanny about him—he understood her better than all her other brothers.

"Yonie!" she said again, unable to hold in her laughter.

"Ach, I should know you're up in the haymow, Annie. If ya want to talk, then ya best be comin' down."

She shrugged. "Well, you must have eyes on top of your head, brother."

"Nope, I ain't at all like Daed who sees and hears everything . . . nearly like almighty God." Yonie's head popped into view as he climbed up the ladder. He grinned at her, a long piece of straw stuck in his mouth. "If I was, maybe I'd already have me a girl to hitch up with."

"You shouldn't have a speck of trouble findin' a girl to marry." Annie figured her brother had plenty of time to find the right bride. After all, the boys could marry a girl several years younger . . . so if this year's crop of sixteen-year-old girls didn't take his fancy, then maybe next year's would.

Yonie sat on the edge of the hay hole, swinging his legs. "Well, look at *you*, Annie. I thought you'd be wed by now."

Climbing back up the hay bales, Annie reached for the long rope. She swung across the expanse of the loft, her legs tight against the rope so her dress would not billow out. Her feet were so callused from going barefoot early spring to late fall, she was able to cling easily, though her toes strained upward. "You goin' to the next singing?" she asked, riding all the way up . . . up toward the rafters and then back.

"Well, if you are, I guess I *have* to go and drop you off, now don't I?" His eyes shone with tomfoolery.

She laughed, keeping her back straight as a board as she flew. "Seems to me you could go and stay a mite longer than five minutes. That way you might actually meet a cute girl to take out ridin'."

He shook his head. "Got no interest in Amish girls just now."

"Brave soul, you are."

"And . . . I have some plans, comin' up soon. But Daed knows nothing 'bout it, so keep quiet."

She let the rope take her across the loft once again. "Bet I can guess."

"Like fun you can." He patted his straw hat. "Unless you've been eavesdropping."

"Oh, I figure you're not long for here . . . that's what. Soon as all the plowin's done, you'll head out to do some hunting in the woods somewhere with your friends. Ain't so?"

"Well, if that don't beat all. How'd ya know?"

"I heard nothin'. Honestly."

"Well, then, you're a strange one, 'cause that's exactly what I have in mind to do."

Still holding the long rope, she said, "There's plenty of deer comin' down to the hay fields, nearly every evening now. Seems you wouldn't have to leave home to bag yourself a buck or doe."

Yonie frowned. "I've thought of spending daylight in a tree stand, but the deer can spot you a quarter mile away. Honestly, though, just gettin' away might do me good . . . for now."

"Well, if ya have to go, fine and dandy." She made her way down off the hay and joined him by the ladder. "I need to ask you something first, though." Quickly she told him about Louisa's hope to visit. "What should I tell Daed?"

"Do like I'm gonna do. Tell him right out."

"But I'm a girl."

He pulled the straw out of his mouth. "That's where you're ferhoodled, all mixed up, if ya think you can't speak your mind. Like Mamm does. I daresay he might just listen if you don't hem and haw . . . the way you do sometimes."

She thought on that.

But before she could say more, Yonie spoke again. "Daed likes folk to get to the point and be done with it. So if you're gonna ask him anything, do it with confidence—I know you've got it in ya."

She realized if Yonie was going hunting, then Louisa could have his bedroom upstairs for a week or so maybe.

"You go 'n' bring in the herd. I'll find Daed," she said, practicing speaking up to a man this minute, bossing her brother but good.

"Thataway." Yonie shooed her out of the barn, chuckling.

She ran hard as she could out to meet her father, who was walking her way, wearing the caked-on dirt from the field on his work boots and the bottom of his pant legs, looking like he could use a good hot meal and a warm bath. But the big galvanized tub wouldn't be brought indoors till Saturday night, like always.

Glad that Luke and Omar were nowhere near, she blurted her request when she reached him. "I'm hopin' you won't mind if my pen pal comes to stay with us for a while."

"What's that you say?"

"You know . . . my English friend, Louisa? She needs to soak up some of the peace here, I'm thinkin'."

"Why's a fancy girl want to come to Lancaster County? Is she lookin' to be Plain?" Daed's face grew more serious, and he reached up to tug on his long beard.

"Well, she's never written that." *Of course not. Louisa would never give up her art,* she thought suddenly.

His eyes were softer now. "Does she need a place to stay? Is that what you mean?"

"She just wants to visit."

"And what do her parents say?"

"I don't know."

Daed frowned suddenly. "Have ya given any thought to where she'd bed down? We've got a houseful of boys . . . 'cept for you and Mamm." He paused, then he continued. "And what would she do durin' Preaching service? And there are plenty of weddings comin' up, too."

She couldn't mention Yonie's plans to be gone till he shared that with Daed himself. As for her father's other concerns, she honestly couldn't say. "I'm not sure 'bout church and the weddings." But just then she realized her chance, a way to make some sense of this. "Maybe she'd want to go along to church and the weddings and whatnot all. Might be interesting for her, don't you think?"

"A fancy girl would find a three-hour meeting, perched on a wooden bench, quite trying, Annie. Not interesting. And she won't understand much of what's goin' on." His eyes were serious. "You're not thinking sensibly, I can see that. And I best be warnin' ya, too . . . there'd be no shirking your chores with Mamm nor your work over at Cousin Julia's, you know."

She sighed, still hoping he might surprise her and say that Louisa could come.

He continued. "Honestly, I don't know how I feel about it, especially with my daughter still so apathetic toward the church. This girl might lead you astray, Annie."

"But I've been writin' to her all these years," she said without thinking. Then she bit her lip. "I'm sorry, Daed. I didn't mean to be rude."

"I'll be thinkin' on it." He looked away. "Don't ask me again. . . ."

She wanted to groan, but she squelched it. Besides, he had a point. She was at high risk for the world, the flesh, and the devil. If the people knew the truth, they'd think she was a hardened sinner already.

She shrugged off the annoying thought. It was much more pleasant to hope that she and her family might impart the peace Louisa was desperate for instead of dwelling on her own transgressions.

# Chapter 9

Jesse watched his daughter hurry through the half-plowed field, making a beeline toward the barn. *She won't leave a single stone unturned,* he assumed.

He had not shown an iota of interest in Annie's pen pal through the years, and he didn't feel he'd been kept in the dark by either Annie or her mother. Still it was hard not to wonder about the young woman's motives. Was Louisa simply curious, as were the gawking tourists?

Thirsty now, he began to make his way across the furrowed soil, turning his thoughts to Caleb Esh's comments about Annie and Rudy. He hadn't been able to dismiss them, even though the grapevine was entirely unreliable. Yet knowing Rudy as he did, it was perplexing why a staunch young man had not been able to persuade Annie to marry. It didn't add up. *Something's peculiar with that. . . .*

Then it dawned on him—Annie was surely stronger-willed than her former beau, and maybe more so than a good number of the young men in the church district. He found this realization not only startling but secretly a bit satisfying. Annie knew her mind, that was clear. Having seen the earnestness in her eyes regarding her English friend's visit, for instance, Jesse thought he might at least run it by the other preacher, Moses Hochstetler, Zeke's elderly uncle. Then, if need be, he'd work his way up to the bishop.

*We'll just see what's what.*

All-in from the day, he made his way through the barnyard toward the road. When he came near to the back door, he caught a whiff of what smelled like beef stew and hurried inside to investigate.

*A fine meal by the best cook ever*, he thought, going and slipping his arm around his wife's stout waist. Accustomed to his furtive interest prior to meals, she lifted the kettle lid. Jesse leaned into the fragrant steam, eyes closed, breathing in . . . then turned to the woman he loved and planted a kiss on her soft face. "Keep this simmerin' a bit longer," he said, winking.

"Why, sure." She smiled knowingly, leaning toward him.

"I'll be makin' a quick trip out."

"All right then, love," she said. "Stew and corn bread will be waitin'."

With the memory of the mouth-watering aroma lingering, he hurried out to hitch up his fastest driving horse to the family carriage.

Annie found Yonie already starting the afternoon milking. She stood near the center aisle of the milking area, seeing two rows of cows' hind parts and tails, and below, the manure ditch. She waited for Yonie to see her, and when he did, she motioned to him.

He sauntered over to her once all the cows were hooked up to air compressor-run milkers. His hazel eyes were bright with the question. "Well?"

"I did what you said. But Daed's goin' to think about it. So who knows."

"You worry too much." He flashed an infectious grin.

"Seems to me I'm allowed to fret a bit. *You* haven't spent nearly a lifetime writing to Louisa Stratford. This might be my only chance to meet her."

He frowned momentarily, and then there came the twinkle in his eye. "Hmm. Stratford. Sounds like a high and mighty name for a *best friend*, ain't?"

She didn't know where on earth he'd gotten the idea Louisa was that close to her. Not unless Mamm had mentioned something, which was unlikely. Other than their mother, nobody knew of Annie's close friendship with Louisa except . . .

"Wait a minute! Have you been talkin' to Mrs. Zimmerman?"

Yonie grinned. She'd caught him. "That's for me to know and for you to find out."

"Well, I just did!" She should've put it together the instant Yonie had declared Louisa as her best friend. Mrs. Zimmerman was their busybody mail carrier, and her daughter, Dory, was one of the prettiest English neighbors around. So Yonie was interested in the local girls—just not Amish ones.

Yonie suddenly looked sheepish.

"Aha!" Annie exclaimed. "I'll keep your secret if you keep mine. Jah?"

"Nothin' to keep, you silly." With that he turned back to attend to the milking.

*I know better,* she thought, for she'd seen the blush of embarrassment on his face. Well, no wonder Yonie wasn't so keen on attending singings and other youth activities. She just hoped he didn't do something stupid, like fall hard for the wrong girl . . . like Louisa had surely fallen for the wrong fellow.

She headed back to the house, hoping to hear something soon from Daed, trying to remain optimistic.

"As a father, I'm concerned 'bout Annie's worldly friend," Jesse told Moses Hochstetler at the elder minister's kitchen table, where they drank their coffee black.

"What's that?" Moses asked, struggling to hear.

Jesse thought of writing down what he wanted to discuss, that his daughter's pen pal wished to come for a lengthy visit. And he sure wouldn't want to tempt his youngest sons with a modern girl in the house.

He moved closer to the elder minister and proceeded to speak directly into his ear. "Our Annie's got herself a worldly friend who's lookin' for a dose of the simple life."

A glint of recognition passed over the furrowed brow. "Ah, jah, she's a right good one . . . your daughter."

"I'd like to keep it that way," Jesse muttered.

As if Moses had heard, he adjusted his glasses, studying Jesse. "What's this 'bout an Englischer? She's not comin' to spy, is she?"

Jesse reiterated that the girl, as far as he knew, was looking only for some respite from the world.

"Well, sure. Why not have her come, then?"

"I've got myself three sons still in the house. It wonders me if it's such a good idea to bring a fancy girl under my roof." He pondered Yonie, especially, who seemed to be working his way toward the fringe. "Sure wouldn't want my boys taking a shine to Louisa. We can't be losin' any more of our young folk."

Moses cupped his ear with his gnarled hand. "In all truth, the Englischer might just be the thing to push Annie off the fence, so to speak. Could be a wonderful-good idea."

Jesse couldn't imagine such a thing.

"Well . . . I know we must be patient with our youth."

Moses nodded his head, as though pondering further. "This worldly girl might be a godsend, the answer to your problem. Might move Annie closer to joinin' church, her friend bein' so interested in our way of life."

"Hadn't thought of that."

"But I hope the outsider won't cause any confusion in our midst, 'specially in your house, but that she'll receive the peace she seeks," Moses said. "I would also hope she might fit in with the womenfolk here . . . go along with Annie to market, quilting bees, and such."

Jesse finished his coffee, still thinking of Annie, who was not past her Rumschpringe. He wished she would continue to attend the youth activities and find herself a new beau.

Getting up from the table, he waved his hat, thanking Moses for the coffee. He hurried out to his horse and carriage, anxious to return to his wife's delectable beef stew.

Riding along the countryside, Jesse waved at acquaintances in several passing buggies. Then, once he'd passed the most worrisome intersection, he leaned back, contemplating Moses' agreeable nature. Such a compassionate, upstanding man he was, but his days of prophesying were surely a thing of the past. Since taking a hard fall on the ice years back, not only had his hearing been greatly affected, but his ability to stand long enough to deliver the main long sermon had, as well. Old Moses, as some of the People referred to him, could no longer remember the required sequence of biblical stories and Scriptures to accompany them. So, then, was it even possible he was right? That spunky Annie might simply need to encounter firsthand a worldly friend to nudge her closer toward making her lifelong vow to God and the church? Only time would tell.

# Chapter 10

On Friday Annie made haste to Cousin Julia's. Once her work was done, she would have more time this afternoon to paint, since she'd finished up every piece of ironing last Tuesday. Still holding out hope for Louisa's visit, she thought of her present painting in light of her friend's artistic achievement. Far as she could tell, the scene depicting the setting of the kidnapping was her best work yet. All that was left was the highlighting of tree trunks and branches, as well as making sure the sunbeams skipped off the creek water as it made its way past the old bridge.

*I want Louisa to see it*, thought Annie.

As she walked, she thought of all the places she wanted to show her friend, but most of all she wanted to share with Louisa her private little artist's sanctuary. *She's heard all about it in my letters . . . and she'll keep my secret, for sure!*

When Annie reached the Ranck home, she caught sight of James and Molly playing "horsy and buggy" in the side yard, where James had his little sister tied to a cardboard box, with the rope "reins" in his hands. Molly appeared to be quite a lot better, and Annie was glad of it.

"What's that you're doin'?" she called to them. "Seems to me Molly ought to be the one riding in the carriage, and James, you could be the big strong horse."

That got big smiles from both children, and right away James began untying and switching the horse and driver. "Molly's bumps aren't so itchy no more," he said, pointing out several on his sister's arm to show Annie.

"Jah, I can see that." She stood there, watching James work the knots out of the slender rope he'd put around Molly's little arms. "You must think you're Amish today, both of ya."

"That's right," Molly said, eyes sparkling with excitement. "We're just like you."

"But you never bring your father's horse and buggy over here, do ya, Cousin Annie?" James never even looked up at her, just kept untying the rope.

"By the time I hitched up, that would take a good thirty minutes, so why not just walk over here in the same amount of time?" she explained.

"Or you could hop in a car, like we do, and get here even quicker."

She tousled his hair, thinking he was mighty smart for his little britches. "Jah, there's a lot of things one could do, I 'spect. But we Amish do what we do for a reason."

"What's that?" Molly said, obviously glad to be free and on the other side of the box now, holding the reins big as she pleased.

"Well, we obey our church rules. And, besides, it's much better for us to walk when we *could* be riding. Even better is to hitch up horse and carriage than to drive a car. It keeps us slowed down some . . . not in such an awful hurry." She thought she might be stepping on some toes, so she stopped right there. After all, the Rancks were as fancy as anyone around here, being Mennonite and all.

"I wish we had a horse and a buggy," James said, moving his head as if he were a prancing steed.

*The grass is always greener*, she thought.

James was off running now, with Molly behind him, hurrying to keep up. She smiled over her shoulder at them . . . so adorable. She thought again of Rudy and what a fine father he might have been. But he was off going to sing-ings and taking someone else home, and rightly so.

Refusing to fall into a quagmire of self-pity, she hurried toward the house and got right to work redding up the children's rooms upstairs. Then she set about cleaning the large bathroom, thankful not to have that chore to do at home. With an outhouse, there was much less upkeep, she decided, although there were plenty of times, especially in the winter, when she would have liked to close the door on herself and the large tub Daed brought into the kitchen from the shed, where she and Mamm got the Saturday night bathing routine started. At least she was usually first or second, not nearly as grimy as the boys and Daed always were. Of course, she and Mamm often took sponge baths in the privacy of their rooms, using a large washbowl and a kettle of hot water. Same thing her grandparents had to do, because they were too frail to get in and out of a tub anyway. The boys and Daed would slip out to the makeshift shower in the barn and rinse off every other day, though they complained of it being cold as ice in the wintertime. Still, there was nothing worse to Annie than feeling dirty.

She and her sister-in-law Sarah Mae had often had conversations about such things. And now, Sarah Mae and Jesse Jr. and their children lived in a farmhouse with two large bathrooms—approved by the ministers, because they were merely renting the place. Occasionally Annie had even hitched up the team and gone over to enjoy their bathtub in the heat of the summer, soaking away the cares and soil of the day. Sometimes, too, Sarah Mae let her use her very own bubble bath, which was a special treat.

*Ach, no!* She was nearly aghast at the thought of Louisa, who was used to taking as many as two showers a day. *Oh, goodness! Shouldn't I write and tell her?*

But she would do nothing at all to discourage Louisa from coming, if Daed allowed it. Annie found herself grinning. *Louisa might just wish she'd never longed for the simple life!*

Exhausted from precious little sleep, Esther felt her muscles beginning to relax now as she tucked in both Zach and John for, hopefully, a long afternoon nap. Little John had awakened with an asthmatic attack at midnight, and she had held him while sitting up in the rocking chair in his room, making sure he was breathing. Making sure his struggling cries would not awaken Zeke, too.

Now she sat on the double bed, reaching over to put her hand on John's tiny forehead. "Close your peepers," she said to both boys, and they blinked their eyes shut obediently.

Sitting there, she gazed down fondly at them, nearly like twins in looks, and so close in age, but quite different temperamentally. Zach was similar to big sister Laura as a young one, easygoing and anxious to please. Baby John, on the other hand, was restless and more apt to have upset stomachs, like Esther herself was these days. He had started out quite frail due to his breathing problems—*a predisposition to upper bronchial problems*, the Strasburg pediatrician had told them early on.

She realized how awful small her little boys looked in their big bed. "Sleep tight," she whispered, absently touching her abdomen, where yet another baby grew. She left the door open enough to hear John should he begin to wheeze again.

Sighing, she tiptoed to her bedroom, in desperate need of rest before Laura arrived home from school. The thought of standing and making supper was beyond her at the moment, and she dismissed it till later. She wished she might simply slip into her nightclothes and sleep soundly, dead to this world, and absolutely irresistible was the urge to do so. Yet she shuddered at the thought of making herself too vulnerable. Two other times she'd done so, but no longer. These days she kept all her clothes on, including her long apron, even on the hottest summer day during a rare short nap. Today would be no exception.

She turned to close her door but thought better of it, still on edge from last night's frightful spell. Not knowing if their wee boy would live to see the light of day had caused her an ongoing heartache. Yet he had, and she attributed his recovery to the inhaler she kept near for such alarming occurrences, although five months had passed since the last episode. What a true relief the rather long reprieve had been. Still, her heart feared there might come a day when she would merely sleep through his nighttime attack.

But, no, she had some confidence that young Zach would be aware, sharing the same bed, and come to get her help. On the other hand, her husband, once asleep for the night, was out so soundly that not even a lightning strike could shake him awake. She knew this to be true, as he'd slept through a deafening thunderstorm not so many years back, their barn hit by lightning in the night. In some ways, her husband's unusually deep slumber was a blessing, but in the case of their youngest, it was a tremendous point of ongoing concern.

She walked to the window and sat on the small cane chair, one her father had made for her hope chest the year before she met Zeke. *I miss you, Pop,* she thought, wishing her father might have lived to see the births of Zach and John, and the new little life she was now carrying. She had never forgotten his grandfatherly delight over Laura, as a brand-new babe, despite the fact Esther knew he suspected baby Laura too hearty an infant to be called premature. But he and Mamma had never questioned that, were never outwardly skeptical.

She had yet another reason to wish Pop had survived his heart attack. A terribly selfish one. Even so, had he lived, she wondered if even he would have seen fit to help her, since all men were considered ordained of God, the sovereign head of their families. And, invariably, what they wanted they got, no questions asked. She'd never had the nerve to ask another married woman, not even Mamma, only silently observing those whose expressions were consistently cheerful and those who were merely marking time, as she was.

*Waiting for my number to be called,* she thought woefully, staring at the woodshed and the outhouse beyond. *Why was I born a woman?* She was convinced if she were a man she would not treat anyone—human or beast—the way Zeke treated her. But, of course, that was a futile thing to ponder. Truth was, the Creator-God had seen fit to make her a woman. A woman whose needs were ignored by a man who did lip service to cherishing her but who never once considered her hopes and wishes. Such thoughts made her feel terribly guilty, as though she were going against everything she knew she was called to do—under God and man. *Submission is my only choice.*

Since childhood, she had been taught compliance, observing it in action. It spilled into all areas of their lives, including acquiescence to the ministers, who ruled as they deemed best. So the façade of peace saturated the community, but she knew better.

Hearing John's sudden cries, she rose and went to him. As if by some punishment for her lamentable contemplation, her time of rest had been cut short.

Not to awaken Zach, she went around the side of the bed nearest the wall and picked up whimpering John. She carried him to her room and closed the door.

Walking the length of the room, she felt too weary to calm him. "Shh, I've got ya . . . Mamma's right here," she said, fighting her sad little tears as she held him near.

# Chapter 11

*Saturday morning, Nov. 5*
*Dear Louisa,*

*I'm so excited!*

*Oh, before I get carried away with my news—how are you? I hope you're doing all right and not second-guessing your decision to back away from your marriage plans. Honestly, though, I've been doing some of that here, but for different reasons, of course.*

*Well, here's why I'm so happy. My family wants you to feel free to stay with us for as long as you wish. My brother Yonie is going off hunting, so he'll give up his room for the time being. If you decide to stay for longer, there are two empty bedrooms in our Dawdi Haus, if you don't mind my grandparents. That's entirely up to you. Just let me know so we can have everything shiny and clean for you!*

*I must hurry off to a quilting bee. We're making a wedding quilt for my eldest brother's niece (his wife's niece, that is, but here we're all family, no matter by marriage or just what).*

*I'm looking forward to seeing you, face-to-face!*

*With love,*
*Annie*

She was thrilled to be able to send the written welcome to Louisa, indeed. She pushed the stamp onto the envelope and then quickly wrote the address. She headed down the stairs and out the front door to the mailbox at the end of the lawn. Daed had been as agreeable as she'd ever known him to be, which seemed to delight Mamm no end.

"That's good . . . keep everybody happy," Annie said, pulling up the little red flag on the hefty mailbox. "Not the easiest thing in the world."

❖

By the following Tuesday, on her early morning walk to Cousin Julia's, Annie had what she guessed might be a brain wave, as Yonie liked to say of a sudden—and terrific—idea. And when Julia agreed that she most definitely could eat her lunch in the attic, Annie took advantage of her time to paint.

Studying the canvas, which was still resting on the easel, she knew exactly what she must add to the picture. *The final touch . . .*

The account of the small boy's disappearance was quite clear in her mind, and she was convinced the tale was incomplete without the peach stone. A boyish token, of sorts. As a young girl, she'd heard other children talk of squeezing a peach pit hard enough and long enough, till it would eventually sprout. A made-up story, most likely. But little Isaac, long presumed dead, had carried the stone with him everywhere, as she recalled from hearing the details of his kidnapping time and again. She'd known this firsthand, as well, from having spent many happy hours in the company of the imaginative boy.

*Isaac, my little friend . . . lost forever.* The thought never ceased to put a grind in her teeth, this fiery anger she'd never voiced.

So solemnly, even crossly, she painted a tiny oval-shaped peach pit on the board of the long tree swing. Hard as it was to spot in the picture, she impulsively brush-stroked a pale yellow ray of sunshine falling on it.

*Now the painting's complete,* she thought.

Minutes later when Julia brought up a big slice of apple pie, she was so taken by the image on the canvas, she stood there and stared.

"Is something the matter?" Annie asked.

"My word, no . . . this is beautiful. I never would've guessed you could paint such splendor." Julia's smile was as radiant as the sunbeams shining on the locust trees and the stream. "Wait here just a minute . . . I have an idea." With that, she turned and hurried back down the stairs.

*Where's she going?*

But Annie wasn't worried what Julia was up to, for the woman was as keyed up as anyone she knew. She could burst out laughing at the most unpredictable thing, and Annie believed because of this, young James and Molly were the most contented and carefree children. Even more so than her own nieces and nephews. No, there was truly something remarkable about spontaneous laughter in the home, and Julia had a corner on that happiness, for sure. She was also quite eager to extend herself to others—taking meals to sick neighbors and driving elderly folk to doctor appointments. A true friend, indeed.

In no time, Julia was back and waving a paper that looked to be clipped out of a magazine. "Here now, and don't say no till you hear me out," she said. "In fact, why don't you sit right down a minute and I'll read it to you."

Annie did so, listening as Julia read about an "artistic opportunity," where the first-place winner would receive some classes with an experienced artist.

"Now what do you think of that?"

Annie had no idea what she was getting at. "I just don't know. . . ."

"I'll take a digital picture of your painting and submit it for the contest."

She could see Julia was convinced. "Then what? If I should win—which I know I won't—what then?"

"Well, it says here the first-place winner will be featured on the January cover of *Farm and Home Journal* and will receive three art lessons by a master artist. Oh, Annie, you'd finally have the chance to study art."

Annie shook her head. "No, no, this is a bad idea." *Such education smacks of headiness and high-mindedness . . . frowned on by the People.* "I don't have a scholarly bone in my body."

"That's where I think you're wrong. You know I believe in your work. This is a wonderful opportunity for you. It's a fine magazine; Irvin and I have read it for years."

"Well, it may be good 'n' all, but that's not what I'm concerned 'bout."

Julia's face grew more serious. "What, then?"

Annie gritted her teeth, but she felt sure Julia knew already. "Bein' found out—this place here where I work and all. I wouldn't want anything to change, wouldn't want my father to know what I'm doin'."

"Honestly, Annie, you're taking a risk every time you come up here. But you haven't joined the church yet, so why's this such a concern?"

Julia had a point. "Still, I haven't made my decision on that."

Julia reached out a hand. "In your heart you're just not sure, Annie. . . ." She paused, tears welling up. "Maybe the Lord has something more for you."

Annie inhaled slowly. She knew what Julia believed—that a person could know the Lord in *an intimate way*, as she liked to say. Annie sighed. "I've never said I wasn't going to make my church vow. If it weren't for my art it would be ever so easy . . . I might have already. But my first love tends to get in the way."

Julia nodded. "I know you want to improve and keep working on your craft, getting better with each painting, just as Irvin and I see you doing every time you come here."

She offered her thanks, grateful Julia hadn't pushed with all her talk of salvation, as she had in the past. "You've been so kind to me, and I appreciate it. Really I do."

Julia's bright eyes held Annie's gaze. "What's to lose if you let me submit your painting to the contest? I'll even pay for the fee."

*I'll never win anyway,* thought Annie.

"Pretty please let me do this for you?" Julia entreated. "At least for a chance to have a few pointers from an instructor."

Annie suddenly thought of Louisa. "My pen pal is comin' to visit, and she's an instructor, but that'll have to be kept quiet, I'm thinkin'." She went on to say how Louisa even held exhibits for her students and was doing so this very week.

"Well then, if you should happen to win the prize, your artist friend could go along with you to the classes. Maybe so?"

"I don't know. . . . I can't see myself taking classes out in public. Besides, as I said, there's no way on earth my painting can possibly win."

Knowing Julia as she did, she would be trapped right here in the attic today unless she agreed. Even if she didn't, Julia might simply snap the picture with her fancy camera and send it off on her computer—by something called email, which both she and Louisa knew all about—and submit her painting anyway.

She rose and went to look at the image once again. Closing her eyes, she cleared her vision. Then, opening them, she attempted to look at her own work through different eyes. She had in mind that her paintings should have a purpose, but just what she didn't know. Surely it was not to vent her anger over Isaac's long-ago disappearance? *I must forgive whoever took Isaac away. . . .*

"All right, dear cousin," she whispered, "if you must. But I'll be payin' the fee."

Julia hurried to her side. "Oh, this makes me so happy! Wait till I tell Irvin. He'll set up some lights in here and we'll use the digital camera until we get it just right."

"Best not let the word slip out," she reminded her. Constantly she felt she was repeating herself about this secret . . . this beloved place. "Promise?"

Julia nodded, pushing the paper in front of Annie's nose once again so she could sign her name. Once that was done, she grinned at her. "You won't be sorry. I just know you have a very good chance!" Then she disappeared down the steps.

Annie leaned against the far wall, looking at the painting, at the swing hanging from the tree. She stared so hard at it, for a split second she thought it had moved slightly, but that was impossible. The painting was as real to her as her memories of her childish bond with the missing boy.

She hoped Louisa might not be troubled if ever she were to hear what had happened. But Annie knew she would not be able to keep the tragic story from her good friend, especially when she showed Louisa this painting. *We won't visit this spot right away,* she thought. *No sense starting things out on the wrong foot!*

# Chapter 12

Louisa wondered when she might have the opportunity to recharge her smart phone, since Annie's family lived without electricity. She took her time going over her address book and calendar, making note of the date, Saturday, November 12, and checking on the weather forecast while riding in a cab from the Harrisburg airport to Lancaster County.

*A red letter day. Paradise, here I come!*

She called home to let her mom know she had arrived safely and then put her cell phone away. Glancing at her laptop in its case, she wondered how often she would get to use it, wanting to keep in touch with her art students by email. Some by instant messaging. She longed for a less complicated life, but she could not leave behind her ability to communicate, which was essential to her work—even if Mother's voice *had* been cold when Louisa let her know she had arrived safely. At least she hadn't pulled the martyr routine . . . yet.

Louisa wished now she hadn't given out Annie's mailing address. *Too easy for letters from home to reach me. . . .*

Looking out at the farmland whizzing by, she replayed Michael's outrage at her supposedly "playing runaway bride for effect . . . nothing more," as he so angrily had said. Mother, of course, had had her say, as well. Interestingly, though, her dad had not voiced displeasure, but his squinted eyes had exposed his annoyance.

As for the pre-wedding expenses, Louisa had offered to pay her parents back, over many years' time. *At least the next twenty or so.* But Mother would not hear of it, most likely because she assumed Louisa might snap out of it and return to Michael's waiting arms. To put that belief to rest, Louisa insisted on canceling everything herself, from the Brown Palace reservations to the white stretch limo.

At this moment, she felt more relaxed than she had in months, and much of it had to do with Annie putting out the proverbial welcome mat. She was bemused as to how the Zook family could have possibly understood her wishes, that she needed a clean break from Michael, not to mention some distancing from her parents, as well as hoping to infuse herself in the simple life for as long as possible. Annie's open-ended invite proved once again her opinion that she and her Amish pen friend were on similar wavelengths, having shared rather confidentially in their letters.

Leaning her head back, she spotted a billboard for the Rockvale Square Outlets. *Discount malls abound even in Amish country.* . . .

But most alarming was seeing firsthand precisely what Annie had been writing about for years, that the business sector was encroaching on precious farmland. Too many non-Amish farmers were selling their land to developers. Town houses, patio homes, and large custom homes were rising up out of the world's most fertile soil.

*Stunningly sad,* she thought. *Actually stupid!*

Having grown up in Denver, she might easily have viewed all the new development as a nonissue. But because of her close relationship with Annie, she had some empathy for "the People," as Annie liked to refer to her church community, and their problems.

*No wonder the Amish are searching for land elsewhere!*

Well, there was certainly ample land in other states. Take Colorado with its wide-open spaces such as the sprawling ranches situated between the small cities of Monument and Castle Rock. And thousands of acres of grazing land stretching out to the east, toward the Kansas state line. But the semi-arid climate and high altitude were not conducive to the array of crops Annie's People were accustomed to growing.

She leaned up to ask the taxi driver, "How far to Paradise?"

"Oh, a good ten miles or so, miss."

*Miss.* The bleak realization hit her once more. The sadness, no, the deception hurt the most.

Shaking her head, she found herself exasperated anew at her father's interference in her life. One of the reasons she had desired to come to Pennsylvania was to sort out her feelings. She needed to put things together in her head . . . and in her heart. Remaining in Colorado had not been one of the options she allowed herself. Except for her enthusiastic students, nothing held her there any longer. She had seen to it that they each had plenty of assignments to keep them busy. That way if she decided to be away longer than a month, she was set.

She stared down at her "Palm," the minicomputer, organizer, cell phone, and camera all rolled into one very cool gadget, and wondered how she would ever manage without it, along with her fabulous car, her favorite DVDs, and her many jazz CDs. Despite any small misgivings she felt now, she couldn't wait to see Annie, to talk with her in person. That alone she hoped would make up for the abandonment of all her high-tech toys.

*Weird,* she thought, *having such affinity to a Plain girl.*

Next to her on the seat, in the pet carrier, Muffin opened his kitty eyes and looked at her through the mesh window as if to say, *Where are you taking me?*

Leaning over, she whispered, "You'll have lots of company where we're going." She almost laughed, but smothered it so as not to call attention from the driver, who had been noticeably surprised when she'd given the Paradise Township address. *"Isn't that Amish farmland?"* he'd asked, and quickly she agreed that it was, saying no more.

She closed her eyes, weary of the day, having gotten up at three that morning to shower, shampoo, and dress in order to catch the first flight out of DIA. Then there was the mad rush to the connecting gate at Chicago's O'Hare. She was glad to be this far into her travels and could hardly wait for some of Barbara Zook's home-brewed coffee!

Annie pushed a wet rag deep into the corner, back where the bed hid the floor from the doorway. After dry mopping, she had taken great care to get down on her hands and knees, making sure all stray dust bunnies beneath Yonie's bed, or anywhere else, were gone. She had also given the front porch a good strong sweeping, very glad the potted mums were still blooming due to no frost yet, a rarity. She had even done something rather "fancy" by bringing in the pots at night, hoping to preserve their beauty for Louisa's arrival.

Just now she wondered about the time and excitedly ran downstairs to check the wall clock in the kitchen.

She asked Mamm about the apple dumplings. "Are they done yet?"

"Ach, calm yourself, dear."

One look at Mamm and she knew they were *both* wound up. The whole family was. Yonie, of course, was out deer hunting with friends over the weekend and most of next week, but Luke and Omar would be around and grinning to beat the band. Jesse Jr., Christian, and Abner and their wives and children, too, would meet Louisa after Preaching service tomorrow. No question, her pen pal's coming was a first for all of them.

"I made sure Yonie's room was spotless," she told Mamm, hurrying to the front room to look out the window.

Her mother followed close behind. "Why don't you give me that rag?" Mamm held out her hand. "And why not comb through your hair once? Worry less 'bout the cleanliness of the house now and be thinkin' how ya want to look yourself."

*I'm all mussed up*, she thought, recalling the only other time Mamm had ever spoken to her like that. Back when she was a little girl and not even close to being ready to leave the house for Preaching.

Now she considered tomorrow's house church meeting. How would the People react to Louisa sitting in their midst? And would her friend even want to join them?

*I'll know soon. . . .*

Louisa released her seat belt and stared at the Zooks' property—the old two-story barn with its picturesque windmill to her right. And the tall white farmhouse with distinctive black shutters on the other side of the road, the south-facing porch dotted with clay pots of gold- and bronze-colored mums. A lofty willow, minus its leaves, hovered near the back of the house, gracing the yard. The distinct vision she had formed in her mind since childhood had been merely a reflection of the real thing. Now, here she was.

*This is Annie's world!*

Nearly speechless, she jumped when the cabbie announced the fare. "Oh, sorry," she said, digging into her purse for a wad of cash.

When her suitcase and matching overnight case were unloaded from the trunk, she thanked the driver again. Then, hooking the two pieces of luggage together, she rolled them across the road, carrying Muffin in his pet tote up the dirt lane leading to the house.

She heard the first little squeal of glee and looked up to see Annie running toward her, arms outstretched, long skirt flying as she came. "Ach, you're here, Louisa! *Willkumm*, friend!"

Letting go of her luggage, she set down Muffin in his carrier just in time to receive the warm and welcoming hug. "It's great to see you," she said, feasting her eyes on her friend. "You're so pretty, Annie! You didn't do yourself justice in your descriptions through the years."

They locked eyes on each other, and Annie said, "I'd have to say you look just like the picture you sent."

"The engagement picture or the one with my art students?"

"Well, both. I'd know you anywhere."

Before she could stop her, Annie grabbed her luggage, talking all the while. "I'm so glad you're here safely . . . flyin' on an airplane and all . . . what was that like?"

Louisa smiled at her exuberance. "Oh, it's really lots safer than driving a car, according to statistics."

"But how's it feel to go so fast?"

"Surprisingly, you don't realize the speed, except for the takeoff and landing. You mainly sit in a chair, buckled in, of course, and if you're like me, you pick up a magazine and read. Some people actually sleep through the entire flight, if it's not too choppy, which it certainly can be flying out of Denver." She explained the updrafts and stronger currents near the mountains. "One of my friends flies a small aircraft—a four-seater—and she nearly crashed it because of the bizarre wind currents out there."

Annie's blue eyes twinkled. "Did you say a girl flies the airplane?"

"Well, she's my age . . . a year older."

"Ach, what a life, goin' ever so fast!"

*No, this is the life . . . right here,* thought Louisa as she walked with Annie, as energetic and delightful in person as she had always been in letters.

They walked through the well-landscaped side yard, around the house to the screened-in back porch.

Annie's mother met them with a winning smile, as overweight as Annie was slight. "Come in, come in, Louisa. Make yourself at home," Barbara Zook said, wiping her hands on her long black apron.

"Thank you, Mrs. Zook. I'm so pleased to meet you at last. Annie's talked so much about you . . . well, written about you, anyway."

That brought another cheery smile. "Oh, you mustn't call me something so formal sounding. Honestly, Barbara's just fine," she said. "How was your trip in?"

"Uneventful . . . a good thing, thanks. It's really wonderful to be here." Louisa took in the unique surroundings and wondered how the large kitchen with its massive black wood stove and long table with wooden benches on either side would have looked to her today if she hadn't already visualized this house from Annie's letters. "What a beautiful place," she said, as if standing in the middle of a dream.

But it was Annie's demeanor, composed and demure, that struck her. She was as attractive as any of Louisa's friends. Simply remove the head covering and the long cape dress, and she could pass for a modern girl. But Annie's remarkably blue eyes grew suddenly wide as she caught a glimpse of Louisa's long earrings.

*Annie is startled at the sight of me,* Louisa thought, wishing she hadn't worn either her pencil-thin jeans or her jewelry.

# Chapter 13

Annie sure hadn't expected Louisa to be dressed the way she was. She honestly wasn't sure how she'd expected Louisa to look, really. She was quite sure Daed would be distressed, though, once he came in from the barn and met their English visitor.

A mite taller than Annie had anticipated her to be, Louisa also looked much too skinny. Like the painfully thin catalog models in tight-fitting blue jeans and hyacinth-colored linen shirts over matching camisole tees. She knew of such descriptions and colors only from having paged through the ads at Julia's. She had no idea why the catalogs came in the mail there, since her cousin sewed all her own clothes, as well as little Molly's dresses and nightgowns. Still, it was interesting to see the different types of shoes and purses and whatnot. She'd even peeked at the fine jewelry section—rings, bracelets, and necklaces—knowing she'd probably never wear such things, but they were awful easy on the eyes.

"Come, I'll show you where you'll be sleeping. Yonie's out hunting, hopin' to get his first deer this year, so you'll have his room for the time being." She started up the stairs, still holding the two pieces of luggage, the nicest-looking suitcase and tote she'd ever seen, and motioned for Louisa to follow her.

"Hey, I'm not helpless," Louisa said, trying to wrestle away the suitcase while still carrying Muffin.

Annie laughed. "If you want to help so much, then you can finish washing and drying all of Mamm's dishes for tomorrow's noon meal. We'll feed about two hundred and fifty people, how's that?"

"That's a bunch."

"Well, wait till you see how many attend our weddings." She stopped at the top of the stairs and waited for Louisa to catch up. "Ach, I'm sorry to mention that right off."

"Don't worry, Annie. I'm not super sensitive about it."

"Well . . . you know. I think we both need some pampering, jah?"

"For sure." Louisa smiled.

"By the way, breakfast comes early on Sunday mornings, 'specially when we have Preaching here."

"I'll be awake in plenty of time," Louisa said. "Remember, I'm a morning person . . . like you."

"But your body clock's two hours behind us here, jah?"

It was Louisa's turn to laugh. "I'll just set my Palm to go off before dawn." Then she seemed to remember something. "Oh, no! That won't work."

"What won't?"

Louisa shook her head. "There's no place to recharge, right? No electricity here. Duh . . . I should know this!"

"Unless you want to head down to Cousin Julia's right away. She and Irvin have electric," Annie said. "But, honestly, you won't have any trouble wakin' up. Our peacocks have a built-in alarm clock, trust me on that."

She led Louisa down the hall, stopping to point out her own room. "See there? That's the desk where I write to you."

"Sweet." Louisa hurried into Annie's bedroom, cat carrier and all.

Annie set down the luggage and moved the desk out from the wall to show the date and initials carved into the back.

"Your dad made this?"

"It was a big birthday surprise when I was twelve. I got spoiled that year." Annie watched her friend sitting on the chair where she'd pondered so often what should or shouldn't be shared in her letters to an outsider.

Just then, Louisa turned and looked up at her. "This is so wild. I've tried to picture you, your room . . . everything. You have no idea how terrific this is."

"Ach, I feel the same way, havin' you visit." Annie suddenly thought of their bath routine tonight and cringed. *What'll she think when she finds out about Saturday night baths? Will she turn right around and make a beeline for home?*

But she didn't reveal the bath routine. She just kept smiling, and Louisa did, too, like they were long-lost friends; except they knew they weren't that at all.

"Come, let's get you settled."

Annie was amazed at the "slide show" in Louisa's Palm, as Louisa called it—one image after another of the watercolor and oil paintings in the recent exhibit.

"You must be so happy 'bout your students," said Annie, looking intently, and then holding the gadget when Louisa handed it to her. "What do I do with it?"

"Just watch."

"It goes all by itself?"

"Yep."

She'd heard of some of the womenfolk in other church districts being allowed to own cell phones, but she'd never seen anything like this. "It's hard to believe . . . such clear pictures in a little device." She looked at Louisa. "What will your students do without you while you're here?"

"Oh, don't worry . . . they have plenty of assignments."

"A whole month's worth?"

"At least." Louisa turned off her Palm. "That's enough for now," she said. "Want to help me unpack?"

"Sure." But as Louisa removed her colorful clothes from her suitcase, Annie was quite surprised. There were a number of outfits, and for all different occasions, it seemed—dress up, work, play, and everything in between. Foreign as anything she'd ever seen, as fancy as the catalog pages at Julia's. There was even a separate pull-out case for Louisa's bracelets, necklaces, and earrings.

Annie bit her lip, wishing she might persuade her friend away from such ornamentation while she was here, at least. Contemplating the potentially awkward situation, she continued helping Louisa organize her clothes.

Out of the blue, Louisa stopped what she was doing. "It's surprising that you and your family would open your home to me. I'm really grateful."

Annie touched her arm. "You're truly welcome." She leaned over to line up Louisa's shoes beneath the wooden wall pegs. "We enjoy havin' company, believe me. My mother loves to cook . . . likes havin' lots of feet beneath her dinner table."

"Cooking is one of *my* passions, too. Sometime while I'm here, I'd like to treat all of you to one of my favorite recipes. Deal?"

"I'm sure Mamm will be more than happy to take you up on it, but we'll help you with the wood stove, of course."

"Oh, I didn't think of that." Louisa's eyes were mischievous. "I might present the family with a burnt offering, which would never do." She reached down and unzipped the pet carry bag. "I hope my kitty's welcome to stay . . . here in the bedroom. Is it all right?"

Annie wondered when Louisa might mention Muffin. "Well, since he's a city cat he must be used to lots of pamperin', jah?"

Lifting out the lump of grayish-blue fur, Louisa snuggled her nose into his neck. "There's my sweet boy. Aw, such a good traveler you are."

"Our mouse catchers in the barn never had it this fine." Annie laughed, enjoying the sight of Louisa and her cat. She'd heard so much about "precious Muffin this," "darling Muffin that" for the past year or so, since Louisa had gotten her new place after college graduation.

Louisa set her kitty on the floor, and immediately Muffin disappeared beneath the ruffled white bed skirt.

For good measure, Annie hurried to close the door. *In case he decides to make a run for it.* Returning to sit on the bed, she decided now was a good time to tell Louisa about the evening's activities. "Since we're hosting the Preaching service tomorrow, there'll be a group of men comin' later this afternoon to remove some of the interior walls—to make an open space large enough for the meeting. The bench wagon will arrive soon after."

Louisa nodded. "I'm fascinated to see how everything is set up."

"Well, some of Mamm's helpers will start arriving at seven-thirty tomorrow morning. It gets awful busy round here on Preaching days."

"I don't want to be in the way," Louisa insisted. "Just tell me what to do and when."

*Should I say something about fitting in just yet?* Annie wondered, not wanting to stare at Louisa's shiny pink lips or her dangling earrings. Rather, she zeroed in on her thoughtful aqua blue eyes, but even they were made up too much.

Then, as though sensing her concern, Louisa said, "I brought along several skirts and dresses. Wouldn't want to stick out like a sore thumb here." Promptly Louisa held up a bright red shirtdress, a tiny flap-style pocket on the upper left bodice. The other dress she showed Annie was a solid lime green, a bit low cut, and the color shouted, *"Lookee here at me!"*

Annie held her breath. The dresses, if they were Louisa's only choices, were much too loud for Preaching service.

"Knowing your people as you do, Annie, which would be best for church tomorrow?"

*Ach, neither one!* She was at a terrible loss for words.

Right away, Jesse was in a quandary, seeing Annie's friend enter the kitchen looking like Jezebel herself.

*What have we done?* Even as he thought this, he scooted his chair back from the head of the table. He felt strongly the importance of showing respect to their guest even though she was bejeweled, made up to kingdom come, and wearing fancy clothes . . . a man's pair of trousers, in all truth.

"Welcome to our house." He extended his hand.

"Thank you, uh . . . Mr. Zook. Well, Preacher Zook is better, isn't it?" She shook his hand and smiled.

He could see she was trying hard to be polite, though he was also mighty sure she was terribly uncomfortable. Still, he recalled the curious words spoken by Preacher Moses regarding Annie and her visitor and hoped that just maybe Louisa's coming might prove to be providential indeed.

Annie insisted on Louisa sitting next to where Mamm always sat at the table. Louisa offered repeatedly to carry over the serving platters, but Mamm was adamant about her being "waited on" for the first meal with the family.

Meanwhile, Dawdi and Mammi Zook came over from the Dawdi Haus, the connecting addition to the main house, Mammi leaning on both her cane and Dawdi's arm. "Well, who do we have here?" she asked, eyes bright as she leaned forward, wobbling a bit.

"Louisa Stratford has come to stay awhile," Daed spoke up.

"Well, it's very nice to meet you, young lady," Mammi said, nodding her head and smiling.

"Where'd you come from?" asked Dawdi, his pure white beard touching his chest.

Before Louisa could answer, Annie volunteered. "She's all the way from Denver, Colorado." *Not from Mars!*

"Well, now, I hope ya didn't walk," said Dawdi, a twinkle in his eye.

Louisa shook her head, smiling. "Two thousand miles is a long way."

"She flew on a plane," Mamm spoke up. The comment put a slight damper on things until Luke and Omar wandered in from the barn, looking disheveled. Annie waited till both had washed up at the sink, and then she introduced them to Louisa, as well.

Luke blushed and muttered "hullo," as though he ought not to be looking at such a fancy woman.

But Omar stuck his hand out and smiled big, his brown eyes shining. "Nice to meet ya."

"And you, too," said Louisa, smiling back.

When they were all seated, following Daed's silent mealtime prayer, Mamm carried the conversation, asking Louisa about her family. To this Louisa summed up her father's work, saying merely that he was a busy attorney and that her mother kept occupied with her social groups, including a monthly book club.

"Oh, a book club, you say?" Omar's eyes shone. "I'm curious 'bout that."

Mamm clammed up quickly, casting a glance at Annie, a question mark on her face.

Louisa continued on. "Last count, there were eight bookworms in the group. Two men, the rest women. They choose a book to read each month, then meet for coffee and dessert at someone's house and talk about it."

"Sounds interesting," Daed spoke up suddenly. "What sort of books?"

*Here we go,* thought Annie.

Louisa shrugged. "Oh, all kinds. This month it's Grisham's latest novel."

"Who's that?" Omar asked, his left suspender drooping off his shoulder.

"The author, John Grisham, writes courtroom thrillers, for the most part." Louisa said this with such certainty that Annie was sure Louisa had also read them. "My mother's book club reads everything from CIA suspense to alternate reality," Louisa added.

Daed frowned, clearly mystified. "I can't say I've ever heard of this alternate reality. What do you mean by it?"

Louisa paused, reaching for her water glass. She looked so peculiar with her eyelashes long and dark, as showy as the English tourists who visited the quilt shops and the many roadside stands up and down Harvest Road. "What if you could wake up and discover the dreams you have at night are actually real—your *true* life? So you're walking around in your dream, but it's really your life."

Luke chuckled and put his head down quickly, but Omar latched right on to Louisa's comment. "I could go for a book like that, really!"

Everyone laughed, including Daed.

"I could go for 'bout any book if I could see the print," Dawdi added.

Mammi wore a sly grin. "Oh, go on with ya, Pop."

Annie felt herself relaxing a bit. Her family was attempting to make Louisa feel comfortable. Still, a downright awkward predicament, to be sure.

# Chapter 14

Louisa was bowled over when Annie said she could be first for the Saturday night bath in the kitchen. "You mean you all use the same bath water?"

Annie grinned, though it was apparent she was trying her best not to. "It's the fastest way to get done."

"Well, that's nice, but . . ." She felt positively speechless. *What was I thinking . . . leaving my Jacuzzi tub behind?*

"You all right?" asked Annie as they talked in the privacy of her bedroom.

"Oh, sure." But Louisa was convinced her mascara was smudged and her face oily from the humidity here and the long day of travel. A brisk scrub or even a facial would be wonderful if she could actually see what she was doing. *No large mirrors?*

Annie explained further. "For the baths, the kitchen is closed off, really 'tis. We simply hang a big curtain between the kitchen and the adjoining room. We tape cardboard up on each of the windows so no one could possibly see in."

"I guess I'll adjust." But Louisa wasn't certain the required adjustment would kick in within the next few hours. So . . . this was the real introduction to the simple life she had been craving.

The next shocker awaited her in the outhouse. Her eyes watered at the horrendous smell, and she refused to sit down on the wooden opening. *I'm going to have to expand my lung capacity immediately!*

Louisa lathered up with the scratchy bar of oatmeal soap, unquestionably homemade, resisting the slightest urge to relax or soak. Sitting knees up in the tub, she wondered wryly what her friends would say if they could see her now.

Thinking back to supper, right here in this room, she recalled the flabbergasted looks on each of the Zooks' faces. *I must seem like an alien!*

Following the inelegant bath, she was glad for the warmth of the grand old cookstove and wrapped herself in a thick towel. She fought off the lingering concern that Luke or Omar might forget and walk in on her, and dried off quickly.

Putting on the long pink bathrobe from home, she thought, *I must be nuts to stay here longer than a few days!* Laughing softly, she slipped her well-pedicured feet into matching slippers.

She remembered Annie had said her mother would be the third to bathe after Annie, followed by the preacher and so on down the line of boys. Annie had also reminded her that since Yonie was out hunting, there was one less person using the communal tub this night. Lucky Omar would be the final one to wash off in everyone else's dirty bath water.

The thought repulsed her, but she tried to distract herself by fluffing her hair with the towel, missing her blow dryer. *No wonder Annie gets by shampooing only once a week . . . her hair is covered up!*

Still feeling exposed, she peeked through the curtain. Seeing no one, she dashed to the stairs, hair still dripping. Upstairs, she knocked on Annie's door to say it was *her* turn.

"Already? Goodness' sake, you're fast." Annie smiled, her gaze falling on Louisa's pink robe. "I'll hurry, then we can talk, jah?"

"Sure, I'll go dry my hair."

Annie smiled. "Sorry 'bout that. We use the air, ya know."

"So do I—only forced air . . . all at once." She laughed.

"I won't dawdle," Annie said, heading down the hall to the stairs.

Louisa went to her room and closed the door. She swished her thick hair around, patting it with the towel and combing through it with her fingers.

Going to the tall bureau, she picked up her Palm where she'd left it on. Not expecting to see any messages, she was actually pleased to see four. *Who's thinking about me? Maybe Courtney or one of my students?*

Sitting at the window, on the only chair in the room, she punched in the numbers for her code, then listened for the first message. "Louisa, we need to talk. . . ." Michael's voice jarred her.

"We have nothing to talk about," she whispered, deleting his message and going to the next.

"I have an idea, babe. Please call!" Another from Michael.

*Yep, I have an idea, too. Get over yourself!*

But hearing his voice made her feel miserable. She really hoped all four messages weren't from him, because she wanted to fall asleep in the stillness of this stark bedroom, not with Michael's desperation ringing in her ears.

Sighing, she listened to the third, finger poised to skip over it if she heard his voice again. But this time it was someone else. Cybil Peters, one of her newest students, was calling to say she'd sold an oil painting from the art show. "It's my first, and I owe it to you, Louisa. We definitely have to keep in touch while you're on your sabbatical."

*Sabbatical? Did I say coming to Amish country was that?* She didn't recall, in the midst of all that had transpired prior to her flight to liberty.

She pressed to return the call and was thrilled to hear Cybil's perky voice. "Hey, there!"

"Cybil? It's Louisa. Got your message . . . and I'm so jazzed. This is great news."

"Don't I know it? And guess who bought it? You remember that older gentleman, the one who kept circling back to stand and stare at my painting? Well, he's the one. I got a whopping three hundred bucks . . . so I'll be hitting Aaron Brothers tomorrow, to stock up on art supplies." Cybil continued chattering, and Louisa was more than happy to oblige her by listening.

After a few minutes, Cybil said, "Well, it sounds like you've got another call coming in, so I'll let you go."

"Hey, keep in touch," she said. "See ya!"

Catching the incoming call, Louisa was surprised to hear her father's voice. "Honey, we miss you. I know you're upset, and so are we." He paused. "Frankly, this whole thing with Michael can be unraveled."

"No, Daddy. Marrying Michael would have been a mistake." The lump in her throat threatened to choke her words.

She heard him sigh. "Your mother and I think—"

"I can't do this now," she interrupted.

"Listen, we need to discuss this. I see it as essential, Louisa."

*Essential?*

"I'm losing power," she told him. "I really need to go. 'Bye, Daddy."

She pressed the off button. It was true, the Palm needed recharging. *Perfect . . . I'll be unavailable for a while. . . .*

There was another voice message to check, but she turned off the power, not in the mood for more pleas from either Michael or her parents.

Going to lie down, she was happy to see Muffin jump on the bed and come purring toward her. "Oh, you . . . hiding again?" He snuggled down on her stomach, curling up like a kitten. "What would I do without my kitty?" she whispered. "You don't know it, but tomorrow's going to be a busy day. So I hope you'll be a good boy and stay right here in this room."

She considered the church meeting tomorrow, but not so much the length as the awkwardness of it. *Will I feel as out of it as I did at supper?* She couldn't stop thinking how strange it felt to be looked at with such curiosity. *Like Annie and her family must feel when they're in the minority.*

Lying there, it struck her that she was free of any home ties—especially those connected to Michael. She stroked her cat, aware of his persistent strong purring. "I think you must be as contented here as I am," she whispered, playing with his crystal ID tag.

Smiling to herself, she reveled in the solitude, thinking of Cybil's excitement at selling her art, recalling her own first sale ever. It had happened the fall semester of her sophomore year at California School of Art. The acrylic painting had been dear to her, inspired by a trip to Hampton, Virginia, when she was twelve. She had spent a few weeks that summer with her single great-aunt on her father's side of the family. Margaret Stratford was the only person Louisa had ever known to talk somewhat casually about God . . . as if she met Him often for espresso and pie.

Although she did not see Aunt Margaret after that summer, not until years later at her funeral, Louisa had never forgotten her tender, even intimate prayers, offered at mealtime and other times of the day. Seemingly insignificant things brought out her aunt's eagerness to chat with divinity. Margaret would blink back tears at the mention of Jesus and "that black and heartbreaking day—Good Friday," as she referred to it, when her dearest friend was mutilated and killed . . . a criminal's crucifixion.

At the time of her work in progress, Louisa's heart was fiercely bound up in the painting, fondly recalling the one-time connection with soft-spoken Aunt Margaret. The Virginia seascape was the ultimate inspiration, set at Grandview Beach at the nature preserve, where she and Margaret walked the two-mile stretch of beach. In Louisa's mind, the lovely woman in the picture, gazing out to sea, captured perfectly her devout aunt as a young woman "communing with the Creator," as she liked to say.

Terribly attached to the painting, Louisa kept wishing she might have set the price higher on the opening night of the show. Ridiculously high would have been much better than being forced to sell, but when a serious buyer approached her with cash in hand, ethically she had no choice.

Ironically, the easy sale opened wide the door to romance. The buyer, a captivating man five years her senior, wined and dined her often. Quickly she was caught up in the exhilaration of his keen attention and his admiration for her artistic talent. But the relationship distracted her terribly from her studies and her painting, so when he talked of opening an art gallery on London's posh Cork Street, she let Trey Douglas walk out of her life without even so much as a dispute.

After he left for Europe, she turned all her attention back to completing school, often wondering how her first love was doing. Was he happy in Europe? Had he found his niche?

The next year, Michael Berkeley entered her life with grandiose and surreptitious plans. . . .

Louisa was lifted out of her reverie by a tapping on her door. "Are you still awake?" Annie called softly.

"Sure, come in." She sat up, still holding Muffin. "I've been thinking. . . ."

"Well, that's a good thing to do!" Annie laughed.

"Seriously, do you happen to have an extra dress I could wear for tomorrow?"

*Glory be!* Annie squelched her enthusiasm. "Just a minute." She hurried to her room and chose from the wooden pegs two of her best and newest cape dresses. One blue and the other purple.

She took them to show Louisa. "Which one of these do you prefer—the color, I mean?"

Louisa looked at one, and then the other, and back again. "Umm . . ."

"Well, which?" Annie pressed her, trying to keep a straight face.

"Both are nice solid colors." Louisa seemed unsure. "We'd look like twins!"

"And what would ya think of that?"

"Well, it might be fun. The perfect way not to stick out, jah?"

Annie giggled a little at her use of the Dutch. "I can see havin' you here will be loads of fun. You'll be talkin' like us in no time."

*Hopefully not the other way around!* thought Annie.

"Which one did *you* plan to wear?" Louisa asked.

"No, no, you pick."

Louisa reached for her purse on the bed and rummaged inside. She pulled out her wallet and found a nickel. "Here we go! Heads it's blue, tails it's purple. Deal?"

"Deal," Annie said, using Louisa's word. She watched her flip the coin high into the air, letting it fall *kerplink* on the wide plank floor. Her brothers had often done this very thing, but mostly to decide which team would serve first in volleyball.

"Tails!" Louisa leaned down to retrieve the coin. She rose and pointed toward the purple dress. "That's the one. Mind if I try it on?"

"Sure, let's see if it fits." She removed the hanger from the dress, hand-sewn just last week, glad Louisa had picked this one. Especially since it hadn't been worn except while Mamm marked the hem for her.

Louisa had already kicked off her slippers and was untying her robe when Annie said, "You know what? I'll leave ya be."

"Oh, I'm fine . . . stay."

Even so, she felt nearly pained with her friend undressing right here. When Louisa's pink robe fell to the floor, Annie's face burned in embarrassment and she huddled in the corner, waiting for Louisa to request help if she needed it. Pinning the *Halsduch*, the cape part of the dress, to the waistline was a real chore.

"I guess you read my letters right close, then," Annie joked. Louisa seemed to know all about the pile of straight pins required for securing the cape to the skirt. She picked up a few and began pinning the front of the skirt.

"I read every word, silly." Louisa stood tall and still while Annie began pinning the back.

"This is my least favorite part of gettin' dressed," Annie admitted. "Takes a bunch of pins, as you can see."

"Ever stick yourself?"

"Honestly, I never have, but my friend Esther Hochstetler—oh, and you've got to meet her tomorrow—she's stuck herself by mistake. She's my closest Amish friend, I'd have to say."

"You wrote me once that you feel lonely sometimes with only brothers," Louisa said suddenly.

Recalling that, Annie replied, "Mamm and I are closer than some daughters and their mothers, prob'ly. But with three sisters-in-law, I'm not the only young woman in the kitchen at family gatherings, that's for sure."

When the final pin was in place, she said, "There. You look like one of us, 'cept for one thing yet."

Louisa's eyes widened. "Don't tell me . . . you're going to pull my hair back in a bun?"

Annie nodded. "Let's do this right. I'll be back." She headed to her room to get an extra head covering, terribly excited that Louisa should consent to this much Plain dressing.

Returning, Annie displayed the white netting heart-shaped cap. "This goes over your hair, and the strings are tied for church but no other time."

Louisa appeared to enjoy the process, while Annie took care to twist the sides of Louisa's parted hair, keeping any strays from escaping the tight, low bun.

When they were finished, Annie reached for a small hand mirror and held it up. "See?"

"Wow . . . I look like you. Well, sort of."

"No, you actually *do*," Annie said, wondering how long this new look would last with Louisa.

# Chapter 15

Though it was late and Louisa was tired, she joined Annie in her room after changing out of the purple dress and into her pajamas. She remembered how strange it had felt wearing Annie's clothing. But there was something else, too . . . something incredibly positive about the Plain attire. She'd felt stripped of all pretense. Truly uncomplicated, just as she had longed to be. And now, wearing her pink and silky shorty pajamas, her damp hair brushed straight back, away from her face, she actually missed the mega modest dress . . . missed how she had felt in it, too. Like she was someone other than a member of the Stratford family. She wouldn't have known how to explain the feeling to anyone, being a thoroughly modern woman from the soul out.

Not wanting to stare, even though she was, Louisa couldn't get past the conspicuous contrast between herself and Annie now that they were dressed for bed. Her Amish friend looked almost childlike in her white ankle-length, high-collared nightgown, her golden-blond hair parted down the middle with loose waist-length braids. Louisa felt like a schoolgirl again, sitting there with Annie on her bed, happily whispering together. *An old-fashioned sleepover!*

"What's your favorite memory, besides Christmas or your birthday?" Annie asked unexpectedly.

"Let's see. . . ." But Louisa didn't know, couldn't think of an answer. "What about you? What's yours?"

"I believe it was the day I finished an entire painting—the first time I did—back when I was fourteen. It was a Friday—I go to Cousin Julia's to work on Tuesdays and Fridays." She paused, reminding Louisa of the attic room. "I can't decide which is my favorite memory, really. It was either that day or the first time Rudy asked me to ride home from a singing with him. Oh, Louisa, he was so awful cute. And he still is, but . . ." Annie looked like she might cry, but she composed herself quickly. "I remember my heart sure did flutter fast."

Louisa knew too well the feeling of exhilaration. "Torn between two passions?" She couldn't fathom having to choose between romantic love and her enthusiasm for her art. In fact, if she wanted to have both, she could. That was not the struggle of *her* life.

Annie leaned back on the bed, staring up at the ceiling. "You know, I never thought things would end up the way they did between Rudy and me. I thought for sure we'd be married, somehow or other. I loved him, really I did."

*Still does*, Louisa realized. "You're not telling me anything. It's excruciating letting go. It would be way harder for you, though, having been in a courtship for three solid years like you were." She pondered the many dates Annie and Rudy must have had, even though Amish couples saw each other rather infrequently—every other Saturday and the opposite two Sundays each month. The only other opportunities were flirtatious exchanges across the room at Preaching service or if they happened to be seated near each other at one of the many wedding feasts from November through March. Annie had written that since fewer farmers were raising tobacco currently, more time was freed up, and the bishops had extended the wedding season by three months. A good thing in the grand scheme of things—the more couples "hitched up," the more babies born. This, as Louisa understood it, was the way the Amish propagated themselves, not by seeking out new converts.

"Poor Rudy," Annie said suddenly. "He got awful tired of bein' put off. And who's to blame him? In the end, I refused to submit . . . turned him down."

Louisa wanted to divert the conversation. It was way too easy for both of them to get caught up in the "woe is me" thing. So she attempted to change the subject and asked about Annie's lovely walnut hope chest.

"Sure, I'll show you." Annie went to the foot of the bed and opened it wide. She removed a heart-shaped pillow with a tatted edge and held it up for Louisa. "Sarah Mae, my first sister-in-law, made this for me." Next she presented a set of starched white doilies. "Nearly all the gifts here were given on my sixteenth birthday." She took out a long tablecloth, neatly unfolding it and pointing out embroidered delicate pink roses. "This one's so colorful, ain't so?"

*Ain't so.* Louisa pursed her lips to make sure she didn't smile too broadly. Annie's exuberance was infectious, no question. She was incredibly excited about life in general and more specifically about making Louisa feel quite at home here, even though Annie was still terribly wounded, Louisa knew.

Watching Annie display one cherished item after another from her hope chest, Louisa realized suddenly she was quite okay about not returning Michael's persistent calls. In fact, she could not summon even the smallest fleck of guilt, entirely content to relax here in this room. A world apart.

Upon first arriving and sitting at the desk made by Preacher Zook, Louisa had noticed how sparsely furnished Annie's room was. A double bed with a solid maple head and footboard, two large multicolored rag rugs, a wide maple bureau—without a mirror!—and the petite writing desk in the opposite corner graced the room. Other than that, there was a single cane-back chair situated near one of the windows.

Definitely exhausted, she felt this first evening in Amish country seemed perfect, almost surreal . . . like being a character in one of the alternate reality books her mom's book club had read and discussed. Like dreaming you were in Amish country and waking up to find it was quite true!

*Maybe this is my favorite day ever. . . .*

Tears rolled down Esther Hochstetler's face as she lay on her side in bed, facing the door. She willed herself to take only shallow breaths, not wanting to awaken her husband.

*Has he forgotten what it means to be a child?* she wondered. *Poor little Laura. Her heart must be broken, for sure.*

It was all she could do to lie still next to him, her back toward his. He preferred to sleep like two spoons nestled together amidst warm layers of heirloom quilts. But she had made it a point to distance herself from his wrath, silently accepting some of the blame.

She had been frightened to intervene this time, as she always was. A submissive woman under God was not to question her husband's methods of discipline, according to their upbringing. The womenfolk toed the line without reservation or animosity toward their husbands or the church brethren. This was expected.

*What's wrong with me? Why do I question Zeke's authority?* She asked herself such questions nearly every day.

Earlier tonight, young Laura had simply rushed out the back door alone, making a beeline to the outhouse. Something she'd eaten had not set well. This had been the childish excuse given. Esther had believed her daughter's confession, for she'd seen her little one's ashen face soon after the supper hour.

Laura's transgression had occurred once the house had fallen quiet, several hours past dusk. Ignoring the standing rule, made when Laura was a mere toddler, her girl had not stood at the bedroom door and called out to awaken Esther. After dark, the children were required to have either Zeke or Esther accompany them everywhere. Other fathers amongst the People had imposed similar expectations for a good number of years now, as well.

*Who knows what may lurk in the darkness,* Zeke uttered all too often, but oddly enough, his urgings no longer put the fear of God in Esther.

Always before tonight she had managed to bite her tongue and keep her peace.

*Honestly, I couldn't wait, Dat. I had to hurry. . . .*

Little Laura's pleas ricocheted through Esther's memory now—her pleadings for Zeke not to whip her were followed by high-pitched screams that ripped through a mother's tender soul. Esther concluded that Zeke's heart was hard as stone, for Laura's cries had touched him not one iota. He had taken their wee girl out behind the barn, made her raise her skirt, and thrashed her with a willow switch, leaving welts up and down the back of her legs.

No longer able to stand by, Esther had gone out and hollered at him, "Stop hurting her, for goodness' sake!"

By some miracle, he had stopped, his face all flushed red, anger spent. Looking at Laura with glistening eyes, he pushed her back toward Esther. "There, now that you've learned your lesson, go to your mamma," he said, his voice cracking with a hint of remorse.

But now in the dark room she agonized anew. *Why must he be so?*

Boldly, she had ordered something by mail, from an ad she'd seen in *The Budget* a few weeks back. And lest she be found out, she'd watched the mail like a hawk till the order arrived. Yesterday! Oh, how eager she was to see if it would work. Starting tomorrow morning, and every day after, she planned to steep the tasteless herb into Zeke's black coffee. *This is desperation,* she thought.

Suddenly he turned and reached for her in his sleep. Her body shuddered at his touch, and she held her breath, frightened that he might awaken fully.

She lay there in the stillness, pondering her resentment. How could Zeke be kind, even understanding, one day, only to pester and belittle his family the next? He had already started in on young Zach, who, if childishly forgetting one of the rules—misbehaving in the least—was humiliated no end. Sadly, she was most perturbed by the helplessness she felt at her inability to protect her own offspring.

Her animosity was devouring her love, as each year passed. *Yet I will bear another baby for my husband this winter.* Her muscles tensed at the thought of one more innocent life having to endure the domination of such a moody and volatile parent. She hoped the new babe might be another boy, and a brawny one, to be sure. One who could stand his own against his father if ever things should come to that.

*How did I ever fall for such a man?* she wondered.

But she knew all too well and could not blame anyone but herself.

Outside, the late September day had been perfect in every way—full sun, warm breezes, and nary a cloud on the horizon. Inside, however, Essie was scared speechless as her heart pounded at the thought of mingling with young men at the church-sponsored youth activity. Her older brother had taken her in his open carriage, as good brothers did, to her first Sunday singing.

A buzz of voices wafted her way as she stepped out of the buggy and wandered toward the two-story barn. The sound of so many youth in one place—boys and girls alike—filled her heart with dread and her head with visions of being passed over.

Soon she and all the others were singing the "fast songs" in unison. At one point, she looked down the long row of young men on the opposite side of the table from her and a host of other girls. Like a magnet pulling hard on her, she caught the unexpected gaze of a boy she'd never seen at Preaching. He was staring and smiling at her, and making no bones about it, either.

Quickly, she looked away, her face burning with shyness. Try as she might, she could not continue singing, her mouth so dry and her brain so befuddled.

It turned out the boy with light brown hair and shining brown eyes must have kept his gaze focused squarely on her the entire time of singing and table fellowship, although she did not once look his way again.

When later she stood to talk with several girls, she was astonished by his haste, and even his courage, in approaching her. She had turned only slightly and there he was, standing a smidgen too close. The girls who were with her revealed a certain alarm in their eyes, or perhaps it was astonishment. She didn't know which.

"You're the pertiest girl here" were the first words out of Ezekiel's mouth.

From that moment on, she was smitten with the good-looking boy from out of town, who had just happened to come for no apparent reason. His striking confidence in what he seemed to want, her as his *Aldi*—girlfriend—made her feel ever so good about herself.

After a mere two rides in his courting carriage, she embraced his wonderful-good declaration of her as "my precious little dove." He was constantly saying how he would take such good care of her all the days of her life. She believed him, deciding then and there this handsome, caring Zeke was the man of her dreams.

When they had been engaged for a short time, her father somehow found out and stepped in, pleading with Essie not to marry outside her church district. Preacher Zook also went to her father privately and strongly urged him not to allow her to marry Zeke, never giving any solid reason for the opposition. But she insisted she could not turn her back on her fiancé.

Zeke had spent his most recent years in Honey Brook, and he made it known he was not so keen on living in Paradise, though he had been originally from the area. A topsy-turvy time, to be sure.

Eventually Zeke was persuaded to change his mind about where they would live, and in the end, agreed to settle near Essie's parents' farm, accepting a thirty-acre parcel of land.

Without a doubt, Esther was quite sure they would be living far from here instead of a close distance to her now widowed mother had her father not intervened and convinced Zeke in the end with the whopping-good dowry.

Sighing now, she felt painfully hemmed in, wishing she could move away from the confines of her husband's unconscious embrace. But the slightest movement might set off an alarm in his brain—trigger his own persistent nightmares—so she kept her upper body completely motionless. Slowly she slid her legs down, stretching them carefully, glad for the coolness of the sheet against her skin.

*Who can I talk to? Who would even begin to understand?*

Esther wished she dared slip out of bed, if only for a moment, to comfort her wounded little girl. She longed to hold Laura close, soothing her with gentle strokes and kisses. Sleep evaded her as the muted sniffles of her firstborn echoed down the hall.

# Chapter 16

At Sunday breakfast, Jesse nearly fell off his chair when Annie and Louisa strolled into the kitchen arm in arm. The Englischer looked every bit as though she belonged in the family, decidedly Amish. Aside from the unusual color of her bluish-green eyes and brown hair, she might even have passed for Annie's sister.

*I worried for nothing, indeed,* he thought, amused. In all truth, he was pleased at Annie's transformation of Louisa Stratford, because his heart had sunk instantly at seeing her saunter up the lane yesterday, modern as the day was long in such brazenly tight jeans and that loud shirt and gleaming gold jewelry.

But now, at this minute, Louisa's expression was nearly as soft as Annie's own. He thought of his mother—dear Mamm, who was cooking breakfast next door because Dat was ailing this morning. Still, Jesse recalled her words of long ago: *The way in which a child is dressed reveals a mother's true heart.*

Annie couldn't help but notice her brothers' reaction to Louisa's purple dress and full black apron as they settled into their places at the breakfast table.

"Didn't expect you to be lookin' so, uh . . . Plain this mornin'," Omar said, eyeing Louisa's head covering. "You oughta come along to the singing tonight over at Lapps' barn. Ain't that right, Annie?"

She hadn't yet mentioned anything to Louisa. "We'll see." She poured freshly squeezed orange juice into each glass, wondering if Louisa might be curious to see from afar who Rudy Esh was, having heard so much about him. After all, Louisa had been fully aware of Rudy and Annie's courtship from the very first night on. *Might be the only reason she'd want to go,* Annie thought, sensitive to her friend's own emotional state.

Severely disappointed in love, Louisa would not care to meet new young men. Not even the cutest fellows that hung around the singings, probably. Annie seriously doubted she would want to go at all, and now, seeing the distant look in her eyes, she wished Omar hadn't brought up tonight's singing.

Two sermons, one much longer than the other, were given in High German, followed by a few testimonies in Pennsylvania Dutch, a dialect of German. As a result, Louisa didn't understand what either the preachers or the deacon were saying, but she did manage to turn around and kneel in silent prayer at her seat whenever Annie and her mother did, which happened twice during the meeting. She also rather curiously observed the rise and fall of Preacher Zook's rhythmic discourse, noting the way both he and the other minister folded their hands beneath their long flowing beards, as if in perpetual prayer while they stood preaching to a packed house.

*A unique subject for a painting*, she thought, wishing she had the nerve to bring along a sketch pad to church in two Sundays, when the next meeting was to be held at Rudy Esh's parents' house. Annie had whispered this tidbit of news as they filled the feeding trough with a combination of cracked corn, cat food, and game bird food for the enthusiastic peacocks earlier this morning.

Louisa had awakened later than planned, and it was no wonder, since she and Annie had stayed up late talking. Even so, she had wondered why Annie hadn't knocked on her door, so she hurried out of bed, made it quickly, and peeked into the hallway. Annie was already coming with a pitcher of warm water for her washbowl and an extra hand mirror. "This'll help some, maybe," Annie said, all smiles, handing over the mirror first thing.

The second mirror *did* help, at least somewhat, although she still had no definite idea how she looked in her getup. But she certainly felt strange with her face pulled wide at the temples, the way Annie twisted the sides of her hair and then pushed all of it into a tight bun. She wondered how long before she would get used to this terribly simple hairstyle but was very glad it had worked out for her to appear this way, as Annie's sister or cousin, here today. She couldn't imagine which would be worse, however: wearing her own modern version of a simple dress and calling attention to herself in a sea of Amish women, or wearing this midcalf-length purple dress of Annie's with its full-length apron and dozens of straight pins poked into the waistline, holding everything together.

As for the lack of makeup, if she were to admit it to herself, it felt surprisingly good to go with a fresh face, although she'd never gone anywhere without her "lips." Lipstick made the world go round, and here she sat with scarcely any color on . . . only a bit of gloss.

At the moment, though, Louisa was becoming more preoccupied with the lack of padding on the seats than the fact that her eyelashes were mascara-less or that her lips were practically au naturel. The backless aspect to the wooden benches made her wonder how the four- and five-year-old children sat quietly for so long on either their parent's lap or next to them—girls with their mothers on one side of the room and little boys with their fathers on the opposite.

Not meaning to stare, she spotted a woman using a simple handkerchief to keep her preschool-aged daughter occupied. Soon a tiny cradle with twin babies in the center appeared from the hankie, and Louisa had to be careful not to smile too broadly, for she had never seen such a thing. Next, the handkerchief was transformed into a series of knots that, when the ends were pulled, gracefully vanished, bringing a look of surprise each time to the pixie-faced child.

All of a sudden, a flash of gray caught Louisa's eye, and she wondered if it was merely her imagination. But soon she heard a steady stream of meows.

*Muffin . . . oh no!*

Annie's eyes widened and she mouthed to Louisa, "Your cat?"

Louisa nodded.

"Just leave him be," Annie whispered back.

Muffin skulked down the narrow space between the rows of benches, back hunkered low, tail high, in prowl posture. Hemmed in as Louisa was, she couldn't get to him, but she leaned over, snapping her fingers gently, whispering the cat's name, desperately trying to divert his attention. But Muffin was headed straight for the front of the meeting—toward Preacher Zook, who seemed unaware of a cat approaching him despite the muffled spattering of *achs* from his congregation.

*What's gotten into Muffin?* Louisa wondered, mortified.

One of the bearded men up front rose from his seat and clapped his hands, which was the wrong thing to do to get a feline's attention, especially her cat. Perhaps the man was attempting to scare Muffin out of the room.

However, Muffin remained planted where he was. In fact, he was now poised for attack only a few inches from Preacher Zook's black shoes.

Annie's father paused suddenly, abandoning his German. "Well, now, seems we've got ourselves a visitor . . . though not such a saintly one, I daresay."

Louisa bowed her head, completely embarrassed. "I'm sorry," she whispered when Annie touched her hand.

"Not your fault."

101

*I forgot to latch the bedroom door,* she recalled.

Preacher Zook spoke again, this time chuckling as he declared the entice-ment for Muffin's humorous entrance into the house of worship. "Seems my shoes tracked in a small temptation for this mouse chaser."

Louisa looked and was shocked to see Annie's father holding up a peacock feather.

"Well, for goodness' sake," Annie said softly, followed by a stymied giggle.

Laughter rippled through the large room where yesterday, minus its removable walls, a living room, sitting area, kitchen, and bedroom had been well defined.

When Louisa looked again, Muffin was gone from view.

Scarcely skipping a beat, Annie's father resumed his sermon-making, and the People were lulled back to reverence by his singsong tone.

An hour later, Louisa was still contemplating Muffin's whereabouts, hop-ing he hadn't completely disappeared into the cat population residing in the Zooks' barn.

Nearby, a little girl strained to look under the bench ahead of her. *Is Muffin hiding there?* Louisa wondered. She could kick herself for all the commotion. *My first Sunday with Annie . . . and this happens!*

She was somewhat reassured by the way Annie's dad had handled the situation with a proper though quite ornery English cat in the middle of their sacred service.

Sighing, she was again taken by the incredibly close proximity of all these people—two hundred and fifty, give or take a few dozen—as Annie's mom had stated earlier, at breakfast. All of them smashed in like pickles in a jar. Louisa considered how good it was they took their baths the night before these Sunday gatherings. Half of the church district was made up of teens, children, and nurs-ing babies, and she had already counted more than a hundred young people—a way to pass the time until she would help Annie and her mother serve the cold cuts and other food items for the common meal, as Annie had called it.

Thinking back to the rare times she had attended church with her parents, Louisa recalled a soft kneeling pad, pipe organ music, and stained-glass windows at the big community church in Littleton, Colorado. She remembered thinking the parishioners seemed distant somehow. Close vested. Far different from this quaint church experience, but Annie had addressed the closeness in one of her early letters, attempting to describe their concept of unity. Not until now did Louisa begin to understand that letter—the idea being fleshed out before her eyes. *A tight-knit group of people . . . close to each other and to God,* she thought as the final hymn was being sung.

Louisa still had not located Muffin by the noon meal, when she was to help Annie and her mother with the distribution of food. Deciding she had no real option but to wait—accepting Annie's assurance that "Muffin will come back"—she cut through dozens of pies, having never seen so many kinds in one place. She also helped set the tables, marveling at the number of people who would enjoy a lunch of bread, cheese, cold cuts, jams, red beets, sweet and sour pickles, and hot coffee here in the Zooks' old farmhouse.

The ministers, both the local and visiting preachers and deacon, along with the eldest church members, sat down to eat at the first table setting. The children ate at the fourth and final setting, and Louisa was surprised at how polite and self-sufficient they were—the older children helping the younger ones.

By the time the massive cleanup was underway, she had lost count of how many introductions Annie had made on her behalf. Funny, because none of the women had ever heard of her before today. Not even Rudy Esh's sister, who looked eager to come over and get acquainted. Rhoda also went out of her way to tell Annie that Susie Yoder was at home, sick with a cold, the reason she hadn't attended the corn-husking bee, either, she said.

Louisa wondered why it was necessary for Rhoda to explain, but Annie seemed to take it in stride. Most interesting to Louisa was the secret Annie had evidently kept all these years . . . that she had a pen pal relationship with a non-Amish woman. *Wouldn't they be surprised at her other bigger secret?*

One after another, women came up to Louisa, repeatedly saying such things as, "Nice to have you visit—what church district did you say you're from?" or "Are you in from a long ways?"

To this, Annie's eyes sparkled with mischief as she apparently enjoyed setting them straight. "Louisa's from clean out west in Colorado. She's actually English, wearin' my for-good clothes."

*Trying to fit in,* Louisa thought with a smile. Yet Annie avoided any mention of their years of correspondence.

Once all the dishes were washed, dried, and put away, Annie, her mother, and all three sisters-in-law, as well as several other women appointed to help, stood around the kitchen chatting. At one point, Annie grabbed Louisa's arm. "Come, I see Esther Hochstetler."

Louisa followed willingly to the corner of the kitchen, where Esther was standing, swaying with a toddler-aged boy asleep in her arms. She recalled having read letters about someone named Essie who had later returned to her given name, Esther. Annie had always indicated Essie was her dearest friend among the People.

"Hullo, Esther," said Annie, giving her a big smile. "I was hopin' I'd see ya today." She turned to Louisa. "Meet my friend Louisa. Doesn't she look ever so Plain?"

Esther cracked a smile. "Louisa's an awful perty name."

"Thanks," said Louisa. "Nice to meet you."

Annie reached over and stroked the sleeping boy's hair. "This is Esther's youngest, John. He's got an older brother, Zach, and a big sister, Laura." Annie went on to say how "awful sweet" Zeke and Esther's little ones were.

Louisa listened, intrigued by the dark circles under Esther's eyes, as well as the pallor of her face. She appeared to be six or seven months pregnant.

"You're comin' to the quilting this week, I hope," Annie said.

"Well, I wasn't plannin' to," Esther was quick to say.

"Ach, you should. I'm goin', and so is Louisa, if she wants to."

Louisa was fascinated by the interplay between Annie and Esther.

Annie continued. "Connecting with the womenfolk, well, it's the only way to make it through . . . at times, ya know."

"S'pose you're right, but I can't get away," Esther replied.

"I'll miss seein' ya, then. Honestly, I will."

Esther nodded, and Louisa thought she saw a glint of a tear in the woman's eyes.

"Take care of yourself, Annie," said Esther. Then to Louisa—"Have a nice time while you're here visitin'. It's good to have you."

"Thanks, Esther. It was very nice meeting you." She wished she might capture on canvas the pathos on the face of the saddest woman she had ever encountered.

# Chapter 17

The first order of business, once the house was vacated of so many people, was to find Muffin. Annie helped with the search, suggesting the barn first, and to this Louisa cringed, visualizing mud and manure caked on Muffin's paws. She had taken care to have him freshly groomed for the trip here.

Climbing up the long ladder to the haymow, she suddenly missed wearing jeans for the first time since arriving here. But she kept up with Annie, following her to peer behind the square hay bales with a flashlight, calling for Muffin. They looked in the lower level of the barn, in the milking area, as well as the bedded areas, and last of all, the milk house, behind the milk tank and the cleaning units.

"He has to be frightened by now," Louisa said, hoping she hadn't seen the last of her pedigree cat.

Annie nodded. "Maybe so, but he's not lost . . . 'least not for long."

Louisa was concerned, but she didn't want to be priggish and mention the cost involved in purchasing such a well-bred cat.

"Have you looked in your room?" asked Annie

"Several times, yes." Louisa thought of Muffin's playful nature. "He's been known to entertain children, so I hope he didn't follow one of them home. Except he's very intelligent, so I doubt that."

"I've never met a smart cat," said Annie.

"Then Muffin's the exception."

"Well, let's think like a cat," Annie said, making a decidedly feline smile. "She has a permanent smirk on her kitty face."

"It's one of the features of the Russian Blue breed," Louisa said. Then she heard a squeal—a catlike one.

"What on earth?"

"That's Muffin!" Louisa announced, relief washing over her.

"It's coming from the cellar, I think."

Quickly, Annie led her down the wood steps to what they called the cold cellar, where hundreds of quarts of vegetables, meats, and fruit were lined up on neat shelves. When they heard the squeal again, they followed the sound to find Muffin—his head stuck in an empty jar.

Louisa quickly knelt, making a fuss over her precious pet.

"Poor thing. He's stuck," Annie said, joining Louisa on the floor.

"This is nuts . . . he's never done anything so weird." *Smart cat, indeed.*

Then Annie, getting down to inspect the situation at eye level, saw the real reason. "Your city cat chased a country mouse, that's what. Look, part of the tail's still in the jar."

"Oh, Muffin, what will I do with you?" Louisa laughed.

"I know for sure one thing," Annie said. "We need a hammer."

"You sure we can't get him loose without breaking the jar?"

"Not unless he holds his breath." Annie burst out laughing now, too.

"At least the lost is found." Louisa stayed with Muffin while Annie went to get her father. "You've got the preacher coming now," she whispered, petting his haunches. "You're in so much trouble!"

Muffin peered out at her, his natural smile still evident.

"This is too funny!" Suddenly she wished she could share this with her parents, but the feeling was short-lived, and her Palm had very little power left anyway.

Annie's father came downstairs along with Annie, who had a big towel in her hand. "Well, now, just what do we have here?" He eyed the situation without cracking a smile.

"Can you get him out safely, Daed?" Annie asked.

He advised Annie to wrap the towel loosely around the canning jar.

Louisa helped hold Muffin's lower body and legs while the towel was put into place. She spoke softly to her cat. "You'll be out of there soon, little boy."

Annie's dad raised the hammer and struck the canning jar through the towel. With a muffled crack the jar broke into large pieces. Muffin was out and not even scratched for all his dim-witted curiosity.

"Thank you," Louisa said to both Annie and her father. "Muffin and I appreciate it."

The Preacher smiled and nodded. He looked at Muffin. "Seems this cat's lookin' for a bit of adventure . . . twice in one day, jah?"

Annie covered her mouth, apparently finding her father's comment amusing.

"I'll keep better tabs on him from now on," Louisa promised.

Annie's eyes twinkled with mischief. "Got to keep tabs on the tabby?"

"Aren't you the punny one?" Louisa cradled her beloved cat.

That evening, Louisa and Annie stood on the back walkway waiting while Omar hitched up his horse to his shiny black buggy used for courting. The air was cold, and Louisa was not at all accustomed to wearing a woolen shawl. It reminded her of playing dress-up when she was little.

"Now, Omar, don't be leavin' us high and dry if you find yourself a girl to take home tonight, ya hear?" Annie said, smiling at her brother.

"Well, why not?" He grinned back.

"You know why."

Louisa found the tone of voice Annie used with her brother to be quite curious. For a girl who had been taught submission to male authority, she certainly felt free to banter with Omar.

Annie whispered to Louisa, eyes bright with mischief, "We best be stickin' together, jah?"

"Well, since I don't speak your language—or understand—it could get very weird." She didn't want to be put in the position of having to find her way back here without either Annie or Omar. "I'm not lookin' for a new boyfriend anyhow. The last one was somewhat of a disaster, as you know."

Annie shook her head, eyes flashing a warning.

"What? Did I say something wrong?"

"Come with me." Annie motioned with her head toward the well pump in the side yard. "We never talk 'bout a beau, present or past, 'specially not in front of another boy. Or a brother. That's how rumors spread, and goodness knows, that's not what you want to happen."

"Well, good," Louisa said, trying not to laugh. "I'm glad that's settled."

A few minutes later, Omar called to them. "Time to get goin' if yous want to be on time."

Annie reached for Louisa's hand and playfully pulled her toward the buggy. "Jah, we'll have us some fun tonight. It's 'bout time. . . ."

Louisa felt hesitant, but she was also interested to see firsthand the social scheme of things from the Amish perspective.

*I can't believe I let her talk me into this barn singing,* she thought, raising her skirt just enough, as Annie did, to get into the open carriage on the left side.

Omar sat on the far right, looking a bit impatient as he held the reins, but Louisa somehow sensed he was enjoying himself. Even though Annie kept poking fun at him.

Once they were on the road, Louisa asked, "Do you think I could ever learn to drive the horse and carriage, Annie?"

Omar leaned forward and looked at her. "I can teach you, easy."

"So can I!" Annie sat straighter, egging Omar on.

"That would be right nice," Louisa said, bringing a pert smile to Annie's face and a chortle from her brother.

They rode for more than a half hour, and as they did, Omar ribbed Annie with his words, looking over at Louisa every so often, no doubt trying to include her in the conversation.

At one point, Louisa asked about the theme of the morning's sermons. "It seemed like the ministers, including your father, were making eye contact with the young people. At least it seemed that way."

Annie spoke up right away. "You're quite right on that. Both sermons were about obedience . . . it's the theme of the day."

Louisa wondered why that should be. "What's up with that?"

"Well, I don't know 'bout up, but there is a downside to not following the Scripture and the Ordnung," Annie said. "For sure."

Omar piped up. "You can say that again."

"Well, like what?"

"For instance, there are several boys in the church district who are known to be runnin' with a wild crowd," Annie explained. "They call themselves the Mule Skinners and have guitars and carry on at Saturday night dances . . . nothin' like the expected behavior at our Sunday singings, I can tell you. If they were baptized church members and actin' like this, they'd be put under the shun."

"Most definitely," Omar said solemnly. "They don't care how they hurt their parents and younger siblings with the fancy clothes they wear and their English hair cuts 'n' all."

"More than likely, that's the reason for all the preaching on submission to God and the authority of the People," Annie said. "Nearly *every* meeting, here lately."

"*Authority of the People* . . ." Louisa considered the idea of kowtowing to the expectations of an austere group. Even Annie was struggling, and Louisa knew this to be true. All these years of hiding her artwork, Annie had been disobeying or "sinning," as she always called it in her letters.

The buggy ride afforded plenty of time to think—an evening for some hard thoughts, continuing with the jolting impressions she had experienced while enduring the hardness of the church benches earlier. One of the more positive things about Annie's people was their connectedness. Louisa didn't have to understand Dutch to get this. They cared for each other with unusual compassion, including their very young and their aged. High regard was given to the elderly men and women at the large church gathering, evidenced by their being served the noon meal first. But it was the concept of an integrated sharing community—putting everything into a common pot—that shook her to the core.

*If only my mother might understand this, if not witness it for herself.*

Such a perception was foreign to Louisa's upbringing. Instead of hoarding wealth or spending it on oneself, a person could supposedly lay up treasures in the hereafter by demonstrating kindness and extending love and thoughtfulness, as Annie had explained with great enthusiasm following the church gathering. She described a community where people shared not only their finances but also time and energy. Annie said this was one way to carry out God's will on the earth, helping one another. Even to the point of sacrifice, if need be.

The thought made her eyes swim, and she had an irresistible urge to continue dressing Plain. *I might even ask to borrow one of Annie's cotton nightgowns,* she thought, not understanding this new and peculiar yearning but wanting to follow wherever it might lead.

The tranquility of the buggy ride was eventually replaced with noise and laughter coming from a large barn as Louisa and Annie stepped down from the open carriage.

"I'll wait for you two," Omar said, tying the horse to the post.

"Well, you better!" Annie called over her shoulder.

Louisa was amused. "You and your brother are a hoot."

"You think so?"

"Omar enjoys throwing barbs, I can tell. And you give it right back."

Annie nodded. "Well, you haven't seen anything. Wait'll you meet Yonie if you think Omar's that way. Yonie and I are constantly carryin' on . . . never get our feelin's hurt, though. My brothers would be the first to defend me, I know."

Unable to relate to sibling camaraderie, Louisa was quiet as she followed Annie into the barn. She took in the curious scene, aware of not only the sights but also the noticeable farm scent, which her college friends would describe as a stench. None of which seemed to deter the crowd of Plain-garbed youth milling about, some in the lower area, near the stabled animals, others up in the haymow, swept clean for the gathering.

She heard the strains of country music. "Hey, check it out."

Annie leaned forward a bit . . . then frowned. "Someone's goin' to be in trouble. It's got to be a radio or a CD player, one of the two."

For a moment, Louisa wondered why an Amish barn would be rigged for electricity. "Must run on batteries," she said.

"Always batteries. Still, we're not s'posed to have radios at singings. My father's spoken out on this at Preachin' plenty of times." Annie began to explain the different groups of kids, called "crowds." Some who pushed the boundaries and were considered liberal, some who were more middle of the road, and about five different groups like the one assembling here, who were more likely to toe the line. "Even still, there's often a rowdy one who tries to influence everyone else."

Louisa had never had a reason to question the rank and file of Amish youth. She assumed they were all similar to Annie, merely wanting to have a good time mingling with the opposite sex, and ultimately, making a decision about their future. She had not expected to hear Kenny Chesney crooning "When the Sun Goes Down." Not here. And looking up, she spied the culprit perched high in the rafters. "Look, Annie." She pointed at the portable CD player.

Annie craned her neck. "I wonder how it got up *there*."

"Got a gymnast in this group?"

"Jah, it takes all kinds." Annie stopped walking and turned toward Louisa. "Don't stare, whatever you do, but over yonder's my old beau."

"Auburn hair, right?" She remembered from Annie's description in her letters and had already spotted Rudy standing with several other boys.

"Uh-huh."

*He's gorgeous,* she thought. *Amish or not.*

"Oh . . . no," Annie sputtered.

"What?"

"He's lookin' this way."

Not only looking, but Rudy was walking toward them. "Don't freak," she told Annie softly. "Be cool."

Rudy strolled right up to them. "Hullo, Annie. Nice to see ya." Then he smiled at Louisa, removing his straw hat. "You from round here?"

Annie spoke up. "This is Louisa Stratford, a friend of mine from Colorado."

Nodding, Louisa said, "Hey. How's it going?" But by the surprised look on his face she realized she'd said the wrong thing, the wrong way. *Too forward for a girl who looks Amish.*

Rudy frowned, scratching his head and eyeing Annie. "Stratford? Never heard of that one."

"That's because Louisa's English," Annie said.

"But I sure don't look fancy, do I?" Louisa couldn't resist, and it was all she could do not to burst out laughing. This Rudy was a wreck, absolutely on edge around Annie.

"You're as Plain as any girl here." He offered a quick smile at last. With that he waved, especially at Annie, then put his hat back on, turned, and marched back across the barn to the other young men.

"Oh," Annie groaned.

"Yeah, I see what you mean. He's cute." She studied Annie, obviously still pining. "Why not get back with him again? It's not too late, is it?"

"No . . . no, you don't understand" came Annie's woeful reply.

"Well, I'm not blind. I can see how miserable he is without you." She was convinced of this . . . she'd seen the way he looked at Annie.

"I can't have it both ways—Rudy *and* my art." Annie sighed, turning away from the growing swarm of boys. "In order to ever marry at all, I would have to turn my back on my drawings and paintings."

"Bummer," Louisa whispered.

"Time's running out for me . . . and the pickin's will become slim once I turn twenty-one. Most fellas get hitched up pretty quick once they eye the new batch of sixteen-year-old girls each year." Annie began to walk toward the barn door, swung wide for the evening.

"Sixteen? Wow, that's young."

"That's when we start courting, lots of us girls do."

Louisa shook her head. "Well, how can anyone possibly know who . . . or what . . . they want at that age? At twenty-two, I nearly made a huge mistake marrying the wrong guy."

"I know girls who marry and are expectin' their first baby by the time they're turning just eighteen."

"That's way too young," Louisa said again.

"It's our way."

*Makes no sense to me.* Louisa looked at the dark sky, glad to have escaped the din of the barn. Several lone stars cut through the blackness, and she sensed Annie's dire frustration—being trapped between wanting her art and wishing to be a wife and mother someday, which suddenly united with Louisa's own very discouraging position.

# Chapter 18

Jesse was mighty glad for a morning without a single wisp of a cloud, and this being wash day, his wife would be, too. As for his own work, he had offered to help one of the older farmers, Al Fisher, extend a field by digging up a section of pastureland. Luke and Omar were going to lend a hand to yet another farmer—finishing the plowing—so the three of them would leave for the day soon after breakfast. Once Omar cut their hair, that is. Jesse was glad not to bother Barbara with the chore. *Anything to ease her duties. . . .*

Luke's and Omar's absence later today might benefit Barbara and Annie in that they could forget about cooking up a big meal at noon. Of course, with Louisa there they still might make themselves a nice hot meal, with plenty of leftovers for the evening meal, he hoped.

While Barbara cleared the table and put away the leftovers, Jesse sat mighty still as Omar snipped away at his hair. "Keep it just below my ears," he advised.

"Jah, Daed, I will," Omar said. "It got awful long this time. Your bangs, too. Nearly in your eyes they are!"

Luke sat in the corner drinking coffee while he waited his turn. Jesse let his mind wander back to his sons' toddler days . . . how the three of them had come all in a row. Annie, too, being the only daughter—sandwiched between three brothers on either side. Barbara had been overly protective of Jesse Jr., Christian, and Abner. For all good reason, he supposed. There had been no more kidnappings in the area, and for this Jesse was most grateful. But he had never stopped thinking that if Daniel Hochstetler had not exerted his own will against that of the Lord God's, they all would be waiting for Isaac to make his baptismal vow and join church about now. *Just as someone else ought to be doing,* he thought.

When Omar was finished with him, Jesse hurried outdoors and quickly brushed the hair snippets off his neck and shirt. He could hear Luke grumbling about being next, the typical protests that occurred every six weeks or so, when haircuts were in order.

Later, while making his way south toward the far edge of Paradise Township—to a field near the Strasburg railroad station—Jesse contemplated the contents of his sack lunch. Annie and Louisa had made a fine one for him, and he'd overheard them whispering as they buttered bread enough for two sandwiches, then spread the dressing nice and thick, sliced the liverwurst and dill pickles and topped both sandwiches with lettuce. A hefty helping of potato salad awaited him, along with a fruity Jell-O salad and four oatmeal raisin cookies, his favorite. He'd taken note of Annie's exceptional cheerfulness—a distinct shift from her attitude prior to Louisa's arrival. Just why that would be, he had no idea.

He had much back-breaking work ahead of him today, so he must save his energy and let the women fuss over lost love and whatnot all.

Halting the field mules, Jesse set down the handheld single-bottom plow to pause a moment, mopping his brow. The sun was exceedingly warm for a November day, its rays bouncing off the silo in the distance. With more work to be done to smooth out this section of the former pasture, he was relieved to see one of Al's daughters, Becky, running across the field toward him, carrying a thermos.

*Something to wet my whistle.*

At the edge of the field, Al was trudging along, working another handheld plow, and moving at a slow but steady pace. By midafternoon, Jesse figured they'd have this section of land plowed and fertilized with plenty of manure, ready for planting come spring.

"Would ya care for a drink, Preacher?" Becky asked shyly, her cheeks bright pink.

"Denki," he said. "'Tis good of you."

She opened the lid with clean hands and poured the ice water, offering him the red plastic cup. He drank the water straight down, then another cup, and at last, a third.

"Be sure 'n' take some over to your pop. He looks all in." Jesse wiped his mouth, and Becky turned to leave, thermos in hand.

Refreshed some, he resumed the mind-numbing work and eyed the double hitch, as well as the four hard-working mules ahead, making well-defined furrows in the soil.

He pondered yesterday's sermon as he steadied the plow. All day Sunday he hadn't been himself, although not physically ill; he knew that much. Too much of his time was spent in wonderment, pondering his daughter's standoffish attitude toward church membership. Preacher Moses and Bishop Andy had both urged him to give the long sermon, but had they known of his malaise, they would not have pressed him to stand for the two hours necessary to give the biblical account of Adam's fall to Abraham's faith, followed by an even longer retelling of the life of John the Baptist to the close of the apostle Paul's numerous missionary journeys. Jesse had known something was terribly out of kilter that morning. Then, of all things, Louisa's feisty gray cat had appeared, ready to pounce on his shoes, which further added to his distress, even though he thought he'd concealed it well.

Inhaling more slowly now, he was aware of the sun beating hard on his back, but he would not let the unseasonably warm afternoon deter him. He kept his gaze on the ground, watching the grassy chunks of sod turn over as the plow loosed and aerated the soil.

In the middle of the row, a flash of something light caught his eye in the dark soil. *Bone colored.*

Halting the mules, he let go of the plow and leaned down to look, thinking this must be a decomposed animal, nothing more. But as he moved away the dirt, he drew in a quick breath.

There before him was a partial section of what appeared to be a skeleton sticking out of the earth, which did not resemble that of an animal. Suddenly, he was compelled to dig deeper, using his gloved hands to burrow out the buried remains.

A human child. Small, yet complete, the frame was perfectly undamaged.

He recoiled at the sight, unable to speak. *O Lord God and heavenly Father,* he prayed silently.

He opened his mouth to holler at Al, but on second thought stifled the urge to call the man over. Indecisive, he wondered if he should leave the remains as they were and hurry to the bishop or attempt to bury the bones even deeper and simply keep mum. Never to speak a word of this.

But if his assumptions were correct, he would like to have more to go on than simply the size of the skeleton, which prompted his thoughts toward the small boy who'd disappeared years before. Emboldened now, he searched further, on his hands and knees beneath the plow.

Lo and behold, his right hand bumped something small and round. Scraping it out of the earth, he saw the lump to be mud-caked with hints of gold shining through. He removed an old work handkerchief from his pants pocket and warily wiped the face of a pocket watch, searching for a set of initials, unaware he was whispering to himself, heart pumping hard. "Anything . . . *anything* to go on."

But look as he might, there were no recognizable decorations or markings to point definitively to the missing child. Even so, a dozen thoughts flooded his mind, not the least of which was "Ichabod," and he knew beyond any doubt he must pay a visit to the bishop immediately.

Esther sighed, leaning against the doorjamb between the kitchen and the sitting room. Fondly she observed Laura, who was sitting on the kitchen floor, entertaining her brothers. She was building with a combination of wooden blocks and checkers, creating what looked to be a small village, while Zach and John watched.

Remarkably, little John had not swung his dimpled fist to knock down the creation as of yet, but he *was* wide-eyed and intent on Laura's placement of the final red checker.

"There we go," said Laura. "See? This is Dat's big barn and there's the woodshed."

"Big barn." John echoed, his babyish voice so cute.

"*Two*-story barn," Zach added, pointing to the second level.

Laura smiled, nodding broadly. "That's right. Dat's barn has two big stories."

"Wanna story." Zach got up right quick and hurried to her. "Story now, Mamma?"

Jah, she wished she might sit and rest alone. But with Zeke over chewing the fat and having coffee with their neighbor, now was as good a time as any, she guessed. Soon it would be bedtime, and she was all done in from the long day of washing and hanging out clothes. Tomorrow she would iron every single piece.

She thought of asking Laura to make up a soothing tale for the boys. But, no, Laura had spent quite a lot of time with her brothers already while Esther redd up the supper dishes. Young Laura needn't have so much responsibility thrust on her just yet, even though it was inevitable what with another baby brother or sister on the way.

Tonight Esther would do her best to recite a Bible story, hoping she wouldn't leave out anything important like last time. "I'll tell you a true story, 'bout baby Moses," she said, which got both Laura's and Zach's attention. "Come, let's sit together."

Going to her husband's rocking chair near the wood stove, she took John onto her lap, while Zach and Laura sat at her knee.

Laura's eyes sparkled with anticipation, and once again Esther was reminded of her daughter's sweetness. The Amish midwife who'd helped deliver her had declared the little bundle a "perfect baby . . . with nary a single flaw." And now as Laura reached over and placed a protective arm around Zach, Esther's heart was filled anew with appreciation for this wee angel of a daughter. The fact that Laura could endure a whipping one day and display such a lovely disposition in spite of it the next was truly a marvel. Esther's own childhood experience with occasional thrashings served not to soften her spirit at all, but rather had borne resentment in her, although she had long since forgiven her father for his quick temper. *As I must Zeke*, she thought suddenly, but there was not an ounce of mercy left in her for her husband.

"Once upon a time, long, long ago, a baby boy was born to a devout and humble woman named Jochebed, wife of Amram . . . daughter of Levi." Esther began the story for her attentive threesome, but this one was especially for Laura, who loved it above all others.

Jesse stood, legs locked, in the most concealed corner of the bishop's barn. "Well, sure, if you think we must keep this in-house, then so be it."

Bishop Stoltzfus folded his knobby arthritic hands and bowed his white head momentarily, exhibiting a well-known determined pose. "I will speak with our neighboring bishop on this, but I'm sure the decision not to call in the authorities will be made. The Hochstetler kidnapping was never reported, as you recall. And that's how it should be."

Jesse remembered, all right. He'd never forgotten the panic of the nighttime search, the days of waiting for news, the family's eventual moving from the area, and the silence lapsing into the stupor of years . . . the yearning to put the reprehensible incident behind them, needing to move on with life, which they all had done to some degree, he supposed. Some more than others. Till now.

No question, the abduction had altered their lives. His own wife's jovial nature and carefree approach to mothering changed overnight. And when

Jesse Jr. married and his Sarah Mae began bearing children, Barbara began to fret and hover over each newborn grandchild, as well.

"'Tis best we keep the police out of this, as we always have," the bishop said.

Jesse had never questioned the ordained man. Bishop Andy's way was best, prompted wisely by the Lord God, he knew. But it was the other minister, Preacher Moses Hochstetler, whose decision-making processes concerned Jesse. That and the fact he was related to Zeke Hochstetler and poor dead Isaac. Besides, Moses was as frail as any of their elderly church members. "Will you be sharin' any of this with Moses?" asked Jesse.

The bishop paused, clearly contemplating what to do. "I'll have to think on that," he said at last. "The cat is so easily let out of the bag, you know."

*Jah, which means the womenfolk need not hear of this*, thought Jesse.

"Mum's the word, I daresay," Bishop Andy stated. The two men locked eyes, considering the seriousness of the situation.

They continued talking quietly for a while longer in the solitude of the barn, bringing up the need for a suitable burial.

"You covered the bones up adequately, you say?"

"For the time being, at least." Jesse lowered his voice. "I marked the spot by countin' the paces to the cemetery. I can easily return to the location."

"By all means, get over there later on tonight. I'll meet you behind the stone wall . . . somewhere safe, where no one will ever notice a freshly dug hole."

Agreeing with the bishop's plan, Jesse contemplated what must have happened that fateful night. "The little fella surely put up a fuss—a feisty one, he always was, remember?—and the kidnapper must've dumped his body in that pasture at the time, on his way out of town."

"Just can't figure why a killer would seek out our farmland for such a burial," the bishop said, his brow crinkly now.

"In some circles, Amish land is considered to be hallowed ground . . . 'least by the English," Jesse said. "And this isn't the first time, either." He cited several cases where, over a period of years, Amish soil had been chosen as burial plots for victims of serial killers.

The bishop's eyes were suddenly bright with tears. "The pitiable family . . . what they surely have suffered all these years since. Ichabod included, poor fellow, not knowing what happened . . . aside from God's sovereign judgment." He sighed audibly. "But, then, we still don't know, do we?"

"Has anyone kept in touch with the family?" asked Jesse.

"As I understand it, not even the eldest son knows their whereabouts, sad to say."

Jesse shook his head, not in disgust but disbelief. It was impossible to imagine any of his own children abandoning family and faith. Not even Annie. "Knowing *something* just might bring some finality to the parents, jah?"

Bishop wiped his eyes and face with a blue paisley handkerchief. "I'll see what can be done. But this must not leak out amongst the People, mind you."

Indeed, Jesse would heed the older man's admonition. After all, such a bleak report would only stir up more sorrow and foreboding.

# Chapter 19

Annie studied Louisa intently. They were sitting at the writing desk drawing each other's profiles, making a game of it, to see who could draw most accurately and most quickly. Louisa, seemingly anxious to do some sketching again, was all for it, and she held her kitty on her lap as she did.

So far the outline of Louisa's eyes looked just right on the paper, her thick and slightly curly eyelashes nearly exact. Several times Louisa asked if Annie could turn slightly, not blinking.

*This is such fun!* thought Annie.

As she worked, she experienced a sense of purpose and even peace, right here in her own bedroom. Doing something she never would have dared to do had Louisa not come. She knew she was terribly brazen, but who was to know? "Who would've thought we'd ever be doin' this . . . working together?" she said.

Louisa agreed. "Funniest thing. I never considered visiting you until . . . well, you know."

"Perfect timing, jah?" Annie knew what Louisa meant. "Daed often says 'God works in mysterious ways.' And I s'pose this could be one of those times."

"Well . . . I'm not sure how I feel about that," Louisa replied, her face more serious now. "God may be okay for other people, I guess."

"I'm not at all sure what I believe and what I don't," Annie said, then clammed right up, not wanting to discuss such things within earshot of Mamm, who was resting in her own room down the hall.

She turned her attention back to getting the curve of Louisa's brow just so, as well as the shape and length of her cute nose.

119

Some time later, a knock came at the door, and without thinking, Annie said simply, "Come in," only to see that it was Mamm standing there.

"Girls?" Her mother came closer, peering down at their sketchbooks, eyebrows high. "What's this?"

*Too late to hide the truth*, Annie thought glumly. "We're tryin' to draw each other" was her reply.

"Jah, I see that . . . and these are ever so good, I daresay." Mamm stepped back a bit.

Annie could hear Mamm breathing hard, and she cringed, waiting for the words sure to follow.

"I didn't know you could draw like this, Annie."

Louisa's eyes locked on her. *What to say?* The heat rushed to Annie's head and neck. At a loss for words, she blinked, too aware that she was holding her breath.

"I have a group of students back home," Louisa volunteered, speaking up, yet sounding hesitant. "But Annie and I, we're just practicing now, that's all."

Mamm sighed audibly. "Well, your father better not catch you, Annie Zook." With that she stood shaking her head and muttering something about never having heard that Louisa was a teacher. Then she turned and left the room quickly.

Annie felt frozen, her muscles taut as can be. She even wondered if her mouth had gaped open, like a fish. But she waited to speak to Louisa till Mamm's footsteps faded in the hall, and then in only a whisper. "We can never let this happen again. *Never.*"

"I'm so sorry, Annie."

"No . . . no, it's not your fault." Annie closed her sketchbook. "Tomorrow, when we go to my cousin Julia's, I'll show you my art studio. You'll love it as much as I do. And there's no chance of bein' found out there."

Louisa frowned briefly. "This is a huge problem for you, I can see that. I can't imagine not being able to express myself artistically."

"Jah . . . a problem's putting it mildly."

"I don't want to cause further trouble for you." Louisa was frowning now, glancing back toward the door. "Your mother is obviously upset."

"At me, 'specially. So not to worry. Promise me ya won't?" Then she gasped, remembering Julia's insistence on entering her painting in the upcoming magazine contest. "Ach, no . . ."

"What?"

In all the excitement of having her friend visit, Annie had completely forgotten this secret tidbit. Now with Mamm's stern warning, and the likelihood of her father being told, Annie dreaded the possibility of word getting out—whether she should win or not. *I never should've let Julia twist my arm!* she thought.

"What is it?" asked Louisa. "You're suddenly pale."

*Can I even trust my cousin to keep quiet?* Annie inhaled sharply. "You'll never guess what dumb thing I did. . . ."

After Annie had turned in for the night, Louisa lay awake. It was hours before her usual bedtime and she couldn't fall asleep. So she crept down the hall to Annie's room, careful not to wake her. There, she set the old framed self-portrait of Annie on the dresser. Stifling the urge to giggle like a schoolgirl pulling a prank, she tiptoed back to her room and slipped into bed. Still, she was too wired to close her eyes, too worried about Annie. What would Barbara Zook tell her husband about her discovery tonight? And what would Preacher Jesse do about it?

Turning in bed, she was conscious of an owl's persistent hoot. *Right outside my window?* she wondered.

Curious as to the location of the loud and immediate call, she again left her curled-up cat and went to the window. She raised it easily. Then, deciding to remove the screen, she did so and poked her head out.

The night was a silent, glowing basin before her, as the moon lit the pastureland and plowed fields in all directions. She listened, straining her ears.

Once, as a little girl, she had gone with her grandfather into the woods on a full-moon night, as he had called it. Enthusiastic about seeing the wide-eyed swivel-necked creature in the Connecticut woods at Christmastime, she had been intimidated by the size and grandeur of the black forest. But she had been equally intent on the owling adventure. In the space of a mere hour, they had thrilled to the eerie call of several owls but had not been successful at spotting a single one. Even so, the memory of the breathtaking experience remained all these years.

Less than two minutes had passed since throwing open the window. Suddenly, as if on cue, Louisa felt a brush of air against her face. The realization was nearly jolting.

*Where is he?* she wondered, looking . . . looking.

Then she saw the extended graceful wings, silver-brown in the moonlight, thrust straight out in a thin, silent line above the open field. She memorized the longed-for image, wishing the owl were flying toward her instead of away.

Tears sprang to her eyes, and she struggled to see as he flew with seemingly little effort, gliding over the harvested cornfield.

*After all these years, is it a sign?*

Suddenly from below, she heard a door open and there appeared Annie's father heading for the road, a shovel slung over his broad shoulder.

She stood there staring down at him until he disappeared into the shadows. *What sort of Amish work is required so late?* she wondered.

Esther was sitting reading the old German Bible by the cookstove when Zeke came into the kitchen, looking for seconds on pie left over from supper. He sat down at his usual spot at the head of the table, as if planting himself anywhere else might give the wrong notion to Esther . . . that he was loosening the reins even for a moment. She was probably wrong, but she sensed it all the same, the unspoken aspects of his dominance.

Closing the family Bible, she leaned her head back, aware of the smack of Zeke's lips as he enjoyed the pie. She couldn't stop thinking of Annie's introduction yesterday . . . of her English friend, Louisa. And she found it ever so curious that the preacher's daughter should be entertaining a worldly girl, one who'd been kept very much a secret from the People, evidently, although Esther remembered Annie had mentioned a pen pal back when she and Annie were schoolgirls.

Still, there was something terribly enticing about Annie's way. At times she had observed Annie in the line of young single women waiting to enter house church on a Sunday morning. Invariably, she would be the only girl with her hand perched on her hip. Not that Annie wanted to be bad-tempered, no. Neither was she known for being defiant. Even so, Esther thought she knew what made her tick, deep down. Preacher Zook's only daughter had some difficulty with the idea of wholly submitting. Rudy Esh was only one case in point.

Esther thought again of Annie's enthusiastic invitation to the quilting bee this week. Just the talk of work frolics and such left Esther feeling nearly overwhelmed. Too many prattling women sitting round a quilt frame gave her the jitters anymore.

Truth was, she enjoyed the company of the other women, but she felt out of step with them. As though *they* were doing what was expected and she was not. She privately questioned the whys and wherefores of submitting to male authority. It was impossible not to. She hadn't had the luxury of being born with the desire to simply say *jah*, like her female counterparts.

She sighed, acknowledging to herself that she made a consistent effort to put her best foot forward nearly all the time—at least giving the appearance that all was well. Yet she knew otherwise and was beginning to suspect that Annie may have been sensing it, too.

More often than she cared to admit, even to herself, she imagined rising up and shaking her fist at a man. Especially at Zeke.

She wished he might hurry and finish his snack so she could clean up after him. *Yet again.*

Rocking harder now, she clenched her fists, her breath coming faster as she stared a hole in the back of his head. She might have blurted out a terrible thing if someone hadn't come riding up the lane right then.

Zeke got up and looked out. "Well, I'll be. The bishop's dropped by," he said and hurried out through the back porch.

"Hullo, Ezekiel," she heard the minister say to her husband.

But the men's words faded quickly, and Esther rose and went to stand near the window. Curiously, she watched the two of them mosey out to the barn in the fading light, wondering what was up, even though it was not her place to know or to inquire.

When the bishop reached over and placed a hand on Zeke's shoulder, she knew there was definitely something off beam. *What on earth?*

# Chapter 20

Waking up the next morning, Annie was thankful for a few minutes to stretch and relax beneath her colorful quilts before getting up for the day. She snuggled down in her warm bed, staring at the window across the room, noting the slowly-shifting glow as dawn inched its way into daylight.

Eyes fixed on the light, she pondered Louisa's visit thus far. She knew one thing sure, she was beginning to see her own surroundings through her friend's eyes . . . grasping a glimpse of the peace she and the People seemed to take for granted. Right along with the rigid expectations weighing her down at times, though she attempted to conceal any negativity from her family.

She thought back to Sunday night, following their buggy ride home from the singing, when Louisa had said the most surprising thing: "The peacefulness here . . . it's like a sort of blessing hangs in the air."

*Funny, hearing Louisa say such a thing. . . .*

Louisa had never expressed this before, and Annie hadn't ever thought of Paradise that way. But she guessed the immense contrast between city living and Amish country was rather severe to Louisa. The farthest she had ever ventured into the populace of Lancaster was to the town of Strasburg. Which was enough of a jolt to her, what with tourists driving here and there, milling about, and in and out of the quaint little shops on the cobblestone sidewalks.

Today, though, she was anxious to accomplish her home chores quickly and head to Cousin Julia's for the remainder of the day. Still upset at Mamm's discovery of the two artists at work, she decided it would be nice if her friend could possibly paint to her heart's content in the attic studio while Annie did her housework for Julia.

*A wonderful-good surprise*, she thought, slipping out of bed and hurrying to put on her house slippers and long white cotton robe.

She went to the dresser and picked up the small hand mirror. Pouring a bit of water from the pitcher to the ceramic basin, she began to wash her face in the cold water. Quickly, she patted her face dry with an embroidered linen towel.

Just then she spotted a gold-framed picture Louisa must have left on the corner of the dresser. "For goodness' sake!" She studied the long-ago drawing of herself. *I hope I've improved since this*, she thought, knowing without a doubt she had. The early morning surprise brought a smile, and she could scarcely wait to thank Louisa.

*Best not have this on display anymore!* She placed the picture in her bathrobe pocket and tiptoed over to Louisa's room.

Jesse rose earlier than usual, still both mystified and shaken by the unearthing in Al Fisher's pastureland. The bishop had been quite prompt in meeting him last night, and together they'd decided upon an out-of-the-way spot for the suitable burial—a safe distance, deep into the walnut grove, behind the Amish cemetery, where they left no grave marker to signal the shared secret.

As for the bishop's plan to visit the Hochstetler farm last evening, Jesse speculated how Zeke had taken such hard news. The headstrong man was also known to be quite outspoken. But Jesse had always assumed the fiery nature had more to do with Zeke's inability to forgive himself for his brother's disappearance than anything else.

Jesse shuddered and considered how such information would have affected him . . . *if I were the son of Ichabod*. . . .

Then and there, he purposed to reach out to the younger man, the first chance possible.

For now, though, he best get himself across the road for milking, because following breakfast he must head to an all-day wedding, where he was expected to give the *Anfang*, the opening comments, prior to the bishop's main sermon. He also must shake off his impending feeling of doom, wishing to convey a cheerful countenance on behalf of the bridegroom and bride.

Annie offered to take the horse and buggy over to Julia's, but Louisa insisted they walk, just as Annie always liked to. "Look over there." She pointed to their neighbors' farmhouse as they made their way along the road. "That's where the girl lived who first requested you as a pen pal. See how the electric lines run right up to their house and barn?"

"So *that's* how you know who's Amish and who isn't?"

Annie laughed softly. "Well, it's one way. You also have to watch for horsey apples in the lane."

This got a sniggle from Louisa, who looked as Amish as Annie was, except she'd twisted the sides of her hair looser than Annie ever would have. *At least she's learning.*

"What's Jenna Danz doing these days?" Louisa asked. "Haven't heard from her in years."

"If you'd like to, we could stop by the house and ask 'bout her. The Danzes are ever so friendly."

"No, I'm here to hang with you." Louisa was lugging her laptop in a leather case, evidently ready for some connection with the outside world.

"So . . . does hanging with someone ever hurt?" Annie tried not to giggle.

Louisa wrinkled her nose. "You're as bad a tease as I am."

"That's for sure." Several horse-drawn buggies went by, and Annie waved at each one.

"Where's everybody going?"

"It's Tuesday, so I'd have to say they're headed for weddings. Most families get multiple invitations. They might have relatives in other church districts, so they must decide which one to attend . . . a busy time." She hated saying it, worried that another mention of a wedding might upset Louisa.

"How many in a single day?"

"Oh, oodles, really."

"Do you ever stay home," Louisa asked, "just skip going?"

"Most of the weddings in the past few years have been for my first cousins—close in age—or friends of mine." She sighed, not sure how to explain that it was beyond rude not to attend. "For me not to go would be similar to shunning someone for a whole day. It's just not done." *No matter how difficult,* she thought, aware of the wrench in her heart again, relieved that the couples marrying today were not close kin.

"Fascinating . . . to set aside a time of year just for weddings," Louisa replied. "Like we moderns have our June weddings . . ."

Annie smiled. "My father's glad to be finished with plowing, 'specially with his responsibilities for tying the knot for quite a few couples. He'll be busy for the next few months."

"Well, he certainly looked busy last night, too."

"What are you talking about?"

"I saw him carrying a shovel . . . out to the road. Must've been round nine o'clock."

Annie shook her head. "You must be mistaken. Daed always goes to bed with the chickens."

"Say what you like, but I saw what I saw."

"And you also must've spotted an owl, too, jah?" Annie covered her mouth, stifling a laugh.

Louisa pulled a face. "As a matter of fact, I did! Didn't you hear him?"

"I heard him, all right. I almost got up and went downstairs. Sometimes I creep out into the night and shine a flashlight on them. Daed's caught me several times."

"I felt the silent flap of his wings and saw the hind end of him. Amazing. So . . . can you guess what I plan to draw the moment my peacock painting is finished?"

"My father chasing an owl?" She couldn't help it, she burst out laughing.

"Very funny, Annie."

Annie was exceptionally surprised about Louisa's encounter with the owl—hindquarters or not. But she wasn't about to reveal the common superstition: if a person sees an owl up close it sometimes points to a death. No sense causing Louisa to freak out, as she liked to say. Still, the *bird of death* had flown over them.

They walked farther, soaking up the sunshine and enjoying the fresh air as the tension between them subsided.

Louisa brushed off her apron. "Does your cousin have an indoor bathroom? I would love a shower!"

"Sure. Julia won't mind at all if you shower there." Annie found Louisa's need for soap and water interesting. Not even half a week had passed since their Saturday night baths!

"I've been thinking about something else, too, Annie. If it's not a problem, would you care if I washed my hair more than once a week? I don't think I can stand it for more than three days, which it is today."

"Oh, you can shower at Julia's on Tuesdays and Fridays, take a bath at my house on Saturday night . . . and, in between, there's always the makeshift shower Daed and the boys use out in the barn. Goodness' sake, you'll be the cleanest girl round here!"

They counted fifteen more buggies coming their way, and at one point Louisa said, "I've never felt so strangely miserable and wonderful at the same time. Except for maybe the summer I spent with one of my aunts."

"Why's that?"

"I think it comes down to the basics, and I'm not talking baths or showers or indoor plumbing." Louisa slowed her pace. "Sure, I miss all the conveniences of my home, yet I feel somehow closer to all that is good."

"To the Lord God, you mean?"

"I don't know." Louisa turned to look at her. She had an almost sad expression. "Do you ever wish, sometimes, that there was something way more tangible to believing? I mean, than just a bunch of one-way prayers?"

"Well, my cousin Julia has conversations with the Lord. I'm not kidding, she honestly does." Annie wondered if she should go on, but she forged ahead. "I say silent rote prayers first thing in the morning and the last thing at night. I've never considered addressing God the way Julia does."

"Really? You don't *speak* your prayers?"

"Never."

"Well, then, I'll have to get acquainted with this cousin of yours."

A lone horse and carriage was coming their way, and at a fast clip. When Annie spied Susie Yoder and her older brother, a surprising lump caught in her throat. Instead of calling out her usual cheerful hullo, she merely raised her hand to wave.

Susie, wearing her for-good blue cape dress and white apron, was quick to return the wave, smiling and glancing at her brother who held the reins, wearing his best black suit and bow tie. When Susie looked back at Annie, there was a noticeable twinkle in her eyes and a radiant smile on her dimpled face.

*She looks too happy not to be in love. . . .*

Annie's heart sank like a millstone. *Oh, what's-a-matter with me?*

After all, it was to be expected that Susie would spend the afternoon and evening, following the all-day wedding festivities she was apparently headed to, playing games and attending a late-night barn singing with Rudy, along with many other courting couples. There was no other reason for Susie's big brother to be driving her today otherwise.

Annie swallowed hard. *Since I refused to marry Rudy, why should I begrudge Susie her happiness?*

Momentarily she wondered what it might be like to somehow get Rudy's attention back for herself. To abruptly abandon the near-delirious joy of mixing colors, painting whatever her heart desired. But such thoughts troubled her greatly. No, she could not substitute a man—not even Rudy—for her dearest love.

# Chapter 21

Esther did not know what to make of Zeke's peculiar behavior. Nearly all day he stayed close to the house, except for doing necessary barn chores. He was spending more time with their boys than any other weekday she ever recalled—playing with them indoors, in the yard, and even washing their faces after the noon meal.

But each time she looked at her husband this day, she was keenly aware of a painful softness around his eyes. Something she hadn't seen in years. Was it the herbal potion she furtively mixed into his coffee each morning? Or was it linked to the bishop's surprise visit?

*Is someone dreadfully ill? Or has Zeke's father gotten in touch with him at long last? If so, wouldn't Zeke say something?*

She couldn't stop thinking about the bishop's mysterious visit, the good half hour he spent alone with Zeke in the barn. To get her mind off whatever it was, she set about baking an angel food cake for their supper tonight. *Zeke's favorite . . . and Laura's, too.*

"Cousin Julia!" called Annie at the back stoop and let herself in, holding the door for Louisa.

Molly and James came running to meet them, and the sight of the children cheered Annie's heart. "I've brought along my very good friend today," she told the smiling youngsters. "James and Molly, can you say hullo to Louisa?"

129

James grinned, showing his little white teeth. "Hullo, Louisa," he said, mimicking Annie. "You look just like Annie."

"Well! I'll take that as a compliment."

Molly reached for Louisa's hand and smiled shyly. "Molly . . . that's me."

Louisa was clearly taken with the little girl. "It's nice to meet you, honey. Your long braids are beautiful."

Nodding, Molly reached up to touch her hair. "Mommy makes 'em."

"She does good work," Louisa said, touching Molly's head.

Soon, Cousin Julia hurried into the kitchen, face aglow at seeing Louisa.

"Julia, I want you to meet my English pen pal." Annie quickly explained that she wanted to "be one of the People, at least in looks, for the time bein'."

"How thoughtful!" Julia extended her hand to Louisa.

Annie was most grateful for the warm reception, especially since she'd never told Julia about this peculiar friendship. And once the children had gone outside to play, she asked if it was all right for Louisa to have a shower or bath sometime today while they were here.

"Oh my, yes. Help yourself, Louisa . . . anytime, really." Julia's eyes twinkled when she smiled. "I see you've brought your laptop along, but if ever you want to simply use our computer, you can do that, too."

"I appreciate the offer," Louisa said, looking a bit surprised. "So . . . then, you're permitted to use computers?"

Julia nodded. "Well, yes, we are. You might not guess by looking at us, but many Mennonites embrace the whole gamut of technology. We are more conservative than some, but even our little church has its own Web site as an outreach ministry."

They stood and talked awhile longer, and then Julia gave Annie the list of chores for the day. Louisa offered to help, but Annie insisted she should get her shower done. They argued jovially about that, but Annie finally said she could have the ironing out of the way by the time Louisa finished upstairs.

"Well, if you're sure," said Louisa.

"Oh, jah, I am . . . now go and get yourself cleaned up."

Louisa shrugged and smiled, then followed Julia upstairs to the only bathroom in the house while Annie set to work ironing, realizing anew how much easier this task was with the use of an electric iron. But as she pressed Irvin's Sunday shirt, she pushed away envious thoughts, including what fun Susie would be having with Rudy tonight.

She thought instead of Louisa, ever so eager to show her the attic art studio.

*I'm truly gaining a sister, of sorts*, she thought. *If only Mamm hadn't caught us drawing. . . .*

"Come, it's time for you to see my studio," Annie told Louisa once the ironing was finished . . . and when Louisa's hair was dry from her shower, hanging loose over her shoulders.

"Well, hey, you've described it to a tee in your letters, but I'm dying to see it with my own eyes."

Annie motioned for her to follow. "I need your opinion on something else, too." She wanted to know what Louisa thought of her painting, the one featuring the London Vale covered bridge, the cluster of locust trees, and the nearby creek.

When they arrived at the top of the attic steps, Annie reached for the skeleton key high over the doorjamb and unlocked the door. "Have to keep this locked, for obvious reasons," she explained.

"Wow . . . this *is* a top-secret room."

Annie stepped aside. "You go in first."

Louisa walked into the room and slowly moved toward the center. She stood like a slender statue, simply staring. Then, slowly, she turned around, taking in every nook and cranny. Pursing her lips, she said, "What a place. It's terrific."

Annie felt like she might burst. "I want you to spend the rest of today painting here . . . if you'd like."

"You mean it?"

"Well, since you can't just turn it off or on . . . sure. It's been a while since you painted . . . since comin' here." She smiled at her dear friend.

"This is too cool, Annie. I love it!"

Annie paused. Was now a good time to reveal the painting that had been driving her lately? "Uh, just real quick, I want to show you something I've been working on."

Louisa went to stand near the empty easel. "I traveled a long way for this, Annie."

Turning to the artist's desk, Annie gingerly carried the dry canvas, setting it just so on the easel. "This painting has a sad, sad story behind it. For the longest time, I wasn't even sure what to call it."

Louisa stepped back, studying the picture. Then, finally, she said softly, "This is very good." She paused, tilting her head a bit sideways. "You have some really wonderful contrasts here . . . and I can feel the mood. It's an undertow of something portentous. Bravo, Annie."

"You honestly sense something?"

"Absolutely! It pulls me right in."

"It's titled 'Obsession.'"

Louisa turned to look at her. "Meaning what?"

"I'll tell you tomorrow. We'll go up to the covered bridge and walk around."

"Now you have me riveted. I can't wait."

"Well, since Julia's not payin' me to stand here and yak, I need to get busy." She turned toward the stairs.

"So, just like that, you're going to leave me hanging?"

Annie wiggled her fingers in a dainty wave. "You like 'hanging,' remember? Besides, I'll be anxious to see what you paint today!"

With that she headed back to her domestic work, most excited about Louisa's response to the Pequea Creek painting. Yet, once again, she was torn by what the People would think of her if Mamm's discovery got out . . . how disappointed Daed would be. She hated letting her parents down.

*The Lord God must be terribly displeased, too.*

Louisa sat quietly in bed snuggling with her sleepy kitty long after Annie had left the room for the night. They'd talked about their day, and Annie had been quite elated over Louisa's colorful peacock painting, saying she "just knew" this would capture her imagination.

But it was not her own sketching and subsequent painting that intrigued Louisa. Annie's startlingly real depiction gripped her even now as she propped her head up higher with an additional pillow. She wished for a way to offer Annie some technical pointers—to share a wealth of knowledge she had gleaned in L.A. at art school—although Annie was unmistakably on her way to becoming a superb artist under her own steam.

*Remarkable . . . considering her humble background,* she thought. *Shoot, no one even knows!* Except now Annie's mother was on to Annie's talent. . . .

Louisa contemplated what Annie's mom might do at having accidentally discovered Annie's ability—at least in part. It was bad enough for the Zooks to innocently open their home, let alone allow Louisa to influence Annie.

Her eyes roamed the wide plank floorboards to the windowsill, the flush of a full moon all around, and she was taken with the pronounced difference in the wispy, nearly ethereal light she experienced here in this country setting. It was as if she were nestled on the edge of the world as she knew it. Annie's world. Nothing at all like the glaring light of Denver's metropolis.

*Annie was born into this, so how can she possibly appreciate what she has?* wondered Louisa.

But she also pondered the flip side. *What if Annie were to leave the only life she knows?* Louisa shuddered, aware of the fierce competition within the artistic community. *How could an Amish woman possibly survive?*

Louisa decided quickly that Annie was probably better off staying here . . . that is if she would even be allowed to remain for much longer. From everything Annie had shared regarding the strict denial of individual self-expression, Louisa didn't see how Preacher Jesse would allow Annie to stay past a certain age, barring some unexpected turn. And if Annie's pull toward art was as strong as Louisa's own, which she surmised it was, how could Annie simply walk away from that?

High in the cozy attic earlier today, Louisa had gotten so completely lost in her peacock painting she'd forgotten to charge up her Palm. She'd even snoozed checking her email or connecting with her students by IM, too. *Friday's soon enough,* she thought, relishing the hours spent in Annie's delightful studio. *Unless Preacher Zook sends me packing before then!*

Jesse cradled his wife in his arms as they talked in bed, careful to keep his voice low. "I wish I'd known years ago," he told her. Hearing that Louisa was an art teacher did not set well with him. Nor did his wife's recent discovery— Louisa's teaching Annie how to draw. Had Annie tricked all of them, bringing Louisa here? "You were right to tell me, love," he said.

"I do wish you might've seen what I saw. I think you would've been quite surprised. Our Annie, I daresay she may have a gift."

"Now, Barbara . . ."

"No . . . I mean it."

Her words troubled him greatly.

"The best gifts are compassion, serenity, and joy. You know that. Patience, gentleness . . . self-control. And surrender to God, the Ordnung, and the ministry." He paused, thinking how he ought to say further what was on his mind. "Annie's gifts dwell within the confines of the church, not in self-expression." He felt her body tense. "No matter how much talent you may think our daughter has, you cannot encourage Annie in this. We must, all of us, offer ourselves up to God as a community—pure, unspotted, and without blemish. Nothing less will do."

Barbara's breathing came more slowly, yet she did not verbally agree to abide by his wishes.

"Have we made a mistake, bringing the blind and perverted world to our doorstep?" he said.

"Well . . . maybe so." Barbara's voice quivered, and for this reason sleep did not come to Jesse for another wretched hour.

He could not bring himself to think about Annie rejecting the faith, yet he could see she was most surely on the path right out of the community. And having Louisa to talk to and spend an inordinate amount of time with, well, he could kick himself for agreeing to invite Louisa here. Beneath the façade of Amish attire and head covering, she was no more interested in the Plain life than any ungodly outsider. He'd heard her talking on her little phone late into the night, even thought he heard her singing threads of a worldly song alone in the room. Aside from all that, it was rather remarkable how she had made an attempt to fit in. *To please Annie, no doubt.* Despite Moses' prediction, Jesse could see no evidence of Louisa's visit moving his daughter closer to joining church.

*I ought to give Annie a time limit,* he thought. *At what point does a father simply give up hope?*

# Chapter 22

First thing the next morning, Annie tiptoed to Louisa's room. She knocked lightly and whispered, "You awake?" Aware of a small groan, she inched the door open and peeked in. "Psst! Louisa? All right if I come in?"

"You're halfway in already, you goof."

Annie sat on the bed, smiling. "I want to show you around today."

"What about chores?" Louisa sat up and stretched her arms. "And when's that quilting bee you talked about?"

"You'll see how quickly chores get done . . . and we'll even sew you up a dress or two before noon." She was surprised Louisa had remembered the comment made to Esther about the quilting bee. "The quilting's tomorrow—would you like to learn how to make the teeniest tiniest stitches ever?"

Louisa looked at her, a sleepy haze still evident on her pretty face. "That's why I'm here, right?"

"Oh you!" Annie plopped down on the pillow next to Louisa's; her cat came right over. "What did I ever do without a sister?"

"Aw, you're too sweet, Annie."

"I mean it."

"Well, I feel the same way. *And* I have so much catching up to do if I'm going to be a *good* big sister . . . starting with you showing me how to cook on that funky stove of yours."

"Honestly? You want to make breakfast today?"

Louisa nodded, reaching for Muffin. "I'll give it my best shot."

"Sounds like Yonie and his hunting adventure . . . probably shooting everything in sight."

Beverly Lewis

"I'll need time to de-feminize the place so he doesn't freak when he returns." Louisa glanced at the room.

"No matter what, you'll have to open the window and air it out." Annie laughed, but she meant it.

"Hey," Louisa protested, "I told you I wanted to bathe more often!"

"I didn't mean it like that—it smells far too perty in here, that's what."

"Mm-hmm, sure. . . . So, what did you want to show me today?"

"This afternoon, I'll take you to Pequea Creek, where little Isaac disappeared." She paused, looking over her shoulder to see that the door was securely shut. "And we'll smuggle along our sketchbooks, too, if ya want."

Louisa raised her eyebrows. "You're one rebellious chick."

*Chick?* "So now I've been reduced to a fowl?"

"You crack me up, Annie. Go get dressed."

"I'll meet you downstairs in ten minutes." Annie headed to the door.

"Too short. I need time for a sponge bath."

Annie gave a little laugh. "You showered at Julia's yesterday. How clean must ya be?"

Louisa shook her head, feigning a pout.

"Okay, I'll bring up some heated water in a bit."

"Thanks, Annie. Maybe I'll actually be able to live with myself now."

Annie wasted no time giving Louisa a thorough lesson on how to cook on a wood stove. She began by talking about a good grate and how important it was to have a tight fit when it came to tending a fire, as well as keeping it from smoking up the house. "The fire is the focus of your attention, really. Once you get used to how hot you need the surface to be, you'll be fine." She paused, watching Louisa's expression.

"Want to help me get the fire started?" Louisa asked.

"This time, sure. Next time, you'll be ready to do it yourself." Annie pointed out the vents, ash box, and dampers and explained their functions. "Actually, a firebox this size is wonderful-good, 'cause it can hold a fire longer and requires less tending."

"I've read that food cooked or baked on a wood stove tastes better."

"Prob'ly so, but I haven't had much experience otherwise." Annie remembered eating at Cousin Julia's and, once in a blue moon, when she and Rudy were courting, she'd enjoyed supper at Harvest Drive Restaurant, as well as at Dienner's.

"I'll try to remember everything." Louisa reached for the big iron skillet and set it on the counter.

136

"Do you want to gather eggs or set the table?" Annie asked, curious to know which Louisa would choose.

"You're way better at the egg thing, so have at it."

"Ach, you'll be doin' that in your sleep by the time Christmas comes." And then it dawned on her: if Louisa stayed put, she could attend the annual school program at the one-room school, along with all the other fun holiday activities.

Louisa was studying her. "You think I'll ever gather eggs without getting pecked to death by defensive hens?"

"Maybe not." She offered a smile. "When I return from the henhouse, I'll show you how to test the stove's surface for adequate heat, with water droplets. All right?"

Louisa nodded, smiling, and turned to wash her hands. When she'd dried them, she pulled out the utensil drawer and counted eight place settings, including enough for the grandparents next door. "You must be laughing at me, Annie."

"Now, why's that?"

"I must seem nearly helpless in the kitchen . . . at least to your way of doing things."

Annie looked her over good. "I daresay you definitely need another dress or two. That one's got a telltale sign on it, by the way—paint from yesterday's visit to the attic." Here, she lowered her voice to a whisper.

Louisa grimaced. "An apron will remedy that, jah?" She went to the back of the cellar door and removed Barbara's work apron off the hook. "There. Ta-dah!"

Annie had to laugh. "You've come a long way in a few days, Miss Lou. You look and cook Plain, and you talk our first language." With that, she headed for the mud room to put on her work boots.

*Miss Lou? Hey, I like that.*

Louisa watched Annie leave the house, then went to the trestle table and, remembering precisely where each person always sat at mealtime, she began to set the table. "If my mom could see me now. . . ."

At that instant, a little furry creature appeared from under the cellar door and skittered across the width of the kitchen floor. Louisa stifled a squeal, looking around for safety. The mouse ran toward the sink and hid in the shadows. In turn, Louisa dashed to the long bench pushed against the table and hopped up.

Shaking with fright, she spied the rodent running the length of the counter. Then it zipped behind the cookstove. Louisa got up on the table and sat cross-legged there. *This would never happen in my apartment!* she thought.

She contemplated the contrast between the black-and-white checkerboard linoleum floor here and her own high-end ceramic-tiled kitchen with its state-of-the-art Sub-Zero fridge and stainless steel sink. *Definitely no mice!*

Her pulse pounded in her head, because more than anything, she despised rodents—filthy, disease-ridden critters. She leaned down, putting her hands over her face, and groaned. Her mother would be appalled and Michael would be splitting his sides with laughter. Yeah, they were so sure she wouldn't last here, and at the moment Louisa couldn't see herself ever getting down off this table. *Never!*

Without a warning, Annie's grandma wandered over from the Dawdi Haus. "Mornin' to ya, Missy," she said, her head covering a bit cockeyed as she stared at Louisa. "You city girls do yogurt exercises on tables?"

Louisa squelched a nervous laugh. "Uh, no, this isn't exactly yoga." She hated to reveal what a total wimp she was. "I . . . er . . . saw a mouse." She felt ridiculous, but she was too freaked to budge.

Grandma flashed a smile. "Well now, that explains it." She stood there staring. "Did I hear voices a bit ago? Annie's, maybe?"

Nodding, Louisa glanced at the floor. "I had a cooking lesson . . . before the mouse showed up."

"Annie's got you workin', does she?"

"I'd like to pull my weight around here." That struck her funny, and she imagined how strange she must look perched up here.

Grandma Zook shook her cane about, as if shooing away the unwelcome visitor. "There. I daresay it's safe for you to come down now, if you've got your wits 'bout you."

That was definitely her cue to start acting like the empowered young woman she believed herself to be. She unfolded her long legs and hopped to the bench, standing there for a second before entrusting her feet to the floor.

"Quite a morning, already, jah?" Grandma teased.

"I'm still getting acclimated to the country," she said with a smile. Then— "Any mousetraps around here?"

"No need, really, with all them barn cats. And your Muffin . . . where *is* that feline when he's needed?" Grandma's eyes twinkled with mischief.

Cringing at the thought of her beloved kitty's paws getting anywhere near another disgusting mouse, Louisa went immediately to the sink to wash her hands. Then, returning to the table, she folded the white paper napkins and placed one beneath each fork.

The older woman smiled broadly, nodding deliberately. "Annie will have you cookin' all the time, if you're not careful. She's a good teacher . . . but not much interested in domestic chores, seems to me." She hobbled over and sat in the chair at the foot of the table. "My granddaughter's got other things takin' up space in her head . . . ever since she was a wee girl."

Louisa kept her eye out for a return of the mouse.

Grandma Zook continued. "We just don't know 'bout that one. Good-hearted, for sure and for certain, but our Annie thinks her own thoughts." She shook her head in short, quick jerks. "If you have any sway over her, I should hope you can steer her in the right direction."

*That's a tall order*, thought Louisa.

"Her Dawdi and Daed are both worried, 'tween you and me."

Louisa perked up her ears. "Why would that be?" She wasn't playing dumb. She really wanted to know what this little demure grandma was thinking.

"It's a cryin' shame for Annie to snub her nose at the Good Lord." Sighing, Grandma continued. "Seems to me she should've been first in line to join church when she turned courting age, or soon after. Just makes not a whit of sense."

Louisa found it interesting that Annie's grandmother, whom she scarcely knew, felt comfortable opening up like this. "Well, I'm sure Annie will eventually do the right thing."

"I should hope so . . . for the Good Lord and the People," Grandma was quick to say with the fire of sincerity in her eyes.

When Annie returned to the house, Louisa was amazed at the large quantity of eggs in her wire basket.

Annie smiled big. "'Mornin', Mammi . . . I got me a perty big batch."

"Well," said her grandmother, staring at Annie. "You missed all the excitement."

Louisa shrugged, wishing to forget the appearance of the mouse. And when Grandma didn't attempt to tell on her, Louisa was rather pleased . . . as if the older woman and she shared a small secret.

Annie looked somewhat confused. Not inquiring, she motioned for Louisa to go to the sink for some water. "See if the droplets bead and roll . . . and hiss on the stove. You try it."

"Jah . . . bead, roll, and spit. Bead, roll . . . spit," chanted the elderly woman.

When Louisa tested the heat, the water did precisely that. "That's cool," she said.

"No, that's hot," Annie said. "You're ready to scramble up some eggs."

"Mustn't forget the bacon." Grandma Zook came over to observe.

Louisa welcomed her presence. She wasn't hovering the way Louisa's mom typically did. The woman, oddly enough, was most supportive and encouraging, though she merely nodded her little gray head, folding her hands now and then.

But in a few short minutes, even though she tried to keep ahead of the fire by continually scraping the eggs from the bottom of the cast-iron frying pan, Louisa had burned the eggs to a crispy mess. Chagrined, she wished she had attempted fried eggs instead. "I'm so sorry," she said, looking to Annie. "I'll have to start over. What about a back-up plan?"

"Such as what?" asked Annie.

"Peahens' eggs?"

Annie covered her mouth, trying not to laugh, but her eyes told the truth. "No . . . no, *those* eggs are our future peacocks and peahens."

Even Mammi Zook had to hold herself together, she cackled so hard.

"Maybe I'd do better with pancakes," Louisa suggested, hoping so.

Annie quit laughing long enough to say she'd help Louisa figure out when to flip the pancakes.

At that moment, Annie's mother entered the kitchen, looking quite stunned at seeing an Englisher standing at her cookstove. *And a worldly artist, at that!* Louisa was sure Barbara held her at arm's length and would continue to do so. And no wonder.

Annie offered no explanation but quickly began to mix up the pancake batter. Her mother, who must have sniffed the burnt offering, set about making coffee.

It was Mammi Zook who nodded her head silently, patting Louisa's arm before heading over to the table to sit. *What a sweetheart,* thought Louisa, wondering why the older woman hadn't coached her earlier. *Learning by doing.* A concept her own mom had ignored early on as a young mother, too eager to step in and do things herself instead of allowing Louisa to try and possibly fail.

*Part of why I love this place*, Louisa thought. *I'm free to fall flat on my face.*

Thinking ahead, she had difficulty envisioning the process of cutting out a cape dress and sewing it up in a few hours. But then, a few weeks ago she never would have believed she'd be running from an Amish mouse *or* wreaking havoc with breakfast for Annie's family!

Louisa was heartened by Annie's patience toward her . . . stretching the measuring tape from nape of neck to waist, and waistline to hem, as well as all the other vital measurements . . . to marking the hem. "Good thing we're sewing another dress for me. I have to admit, I have a hard time wearing something more than once. And it might be nice to have a nightgown, too. If you think I can sew one of those."

"Oh, well, if you really want to sew your nightclothes, that's fine, but I usually get mine at Wal-Mart."

"No kidding?"

Annie smiled playfully. "They have a hitchin' post out behind the store for us horse-'n'-buggy folk."

"Wow . . . interesting."

"Yeah, we show up every so often in pictures on the pages of the *Lancaster New Era*, one of the local newspapers, I'm told."

Louisa was captivated. "The juxtaposition of the old ways and the modern high-tech world is really quite a clash—nearly startling, actually. Who would believe that people live this way . . . in the twenty-first century?"

She tried to focus on Annie's instruction. It was as if she were in seventh grade home ec class all over again. Except she'd never seen a treadle sewing machine, let alone operated one. It was so tricky to get the rhythm of her feet pressing back and forth. She felt absolutely inept.

"Here, I'll show you once more," Annie offered. "It's like eatin' watermelon, spitting out the seeds, and walking at the same time, jah?"

"I feel like such a klutz."

"You mean clumsy, jah? Here we say *dabbich*."

Louisa repeated the Dutch word and smiled. "I'm slowly building my new vocabulary."

"That you are." Annie's feet worked the treadle, smooth as satin. "It takes some doin' . . . you almost don't want to think 'bout it too hard, though."

Louisa watched and was soon ready to try again. "Your grandmother said you're a good teacher, and you're proving it to me."

"Did she also remind you that I taught at the one-room school for several years?"

"No, but I remember *those* letters back then. You were waking before sunup to crank up the ol' wood stove so your students—all eight grades together—wouldn't shiver during the first hour of school."

"But I quit the second year Rudy was courtin' me. It looked as if I might be getting married that fall, but as you know, I didn't. By then, another girl had taken my spot as teacher." Annie explained how once she graduated from the eighth grade she was immediately eligible to instruct the younger students. "But the minute you're married, you're out."

"How come?"

"A bride is expected to put all her attention into makin' a home for her husband and preparing to bear many children."

"So you couldn't have gone back to teaching even if you wanted to?"

"*Nee*, wouldn't think of it," Annie said. "Such would set me up for tongue-waggin'."

Not wanting to press further, Louisa could read between the lines. Preacher Jesse's daughter was a conundrum to the community. Big time.

*And my coming adds even more fuel to the fire*, Louisa thought. Yet she felt no urgency to abandon Annie and cut short the visit. If anything, she was even more determined to stay and encourage her friend to follow her heart.

## Chapter 23

The first thing Louisa noticed when they arrived at the covered bridge on Belmont Road was how very much it looked like Annie's painting, except for chips of missing reddish-brown paint from several roughly-hewn boards nearest the road. She recalled clearly the way Annie had set the tall craggy trees back away from the road in her picture—the locust grove gracefully bordering the creek—and the way the gray stone abutment seemed to vie for equal attention. The entire setting had been pinpointed precisely in the exquisite painting.

"Talk about quaint. This is definitely it." She and Annie strolled together, arm-in-arm, to the base of the first tree, carrying their sketchbooks.

"I've always heard the black locust seeds are poisonous," Annie said as if her mind had wandered.

"You must feel plagued by this place. Is that why your painting is called 'Obsession'?"

"In more ways than I can say." Annie pointed out the dark trunk furrowed with interlacing bark. "Ever see thorns like this on a tree?"

"Kinda creepy."

"And dangerous, if ever you've tried to climb it. Thorns are all over the limbs and on the trunk."

They stood there silently, peering at the grove.

Suddenly the light left Annie's eyes, and it looked as if she might start to cry.

"As pretty and serene as this is, it does have a haunting feeling," Louisa said.

Annie looked the other way for a moment, composing herself, no doubt. Then, she said softly, "My friend, Esther Hochstetler—you met her Sunday—well, her husband was the last person ever to see the boy who disappeared. Right here, where we're standing. Isaac was Zeke's little brother."

"Really? Well, what happened that night?"

"Truly, Mamm's the best one to ask, but I can tell you what I know at least."

Standing beneath the airy umbrella of branches, mostly devoid of leaves, Louisa listened as Annie began her story. "Something this awful had never happened round these parts . . . I can tell you for sure. Folk came and went—Amish and English alike—never thinking twice 'bout locking doors or being suspicious of strangers and whatnot. Never." Annie put her hand on her chest.

"If it's too hard to—"

Annie shook her head. "No . . . I'll be all right." She sighed loudly. "Every mother lost sleep, Mamm told me. Some parents were so fearful they got permission from the bishop to get indoor plumbing . . . abandoned their old outhouses and whatnot."

"To keep tabs on their kids?"

"Oh, jah."

"And what about Zeke? He must've totally freaked out, losing his brother like that."

"That's the truth. Esther's husband was hit terribly hard emotionally, I'm told. He was just a youngster, only eight when Isaac vanished into the air. He and Isaac had left the house after dark to bury their dead puppy. But Zeke acted against his father's will, sneakin' out of the house after supper when no one was looking." Annie paused, not saying more for a moment.

"Heavy stuff."

Neither spoke for a time. The air became eerily still before Annie began again. "Esther told me once that Zeke's father refused to forgive him and belittled him all through his growing-up years. Made a point of telling everyone the kidnapping was the worst possible punishment to befall a disobedient son, meaning Zeke, but that the harsh, even divine judgment had come for a reason nonetheless."

"But *Isaac* was the one who was lost," said Louisa. "Surely the father didn't believe that the so-called punishment for disobedience was to rest solely on his *eight-year-old* son. Seems unnecessarily cruel."

"And Zeke was, no doubt, already bearing the weight of blame."

*What a horrendous guilt trip to put on a person, let alone a kid.* Louisa was truly aghast.

"To this day, no one knows what happened to Isaac Hochstetler." Annie's eyes shone with tears. "Ach, not sure why this bothers me so."

Louisa reached out a hand. "Well, you're softhearted, Annie. One more reason why you're an incredible artist."

She nodded slowly. "Maybe so."

"You may talk big, but you're sensitive on the inside."

"I s'pose I am."

"Well, we both are," Louisa admitted.

She followed Annie down to the creek, where they stood silently and watched the water surge beneath the covered bridge.

Then they turned and walked down the creek a bit and, later, back again to the first tree. "In case you're wondering, the rope swing in my painting is long gone from here. My mother says it was taken down after Isaac went missing. But I have no idea who would've done that."

"Maybe Zeke's father?"

"Could be, but I never heard that."

"But you put it back in your painting . . . where it belongs."

"At least in my heart it's there." Annie glanced at the sky, then back at Louisa. "So, you see. Our village of Paradise hasn't always been as peaceful as you might think."

She felt inadequate to offer the slightest measure of sympathy. "I can only wish that Zeke's brother had never disappeared."

"Isaac would be getting married 'bout now, prob'ly." Annie forced a smile. "I remember playing there in the creek . . . his brother and my brothers, too. We were such good little friends."

"How do you remember what happened when you were so young?"

Annie shrugged. "Mamm says I remember things clear back to when I was only three. So, jah, I have a right clear memory of Isaac. It was just the most terrible thing when he was kidnapped. I even wondered if something like that could happen to me."

"Is it possible he simply wandered off—got lost in the night?"

"I don't see how, not with his brother right there. Every inch of the township was searched—the little waterfall across from the old stone mill, and the Eshelman Run, all through the community park and the fields. It's a nightmarish mystery, that's what."

"Did the police question Isaac's family . . . all his relatives?"

"I don't know." Annie frowned. "The church brethren handle things their way, so I doubt he was ever even reported missing."

Louisa was stunned. "You've got to be kidding!"

"It's the way we do things, that's all I can say."

"And the brethren? You mean all the men in your church?"

"Our *ministers*—one deacon, two preachers, and our bishop."

Louisa pondered the curiously unexpected answers. She couldn't imagine a child vanishing in the area of Colorado's Castle Pines without the authorities being called in. For that matter, she couldn't conceive of it happening that way anywhere on the planet. "How long ago was this?" she asked.

"Well, I was the same age as little Isaac when he disappeared . . . so sixteen years ago."

"An eternity for the family. . . ." Louisa couldn't begin to think how she would feel if one of her own family was taken . . . and a mere child, too.

Annie brushed a tear from her cheek with the back of her hand. "Plenty of folk put their lives on hold right along with the Hochstetler family," she said. "But Isaac's family didn't stay put here for long."

"You mean they left because of what happened?"

"Jah, never returned. They cut themselves off from the very church of their baptism and, eventually, from their son Zeke."

Foregoing their plan to sketch there, its beauty now overshadowed by somber thoughts and images, Annie and Louisa walked back to the waiting horse and buggy.


When they returned home, Louisa was surprised at Annie's insistence in discussing the topic of the kidnapping with her mother. Annie seemed to take advantage of the kitchen being deserted and began to pour lemonade into three glasses. Then she boldly suggested they all sit at the table "for a little while."

Louisa cringed inwardly, but at Annie's urging she reluctantly brought up the long-ago incident. "I was just curious about the events surrounding that night." Louisa went on to say that she and Annie had gone to the creek to look around. Nothing was said about Annie's painting, of course.

Barbara's round face became quite flushed, and she began to blink her eyes as she looked first at Annie and then back at her lemonade. It was obvious she was reticent to discuss what she recalled, at least with an outsider. Either that or she was still peeved at Louisa, especially, for the profile-drawing session two nights ago.

*If I'm not careful, I'll get booted out and fast. . . .*

Louisa immediately felt apologetic. "You know, that's all right," she spoke up. "You don't have to talk about this now, or at all."

"No . . . no, I want Mamm to tell you what she knows," Annie interjected. "Besides, it's been a long time since I've heard the story." She leaned forward at the table, eyes fixed on her mother.

"Well, all I'm goin' to say is that the perpetrator—the person who stole Isaac away, prob'ly killed him, too—will certainly be required to answer to almighty God for the treacherous deed." Annie's mother turned to look directly at Louisa. "And, I believe the Lord God and heavenly Father looks not so kindly on *anyone* who purposely sets out to harm one of His own."

*Jeepers, I've been told.* Louisa felt the heat of embarrassment rise in her face. Before she could make an attempt to excuse herself, Annie's mom said rather pointedly she wanted to speak with Annie "right away." Translated to mean—and Louisa was absolutely sure—that she personally needed to get lost as soon as she finished her lemonade so Annie could get an earful in private.

Frustrated and aghast at Mamm's pointed approach, Annie shifted in her seat. Her mother had never reacted in such a way, that she recalled. "You're terribly upset," Annie said softly.

Mamm sat solemn-faced, fanning herself with a corner of her apron, even though it was anything but warm in the kitchen. "I'm glad you're having a good time with your friend, Annie, but you daresn't be tempted by the fancy drawings she makes."

*Tempted?*

"Louisa's drawings are wonderful-good. Did you see how close to perfect her profile was of me?"

"Now, Annie."

"No, I'm serious. She has an amazing gift."

Her mother's face softened quickly, and she reached a hand over to touch Annie's arm. "Dear one, you must not allow Louisa's talent to draw you in . . . to entice you away from the People."

*It already has. . . .*

"Havin' Louisa here has been the best thing for me, Mamm. You just don't know." She bit her lip thinking about her breakup with Rudy just then, but she caught herself.

"I see in your eyes how happy you are, but Louisa certainly isn't Amish and won't be stayin' here forever. So you need to be thinking 'bout your future . . . who you'll settle down with and marry."

Annie shook her head, taking quick short breaths. "Well, you best enjoy your grandchildren from my brothers, 'cause honestly, I don't see myself becoming a bride now." It wounded her to admit it, but truth was the boys her age were all getting hitched.

Mamm's face fell. "You can't mean it."

Once the difficult words were out in the air, Annie felt some better. Now Mamm would stop bringing up this painful topic, just maybe.

"Well, it hurts me to think . . . another baptism season has come and gone already."

*Jah, Annie, you've missed out on joining church yet again!* Annie grimaced at her own thoughts. "Well, why's everything all tangled up with what's expected of me?"

"No . . . no, you mustn't be thinkin' on it that way. It's what is good and right and true, Annie. That's what." Mamm sighed loudly, her face ever so serious. "You may not know this, but there's much more to the story of little Isaac Hochstetler, and what with our talk about your future 'n' all, it just might be time for you to hear it, lest you yield to temptation yourself and turn your back on all that is right."

Annie hadn't the slightest idea what her mother meant.

Mamm began to explain. "Isaac's father committed a deadly error . . . no other way to say this." She paused, placed her hand over her throat, and then continued. "You see, Annie, the divine lot for Preacher fell first on Daniel Hochstetler one month before the kidnapping occurred. He out and out refused to accept the ordination."

Annie could not believe her ears. A terrible, bad omen. . . .

"'Tis a decision unto death."

"Oh, Mamm . . . I never knew of this."

Her mother nodded, face drawn. "It's scarcely ever talked about, even in a whisper, for all good reason. So . . . your father was God's second choice for preacher . . . no getting round it."

"I never would've guessed someone would be so unwise . . . turning away from the drawin' of the lot," Annie said softly.

"The People called him '*Ichabod*—the glory of the Lord has departed,'" Mamm whispered. "It was nearly like a shunning, and some of the brethren *did* banish him. Then, not long after, the family up and left, only to be heard from again when Ezekiel returned and wed Essie."

Annie listened carefully, wondering why on earth Mamm was sharing such ominous news.

But then quite suddenly she knew. Sure as a mackerel sky means rain, she knew.

Jesse accepted a mug of coffee from Esther. Then, when she'd left the kitchen, the little boys in tow, he looked at Zeke and motioned toward the back door with his head.

Zeke followed willingly, carrying his own coffee and talking all the while about the nice weather "this late in the season."

In the barn, Jesse offered Zeke a cigar, but he shook his head, saying he never cared so much for the odor. "Well, just thought I'd . . . pay you a visit," Jesse said, stumbling over his words. He felt downright awkward, but he wanted to know how Zeke was doing. "I'm awful sorry . . . 'bout your brother. Such a terrible shame."

Zeke stared a hole in him. He was silent for a time, taking one gulp of coffee after another. At last, he spoke. "Where's he buried?"

Shuffling his feet, Jesse hadn't expected this. "The bishop and I took great care to find an out-of-the-way spot for your brother's bones. Bishop wants it kept quiet."

*Eight big steps past the edge of the cemetery, four short ones past the first tree*, thought Jesse.

Zeke ran his hand through his light brown beard. "I beg to differ with that. He's my kin . . . I have the right to know!"

"S'pose you do."

"No supposin' about it, Preacher. I want to pay my respects."

The fire in Zeke's eyes could not be missed, and Jesse wondered if he'd made a mistake by coming here. "I say we follow the bishop on this," he stated flatly. "No need to argue with the man of God."

Zeke shook his head slowly. "Well, seems a man ought to be able to quietly go and say good-bye to his own brother."

*Seems so*, thought Jesse. But he wouldn't budge where Zeke was concerned. The man was as volatile as any of the farmers he'd ever known. As headstrong as Zeke's own father had been. "The womenfolk . . . that's what the bishop's most concerned 'bout. Such an upheaval your Isaac's disappearance caused amongst the People. No need in stirring all that up again."

Zeke eyed the spare cigar. "I just might take you up on your offer, Preacher," he said, pointing at his pocket.

Jesse pulled out the cigar and handed it to the distraught younger man. "I best be headin' on home. Always plenty of chores to tend to."

When Zeke lit up and puffed some, but didn't say a word for a good long time, Jesse figured he was ready to get back to work, too. But Zeke followed him all the way out to the horse and buggy, and as soon as Jesse was settled in the front seat, reins in hand, Zeke said, "You ain't heard the end of this, Preacher."

Jesse looked at him, this man who'd suffered such torment his whole life.

To think that selfsame misery had turned to a stone wall in the end—something Zeke could not get past and apparently needed to.

"It's time to put this to rest," Zeke said, his voice cracking.

Compassion swept through Jesse. He couldn't just ride out of the man's lane without giving him something to go on, at least. "All right, then. I'll talk to the bishop for you."

"And I won't rest till I hear back," Zeke said. "Gut day!"

Jesse directed the horse forward slowly, and not even when he made the turn onto the paved road did he hurry the steed. *Such a can of worms!* he thought, hoping Zeke might simply forget and go about his farm work. Because there was no way he was going to get Bishop Andy to budge on this matter.

# Chapter 24

Following breakfast and kitchen cleanup on Thursday, Annie hitched up the team with some help from Luke. She was anxious to take Louisa to the quilting bee, along with Mammi Zook, who required extra care getting in and out of the family buggy. Mamm had decided to remain at home in case Yonie returned from his hunting trip with a deer, so Annie headed out to Sarah Mae's with her grandmother and Louisa filling up the front seat.

The cold seeped into the enclosed carriage despite the heated bricks she'd placed on the floor, as well as the lap robes, to help ward off the nip in the air. Her nose became quickly chilled, but the tips of her ears were well protected with her black "candle-snuffer" style hat. She was amused, looking over at Louisa . . . the three of them looking rather alike in their winter bonnets. *Such a good sport is Louisa, dressing as if she were truly Plain!*

It turned out that Esther did not show her face at the quilting frolic, just as she had indicated on Sunday. But a dozen or so other women were on hand—half of them were married first cousins of Annie's; the others were hoary-headed seasoned quilters.

When it came time to sit at the enormous frame, Louisa planted herself next to Mammi Zook. She seemed determined to imitate the smallest stitches, listening to the storytelling while heeding Mammi's gentle instruction. Louisa appeared to be quite taken by the bold reds, purples, and greens of the Center Diamond quilt. Annie wasn't surprised at all, for it had always been one of *her* favorites.

The only Mennonite woman present—a cousin of Julia's—commented that several women in her neighborhood had formed a "Scraps R Us" group, creating comforters from leftover fabric. "Some of our husbands are helping cut the squares," the woman explained, "and the youngsters tie the knots on the comforters."

Mammi Zook perked up her ears. "Well, I have hundreds of pieces—I'd be glad to donate 'em."

The Mennonite woman smiled and thanked Mammi, returning her attention to making careful stitches. Annie was content to sit across from them, concentrating on the process of quilting, saying precious little. Rhoda Esh and Susie Yoder were on hand, as well, and it was rather clear that Rudy's sister and his new girl had gotten themselves on much better footing these days.

*Time heals. . . .*

Annie couldn't stop thinking about Mamm's startling revelation last evening. *Isaac's father is Ichabod. . . .*

She shivered with the ominous feeling, the knowledge that one of their own had rejected the divine appointment. Could time heal such a thing as *that?*

The next day, Louisa worked diligently on her colorful peacock painting in the attic studio while Annie cleaned Julia's downstairs. Louisa didn't have to remind herself to charge up her Palm. She was beginning to feel somewhat out of touch and was ready to make contact with the outside world. *I need to remember who I really am*, she thought as she mixed blue with green on the palette.

Julia knocked softly and entered, bringing a cinnamon roll and a cup of tea. She placed the tray down and stepped over to the easel, eyes wide with delight. "Oh, Louisa. What a wonderful talent you have! God certainly has given you a great gift."

"Well, thank you. I've never quite thought of it that way." Louisa paused, realizing this woman was absolutely sincere. "Do you really think God gives people certain abilities?"

"Oh my, yes. The Lord is the ultimate artist, you know, creating each one of us with special gifts. I should say so."

Louisa was stunned. Julia wasn't kidding . . . she believed this.

"There are gifts such as musical ability, as you know, writing gifts, and gifts such as friendship, loyalty, and courage. Honestly, the list goes on and on. I'm sure if you think about it, you'll realize this in your own life . . . and others."

Louisa thanked her for the "sticky bun," as the breakfast rolls were called here, and the honey-sweetened peppermint tea before Julia slipped out nearly as silently as she had come.

During lunch Louisa checked her email on her laptop, corresponding with Cybil Peters and several other art students, smiling at their waiting remarks about her abandoning them for Amish country. *They would snicker at my Plain getup*, she thought.

While she was online, Courtney sent her an instant message, reminding her unnecessarily that today was the eve of her once-planned wedding. "I'll be thinking of you—especially tomorrow. Just want to make sure you're okay, girl." She replied to Courtney, assuring her she was fine and happy to hear of her latest date to *The Phantom of the Opera*, at the Buell Theatre in downtown Denver. Louisa experienced a twinge of melancholy, having seen the musical years before on Broadway with her parents. Suddenly she decided to send individual email messages to her mom and dad, which triggered an interesting thought: *Am I becoming latently homesick?*

When her Palm was completely charged, she listened to all of her new voice mail. Starting at the beginning, with the call she'd snoozed the last time, she was surprised to hear Trey's voice in her ear. *Hey, Louisa . . . I just sold a large Joseph Bohler painting—man, what a style . . . earthy and honest. Anyway, Joe's work made me think of you. Maybe we can do Denver again sometime. Call me!*

Hearing Trey's voice did crazy things to her. She pressed "9" to save his message. When she'd heard each message, including three from Mother and two more from Michael, she replayed Trey's, savoring the rich tone of his voice, visualizing him making the call from London, within the confines of his fabulous art gallery.

*Why did we disconnect so thoroughly?*

But she knew. She had wanted to finish her degree at the California School of Art, and he was ready to get on with his life, having completed a master's degree in business management, his undergraduate degree in fine arts with an emphasis in art history, theory, and criticism. The perfect combo for an art dealer.

She humorously recalled his aversion to high tech anything, never having asked for her email address and avoiding the Internet as long as possible. If she could have reduced Trey to a two-word definition, it would have been *earthy sophisticate. But minus the deception*, she decided, smiling at the perfect description for her first boyfriend.

*Why should he contact me now? Does he know about my split from Michael?* She also wondered if he had ever known of her engagement.

She recalled her many dates with Trey, the way he seemed to enjoy treating her special—like a lady. Rushing around the car to open her door, insisting on paying for her expensive dinners, ordering for her . . . things most men overlooked, or women didn't value, being liberated and empowered these days. Trey appreciated fine quality and nice things, but he had always been just as comfortable in jeans and a sweater as he was in an expensive suit.

All day she contemplated his charming phone message, growing more introspective of their past romance as the hours ticked by. Even at supper that evening, Annie attempted to pry Louisa out of her blackout, asking occasional questions about Denver, her college years . . . as did Annie's mom, uncharacteristically so. But Louisa was preoccupied with Trey, struggling with the strong tug toward him yet somewhat stunned by the uncanny timing of his reappearance in her life.

During the evening prayers—always silent rote prayers, so she never really knew what the Zooks were saying to God anyway—Louisa considered returning Trey's call . . . perhaps in a few days. *I'll give myself more time to think. . . . But, no, we called it quits. It's over.*

Kneeling before the plain sofa next to Annie and her family, Louisa was so conflicted regarding Trey. She wondered if her back-and-forth state was itself a clue. *Should I pay attention to that alone?* In the past, she'd often listened to her psyche, making sure all systems were go, especially when it came to relationships with guys. So many things could go wrong, she had quickly discovered.

But since hearing Trey's voice, her old feelings continued to resurface. She wouldn't tell Annie, when she asked what was bugging her, in so many words . . . but Trey *had* been the all-time best kisser ever. A truly affectionate man. Was that *his* gift? she wondered, smiling and recalling Julia's strange remarks. She wished she'd thought more than twice about possibly following him to London. Had she agreed to go with him, she might have easily transferred her credits to the Sorbonne in Paris, where two of her girl friends had gone. If so, she would never have been around for the blind date setup with attorney Michael Jackanapes Berkeley!

The next morning, Yonie returned home without a buck to show for all his hunting. There was one good thing about his recent disappearing act—he seemed more relaxed, Annie thought. They promptly resumed their fun-loving bantering, including his comments about Louisa's "powerful cologne," which Yonie insisted still permeated his bedroom even though she'd aired it out but good. He hadn't seemed to mind Louisa staying in his room, however. If anything, he was intrigued by an English girl dressing in Amish clothes.

There was a decided spring in his step, so Annie guessed he'd also paid a visit to Dory Zimmerman en route home.

As for housing Louisa, Mamm was surprisingly agreeable, allowing her and Annie to move to the large upstairs bedroom in the Dawdi Haus, which put a surprisingly big smile on Mammi Zook's wrinkled face.

As Annie unpacked a box of her things, she ran across Louisa's wedding invitation—the fancy wedding that had been scheduled to take place at high noon today. She slipped the invitation into the bottom of her drawer, thinking Louisa didn't need the reminder, especially considering how quiet and preoccupied her friend had been lately.

In the weeks that followed, various works of art began to emerge from both Annie's and Louisa's keen imagination onto the pages of their individual sketchbooks and the canvases in the sequestered attic. Louisa insisted, however, on taking time off to show Annie some advanced techniques, saying her brain needed time to be "re-inspired" between projects. Annie soaked up the instruction, which involved highlighting to set a mood, layering and glazing colors—moving from light to dark values in watercolor and pastel chalk—and the power of shading accents with pencil drawings. Louisa worked frequently with Annie to help her transform her simple still lifes into a three-dimensional look. But Annie needed less help with her landscape paintings—which popped right off the canvas—and Louisa focused on their fine details by using unexpected spots of color.

Annie savored these educational, yet creative hours, but had the growing conviction that they could not last much longer. Although she didn't breathe a word to Louisa of Mamm's revelation about Isaac's father's refusal of the divine lot, she frequently brooded about it, wondering what consequences might befall her, too, for refusing to submit to the will of the People.

She also found herself finishing her household chores for Julia more quickly than she had in recent months. And even though Louisa offered to assist with the work, Annie continually refused, urging her to "make good use of the time," knowing they must not risk a further run-in with Mamm at home.

Preparations for a Thanksgiving feast were in progress with oodles of baking—a half-dozen pumpkin pies and the same of mincemeat—which meant less time for drawing at home. Annie was actually glad none of her cousins were scheduled to marry that week, otherwise they would have been planning to attend the all-day wedding celebration instead of happily inviting all of her brothers and their families for a big get-together.

Later, when Louisa brought up the possibility of renting a car "for a few days" for the purpose of purchasing additional art supplies and exploring the art galleries nearby, Julia offered to drive her to several locations, including the Village of Intercourse. In short order the completed peacock painting and the ethereal owl in flight, as well as one of surrounding farmland, including Preacher Zook's barn, were quickly snatched up on consignment by a small art gallery and craft shop situated on Route 30, near Leaman Place Furniture.

Annie was delighted no end at Louisa's success in placing her realistic paintings where, given the heavy tourist trade, they could enjoy a wide audience of potential customers. Of course, Louisa's appearance, looking as if she were Amish, had an appealing influence on the owner, as well. Louisa was quick indeed to set the record straight, revealing that she was actually a modern young woman, though residing with an Amish family "for the time being." Annie was fairly sure the English owner didn't believe this for a single minute.

Annie secretly wished she, too, might sell her work. But that was out of the question for now.

❖

One Saturday morning, Louisa, Annie, and Julia, along with her children, headed out by car to the Old Country Store in Intercourse. There, Julia shopped for precut fabric, color-coordinated in packs, ready for quilting.

Meanwhile, Louisa and Annie walked around, looking at the various hand-made crafts—the embroidered items especially interesting to Louisa. "I can't believe someone actually makes this stuff by hand," she commented softly to Annie. "You know, it's really an art form—check out the colorful arrangements and the unique designs."

"Well, the whole upstairs is a quilt museum, if you want to see more," said Annie. "Quilts made before the 1940s."

Louisa glanced toward the stairs. "I'm in!" Then she ran her fingers over the intricate flowers in a basket stitched onto the wide hem of a pillowslip, studying the needlework. "Do you embroider like this?"

"Jah, all the womenfolk do . . . 'specially during the winter. Some are better at it than others, though."

"Well, this is a talent, too, Annie, like painting. A gift, Julia would say."

Louisa became aware of two "English" women near the piece goods, looking their way and talking none too quietly.

"Look, Cari, they're Amish," said one.

"Oh, you're right," said the other. "Have you ever seen dresses like *that?*"

Louisa rolled her eyes and moved away. *They must think Annie and I can't hear them with our bonnets on! How rude!*

There was a sudden flash, and Louisa turned and came face-to-face with one of the modern tourists, now wielding a camera.

"Smile!" the woman said, with one eye squinting.

Louisa put her hand in front of the lens. "Excuse me. What you're doing is impolite," she spouted, glancing now at Annie, who looked nearly as stunned as the tourists.

"But you're both so *cute*," the too-blond woman cooed.

"Your camera's not welcome here," Louisa said, stepping between Annie and the tourist like a shield. She stared at this pushy, insensitive person, the first bejeweled, made-up woman she had seen since coming to visit. *Was I ever that rude?* she wondered. *I hope not!*

She took a deep breath, suppressing the urge to speak up again.

Annie marched off, keeping her face from view. And Louisa followed suit, mimicking her Plain friend, quite proud to join ranks with Annie.

During afternoon milking, Annie mentioned to her father that Louisa had seen him out quite late one night, carrying a shovel. "I told her she must've dreamt it, Daed."

But it was peculiar how he did not return her smile. His eyes took on a serious, even stern expression. "No need talking 'bout this," he said flatly.

"Then I guess Louisa wasn't dreamin' after all."

"Ach, Annie . . . church business."

She knew by that she best hush up. Because whatever it was, Daed had no intention of revealing it to her. And now she was ever so curious.

# Chapter 25

Toward the end of the fourth week of Louisa's visit, an important-looking letter arrived in the mail. Glancing at it, Annie noticed the inscribed address for the law offices of Louisa's father.

Dashing across the road, she found Louisa pitching hay to the mules with Luke and Yonie. "Mail call!" she announced, holding out the elongated envelope.

Taking a moment to study the envelope, Louisa promptly folded it in half and stuffed it into her dress pocket. "This can wait," she said softly, shrugging a bit.

But after supper, Annie sat on the bed with Louisa in their shared room in the Dawdi Haus. A small but cheery sitting room separated their bedroom from Dawdi and Mammi Zooks'.

"You're upset," she said, aware of Louisa's gloom. "Anything I can do for you?"

Louisa held the letter in her hands, staring at it, a wistful frown on her face. "My father wants me to come home—especially since I stayed here through Thanksgiving. They're thinking of having a family reunion, I guess you could call it, before Christmas. A get-together of sorts to take the place of my canceled wedding."

"Did he say *that*?"

"No, but it's implied, trust me. If I return, they'll fly the extended family out. If not, they'll skip it. So the burden rests on me."

Annie felt sad, knowing how terribly she would miss Louisa, who had become her dearest sister-friend. "Must you go already?"

Louisa returned the letter to the envelope. "Well, I doubt my parents would appreciate my Amish dress and apron. . . ."

158

This made Annie smile. "Then why not stay for Christmas?"

"You know, Annie, I have to say for as out of place as I felt when I first arrived, I can't seem to get enough of your Paradise."

Annie was heartened at this. "Have you considered stayin' for longer . . . like a full year? What would ya say to that?"

"I think I do need more time here. . . ." Louisa looked intently, even longingly, out the window. Her head covering fit her face and hairline quite perfectly.

"Then it's settled. You're stayin'."

Louisa's eyes brightened again. "If I can make all the arrangements—and if your parents consent to it—I'll take you up on your suggestion."

"Oh, this is such good news!"

"Let's not count our chickens before they're hatched," Louisa said, which got Annie laughing. "I'll have to sublease my place, and I need to touch base with each of my students. And to keep painting at Julia's and selling my art, too, if possible. I'm not a freeloader."

Annie wondered why Louisa hadn't mentioned contacting her parents. "I'll cross my fingers and hope real hard that everything falls into place." Blissful at the thought of Louisa staying on, Annie also knew this might well be her last year in her parents' house. She suspected the brethren of having spoken in private on the knotty problem of her hedging about church membership. If she didn't sign up for baptismal classes by next spring, there would be more to deal with than a multitude of raised eyebrows.

Leaning her head back on the bed, Annie stared at the ceiling. Then, sighing, she looked over at Louisa. "You goin' to answer your father's letter?"

"When I know for sure what I'm doing," Louisa said quietly. "Meanwhile, I think I might like to talk to your cousin sometime."

"'Bout staying put here?"

"No, other things. Julia seems like a person who's actually interested in reading the Bible. That blows me away, because it's such a dry sort of read, from what I remember. But your cousin's got her nose in it a lot." Louisa paused for a moment, then continued. "There's just so much about God that I don't get. Ever feel that way?"

Annie definitely understood. "Jah, more than ever."

Annie was sitting toward the back of the kitchen, closest to the sunroom at Deacon Byler's house, during the common meal. She was mulling over the sermon her father had given. Often she contemplated the way he told the story, as if attempting to communicate the Old Testament accounts in such a way as to draw in the young people more fully. And he'd certainly done that today. Sometimes she felt as if she were seeing a side to her father she rarely saw, except on Preaching days, and she savored the feeling.

She was so deep in thought she literally jumped when Esther came over and tapped her on the shoulder. "When you're through, can we go walkin'?"

"Why sure." Annie pushed her dessert aside. "Let's go right now."

"No . . . no, finish your pie." Esther's face was drawn and she looked to be sleep deprived, the way she often looked lately.

"I'll tell you what . . . I can easily take it along." Annie scooped up the pumpkin pie and placed it on a napkin.

"Will Louisa be all right?" asked Esther.

A quick glance up the table and Annie could see Louisa well occupied with Mamm and several of Annie's aunts. "Looks like she's busy talkin' for now."

They headed out the back door and down a stony walkway. Annie asked which way she wanted to go, pointing out the narrow farm road as well as the paved but little-traveled road out front.

"Back road's best, I think."

By this Annie knew Esther had something personal on her mind. "I'm glad you asked me to come walking. You feelin' all right?"

Esther pulled a hankie from her pocket. "Oh, Annie, I've wanted to talk to you in the worst way. . . ." Her voice quavered. "Things have gone from bad to worse 'tween Zeke and me."

Annie didn't know what to say, having only suspected something amiss . . . never knowing what, at least not from Esther directly. There had been some things dropped now and then from Annie's mother to Sarah Mae, but nothing substantial. "I'm so sorry, Esther. How can I help?"

Esther stopped beneath a tree, gathering her shawl about her. "My wee babe's comin' soon, but something keeps tellin' me to run away. I even have dreams 'bout taking Laura and the boys and leaving Zeke."

Annie was aghast. "You'd do that?"

Esther hung her head. "Some days I want to disappear just like Zeke's little brother did back when. Other times, when Zeke's right kind, even thoughtful, 'specially toward the children, I wonder what the world I'm thinkin'." She reached for Annie's hand. "I believe I've come to my wit's end. Is it just me, or am I truly losin' my mind? Are things so terrible wrong at my house?"

Annie inhaled deeply, gripping poor Esther's hand. "Maybe you'd better tell me what you mean."

Esther's lower lip trembled. "Well, to start with, I need to know something." She took a great deep breath. "Does your father ever lay a hand on your mamma in rebuke?"

"Never in anger, no. But then Mamm respects and obeys him, no question 'bout that."

"Are you sayin' it's all right for a man to strike his wife if she doesn't?"

Annie thought on that. "Well, we both know there are plenty of men who demand submission . . . and they use the Ordnung to back that up." She was thinking of her grandfather Zook and some of his brothers, much too harsh in some ways. There were rumors, too, that Deacon Byler and some of his married boys were awful hard on their women, including the younger girls. "Usually, the men say it's the woman's fault. . . ."

"But I need answers, 'cause I feel like I'm walkin' in the dark." Esther let go of Annie's hand, moving slowly now.

"There aren't easy solutions, I don't think. But if you're ever in danger, you know where you and the children can come for safety." Annie meant this with all of her heart.

Esther shook her head. "I could never take you up on that. I doubt Preacher Zook would tolerate such a thing. He'd say I was diggin' in my heels, not yielding to my husband." She grabbed hold of her shawl again. "Truth is, one of these times, you just might not see me round here anymore, Annie."

"Honestly, you'd up and leave?"

"I'd find myself some peace, that's all. It's not like I *want* to go away. . . ."

"So it's your husband you'd run from, not the Lord God?"

Esther blew her nose as they continued walking. "Don't you see? I feel I may be in danger . . . and the children, too." She put her hands on her protruding stomach. "With the next baby coming, well . . . I just don't think it's a good idea to stay put."

Annie was at a loss to know what to say. "Are you afraid of Zeke?"

"Jah, awful much." Esther sniffled and began to cry. "He's impossible to understand, truly. I don't know what he's capable of doin'." She rambled a bit, telling tidbits about the ups and downs of her husband's moods.

Then her voice grew stronger. "I found the oddest thing here lately, while doing a bit of sorting. It was a small burlap bag . . . with dozens of peach pits inside. They looked to have been washed clean and set out in the sun to dry and bleach a bit."

"Sounds like Zeke's still grieving his brother's disappearance."

"Well, I've heard him whimpering in his sleep the past month . . . more than ever before."

Annie's heart went out to both Esther and Zeke. "Too bad there isn't some way for one of the brethren to talk with him . . . to let him pour out the bitterness somehow."

"Funny you say that, 'cause Bishop Andy came over one evening some weeks back. He and Zeke hurried out to the barn. The next day, Zeke was ever so kindhearted toward our little boys while Laura was at school. But then, later that night, he turned ugly again."

"Does he drink, do you know?"

"I've smelt it on his breath some."

Annie pondered what to do. "Would you want me to say something to my mother? In confidence, of course."

Esther's eyes flashed disdain. "Well, why would you do that?"

"Only that she would talk to Daed . . . see if something can be done."

Turning, Esther looked her square in the eye. "If I wanted to tell a preacher, do ya think I'd be whisperin' all this to *you?*"

Annie felt terrible. She'd said the wrong thing, she knew . . . hurt her friend's feelings. "Ach, I'm awful sorry. I just want to help if I can."

"I daresay you must want to tell it around, that's what."

"No, now listen, Esther. You have my word. I'll keep your secret . . . but is that the right thing? For you and your coming child? For Laura and Zach and little John? Is it?"

"I should've kept quiet, looks to me like," Esther said softly.

Annie felt empathy, as well as a good measure of anger at being misjudged. "Well, I'm warning you now, if I ever see you with a black eye or other bruises, I'll be goin' straight to my father. Hear?"

Esther shook her head, tearstains on her face.

"Look," Annie challenged, "do you believe the Lord God gave us women the ability to think or not?"

"Maybe so. . . ."

"I say don't let any man trample you into the ground. Who cares how some of the menfolk treat their wives and daughters, or how our great-grandfathers did back when. It's time Zeke started showing you and your children the kindness and love you deserve, Essie!" She couldn't believe she'd just spoken Esther's old nickname.

Letting out a little gasp, Esther turned away. She didn't even bother to say good-bye, just trudged back toward the barnyard on the rutted dirt path, the fringe of her black wool shawl bouncing as she went.

*Well!* Annie crossed her arms and took several slow, deep breaths lest she holler one final remark and cause even more strife in poor Esther. *Maybe it's good I'm not getting married anytime soon. Even if I ever meet a man who measures up to Rudy.*

# Chapter 26

M uch of the night and now this morning, too, Annie had been stewing over Esther and their impulsive conversation. Esther's comment about wanting to disappear upset Annie horribly. *Surely she won't lose her head and do something stupid!* Yet Esther had been clearly distraught out on the farm road.

Annie's thoughts were jarred by Yonie's voice as the two of them worked together, milking the cows before breakfast. "How do you expect your fancy friend to be content at all if she doesn't have any wheels while she's here?" Yonie asked her. "Louisa's used to drivin' a car, ya know."

Annie considered that. "Well, on one of her first days here, Louisa did say she wanted to learn how to drive the team. Both Omar and I volunteered."

"So, did ya teach her then?"

"Haven't yet."

"What're you waitin' for?"

She smiled. "Christmas, I guess."

"Which is almost here." He patted the backside of a cow.

Annie watched Yonie move from one cow to another, so at home with the farming routine. She was dying to ask him about his English girlfriend, but she thought better of it, aware that both Daed and Luke were coming and going, hauling five-gallon milker buckets between here and the milk house.

"You say Louisa's plannin' to stay longer." Yonie removed his black work hat and scratched his head where it was flattened and oily. "But if she does, it'll be right surprisin'. I can't imagine her giving up her car for too long. Downright odd."

She had to speak her mind. "You've got cars on the brain, ain't so?"

"Aw, Annie, why would you say that?" He looked sheepish.

"You're smitten with talk of wheels, that's what." But there was more to it. She'd heard through the grapevine that not only was Yonie taking joy rides with Dory Zimmerman, but that she was teaching *him* to drive, too.

He eyed her, holding her gaze. "I'm not ashamed of running around. If this is the worst thing I do, well, then . . ." He put his hat back on. "Besides, I'm doin' what I want to, just like you."

"What's that s'posed to mean?"

"Don't play pretend. You have your secrets."

Her heart was hammering. *What's he know?* "I think you'd better tell me what you're accusin' me of, Yonie-boy."

He looked over his shoulder and all around the milking area. Then, leaning closer, he said, "Where'd ya ever learn to paint a picture, sister?"

Her breath caught in her throat. *Who spilled the beans?*

"What picture?" she replied, trying to keep her composure.

He took his time answering, shuffling his feet a bit and looking away, as if he were in trouble. "Well, I've been spendin' a lot of time at the Zimmermans', to tell you the truth, and you best be keepin' what I'm going to say quiet, ya hear?"

"I won't say anything. What picture?"

He looked relieved and continued. "Just listen. Dory's father lets me sit in his office there at the house and read."

"What're you gettin' at?"

"Yesterday, I was sitting and soakin' up the sun, on such a cold day. And I happened to be poking around in one of his new magazines, and, well . . . your name was listed on the inside cover, as a winner in an art contest."

She gasped inwardly.

"There you were: *Annie Zook of Paradise, PA.*"

This was the last thing she'd expected to hear. "You're pullin' my leg, Yonie, I just know it."

He studied her curiously. "No, I think you're pulling *mine*."

"What do you mean?"

"It seems you've won yourself a place on a magazine cover."

*This cannot be!* She froze, scarcely able to breathe.

His probing gaze held hers. "Unless there's another Annie Zook round here . . ."

She wouldn't lie. Yonie would see right through her.

*Such horrid news!* And, right then, the tiniest possible thrill, the joy of winning something, vanished completely.

Even so, on some uncanny and wonderful level, this was lovely news to her ears. Someone besides Cousin Julia and Louisa was now aware of, and appreciated, her work.

All of a sudden, the terribleness registered in her brain. *My painting will be seen by all who subscribe! My lifelong secret will be discovered.*

She leaned down and reached for a three-legged stool nearby. Daed's eyes would offer a stern yet silent warning at first, if found out. Then he would open his old Bible and read slowly, thoughtfully. If she did not adhere to the Ordnung and abandon her artwork, she would be asked to leave home.

"You all right?" Yonie frowned.

*I'm sunk, that's what.*

He squatted beside her. "What's-a-matter?"

"How large is the print—for my name?" She wiped her face with the hem of her black apron.

He looked at her with disbelief. The truth had definitely registered. "So it *was* you. Annie. What's this about? You lead a secret life?"

Slowly she began to explain how someone had talked her into entering a painting in the contest. She didn't say "one of her paintings," because she must keep him in the dark for as long as possible. "Being a first-place winner is a curse, for sure and for certain." She eyed him now, hoping he might understand her next request. "You must keep this under your hat. Promise me!"

He nodded. "And in return will you do a favor for me?"

"Say the word."

"Tell no one 'bout my visits to Dory Zimmerman, all right?"

"That's easy." With the mention of the mail carrier's daughter, the wheels began to spin nearly out of control. "Wait a minute! Which of the People subscribe to that magazine round here? Any idea?"

He shrugged. "Sure seems more geared to the English."

"Jah, good," she said, still thinking ahead. "But how can we know for certain? There's got to be a way, what with Dory's mother delivering the mail. Mrs. Zimmerman has a wonderful-good memory. . . . I daresay if she sees it, she knows."

Yonie nodded, then he hurried to empty one of the milkers, pouring the contents into the tall milk can. "I take it you want to find out . . . and soon. And you want Mrs. Zimmerman's help?"

"No, not hers . . . Dory's."

Just then, they heard their father returning from the milk house. "I'll tell ya what." Yonie leaned closer and whispered, "I'll talk to Dory tonight. See if I can figure out a way to get you out of this jam."

"Thanks, Yonie. Let me know what she says."

Annie made her way down the center walkway, cow tails flapping on either side. Between her and Yonie, they were a good team, and they might be able to save the day. *Just maybe.*

Letting her mind wander unchecked, she imagined confiscating next month's issue of *Farm and Home Journal* from rural mailboxes. Of course, she wouldn't actually consider committing a crime. Still, her mind was working overtime to devise a way to keep her father and the brethren from knowing of her secret hobby.

But what could she do? The December issue was already out . . . with her name on the inside cover, along with other artists, although Yonie had said the print was rather small. Still what were the chances of *that* being missed? These farmers liked to read every word!

Feeling glum, she headed through the barnyard, buttoning her old brown work coat, glad for it, as well as her holey gloves. She contemplated all the happy days surrounding Christmas and knew she must enjoy them to the hilt this year. Because unless she and Yonie could cook up a plan to thwart the arrival of the magazine in neighboring mailboxes, the end of her artistic pursuit was clearly in sight. Maybe her future here, too.

*Thank goodness Louisa's here!* she thought. *My one supporter.*

She was also grateful for something else: Yonie had not asked where she'd hid out to do her painting. She was not ready to divulge that information anytime soon.

*Talk about wanting to disappear!*

The spare bedroom in the Dawdi Haus was large enough to accommodate two beds—a firm double situated between two windows, the other bed a plump three-quarter daybed pushed against the far wall. Annie had given Louisa first choice but then nearly insisted she take the larger bed with its attractive four posts after Louisa had picked the smaller. Now that they had been settled in for several weeks, Annie was rather glad to have the daybed, where she occasionally snuggled with Louisa's gentle and friendly kitty-cat. She and Muffin had become good pals, but only if Louisa was nowhere in sight. Then, and only then, was Annie a close second.

Tonight though, Muffin was nestled in Louisa's arms. Annie watched the kitty's eyes go half-closed each time Louisa stroked his little head. "Did you ever write back to your parents," Annie asked, "about the family reunion?"

"I wrote a long letter, but I haven't heard back. I'm sure they're peeved at me for snubbing my nose at their idea. No doubt I'm a total washup in their eyes."

"Well, I'm awful glad you're staying." Annie plumped her pillow. "How would you like to go ridin' tomorrow after we get home from Julia's?" she asked. "I think you need more fun in your life."

"Don't be silly." Louisa lifted the cat close to her face. "I'm having the best time, Annie. Do you think I'd want to stay longer if I wasn't?"

It was surprising to see how relaxed and cozy Louisa looked under several of Mammi Zook's heirloom quilts.

"Where do you want to go tomorrow?" asked Louisa.

"Anywhere, really . . . but with *you* holdin' the reins. It's time, don't you think?"

Louisa leaned forward, eyes alight. "You mean I finally get my first driving lesson?"

"Jah, it'll be you, me, and Yonie."

Louisa smiled at that. "He's nice . . . all of your brothers are."

"Yonie's fun loving, that's for sure."

Louisa asked if it was a good idea for her to be in control of a horse, "out on the road, I mean."

"No worry. Yonie can take over quickly if need be."

"Probably a good idea," Louisa admitted.

They talked briefly about the weather, that a cold front was coming in and what they might do if a snowstorm hit during the night. Annie hoped they could still go, all bundled up with mufflers and foot warmers . . . with the horse hitched to their small sleigh.

Later, when Louisa was still second-guessing whether or not she ought to try directing a horse, Annie simply said, "If you can fit in round here like you do, I don't see why you couldn't manage to drive us over to stock up on some candy for the holidays, maybe."

Louisa's smile inched across her tired face. "That could be interesting. But you might never want to ride with me again."

"I thought we could go to Sweets for Sweeties—you'll like that shop. They have every imaginable candy and then some," Annie said, recalling that Mamm had been asking for a purchase of some hard candy to give to the grandchildren at Christmastime.

Finally, she got around to telling Louisa her news of having won first place, although she was reluctant, not wanting to sound bigheaded. "I'm shocked, truly."

Louisa leaped out of her nest of quilts, coming around the bed to sit on Annie's. "This is so cool! How did you find out?"

"Oh, from the grapevine." She was stuck, had spoken much too soon. Yonie would have her head if she said more.

"Come *on*, Annie . . . don't be vague. How did you find out without me knowing it? You're with me twenty-four-seven!" The green in Louisa's eyes by some peculiar means seemed to overtake the blue suddenly. Annie had noticed this once before. Whenever Louisa became overly excited, the color in her eyes would change.

"You'll see for yourself the next time we go to Julia's." That was all she cared to say. She knew better than to say more. With Yonie working on his plan, whatever it was, she could not risk implicating him.

Louisa continued to stare at her. "So you're not going to cough up the full story? I'm dying here. I'm so excited for you!"

She'd never known Louisa to be this demanding. "It'll have to wait. I've said enough."

"I don't get it." Louisa shook her head, looking awfully befuddled.

"Well, it's late, that's what." Annie scooted past Louisa on her bed. She went to the bureau and reached for the gas lamp and blew it out.

"Congratulations, anyway," Louisa said in the darkness, finding her way back to her own bed.

Annie wished she'd kept the news to herself. *What was I thinking?*

# Chapter 27

The bejeweled ice pattern on the windowpane was so thick the next morning Annie had a difficult time finding a clear enough spot to peer out. As the sun rose past the horizon line, over distant sticks of trees, she found a singular transparent circle on the glass, through which she glimpsed the barnyard below. "Goodness' sakes, what a lot of snow. It's a blizzard out there!"

She heard the rooster crowing repeatedly and remembered how Daed's father, Dawdi Zook, sometimes said the changing of seasons was a fearsome thing. The beginning of something, as well as the end.

Feeling the cold air whoosh through the space between the base of the window and the sill, she couldn't stop thinking about the astonishing first-place announcement. The news had wormed its way into her dreams last night, as well. *A startling end, and yet a beginning in some ways, too. The end of my terrible deceit . . . forced upon me.*

Across the room, Louisa stretched in bed, and Muffin moved from his spot near the double lump that was Louisa's feet and yawned widely before moseying up closer to the pillow. "This bed is so comfy," she said sleepily.

"My first nephew was birthed right there," Annie said.

"Argh! That's TMI!"

"What?"

Louisa laughed. "Too much information, Annie."

"Well, it's true. Jesse Jr. and Sarah Mae stayed in this room for a while after they were married." Annie turned her attention back to the window, peering out. "Too bad, but I'm afraid your driving lesson will have to wait. We'll have to take the sleigh over to Julia's today . . . one of the boys can drive us."

"Horses don't have trouble getting around in the snow?"

Annie shook her head.

"So I guess you never had to miss school for bad weather when you were a kid."

*At least she's not asking about the art contest again,* thought Annie.

She slipped into her bathrobe and made her bed. "I can't remember ever not getting to school, really. 'Least not for a snowstorm."

"Do you typically get tons of snow in December?" Louisa asked.

"We have plenty, jah." She told how the whole family enjoyed sledding, "except for my grandparents, of course."

"Your parents actually go?"

"Well, not every time. But Daed built a toboggan just for the two of them. Mamm squeals all the way down the hill . . . and she loves it."

Louisa nodded, stretching her arms above her head. "I can't imagine my mom doing that! But *I'm* all for it."

"Since Christmas falls on Sunday this year, there should be oodles of fun on both Saturday and Monday. Of course, we'll have Preaching service all morning Christmas, and then the most delicious feast afterward, which will be nothin' like the common meal every other Sunday, with cold cuts and Jell-O, no. It'll be more like a wedding feast with a roast and all the trimmings . . . and lots of candies and cookies."

"Food and feasting is a big part of your church life, isn't it?"

"Yonie likes to say, 'the three *f*'s—food, fun, and fellowship.'" She smiled, recalling that. "As for food, I know of several Amish couples in Lancaster County who make extra money serving seven-course meals to English tourists two or three nights a week. So, I believe we *are* known for wonderful-good home cookin'!"

"I'll probably gain ten pounds while I'm here!"

Annie glanced at Louisa, who was making her own bed now. "A few extra pounds won't hurt you none." She tossed a pillow at her friend, then headed downstairs to heat water for the wash-basins.

Julia opened the side door as Annie and Louisa trudged up the steps. "Hurry inside, girls. Isn't this the most snow we've had in quite a while?"

Annie turned and waved to Yonie, who had been kind enough to bring them. "Looks like fallin' pigeon feathers it's so thick." She spied little Molly, her dress matching the fabric of Julia's, cleaning out a mixing bowl with her fingers, then licking them off. *Cake batter*, Annie guessed and hurried over. "Don't you look 'specially perty in your new dress."

Julia told how she'd found a bargain at the fabric shop. "I guess I really stocked up this time . . . bought enough material to make six or seven dresses. So I made me one, and Molly, too. I'll make dresses for my sisters and their daughters, too, sometime soon."

Annie smiled. "Mamm often does that. Why pay more when you can all look alike, jah?"

Just then, she spied the *Farm and Home Journal* lying on the telephone table over by the window. She didn't mean to stare, though she was anxious to see what Yonie had already mentioned to her.

Evidently the magazine was uppermost in Julia's mind, too, because she marched right over and picked it up. She opened the magazine to the first page. "I'm thrilled to show you something, Annie." Her eyes shone with happiness. "And I can't say I'm one bit surprised, either."

Annie waited, partly eager to see her name in print but dreading the conversation sure to follow.

"Your lovely painting—'Obsession'—has won first place." Cousin Julia pointed to the page and held the magazine out for both Annie and Louisa to see.

Annie looked hard at her name, seeing it for the first time. The recognition alone was more than enough honor, she felt.

Even though Louisa already knew, she gushed all over the place. Then little Molly came and gave Annie a little squeeze around the legs, congratulating her in her own way.

"Isn't it grand?" said Julia. "Here's a letter from the magazine. I imagine it's about the art classes you've won."

Annie nodded but remained silent. She went and sat down at the table, wishing someone else might've won. "It's so hard to believe, really." *Could it be a mistake?* "In the most peculiar way, this is the death of a dream, I'm sad to say."

Julia's smile turned to a quick frown.

"If my father gets wind of this—and how will he not?—I'll no longer be welcome to sit idly by, not joining church. I'll be a thorn in his side . . . forced to make a choice, one way or the other!"

Louisa pursed her lips, looking concerned.

Julia folded her hands. "I never wanted to cause trouble for you. I hope you know that."

Annie contemplated the irony of it all. "Jah. . . ."

"This might seem strange, but I hope this might open the door for you to have a discussion with your parents . . . especially your preacher-father."

*That's absurd,* Annie thought. But to Julia, she said simply, "Honestly, I don't know any woman who does such a thing . . . speaking up to a minister, related or not."

*Women are not to speak up to men at all, and especially not to the ministers.* Anyone knew this.

Thinking on it, though, she recalled one time in particular when *she* had not only talked up to her father, but talked back. She had been one week shy of turning fourteen when Daed caught her sitting on a milk can out behind the springhouse, drawing the redbud trees in full bloom with a handful of stubby colored pencils.

When her father happened upon her, he did not have to stop and remind her of her previous disobedience, no. Without a doubt, this was the *second* time she had been in hot water with him, and they both remembered all too well.

Without speaking, he had reached down to take up her colored-pencil picture, deliberately tearing it into small pieces. Her anger soared beyond the limits of her ability to subdue it, and without thinking she uttered words that never should have been spoken to a parent, let alone a preacher. Still, she felt justified in spouting off, *"What right do you have?"*

Daed had not merely rebuked her with fiery eyes and his words, but he had also struck her, once, as well. He forbade her to demonstrate such outright rebellion ever again. *"You're not old enough for Rumschpringe, and yet you defy me!"* he said, eyes burning with his own fury. It was the first time he had ever raised a hand to her.

That night, all curled up in bed, she felt like a whipped puppy. And in the quietude of her room, with tears falling fast, she made a mental journey, going back to all the times she had drawn or colored little pictures for her pen pal, who seemed to appreciate them each time she slipped one into her letter, Daed none the wiser.

Later that week, when Julia happened to visit, asking Mamm about the possibility of hiring Annie part time, Annie jumped at the chance. But she'd had an ulterior motive from the start—remembering the empty little garret room. *I'll do my drawings there,* she decided before ever consulting with Irvin and Julia. Soon enough the Rancks' attic became the only refuge for her forbidden dream.

"Annie? I hope I haven't offended you," Julia was saying.

*Offend* was too strong. After all, Annie had given the go-ahead, although reluctantly, to enter her painting. "No . . . no. You mustn't feel bad."

Even so, Julia wore a concerned look. "The next magazine will be out in about a month . . . mid-January, I'd think."

Annie glanced at Louisa, who had been very quiet, perhaps deliberately keeping her nose out of it. "Honestly, it's beyond me how my parents *wouldn't* see or hear of this."

"Well, I happen to believe you could make it outside the Amish community, Annie . . . if it were ever necessary, I mean," Julia said.

Annie didn't feel like thinking about a future without the People, nor did she wish to give up her art. What most beginning artists would have longed for, she wished to reject. The glory of winning had scarcely had time to register in her brain, and now it was gone from her altogether.

She could hardly wait to talk to Yonie the following night. Even at supper, Annie kept trying to catch his eye. Finally, she did . . . and her curiosity was piqued even more when he nodded his head toward the door later on while eating Mamm's pecan pie and homemade vanilla ice cream.

*What'll he tell me?* She hoped against hope something could be done to thwart the delivery of the January issue of *Farm and Home Journal* to local subscribers. Or, if not, that Yonie would have some idea how to keep their father's anger to a minimum.

Her hands trembled as she washed dishes, passing them off to Louisa to be dried. As much as Louisa already knew, Annie was almost certain she hadn't noticed the exchange of glances between Yonie and herself. At least if Louisa had, she wasn't commenting. *Thank goodness!*

When the kitchen was sparkling clean, Annie waited for Louisa to slip over to the Dawdi Haus and then headed for the wooden wall rack out past the cookstove. Pulling on her heaviest jacket and then her boots, she was glad for the peace—no one around to observe her leave by way of the back door. She tromped through the snow to the barn, heart racing.

In the lower level of the barn, she found Yonie rubbing his hands together. "It's freezin' out here, jah?" she said.

"So let's make it snappy. I've got good news for ya . . . at least I think you'll agree."

"What is it, Yonie?"

"There are only three farmers in our church district who get the magazine, and Daed's cousins, the Rancks."

"Who are these farmers, and do you think they'll be talking to Daed 'bout it?"

"Not till mid-April, prob'ly."

"What do you mean?"

"Well, one of the farmers is out in Nappanee, Indiana, for the winter, helpin' ailing relatives. The others are down in Florida—snowbirds, ya know?" He was smiling too much, the usual teasing glint in his eye. "I doubt you have much to worry 'bout till spring, Annie-kins."

"You mean it? They won't get their mail for another three months or so?" Oh, this was beyond her best hope. *So wonderful-good!*

"Far as I can tell, no one in our church district, at least, will be notifying Daed." He went on to tell her how he'd discovered all this . . . by asking Dory's participation and keeping it quiet from her mother, the mail carrier.

Annie breathed a sigh. *A bit more time to enjoy my art,* she thought.

"I think you need to know you're not out of the woods on this." His near-perpetual smile had faded.

"What do you mean? I thought you said—"

"The magazine is based near Marion, Kentucky, but it goes out to farmers and others all over the country. Daed has cousins near and far. 'Specially in Wayne County, Ohio, so who's to say someone might not notice your name in the December issue or see your painting on the next?"

She felt her shoulders droop and was suddenly as fretful as she had been at the thought of the magazine winding up in one of their church members' mailboxes. No longer did she care to know what the cover would look like with her beloved painting plastered on it.

*"Be sure your sin will find you out."* Her father's words from long ago echoed in her mind.

"What will I do, Yonie? What'll happen to me?"

He shook his head. "I guess you should've thought of that sooner."

"Well, too late for thinkin'. If I catch it, I'm out."

"Won't be that cut and dried," he said. "But if I were you I'd walk away from this artist thing you're caught up in. Right away."

"Easy for you to say. You're being groomed to be a farmer."

He eyed her. "Well, it sounds like you think that's not such a grand thing."

"It's fine, all right . . . for you. What's expected." She felt bad now . . . didn't want to say another hurtful word. Not to the brother who had gone to some trouble for her. "You know what? I'm sorry," she said. "I don't mean to be sassy. I'm grateful for what you and Dory did for me."

"Good, 'cause I swore her to secrecy, too."

She looked warily at him. "You had to tell her?"

"No gettin' around it."

*Puh! Too many folk know.* . . . She shivered with the knowledge, as well as from the cold. "We ought to head inside lest someone misses us." She thanked him again.

"You owe me," he said as they hurried back to the warmth of the house.

"I keep my promises. Don't you worry none."

# Chapter 28

Louisa had never been involved in making so many cookies of different kinds and shapes in her life. Baking and running errands with Annie and her mother, as well as attending yesterday afternoon's Amish school Christmas program, had taken up much of their time during the past week. Even at the Rancks' there was much to do to help the family prepare for the holiday. There had been little time to be taught to drive a horse and buggy, but she could wait for a better time.

Meanwhile, she had begun a new drawing of the quaint well pump coated with a fresh sprinkling of snow. She could easily view it from her vantage point in the Dawdi Haus bedroom, working without having to camouflage her art as Annie continued to do. Often she felt apologetic because Annie insisted she openly work on her drawings while Annie couldn't—or wouldn't.

*It has to be a pain to hide what you love*, she often thought and sometimes contemplated the apparent incongruity of it—a group of people following stringent rules they imposed upon themselves. The concept of an unwritten system of expectations and required behaviors—expounding what is good or evil, although discussed by the ministers and voted upon by the church membership twice yearly—was mind-boggling. Had she not come here to experience it for herself, she never would have perceived the riddle of the Amish from Annie's letters. The freedom she had always envied, which she believed Annie had managed to take for granted, seemed to come at an exceedingly high price.

The thing most amazing about deciding to stay on here was the notion that her coming may have bought some creative time for Annie. But now, with Annie's worry of being found out by her father—and she fumed over this constantly, even whispering late into the night—Louisa wondered if it wouldn't be a good thing if her friend's secret *was* discovered. That way some understanding could possibly begin. *Either that or she and I will be looking for an apartment somewhere off Route 30!* But she knew she'd never encourage Annie to leave her roots. What was the point? Her life was all wrapped up in being Amish.

Louisa still had not deciphered how Annie had known of the first-place win before ever going to Julia's. But she had more than enough on her mind today—up to her proverbial earlobes in cookie dough and chocolate frosting.

In the middle of the morning, a knock came at the front door. Annie and her mother and three sisters-in-law turned their heads to look in unison, appearing quite startled, as nobody, except outsiders, ever used *that* entrance!

Annie hurried off to answer it, and when she returned carrying a large vase of red roses, Barbara Zook let loose with a string of astonished Dutch. Soon, Sarah Mae was chattering, too, and all of them were observing Louisa, as if they knew instinctively this bouquet was not intended for Annie.

"These are for you." Annie held the vase up.

Amazed, Louisa couldn't imagine who would be sending her flowers *here*. A dozen at that.

Annie went with her to the table, where Louisa carefully placed the glass vase in the center. "Look, there's a little card with it," said Annie, seemingly eager to know what Louisa herself was curious to see.

*This must be from my parents . . . or Michael.* She pulled the small card from the plastic holder, opened it, and read: *Merry Christmas with fond memories of us. Thinking of you, Trey*

"Michael or a secret admirer?" Annie whispered, wide-eyed.

"Not so secret now." The surprise overwhelmed even her—the thought of Trey doing something like this. And how had he known where to send the roses?

*Unless . . . did he contact my parents?* That was the most likely scenario. Trey had not received a return call from her, so he'd called her parents' home. *Too weird.*

"Roses are for love," Annie whispered later in the day, when she was admiring them on the bedroom bureau. "Are you *sure* there isn't something still 'tween you two?"

*Could there be? Impossible!* Too much had passed since they'd parted ways. Besides that, she was on a quest for peace and understanding far from city lights and metropolitan madness, whereas he had gone to seek all the exhilaration one London town could offer.

"Trey was always very thoughtful, that's all it is," she said. "Probably . . ."

❖

Louisa was amused at Annie's attempt to bundle them up for the ride once they were settled in Yonie's courting buggy. "Must be miles away to Esther's," she said while Annie continued to tuck lap robes around them.

"Oh, trust me, you'll be ever so glad for all these once we get goin'," Annie said as they waited for Yonie. "Your driving lesson's long overdue, ya know."

Louisa felt terribly restless now that she sat here staring down the long back of the enormous horse. "I had no idea we were going out this afternoon . . . with all this snow."

"It'll be fine, you'll see. There's little or no traffic out here, so we'll be safe from cars. The snow will be plowed to the sides of the road, but if too many cars get behind us, we'll pull off and let them pass. Then, when we return home, we'll all go ice skating on the pond behind our neighbors' barn."

"Danz or Lapp?"

"The Lapps . . . . 'cause we have a standing invitation from them anytime we want to skate," Annie said. "Awful nice, jah?"

Yonie came dashing across the yard, making boot-sized holes in the snow. "All right, let's go!" He climbed into the buggy next to Annie, but to Louisa he said, "All set?"

"As ready as I'm going to be."

"Well, if you want the horse to know you're in charge, it's best to hold the reins with confidence," he advised.

Louisa had no idea how to make the difference, but she sat up straighter and the reins became slightly taut. "Like this?"

"Much better." He was nodding and smiling. "That's just right."

"Now what? Should I say *gee?*"

Before Yonie could reply—and even with her rather soft directive—the horse began to move forward. "Wow, I didn't realize how easy *that* was." She laughed at herself, still as nervous as she'd ever been.

"This horse is very responsive," Yonie said. "Besides that, you're a natural, Lou."

*Lou? There is it again*, she thought. The nickname sounded so right somehow. "Do you really think I'm a Lou?"

"Seems fine to me, jah," Yonie said.

Annie nodded. "A good fit it is."

"A big departure from prissy Louisa," she admitted.

"Well, I like both names equally well," Annie said.

Louisa snickered. "Lou is much less fancy, jah?"

Now Annie and Yonie were the ones to laugh. "It strikes me funny when you say *jah*," Annie said, her breath releasing little white puffs into the air.

"It's such a cool way to say yes, you know? And I think I do like being called Lou . . . it's new. A nice change."

"Hey, Lou is *you*," Annie sang. "The new you!"

*The new me.* . . . She wondered if being called something different from her given name was a way to distance herself further from her modern life, to turn over a new leaf. Not that she was becoming enamored with the Plain culture, because being born into this subculture was the only real hope of successfully fitting in. Although Annie had told of a handful of folk she'd heard of, especially in other communities, who had attempted to join the church out of sheer frustration with the stressful life of the modern world. Most outsiders failed in such an endeavor, largely because they did not attempt to learn the language—Pennsylvania Dutch. The grueling work schedule also had a tendency to discourage them.

On the flip side was the idea that a Plain person, such as Annie, could make it on her own in the hubbub of the high-tech world. Louisa suddenly thought of herself, wondering how difficult it would be to reemerge into her former life . . . *when* she was ready.

*A girl named Lou would not mesh so well in a complicated world.* She smiled to herself, holding the reins for not only this powerful horse but for her own life, at least for this season of time. *I'm in charge . . . and I like it!*

"You're doin' just great," Annie said, instructing her to tug on the right rein just a little before the next intersection. "Then, after that, it won't be but a mile or so more before you'll see the Hochstetlers' driveway."

Louisa was careful not to move the reins too much, but when it came time to say *gee* and pull on the right rein, she did it with as much poise as she could muster, her body stiff. She held her breath, watching the horse strain on the harness as it made the turn.

Once they were headed on the next road, Yonie announced that she looked like "an old horse hand."

"If both of you weren't cheering me on, there's no way I'd ever want to attempt this," she confessed. "Way too much power at the other end of these reins."

"That's right," said Yonie. "You don't want to take a horse this size for granted, but I picked our gentlest and oldest for today."

"Well, thanks." She leaned up a bit, glancing his way, feeling edgy about moving around too much. The experience had taught her some interesting things, but after they made their cookie exchange with Esther, she would gladly give up the reins to either Yonie or Annie for the ride home. But she *would* like to try again on a road minus the snow pack.

Upon their arrival at the Hochstetlers', Louisa couldn't ignore Esther's swollen red eyes and suspected something was very wrong. She assumed Esther and her husband were having some conflict, because as soon as they headed into the house, he hightailed it out the back door, presumably to the barn. In turn, Yonie followed behind. Louisa had quickly discovered that most Amish males spent much of their time working outside. *Better than in bars,* she thought, wondering what could be troubling the tall man with haunting brown eyes.

Awkwardly she stood in the kitchen, much of it in disarray. Dishes were stacked high in the sink, and a bucket of sudsy water provided a needless obstacle in the middle of the room. The mop lay willy-nilly on the floor, while the youngest boy toddled around the bucket, leaning into the water to splash and cackle, oblivious to his mother's melancholy. One end of his diaper dragged behind him.

Louisa spied the older boy playing quietly with a mere five blocks in the sitting room, between the kitchen and the front room, talking to himself.

*What happened here?* She looked to Annie for clues, hoping Esther was not a victim of spousal abuse.

Annie, too, must have sensed something amiss, for she put her arm around Esther and guided her to the table, where they both sat and whispered in their first language.

Louisa wasn't sure where to put the several dozen cookies she'd carried in, so she set them inconspicuously on the far end of the table. Then, removing the plastic wrap, she chose one on top, with a big glob of frosting on it, to give to the little boy with the droopy drawers.

"Ach, no," Esther said quickly, turning toward her. "Little John's not to have much sugar."

"Oh . . . sorry."

"He has bad asthma," Annie volunteered, sitting close to Esther. "And sugar seems to feed the problem."

Suddenly feeling useless, Louisa set the cookie back on the table and went to the wood stove to warm up, watching the little tyke mumble to himself as he continued making his futile yet contented circle around the bucket.

Annie and Esther eventually switched to speaking in English. And even though she had no interest in listening in on their muted conversation, Louisa wondered if this was Annie's way of including her. She couldn't quite understand why that would be, however.

But she could not ignore what was being said, that Esther was troubled . . . something about her husband threatening her with "the shun" if she didn't stop talking about a "newfound friend." Whatever that meant, Esther's tone of voice triggered a deep-seated alarm in Louisa.

From everything Annie could gather, Esther had stumbled into Cousin Julia, of all things, this past week at the Progressive Shoe Store. Esther was adamant now that their chat was "ever so providential." Talking with "this most wonderful-good woman" had raised her spirits, at least for a time, Esther said.

"Another dose of your Mennonite kin was just what I needed." Esther's blue eyes began to sparkle now with each mention of Julia. "She shared things I must admit to never havin' *ever* heard. Oh, I honestly ate up what she was sayin'." She lowered her voice, even though it was only Louisa and the boys hearing what she had to say.

Whatever had transpired between her cousin and her close friend, Annie felt at a loss to understand. Having known Esther her whole life, she wondered now why Esther had paid such little attention, if any at all, to *her* advice. And the more Esther talked of "saving faith," Annie experienced an empty sensation, wishing she might have been the one to help Esther instead of a Mennonite interfering, whether Esther thought it Providence or not. It was altogether clear that Julia's words had affected dear, distressed Essie.

"Why the tears before?" Annie asked her.

The sound of splashing of water ceased as wee John sat down on the floor patting the leather boots beneath Louisa's Amish dress. With the kitchen too quiet all of a sudden, Esther simply shook her head.

"C'mon, tell me," whispered Annie, reaching for her hand.

Esther looked about, then leaned forward, her nose bumping Annie's ear. "Zeke threatened to report me to the brethren," she confided.

*Report her?*

"Why on earth?" Annie whispered back.

"Oh, but he's right, ya know." Esther's face fell again, and tears sprang to her eyes. "The People will look on me as ever so haughty . . . jah, the sin of pride, they'll say. For sure and for certain."

Annie's heart was in danger of breaking. *Ach, she believes she's got herself saved!*

The lanterns rimming the shoreline were mesmerizing as Annie skated around the far rim of the Lapps' large pond. Louisa was close behind, doing "ice laps," as she jokingly called her everlasting loops. Annie wasn't sure, but she thought Miss Lou just might be determined to ignore Trey's kind gesture of the bouquet of cut roses. *What a shame to waste such pretty flowers!* she thought, skating much more slowly now as Louisa whizzed past.

She had heard once, when she was a girl, the notion that if you wanted a boy to fall in love with you, a rooster's tail feather would easily do the trick if you pressed it three times into your beau's hand. That alone was supposed to make him love you forever. The old tale was the most outlandish she'd ever heard. Yet pondering romantic love made her wonder how Louisa's former beau had happened to resurface here and now, via the roses.

As for Annie, there was plenty on her mind to make her want to skate "till the cows came home," which had already happened twice today, as she'd helped put milkers on a good two dozen of the herd earlier this afternoon, following their visit to Esther.

Louisa slowed her pace and came over to skate alongside Annie around the rim of the pond. It was clear that she, too, had something on her mind. "What's with Esther and her husband?" she asked. "Is she always that upset?"

"That's between them."

"Well, what's he doing to her? Do you know?"

"Not for sure."

"But you must suspect something's wrong, don't you?"

Annie looked at Louisa as they made the turn at the lake's narrow end. "The women are to mind the men. That's what we're taught." She had promised not to spill the beans on Esther.

Louisa continued to press for answers. "Are you saying . . . even if you knew for sure Zeke was beating Esther, you wouldn't contact the police?"

"Never the police. It isn't our way."

"Then, what *is* your way?"

"Well, God's way, according to the church."

"So . . . let me get this straight. You simply turn a blind eye when husbands abuse their wives?"

Annie felt the sting of cold . . . and the harsh words.

Louisa must have noticed and quickly apologized. "I'm sorry, Annie. I know you care deeply about Esther . . . and you would help her if you could. I'm sure you feel quite helpless."

"Jah, 'specially when she looks so pale and exhausted . . . and expecting her baby soon."

Indeed, her befuddled friend's eye-opening disclosure weighed heavily on Annie's mind. That and the fact that Esther seemed to be losing the ability to keep up with her chores and her children. To help her catch up some, Annie and Louisa had finished mopping the floor and doing the dishes while Zach gathered up the toys in the sitting room at Annie's request. Annie even picked up little John and put him in a clean diaper, then into Esther's arms for a quick nursing. Esther had nearly weaned him, knowing full well she'd be kept busy with the new baby here before long. Besides, young John's baby teeth were becoming a problem, she'd said quietly.

*Hemmed in on all sides*, thought Annie.

Skating over a stray willow twig, Annie put out her arms to steady herself, then kept going. She considered Julia's involvement with Esther, which still flabbergasted her, in spite of Essie's ongoing struggle. *What right does my cousin have imposing her religious opinion on Essie?*

Oh, there had been occasions when Julia had talked about the Lord or heaven or what she liked to call "the gift of God—eternal life." But for the most part, Annie had paid little attention, letting it go in one ear and out the other. It wasn't that she wouldn't have been long-suffering enough or willing to hear Julia out; she just didn't see why she should compound her problems with unknown doctrine, or whatever it was her cousin was spreading around. Her own problems, though suppressed at this moment, were big enough to keep her up pacing the upstairs sitting room at night.

*How long before one of our cousins in Ohio sees Annie Zook of Paradise, PA, is painting in her spare time and says to himself,* Well now, isn't that Jesse Zook's girl back East?

Annie could hear it now, the ruckus such a disclosure would raise with her father first and foremost. Then it would filter into every crevice of the church district. People would wag their tongues like dogs catching flies. *That awful wicked girl . . . doesn't she know better?*

Annie had been noticing Louisa nearly every night sitting and drawing in her sketchbook in bed. Sure, she'd urged her friend to feel free to do so, but she hadn't thought Louisa would quite so often. Not with Annie propped up in her own bed nearly pining away for a graphite pencil and her own artist's pad. She often imagined what it would be like to openly convey her ideas on paper . . . or to sell her drawings unframed in small bins where customers could simply look through and discover a special gem. Louisa had recently sold several more paintings to the art gallery on Route 30, and Annie had decided to give Louisa the art classes she'd won as a special Christmas gift, since there was no way she would ever go.

*What would it be like not to have to sneak around?* she wondered.

Then it struck her like a brick out of the sky. *If the People would shun Esther for simply being led astray, what would they do to the preacher's willfully disobedient daughter?*

# Chapter 29

Annie's stomach began to gnaw and rumble during the final hour of the second sermon on Christmas Day, and she couldn't resist breathing deeply to get a whiff of the roast and all the fixings warming in the bishop's old black cookstove. Each family remaining for the special dinner had also brought along a tempting dish. Some brought more than one. She only knew of a few who would be heading home for their own family dinners, so there would be a big crowd staying put at the bishop's big farmhouse today.

Smelling the delicious food, she was more than ready to hear from Deacon Byler, who rose to announce the location of the next meeting, as was customary. Then he continued. "Our brother Rudy Esh, along with our sister Susie Yoder, plans to marry next month, along with several other couples."

Annie paid close attention, although the words did not register immediately. Yet she had been expecting this "publishing" of the wedding news for some time now . . . and here she was, on Christmas Sunday, witnessing what might have taken place for herself and her former beau. *They're thick on each other, so they ought to marry,* she told herself.

Next thing, Susie's father walked to the front and stood before them, announcing that a January tenth wedding—"on Tuesday"—was to take place for his daughter. "Those of yous sixteen and older are invited to attend the wedding service at our place."

*In no time at all, Rudy will be a married man.* Annie realized at that moment she was quite all right with the announcement. She actually had pleasant thoughts for the couple . . . not feeling regretful at all. Thankfully so.

Following the preaching service, Jesse situated himself among the group of older men just inside the barn, waiting for several of the younger men to move the benches around in the house, creating long tables for the common meal. He glanced up and noticed Zeke Hochstetler hurrying across the snow toward him.

*Will he cause a scene on Christmas Day yet?* Jesse wondered.

He anticipated what he would say if Zeke threatened to go to Bishop Andy with his malarkey. Truth was Jesse hadn't bothered with Zeke's request at all. It made no sense to speak to the bishop when he knew precisely what Andy would say. *What's done is best left alone*, he thought.

Zeke came right up to him and asked if he could have "a word" with him, and Jesse nodded, stepping out from the group, none of the men taking much note. "What's on your mind?" He almost slipped and said *son*, which would have been a bungle.

"I've been wonderin' where you've been." Zeke looked right at him. "I thought we had an understanding," he muttered.

Jesse wouldn't stir the fire by making an offhand remark. Instead he said, meekly as possible, "It's best all round to leave it be."

Zeke grunted. "No, I'm not going to rest till something's done. If you can't get the bishop to move on this, then I will. And I won't wait."

"Well, I see no need for anything rash."

Looking around, Zeke's jaw was set in a dogged clench. "Where's the bishop now? I'll talk to him myself."

"I'm tellin' ya, Zeke, this is unnecessary." He reached out a hand.

Zeke brushed him away. "Isaac's dead, and I want the murderer caught." Lowering his voice as he looked around, he said, "I want some justice for the blood of my brother."

Jesse heard the misery seeping out. There was no getting around it, Zeke was unable to manage his grief or the knowledge of the boy's death. "Ain't our way, and you know this. We don't press criminal charges . . . or any for that matter."

"Well, this is the exception to that rule!" Zeke's words were biting now, and his eyes glowed with pain.

"It's best if we not bring the English world into our own. It is imperative."

But Zeke continued to urge, only for Jesse to put him off. "It is *always* best to err on the side of obedience. And that is my final answer," Jesse said. "It is Christmas Day, Zeke. Let's rejoice together in the advent of God's son."

Downtrodden as ever he'd looked, Zeke turned and clomped back through the snow, away from Jesse. *Will he bend his will and come under?* Jesse could only speculate, quite concerned that Zeke might do something foolish. Something to jeopardize all of them.

Louisa had charged up her Palm on Friday at Julia's, and by keeping it turned off since then, she had enough power to place several Christmas calls. She was hesitant to use it within earshot of Annie's church friends, all of them still hanging out at the deacon's place following the Preaching service. She'd kept the device tucked away in her dress pocket during the service, aware of the lump in the cotton fabric.

While the other women were preparing for the common meal, Louisa stepped out onto the porch and speed-dialed her home. She was relieved when her dad answered. They talked casually, and he did not once mention Michael's name this time. "We miss you, Louisa, but hope you're having a good Christmas there." Then, when he'd said "Good-bye, dear," he put her mom on the line, and even she was not pushy. *They've backed way off,* she thought while her mom rattled off about this function and that they had attended. "How *are* you, Louisa?"

"I'm doing well." *A safe answer.* "Thanks for the Christmas present. . . . I didn't buy any this year . . . needed a break from the mall scene. And, well, that whole shopping nightmare."

"We thought you might need a new watch, dear."

"It's beautiful," she replied. *But I won't wear it here.* She wondered if this was her parents' way of alerting her that it was *time* to get over her little fit and return home.

"Thanks for thinking of me." She wanted to be polite. Well, she did, and she didn't. The purchase of the diamond-studded watch was not the best choice for one who wished to loosen her grip on material possessions.

"Are you eating healthy food?" Mother asked.

"Straight from the moo to you."

Mother actually laughed into the phone, almost too loudly, too freely. And then Louisa realized why. They had been drinking, probably a few too many glasses of wine with Christmas dinner. *Dinner alone . . . just the two of them, and why? Because their only child had abandoned them. Perfect reason to get sloshed!*

"I hope you both have a Merry Christmas," she said.

"You have a nice time there, too, Louisa . . . with your Amish friends."

"Well, 'bye, Mother."

"Good-bye, dear."

*Wow, Mother didn't fight to keep me on the phone. Weird. New tactic?*

She didn't know, and she really didn't care to analyze the conversation to death. Instead she called Courtney and was oddly relieved when her friend didn't answer. Somehow she knew Courtney would give her grief about jumping ship. She left a cheerful Christmas greeting on her voice mail and disconnected.

Then she pulled her sleeve back and looked at her simple watch with its plain brown leather band. She calculated ahead five hours from eastern standard time, assuming Trey probably wouldn't be having supper yet at six o'clock his time.

Annie stepped onto the porch, startling her.

"What on earth?" Annie said, eyes blinking and very serious. "Best not be takin' any chances."

She'd pushed her limits. "Oops, sorry. . . ." Not wanting to cause further alarm in Annie, she eyed the area of the springhouse and set off tramping through the snow to the more private spot.

Louisa checked for Trey's current cell number, stored in her incoming list of calls. It was the polite thing to do to call, to thank him. A dozen roses of that quality—roses that actually opened beautifully—didn't come cheap.

He surprised her by answering on the second ring. "Trey here," he said, sounding nearly British.

"Hey, merry Christmas. It's Louisa."

"Well, it's great to hear your voice."

"Yours, too." It certainly was, and she was quite glad she'd found a quiet spot to chat. "The roses were so gorgeous . . . well, I mean they *are*. Thanks."

"I had the hardest time tracking you down, girl. What are you doing in Amish country?"

She laughed. "So you must've called my parents?"

"Your mom told me about the wedding. I'm truly sorry, Louisa."

"Don't be. I'm having a blast here . . . sorting out some head junk."

"So, let me get this straight . . . you ran away from the wedding altar to go and hang with your Amish pen pal?"

"Uh, close."

"Which part?"

"I didn't exactly bail at the altar." She paused a moment. "Let's just say I would've been out of my mind to take that plunge."

"I can't say I'm disappointed," he stated, followed by an awkward pause.

Then—"I understand you're living in an old drafty farmhouse . . . probably not much different from the old digs I rent. Man, the winters chill straight to the bone here."

She smiled into the phone. "Yep, I wake up to the sound of peacocks, roosters, and cows every morning. Bet you can't believe that."

"It is surprising, Louisa . . . knowing you."

Not wanting to go there, she quickly asked, "How's the art business?"

"Booming . . . you'd be surprised. Actually, you wouldn't." He paused. "I hope you're still painting—you have the magic, girl."

"Well, I don't know about *that*," she said, beaming inwardly. "I do have a buyer for my work, though, here in Lancaster County."

"At a gallery?"

"Yep."

"Sold anything lately?"

She gladly filled him in, and he responded with the enthusiastic support she remembered so well.

"Well, let's keep in touch, okay?"

She warmed to his words. "You have my cell number now, but I don't have electricity here at Annie's. I charge up twice a week down the road."

He chuckled, that deep and jovial laugh she'd always enjoyed. "I hope you're kidding."

"Actually, I'm not."

"Really? No electricity?"

"None."

"Running water?"

"Some."

"This *is* interesting. Too bad you're not a writer. You could turn this funky experiment into a novel."

She let out a little laugh, feeling terribly vulnerable . . . the way his voice gave her goose bumps. "I just might, at that. But it's really not an experiment. It's a most needful thing." She'd picked up on this phrase at Julia's one day and liked it. Trying it out now seemed both strange and truthful somehow.

"Merry Christmas, Louisa. Terrific connecting with you."

"Same here. And a happy New Year, too."

"I'll call you soon."

"'Bye."

She scarcely noticed how rough going it was getting through the snow back to the house or how she'd begun to shiver. All she wanted to think about was the fantastic conversation she had just had with a most amazing guy, who, it seemed clear, was still interested in her.

*I forgot to ask for his email address.* She laughed at herself, questioning her own motives. *No, I won't chase him,* she decided.


Jesse sat enjoying his second dessert of carrot cake in Deacon Byler's kitchen, where a number of the older men had lingered following their Christmas feast.

He bit the inside of his cheek as he noticed Zeke making his way toward him, this time with Esther in tow. *What's this? Has he already blabbed the secret to his wife?*

"Esther here has somethin' to say," Zeke said, not pulling any punches.

Jesse got up from the table and motioned for them to follow. *Where could they go for privacy with a houseful of people?* He eyed the stairs and headed there.

When the three of them were shut away in the smallest of the upstairs bedrooms, Zeke blurted out, "Esther, go on . . . tell the Preacher what you did."

The young woman blinked her pretty blue eyes incessantly, cradling her swollen stomach. She looked at her husband, then back at Jesse, clearly nervous. "I . . . well, it's awful hard to explain."

Jesse was moved with sympathy and touched her elbow, guiding her to the only chair in the room. "Rest yourself," he suggested, and she quickly did so.

"Now, go back and start at the beginning." Zeke kept his distance, standing near the door.

"I've known a few Mennonites since I was a little girl," Esther said. "But this one lady, not so far from us, well . . . she's always been kind to the children and me. Seems to seek me out . . . as a friend, Julia Ranck does." She continued, reciting the various occasions she had encountered Jesse's own kinfolk.

Zeke became impatient and raised his voice. "Get on with it, woman. Tell what wrong thing you did!"

Esther immediately looked down, biting her lip. Jesse had a hankering to interfere, once again aware of the intense conflict between the two. But he waited, his heart entirely too soft to this lily of a woman who had often spent hours with Annie under his own roof.

"It's just this. Only this," she whispered. "I've found the Lord, at long last. Or maybe I should say He's found me."

"We are *all* followers of Christ and His church," Jesse replied.

She was shaking her head now. "I'm not talking 'bout man's rules."

Zeke spoke up, "She's fallen for this like a boulder in a fish pond, Preacher."

Jesse indicated with his hand that Zeke should calm down and be quiet.

But when Zeke continued to rant, Jesse knew he had a larger dilemma on his hands. Not only was the man itching for conflict, he had more than one ax to grind. Jesse must firmly address the issue at hand and hope, it being Christmas, that Zeke's urgency for hunting down Isaac's killer might diminish.

Esther spoke again, eyes bright with tears. "I believe what my friend Julia reads from the Scriptures. I'm not ashamed to say I'm a follower of the Lord Jesus."

Zeke snorted a laugh. "See? Didn't I tell ya, Preacher?"

"I see no reason to ridicule your wife." Jesse turned to Zeke, putting a hand on the man's shoulder.

"Well . . . go ahead. Ask her!" Zeke was close to shouting, rebuffing him. "Ask her if she's saved."

Before Jesse could do so, Esther was bobbing her head. "I have nothin' to hide . . . and nothin' to lose, neither one. I've given over my sins—my very life—to the Lord. I'm redeemed by His blood."

All kinds of buzzers were going off in Jesse's head. He had only once encountered such a problem with a church member. *Embracing an alien belief,* he thought, suddenly feeling less merciful. "Well, now, ya know declaring yourself saved is the most prideful thing a person could possibly do, don't you, Esther?"

Zeke nodded his head fiercely. "Oh, she knows, all right. She's testin' ya and she's mighty good at it."

Apparently there was no limit to Zeke's smart-aleck approach. "I'll be talkin' with Preacher Hochstetler and Deacon Byler on this," Jesse said, presently feeling the need to distance himself from the couple.

"Well, and while you're at it, be sure 'n' see Bishop Stoltzfus 'bout that other important matter we discussed," Zeke demanded.

Jesse held his peace, but what he truly wanted to do was to cut loose on the younger man. But he squelched the impulse for a full-blown confrontation with their mouthiest church member. "You'll be hearin' back from me—both of yous." But he had no intention of squabbling with the bishop.

Turning toward the door, he opened it and walked as confidently as he could muster into the hallway and down the stairs.

# Chapter 30

A gray smothering of clouds was suspended near the earth the whole week following Christmas, and although the atmosphere seemed conducive to snow, none fell.

The People marked the New Year by going from one relative's house to another, visiting extended family near and far. Some of the aging parents with more grandchildren and great-grandchildren than they could count knew they would still be having so-called Christmas dinner get-togethers come Easter. And many of those same youngsters displayed their Christmas gifts in the sitting room for visitors to see, especially teenage girls who had received a first "good china" cup and saucer or floral dish for a hope chest.

It was nearly Epiphany, the day often referred to by older church members as "Old Christmas." Annie's father asked her to pick up a new harness at Cousin Irvin's tack shop. Louisa hadn't been feeling well, because she'd caught a nasty head cold and was nursing a fever, as well. So Annie headed out alone with the team.

Her younger brothers were busy helping slaughter steers three farms over, and Daed was tied up with the ministers over at the bishop's place. Annie was glad the majority of the pre-Christmas snowfall had turned to slush, at least on the main roadways.

Finding herself with the only horse left at home, one of the slowest driving horses Daed owned, she figured she might as well take her time to get where she was going. She settled into the front seat, glad for all the weight of the lap robes, as well as several heated bricks Mamm had given her for the trip.

Her thoughts meandered back to Christmas dinner—of observing Zeke coercing Esther to speak with Daed. Poor Esther's eyes were terribly pained and her big belly protruded like she was surely close to her time of delivery as she and Zeke followed Daed up the long staircase. Annie guessed Zeke was urging her to confess those things she'd already told Annie—of having found a friend in Jesus, in so many words.

*Perhaps this is also the reason for Daed's meeting with the brethren today.* She shuddered to think of her long-time friend being put under the *Bann*, if only for a few probationary weeks. Even still, knowing the tenacity Esther was willing to exhibit—rare for a woman—Annie wouldn't put it past her to endure the punishment without coming under the Ordnung. No, if anyone could hold her ground against the ministers it was Essie Hochstetler. *And her best sidekick . . . me.* Annie stifled a smile, knowing she ought not to be at all proud of it and wouldn't think of saying so to anyone. Least of all her father.

In the small parking area outside the harness shop, designated for horses and buggies, Annie tied her father's horse to the hitching post and headed inside, aware of the jingling bell on the door.

The first few days of Ben Martin's new job had blended uneventfully with the instruction Irvin Ranck had so kindly offered—the cleaning and refurbishing of harnesses. Ben enjoyed watching Irvin lay out the inventory of leather, using patterns to cut out and sew up harnesses. Some were quite ornate, as in the matching sets of six for a team of Belgian horses. He hadn't needed extensive training in the trade, having kept himself busy with horses in Kentucky—especially at the Saddle Shop near Marion, where he had been employed since high school graduation. A lover of horses and racing, he had spent many summers as a groom at Churchill Downs, home of the Kentucky Derby, and filled his other leisure hours with stints as assistant coach for the local high school's football team.

The obnoxious dinging bell alerted him to the next customer, and when he looked up, he saw a blond Amish girl coming through the door. She was so pleasing to look at he was caught off guard . . . failed to call out his usual greeting. He could not overlook the confident tilt of her head and the purposeful way she carried herself. She was now walking toward him, and he had to remind himself to breathe.

When he found his voice, it was excessively strong. "May I help you, miss?"

"Hullo. Well, I hope so," she replied, smiling, "'cause it sure was a long ride over here in the cold."

*Is she merely mischievous?* He didn't know. Certainly not flirtatious, he didn't think, although there was a curious twinkle in her eyes. *Blue . . . they're definitely blue.*

"Cousin Irvin must've needed some help round here, jah?" she said.

He nodded, captivated by her demeanor . . . the fact that she did not seem put off by his being non-Amish and her being every bit as Plain as the four hundred or so horse-and-buggy-folk who'd settled in Crittenden County in Kentucky, where he had grown up.

"My father's in need of his order, and I s'pose you know what that would be."

"I'll look it up. What's the name?"

"Preacher Zook," she said. "That's not me, of course. My father's one of the ministers round here."

*A preacher's daughter,* he thought. And this one was made of pure spunk.

He pulled his grin into check and hurried off to look up the order for a Zook. He hadn't recalled a farmer with that name coming in to drop off a harness since he started the day after New Year's, but there had been so many unusual surnames floating around. Glick, Stoltzfus, Lapp . . . and more.

*So . . . how does a guy go about getting a date with an Amish chick?* he wondered, answering himself promptly, *He doesn't, nut head.*

Returning with the newly refurbished leather harness, he rang up the bill, aware of her fragrance there in the midst of leather and oil. Not the earthy, soil-beneath-the-fingernails kind of aroma he expected, but the spring-fresh smell of a young woman. Not more than twenty, if he was correct. He didn't care to analyze that his mouth had gone ridiculously dry, but he knew he had to at least discover her name.

"We checked the stitching, replaced what needed replacing, and made the harness as safe as possible," he said. "Here you are." He handed her the bill.

"Oh, just put it on the tab . . . that's how Daed always does it."

A dozen lines flew through his head. How to get her to introduce herself? "Who should I say made this request of the outstanding charges?" he asked

Her soft blue eyes put darts in his toes. "Just tell Irvin his cousin's daughter was here . . . he'll know by that." She turned to head toward the door.

*No . . . no, wait,* his brain was saying. But he refused to make a fool of himself. He stood and watched her push open the door and head into the daylight.

The thought crossed his mind that he might not see her again. So the memory of the jangling bell was all he had of her.

On the ride home, Annie considered Cousin Irvin's hiring someone outside of his own conservative circles. It made no sense, because she could see the young man wasn't even remotely Plain . . . no outward indication, at least. With her Mennonite cousins being devout in their strict beliefs, she was baffled why that would be.

The hired help had seemed to have trouble keeping his eyes off her, which was a bit surprising because she'd never considered herself pretty. *Maybe he hasn't seen many Amish before,* she thought. *But, no, how can that be?* He would have to wear blinders on those irresistible brown eyes not to have seen the likes of her . . . head covering, cape dress, apron, and all.

But even if her initial impression was correct, she had little hope of speaking with him again, unless she volunteered to run errands for Daed and maybe even her married brothers, too. But that was absurd. *Why should I be thinking this way? He's an Englischer, for pity's sake!*

On the morning of January tenth, Annie sat straight and tall, keeping her full attention on the bride and groom as they stood before Bishop Stoltzfus.

Lou, who was feeling much better, sat next to her, far less fidgety than she had been during Preaching services. Annie guessed Lou found this wedding quite foreign to the extravagant plans made for her own wedding day last fall.

Mamm sat on the other side of Annie, nodding off from time to time, probably because the house was much too warm. Three hundred people provided too much body heat, packed in as they were.

At the feast, though, Annie was seated across from Obie Byler, the deacon's cutest son, but she did not care to engage in much conversation with him. Each time she looked up, he was smiling over at her, though, showing his teeth like he was proud of how straight they were . . . *like a horse, nearly*!

Truth was, she kept thinking back to her encounter with the new fellow at the harness shop, wondering what her father's cousins were thinking, being "unequally yoked" as they liked to say, between themselves and a modern employee. Mennonites came in all shapes and sizes, just as there were a myriad of Amish groups. Maybe the young man with eyes as big as a cow's—and an intense gaze to match—*was* actually one of them.

*Ach, maybe he's someone Lou would enjoy getting to know.* The thought crossed her mind just as she was putting her fork into her slice of apple pie. But perhaps Louisa was having more than her share of male attention presently, what with Trey's long messages on her cell phone every few days and Michael's enormously long letter through the mail.

Annie craned her neck to see where Lou had ended up, and when she found her, she wiggled her fingers in a quick wave and smiled at the interesting combination she witnessed down the table from her. Louisa was sitting across from Rudy's first cousin, Noah, who wore a noticeably deadpan expression, quite clearly aware he'd been paired up with a worldly girl in sheep's clothing.

# Chapter 31

The clutter of her sketchbooks was beginning to annoy Louisa. She dry mopped the bedroom, and when that was done to her satisfaction, she sat cross-legged on the hardwood floor and began to organize. "Who would've thought I'd use up so many pages drawing here," she said more to herself than to Annie, who was cleaning her own side of the room.

Annie looked over, pushing several stray hairs behind her ears. "Is it more than you draw at home?"

"Hard to estimate . . . besides it's been two months since I left." She continued what she was doing, glancing over at Annie every so often, wondering how she was feeling with Rudy having given his heart publicly to Susie Yoder a week ago. "You okay?"

Annie nodded, coming over to sit on her bed. "You're talking 'bout Rudy and Susie, ain't so?"

"Whoa, that's scary. We're starting to think alike."

Annie's face lit up. "I like that part of bein' sisters with you, Lou. So, I guess you can never go home."

"Hmm . . . I don't know about *that*." She studied Annie and decided she looked tired. "You didn't think you could keep me here forever, did you?"

Annie's eyes were bright with some help from the blue light of dusk shimmering through the windows. "We both know this isn't permanent. And I won't be sad when you say you've had your fill."

"Promise me that?"

Annie laughed right out. "Ach, I doubt I should say such a thing. Who's to know how I'll feel when that day comes, really."

198

Before arriving here Louisa had never been much for asking pointed questions. Of course she had posed plenty to Michael the night of their breakup. But other than that, she hadn't recalled expressing herself so fully with another person. Not her parents and not even her almost-maid-of-honor, Courtney. "So . . . do you think Rudy and Susie are a good match?" she asked.

Annie took her time replying, removing her head covering and pulling the hairpins out of her bun. "It's not so much 'bout them being suited for each other as whether Susie will be a good housekeeper and cook, and if Rudy will be a good farmer who can make some basic furniture for the house. That's the real question. And knowing Rudy, I'm sure he'll be all of the above."

Louisa hadn't considered that the newlyweds might *not* be well suited. Wasn't everyone in the Amish community raised similarly, therefore a good match? She asked this of Annie, who was quick to shrug.

"We don't ponder ourselves silly over personality types and such . . . I happen to know 'bout this from the magazines I sometimes read at the doctor's office or at the library . . . well, I did back when my father let us go and check out books."

"No more?"

"Most everything's getting too worldly, he's decided." Annie's hair hung down over her shoulders, and she rose to get a brush from the top drawer of the bureau.

"Well, those 'winner's' art classes I took—thanks to you—weren't at all offensive. You easily could've gone."

"You know why I didn't go," Annie retorted.

"Yep, and you didn't miss much, as far as I'm concerned."

Annie frowned. "You must not have enjoyed it."

"Oh, I did. But I'm so not into abstract. You just never know, though. It might hit me someday." Louisa thought of Trey again. He adored abstract art—color-field painting and neoplasticism, especially Piet Mondrian's "Amaryllis."

"I would've been lost in a class like that," Annie admitted, staring at her now and then breaking into a big smile. "Do you realize you keep your head covering on till you slip into bed? And there's no need to, really. Once we're up here and the door's closed, it's all right to dismantle yourself back to bein' English."

The way Annie said it struck Louisa funny, and both girls broke out in peals of laughter.

When they'd composed themselves, Annie said, "Here's something to think 'bout . . . but I doubt you'll even crack a smile." She looked more serious as she brushed her hair. "There's an interesting fella you ought to meet . . . workin' for my cousin Irvin, Julia's husband."

"Yeah, I'm laughing. *Not!*" Louisa didn't care to tell Annie how weird it was to read a novella-sized letter from her ex-fiancé the same week as Trey's sweet-sounding words filled her voice mail.

"I'm not kidding, Lou. There's something special 'bout the guy."

"What's his name?"

"Don't even know."

Louisa eyed her. "So . . . he's not *your* style, is that what you mean?"

"He's English, that's all." Annie shook her head.

*She's curious, though,* thought Louisa. "When do you want to go back over there? Huh . . . huh?" She couldn't help it. Annie was so much fun to tease.

"Well, maybe Daed will have another errand for us to run for him. I'll see." Annie said this with a straight face—as naïve and guileless as ever.

*She does like him!* thought Louisa.

Her husband was in the process of rounding up the excess barn cats, and he might've shot them all in the head, in spite of what Esther had firmly suggested to do with them—put out a sign on the road: *Free Kittens.* And if Laura hadn't come wandering out to the barn just as he was loading his rifle, he might have done just that.

"Dat? What's that you're doin'?" their daughter asked.

The instinctive fright on her sweet face sent Zeke back to the ledge where he kept his gun. "Can you help me gather up some of the kitties to take to one of the farmers' markets—the Green Dragon, maybe?" He glanced disdainfully at Esther.

She ignored his glare, focusing instead on Laura, who nodded her little head and beamed a smile. "I'll go right now, Dat."

There was something that attracted cats to Laura. All animals, really. It was her gentleness and innocence, no doubt. Esther was secretly grateful Laura appeared when she had. Off Laura went to climb the haymow ladder, which was a good thing, because not but five minutes later, here came Deacon Byler in his family buggy, a long expression on his ruddy face.

"Zeke . . . Esther," the deacon said, removing his black winter hat. "I'd like a word with yous."

"Right away," Zeke said. He was raring to go, she could tell . . . mighty ready to have his whippersnapper wife shamed into repentance for *"all this twaddle about being called by the Lord Jesus,"* as he'd rudely stated right to her face a few hours before.

Ben Martin was unduly smitten. Preacher Zook's daughter, whoever she was, had his emotions by the throat, and he could only think of the next time he might glimpse her across the road, or far better, she might march back into the tack shop.

*Or is there something I need from her father? I'll drive right over there. A good dose of religion, maybe?*

He laughed at his own private joke as he worked, switching the hame strap on the front end of a harness. After all, if it was organized religion he was after, he would have nailed it by now.

During his short break time, he headed out through the snow to get a can of soda from the cooler he kept in his car. He inhaled deeply, taking the cold air into his lungs, totally jazzed to have signed a one-year lease on a 900-square-foot bungalow several miles from the harness shop. *Kentucky Ben walking on foreign but appealing soil, a long way from home,* he thought.

But where else could a guy work for an upstanding businessman like Irvin Ranck? Precisely the sort of man Ben had always wanted for a boss. None of the nonstop male chauvinistic blather punctuated by profanity, like at the last tack shop, his first job. Meek almost to a fault, Irvin was a man of few yet profound words . . . the most conservative man Ben had ever met. And he treated his wife like a queen.

Ben believed it to be sheer luck, among other things, that had brought him to work in this little harness shop in a Podunk place called Paradise.

Taking a swig of his soda, he recalled looking out at the Amish girl's horse and carriage, wondering which direction she was headed. *This is silly,* he thought, picking his way back to the shop. But he shook the door enough to jingle the bell repeatedly, for the pure adrenaline rush of it.

She was out on her ear, or so Zeke seemed determined to remind her. Even after Deacon Byler left, Esther sat alone in the stillness of the kitchen, tears refusing to dry up. She had fully known what was coming, for she had been raised in the strictest of households, her own parents most mindful of the Old Ways. To think she had turned her back on the rigid expectations of her own church . . . *my own people.* And just today she'd been given yet another chance to renounce her new walk with the Lord. *How odd that embracing the assurance of salvation through God's Son is so frowned upon!*

Her lot in life, at least till such time as she "came to her senses," was for her to be separated from her own family while living under the same roof . . . here in this house where she and Zeke had made their home. Here, where she had been the ever-dutiful wife and loving mother.

She rose and moved slowly toward the stairs. Painfully she made her way to the bedroom where she'd shared all her married days with Zeke. But no more. If she was to be so arrogant as to declare herself "redeemed," then she was forbidden to engage in marital intimacy. *Who's going to check up on that?* She allowed the sarcastic yet comical thought to hold sway momentarily. *The deacon? Preacher Zook? Just who?*

She sat on the bed, collecting her wits, not wanting to be seen moving her personal items and clothing to the far end of the hall, to the tiny bedroom set aside for a toddler's nursery . . . where her next baby would reside, along with its mother, as she did not see herself bending her knee before the People. Not when what she fully believed was ever so right and good . . . and heaven sent, just in time.

*I won't turn my back on this wondrous thing,* she determined in her heart, unsure what the ramifications might be for her precious children. Not taking into account Zeke's husbandly needs and wishes, she must follow the shunning requirements, and what a pleasant respite . . . at least for a time. Zeke would surely hold her to the *Bann,* imposed by his own will and the church's. She shook her head, aware of the irony.

Esther held her stomach, so large now she could not see her own knees, let alone her ankles. A wave of sudden sadness, beyond the pronouncement of an impending permanent shun, was the stark realization that this child she was carrying would be her very last. And in her despondency, she prayed it might be a girl. If so, she would name her Essie, after her own lost innocence. That is, if Zeke deemed it acceptable.

When Louisa checked her voice mail, she was dismayed to hear Michael's voice. *Again!* Only this time he said he was booking a flight to Pennsylvania for this week—didn't say what day he planned to arrive—only that he was indeed coming.

"Oh, this is so lame!" she said while she hung out in the barn with Annie, who was inspecting the bridle and other parts of the many harnesses, in response to her father's request.

"What's lame?" Annie asked.

Sighing, Louisa groped for the right expression. "All right. It's the pits," she said. "Michael's determined to bust his nose in here and talk turkey."

"Himmel, not *that*!" Annie smirked. But then she must have realized the gravity of the situation.

"He says he has a new angle he wants to present in person." She wanted to have a royal fit—pull out her hair bun or throw something. But if she looked Plain, she ought to act it.

Annie looked at her stunned. She obviously didn't get it. "Well, why'd you say he could visit? Tell him to stay home."

Lou shook her head. "He left all this on my voice mail. Michael's like that. He doesn't wait for an answer . . . just barrels his way through."

"Honestly, I like a man like that," Annie said, surprising herself. "But is there anything he can do or say to change your mind, Lou, really? And if not, then it's a waste of money and time."

"Nothing will change my mind."

"Tell him to stay put, then." Annie could talk big. Louisa wondered if Annie would actually have done this if Rudy had decided to pull out all the stops after their breakup.

"Sure, I can do that. For the zillionth time," Louisa said. The last thing she wanted was Michael walking around here on Annie's turf. The thought of it made her livid, like it might desecrate the soil or worse. "I hope my Palm has enough power left for me to call him."

"If not, we'll go 'n' get some quick-like. We'll take Daed's fastest horse and the buggy and head straight to Cousin Julia's."

Louisa saw through Annie's suggestion. "By way of the harness shop, right? Hey, I know what you've got on *your* mind."

Annie blushed crimson, shaking her head all the while.

"I see right through you, Annie-girl." She was amused now. "I guess it's time for me to check out the harness shop dude for myself."

Annie blinked fast, and then gave a frown. "Dude?"

"Well, he'd have to be one if he's a modern boy hanging out at a tack shop, right?" She wasn't about to check the power on her cell now. "Come on, let's get going. I have a call to make!"

203

# Chapter 32

Michael picked up immediately, and Louisa sensed he was at work.

"I want you to listen to me." She sucked in a deep breath.

"Hey! I'll be seeing you soon, Louisa. We can talk face-to-face."

He was not listening. He was railroading his way over her, the way he presented closing arguments in court. "No. The answer is no, even though you never bothered to ask," she said.

"What's wrong, babe?"

"Don't you get it? I'm done. We're finished. Cancel your trip."

"So . . . you've already hooked up with someone else?" This surprised her.

Immediately she thought of Trey . . . but that was so strange it was a sort of nothing on her radar screen right now. The fact was she'd found what she had craved: freedom to live her life.

She glanced over her shoulder at Annie, who was helping Julia in the kitchen. "It's not about another guy, which is really none of your business anyway."

He went silent on her, but she braced herself for the comeback. Definitely, there would be one. But *no*, she wasn't going to brace and she would not wait. "I'm going to hang up now," she said. "Good-bye, Michael."

*Click!*

*Almost too easy*, she thought, congratulating herself. And she knew Annie would be proud of her for standing her ground.

Ben followed the scent of woodsmoke, going to the door of the shop to look out. A quarter mile or so away, near Irvin's house, a lone Amish buggy was parked in the driveway.

Certainly he had work to do, but his feet were firmly planted as he waited and watched, curious to see who might emerge from the Rancks' door.

The phone rang a moment later, and he turned reluctantly. Answering, "Rancks' harness shop," he carried the portable phone over to the door and stood there, watching.

Paying attention to the broken English of the decidedly Amish customer on the line, he made a mental note. "I'll check on that order right away, sir. Have yourself a fine day," he said and hung up.

*Fine day, indeed.*

It was then that the horse began to rear its head, and one by one, the small pickets from the fence began to fly into the air. "He'll rip it to pieces," he muttered.

Grabbing his jacket, he hurried out the door. He considered driving the car over but quickly changed his mind, thinking the engine might scare the horse further.

*Forget that,* he thought, running across the wide field.

Annie heard the horse making a racket and excused herself from the kitchen, where she and Julia had been organizing all the lower cupboards and shelves while Louisa checked her email.

"Well, what's going on out there?" Julia asked.

"I'll go see." Annie said as she dashed to the door.

There, down on the driveway, the harness shop "dude" was attempting to steady her father's horse, and doing a fine job of it, surprisingly so. He had a hold of the reins and was stroking the horse's long nose and apparently talking to him, as well.

*He's got a right gentle way,* she thought, heading down the stairs to thank him.

"Hullo, again," he said before she could say it first.

"Well, now, looks like you just spared Cousin Julia's fence. Maybe she won't have to replace the whole stretch of it . . . 'cause of you."

He nodded, extending his hand. "Glad to help. Any time."

She shook his hand, aware of his strength. "Thanks ever so much."

"I'm Ben Martin . . . and you are?"

"The preacher's daughter."

He handed her the reins, ignoring her impertinence. "This is one feisty horse," he said with a sly grin. "So then, you have no name?"

"Perty much," she said. And had it not been for Louisa coming down the back steps right then, Annie might've stood there wondering what forthright thing to say next, to keep this fellow's eyes from lighting up like an English Christmas tree every time she even uttered a word. But here came Lou, waving to them and smiling for all she was worth. "This is my good friend Louisa . . . she's decided she likes goin' by Lou, though. Say hullo to Mr. Ben Martin."

"Nice to meet you, Lou," said Ben, nodding politely.

"Same here. You're not from around here?"

"Good ol' Kentucky's my home. Fine horse country . . . you may have heard."

Annie had noticed the slight southern twang and was intrigued by the thoughtful drawl of his words. "Well, what brings you to God's country?" she asked.

That brought a laugh all around. Then, Ben seemed to focus his attention on her once again, which made Annie feel peculiar. "It's a long story how I ended up here, but for now I need to get back to the shop. Need to keep the customers satisfied."

She smiled, relieved to see he wasn't going to stand there and stare at her all day. "Cousin Irvin always says, 'The customer is king.'"

"And I agree. Nice meeting you both," he said, then turned to leave, patting the horse and whispering something to the animal before heading across the field back to the harness shop.

"Now there's a hottie if I've ever met one," Louisa whispered as the two of them stood watching him go.

"Oh, you and your English slang." She wondered if Louisa was at all intrigued by the newcomer. If so, too bad she'd decided to dress Plain while here. *Because Ben must surely assume she's Amish like me!*

*So . . . she wants to remain anonymous!* Ben was intrigued by such an outspoken girl and Plain, at that. He hadn't been in *such* a hurry to return to the shop. He'd used it as an excuse to hightail it back to privately consider the spark that had ignited when he touched the preacher's daughter's hand.

He wanted to see the Zook girl again. But he wondered what dark-haired Louisa was thinking . . . looking as if *she'd* like to go with him to Starbucks.

He knew he would probably second-guess this thing to death. No doubt the girl who made his heart pound like a jackhammer was probably already engaged. Nothing was ever this easy. . . .

Getting back to work, he decided to dismiss his ridiculous notions. What would an Amish girl want with an outsider anyway?

❖

They quarreled bitterly prior to retiring for the night, Esther pleading with Zeke not to raise his voice lest the ranting rise to the ears of their little ones who were supposedly asleep. But Zeke kept insisting she must "give up her silly little game."

"My devotion to God has nothin' at all to do with playing a game."

But, sadly, at the end of their disagreement, Zeke was more concerned about being without her in their bed. "Your punishment is mine, too," he stated fiercely, his fists clenched.

Her head throbbed with the knowledge of his anger. By her sheer ingenuity she managed to get away from the stinging words that spewed forth near endlessly. It wasn't that she lied to do so, not at all, for she surely *was* nauseated, even concerned with her baby coming in a few weeks. The stress of his confrontation was terribly taxing, and she needed a reprieve quickly. So she told him she must get some rest . . . "lest the baby come early." This seemed to help the situation, although he was surly all the way up the stairs.

*His punishment, indeed,* she thought, settling into the small bed in the corner room of the house.

Pulling up the layers of quilts, she knew that yet another punishment for her was the way the cold crept into this particular room, far from the heat source below them on the other side of the house. The lingering fires of the cookstove were located in the center of the kitchen, the warmth rising to the large bedroom where Zeke would sleep now, alone. And the only portable propane heaters they owned were situated in the children's rooms. Rightly so.

It was her darling children who encompassed her every dream this night, away from her marriage bed. First Laura, her oval face beaming with joy over the cuddly kitties she cradled in her arms, sparing them from a swift death. Then it was Zach and John pulling on a thick rope, laughing so hard they cried as they tugged . . . pulling . . . straining in their play. In helpless haziness, she was very aware of her dear threesome, and the baby growing within, in the vignettes of her many dreams.

Later in the deep of night, when she dreamt of her littlest boy struggling to breathe, she wakened with a start, sitting straight up in bed, wringing wet with perspiration.

Listening, she heard whimpering. *Am I still sleeping?*

Gingerly she raised her swollen self out of the foreign bed, rising as if in slow motion, unable to feel her bare feet on the floor at first. Then the familiar smarting—the sting of cold shot straight to the bone.

She moved about, attempting to locate her house shoes with her awkward feet, and quickly lit the lantern, keenly aware of Laura's small voice, calling . . . pleading for help.

*Zeke sleeps through everything,* she thought, shuffling herself along the long hallway, following the sound of Laura's voice.

"Mamma! Come help . . . Mamma, do come quick!" Laura called softly, having been programmed not to holler.

Then it was Zach's pitiful voice she heard. "Where *are* you, Mamma?"

The children knew better than to ever knock or call at the door of the main bedroom, lest they pay dearly for it.

Finally she stood at the door of Zach and John's room. What she saw made her gasp. There on the bed, being looked after by both his older sister and brother, was sweet little John, arms out at his sides . . . a frightening blue-gray pallor on his tiny face, evident in the lantern's light.

*Oh, dear Lord, let him be alive!*

She rushed to his side as fast as her weighted body would allow, and she leaned her ear down to his pale lips. Horrified, she began to press her own mouth over his, gently blowing a stream of her breath into him.

"Where were you, Mamma?" Laura's face was wet as she clung to her. "I was callin' ever so long."

Again she breathed for her wee son. And yet again. She could not simply let him slip away.

"Mamma . . . Mamma," Zach cried softly, hovering near them.

*Live, my child . . . oh, you must live!* She continued to coax air into his tiny round mouth . . . willing John to breathe.

At one point, between ragged breaths, she lifted him to her bosom, praying her nearness might revive him. *Somehow it must.*

"I'm here," she said to all her dear ones. "Mamma's here."

# Chapter 33

Louisa awakened in the night, perplexed by her dreams. She and Ben Martin were riding bareback on a single horse through an open meadow of gleaming blue wild flowers, the wind in their faces and hair. She was no longer wearing Amish attire . . . she was back in her designer jeans and boots, encircled in Ben's arms.

*Good grief*, she thought now that she was fully awake. *What's that about?*

She had gotten up to use the chamber bucket beneath the bed, but on second thought she decided to pull on one of Annie's heaviest bathrobes and make her way outside for some fresh air.

The lingering visions remained even as she donned Annie's work boots and clumped out through the snow the short distance to the outhouse. The moon was bright enough to mark the way, and she smiled sleepily, wondering what could have triggered her subconscious to serve up such a weird dream. Sure, the blond-haired guy with inquisitive brown eyes was a hunk. But not her style, was he? And even if he was, he had eyes solely for Annie, of that she was convinced.

*Maybe he's a temporary answer for her,* she thought, even though Annie had assured her she was no longer hurting over Rudy. Maybe this Ben guy could be her transitional man, someone to soothe her wounds and make her feel good about herself again. Like anesthesia.

*Is that what Trey is to me?* She surprised herself with the thought. And she knew better. Trey wasn't someone who was just filler in the larger scheme of things. He must have genuinely cared for her . . . simply stepping back while she completed art school, although he'd never stated this as his intention when he melted into the European woodwork back when. Now he was back in her life in a big way, calling several times a week, talking about a rendezvous in Colorado or even here in Pennsylvania. Emotionally, she felt she was keeping him at a safe distance. Even now. She wanted to be sure this time, wanted no residual stuff floating around. Nothing to get in the way of a new yet very warm former relationship.

On the way back from the drafty outhouse, where she'd encountered spiders galore earlier in the autumn—not so this time of year, when things were good and frozen beneath that disgustingly smelly place—she happened to see a car parked out on the road. She stopped walking, pausing against the cold. If she wasn't mistaken, one of Annie's brothers was leaning against the car, locked in an embrace with a girl. His silhouette—with a black winter hat—was stark against the moonlit snow.

*Whoa . . . interesting.* She was captivated by the thought of Yonie or possibly Omar sneaking around with an English girl, which it had to be, otherwise where had the car come from? Unless, perhaps, he owned a car and hid it from the eyes of their father, as Annie said some of the boys did during their running-around time. That, too, was another eye-opening concept. To think Amish parents allowed their teens to go pretty much their own way, offering freedom in the hopes of retaining them for the church. *The illusion of being given a choice,* she thought.

Shivering now, she made her way down the walkway and into the house, surprised that someone had been up and put extra logs in the belly of the wood-stove. *Probably Annie's dad,* she guessed, wondering if he was also up checking on his absent son. She would ask Annie in the morning about what she'd seen tonight. *Love must be in the air!*

"Zeke! Wake up." Esther called to him repeatedly, even daring to shake him. "I need your help!" She was hollering now at him, Zeke lying there rather lifeless himself.

She heard Laura crying in the next room, where she'd left John and Zach. Now, attempting to rouse her husband, she called to him again, touching his face, his chest.

Getting down right close, she happened to detect the scent of alcohol. *Ach, no!* For the longest time, she'd felt he was staying away from his whiskey, but evidently whatever troubled him of late had gotten stronger footing once again.

Failing to wake him, she waddled back to the children, praying silently all the while, and feeling as panic-stricken as ever she had.

She lay down in the bed beside her tiny John, holding him near, praying aloud and asking the "dear Lord Jesus to return life to this child, just as you did to Jairus's daughter so long ago. This I pray, humbly . . . and not for my own sake. Amen."

She continued to cradle him, putting all her trust in the heavenly Father's love for her and her family.

Feeling a strange warm calm come over her, she placed her fingers beneath his chin, checking for a pulse. "Oh," she said, feeling the faintest beat. "Denki, dear Lord . . . oh, thank you."

"Mamma, what is it?" Laura tugged on her bathrobe.

"I believe your little brother is alive!" she said, looking into Laura's near hollow eyes.

Zach snuffed his nose and rubbed his face.

She sat John up and patted his back, talking softly to him, half praying, ever so near. He opened his small eyes, his long, thick lashes brushing his eyebrows, and he began to heave and cough . . . a deep, ragged rasp, spitting up as he did. The harsh yet all too familiar sound sent more shivers up her spine, but she was relieved to hear the coughing, which meant John was breathing indeed.

Going to the bureau, she opened the first drawer and took out his prescribed inhaler. Now that he was breathing, she would attempt to administer it.

She was determined to keep watch over her frail boy. *I'll put him right in bed with me!*—where she was now intended to slumber alone, for as long as she did not repent of finding the joy of her dear Savior and Lord.

*O Jesus, it was you who spared my little one this night. I am ever so grateful!* She prayed this silently as tears spilled down her cheeks.

Annie had something of a predawn ritual upon awaking each morning. If Louisa was even conscious that early she would sometimes drowsily observe Annie staring at the ceiling, as if contemplating her life. Or perhaps she was "saying" her silent rote prayers. Then, after a time, she would sit up in bed for a few minutes before slipping out from beneath the mound of quilts, going to the window to stand and look out.

This morning, however, Louisa did not wait for Annie to swing her long legs out of the bed and onto the ice-cold floor. She simply brought up what was on her mind. "I think one of your brothers has a girlfriend . . . and she doesn't look very Plain."

Annie was nearly angelic looking in her high-throated white nightgown. "He might just be pushin' the boundaries, but most of our boys do that."

"Well, there was lots of kissing going on, and I don't mean pecks on the cheek."

"Oh, that." Annie paused. "We're s'posed to just talk on those all-night buggy rides, ya know. But, honestly, many of the young people do way more than that."

"Don't we all."

"The main thing is gettin' all this out of your system before joining church."

"So, then, you must know for sure your brothers will." She was curious what Annie might say.

"Well, I'm perty sure they'll come to their senses."

"Like *you* will?" She had to say it . . . had to know what Annie was really thinking about her future as an artist.

Annie was on her feet all of a sudden, pushing her toes into soft slippers. "The difference 'tween a boy in love with a girl and . . . well, what I'm passionate about is awful easy: loving something that's not fickle. You know, like art. It's always there. Never betrays, never disappears, jah?"

She smiled at Annie's desperate attempt at honesty. "Hey, you don't have to convince me." Creating was such a big part of her life, she couldn't imagine having to choose art over a guy . . . or worse, over a belief system. "I'm not sure how you've managed to stay Amish this long, Annie."

"Well . . . it's the belonging . . . being connected to the community of the People." Annie patted her chest. "I know it in here. Like my father's faith in God."

*What's faith anyway?* Louisa thought. This was the hang-up of her life. The faith thing was so real and powerful and good that people from all walks of life embraced it on some level. Your "higher power," the AA folks called it, a confidence in something beyond oneself. But did it have to be all wrapped up in what *others* believed?

Whatever faith was, she didn't possess it. And she wasn't about to bring up the topic, not when Annie was eyeing the window again, preparing to race the dawn.

*Work takes precedence over reflection in Paradise . . . most of the time,* she decided.

Annie wasted no time talking to Yonie out in the barn. "You *Dummkopp!* Lou saw you with Dory last night!"

"How's she know it was me?"

"Well, she doesn't know for sure."

He squinted at her. "You didn't own up to it, did ya?"

"No, but even if I did, what would it matter? Lou won't talk it around."

He looked discouraged now. "We made a promise, remember?"

She nodded. "Louisa thinks what she saw was *one* of my brothers . . . and an English girl. Don't worry."

Yonie helped her pour the fresh milk through the strainer in the milk house. "You really have no room to talk, Annie . . . you sneak round, too."

"We aren't talking 'bout me, in case you forgot."

"All the same."

"I was only tellin' you so you'll be more discreet maybe."

Grinning, he said, "Well, now, aren't you quite the scholar? I've never heard you use such words."

"Seems to me, hangin' with Lou is one of the smarter things I've done."

Yonie walked with her back to the barn. "Just so she keeps her mouth shut 'bout what she sees past twilight."

They couldn't discuss this further, because Daed, Luke, and Omar were within earshot, getting ready to haul more milk cans to the milk house. For now she would take Yonie's remark at face value. Of course, Cousin Julia might call Lou's coming a blessing. But in *her* mind, having an Englischer visit here had opened her eyes to more things than she could begin to say.

Then and there, she purposed to make all their time together extra special, till that sad day when Louisa decided her "experiment" was over, that she'd had enough of country living and was ready to return home.

# Chapter 34

Esther awakened to see Zeke leaning over and staring at her and little John nestled against her like a limp little lamb. She spoke softly, saying how grateful she was that John was better now, explaining what a horrid thing had happened—"our littlest one nearly gave up the ghost last night," she admitted, reliving the trauma.

Zeke frowned, shaking his head. "You mean you nearly let him die?" He straightened, and she realized how very tall her husband was, frighteningly so. He turned and paced the floor, then went to stand at the foot of the bed. "Sit up when I'm talkin' to you!" he demanded.

She trembled but quickly did as she was told, relieved to see John still resting, eyes closed, with a spot of color in his cheeks.

"If you'd slept in my bed, where you rightfully belong, instead of getting yourself put under the ministers' discipline, you would've heard John coughing and sufferin'. So it was your fault." Again he shook his head, looking down at the bed quilts before raking his big hand through his shock of brown hair.

His words cut through her, yet she refused to defend herself. Not with their little one lying here asleep, hair tousled, hands relaxed against the pillow.

"I hope you know it would've been your punishment—on your head—had our son died."

She did not respond, either in word or deed. He was picking a fight with her, she knew this well. Praying she might escape his wrath somehow—even this morning—she did not make eye contact with him further but turned to get out of bed. Reaching for her house robe, she lifted it and would have put her arm through the sleeve, but Zeke moved quickly to her side, as if he might help her do so.

Instead, he reprimanded her yet again. "How dare you disregard your own husband."

*A soft answer turneth away wrath. . . .*

In the case of Zeke, there was no indication that such an approach to communication worked at all. Evidently King Solomon had never met the likes of Ezekiel Hochstetler when he penned those words. In her daily experience, living with this oft-crazed man, no matter what she did lent itself to conflict. *It's no use trying*, she thought, no longer grieved but as angry as ever she'd been. But she contained her rage, breathing slowly.

She did not see it coming. In an instant, he raised his hand and slapped her hard on the face, the force of it pushing her whole body against the wall. "You will answer me!" he shouted.

Little John began to whimper, and she feared for him, as well. Her cheek smarting, she tenderly held her left side, worried she had hurt the babe within her.

Knowing from past incidents that she must respond or become the brunt of even more mistreatment, she nodded penitently out of sheer necessity. "Jah, Zeke, I do heed what you say."

He huffed and snorted like an enraged animal, and when she sat on the bed near her boy, Zeke miraculously exited the room.

The day she'd feared had come. *I must get away from here*, she thought, aware of the throbbing pain.

"Come here to Mamma." She gathered John near. "You gave me an awful fright last night."

"*Millich*," he said softly, eyeing her bosom.

"Jah, 'tis nearly time for breakfast." She felt so terribly weak . . . too shaken to stand and cook. She longed to lie down and simply wallow in her pity like the big black and white hogs Zeke raised out back. But she was anything but lazy and wouldn't think of shirking her responsibility, not when she was so needed.

Filled with tremendous sadness, she opened her nightgown and lovingly offering her sweet breast milk to John as she rested against the pillow.

Setting the table for breakfast, Esther imagined herself knocking on Julia Ranck's door while the children waited in the buggy. *My only refuge*, she thought of her Mennonite friend.

Annie's house had never been an option, not really. For all the conclusions she'd drawn in her head . . . and for the reasons she'd given Annie the day they had been so plainspoken with one another, she simply could not flee to Preacher Zook's house. Neither was her widowed mother someone she could run to, because hers would be the first place Zeke would set out to look. She and the children would be welcomed at Julia's . . . safe, too.

*For a time. . . .*

Once there she could simply let the horse gallop home, pulling the empty carriage back to Zeke. That way he would have his best driving horse back and the family carriage.

On the other hand, Laura could easily walk the short distance to the one-room Amish schoolhouse, possibly attend tomorrow. Zach would entertain himself playing with James and Molly, and Esther could watch John closely. She'd thought of trying to have their doctor take a look at John first thing, but she knew why his asthma had gotten out of control and what to do to prevent it in the future. Such a thing would not happen again; she'd see to it.

As for birthing her baby, Esther knew that Julia would gladly, *lovingly* assist. Beyond that, she had no idea, but she wouldn't allow herself to worry over the future.

*Not today. I'll put one foot in front of the other, nothing more. . . .*

❖

After Annie helped finish her milking chores, she hurried indoors to help Mamm with breakfast. Today it was fried eggs, apple fritters, leftover pumpkin nut bread, freshly squeezed orange juice, and black coffee.

The kitchen already smelled of her mother's dusting powder, which she patted on daily, even on the coldest winter days. That coupled with the frying fitters created a kind of fragrant cloud around her.

"Where's Lou?" Annie asked Mamm, who had set out the utensils already.

"Took off walkin' not more than twenty minutes ago."

Annie hurried to the table and began to place all the forks around, as well as the paper napkins and their biggest plates. "Did she seem all right?"

"Wasn't upset, if that's what you mean."

*That's good,* she thought, assuming Lou was perplexed, maybe even a bit stressed, too, over the many messages left by Trey.

"Are you girls plannin' to attend the quilting bee next Tuesday?" Mamm asked, flipping over the first fritters in the frying pan. "It's at Sarah Mae's this time."

"I'll go . . . but I'm not sure 'bout Lou." Honestly it seemed maybe her friend needed some time to herself, but Annie wouldn't mention it. Mamm had enough on her mind, what with taking oodles of baked goods to various markets several days a week.

Annie had also been thinking quite a lot about her best painting. Since she believed herself to be on the brink of being found out anyway, the least she could do was get her favorite work framed. She'd decided to ask Julia to drive her to the art gallery where Louisa had been successful in selling her own paintings. Since the magazine judges had chosen Annie's work for their cover, then, just maybe, the painting *did* have some merit . . . and she wanted to see it framed.

"Does Louisa ever seem homesick to you?" Mamm asked.

Annie sighed. She should've known a question like this might emerge at some point. Fact was, Louisa had settled in quite nicely . . . *for a fancy girl*.

"You'd think her parents would miss her something awful." Mamm was pushing for some kind of response; and out of respect for her, Annie knew she ought to speak up.

"Lou hears from her family some. She charges up her phone at Julia's and calls them now and then."

"She has no other close relatives . . . no brothers or sisters, jah?"

Annie shook her head. "Sadly, no." But her mother had known this for a good many years now . . . from all the letters.

"She must feel like she has a sister in you." Mamm forced a little smile, staring at the frying pan as if contemplating what she might say next. It was mighty clear Mamm had a talk on.

"Oh, we're sisters, all right. We've felt that way right from the start."

"And she shares her knowledge of art with you, as well?"

*There it was! The thing Mamm was worming her way to.*

"I watch her draw sometimes" was all Annie cared to admit. No sense volunteering more. The woeful day was coming, she knew, and she often had nightmares about it—Daed pushing her published art before her eyes, forcing her to behold her own sin, his eyes pinning her soul down but good.

Mamm turned and looked at her. "S'posin' I ought to rue the day your father ever agreed for Louisa to come here . . . but, Annie, I have to tell ya—'tween you and me—I'm rather fond of her."

"Jah . . . I've sensed that." Annie felt a tender pull toward her mother.

"Louisa certainly doesn't have to contribute money, and you must tell her this." Mamm was referring to Lou's sale of art, but Lou had never told them the origin of the money.

"Well, she's not one to wear out her welcome. She wanted to pay her way from the outset here."

"Oh, but she's been more than generous. She doesn't owe another cent."

Annie smiled. "Might be hard to get that through her head."

Their conversation turned toward the day's snowy forecast, and just then Annie recalled having heard from her brothers that the hill behind the meadow was "right slick and good for sleddin'."

Her mother remarked, "I trust you won't let Louisa's friendship lead you astray, dear one."

*She feels she has to repeat this. . . .*

Quickly, Annie set about making toast and then buttered it. "I'll go over and see if Dawdi and Mammi Zook are ready to eat," she said, looking for an excuse to slip out of the kitchen.

The smell of fresh-brewed hot coffee tempted her, and she could hardly wait to have some. Mamm's was the best. *I'll have it black,* she thought, as if coffee void of sugar and cream would alone serve to quell her apprehension.

Yet she would not allow her worries to overtake her. She must move forward and explore the possibility of getting her best painting framed.

*Hopefully today. . . .*

Esther sat down at Julia's lovely table to eat homemade potato soup and chicken salad sandwiches. She had gotten her own children settled into their chairs, with John perched in Molly's former high chair. Besides Zeke, Julia's husband was the only one missing at the meal, out on a company-related sales call in Allentown.

Julia bowed her head and said a heartfelt blessing, mentioning Esther's name as well as Laura, Zach, and little John. "And, Lord, please pour your abundant grace into the hurting places of our lives," she continued.

Esther held Laura's hand during the prayer, squeezing it and offering a comforting smile when Julia finished, saying "amen" in a hushed and reverent tone.

On the buggy ride here, Esther had said very little to the children, mainly that they were going for a visit to "Auntie" Julia's, even though they had never met either Julia or her husband and children. Laura had been full of questions, as always, asking if this was a day off from school . . . and why wasn't Dat coming along with them. Esther had not fibbed, however, careful not to alarm either her eldest or Zach and John, who seemed to be quite happy to get out in the "snowy land," as Zach called it.

Having kept an overnight bag packed and hidden for several months now, Esther had been able to gather her wits, her bag, and the children in record time, her heart in her throat, while Zeke was gone visiting at the neighbor's for his midmorning coffee break. All during the time of her escape, she'd prayed both silently and under her breath, mindful to carefully bundle up John, who looked surprisingly fit for having nearly suffocated in the night. She realized that if she should fail to escape this time, she might never have another chance. Zeke would see to that. Even her stay at Julia's was risky business.

Still, she felt justified in leaving, needing a safe place to deliver her baby. *My helpless wee baby must come first.* She did not know what the next permanent step might be, for it would be presumptuous for her to think she could stay for an extended period at Julia's.

Handing the large soup tureen to her, Julia said, "Help yourself to plenty. I made a double batch . . . one for our shut-in neighbors, too."

"Denki," whispered Esther, still stunned she'd made it this far into her unknown journey. She dipped the ladle into the thick soup, putting a small amount in Laura's bowl, then into each of the boys'. Last of all, her own.

The kitchen was pleasant, situated where sunshine could flood the eating nook as they all sat, the drop-leaf table extended out to accommodate all of them. With its refinished oak hardwood flooring, white cupboards and apothecary knobs, and hard rock maple butcher-block countertops, Julia's kitchen was more modern than anything Esther had ever seen. Bright touches of red cookie jar, sugar dish, and salt and pepper shakers, and the deep yellow sunflower toppers above the windows, made for an appealing room.

She felt her muscles relaxing as she ate each bite of food, not realizing until this moment how hungry she'd been. She enjoyed the simple offerings of tasty soup and sandwiches.

Later, when she was helping dish up the fruity Jell-O for Zach and John, she felt the sharp cramping of another contraction. Not wanting to upset the children, she would not let on.

After the children were finished with their cookie munching, she felt she ought to lie down, hoping to stave off the onset of contractions. She whispered to Julia that she was "all in," and Julia encouraged her to take the spare room, away from the traffic of the house, "back in a little corner, here on the first floor," said Julia. "I'll tend to the children. You rest."

Ever so relieved, Esther rose and thanked her for the good meal. Picking John up, she turned to Laura and Zach. "Be sure to mind Auntie Julia, ya hear?"

Laura's eyes were focused on her, but her daughter said nothing. Esther smiled back, wanting to ease any fears her too-perceptive girl might have.

"You go on, Esther. It's nice and peaceful back there," urged Julia.

"Thank you ever so much." She felt so appreciative of her Mennonite friend and longed to rest her weary bones . . . and to have little John near to keep a closer watch on him. "Come, let's get you washed up." She kissed his sticky face.

*Dear Lord, be with my wee unborn babe!* she prayed.

# Chapter 35

Annie was bursting at the seams to share with Lou her sudden yearning—to frame her painting. But Omar was at the reins, having been kind to offer to drive them to Julia's. *This will have to wait*, she decided, trying to picture what such a large canvas would look like professionally framed.

And she couldn't wait to see the choices of beautiful frames. Of course she would be taking her chances at being seen out in the English world, but far as she knew there were scarcely any connections between herself and the fancy life here in Lancaster County. Next to none.

She kept still and listened to Omar and Lou chatting about upcoming farm sales, which Omar—and Yonie, especially—were always happy to talk about.

"What sort of things are sold at auction?" Lou asked.

"You name it . . . it's there." Omar was keeping a straight face, but Annie knew he was smiling inside. Anytime anyone wanted to talk about the sale of cattle, mules, driving horses, shovels, rakes, and all kinds of farm equipment, Omar was more than willing. "You oughta come along sometime. It'd be quite an experience."

"I'll say," Annie spoke up. "An all-day thing, with baked goods, quilts, and such for sale, and just like Omar said, everything under the sun, truly."

*But not a speck of fine art*, Annie thought.

By the time they arrived at Julia's, Annie could scarcely keep mum. But she waited till Omar had turned the horse and carriage around and headed toward the road before saying what was on her mind. "I want to tell you something, Lou."

"What's up?"

"I'd like to buy a frame for my painting."

"Hey, that's a terrific idea!"

"You don't think I might be seen there with it, do you?"

Lou shook her head. "I've never noticed any Amish people in that gallery. So . . . go for it." She opened the side door to Julia's house.

"All right, then. I'll do it today . . . if Julia will take me." Annie stepped inside the house, and right away she heard Laura Hochstetler's voice. "Well, what the world?" she whispered, going to investigate by peeking around the corner.

There in the cozy nook off the kitchen sat Esther's children with Julia, James, and Molly. "Well, hullo . . . we're late in coming today," Annie apologized first thing.

"No problem at all," Julia said. "As you can see, I have some houseguests."

*Goodness' sakes! Has Esther suffered the last straw? Has she left Zeke?* Annie went to Laura and touched her pretty hair, then leaned down to talk to her and Zach. "Looks like you had a nice lunch . . . here with Auntie Julia."

Laura smiled up at her, no worse for the wear. "That's just what Mamma calls her, too."

*Poor little children.* Annie stood up, thinking what an odd situation she was observing. *How will Lou occupy herself while I clean?* But she did not say what she was thinking, that the attic studio was surely off limits now. Instead, she asked, "Is Esther resting?"

Julia came over and guided her into the small front room, speaking in soft tones. "Oh, Annie, dear Esther needs our prayers . . . and some good rest, too."

"Well, I'll get the housework done right quick," Annie said. "And get out of your way."

"I'm glad you and Louisa came when you did. Is it all right with you . . . can you get the children tucked in for naps?" Julia explained she had a quick errand to run, out on Route 30, not far from Paradise Lane.

*Right where I'd like to go!* Her face must've dropped with disappointment, because Julia asked, "Annie? Did I say something wrong?"

"Ach, no . . . not at all. It's just . . . well, I have an idea . . . 'bout my painting."

"Oh, that reminds me! With Esther coming, I almost forgot." Julia looked mighty pleased. "Irvin's copy of the new issue of the *Farm and Home Journal* arrived today. Come look."

Annie felt every possible emotion, from elation to sadness, as she held the small magazine in her hands. "This scene, by Pequea Creek . . . it just looks so real," she said softly, feeling as though she could fall right into the cover—*my own painting!*—and be right there, standing where she had so many times over the years.

Louisa paused at the window in what Julia always called the "front room," watching Annie carry her original painting, wrapped carefully in many pieces of newspaper, out to Julia's car. Julia lifted the trunk and the two of them lifted the "Obsession" painting inside.

*She's hung up on that place . . . and the secrets behind it,* Louisa thought.

Sighing, she hoped her friend might not freak under the pressure of her own enormous secret.

*Whim or not, she's painted herself into a corner. . . .*

She went to look in on the children, who were soundly asleep in two different bedrooms, except for little John, whom Esther had taken in with her. Then she wandered to the kitchen, where she sat at the sun-strewn table with her sketchbook and a handful of colored pencils. Annie had indicated, in whispered tones, to avoid going to the attic to work today. *That will definitely have to wait,* she'd told her, and Louisa agreed. But it wasn't as if Annie's secret was secure anymore. The second hand on Annie's life clock was moving fast toward midnight.

Louisa turned her focus to her drawing, deciding to sketch Trey's handsome face from memory, only doing more of a caricature than the real thing. Casually she gave him a black Amish hat and brown beard, smiling at the juxtaposition of his modern attitude—evidenced by the wry grin and the charisma in his eyes—and the imposed plainness.

After a while, she rose to get some tap water at the sink and happened to glance out the window. She saw an Amish man rushing toward the side door. Bent forward, he was either angry or coming for help.

*Zeke?* she wondered. Thinking back to her only visit to Esther's house, Louisa couldn't recall what Zeke looked like. She'd only caught a glimpse of him before he disappeared into the barn. Besides that, the untrimmed beards and identical attire Amish men wore gave them the illusion of sameness.

In a few seconds the man was pounding at the side door. She felt nervous, being the only person fully awake in the house. *Should I even go to the door?*

She shoved her fear aside and walked through the little sunroom-sitting room, past the mud room, to the side door.

"Oh, I wish you'd have brought along the magazine," Miss Sauder, the gallery owner, was saying in response to Julia's cheerful prompting.

"Well, it's back home on the lamp table," Julia said quickly, looking at Annie. "But you have my word . . . she's a *very* good artist."

Quite embarrassed, Annie spoke up. "I'm interested in seeing some frames." She looked down at her painting all wrapped up, hidden from view.

The woman smiled kindly. "Come with me, I'll show you what we have in stock, as well as what can be ordered."

"Thank you," Annie said.

"Tell me again about your first-place award, please." The owner directed her question to Annie, but Annie deferred to Julia, since she seemed to derive such joy from sharing the news.

By the time Julia had described the contest in great detail, Miss Sauder was setting Annie's unwrapped painting up on a tall easel. She stood back and looked at it from all angles. "I've seen this place . . . I know I have," the woman said.

Annie glanced at Julia. "You have?"

"Oh my, yes."

"It's north of here, just down the slope from London Vale covered bridge," Annie told her.

"My sister and her family live a short distance from there." The woman turned to Annie and surprised her by asking if she might ever consider selling it. "I believe I may have a buyer for it, even now."

Annie didn't have to think twice. "Why, no. It's not for sale."

"Do you have other work, perhaps?"

The question took Annie by surprise. "I do . . . but I think I might need some time to think on that. It's very nice of you to ask." Talking about selling something with her name on it gave Annie a dreadful sinking feeling. Like she was doing something unforgivably wrong indeed.

When the woman placed on the long counter the frame samples—traditional woods in classic and antique styles, composite moldings, and aluminum frames in twenty colors—Annie considered each one carefully. With Julia's good help, and taking up quite a lot of the owner's time, the three of them came to an agreement upon the best frame to "enhance the feeling of mystery," as Miss Sauder said.

*Jah, mystery,* Annie thought. *If only she knew. . . .*

Louisa stood at the door, looking into the face of the man who said he was Ezekiel Hochstetler, who babbled on about his horse and carriage having been returned by a young man. One Ben Martin. Evidently the horse had made the turn into the long lane leading to the harness shop, and Ben recognized the newly made harness as one he had created for Zeke himself. "That's why I'm thinkin' you've got yourself some visitors here," he said, frowning.

Before she could answer, Zeke turned and spit tobacco juice out the side of his mouth. "I need to see my wife," he said.

"She's asleep . . . can you return later?" Louisa felt she ought to say this, not knowing the real reason why Esther and her children had suddenly shown up here. She suspected something was quite wrong though, for a pregnant Amish woman to come with three children in tow, and a rather large overnight case, as well.

"No . . . I'm here now. I want to see Esther." He raised his voice slightly, his face growing ruddier. "You're Annie's friend from Colorado, ain't so?"

"That's right."

He shook his head, his mouth twisted in a sneer. "I don't understand why you want to dress like the womenfolk round here."

"I don't see how that's anybody's business but mine."

"Look, missy. . . ." He shoved his foot in the door and pushed his way inside. "Now, how about you get my wife for me!"

Her heart was pounding as she eyed the portable phone in the kitchen. Moving away from the door, she rushed to it, snatching it up. "Stay right there . . . I'm calling the police!" she told him. She began dialing: 9-1-1.

Zeke backed up and shook his head, waving one of his hands in surrender. "No . . . no, that ain't necessary. Put your telephone away." He eyed the sofa. "I'll sit over there while you go and tell Esther I'm here. I won't cause no trouble."

She aborted the call but gripped the phone nevertheless, wondering what this man might be capable of. "I *will* call the cops, if you even twitch an eyelid."

He went and sat on the couch, and she scrutinized him to determine if he could be trusted here in the house. She wasn't entirely convinced, but she found it startling when he turned to look at the lamp table. He let out a gasp, and she witnessed a cloud of sudden horror cross his face. He had reached for the magazine featuring Annie's painting on the cover.

She couldn't just stand there worrying that he might notice Annie's name printed in the lower right-hand corner. He was preoccupied now, though glowering at the magazine. Quietly she slipped away to the small back bedroom.

The door was cracked enough to peer into the room, and what Louisa saw took her breath away. Esther was resting peacefully with her little boy. Such gentle souls, no doubt having endured verbal abuse—if not worse—from the contemptuous man in the living room.

*There's no way I'm disturbing her!*

Tiptoeing back to the living room, she found Zeke with his hands over his face. "I'm sorry, but your wife is asleep, and little John is resting quietly, too," she said softly. She didn't care to have a ruckus on her hands, so she went promptly to the front door and opened it. "Why not return when she's expecting you? Tomorrow, perhaps?"

He looked up at her, his eyes shooting darts. "You don't understand." His voice was much too loud. "I want to talk to my wife, Esther. I need her back home."

*Want . . . need. Big difference*, she thought.

She wouldn't push too many of his buttons, because this guy was clearly a control freak. She had encountered enough people like this, and now she felt more certain than ever that Esther and her children had needed to escape from him.

"Good-bye," she said, glad for the phone still in her hand.

"Esther!" He planted himself in the middle of the room and hollered. "If you hear me, I mean to take you home with me. Ya hear?"

"No . . . get out!" Louisa raised the phone as a threat but intended to use it.

He caught her meaning. "Well, little missy, I'll be back!" He trudged out the door.

"I think you'd better stay away," she called after the brute.

# Chapter 36

Louisa went around to the side door off the kitchen, making sure it was latched and locked. She felt uneasy here as guardian of this house, especially with all the little children . . . and a very pregnant woman, to boot.

*Will Zeke return?*

Pacing the length of the kitchen, she thought of Aunt Margaret, who had "talked to the Lord," whether it was out of concern or gratitude. *"Don't wait until you're in hot water to call on His name,"* she'd said.

"I'll bet Julia might say the same thing," Louisa muttered, returning to the living room. She caught her breath, glancing at the small maple table. In that moment, she saw that the *Farm and Home Journal*—the January issue—was gone.

*What's with that?*

She recalled how Zeke had been visibly affected by the cover. Most definitely so. She cringed at the thought of his causing trouble for Annie.

The house was peacefully still—so quiet, in fact, that when Esther called out suddenly, Louisa started and dropped her pencil.

"Julia? Julia!" Esther called urgently and Louisa hurried to explain that Julia had gone to run an errand and would be back shortly. "But the baby . . . it's coming . . . coming fast!" Esther clutched her abdomen and groaned.

Louisa took little John from Esther's bed and carried him in to Laura, where she, James, Molly, and Zach were already looking at picture books.

Esther cried out again and fear shot through Louisa, but she knew she must remain calm.

Her heart in her throat, she called 9-1-1, but the dispatcher said all the ambulances were out at the moment and it might be as long as another half hour until someone could get there. Completely ignorant about delivering babies, she did *not* want to handle this alone.

*Oh, what can I do?* She went to the window, on the verge of talking to Aunt Margaret's God. And in that unnerving moment, she spotted the harness shop, way across the field . . . and the car parked in the driveway.

Yes . . . Ben Martin's car!

She dashed back to check on the children—Laura was reading a story to all of them, holding little John in her lap now. "I'll be right back," she told them. "Stay right here. Promise?"

Laura nodded.

Hurrying back to Esther's room, Louisa gently told her to "hold on . . . you're going to the hospital." *For sure!*

It was an hour before quitting time. Ben was busy rubbing down a leather harness with oil when the door opened and there was Lou. He stood up, glad to stretch his aching back. "What can I do for you?"

"Oh, I hate to ask, but I really, really hope you can help me . . . well, *us*." Her face had turned to crimson and she was out of breath. "Would you mind if I borrowed your car? I need to drive a friend to the hospital right away!"

*She drives?* he thought, surprised.

"A friend visiting Julia . . . is on the verge of having a baby. Julia's gone and I know absolutely zip about this."

*Zip?*

Ben removed his heavy work apron. "I'll drive you back over to the Rancks', then on to the hospital," he said, wishing he had time to scrub his hands clean. But he could see the panic on Lou's face, so he grabbed his jacket and they hurried out to the car.

When they arrived at the Rancks' house, Lou jumped out and rushed inside, leaving him to follow behind. "She's freaked," he said to the air, wondering why the birth of a baby should be such a troubling thing for a Plain country girl.

Inside the house, he heard a woman moaning and went directly to the kitchen to scour the leather oil off his hands. Then, waiting for Lou to return, he was suddenly aware of a stream of small children: preschooler James and toddler Molly—whom he'd met only once or twice—and three more he hadn't seen before . . . all coming into the living room.

*Wow. . . . Who's going to watch all these little people?* He stood in the middle of the living room and Molly tottered over and grabbed him around the knee, looking up at him with a grin.

In a few minutes Lou reappeared in the doorway, wringing her hands. "Esther's baby is coming *now*! There's no time to go to the hospital."

"If it's any comfort, I've helped birth dozens of foals," he said, wanting to reassure her. He hoped he didn't sound as nervous as he suddenly felt.

"Foals? Well, that beats anything *I* know." She looked at the children encircling him. "So . . . how about I watch the kids while *you* see if there's anything you can do to help Esther?" Her eyes were blinking ninety miles an hour.

He agreed, but for all his bravado, his heart began to pound and his hands felt clammy. He followed her to the bedroom where the woman lay, startled, no doubt, to see an English stranger—not to mention a guy—enter the room.

"This is Ben Martin, Esther . . . an employee of Irvin Ranck. He knows how to help you."

Ben sure hoped *that* was true.

"And, Ben, this is Esther Hochstetler . . . one of Annie's friends."

"Call me Essie," the woman said, her face flushed, her body covered with a thin blanket.

"Essie it is," Ben said, somewhat confused. *She must be Zeke's wife. So why would she send her horse packing without a driver?* Something was weird about that, because he had seen the same horse and carriage he'd returned to the Hochstetler pig farm show up later, here at the Rancks', with Zeke at the reins. But he didn't have time to think about that now. He must figure out how to help this woman.

Lou wrung her hands, clearly flustered.

"Listen, why don't you go hang with the kids," he told her. "I'll call you when I need you."

Jesse took pleasure in watching Yonie decorate his horse harness with chrome and a few brass buckles. Perched on an old barn bench, Jesse rubbed his hands together, blowing his warm breath on them.

Yonie looked up. "We've got ourselves an understandin' bishop, jah, Daed?"

"Well, he does seem to recall his young days better than some ministers."

Yonie continued fussing with the harness. "So if a bishop's got a good memory, then he doesn't mind us fellas deckin' out our horse harnesses so much, then?"

Jesse nodded. "Must be." He recalled his own Rumschpringe days, shining up his courting buggy and whatnot, mighty eager to meet some nice girls at the barn singings. Pretty Barbara had caught his eye along about the second singing, but she had been seeing another fellow at the time. He remembered *that* even now.

"What were your running-around years like, Daed?"

"Oh, 'bout like yours, I s'pose."

Yonie laughed. "Now, how can ya say that?"

"What . . . you got something to hide, son?"

"Nothin' that most boys aren't doin', seems."

"Well, I don't have to tell *you*, now do I?" Jesse paused, not wanting to sound so overbearing as to shut Yonie up for further father-son talks. "It ain't the smartest idea to follow the crowd, is it?"

"How's a body goin' to know what they're missing then?"

Jesse stifled a smile. "Guess if a body's got to know everything he's missin', then he's not much of a leader but only a follower." He sighed. "I don't see you as the latter, Yonie Zook."

His boy looked at him. "Honestly, Daed, do you see me as a leader?"

"Since the day you came out squalling like a stuck pig."

"Well, then." Yonie squared his shoulders and twirled the shiny buckles on his new harness.

They heard the sound of a horse and carriage, and Jesse asked Yonie to go and have a look-see. Yonie poked his head out of the barn door, then came right back. "Ezekiel Hochstetler's here."

Jesse got up, his ankles cracking loudly, and did several upper torso stretching exercises before heading out to greet Zeke. "Better make yourself scarce now, son."

When he opened the wide barn door and marched out, Jesse waved when he caught Zeke's eye. Not that he cared to, really. He could feel in his bones this was going to be another unpleasant meeting. "Too cold out in the barn," he said, motioning him toward the house, in hopes Zeke might not cause such a ruckus round Barbara and all.

The two men walked together, crunching old boots through the fresh snow. "I want to know where you buried my brother," Zeke started in. "I want to know *now*."

"Snow's much too heavy to go lookin'."

Zeke snuffed his nose. "Don't matter none to me."

"We've talked this to death."

They were inside, in the enclosed porch now, removing boots, scarves, and coats. "I'm plenty tired of waiting," Zeke said.

"No changin' my mind."

"So you're goin' to keep stonewallin' me?"

"Call it what you will. . . ."

Zeke snorted like the pigs he raised. "Well, then, I have something to show you, Preacher." He reached in and pulled a magazine out of his shirt. "Here . . . take a good look at this." Zeke shoved it into his face.

"What's this got to do with anything?"

"Your daughter, that's what."

Jesse had no idea what he meant.

Zeke was adamant. "Annie painted the picture on this here cover . . . see?" He pointed to her name. "And if ya don't believe me, then ask her yourself."

Jesse stared at the picture. *Annie Zook?* "How many women with that name in Paradise?" he muttered, half to himself. "Must be dozens. . . ."

"Well now, Preacher, I guess that's for you to find out."

Zeke was heckling him, and it was all he could do to keep from rolling up the magazine and bopping Zeke with it. Even so, he was drawn to the picture—the way the sun spotlighted a single peach stone there on the swing. He looked closer and saw that peculiar symbol of hope, unable to forget all the village talk following Isaac's disappearance. How many times, years later, had Annie asked about the boy's fascination with a peach pit? The odd way little Isaac had carried it with him in his pants pocket. . . .

*This is Annie's work, all right.* But he wouldn't let on, so Zeke couldn't use it against him. Yet Zeke would, knowing him.

"Go ahead, Preacher . . . look at your own cousin's name on the address label." Zeke poked his finger on the name: Irvin Ranck.

*Irvin and Julia. . . . Jah, they might just know something about Annie's artwork.* But he wondered if he was jumping to conclusions.

"It's your daughter that'll be your downfall," Zeke taunted. "And you know what I mean to do if you keep mum about where you and the bishop buried my brother." He snatched the magazine back.

Jesse resisted his ire. "I'm following the bishop's bidding."

"Well, then, I'll be takin' this here magazine all round, first to the bishop, then to Uncle Preacher Moses and Deacon Byler . . . see what *they* say 'bout your daughter's hobby."

He despised what Zeke was doing, putting him between a rock and a hard place. "I daresay you'll get yourself shunned yet, Zeke. Just like your wife."

Zeke scowled, mumbling under his breath.

"You wouldn't want to lose your pig farm, would you? Your ability to make a livin' for your family?" He could see he was making some headway, and right quick, too. "Better be thinking 'bout what you want to do." Jesse eyed the magazine. "And best be leavin' that here with me."

Zeke wilted, relinquishing his hold on the *Farm and Home Journal*. And seconds later, when it came to accepting Barbara's offer of coffee, he flatly refused. Donning his coat now, Zeke made an excuse about needing to get home.

Jesse put a firm hand on the younger man's shoulder. "Jah, you do that."

Annie led the way to the house, as Julia had insisted on carrying in her own purchases from the fabric store. They had made several stops following the interesting visit at the art gallery.

She noticed a car parked off to the side. "Got yourself more company?"

"Oh, that's Ben's car," Julia said. "He sometimes parks it here and walks over to the harness shop."

So Annie thought nothing of it, stopping at the side door, accustomed to it being opened. But she found it to be locked. *How odd!*

A little chill went up her spine just then, the slightest premonition. But she brushed off her jitters and waited for Julia to come and unlock the door.

Julia opened it and let Annie go in first. Right away as she entered the house, she heard a loud holler coming from the back room. "Hurry, Julia," Annie called. "Esther's cryin' something awful."

Julia rushed into the house behind her.

Annie hurried into the living room and found Louisa there, sitting on the floor and playing with Esther's three and James and Molly, too. "Who's with Esther?"

Lou got up quickly. "You'll never guess in a million years."

As if on cue, Ben Martin appeared in the doorway. "Oh, good, Julia . . . you're back. Your help is eagerly requested."

Lou was obviously relieved, as well, smiling almost too broadly. "Annie, I was so freaked. You have no idea what excitement you missed."

Julia had disappeared to assist Esther, and Annie felt Ben's scrutinizing gaze on her once again. "I'm going in to be with Esther," she said, hurrying past Ben.

Esther's face was wet with perspiration when Annie entered the guest room. But Esther's eyes shone with happiness as Annie came near. "Oh, I'm so glad you're here, Annie. It won't be long now . . . I'm ever so sure."

Clasping her hand, Annie apologized. "I'm so sorry . . . we never should've left you."

"Don't let go of my hand," Esther said, another contraction coming.

Soon, Annie witnessed the tiny life emerge into Julia's capable and loving hands, and the newborn's high-pitched squeal rang out.

Later, when the precious bundle lay resting in Esther's arms, Annie whispered, "She's so little . . . so sweet. I'm glad I was here right when she came."

"I'm awful glad, too." Esther nodded and smiled. "What do you think of Essie for my baby's name?"

"Sounds right fine. I daresay she's an Essie, through and through."

"And the dear Lord Jesus sent His angels to help . . . I just know He did." Esther's eyes were shining. "And Irvin's friend, Ben Martin, who was such an encouragement . . . and helped me stay surprisingly calm."

Annie didn't know what to make of Esther's remarks about the harness shop worker. She leaned down and kissed the wee babe's damp brow. "Honestly, Esther, I had no idea your baby was comin' so soon."

"Everything happened fast. I'd fallen right asleep, even before you and Julia left. It was after Zeke came and was so awful loud, that's when I was jolted awake and things started to happen."

"Zeke was here . . . in the house?" Annie's heart nearly stopped.

"Ach, I was scared he might come marchin' back here and haul me home."

"Aw, Essie, I feel just sick 'bout this."

"Well, don't fret. Your friend Lou sent him on his way. A tough one she is. Then she brought Ben to help. . . ." Esther's tears were not for pity but from exhaustion, and Annie wiped them away with her own fingers. "I'm ever so grateful for a healthy baby. That's what matters, Annie. Thanks be to the dear Lord."

"Well, now, you rest. Jah?"

Esther closed her eyes briefly, then blinked them open. "Do you really think this one looks like an Essie?"

Annie studied the tiny face. "Well . . . I'm not so sure now. Maybe a middle name suits her." She pondered several. "What 'bout Essie *Mae*?" she asked. "That way we won't get her and you mixed up."

"I like Ann better—after you, Annie."

"Essie Ann. Jah, I *do* like it."

Esther's lip quivered. "I just pray my baby girl might grow up more carefree than her big sister, you know?"

Annie's heart went out to her dear friend, and she let Esther squeeze her hand ever so hard. "I know you do."

# Chapter 37

Ben backed his car up and headed over to the harness shop, whistling all the way.

*Annie Zook.* The name had a distinct lilt to it. He even found himself wondering what her middle name might be.

"This is nuts," he said, returning to work. He breathed in the strong smell of leather and oil, taking it deep into his lungs, relishing the odor. He finished up the harness he'd begun before Lou had come bursting in two hours before.

Then he laid out the next harness on the big table, replaying the time at the Rancks'—observing and getting to know Lou better, and what an interesting Amish girl *she* was. He almost had the feeling she was playacting, going through the motions. The way she expressed herself really threw him, but then, he'd heard that some girls went a little crazy during their so-called "sowing wild oats" days. He wondered if Lou had been hanging out with some non-Amish friends, trying to pick up their lingo, perhaps.

Annie was also on his mind a lot. And about the time his thoughts of her seemed to quiet slightly, he would run into her again. Today he had even suspected she might be sensing something, too.

Meeting her had turned his whole world on its head. Never had he experienced anything like this . . . such all-encompassing feelings.

*Annie,* he thought. *Funny how perfectly the name fits her.* He had only known one other person whose name seemed custom-made. His mother, Sandie, with hair the color of a tropical beach and a complexion to match. He already missed his parents, and his four younger siblings, and all of them were great about keeping in touch by cell phone. None of them, especially his next youngest sister, understood why he'd had the urge to uproot so suddenly. And he still felt apologetic about it, all the while enjoying his new work here in Paradise.

He had been oiling down the last harness of the day, staying longer to make up for the time gone, when Lou knocked at the door and waved through the window.

"Come in . . . it's unlocked!" he called.

Lou hurried in, glancing at the many racks of harnesses hanging along the wall. "You know what? I don't think you have any idea how you saved the day . . . over at Julia's."

"I was glad to." He paused. "I must admit, I would have thought someone your age—from these parts—would have been accustomed to helping when babies are born."

"Oh, I'm not from here. I suppose it's okay to say—because everyone in Annie's church knows—I'm actually her friend from Colorado, just visiting. Annie and I, we've been pen pals since grade school . . . that's how we first met."

He listened attentively, wondering why Lou was volunteering this.

"I dress Amish so I don't freak out anyone here . . . especially Annie's dad. He's the preacher-man. Maybe you've heard," Lou continued. "Anyway, I was sick of the complicated world out there—the nutcase rat race. Not to mention materialistic madness."

"Hey, I hear you."

"Well, I just dropped by to say thanks."

"Not a problem." He smiled, not so much at her but with her. He found her story, whatever the rest of it was, irresistible.

"So, how can I ever thank you, Ben?"

He smiled, an ironic thought crossing his mind. He thought of Annie, the way he felt when they were in the same room together. Here in the shop, there at Julia's . . . with such affection for Esther and her new baby.

His mind was doing a number on him again.

"Well," he said, surprising even himself, "there *is* something. . . ." He paused. "What I mean is . . . is Annie seeing anyone?"

"Well, no."

"Would she consider dating someone like me?"

"An Englisher?" She smiled. "You know what? I am staying out of this. I think you'd better ask her yourself."

He nodded. "You're right. I will." *Soon as I work up the nerve!*

❖

235

Annie should have guessed, by the stern set of her father's jaw during breakfast, what was coming. She ate as calmly as she could, making conversation with Louisa and Mamm, both of them eager to talk about Esther's new baby girl. And Annie couldn't help wondering if *that* was why her father looked so angry and disappointed, because she had spilled the beans about Esther's going to Julia's to have her baby. Of course, she'd been careful not to mention Zeke nor to let on that Esther went for any reason other than for help with the delivery, but maybe Daed had guessed the rest.

After redding up the dishes, she and Louisa walked back to the Dawdi Haus as usual. Annie was surprised when her father knocked on the door a few minutes later, saying he needed to talk to Annie alone. *About Esther?* she wondered.

Louisa excused herself and hurried off to the barn.

Then Annie spied the plain manila envelope in Daed's hand and her heart set to racing. *Could it be?* But, no . . . how could a copy of the magazine reach him so soon?

Everything that happened next seemed to Annie like staring through a cracked window—outside looking in. It shouldn't have felt like that at all, she surmised, having been on the receiving end before of such a harsh reprimand.

"You know what this means, don't you?" Daed's pointer finger tapped on the magazine cover. She stared at it, a lump in her throat, not for being caught— the third and worst time by far—but for the fact that her secret lay fragile and bare before her. The evidence not at all appreciated by a man who declared the glory of God and His handiwork each and every Preaching service. This disapproving man, who now stood over her . . . here, where she sat in her grandparents' kitchen, alternating stares between the perplexing landscape on the table before her and the honorable, yet smoldering, gaze of her father.

"You bring shame to our good name," he said.

She flinched, struggling with his pronouncement.

"What do you have to say for yourself?" Daed's finger stayed there, pointing to her name, emblazoned like an announcement from Hades itself.

*I'm guilty . . . I've always been that.* But she dared not express her thoughts in a negative manner. Self-expression had brought her to this moment, after all. This terrible black place. "My art was all I ever had, really. All I ever wanted," she managed to say, as if someone else were uttering the words.

He looked at her, disbelieving. "You never quit drawing, did you? You never stopped all those years ago . . . when I forbade you?"

She would not cower from him. *I must be true to myself.* Yet she could not bring herself to speak.

"You will answer your father, Annie Zook!"

She had forced him across a line. There was something merciless about his eyes now, the angle of his head as he looked at her. "This is who I am," she said softly. "It is not what I do. This painting . . . right here. That's the real Annie. Not who you see sittin' on the church bench at Preaching service or round Mamm's table every day." She patted her chest. "I've tried to be good, honest I have. But I don't have it in me, not if it means I can't draw or paint or study shapes and colors with the eyes the Lord God heavenly Father gave me."

"Be careful, lest you blight your Maker. Pride, after all, is who we are. All of us. Sins entangle us daily. Before Lucifer fell, he could've said to the Lord God, 'This is who I am!'" Daed folded his hands. "It is wrong to align yourself with sin, to say that it is who you are, Annie. You must reject it. Be set apart, as all the People are called to be."

She was crying now, unable to block her tears by sheer will. "To turn my back on my art would be impossible. I know this."

He shook his head but not sadly, she was sure. His attitude was either of righteous indignation or pure anger. "If you refuse to cease . . . if you will not submit to the authority of your own father, and under God, then you must leave the covering of this house."

She was not a baptized church member, therefore she could not be shunned. But many fathers required nearly as strict discipline of their rebellious youths.

Thinking of Louisa, she wondered what her friend would think *now* of the simple life she'd craved for so long. "Lou will leave with me," she said finally. "After all, she came at my invitation."

His eyes registered sudden concern.

*Was he bluffing?* She didn't think so.

"I'll go right away and pack." Looking at the painting on the magazine cover one last time, she rose to leave, even before her father dismissed her.

Upstairs, she opened the bureau drawers and began haphazardly pulling out her clothes, sobbing just as she had over Rudy Esh months ago. She felt betrayed even though she was not.

*I had plenty of chances to obey. . . .*

Hurriedly she folded each piece of clothing. Then, glancing around the room, she realized she owned hardly anything else, except for the contents of her hope chest. Largely, the room's furnishings belonged to her parents, the quilts to her grandmother. The rest was Lou's. Her English friend owned considerably more, in the way of sketchbooks and art supplies, than she. Except for Annie's precious items stored in the studio at Julia's.

*What on earth will Cousin Julia think when she hears?* Sitting on her bed, Annie covered her face with her hands and let go the tears. She felt sorry for poor Esther, and for her little children, and for helpless little Essie Ann, newly born. She felt sad for Louisa, who'd come here searching for something better than the modern world could offer. And she grieved for Mamm, who would be crying her eyes out when she heard what Daed had done.

Just when she felt so bad she couldn't feel a mite worse, right then, she heard a knock at her door. "Annie?"

It was Mamm.

She didn't know if she wanted to be seen this way, the way she surely looked just now, all tear-streaked and disheveled. But she longed for someone who might understand, and if anyone would, it was either Mamm or Louisa. "Come in," she said softly, brushing away her tears.

Her mother entered the room, face red, eyes swollen. Taking one look at Annie, she quickly closed the door. "Oh, you headstrong thing. My dear daughter." She rushed to her side and sat next to her on the bed. "Daed just told me." She didn't say anything at all against him, and Annie knew she wouldn't. But Mamm was clearly upset and sat there, reaching for Annie's hand.

Annie whispered, "I ought to be sayin' how sorry I am . . . but—"

"Hush now. We must keep our wits 'bout us. It won't look so good for the preacher to oust his daughter before she's baptized." Mamm was thinking out loud, which made Annie terribly nervous.

"I must do his bidding," she said. "Lou and I will pack up and find someplace else to live."

Mamm shook her head. "I just don't see how such a thing can be." She turned and looked at Annie, frowning and shaking her head.

"It's my fault . . . I deserve this. I do," she admitted. "I tried to give up my art. But it's got me—it's *in* me, Mamm. That's the best way to explain it."

"But where will you go, Annie?" Mamm asked, her voice quivering.

"I honestly don't know." She'd thought if Esther and her children weren't staying with Julia maybe that would have been an option. She recalled the day when Louisa had suggested renting a car. *Louisa's my answer,* she realized. But she couldn't think too far ahead, because Louisa had made it clear she would return to Colorado in due time.

Mamm wept, fumbling for a hankie in her sleeve. "I can't think 'bout this . . . it's much too hard." She rose and went to the bureau. "You were mighty quick to gather up your things, I see. Are you ever so eager to leave your family behind, dear one?"

"I guess I *do* need some time to think. . . ."

"Jah, we all do." Mamm turned, attempting to smile. "I'll leave you be for now." She made her way to the door, her shoulders heaving as she went.

Annie felt as forlorn as Mamm's dear face looked.

Lou had been outside helping in the barn. Now she came looking for Annie upstairs in the Dawdi Haus. "Can you help find me . . . er, us a place to stay?" Annie asked her right out when she appeared in the doorway.

"What for?" Louisa stared at the piles of clothing on the bed. "And what's all this?"

Feeling emotionally and physically weak, Annie attempted to explain, saying what had happened, how her father had in his possession the magazine with the incriminating cover. "He never said where he got it, but he has it. And he's madder than a sprayed hornet."

"Well, I think I might know," Lou said. "Zeke was looking at it earlier today at Julia's, when he came storming in to see Esther."

*So Zeke came directly here?* she wondered.

"You knew it was a matter of time before this happened." Lou sat on Annie's bed. "I think it's possible some good things can come of it . . . you know, finally getting all this out in the open. It doesn't really matter how freaked your father is right now. The truth is you haven't been honest with yourself."

She was stunned, Lou talking like this. "What do you mean?"

"Well, you say art is so much a part of you—*who* you are. And it is who I am, and everything I want to be." Lou pushed her head covering off suddenly. "But look at me, Annie." She began pulling her hairpins out, her bun falling out quickly. "Is this who I am, wearing my hair in a bun . . . these long blue or green dresses and black aprons? Is it?"

"You aren't Plain, no."

"But you *are*," Lou said. "Through and through. So, is being an artist more who you are than being Amish? I don't think so."

Annie watched Lou shake out her dark brown hair. "What makes you say this?"

"When I first came here, I thought you should follow your heart—your longing for art—but now I'm not so sure. Besides, I can't imagine how you could leave your family and the People behind for the modern world, Annie. I doubt there's any way you'd ever be happy out there . . . on the outside."

"How can you possibly know?"

"You've said it yourself, that you're like a sister to me. We've shared our hearts in letters all these years, and now we're like roommates in a college dorm." Lou got up and walked to the window. "So I guess you'll have to trust me, Annie . . . because I'm not going to let you walk away from here. You have to do the right thing."

"I don't even know what that is."

"Go to your dad . . . talk to him." Lou rose and went to sit on her own bed now. Her kitty came out from under the bed skirt and curled up on her lap.

"So you're not goin' to help me get an apartment?" It was her last effort.

"Listen, I'd love nothing more than to see you spread your wings . . . and for the whole world to witness your talent. But it's not the whole world I'm concerned about. It's *your* world, Annie. The Amish tradition. Right here. *This* is your world—your artist's canvas. You wouldn't be happy away from it—even with all the paint and freedom money could buy."

Annie almost wondered if Daed had taken Louisa aside and asked her to talk straight this way. She watched idly as Lou scratched Muffin behind his ears and stroked his long fur. "Sounds like you've thought all this through."

Lou's expression grew more serious. "I'm probably as surprised as you are—me, of all people, saying this—but why couldn't you express yourself in some acceptable way? Remember the lovely embroidery we saw at the Old Country Store?"

Annie nodded.

"Art is whatever you make it. It's actually a language . . . the way you express your emotions. Just think of the quilt designs and the placement and choice of colors in all those flower beds outside come spring."

"I s'pose you want me to follow the peacocks round, too, watching for the slightest changes in color on their trains, is that it?"

"Sure, why not?"

Annie smiled. "I'll think on it . . . that's all. I won't promise much else."

"Well, good . . . that's progress." Muffin suddenly hopped down off Lou's lap and ran over to Annie, surprising both girls. "See? Even my cat approves of you."

"It's nice someone does." She hugged Lou's kitty, dreading the thought of seeking Daed out.

# Chapter 38

Louisa struggled over whether or not to tell Annie of Ben's keen interest in her, especially with all the upheaval in Annie's life. If she were aware would she entertain even more thoughts of leaving the People and feel justified in dating a non-Amish guy?

Louisa had no clue. Of course, the upside to it was the possibility that Annie might want to stay put, to be in close proximity to Ben . . . if it happened that she was interested in dating *him*. Bottom line, though, Louisa felt strange, knowing she held this romantic secret from her friend, having realized today what an amazing man Ben Martin was. Miles better than Rudy, in her humble opinion.

For someone to come in and do what Ben had done at Julia's—his gentleness in supporting Esther emotionally—was impressive. Not to mention his overall attitude and demeanor. She hadn't ever known a guy like that. And it was funny, too, because she caught herself sizing him up against what she knew of Trey Douglas.

*That's ridiculous*, she reprimanded herself, waiting not-so-patiently in the bedroom while Annie talked with her father downstairs. Louisa *had* laid into Annie, no question, but she truly believed everything she'd spouted off to her friend. *So, would it be wise to let on about Ben now?* Louisa wondered, even though she suspected Annie might be attracted to him, too. She was glad she'd had the presence of mind to tell Ben she was staying out of it and to ask Annie himself. She'd messed with Annie's life enough!

❖

Esther kissed the top of Essie Ann's little head, the peach fuzz tickling her nose. "I'm grateful to you, Julia, and to the Lord in every way," she said, glad for someone of like mind to talk to. "I must say, too, your husband's employee was like a messenger sent from heaven."

"That's the truth." Julia nodded, her soft brown hair beginning to come loose from its bun after the long day. "I can tell you, Ben's a fine young man. Though not a believer, far as we know."

Looking down at the baby in her arms, Esther was filled with love anew for her Savior. "I pray Ben might come to know the Lord, just as I have."

"Irvin shares Christ with him every chance he can." Julia's eyes were soft with tears.

"You all right?"

"Oh yes. Seeing you there, so safe and snug, with this new little one near, well . . . I just want to tell you that Irvin and I have decided you and the children should stay here for as long as need be." Julia pushed back the long stray hairs, her face rosier than before. "Irvin plans to speak with his cousin Jesse, Annie's father, about keeping Zeke away from you and the children. We'll pray something can be done to help your husband in the meantime."

A little sob caught in Esther's throat. "Ach, this takes such a burden off me, Julia . . . you just don't know!"

Julia rose and stood near the bed. "My husband won't allow any more visits like Louisa said occurred with Zeke. Not until you're ready, that is. In the meantime, the men will protect you should he show his face here again."

Esther felt lighter suddenly. "I'll sleep better tonight knowin' this. Denki, Julia. Oh, thank you!"

The afternoon light was fading rapidly when Annie found Daed at the far end of the barn, close to the door where the cows came in for milking. "I need to talk to you," she blurted to him, "'cause I'm all ferhoodled."

He had trouble looking at her, she knew. The anger had diminished some and in its place was great disappointment, that thing she had always wished to avoid.

"I heard you're packing already." His words fell from his lips like broken glass.

"Jah," she said in a near whisper. "But I don't *want* to leave. . . ."

"Well, I won't budge. I'll not have you flaunting your worldliness." His eyes looked hollow, colorless.

"I know this sounds peculiar," she continued, terribly tense, "but I need some time to say good-bye to my work . . . my art. Days or weeks . . . maybe longer."

His brow was deeply furrowed and he stood there, hay fork in hand, looking at her like he hadn't ever truly seen her before. "Cuttin' off a dog's hind leg is much harder done little by little, ain't?"

She sensed how difficult it was for one so deeply rooted in the church. Ever so slowly, she nodded her head.

"You want time to do what . . . dabble further in the world?"

"No, Daed—"

"Well, you're askin' an impossible thing."

She sighed. "I wish you could understand *me*."

He set the hayfork aside and folded his arms across his chest. "Why must this be so hard . . . to lay down your will, as you must, in order to be truly happy?"

She had no answer. They stood looking at each other, father and daughter.

At last, Daed shook his head. "There will be no more discussion on this. I want you to agree to take baptismal classes come summer, to abstain from your drawings and such until then—for a full six months. It's past time to leave your Rumschpringe days behind."

She swallowed the lump in her throat. "I could think on it, jah, but whether or not I can follow through . . . that's another story."

"Must I remind you? 'Where your treasure is, there will your heart be also.'" He took off his hat and began to fan himself. He was worked up again, and she ought to simply walk away—and do his bidding—not cause him this much grief in a single day. "Honestly, Annie, you're a lot like our peacocks when they get their long trains caught under the buggies on the road."

She felt dismayed with his comparison. Already, she'd hurt him enough for a lifetime. Even so, she didn't deserve to be judged against a slow-poke peacock, did she? Truth be known, she'd watched them strut along, unhurried as they were, getting their tail feathers all ripped up, away from the safety of the pen.

"After baptismal instruction, I would then expect you to join church next fall," he continued.

Oh, for his sake, she wanted to say she would. But how? "It would be foolish to make a false covenant," she said softly. "Even dangerous."

He put his hat back on his head and held out his hand. "You ain't a man, but I daresay it might be a good idea to shake on this, Annie. Will you agree to put aside your sin and give obedience a chance?"

She looked down at his callused hand, outstretched to her.

"I could try."

"No, you must cease to try, and simply do it."

*Six months.* . . . She was moved to tears, although she wouldn't dare blink and let them spill down her cheeks. No, she must accept the hand of her father, who was only doing the best he could, for goodness' sake.

Mentally, she marked the moment, wondering if she would recall this promise in her old age, many years from now. And if so, would she remember it with gladness?

Reaching out, she clasped his hand.

Lighting the lantern, Jesse carried it out to the sleigh. Zeke Hochstetler was heavy on his mind and it was imperative to get him hushed up, especially now that Annie wouldn't be leaving, at least not soon. He hadn't seen real signs of repentance from her, and he didn't know how long the promise of their handshake would stick with a free-thinking woman like his daughter.

He stepped into the sleigh and urged the horse down the road, thinking of his side of the family tree. A good and strong branch of it were some downright outspoken Mennonites. Not that they were necessarily an obnoxious lot, but they sure had differing opinions. Irvin Ranck was a strong limb off that particular tree, and from what he had come and told Jesse tonight, on the heels of supper, Jesse figured Zeke Hochstetler was a loose-fitting cork in a pressure-filled bottle.

He contemplated what Irvin had stated vehemently, that they would not allow Zeke to harm Esther or the children. *So Esther's run off for certain,* he thought, not liking it. Far as he could tell, Zeke was merely a loudmouth, nothing more. And if he had ever slapped his wife around, well, then he needed to be talked to. But the way he saw it, Esther was doubly in the wrong . . . claiming salvation and now shirking her domestic and wifely duties.

But there was a larger issue of worry, which was the reason for Jesse's after-suppertime trip to see the bishop. Zeke was a problem for the People as a whole and for Jesse in particular. With Annie possibly settling down some, it would work best all around if Zeke was finally told where his brother was buried. The bishop might not agree, but Jesse felt the distraught and unstable man should be tossed a crumb of information.

*Zeke won't go round stirring up the People over Annie's art.* Of this, he was fairly certain. And he was mighty glad he'd had the presence of mind to keep the proof. This way Zeke had no leg to stand on, except for shooting off his mouth, which he did like clockwork, anyway.

Jesse's greatest fear was the English authorities getting involved. Having followed Bishop Andy's demand from the start, the brethren had never reported the Hochstetler boy missing. *Best to keep it quiet,* the bishop had continually said through the years, whenever the matter was reviewed at the council of the ordained, twice annually. Preacher Moses had always had the biggest beef with it, Isaac being his kin. Which was where the rub came, far as Jesse could tell, yet the bishop had managed to keep a lid on a slow-boiling cauldron. Partly it was because not even Zeke had any idea where his parents had ended up after they left Honey Brook. Some thought they'd gone to a remote part of Ontario, Canada. Others rumored the family had left the Amish altogether.

Turning into the bishop's lane now, Jesse saw a single gas lamp burning in the kitchen window and assumed Andy was reading the German Bible to his wife. When he knocked on the back door, it took a while for the bishop to come and see who was there. Jesse should have called out, announcing himself, but he needed the extra moments to think again what he should say, even though he'd contemplated this visit all the way here in the dark and blustery cold.

"Well, Jesse Zook, what brings you out?" the older man said, ushering him inside.

"Zeke's on a rant." He kept his voice low.

"How's *that* news?"

They stood in the anteroom away from the kitchen. "I don't mean to go over your head," said Jesse. "I'm just wondering if Zeke shouldn't be allowed to know where we buried Isaac."

A gentle smile creased Andy's face. "He must've broken your will. All that flap comin' out of his mouth . . . is that it?"

Jesse wouldn't reveal his daughter's ongoing sin, wouldn't use it as the reason for his request. "Truth be told, if Isaac had been my brother, I might be askin' the same." It was his best defense. The only one.

Andy's jaw was tense, his eyes somber. "What with his missus on a probationary shun, do you think this is a good idea?"

"I see it as necessary." *An appeasement . . . a way to keep Zeke happy during this dismal time,* he thought. "Esther's left Zeke . . . took the children with her." He mentioned that the Rancks' place was her chosen safe haven.

"A whole new can of worms," Andy said.

"I say we give Zeke something . . . the one thing he wants, truly."

By his repeated sighs, the bishop seemed to acquiesce. "If it'll keep him from blabbin' to the police, then maybe so." His eyes lit up. "Jah, that's what you do, Jesse. You give him an either-or. Make him choose not to contact the authorities . . . not to hunt down the killer."

Jesse was surprised; the decision had been accomplished before he'd even gotten his gloves and scarf removed. "If this is your behest, I'll go and tell Zeke right away."

The bishop's wife called to him. "Who's there, dear?"

"Oh, it's Preacher Zook," he said over his shoulder.

"Have him come in for some hot coffee."

The bishop raised his eyebrows. "Care for some, Jesse?"

"Denki, but no."

The hoot of an owl rang out from the trees beyond the barnyard. *Bird of death*, Jesse thought. The cadenced call echoed in his mind as he stared at distant floodlights on an English farm as he made his way through the snow to his waiting horse and sleigh.

*Zeke will get his wish*, he thought. *I hope it's the right thing. . . .*

# Chapter 39

Ben was pleased at Julia's supper invitation, amazed in fact, as she already had a houseful of mouths to feed. But she'd called to urge Ben to join them for a celebration "at the birth of Esther's baby," now that Irvin was home.

He felt she was linking him to the joyous arrival of Essie Ann, and he couldn't take credit . . . wouldn't think of it. But he certainly wouldn't turn down a chance to visit more with Irvin or enjoy Julia's exceptionally good cooking. Not to mention all those cute kids with their contagious smiles.

Annie had not expected to run smack dab into Ben Martin as she was leaving Julia's by way of the side door. "Oh, goodness . . . I need to watch where I'm goin'," she said, backing up and looking at him full in the face.

"I guess we both do." Ben's eyes held her gaze. "You all right?"

She wasn't . . . not really. It had been months since she'd been that close to a man.

Ben stood there, not budging. And now that she'd stepped back, putting a better distance between them, she wasn't inclined to move, either. She did think it interesting that Louisa had chosen today, of all days, to go off by herself, taking pictures of barns and such with her fancy phone and computer gadget— "artistic research," she'd called it. Which put Annie right here in the Rancks' driveway, talking to Irvin's hired man alone, of all things.

"Would you think I'm forward if I asked you to have coffee with me sometime?" Ben asked unexpectedly.

"Are you askin' me now . . . or later *sometime?*"

He smiled and she did, too. She'd been much too hard on this fine-looking fellow. Downright difficult.

"Well, I'll ask now," he said.

She shied away from his shining eyes, instead staring down at her black high-topped shoes. *Doesn't he mind that I'm Plain?*

"I could meet you somewhere if that's easier," he offered.

She thought of the other options. "I doubt you'd want to ride in an Amish buggy. . . ."

He laughed. "And you wouldn't be caught dead in a car with me, right?"

"Better dead than alive," she was quick to say, which brought another chuckle from Ben.

"I didn't expect a Plain girl to have such a good sense of humor. So *is* it against the rules to ride in a car? Would your church fathers frown on it?"

"Well," she replied, "there are both angels and devils in those beards . . . but you never heard this from me."

Her comment seemed to catch him off guard. He looked at her curiously. "I'd like to know more about that."

Just then Julia poked her head out the side door. "Would you like to stay for supper, Annie?"

*How do I squelch my smile? She needs to be more subtle about matchmaking,* Annie thought.

"I can easily set another place," Julia persisted.

"Thanks anyway, but Mamm's waitin' supper."

*So Julia approves of Ben. . . .*

"I know of a wonderful espresso place," Ben said when Julia had disappeared back into the house.

*I shook hands with Daed,* she reminded herself. *I can't go out with an Englischer now!*

She took a breath. "Well, it's awful nice of you to ask . . . but I prob'ly shouldn't," she said. "But thanks all the same, Ben."

His smile slipped a bit. "I understand," he said softly.

Annie gave him a little wave and walked away, already feeling glum.

A dessert of chocolate silk pie was served, and the five youngsters eyed Ben at the table. He had consistently made comical facial gestures at each of them, off and on throughout the meal. He knew he had a way with little kids. His own father had first noticed it years back, when Ben's smile quickly soothed a howling baby on numerous occasions—his colicky nephew, one case in point. His mom and sister often said he would be a "terrific dad" someday. *Finding the right woman is the key,* he thought.

While Julia and Irvin worked together in the kitchen, he got down on the floor with Laura, Esther's oldest, and James. Esther had already whisked diaper-laden John and his infant sister back to the bedroom. Molly and Zach sat out in the kitchen playing with extra-large, toddler-safe Legos at the table.

Thinking how to entertain Laura and James, he pulled something from his pocket, keeping it hidden in his closed hand. "I have a secret hiding here."

"You do? I want to see it!" Laura said, moving right over next to him.

"Me too!" James said, folding his hands under his chin, sitting cross-legged like Ben.

"You have to guess first," Ben said.

"Give us a hint," said Laura, the older.

"Let's see." He closed his eyes, enjoying the tension-filled game. "I know. . . ." He opened his eyes.

"What?" Laura's face lit up.

"Well, you never find it unless you're hungry and start to munch. Then the secret will slowly start to appear. That's the hint."

James looked discouraged. "That's too hard."

Laura's pensive expression changed to a smile. "I think *I* know."

"Then tell me." He loved playing along.

She leaned over and whispered her answer in his ear.

*How could she have guessed?* he wondered.

"What *is* it?" James asked, his lower lip drooping now.

Ben kept his voice low and a bit mysterious sounding. "Here, I'll show you." He opened his hand to reveal a smooth peach stone. "Watch closely." He flicked the pit, fast as a sneeze, between his thumb and third finger. It stood on its end and spun like a little top.

James said a happy *oh*, while Laura wore a wide-eyed look of glee.

"How'd you do that?" asked James.

Ben spun it a second time. "Just . . . like . . . this."

"Do it again!" James scooted next to him, too.

He twirled it again and again, followed by the children's side-splitting laughter each time. At last, when James was called off to his bath, Laura asked to hold the "little top."

Ben placed the pit in her hand, and she looked closely at it. "Ach, it's ever so smooth. Dat's got himself a whole bag of these, but not a single one like this."

*A man who collects peach pits can't be all bad,* Ben thought.

Laura returned the peach stone, and he found himself looking down at it, aware of the overwhelming urge to squeeze hard, and not knowing quite why.

# Epilogue

It would be downright pointless to deny that I'm waiting on pins and needles for the other shoe to drop, as they say—or as *I've* been saying to Lou: waiting for the next suspender to snap. What with my father eyeing me like I've got the plague, there's plenty on my mind.

I recently attended the quilting at Sarah Mae's with Mamm, while Louisa stayed at the Dawdi Haus with Mammi Zook, most recently intrigued by needlepoint. They talked about many things, Lou confided to me, and I know she and Mammi are becoming fast friends. It's interesting to hear Mammi talking in Dutch to Lou now and then.

Julia's in need of her attic to make room for Esther, little John, and baby Essie Ann. Having an art studio ready and waiting for me would be an awful temptation, I confess, so this is a good thing. It's already been more than a full week since my hand has held either a colored pencil or a brush. I can't say it's easy, but I'm taking one day at a time. For Daed's sake . . . and for the Lord God's. When I get the jitters of withdrawal, which is what Louisa calls it, I go and cut quilting squares and arrange them in unusual patterns on the floor in the front room. Mamm must think I've lost my mind, but if it keeps me from sinning, all for the better.

Louisa's friend, Courtney Engelman, says she misses "the runaway bride." I don't know what my father will say about Lou's fancy friend wanting to visit, too, but it'll just be for a long weekend. I figure if I keep myself away from drawing and painting, just maybe Daed will be in favor of yet another Englischer

250

coming to experience the peace of Paradise. And *I'll* find all the satisfaction I need in the acceptable art of my people, as Louisa encourages me to do.

I don't know how many times I've bumped into Ben Martin recently, and not once has it been at the harness shop, not since the first time. For some odd reason, he keeps showing up where I happen to be—making a purchase at the Gordonville Bookstore and at the post office. Things like that. It's downright uncanny, and I have no idea what to make of it. He smiles real big and says, "Hey, Annie," and I say, "Hullo, Ben" back. Secretly, I'm beginning to hope he might ask me out yet again.

Lou's driven me in the buggy over to see Esther and little Essie Ann twice now. Lou's getting quite good at handling a horse, surprisingly so. I keep thinking one of these days she's going to wake up and decide to wear her brand name jeans again, but so far she hasn't. She's careful not to let me see her with her sketchbook and pencils anymore, which makes me kind of sad. There's no reason for her to hide *her* work. But I suppose if she were in the same boat as I am, I'd do the same for her.

Still, I don't know how long I can let her sneak round like that. It doesn't seem fair. She consistently sells her drawings, too. Takes them in for framing every other week. I suspect she misses our little hideaway in Julia's attic, and no wonder. The place was the most delightful location to give our creative minds wings to soar. If Esther decides to live with her widowed mother, the attic studio will become enticing to me once again. And that will be the real test of my will. For now my beautifully framed painting lies hidden there, wrapped up, like my dreams.

Sometimes I can't help but wonder if the Lord God didn't allow all this to happen, in just the way it did, to see what I'm made of. Am I ready to settle down and make my lifelong vow to God and the church? Some days I believe I could be, but then the hankering to draw one of the cow's black and white patterns or to paint the first red sunset of winter tugs hard at me.

Honestly, I'm staying clear away from it. Like an addict who goes cold turkey, Lou says. Nevertheless I *am* mixing paints on the palette of my heart, trying in vain to match the shades of blue in the Creator's ever-changing sky. God's ways, after all, are higher than ours, Cousin Julia says.

These days, my thoughts, even my convictions, seem to shift with the fickle hues of a Pennsylvania sky . . . a blending of what was true for me as the young preacher's daughter with what I now see and know. Is there no way to blend my opposing desires? Will I ever understand all of the shades of goodness, faith, and even someday, love?

# Acknowledgments

I am blessed to have a small glimpse of God on this earth in the efforts and encouragement of some wonderful people. Among them are the following: Carol Johnson, Julie Klassen, David Horton, and Jolene Steffer, my remarkable editors; Dave Lewis, my husband, "first reader," and constant encourager; Hank Hershberger, Monk and Marijane Troyer, Fay Landis, and other faithful, though anonymous, research assistants; Marilyn Stockwood of London, England; Irmi Knoth and Joe Bohler, internationally acclaimed artists; Iris Stuart of Morton, Mississippi; and the good folk at *The Budget* in Sugarcreek, Ohio.

And, yes, the B & B mentioned in Pine, Colorado, is a very real and lovely place.

It must have seemed to my family as if I disappeared at times while musing, scribbling notes, and typing the pages here. But I was always gently nudged back to reality by their patience and love. Special thanks, especially, to Julie, Janie, and Jonathan . . . and to my darling parents, for steady prayer support. And to one prayer partner, in particular, abundant blessings for your faithfulness in lifting my work to the Lord Jesus.

# The Englisher

# Dedication

To
David and Janet Buchwalter,
my cherished cousins.

*C*ircles of sunlight dappled the side of the old covered bridge and the rushing creek below. On the treed slope to the west of the bridge, two children gripped the long rope in a jumble of fear and delight, swinging double. Their hands smelled of twisted hemp and sweat, but neither minded. The warm breeze on their faces, the "tickle in their tummies," as the little girl often said when swinging fast, were enough. That, and playing here in this enthralling place, where their older brothers caught pollywogs in the creek, jabbering in Pennsylvania Dutch and nibbling on soft pretzels all the while.

"I won't let you fall," the boy said.

"You're sure?" the girl asked.

"Here, I'll show ya how." He crisscrossed his black suspenders over the smaller girl and then snapped them onto his britches again. They began swinging higher and higher as the sky opened its arms wide.

# Prologue

*Creative redirection.* That's what my English friend Louisa says I need, though she says it ever so gently. Which is a right fancy way of saying I must be vigilant in finding acceptable ways to express my art . . . my very soul. She and I both know I belong here with the People, so I continually stifle the part of me that once gave me such joy. My never-ending urge to draw and paint.

It must be hard for Louisa to witness this grief of mine, especially as we are ever so close, like sister-cousins. She, too, mourns what she's abandoned, for the time being—her fashionable life in Denver, the modern world that weighed her down. She lives each day to see the beauty in all things Amish, *the art of being,* as she calls the simplicity of our lives here in Paradise, in the thick of buggies, social gatherings, and cookie-making frolics. And Louisa Stratford has experienced a broken engagement, as have I.

It's odd, but nearly the minute I had promised my preacher father I would turn my back on my artistic passions for a full six months, right then, all kinds of new temptations popped into my head like never before. I find myself tracing a design with my finger on my dress, or squinting and eyeing the shape of the cast-iron bell *Mamm* rings for supper. It's as if the drive to create cannot be squelched, neither from within nor without. But I hope, for the good of my word and for the good of my family, I can suppress it long enough to join church. By then surely I will have learned to obey. Without Lou's loving support, though, I can't imagine succeeding.

Nearly as strong as the tug to express myself on paper or canvas is my eagerness to see Ben Martin again. This befuddles me. An *Englischer?* Just as I am free of Rudy Esh, in every way, I am determined to forget about this boy who can be nothing but trouble to my goal of joining church.

Yesterday, out on the road, we happened to run into each other when I was bringing the horse and sleigh home from an errand. Lo and behold if I wasn't alone, which is mighty unusual, as Luke or Yonie, two of my younger brothers, or *Mamm* regularly accompany me.

There he was. Tall and blond, just strolling along in the cold, his strong arms swinging at his sides, his head turned to gaze at distant snowy hills. Well, I didn't even think twice about whether or not to stop the horse—I did so straightaway, sitting alone in my father's buggy, risking being caught talking to Ben in afternoon's brash light.

I felt downright peculiar listening to him talk about his "hope," as he put it. *Jah*, he's determined to change my mind about turning him down for coffee—"we wouldn't be gone but an hour," he coaxed.

Of course, I couldn't even begin to ponder such a thing, and I managed to steer the conversation to something else altogether—the menfolk's local championship game of checkers over at the Gordonville Fire Hall. Ben's eyes brightened and not surprisingly. I've learned that most men perk up at the mention of games: corner ball, baseball, volleyball, and whatnot. So I was glad to have diverted his thinking away from me, at least for a time. Now, if only I can stop thinking of *him*.

We must've talked for a good quarter hour. And without considering the consequences of being caught, I fed his obvious hope, slipping out from beneath my warm lap robe and climbing down from the carriage to talk with him. Right there along the road in the frosty air, where ofttimes I walked in the warmth of a summertime night, breathing in the sweetness of honeysuckle while cornstalks creaked in the field. On such evenings I liked to stare up at the stars, bemused at just how many the Lord God created. Right there, where it struck me anew that if the almighty One had taken time to form all those stars in the vast heavens, then did He also have time to heed a sparrow's fall and the number of hairs tucked under my white prayer *Kapp?*

I stood there and visited with Ben, where any one of the People could have witnessed the intriguing intent in his eyes. I can only guess what my own face—my too-readable eyes—communicated back to him, because my heart was saying some fearsome things to *me*. Things I don't recall feeling toward another man, not even my former beau, Rudy. And if it's true that the Lord God sees everything, He must never again see me with Ben.

Oh, such ill timing! On the heels of my handshake-agreement with *Daed*, yet. First, the pull of art on me, and now suddenly another issue weighs so heavily. *What on earth can I do about Ben?*

Honestly, I find myself sighing loudly whenever I think of this most recent encounter. That and dear friend Lou's kind admonition. *Creative redirection, indeed.*

*Fair seedtime had my soul, and I grew up*
*Fostered alike by beauty and by fear.*

—WILLIAM WORDSWORTH

# Chapter 1

A half dozen blackbirds perched themselves on the makeshift scarecrow on the edge of the snowy garden. The figure wore Preacher Jesse Zook's own black trousers and green shirt, which had already seen better days when twenty-year-old Annie had snatched them up, rescuing them from the rag bag. The long shirtsleeves had been rolled up months before to reveal the straw man's upper appendages. Now the old felt hat and wind-tattered clothing were quite frozen, unyielding in February's blustery gale.

The stark white clapboard farmhouse was a welcoming sight in the fading light as Jesse made his way to the back porch. Stomping his snow-caked boots against the steps before making his way indoors, he was immediately aware of a tantalizing aroma.

*Barbara's zesty veal loaf.*

He hurried to the sink to wash up. "Smells wonderful-good, love."

"It's just us tonight," his wife said from the cookstove, her black apron barely spanning her fleshy middle.

"Oh? And where are the boys and Annie . . . and Louisa?"

Barbara Zook straightened, her face pink from the heat of the old stove. "Well, our sons were each wearin' their *for good* clothes, headed for some business in town."

Jesse nodded and gave a breathy chuckle. "Which means they each have themselves a girl. And Annie? Where's she keepin' herself this Saturday night?"

Barbara explained that a friend of Louisa's was flying in from Denver. "Annie hired one of the Mennonite drivers to take her and Louisa to the Harrisburg airport."

*Another Englischer coming yet*, Jesse thought. There had been nothing smart about his permitting Annie's fancy friend to stay *this* long, either. And now there would be two of them?

Since Louisa Stratford's arrival, Jesse regularly tossed in bed, wishing he had done things differently back when he might've changed the outcome of all the foolishness between Annie and her longtime pen pal, who was, more often than not, referred to as Lou by not only Annie but now Omar, Luke, and Yonie, his three teenaged sons. A young woman with a masculine nick-name—downright peculiar.

Even so, this Lou had kept Annie here amongst the People. She seemed to be something of a balm to his daughter's soul, as well. For that, he was obliged.

He dried his hands on the towel and dropped into his chair at the head of the table. He considered his daughter's promise to refrain from painting pictures such as the one on the cover of last month's *Farm and Home Journal*, which he had prudently hidden away in the barn. When Annie set her mind to do something, she generally followed through. The difficulty was in knowing whether or not she'd been sincere when she gave her word to him some days back.

He recalled the time he'd caught his only daughter drawing in the barn as a wee girl, and her promising never to do it again. Some offspring were mighty easy to know, to have a real, firm connection with—and he certainly had this with his sons. But Annie? Well, they had the typical family rapport, but she was different . . . which was to be expected, he guessed. After all, she was a daughter.

*Put aside your sin and give obedience a chance*, he'd told her. And she had shaken his hand on it.

Now his present appetite for food quelled the jumble in his head, and he was pleased to see Barbara bringing the meat platter to the table and setting it down near him. She returned to the counter for a bowl of creamy scalloped potatoes sprinkled with bacon bits, and there were serving dishes of buttered red beets and of snow peas. When she'd seated herself to his right, he bowed for a silent prayer.

Afterward they ate without speaking, for the most part. No need for his wife to be made privy to those things that caused him continual irritation.

Truth be known, it wasn't just Annie's worldly pen pal that concerned him so much. No, his grim memories of an impromptu burial—the remains of one Isaac Hochstetler, too young to die—also kept him awake at night. Jesse had been the one to handle the small knit of bones while the bishop gingerly pointed the flashlight over the hole as Jesse dug. Then he placed the skeleton in a clean burlap bag, laying it to rest back a ways from the cemetery itself. The knowledge of the lad's remains lying in the undisclosed grave gave him the willies . . . as though he and the bishop had done something altogether deplorable.

With the bishop's agreement, he had told Zeke where Isaac had been laid to rest. Zeke's response had been troubling.

Now Barbara spoke up suddenly as she served a piece of pumpkin pie with a dollop of whipped cream. "I guess Louisa's friend won't be stayin' with us."

Jesse grunted. "Why's that?"

"Evidently Courtney Engelman turned up her nose, according to Annie. Wanted electricity, I guess."

He felt the hair on the back of his neck prickle out. "This one's a *gut* friend of Louisa's, ya say?"

"Well, she must be, 'cause she was goin' to be in Louisa's wedding back last fall."

"So where's *this* Englischer stayin'?"

"That perty Maple Lane Farm guesthouse, over yonder." Barbara forced a smile. She looked down at her generous slice of pie, not speaking for the longest time. "I . . . uh, I've been meaning to tell ya something," she said, meeting his gaze.

He touched her arm. "What is it, dear? You look all peaked."

"Well, jah, I s'pose I am," she said softly. "I've been having dreams—the same one—for a week now. 'Tis awful strange. Isaac Hochstetler's back in Paradise . . . like nothing ever happened to him." Tears filled her eyes and she reached up her dress sleeve and pulled out a small handkerchief, her lower lip quivering.

"Ach, Barbara . . ." He did not know what to say to comfort her. He couldn't just come out with the fact that Isaac could never, ever simply return. His bones were the final proof, although scarcely a soul was aware of them, aside from the bishop, himself, and Zeke. "I'm sorry your dreams are so troubled," he managed to say, stroking Barbara's hand.

Jesse retired to his rocking chair, mentally adding his wife's woes to his own while sitting near the fire. After a time, once Barbara was finished with her kitchen duties and had turned her attention to her needlework, he got up and donned his old work coat, carrying his uncertainties silently to the barn. He went straight for the rolled-up magazine cover, tucked away in the haymow in a safe and out-of-the-way place, where he had also hidden the old rope swing. He'd thought of turning it over to Zeke years ago but could never bring himself to relinquish it. More recently he had thought of simply burning it in a bonfire.

He sat on an old willow chair—his "thinking chair," he liked to call it. His father, a sage if ever there was one, had crafted the now ragged-looking chair in a hodgepodge sort of symmetry. Jesse had helped gather the willow sticks in early spring, when the sap was running, he recalled.

Now he looked at the cover art—Annie's own—holding it in his callused hands for at least the hundredth time, so mesmerizing it was.

*Why would she choose to paint this?*

He huddled against the cold, breathing in the pungent scents of manure and feed. Comforted by the presence of the livestock, he pondered Annie's odd decision to paint the very place where Isaac had been abducted.

*How could she possibly remember him yet? Does Isaac haunt her dreams, as well?*

Louisa and Annie stood near the baggage claim area, across from the rental car counters, waiting for Courtney's arrival. Terribly fidgety, Louisa adjusted her head covering, then went to check the monitor for the second time. "Looks like her plane's late," she told Annie, returning.

"Hope everything's all right." Annie frowned slightly. "But you know more 'bout all this. . . ."

"Oh, it won't be much longer."

Annie excused herself, asking Louisa to "stay put," then headed toward the ladies' room.

Louisa hoped Annie wouldn't have any trouble finding her way back again. But then she realized how easy it would be to spot Annie here in this rather smallish airport with not another Amish person anywhere in sight.

In a few minutes, Courtney came gliding down the escalator, lanky as a model, her carry-on bag slung over her shoulder. Louisa gave a little wave when Courtney got closer, but Courtney kept walking.

"Court?" she called after her, very aware of how pretty her friend's shiny brown hair looked swinging loose around her shoulders. A slight twinge of envy nagged her, but Louisa pushed it away, keeping an eye out for Annie. "Courtney?" she called again.

Turning, Courtney stared at her. Really stared. "Louisa?" She literally gawked, her sea green eyes wide. Then, as if to shrug off her surprise, she said, "Well . . . hey, look at *you*." Courtney held her at arm's length, still studying her while Louisa wondered how she might explain her Plain attire to her longtime friend.

She felt terribly out of place, wishing Annie would hurry back from the rest room. "How was your flight?"

"Fine . . . just fine, thanks." Courtney scrutinized Louisa with a droll expression. "You said you were trying to fit in here, but . . . I had no idea you'd come out in public like this." At once she laughed as if making a joke.

Louisa was instantly glad Annie wasn't near. "You know what they say: 'When in Rome . . .'"

Courtney still looked a bit shocked. And she was speechless now, which was a good thing, especially because Louisa turned and spotted Annie walking toward them. "There's my pen pal, Annie—the one I told you about."

"So that's your famous Amish friend," Courtney said. "I can't wait to meet her."

Annie was smiling as she hurried to Louisa's side.

"Courtney, I'd like you to meet Annie Zook. And, Annie, this is Courtney Engelman."

Annie smiled, nodded. "Welcome. Nice to meet you."

"Thanks," Courtney said, looking Annie over, obviously unable to suppress her interest. "Same here."

When the luggage from the flight arrived, Louisa went with Courtney to pick up her second bag—*with five more pairs of shoes, no doubt*—wondering if it was such a good idea for Courtney to have come after all.

"How long have you been dressing . . . uh, like this?" Courtney asked quietly while they waited at the carousel.

"Since day one. But that's a long story."

"Oh?"

"I'll tell you all about it, Court."

When Courtney spotted her bag, she excused herself, waded through the other passengers and snatched it up.

Together, they returned to join Annie, who waited demurely near the luggage carts in her plum-colored dress, her long wool coat draped over her arm. "We're all set," Louisa said, and the three of them walked out to the curb where their driver was waiting.

"I wish you would have let me in on the dress code before I came, Louisa," Courtney whispered. "I hope you don't expect me to go around like that."

Louisa grimaced.

While they placed the luggage in the trunk, Louisa wished she hadn't said a word about filling Courtney in on her reason for dressing Plain. Suddenly, she felt it was flat none of her business.

❖

Annie sat quietly in a white wicker chair in the upstairs bedroom at the Maple Lane Farm B&B while Courtney got herself settled. Situated in the midst of a wide meadow, near a winding brook, the colonial inn was only a short walk to Amish neighbors, one an accomplished quilter Annie knew.

Courtney gabbed up a storm with Louisa as she plugged in her portable computer and then rustled about to find a place in the empty bureau drawers to put away her clothing.

"How's it going with your roommate?" asked Lou.

"Oh, I've got two now . . . one's a guy," Courtney said, lowering her voice and glancing at Annie.

"Well, when did that happen?" Lou seemed very interested.

Courtney's eyes twinkled. "It's not what you think. We're just sharing a house. And Jared's terrific in the kitchen."

"He cooks?"

"Bakes bread, too." Courtney again glanced at Annie.

Lou mentioned a dozen or more other names Annie had never heard her say before, as Annie curiously observed Lou's interaction with her English friend. It was fairly clear Lou was hungry for information about the outside world, and Courtney seemed more than willing to respond to the many inquiries, filling Lou in on the life she'd so abruptly left behind.

Annie soon began to feel like a fifth wheel but did her best to show interest. Courtney paused from the chore of unpacking and perched herself on the high canopy bed, patting the rust red and white homemade quilt.

Lou glanced sheepishly at Annie, then stared pensively at Courtney's makeup bag. Saying nothing, Lou reached up to run her fingers across the delicate edge of the lacy ecru canopy.

Courtney let herself fall back on the bed, staring up at the underside of the canopy. "Now *this* is elegant stuff," she muttered, looking again at Lou's plum-colored dress and black full apron, which matched Annie's. Courtney's pretty eyes drifted to Lou's white head covering and lingered at the middle part in Lou's hair.

Lou must have sensed the scrutiny and resumed her chatter, asking about Courtney's plans following graduation. Annie felt increasingly awkward, listening in on their banter like a moth on the stenciled wall.

At one point, Lou glanced at her watch. "We need to get going, over to Zooks'," she said.

Courtney frowned. "I should freshen up."

"Ach, you're just fine," Annie said.

"Yeah, let's go," Lou said. "Annie's mom's the best pie baker in the civilized world."

Courtney's eyebrows rose at that.

"Let's not keep her waiting," Lou urged.

Courtney shook her head. "Really, Louisa. I need time to unwind. I feel like I'm still flying. I'll join you tomorrow."

Lou gave in. "All right, I suppose you *do* look like you could use a bubble bath." The way she said it, Annie guessed she might long for one herself. "Glad you're here safely, Courtney. I guess Annie and I'll head home."

"Home?" Courtney gave Lou a curious look.

Annie wondered what her friend would say, but Lou only winked as if revealing a private joke. "You know . . . home for now."

Courtney nodded, then reached to feel Lou's dress sleeve, grimacing as if she'd touched a hot burner. "What sort of fabric is this, anyway?" Lou looked sheepish again, but Courtney's expression turned animated. "I think we've got a lot of catching up to do."

Lou's smile returned.

Annie spoke up, offering to return for Courtney with the horse and buggy first thing in the morning.

Courtney shook her head. "Maybe if I had directions, I could walk over."

"Too far. But if it's any consolation, I'll bring the team over myself," Lou offered.

"You?"

"Sure. I know how to manage a horse."

Courtney raised her eyebrows as if to say, *Now, that's interesting.*

Lou seemed momentarily pleased. "Welcome to Amish country," she said. "Loosen up. Have some fun!"

Annie was surprised by Lou's sudden offhand approach.

"So what time is breakfast?" Courtney asked.

"Six-thirty."

Courtney's mouth fell open. "You're kidding, right?"

"Too early?" Annie asked, stifling a grin.

"And don't forget," Lou added, "church is right afterward."

Courtney groaned. "Uh, that's a really long ordeal, right?"

Annie and Lou exchanged glances.

"C'mon, Court," Lou said. "We talked about this. You'll have a front-row seat."

Courtney sighed audibly. "Fine. A three-hour history lesson."

"Yeah, that's the spirit," Lou said.

"Cool. See ya," said Courtney.

They said their good-byes, but Annie could not shake her unsettled feeling. Not because she wasn't somewhat accustomed to worldly folk but because Courtney seemed to have something up her sleeve. Surely she wasn't here simply to tour the countryside or to visit an old friend.

*Why'd she come here really?*

Years ago Jesse had learned everything he would ever need to know about cows and milking procedures. The practical aspects and the shortcuts allowed by the bishops, including the use of an air compressor to keep fresh milk cooling and stirring in a bulk milk tank, powered by a diesel engine.

But this night, with lantern in hand, he heard only the mooing of Holsteins chained to their wooden stanchions. Milk cows were such an enormous part of his family's livelihood.

The memory of lowing cattle had been planted in his mind for nearly two decades now, since the fateful evening he'd met with Isaac's stubborn father, Daniel, in the Hochstetlers' barn. *"You are God's anointed."* Jesse had been adamant, cautioning Daniel of the dire situation at hand. *"You've rejected almighty God, don't you know? It is imperative that you take up the office of preacher as ordered by the drawing of the divine lot."*

*Imperative.* The word had pounded in Jesse's brain even then. Alas, Daniel had chosen that dark and different path, against the angels of heaven. The first-chosen of the Lord God had stated his decision, slapping his black hat against his thigh for emphasis. *"The deed's done. I've made my bed. Now I'll lie in it,"* Daniel had told him.

Jesse wandered outside, making his way through the snow, strangely drawn to the tall scarecrow over yonder. He stared at it, gritting his teeth. No need to protect a sleeping garden against the boldest of birds in winter, and spring was months away. One look at the arctic gray sky and anyone could see that.

Anger, long suppressed, rose in him and overflowed in one hasty gesture. Marching forward, he set down his lantern and began to dismantle the straw man, first tearing away the cold-hardened shirt to reveal the straw body, then the worn black britches. His gloved hands fumbled repeatedly as he breathed in icy air.

*Helpless Isaac, his life snuffed out like a wee candle. Barbara's dreams fraught with empty hope, when the reality is in the buried truth.*

Jesse thought of his daughter, welcoming yet another worldly outsider into their midst. *Where will it end?*

His disturbing thoughts pushed Jesse beyond the brink of good sense.

The old hat was next to go, and the wooden crossbeam. When Jesse was done, the pieces lay on the desolate ground.

He piled up the scraps of clothing, along with the wooden structure itself. He carried the whole of it to the refuse pile behind the barn, conscious of a pounding in his temples and heat on his neck.

The raucous cawing from the backyard willow made him stop and look up as he made his way toward the house. In the moonlight, he saw half a dozen blackbirds perched boldly on the uppermost branches.

*Predators will come no matter. . . .*

## Chapter 2

Ben Martin had a hankering for a turkey sandwich on toasted rye. He clicked out of the Churchill Downs Web site, having navigated around each location on the site for a solid hour. Stomach growling, he headed to the small galley-style kitchen and opened the fridge and the see-through vegetable drawer for some lettuce and half a tomato. Then several slices of smoked turkey, the all-important mayo, and two pieces of dark rye.

He dropped a handful of ice into the largest glass mug in the cupboard—a gift he'd received for being a groomsman for his good buddy's wedding last year. *Back before everything broke loose. . . .*

When he'd finished making the sandwich, he cut it in half diagonally, as his mother always did. He remembered as a boy lifting the lid on his Aladdin lunch box and finding the sandwiches halved. One of Mom's trademarks. That and the cored whole apple, wrapped in aluminum foil. Why she didn't quarter it and cut out the seeds like his classmates' mothers did, he'd never known.

While eating his lunch, he flipped through his mail, spying an overnight letter from his mom, which included his Social Security card. *Finally*, he thought. He was one step closer to acquiring a Pennsylvania driver's license.

Weeks ago he'd asked her to mail his birth certificate as well, since due to 9/11 Homeland Security measures, two additional forms of ID, along with his Kentucky license, were required. Unfortunately, his mother hadn't had time to unearth it, having moved important files to the attic when their basement partially flooded during a severe storm in mid-November last year. Although she was rather apologetic, it didn't seem she was trying all that hard, most likely hoping Ben would give up this nonsense and return home, upsetting as all this had been to her.

Not wanting to wait any longer, and tired of asking for it only to realize he was rubbing salt in the wound of his leaving, he had decided to apply directly to the Office of Vital Statistics in Frankfort, Kentucky, for another official copy.

Finishing off his sandwich, he began to fill out the application, recalling a long-ago exchange between himself and his sisters. And one mouthy cousin.

He had been trying to get his mom to find some baby pictures for his "Guess Who?" project at school. But his mother had been busy cooking and entertaining their relatives from Iowa at the time. One of the cousins and his sisters had ganged up on him, teasing him mercilessly. "Well, maybe you're adopted," his cousin had said, sporting a mischievous grin.

"Yeah, ever think of that?" said his sister Patrice.

Yet another sister, Sherri, had joined in on the fun at his expense, holding up a mirror to his face. She made a scrutinizing frown. "Here, take a look and see."

He had kidded them back. "Cool! You're not really my sisters then, right?" He eyed the obnoxious cousin, too. "And . . . you? Well, figure it out, cuz."

"Wait a minute," Patrice had declared with seeming disappointment, still holding the mirror. "Your eyebrows have the same arch as Dad's."

"Huh?"

"And you have Mom's nose."

Sherri piped up. "You inherited Daddy's funky annoying laugh, too!"

"Don't forget Mom's morning breath," Patrice added.

"Okay, that does it." He began chasing them around the house, catching Patrice and holding her upside down over the toilet, threatening to douse her, head first.

"I'm gonna die . . . and it'll be . . . your fault," she screamed. "Mom!"

Diana, his youngest sister, had sat in the corner, clapping and egging him on that day. He thought of all four of his sisters now, missing them. He wondered what they would think of Annie if they ever had an opportunity to meet her. But that was a slam dunk. They'd like her all right. *A lot.*

He put down his pen and twiddled it between his fingers. "So . . . have I stumbled onto the girl for me?"

Putting both destiny and love in the same breath was foolish, wasn't it?

Annie was not only Amish, but of the strictest order. He knew this from hearing his employer, Irvin Ranck, speak of Preacher Zook and his family, who were cousins to Irvin. Ben had no business seeking out such a girl. How well did he know Annie, anyway? Sure, he'd enjoyed talking with her on the

273

road the other day, and she kept showing up at the same places as he did. But, hey, this wasn't a metropolis. People were bound to run into each other here.

*But love?*

He dismissed his mood as relating to homesickness. After all, he sometimes felt disconnected from his family, living here instead of in his native Kentucky, having rarely left his hometown—until recently. He spent hours on email and instant messaging each week, keeping in touch with his family.

Still, there was no denying he was captivated by the Plain culture as a whole and always had been. Even the infrequent times he had bumped into a few "horse and buggy" people in Kentucky.

He leaned his head back and reclined against the exceptionally comfortable chair, pleased to have stumbled onto it at a local estate sale. *A great find.* He congratulated himself once more on having negotiated the price down. *Another trait I inherited from Dad.* He chuckled, the correlation leading him to think of a whole list of other qualities the two of them shared.

He cut loose with a nervous laugh in the stillness of his living room, but it did not keep him from pondering, for the umpteenth time, the mystery that had brought him here to Pennsylvania's Amish country.

Daybreak came all too quickly, and Ben stumbled over his boots on his way to the shower. *Too short a night,* he thought, wondering why to this day he wasn't one to sleep in, even as tired as he felt this quiet Sunday morning.

He took his time shaving, combing through his hair, and dressing, all the while considering Irvin Ranck's standing invitation to attend church. But Ben had put him off this long—why change his mind today?

He made enough scrambled eggs to satisfy his enormous appetite, recalling Zeke Hochstetler's recent visit. He, too, had mentioned this Sunday was to be a preaching day.

*Does everyone attend church around here?*

Ben forked into the soufflé-light eggs on his plate, enjoying his meal, thinking about his growing friendship with Zeke. He was one uptight fellow but seemed to enjoy hanging around the tack shop several times a week. It was from Zeke and a few others like him that Ben had learned a great deal about the Amish in a short amount of time, and it didn't take much to imagine a whole group of them assembled at a long table for breakfast.

But fleeting images of such a gathering came almost too easily, as if he could taste the eggs, like the ones on his plate, only with diced green peppers, onions, and bits of ham. He shook it off as he had other mental images since arriving here. He wasn't the only outsider who'd experienced an obsession with these people, strangely set apart, and their staid, family-oriented culture.

He glanced at the digital stove clock. *I'm working too many hours*, he concluded, forcing himself to switch gears, pondering how to win a yes from Annie on coffee or dinner.

Inhaling deeply, he recalled how silent, even obstinate, she had been at the outset of their first meeting. The second time they'd met, too. Or had she been merely cautious? She must have had a safety antenna up her whole life, around strangers at least. *Englishers*, Irvin said was the name the Amish assigned to the likes of him.

*How many Englishers does Annie know?* He thought of Louisa, who was the most mysterious case of all. *What sort of person dresses Plain when she isn't?*

He used his fork to get every morsel and had the last bite of jellied toast. When he was finished, he carried the plate and coffee mug to the sink.

In no way was he interested in attending church today. But he *was* eager for a drive deep into Amish country. . . .

# Chapter 3

Louisa had gotten up extra early to help Annie hitch up the team, and before leaving to pick up Courtney and bring her back for breakfast at the Zooks', she turned on her smart phone—her Palm—to see if she had any messages from London . . . namely, from Trey Douglas.

Sure enough there was one, but as she listened she detected a new urgency in his tone. He said he had "the perfect idea" and wanted to discuss it with her.

After speed-dialing his number, she hurried back to the house to warm up. She stood in the enclosed porch, out of earshot.

"What's up, Trey?" she asked when he answered.

"Hey, Louisa! Great to hear your voice."

He sounded eager, almost too confident, and the more he talked, the more she sensed something big was up his sleeve.

"You said you had an idea?" she prompted. "What is it?"

"Well, for starters, I thought maybe you'd consider flying over to see me. Spend a long weekend here soon . . . I could show you around. It'd be terrific, Louisa." He paused. "You might even think about staying. . . ."

"Well, that sounds like fun."

Then she swallowed, hard. *Staying?*

"So, you ready to pack your bags? Abandon your Amish lifestyle for the glamour of London?"

*I hope he's kidding,* she thought, feeling oddly resistant. She wasn't sure why she wasn't ready to jump at the chance to travel . . . to see Trey again, face-to-face. *Have I changed so much?*

"Louisa?"

"Yep?"

"I really hope you'll think about it."

She sighed. Until just this moment, she hadn't fully come to grips with her feelings. There was no way she could return to their former relationship. Sure, he was nice. Charming . . . and really wonderful, too. He treated her like a lady in public and loved to pick up the tab . . . show her off. But he had no clue about the happiness in something as simple as feeding peacocks or walking beneath a noonday sun, soaking in its warmth on an otherwise brisk day. No, he couldn't begin to understand how it felt to pull on crusty old work boots—too big, so she stuffed in rolled-up socks—to help clean out the manure ditches, holding her breath but getting a real kick out of the earthiness of country living.

"I'd like to pick up where we left off," she heard Trey saying. "I should never have walked away. . . ."

She wrinkled her nose at the thought of getting too intimately involved, especially distasteful after having broken off her engagement to Michael not so long ago. *I wish he wouldn't pressure me.*

"I don't know," she said, suddenly dreading the notion of spending time with Trey. This came as a surprise because she had been enjoying his attention since coming here to Paradise, had even been attracted to him. But now?

His voice was softer now, almost irresistible. "Sure you know, Louisa. Trust me, you'll love London."

She inhaled, slow and long. "No, Trey. It's nice of you to ask, but I'm staying here."

He didn't challenge her but promised to keep in touch. Then, quickly, she said good-bye and hung up.

She smiled to herself when she began to ponder maybe it wasn't only her love of simplicity that had prompted her to refuse Trey's invitation. Maybe it had more to do with Sam. . . .

She hadn't told Annie, but she had exchanged a few *hellos* with one of the young Amish men at the Preaching services recently—Samuel Glick, who went by the nickname Sam. It wasn't that she had a crush on him in the typical sense of the word. But she found herself strangely intrigued by him.

Heading out the back door, she called to Annie, who came running out of the barn to catch up. Then, raising her skirt, Louisa climbed into the right side of the carriage, still finding it amazing she could get in and out dressed like this . . . not to mention handle a horse.

When she and Annie arrived at the inn on Paradise Lane, they found the front door unlocked, and since it was so early, they simply tiptoed upstairs to Courtney's room. There they discovered her sound asleep. They stood at the foot of the canopy bed, observing the mound of covers and the beautiful quilt.

"She's out cold," Louisa whispered. "No way she'll be ready now for breakfast or Preaching. . . ."

"I say we shake her good—that'll get her up," Annie said jokingly.

Louisa considered Annie's suggestion. She wished they could let Courtney sleep off her jet lag, but if so, they would not see her again until much later in the day.

Gingerly she sat on the edge of the bed and whispered Courtney's name. Zero response.

She jiggled against the bed slightly, but again nothing.

Finally she jostled Courtney's arm. Her friend awakened, but it wasn't pretty.

"Hmm? Oh, hey, Louisa. Is it morning already? I had trouble sleeping." She raised her head slightly off the pillow. "I took a sleeping pill around two o'clock."

*Yikes*, thought Louisa, pulling the covers higher in an attempt to tuck her friend back in. "I'll skip Preaching service and come back for you in a few hours," she offered.

Courtney's eyes drooped shut. "Nah, you go ahead. I'll have to sleep this off . . . past noon or so."

Louisa rose, still looking down at her friend. "This afternoon, then?"

Courtney gave no response.

"She's out but good," Annie said softly. "Ain't so keen on church, I take it."

*Neither was I at first*, Louisa realized.

On the way back from the B&B, Louisa hurried the horse, Betsy, enjoying the feel of the reins even more since talking to Trey. The morning was sunny but freezing cold, and she embraced the familiarity of Annie's companionship.

"Too bad Courtney didn't get a good night's sleep," Annie said.

"Yeah, not many people have the chance to attend an Amish Preaching service—and she snoozes it."

"Oh, she isn't the first person to snooze through a preaching," Annie said, grinning.

Louisa giggled, surprised at Annie's joke.

"She might've enjoyed it," Annie continued wryly. "Or at least found some humor, ya know. All the Plain costumes crammed into one room."

Louisa snorted. "She'll get over it . . . jah?"

Annie poked her playfully. "You and your *jahs*."

"It's just so much fun."

Annie leaned forward. "Are you enjoying your time here, really?"

"Well, sure." Louisa looked away, not sure she was ready to share too much. Fact was, as much as she loved Amish country, just seeing Courtney again had made her homesick. It reminded her, too, that she hadn't heard from her parents in the longest time. *Maybe they've given up on me.*

"Nobody's keeping you here, ya know," Annie said, as if reading her. "I wouldn't blame you one bit if you wanted to follow Courtney home. It's been so much fun just havin' you—"

Again, she thought of Trey's sudden invitation. "Annie? Listen to me . . . I'm not going anywhere, unless you're tired of me."

"Oh, you. How could that be?" Annie was quiet for a moment. "And I understand, too . . . how it feels to be lonesome."

Louisa nodded, her thoughts wandering now to Michael.

"I mean to say, no matter how peaceful it seems here, no matter where you grew up, home is always home. I'm sure Ben Martin misses Kentucky, too." Annie gasped and clapped her hand over her own mouth.

"Wha-at?" Louisa giggled. "Where did *that* come from?"

Annie mumbled through her hand. "'Tis hard to say."

"You can't fool me. You like him, so what's wrong with admitting it?"

"Just everything, really."

Louisa jerked her head in a nod. "But why? Maybe it's time you got to know him. Find out if there's any potential there."

"Ach, for goodness' sake . . . potential for what?" Annie shook her head. "You can't be serious."

The Zooks' lane came into view, and Louisa pulled hard on the rein. "I guess it's something you'll never know, then."

Annie smiled. "I have no intention of knowin'. Ben's not for me. End of story."

"Fine. Don't find out. That's cool."

They looked at each other—the sort of knowing glance between close friends—and burst into laughter.

Following the common meal on Sunday, Louisa noticed Sam Glick walking around the long table, heading toward her.

Annie was off chatting with two of her sisters-in-law and several other young women, so Louisa didn't feel quite as uneasy as she might have when he leaned down and asked, "How're you today, Louisa?"

She looked up, aware of the confidence in his gaze, the way his eyes drew her.

"Wanna go for a walk?" His voice was low.

*Doesn't he know who I am?*

She looked around to see if anyone was observing them. Surely Sam knew she wasn't one of them. "Well, if you think it's a good idea . . . I mean—"

"Seems like a nice day for a walk, jah."

She wouldn't laugh. The day was bitterly cold and no one in their right mind would want to go walking in this weather. Yet she found herself saying yes."

Annie couldn't help but notice what a striking pair they made: Lou wrapped in a heavy woolen shawl over her dark blue cape dress and white apron, and Sam, one of Jesse Jr.'s best friends. Sam was taller than Annie had realized till now, looking downright handsome, his broad shoulders filling out his black split-tail frock coat. Still unhitched at twenty-three, Sam was clean-shaven and wearing newly pressed black broadfall trousers. Dark hair clean and shiny as can be, his bangs peeked out from beneath his winter hat as he strolled with Louisa through the slush and snow.

*Ach, interesting . . .*

Louisa had never mentioned Sam during their long nightly chats. Annie *had* noticed, however, that following the last Sunday singing, Sam had sought Louisa out. Just as he had today.

Now Annie watched as they trudged out onto the narrow farm road that led to the vast whiteness of the dormant cornfield behind Deacon Byler's farmhouse.

*Best not to interfere.* Annie stood at the kitchen window, observing Sam's long gait and Louisa's ladylike pace. *I wonder what they're talking about. . . .*

Lest she become too curious, she turned to search for her friend, Esther Hochstetler, and found her rocking infant Essie Ann near the wood stove at the far end of the kitchen.

"How're you and the children makin' out over at Julia's?" asked Annie softly, still thinking how peculiar it was for Lou to go off with Sam like that.

Esther smiled prettily, her blue eyes brighter than Annie had seen them in some time. "This here babe's my big reason for getting up in the mornin'." She went on to talk about Essie's first real smile, the "precious little cooing," and "so many dear, wee things," as if Esther were a brand-new mother. Then, quickly, she spoke of Laura, Zach, and little John. "The children miss their father somethin' awful," she confided in a whisper.

"I'm sure you miss Zeke, too." Annie glanced about her to see if they were being overheard.

"I best be talkin' with you 'bout that here before too long." Esther blinked back the tears.

Annie patted her hand. "I 'spect you're confused . . . understandably so."

Esther sighed. "I miss seein' you. We don't have enough time to, well . . . talk plainly when you come to Julia's to work." Esther lifted the baby onto her shoulder. "I also don't want to wear out my welcome at the Rancks', ya know."

"I doubt that's possible," Annie said, knowing her cousin Julia as she did. "You're mighty welcome to stay as long as need be, and that's the truth. My cousin has said so repeatedly."

"Well . . . I sometimes worry 'bout that. Zeke wanted to visit last evening, but he was so belligerent Irvin had to take him aside, Julia told me later. She said he'd have to be seein' Irvin for coffee every couple of days—for a good long while—before they'd consider letting him spend time with me alone."

Annie reached over to touch Essie's tiny rosy cheek. She thought of the colors necessary to paint such a sweet face, if she were allowed. "You mean to say Zeke hasn't even laid eyes on this little one yet?"

"Sadly, nee—no." Esther looked away, as if to deny more tears. "'Tis his own fault, I daresay."

"Such a hard time it is for you."

Esther nodded her head slowly. "Oh, Annie . . . more than you know."

Annie pulled up a chair. "Well, if Irvin's decided to take Zeke under his guidance, so to speak, that's a wonderful-good thing."

Esther dabbed a hankie at her eyes with her free hand. "I know 'tis . . . jah, for sure. It's just that . . . well, I do miss him quite a lot. In spite of everything." She blinked fast, still struggling. "And to make matters worse, I've got me a bad case of the baby blues."

"Aw, Essie . . ."

Esther's lower lip trembled uncontrollably.

"My sister-in-law says there are good herbal teas to help with that."

"Oh, jah, I forgot. I know just which one I'll brew up."

"Well, I'm glad we talked today."

Esther nodded; then she looked up at her. "I would also like to know what's good for a broken heart. . . ." Her words hung in the air.

"S'posin' if I knew that, I'd be quick to tell you." Truth be known, making

Ben's acquaintance had somehow begun to soothe Annie's own brittle heart, strange as it seemed.

Louisa was surprised when she realized how far they had walked into the silent field. Caught up in interesting conversation with this country boy who insisted on calling her *Freind*—Pennsylvania Dutch for "friend"—she had lost track of time. *And* her good sense, she feared.

"I'm glad we had this chance to get alone . . . if only for a bit." He looked over his shoulder at the distant Byler farmhouse. "Can I talk you into comin' over to the barn singing at my father's place tonight?"

*What's he thinking, asking me out?* She wondered what Courtney would want to do tonight, as well. *Having her here complicates things even more.*

She tried to guess what he might be thinking behind his spectacular green eyes. "I hope you aren't fooled by my Plain dress," she said. "I have no intention of becoming Amish . . . I only wear Annie's dresses and aprons so I'll fit in here for the time being. Don't want to cause trouble for the preacher's daughter."

He smiled and tilted his head to shade it from the afternoon sun. "Seems to me Annie finds trouble a-plenty as it is. All the fellas are still scratchin' their heads over her—well, her and Rudy Esh. 'Course, now he's married to Susie, but Annie really hurt him by lettin' him go and all."

She wasn't about to say she knew much of anything about that. It was not her place and none of his business, and she was fairly sure he would respect that. Maybe he'd brought her out here, far from the homestead, to see what he could get her to say about Annie. "Sometimes it's best if relationships fail. That's all. Rudy looks very happy with his bride." She found that saying *bride* reminded her, once again, of how she'd nearly made it to the bridal altar herself. And she thought again of Trey, how his pushing, even though it was long-distance and via voice mail, really annoyed her.

"That Annie Zook's one fine catch, but no one seems to be able to get her attention much." Sam was still smiling broadly, but it was clear to Louisa that Annie wasn't the girl he was most interested in at the moment.

He told her of his surreptitious stint at Harrisburg Area Community College, on the Old Philadelphia Pike, and Louisa was shocked at his openness. "I had no idea," she said, wondering how he ever would've fit in.

"I didn't dress Plain, mind you. I did my best not to stick out, just as you are doin' here, Louisa."

"What did you study?"

"Business, and I got what I was after. I finished up all my courses . . . graduated with a three-point-eight, but only a few know. The brethren weren't so happy with me, but they figured I was in *Rumschpringe*. You know about that?"

She said she'd heard of the tradition from Annie. "How will you put your studies to good use?"

"Still workin' on that."

They walked a ways farther in comfortable silence.

After a time, she said, "How hard is it for a person to figure out what they really want in life?"

He paused as if pondering her question. "I s'pose it can be easier said than done."

"That's the truth. I can't count the times I thought I was right on with something . . . only to realize I was following the wrong path."

"Things tend to come more easily for some than others," he replied. "My brothers, for example . . . things just fall into their laps. The oddest thing."

She agreed that life's struggles came and went.

He paused briefly. "Would ya want to head on back?"

"Sure, if you do." She couldn't believe such an appeasing remark had popped out of her mouth.

"Well, if it were up to me, I would stand right here and continue talking to you," he admitted.

She tried not to smile. He was so honestly outspoken. Certainly countrified, but smart, too. His interest in higher education was a real no-no, from what Annie had told her, but Sam was anything but pretentious. She knew clearly where he stood on everything from raising chickens to butchering hogs to conservative politics, such as they were, and even how many strapping sons he hoped to have one day. Louisa believed she was forging a bona fide friendship with Samuel R. Glick—no game playing, no pressure. He knew she wasn't staying in Paradise. They were just walking and talking and having fun in this moment.

"What's the *R* in your name stand for?" she asked boldly.

"Family name. But not your typical Amish." He explained it stood for Ranck, commonly a Mennonite name. "There's an interesting story that goes with that."

"I know some Rancks," she said. "Cousins of Annie Zook's father."

"I heard that, too." He pushed his hat forward a bit on his head. "My connection to the Rancks comes from three generations back, is what my father says. My great-grandfather fell in love with an Amish girl and married her. That's how I came to be Amish, too."

*Non-Amish marrying into a cloistered group? How weird is that?*

"I've never heard of that . . . where someone from the outside comes in and joins."

"It's rare, but it happens."

Louisa and Sam turned to walk back toward the deacon's big stone house.

"I hear some of the youth are callin' you Lou," he said suddenly. "But you seem more like a Louisa to me."

"Oh, that's Annie's and her brother's idea. I doubt it'll stick."

"Well, I sure hope not. You're much too perty for a tomboy name."

She felt the flame of embarrassment in her cheeks. "Uh, I think Annie will wonder where I've disappeared to."

"Oh, I'd say she's smarter than that."

"You know what?" she said suddenly, surprising even herself. "I think I might go to the singing tonight."

His eyes lit up. "So I'll be askin' ya to ride home in my courting buggy, then?"

Not to let on . . . and not to be stupid, either, she said, "That's very nice of you, Sam. I hope you won't mind if I think about it, though."

"If you're coming to singing, you've gotta get home somehow, jah?" He smiled broadly.

"I suppose that's true." She left it at that. One small problem, of course. Courtney would *not* be interested in attending a barn singing. Even if she surprised them and agreed to go, there was no way it could possibly work unless Louisa talked *her* into abandoning her fancy clothes and slipping on one of Annie's cape dresses.

*Yeah, like that'll happen!*

# Chapter 4

Not only was Courtney gone from the B&B when Louisa and Annie arrived back at the colonial inn later, but she had taped a note on her door.

*Hey, Louisa!*
    *All that sleeping made me hungry, so I'm out for a late lunch. I figured you and Annie had someplace to be, since it's Sunday. I'll catch you later.*
    *I've got wheels—I called for a cab!*

                    *See ya!*
                    *Courtney*

Louisa slipped the note deep into her dress pocket, and she and Annie made their way down the long staircase. They turned and waved to the smiling owner and headed back outside to the waiting horse and buggy.

"She must've slept in really late," Louisa said, checking her watch. "It's already three-thirty. Guess it was my fault . . . that long walk with Sam."

"You could ask to use the phone here, maybe."

Louisa agreed it was a good idea. They hurried back up the walkway and into the house. After requesting permission, they were led into the large sitting room, near the open kitchen, where she dialed Courtney's cell number. She got the voice mail, left a short message, and hung up. Courtney was probably talking to one of her college pals back home. *But she has call waiting,* Louisa remembered. So Courtney would have known Louisa was trying to get through. *No, of course not . . . she wouldn't have recognized the inn's ID.*

285

Once they were outside again, Annie hopped into the driver's seat. "You'll see her later," Annie said. "Don't fret. Maybe she'll try callin' you soon." She picked up the reins, smiling.

"Well, I guess if I brought my Palm along sometimes that might help." Louisa laughed at herself, realizing that on some level, at least, she had actually begun to dismiss the outside modern world—if only occasionally.

They rode along, crows heckling overhead in the icy air as Louisa settled into the front seat of the enclosed gray buggy for the ride back to the Zooks' farmhouse. Looking over the stretch of drifted white cornfields, she was aware once again of the way the fields literally ran up to the People's front yards. *As if the Plain and the fancy are somehow interwoven, in spite of their differences,* she decided, realizing inwardly that she, too, was an odd part of this intermingling, at least for the present. *A modern woman's soul dressed in Amish garb. The strangest thing I've ever done.* She recalled again Courtney's reaction at the airport.

"Are you planning to go to the singing tonight, Annie?" She hadn't intended to ask quite so abruptly. The question was out, nevertheless.

"Why, no. I just assumed Courtney was comin' for supper." Annie glanced at her, eyes revealing a surprised glint. "Any particular reason why *you'd* want to go tonight, Lou?"

Not wanting to stir up unnecessary suspicion, Louisa simply said, "Just wondered."

"Well, if we did happen to go . . . and we took along your friend, she might cause a stir if she showed up in her trousers, ya know!"

*No kidding,* Louisa thought. Just then it occurred to her—"I hope you didn't worry about *my* coming here. You certainly had no idea I would do my best to blend in. Not beforehand, at least."

Annie shook her head. "Ach, no, your visit was long overdue. Don't think another thing 'bout it."

She found it interesting how accepting Annie had been even from the earliest days of their letter writing. She recalled Annie's prompt replies with Amish sayings printed on a separate page along with sketches of a one-room schoolhouse, Annie's father's black buggy, and other childish drawings. Never had there been any hint that Annie was doing something inappropriate by having an English pen pal, or that she should be careful about what she wrote. No indication, either, that Annie had any problem with Louisa's being "worldly" and Annie, herself, as Plain as can be.

"I say we plan on goin' tonight," Annie said, bringing Louisa out of her reverie.

"You do?"

"Sure, but first let's see what happens with Courtney's plans—whatever they are—before we decide." Annie smiled. "There's been some quiet talk of a square dance."

*Oh, great. Sam didn't say anything about that.*

Louisa's Palm was in the top drawer of the bureau in the Dawdi Haus. She wondered how long before Courtney might actually call. "If we dress her up Plain—" she laughed out loud—"she might end up riding home with a cute Amish boy! Who knows?"

Annie cast a knowing glance her way. "Cute, jah?"

"Well, you know." And she was fairly sure Annie caught her meaning.


"A raw day for a walk, jah?" Jesse said after the common meal when he saw Zeke coming back from the outhouse.

Zeke nodded, his face drawn, his black hat pulled low on his forehead.

Jesse waited for Zeke to get closer before saying what was really on his mind. "S'pose you made it over to the graveyard all right, then?"

Zeke's bearded chin trembled momentarily. He slapped his gloved hands on his arms. "Can't seem to get myself over there, now that I know where you and the bishop buried him."

"Well, no one's sayin' you have to go, Zeke. Maybe it's for the best if you don't." Jesse put a hand on his shoulder. "You've been through some rough waters."

"Jah, my life's out of kilter."

*Rightfully so. A man needs a wife—an obedient one.* . . . "How's the missus?" Jesse asked. "You've visited her and the children over at Irvin's, no doubt?"

"Well, I stopped by there, but my temper's fierce. Awful hard for me to control it anymore." Zeke paused, breathing loudly. "Even still, Irvin's keepin' me from my wife and children."

"Would you want me to speak to my cousin on that?"

"No . . . no. 'Tis best, prob'ly, that Irvin do things his way, since he's the one givin' my family shelter for now."

*For now.* . . .

Jesse wondered, indeed, if the Rancks were getting their grip on Zeke's wife . . . would the People *ever* get her back? Especially with all her talk of saving grace and whatnot. "If she's not back home in a week—and hasn't repented of her pride—we'll have to be talkin', you and I."

"A sorry situation all round. If she'd just stayed home, 'stead of seeking out that Mennonite friend." Zeke scratched his face, looking down at his toes. "I have yet to see my youngest up close."

"A baby girl, I hear," Jesse offered, hoping to raise Zeke's spirits.

"Named after my Esther. And your daughter."

"Oh?"

"Essie Ann's the full name."

Jesse and Zeke turned and walked together, not saying any more as Jesse pulled a cigar from his frock coat. He offered it to the downtrodden new father, who, even though he was known to dislike the smooth, sweet aroma, accepted it gratefully.

Ben had been driving in broad circles around the vicinity of Annie's house for more than an hour, enjoying the wintry countryside, lost in reverie. He decided to drive down Route 30, stopping long enough for lunch at a Bob Evans restaurant.

Resuming his aimless driving, he listened to WDRE, 103.9, out of Philly, all the while stopping frequently on the most deserted roads to take digital pictures of various snowscapes—an old corncrib and wooden windmill, and outbuildings where snow clung to rugged stone structures.

But it was the virtually never-ending fields, stretching away from the road on either side—corn and tobacco fields dormant beneath a foot of snow—that reminded him of home. *I'll give Mom and Dad a call tonight*, he decided.

Having made it a point to know precisely where Annie Zook and her family resided, Ben had driven past the tall farmhouse several times in the space of a few days. A slow-moving peahen wandering onto the slushy road had intrigued him. He had stopped the car to watch the large bird strut in slow motion.

*Annie raises peacocks*, he thought, recalling the interesting tidbits he'd gathered while having supper at Irvin and Julia Ranck's. *Not chickens or pigs, but peahens and their young.*

Now he found himself watching an Amish father pull four small children on a long wooden sled, mesmerized by the man and his plump wife as they picked their way over the plowed roadside, bundled up in their black garb, including the mother's winter hat, a candlesnuffer style he'd seen in parts of Kentucky, as well.

*They must be headed home for milking.*

Later he went in search of the area's historic bridges. He had done some initial checking on the Internet and had printed out a listing of Lancaster

County covered bridges, complete with colorful pictures and descriptions of each. There was the picturesque Pinetown covered bridge built in the late 1800s northeast of Landis Valley on Bridge Road, as well as the Hunsecker Mill Bridge on Hunsecker Road, damaged due to a tractor-trailer hitting the overhead support beam and steel rods, leaving a splintered mess of wood and twisted metal in its wake. Originally constructed in the mid-1800s but rebuilt after Hurricane Agnes destroyed it in 1972, the bridge had been fraught with troubles. Several of his tack shop customers had told hush-hush stories about vandals attempting to cut up the bridge and carry it away. It was the longest single-span covered bridge in Pennsylvania, as well as one of the newest, and was featured on the cover of the state's transportation map, attracting many tourists.

But it was not the folklore of just any bridge Ben was after, nor the fact that it was the two hundredth anniversary of the nation's covered bridges that spurred him on. He believed in his gut he would know the one bridge he had come in search of when he saw it.

Creeping along on Belmont Road, past the weathered wood siding of the Progressive Shoe Store on the right, he slowed the car as a stately covered bridge came into view. He pulled off the road and set the brake. Slowly he surveyed the long expanse of the bridge with barn-red planked sides, spanning Pequea Creek. A *kissing bridge* popped into his mind, and he wondered where *that* had come from.

He reached into his jeans pocket and pulled out his wallet, then removed a folded picture. He opened it and compared it to the landscape before him—the gray stone abutments and the wide creek, now frozen, beneath the wooden bridge. He was also very aware of the stark black grove of trees to the left of the bridge, down along an embankment, although he was uncertain as to why. Everything matched the picture he held in his hands. A picture he'd stared at so often, he actually felt as if he had been here before.

Getting out of the car, he stood with his hand on the door. Then he walked closer and paused in what might have been the shadow of the bridge had a cloud not blown across the face of the sun.

*This is it,* he realized.

He scanned the sloping area to the west of the road, then turned to look into the distance, seeing Queen Road to his left. Quickly he returned to the car and snatched up his Lancaster County map from the seat. He was able to locate the road, *this* bridge—a small icon set on a thick blue line defining the creek—and he decided he had indeed found the match.

He checked and double-checked. Not a question in his mind. This was undeniably the landscape captured in the striking picture he had carried with him ever since first seeing it last Christmas. . . .

He had gone to hang out with a friend at a printshop in Marion, Kentucky, one miserably cold afternoon. The place was so unpretentious no one ever would have guessed a slick-looking magazine was being created on the premises.

"Hey, wanna see how we lay out our cover art?" the pudgy designer asked, motioning for Ben to have a look.

At his first glance at what was to become a magazine cover, Ben felt something of a fist growing in the pit of his stomach. The featured painting, titled "Obsession," rattled him as he observed a reddish covered bridge and a grove of trees bursting with autumn colors. From one of the trees hung a long rope swing.

What jolted him even more was the sunbeam highlighting something unlikely on the wooden seat of the swing—a peach stone—that sent a wicked shiver down his spine.

"Can you make a copy of this for me?" he had asked the designer.

"Sure," his friend said. "This picture happens to be the winner of our first-ever art contest." The man went to print a full-color copy.

Ben hadn't thought to ask who the artist was, only to inquire of the location of the painting.

"Well, I believe it's Lancaster County, Pennsylvania" was the reply.

"Nothing more specific?"

The guy nodded. "Someplace in Paradise. How's that for a name of a town?"

As Ben stared at the painting, he'd felt his friend's curious gaze.

"We've got a few Plain groups around here," the designer continued. "Sure is hard not to gawk at people who look so out of place in the twenty-first century."

Ben had agreed. But how did that explain his fascination with the painting? No Amish folk in it anywhere . . . just an old covered bridge, the stream, and a cluster of trees at peak foliage.

*There has to be a logical explanation*, he thought.

Still, Ben had not told anyone how captivating he found the painting to be, nor that the picture had stirred up a world of visions in him.

Now he stood on the brink of the actual bridge, staring at the frozen creek below. Turning away from the stone abutment, where he had leaned hard for fear he might become ill, he faced the dark tunnel.

The sound of footsteps echoed, and he looked but saw nothing. No one.

An inexplicable sense of danger registered in his brain.

*Turn back! Run!*

Ben's hands were suddenly cold. He had lost all feeling in his fingers. They were as strangely numb as his soul.

*What's happening to me?*

# Chapter 5

Louisa led Courtney up the stairs in the Dawdi Haus to get her dressed for the barn singing. "Annie and I hang out here," Louisa said, opening the door.

Courtney stepped inside and cautiously looked around the stark bedroom. "So this is where you've been holed up," she said.

"Yep," Louisa replied simply, stunned that Courtney would agree to dress Plain. Or that she would consider attending the singing at all.

"Cool," Courtney had whispered so only Louisa could hear. "I'll just pretend it's Halloween."

Annie brought over a royal blue dress and a black apron from the wall pegs, and Courtney rolled her eyes as she slipped into the skirt part of the cape dress.

When Annie ran across the hall to borrow a few more pins from Mammi Zook, Courtney looked at Louisa and shrugged. "How bad can it be? A barn singing, right? Like hillbilly night at summer camp. Remember, Louisa?"

*But this is the real thing.*

Courtney screwed up her face when Annie suggested pulling her thick locks into a low, tight bun. "Is this necessary?" she asked Annie, who was quick to nod.

"Oh, jah, ever so important," Annie attempted to explain. "Without the Kapp, the rest of it is all for naught."

But for bangle-loving Courtney the bottom line was curiosity, most likely. Despite her aversion to the Plain attire, and the fact that her layered hair kept slipping out from the twisted sides and low hair bun, Courtney said she wasn't going to miss out on a "rare chance" to be eyewitness to an Amish barn gathering, especially after sleeping through Preaching service earlier.

Louisa couldn't help wondering what Courtney's true motivation was for going tonight. She suspected it had much more to do with checking up on her, especially in the guy department.

All during the ride to the singing, Courtney kept commenting on how incredibly slow they were moving. Omar, at the reins, said nothing, but Louisa noticed his mouth tighten. Louisa had become accustomed to and now relished the slower pace of things but couldn't imagine Courtney ever giving up *her* wheels. Not to mention her lipstick, mascara, and eye shadow, all of which she was wearing even now beneath her black bonnet. *A peahen dress with a peacock face*, Louisa thought wryly, and grinned.

And riding in a buggy without a heater in the cold—the bone-chilling kind—wasn't something a girl like Courtney would ever forget. Nope. She'd go straight home and tell Louisa's mother how crazy her daughter was . . . living like she was on a Lewis and Clark expedition or something.

When they arrived at the Glicks' home, Omar took care of the horse while Annie led Louisa and Courtney up the slope to the barn, pushing their boots through the snow. The night air was plenty nippy, as Annie might say, and Louisa saw that a large bonfire had been built in the side yard.

"Come along," Annie said, as they went up the snow-covered earthen bridge that led to the upper level of the two-story bank barn. Louisa helped Annie push open the heavy wooden door to reveal a large haymow swept clean enough to see the wide wood planks of the vast floor in the center. Bales of hay had been stacked high on either side.

The young men stood in clusters, their black hats straight on their heads. Some of the shy ones ran thumb and pointer fingers up and down their suspenders, while the girls were prim in below-the-knee-length dresses of blue, green, violet, and burgundy all along the opposite wall. Gas heaters were scattered here and there to ward off the chill. But nervous tension, Louisa suspected, was partly responsible for the frosty atmosphere.

Courtney turned to Louisa. "How do I look?"

"Like a woman on the prowl," Louisa whispered, then laughed.

Courtney poked her in the arm as they stood on the threshold. "I'm in over my head here, aren't I?"

"Just do what Annie does," Louisa offered, hoping that was sound advice.

"Jah, and say what I say, too," Annie added, grinning.

"I'll just say 'jah' all night," Courtney agreed.

"Yeah, and get yourself a ride home with a handsome feller," Louisa teased.

"How exciting," Courtney replied, batting her eyes.

Louisa felt strange encouraging Courtney to come along, even though she herself was still very much on the fringe of this alien society. *Which is where I need to stay*, she thought as she caught a glimpse of tall and smiling Sam Glick. The notion that Courtney might witness firsthand Sam's obvious interest made Louisa uneasy.

*Is it too much to hope she won't notice?*

She sighed, imagining the fallout.

It was past suppertime when Ben called home. His mother answered on the third ring. "Oh, it's good to hear from you. I hope you've changed your mind about staying there."

"Well, I'm not calling about coming home."

An awkward pause ensued.

"You okay, son?"

"Wanted to check in . . . see how you and Dad are doing."

"You have sisters, too, you know."

"Oh yeah. I keep trying to forget," he quipped.

His mom laughed a little, and then he inquired of his dad's health.

"Oh, your father just never quits. Can't get him to rest much at all."

"So he's working long hours?"

"Always."

"How does Patrice like KSU *this* semester?"

"Fine . . . a new start for her. She wants to know when she can hook up with you on instant messaging. She calls here on her cell quite a lot."

*Then she can call me herself and ask. . . .*

Immediately he thought better of suggesting it. He knew if Patrice called, she would ask incessant questions.

He asked about his high-school-age sister. "Is Sherri doing all right?"

"She's standing right here, grabbing for the phone . . . wanna talk to her?"

Well, no, he really didn't, because then Sherri would feel they should pass the phone around the whole family and he wasn't up to that. But he was polite and said, "Sure."

Sherri had frivolous things on her mind, and he wondered why she wasn't blabbing the boy-girl stuff to one of her girlfriends instead. "Hey, I miss you, bro," she said. "When're you ever coming home again?"

"Are you kidding? I've got a good job here. I've moved on . . . in another month I won't even remember your name."

Sherri giggled. "You *better* remember. I've got algebra tests soon, and you're my ticket to an A, don't forget."

"Got my own apartment, sis."

She groaned. "Don't rub it in."

"Come visit sometime," he said, just to see what she'd say.

"Yeah, like Mom'll say yes to that. Well, speaking of homework, Mom's giving me the eye. Better go."

"See ya, needle nose."

"Whatever."

Mom got right back on the phone. "Say, Ben, I read in the paper about a serial killer admitting to some crimes in Lancaster County. Have you heard anything?"

He resisted the urge to groan. Mom had an obsession with true crime stories, gravitating to dubious newspaper articles and TV drivel. Anything sensational.

"Amish farmland has evidently been used by killers before," she continued.

"Oh, Mom. C'mon!"

"No, seriously. I should send you the article."

Ben sighed, ready for a topic change.

"Some folk are saying it must be sacred ground."

"What is?"

"Amish soil . . . where the victims are buried."

"Yeah. Mom? I gotta go."

"When are you coming home, Ben?"

"Mom—"

"All right, fine. But be careful, please?"

"Sure, Mom." He wished Dad were home more often, spending time with her.

She was clucking into the phone. "It's so nice of you to call. We all miss you terribly."

He was ready to say good-bye when he spied the picture of the Pequea Creek bridge on his kitchen table. "Hey, have we ever been to Pennsylvania before?"

A short pause ensued. "Hmm . . . once when you were in grade school."

*No wonder I remember.*

"We came home early from that vacation, though. Got tired of all the people—not the Amish, but the tourists."

He smiled. "The place *is* hopping with sightseers, people dying for a glimpse of the horse-and-buggy folk."

"Well, speaking of dying, you be very careful, dear."

"Hey, did you find my birth certificate yet?"

"Still looking," she replied.

"I needed it weeks ago . . . will you put it at the top of your to-do list, please?" She agreed to.

"Good-bye. I'll call you next week," he said and hung up.

*Serial killers dumping bodies in Amish farmland? Give me a break!*

Louisa recalled instantly what it was that had first forged her friendship with Courtney back in middle school. This girl had magnetic draw. She wore a perpetual winning smile, and she could put a person at ease, make them laugh . . . even disarm them, if necessary. And she was doing it now, mingling, along with Louisa, meeting one cousin or friend of Annie's after another.

Louisa figured the boys were somewhat leery, having met one too many fancy girls clothed by the preacher's daughter. For this she was relieved, glad Courtney would have no interaction with Sam. *I'm off the hook*, she thought. But she wondered how it would go if she didn't end up riding home with Annie. Even so, she wouldn't worry away the night.

*Courtney will only be here for another day or so. . . .*

Some time later, two boys were brave enough to walk over and talk to Courtney, one blushing perfect circles of red on each cheek.

But when someone started playing a guitar, the talkative guy, one Annie quickly informed her was a cousin "once removed," asked Courtney if she wanted to join several other couples in the square. Courtney flashed a look that said, "What're we waiting for?" and followed willingly. Surprised, Louisa would've lost her socks, that is, if she weren't wearing heavy black hose.

Just then Louisa saw Sam making his way through the crowd toward her. She willed herself to breathe, more than happy to see Courtney so well occupied.

"Hullo, Louisa . . . you're way over here? And why's that?" he asked, smiling down at her.

She looked for Annie, who had suddenly disappeared. "I, well . . . Annie and I brought along a guest."

"The made-up girl?" asked Sam, his eyes still on her. "Not from round here, that's certain."

Louisa shook her head. "You're right about that."

Sam did not turn to look at the couples, nor did he show any more interest in asking about Courtney. He leaned near and whispered, "Would ya like to square dance with me?"

Pausing, she wondered if this was such a good idea. *Why did I show up here?*

She felt almost shy as he stood beside her, the sleeve of his white dress shirt brushing against her arm.

*Would Sam be this interesting if he were dressed like any modern guy?* she wondered.

Even so, she did not step away from him, wondering what to do with her feelings.

Then, when the music stopped and more couples joined in, the blond teenage boy caller hoisted himself onto a square bale of hay and announced, "Stir the Bucket," which brought a big round of applause and a few hoots from the boys.

"Now's our turn," Sam said, reaching for her hand. "All right?"

She lifted her hand, surprised how his touch made her blush. *Does he notice?*

Her heart complicated things, too, doing a weird sort of beat. *I can't let this happen.* Even so, she was walking with him, in step, following.

*What'll Courtney say if she sees me?*

Just that quickly, Sam let go, and she got in the line with the other girls. She wanted to shield her hand in her dress pocket, wanting to remember the feel of her hand in his at least for the rest of the evening.

The guitar strumming started again and the caller began the intros with a bit of patter chatter. He called the corner folk to come up to the middle and then back to their places, called "home."

Someone hollered, "Swing your own, 'n' leave mine alone!" which was followed by a long string of Dutch and a burst of laughter by the group.

*Yee-haw,* thought Louisa, glancing up the line and noticing Courtney doing the do-si-do with her own Amish partner. *Too funny! Who would've thought?*

When it was time to meet Sam, lined up across from her with the other guys, she smiled freely, wondering if he might hold her hand again tonight, and not just during the barn dance.

Shaking off the thought, she realized what a fool she was. *What am I thinking?*

After learning many new square dance moves, Louisa and Sam sat side by side in his enclosed carriage. Sam did much of the talking, for some reason wanting to explain that many of the more settled, baptized young men were no longer buying open buggies for courting. They were purchasing the enclosed gray buggies, skipping over the reckless time of youth, planning for their future as husbands and fathers. But he made it clear to her that he had no plans to join the church.

It was as if her reluctance to say much encouraged him to fill in the gaps.

And talk he did. So much so that Louisa wondered if he talked the ears off other girls. Well, other *Amish* girls.

But there was a side to him she found incredibly appealing. The way he drew her into his private circle, his sphere of reality. And when she talked of her family living in Colorado, he wanted to know as much about them as she would share. Unlike Trey Douglas, who, though he continued to send email, did not seem to take much pleasure in her family-related remarks. As for Michael, the only one of her relatives *he'd* shown much interest in, besides her, of course, was her father.

But Sam's focus was nearly entirely on family—his ancestry, the present family tree, and the all-important future one. Yet she wasn't put off by his attempts to woo her, as she clearly knew he was doing. Or trying to.

*Would Annie be freaked if she knew?*

Maybe Annie did know. And maybe she wasn't saying much because she was crossing her fingers . . . as Sam might be, as well.

"That's one fancy friend you've got," he said, sitting on the driver's side. "Courtney sure doesn't look as Plain as you do."

She hoped that was a compliment.

"*Auslenner*, she is," he continued, "decidedly so."

"Uh, back up, Sam."

"Ach, there I go forgettin' you don't know Dutch." He took off his hat. "Your friend's a foreigner. Doesn't much fit in here."

*And I do? Now, that's scary.*

"Well, about now, I think Courtney might be really ticked off at me," she admitted.

"Courtney's upset 'cause I brought you home?" Sam asked. "She and Annie got stuck riding back to Zooks' with Omar and his girl? Is that it?"

She laughed, breathing in the cold air. *That and more.* "Yeah, I'll catch it tomorrow."

"Why's she visiting, anyway?" he asked.

*I wonder, too.*

He smiled. "She's not comin' to talk you into returnin' home, is she?"

Louisa thought she noticed a worried look flicker across his face. "She wants to connect. We haven't stayed in touch much since I came here."

He leaned back in the seat, reins in only one hand. "Why'd *you* come to Amish country?" he asked.

She hadn't told anyone how close she had always felt to Annie, having been pen pals for so many years. She wondered if she ought to tell Sam—test his loyalty. "If I told you something, would you keep it quiet?" She felt suddenly compelled to step out of her comfort zone.

"You've got a secret, I take it?" Sam looked at her curiously.

"Annie and I both do." She forged ahead, explaining their letter-writing relationship. "I'd always wondered what it might be like to spend time with my good friend." *There's so much more to it, but I won't bore him.*

"You weren't runnin' away from anything, then? Just wanted to see Annie in person?"

*Well, not entirely true. . . .*

"I craved a simpler life."

He was silent for a moment. Then he said, "A love gone sour?"

*Man—this guy's good!*

If she changed the subject quickly, Sam would know the truth. If she made up something, she'd be ticked at herself. "Maybe it's best not to talk about where I've been and who I was . . . back then."

*Back then? Who am I kidding?*

"Well, I know you live somewhere near Denver . . . and you were Louisa Stratford then, same as now." He looked at her with serious eyes. "But what're you hidin'?"

*Let it go already,* she wanted to say, but bit her tongue.

He reached for her gloved hand. "Your beau—your man—is he waiting for you to find your way? Is that why you're here for the time bein'?"

She shook her head. "No one's waiting. And I guess I could say I had lost my way. But not anymore."

"*Des gut,* then," he said too quickly. "That's just right fine with me."

*Yikes . . .* Louisa sat back against the seat as the realization hit her full force. *He's falling for me.*

# Chapter 6

On Monday morning, Courtney arrived early enough to join the Zooks for breakfast. Annie observed her reaction to Mamm's overflowing platters: eggs, bacon, and sausage, along with homemade waffles and cornmeal mush, all laid out in a neat row in the center of the table. Or maybe it was not the variety of food that caught *this* Englischer's attention. Still, Courtney's soft green eyes were wide with something that looked like wonder, and she had little to say during the meal, as if she had many more thoughts than words.

Omar and Yonie were exceedingly friendly, almost too much so, Annie thought, asking Courtney about Colorado weather and suchlike. Luke eyed Courtney suspiciously, though, and held back, as was his usual way.

*My brothers must wonder how many worldly women I'm going to invite into the house! Daed and Mamm must be wondering, too,* thought Annie, hoping Courtney's stay wouldn't ruffle too many feathers. Her arrival in Paradise had already raised Mamm's eyebrows, beginning with Courtney's staying at the B&B rather than at the Zooks' home. Still, Mamm had cordially welcomed Courtney this morning, though Annie noted her parents were not overly friendly. Even Mammi and Dawdi were quieter than usual.

Daed's stern words of rebuke were still floating in Annie's head. Goodness knows she was not interested in yet another straight talk from her father. In no uncertain terms Daed had let it be known that her sinning days were to be a thing of the past. And she felt his eyes on her too often.

*Six months is a long time to stay far from my art,* she thought. *But then, so is forever.* She contemplated the life vow she was expected to make to the church come next fall, feeling she had little choice as each day passed. She also knew that her promise to her father would be up in mid-July.

"Pass the bacon, Annie," Daed spoke up.

Quickly she reached for the large plate and passed it to her right, to Luke, who then handed it on. "Would ya like some sausage, too?" She leaned forward, able to see Daed sitting at his usual spot at the head of the table.

"Jah, sausage. *Es gut.*" Her father's gaze caught hers briefly. He wore his black work suspenders and a bright green shirt. "And more coffee, Mamm."

Her mother jumped to her feet. Courtney looked shocked, as if she'd never before seen a woman wait on a man.

*Well, won't she be surprised all round?*

Annie's thoughts flitted back to the first few weeks of Lou's visit, back last November when she'd arrived here in a yellow taxi cab. Late into the night, the first several weeks, they had whispered about the vast differences between the Plain life and the fancy. The role of husbands and wives being one of the bigger discussions, she recalled. According to Lou, worldly men often catered and even kowtowed to their women. And English women, more often than not, were eager to be the boss of the house. Eager, too, to run things in general. *The empowered female*, Lou had kept saying, as if that were the right way to do things.

Annie still found such a thing fascinating, although she had no way of relating to it, mainly because she'd only known one English fellow her whole life. Well, Cousin Irvin was English, too, but he was as conservative a Mennonite as there ever was, so he didn't really count.

But Cousin Irvin's tack shop employee and *her* new friend, Ben Martin, was mighty fancy. No question about that! Even so, Ben had shown no indication of such namby-pamby behavior toward her or Lou, who had often been on hand to witness the interaction between the Englischer and Annie. Lou had been a sort of safety net, but one that Annie was beginning to feel she no longer needed.

"More raspberry jam for anyone?" Mamm asked, reaching for the pint jar.

"I'll have some," Luke spoke up for the first time this meal.

Omar reached over, after Luke had scarcely dipped his table knife into the jam, and snatched it out of his hand.

"Ach, boys . . ." Mamm said, a twinkle in her eye.

"Say, here, we've got ourselves company." Daed's was a more serious tone.

Annie glanced at Courtney, her long and thick eyelashes blinking quickly as she observed the rather ordinary interplay between the boys. *Guess she's never seen homemade preserves, either,* Annie thought, trying not to smile too much.

"Please pass the raspberry jam," Courtney said suddenly.

Annie didn't think she'd ever heard anyone Amish say *please* at the table. Such a fancy sort of word it was, used by the English, which was maybe the reason the People didn't say it, as a rule of thumb. Was their snippy English guest trying to teach *them* manners?

To say they were much too far from home was not an exaggeration. Annie was still scratching her head, trying to figure out how Lou had managed to get Mamm to say Annie could go along to the Rockvale Square Outlet mall, with its 120-plus shops to choose from. *Sugar talk was part of it,* she realized. Goodness, but Lou had even talked Mamm into allowing Annie to skip eating at home so the three of them could go to a restaurant at noon. Annie enjoyed every minute of it, even though the place Lou chose ironically had been the same establishment where Rudy Esh had sometimes taken Annie during their long courtship. *Maybe it was a good thing for me to eat here again,* she thought, taking in everything around her, relieved and grateful she felt no remnants of sadness.

*Has Ben so completely captured my thoughts?*

She hurried to catch up with Lou and Courtney, who were eyeing a pair of blue jeans with an accompanying long-sleeved jacket. "One sweet-looking outfit," Courtney called it. Lou, on the other hand, seemed more interested in the pure white lace blouse beneath the jacket. For Annie, though, the pretty lace and the blue denim didn't go together.

*But what do I know about worldly clothes?* She wondered if the blending of the simple look of the jeans with the fancy lace was likewise how the outlet shoppers must be viewing her and Lou in their Amish dresses and shawls, with Courtney in her tight tan stretch pants and black leather jacket. *Like we somehow don't quite belong together.*

Once again, Ben came to mind. *Unequally yoked,* that's what she'd be if ever she were to give in and go on a date with him. It was as far from being Amish as the modern mannequin Courtney was now pointing to in the shop window. There was simply no middle ground.

"Hey, check out that cool sweater," Courtney said, her gaze on a bright yellow V-neck top.

Lou pulled her black shawl around her more closely, looking over at Annie as if to see how she was doing, exploring this too-modern environment.

"We can go into any store you wish," Annie offered. She did not want to stand in the way of Courtney's desire to *shop till she dropped.* Or Lou's, for that matter.

Annie had made up her mind to enjoy herself, even if it meant haphazardly showing the slightest interest in the modern clothing and whatnot. Even if it meant denying the images of color and design stirred up by surrounding herself with this aspect of the modern English world. Simply stepping foot into a store like Liz Claiborne Shoes was yet another factor in whetting her appetite. It did not serve to discourage her thoughts of worldly Ben either.

*I must hold fast to the Old Ways,* she told herself, following Lou and Courtney into the store. *As best as I can!*

Ben had decided first thing this morning he was going to brown bag it. He'd learned to pinch his pennies from his mom's endless, but gentle, lectures. Replaying last evening's phone conversation in his mind, he contemplated his mother's ability to hide her disappointment. During other conversations she had not been so successful, calling it "ridiculous" of him to leave home for an unknown locality. *She's resigned herself to my absence. . . .*

When the shop door jingled open, Ben scooted his turkey sandwich beneath the lip of the counter as a matter of course. Looking up, he saw Zeke. "Welcome, neighbor," Ben said.

"How's business?" Zeke nodded curtly, then removed his wide black hat. "Slow."

Zeke's golden brown hair was smashed down from his felt hat. He ran a big callused hand through his hair while glancing around the shop. "Anybody here but you?"

"Only the leather and me." Ben smiled, glad for the company. "Help you find something?"

"Well, s'pose I could go for a thick, juicy steak and some mashed potatoes and gravy 'bout now," Zeke said.

"Oh . . . you just missed the kitchen help. They're out for lunch." Ben laughed, and Zeke cracked a smile, unexpected for someone who seemed so hard-faced. But Ben had purposely set out to lighten things up between them.

"Thought I'd drop by, is all," Zeke said.

*A man lost among his own people,* Ben decided.

Appearing more at ease, Zeke went to sit near the long table where Ben laid out the harnesses for polishing. Zeke pulled out a small bag of pistachio nuts. "Care for any?" He held up the bag.

"I was just finishing my lunch here. But thanks." He thought it rather generous of Zeke and not in keeping with his harsh reputation.

"Thirsty?" Ben asked, returning the gesture. "I've got a case of Pepsi out back."

Zeke's brown eyes lit up as if Ben had offered him a tractor, church approved. "That would be right good," he replied, getting up and going to lean on the counter where Ben's simple lunch was hidden, laid out on the back of a folded paper bag.

Returning with a can of cold soda, Ben offered it to Zeke, thinking now he ought to have brought along a large thermos of hot black coffee instead.

Zeke continued to talk. "Our bishop—name's Andy Stoltzfus—and his great-grandson are neck and neck against two other fellas in a checker game to beat all games," he said. "You hear anything 'bout it?"

Ben wouldn't come right out and say Annie told him. "Yeah, someone mentioned it." He paused, observing this man who continued to exhibit all the signs of being a loner—or lonely. He didn't know which it was, though he knew full well that Zeke's wife and kids were still staying with Irvin and Julia.

"Well, there's not much goin' on this time of year, 'cept for mud sales . . . and a few checker games, like I said," Zeke said.

"Anyone play chess around here?"

"I do, but I shouldn't."

"Certain games aren't acceptable?"

Zeke's eyes grew suddenly darker. "In a manner of speaking, no. The fact that it's a war game . . . well, chess causes problems with some of the brethren. Same with playing cards in some of the more conservative circles. Most don't even know why it's forbidden. Just is." He walked across the shop to examine one of the larger harnesses.

"You mentioned mud sales. I'm curious about that."

Zeke turned and broke into a full grin. "Why, they're auctions—sometimes twenty or more auctioneers at once. Some on the back of hay wagons or flatbed trucks . . . some on a makeshift stage in a pole barn quilt room . . . and all to raise funds for our local volunteer fire companies. Last year's sale raised a whoppin' fifty thousand dollars." With a fleeting glimmer in his eye, Zeke continued. "Lots of them take place outdoors, under a big tent. The ground can get mighty squishy with mud durin' the spring thaw."

"So . . . that's how mud figures in." Ben laughed.

"If you ever go, I'd recommend you get yourself some old work boots." Eyeing the ones Ben had on, Zeke said, "Some that are a mite worse off than them there."

Ben smiled. "I'll keep that in mind."

"First big one's comin' up here 'fore too long. 'Bout two weeks from now, over in Honey Brook on Firehouse Lane. Heard it starts at eight-thirty sharp."

Ben was interested. "What things are auctioned?"

"Oh, just everything. Livestock, farm supplies and tools, sometimes brand spanking new pine staircases, rings of Lebanon bologna, manure spreaders—I've seen as many as seventy handmade birdhouses. But if it's the chicken corn soup you're after, go early, 'cause the four hundred gallons the womenfolk bring is usually half sold out by nine o'clock of a morning."

Ben detected Zeke's almost jovial change of attitude. "Next time you come, if you let me know when, I'll bring along some home-brewed coffee," he offered.

"All right." Zeke's mouth turned into another quick smile, then straightened again. "Do they have farm sales down where you hail from?"

"Thoroughbred auctions. I helped a lot at the county fairgrounds in Central City, every third Saturday. Quite a showing of tack, equipment, and fine horses . . . all to raise money to help locate stolen and missing horses."

"What kind of person steals a horse?"

Ben nodded. "I know . . . it's crazy."

Shaking his head and muttering under his breath, Zeke's otherwise ruddy face turned pale. "I daresay there are some wicked folk in this ol' world."

"Can't argue that," Ben said, looking up to see Preacher Zook pulling up to the side door with his horse and carriage. "We've got company."

Zeke spotted the preacher and immediately raised his hand to wave at Ben. "Best skedaddle," he said over his shoulder. "Be seein' ya!"

"*Hatyee*," Ben called.

Zeke turned suddenly, an odd smile on his face. "Ach, now, ya speak *Dietsch*?"

Ben was confused. "Why, what'd I say?"

"'So long.' That's what."

Ben shrugged it off. "Must've picked it up . . . working around all these Amish farmers."

"Jah, s'pose."

Ben waved again, watching as Zeke stopped to greet Jesse Zook before heading outside.

Ben inhaled deeply and stood as tall as he could, glad for the boots he wore today. "Hello, Preacher! What can I do for you?"

Jesse Zook made his way toward the counter. "Oh, I've come for two black hames and the rosettes." He glanced over his shoulder at Zeke. "Do ya often see Zeke round here?"

Ben had a strong feeling the preacher was checking up on Zeke. It wasn't his place to squeal on the man who seemed in need of a friend. "Oh, Zeke was just saying he's counting the days till the first mud sale."

"Oh, jah. That one's a doozy. You should go, just for the experience if you've never been."

Ben was glad for the preacher's seemingly genuine ease. "I think I just might."

Jesse seemed to mentally agree, although he appeared to be somewhat distracted. "What was it I said I was here for?"

"Hames, sir." Ben led the older man to the wooden boxes filled with hundreds of harness accessories.

Esther was much too nervous to meet with her husband alone, even though she was residing in the safety of Irvin and Julia Ranck's home. She had confided her greatest fears to Julia, expressing what a frightening thing it was to be so displaced. Julia kindly agreed that she and Irvin should definitely accompany Zeke upstairs to meet his newest daughter.

Twenty-day-old Essie Ann lay sleeping soundly in her arms. Esther made an attempt to will her heart not to beat so hard, gazing at her beautiful baby girl. "Your dat's comin' up here to meet ya," she whispered in the pink little ear. "He loves ya so. . . ."

Well, she was ever so sure Zeke did love their wee babe Essie—or would. She just didn't know for certain how much Zeke loved her. Not after raising a hand to her. Not after she'd run off to Rancks' to have his baby. Run off and never told Zeke where she could be found . . . secretly hoping he wouldn't find her at all. Yet he'd tracked her down all the same. Came right out looking for her at Julia's, after the horse went trotting over to Irvin's tack shop instead of heading on home the way she thought for sure it would. Had it not been for Ben Martin, Zeke might not have figured out where she and the children were staying for quite some time.

But now she was about to present little Essie Ann to him. The sound of voices downstairs put Esther on edge all the more. *Ach, my life might've been easier if I'd never gone to that first singing seven years ago. . . .*

Mamma had been hesitant about having her go that September evening, the first Sunday following Esther's sixteenth birthday, pleading with Dat to think hard about having their daughter stay home for a few more months . . . "till she's older." Worries plagued Mamma for a full week before the barn singing. "Seems a body ought to know when her daughter's ready to be out alone with

306

a boy nearly all night," Esther overheard her mother telling Dat. But Esther's father wouldn't hear of it. Sixteen was the "appropriate" age when such things were expected to take place. Tradition reigned.

Esther remembered fretting over what to wear and had ended up choosing her plum-colored cape dress, which her mother said made her blue eyes look even bluer, her "perty golden hair" fairer.

She met Ezekiel Hochstetler that night, a boy from Honey Brook, who some of the other youth whispered was "too far away from the Paradise church district to be included." Yet there he was, participating in the activities, along with the pairing up. Ezekiel took one long look at Esther and made it clear he had to have what he saw, and there was no turning back for either of them.

She let herself breathe deeply now, in and out slowly, so as not to awaken the little one who slept peacefully—*innocently*—on her lap.

*I must be calm. Must smile convincingly when I see Zeke again. Oh, dear Lord, I must.*

# Chapter 7

Louisa, Annie, and Courtney stopped at the food court for cookies and a warm soft pretzel at Auntie Anne's Café in the Rockvale Square Outlet mall. Annie was still waiting in line for some hot cocoa, not the smooth espresso mochas Louisa and Courtney had chosen. "We'll grab a table," Louisa told Annie, motioning for Courtney to join her.

On the way to the table, Courtney said, "I wasn't going to say anything, but I think you probably suspect it already."

"What're you talking about?" Louisa sat down.

Courtney's eyes were blinking too fast. "Let's see . . . how do I put this?"

"Just say it."

"I think you're too comfortable here. I mean, what are you *really* doing? Did you have to come to Amish country to run away?" Courtney's face was red, as if holding back a torrent of words.

"I came to see Annie . . . I'd always wanted to visit. And I really do feel settled here."

"Oh, that's just great. You want to become Amish?"

Louisa wished Courtney might have the courtesy to lower her voice, but instead Courtney continued loudly, "You couldn't keep your eyes off that Amish guy last night. What was that about?" Courtney raised her eyebrows. "You're not *really* interested in dating men like that, are you?"

"Like what? Honest, gentle, caring? Men like *that*?"

Shaking her head, Courtney opened a bag of chocolate chip cookies, obviously disgusted.

Louisa forced a smile. "Boy, Court. Why is this such a big deal to you?"

"It's not a big deal just to me, Louisa."

"What's that supposed to mean?"

In place of an answer, Courtney offered a gooey cookie instead. "Here, this will make you think more clearly."

Louisa tapped her cup. "It'll take more than chocolate to change my mind. Trust me." She glanced over to see Annie at the cash register. "Look, this conversation is really pointless."

Courtney stirred her mocha, staring into the cup. "I don't know who you are anymore."

"Well, I guess I don't recognize myself sometimes either." Louisa sighed. "But, to tell you the truth, I actually think I like *this* me better."

Courtney's face registered complete shock.

"For the record, I've found something here. Is that so hard to believe?"

Courtney smirked. "I figured it was just a phase." She chewed carefully, slowly. "But this is nuts. I mean, it's like you need to be deprogrammed or something." Courtney was still for a moment, but when she spoke, her tone had changed to pleading. "C'mon, Louisa. Put all this nonsense aside and come home with me. Your parents would be thrilled."

"No, thanks. I'm learning things . . . I have a long way to go. And I know you'll be shocked, but I'm actually very happy here."

Courtney wrinkled up her nose.

Louisa leaned her elbows on the table, fixing Courtney with a serious gaze. "Why'd you come, Court? To visit or to get me to return home?"

"I came to see you, of course. We've been friends for a long time." Courtney paused, then she said, "Besides that, Michael wants you home."

Louisa leaned back, sighing, squeezing her eyes shut. "So that's it."

Courtney smiled too sweetly. "The guy's still crazy about you."

"He asked you to bring me back?"

"Well, hey, what's so wrong with that?"

"I'll bet he paid for your ticket here, too."

"What if he did?"

Louisa rose and huffed her disgust, heading across the food court, her shoulders squared. She was sick of defending herself to someone who should have understood her.

Annie headed to the table, wondering why Lou had rushed off . . . and where she was going. She sat down with her hot cocoa, glancing toward Courtney. "Louisa's upset?"

Courtney pushed her hair behind her ear. "She's a lot of things right now, I think. Probably offended, too."

Annie suspected Courtney had set Lou off somehow. But she refused to give way to her own anger over this worldly woman's glaring disapproval of Lou. The Good Book said: *The tongue of the wise useth knowledge aright: but the mouth of fools poureth out foolishness.* "It can be an awful frightening thing to lose yourself in the darkness," Annie said softly.

"What do you mean?" Courtney asked, her eyes hard on Annie.

Gathering her wits, Annie continued, "I recall a long-ago sermon my father gave . . . about letting yourself listen to the silence around you—getting in a place where you can actually hear yourself think, ya know? And, well, letting the Lord God make us—each one—into a servant."

"Please," muttered Courtney.

*She's mocking me.*

"No, now listen. Louisa was losing herself in the busy world. She came looking for peace, to make sense of her life." Annie paused. "Guess you might be needin' some of that, too?"

Courtney shrugged and pushed her chair out. "Later," she said, heading off to look for Lou, most likely.

"Something I said?" Annie whispered to herself. She gathered up the refuse on their table and carried it to the trash container.

Esther was aware of Zeke's dark eyes on her as he held their baby daughter. She trembled despite Irvin's and Julia's presence in the small attic room, transformed into a bedroom for her children—six-year-old Laura, three-year-old Zach, two-year-old John, baby Essie—and herself.

"Such a sweetie pie she is." Julia broke the silence, her light brown hair swept back beneath the cup-shaped prayer covering of white netting.

"Jah" was all Zeke said, still creating concern in Esther as he looked from the baby and back to her, meeting her eyes with disdain.

*I've spurned him. . . .*

"The Lord is so good to bless us with another healthy child," she managed to say, linking herself once again to her precious Savior.

Julia came and sat next to Esther, and Esther welcomed her nearness.

"Essie's a droopy one today," Esther whispered, scarcely able to think of anything except that her husband was terribly displeased with her. Not for birthing such a pretty baby, no . . . but for saying she was "saved" and a follower of the Lord Jesus, the reason for her recent temporary shunning. And for running off as she had three weeks ago, leaving him to fend for himself alone without even his children to comfort him with their laughter.

*He must despise me for it.*

Irvin glanced at Julia, an apprehensive look in his blue eyes. "When would be a good time for Zeke to visit again, Esther?" he asked, reaching for his wife's hand.

Esther made the mistake of looking at Zeke, who was already shaking his head in disgust and walking to the window with the baby. *He's ever so angry. But he's always that. . . .*

"I want my wife to return home," Zeke said, his back to them, his feet planted firmly apart. He was breathing hard.

Irvin stood quickly. "We have an agreement on that, Ezekiel. You and I, together, will decide when that's a good idea. And we both know now's not the time."

Zeke turned to face them, still cradling Essie Ann in the crook of his big arm. "Esther's my wife. I say what she does . . . where she lives."

Now Julia rose to stand beside Irvin. "Zeke, please, not with the baby near."

It must have been Julia's gentle way, but Zeke relinquished Essie Ann, who was still sleeping in spite of her father's booming voice. Esther felt herself sigh, glad her husband would be seen out by Irvin—and right quick.

Without even taking time to say good-bye, Zeke followed Irvin to the door.

Esther heard the loud clumping of feet on the stairs, and she waited to speak to Julia, who went to her and held her near. "Oh, Julia . . ." she sobbed. "How can I ever go back to him?"

"You won't . . . not unless he proves himself to be kind and loving. Irvin will see to it."

Esther choked back her tears, for her baby's sake, shaking her head. "There was a time when Zeke was good to me." She sniffled and rose to put the baby in the cradle across the room. "He loved me then."

"Dear Esther, you mustn't say that." Julia stayed seated. "He loves you now. Surely he does."

*Love suffereth long, and is kind . . . love envieth not . . . doth not behave itself unseemly . . . is not easily provoked. . . .*

"Well, doesn't seem so," Esther whispered. "Hasn't for ever so long."

"Trust the Lord that Irvin will minister compassion and help to Zeke, for now," said Julia.

"Jah, I need to trust more." But it was terribly hard when she knew what was in store for her should she succumb to her husband's demands and return to the farmhouse where Zeke now lived alone. A home where first-grader Laura, as well as Zach and little John, would be at the mercy of their father's quick and fierce temper. *And now poor infant Essie Ann, too. . . .*

She recalled the heart-wrenching times when Zeke had yanked their Laura into the pitch black belly of the cellar as punishment for not completing a chore quickly enough. Esther had heard the fearful sobs, knowing too well her little girl was sitting on the tip-top step, her body pressed against the door, no doubt leaning down toward the sliver of light beneath it.

Esther, too, had longed for a thread of hope, when first she'd married Zeke and dared to disobey him herself. Her heart had pounded so forcefully she'd scarcely been able to breathe. *Sent to the blackness,* she remembered with a shudder. *As black as Zeke himself.*

When Annie finally found Lou outside, Courtney was nowhere in sight. "She's off to do some more shopping," Lou explained. "Good riddance, I say. She only came to talk me into coming home. I should've known."

"I'm sure she means well," Annie said.

"But, get this—Michael paid for her to come here. She came at his request."

"Even so . . ." Annie wanted to help. "Wouldn't you want to patch things up with her?"

"What's to patch? She basically said I'm insane to stay here. She has no right to say that."

Annie pondered that. "Jah, maybe so."

Lou looked at her. "Maybe?"

"Well, I daresay all three of us need to separate for a bit." Annie didn't know what else to say. It appeared that Lou was terribly upset at everyone and everything.

"You're right. I think I need to cool off," Lou said. "How will you get home, though?"

"Oh, I'll just call one of our drivers at a pay phone. No problem at all." Annie waved to her. "I'll see you back at the house later on."

"All right." Lou's smile was a thin one.

*She's hurt,* Annie realized, wondering if Courtney really *had* come only to talk Lou into going home. She found it surprising that a modern woman would let a man pay her way, especially one she wasn't related to.

Annie hated leaving her friend there like that, alone and in a right fancy world looking ever so Plain. All the same, she set out walking across the vast parking lot and finally came to the edge of the sidewalk, shivering against the cold and waiting for the light to turn on the busy road.

*Honestly, did Courtney think she could get Lou to return to Colorado by being rude?* Annie couldn't help wondering how close Lou really was to her modern friend.

She pondered Lou's decision to go their separate ways just now as she stood waiting at the pedestrian light. Wondering why it was taking so long, she felt suddenly self-conscious, just as she often did while tending her family's market stand. So many staring faces. She not only felt terribly out of place, but she was freezing.

Suddenly she heard her name rising up over the din of the traffic—"Annie Zook!"

*Am I hearing things?*

Startled, she turned in the direction of the voice and saw Ben Martin waving to her from his car. "Stay right there, Annie," he called and motioned that he would park his car.

She couldn't believe it. How on earth had he found her?

"I mustn't let him persuade me to ride," she said beneath her breath. Yet she wanted to. All the good sense she'd inherited from her Mamm and Daed . . . where was it now? What was she to do in this crucial moment?

But she surprised herself and did as Ben requested, standing there as the light changed. *Er hot mich yuscht fer en Narr ghalde?* "Is he making a fool of me?" she whispered.

*Well, I won't listen to him,* she told herself, wishing she had already crossed when the light changed. But then, wasn't that downright rude?

Groaning inwardly, she grimaced, upset to no end.

"Annie! What are you doing all this way from home?" Ben asked, running toward her now.

She waited till he was closer so as not to raise her voice. "I've been out shopping," she said. "I came with Lou and her friend Courtney—mainly so Lou wouldn't be alone with her Amish dress, ya know."

His eyes searched her face, but she dared not look at him directly. She was much too drawn to this fine and fancy fellow.

"You're not going to walk home, I hope. It's a long way . . . and much too busy a highway, and . . ." He stopped short of saying she'd stick out the way she looked, but his kind intent was evident.

*He's worried for me . . . wants to take care that I get home all right.* And because of this and so many other wonderful things about him, she agreed to ride in his car. "As long as we go straight there," she told him.

She did something she'd promised herself she would never ever do. She let Ben walk her to his car, open the door, and wait till she got settled into the passenger seat. Then he hurried around the car to his own side.

With a contagious smile, he pressed the key into the ignition and the car roared to a start. Annie would not stare, but she was terribly aware that his hand was resting on the gearshift between them, ever so near. . . .

# Chapter 8

Out running an errand after lunch, Ben's heart had nearly stopped when he saw Annie Zook alone near the outlet mall.

*Unbelievable*, he thought. *I must be living right.*

Now here she sat in his car, gripping the armrest as they rode toward the countryside.

"I hope this won't cause a problem for you," he said.

"You drivin' me, ya mean?"

"It won't, will it?"

"Only if someone sees us."

He liked her quick comeback. She pulled no punches, this girl. "Okay . . . just let me know where you want to be dropped off, okay?"

She nodded, keeping her eyes forward, watching the road.

"Is this typical winter weather?" he asked, then cringed at how lame that must have sounded.

She responded politely to his inquiry. "Jah, I'd say so."

When that attempt at conversation fizzled, he was tempted to ask what she knew of the old covered bridge. Was it considered haunted, perhaps? Stranger things had happened. He *had* sensed something there. Maybe from his family's vacation years ago?

Here next to him was a beautiful, smart young woman with a lifetime of knowledge about the area.

*Why not ask her?*

He deliberated without bringing it or anything else up, which he viewed

315

as an outrageous squandering of time, especially since he had been hoping for this very thing: a chance to be alone with Annie.

He turned his full attention to her. "Do you ever go to mud sales?"

She looked at him. "Most everyone does round here."

He mentioned his conversation with Zeke, that he hadn't known of such sales before coming here.

Then they lapsed into awkward silence, terribly aware of each other. Or, at least, he was of her.

Turning off Route 30, he knew the time remaining was relatively short. Inwardly he fidgeted, determined to make this serendipitous meeting count for something.

But before he could open his mouth and shove in another foot, Annie spoke up. "Julia says you've been spending time over there . . . several evenings a week."

*Perfect*, he thought, wondering what other things Julia had told Annie. "Yes, they invite me for supper sometimes. Julia is a fantastic cook, so how can I resist? And those kids of theirs are great fun, aren't they? So are Esther Hochstetler's children. That Laura's a real talkative little gal."

Annie brightened and seemed to relax at the mention of the little ones. "James keeps me laughin' nearly all the time when I clean house at the Rancks'. He says the funniest things, and dear Molly . . . well, she's just a darling two-year-old."

"Takes after her mother, I think."

Annie agreed. "Cousin Julia has the sweetest spirit 'bout her." She looked out the window. "Wonder if it has something to do with her . . . uh, faith," she added.

He found this fascinating. "Why would you say that?"

"Well, Julia—and Irvin, too—seem to think they have a corner on God."

"Maybe not just a corner . . . more like the whole deal," he said.

She looked at him suddenly, her heart-stopping azure eyes wide at his quick comment. "Jah, and just why is it some folk claim to have a full grasp of the Bible and the teachings of God's Son, while the rest of us seem so lost?"

"Lost? But your father's a preacher . . . isn't he?"

She blushed as if he'd caught her in a lie. "Jah, and of course I've learned plenty from Daed at Preaching. I'm hopin' to be taught the High German, too, so I can understand more of the Scripture readings. Still, Julia seems to know so much. . . ."

"Do you mean to say the Bible is read in a language only a few of the People comprehend?" He found this incredible.

"It's always been thataway. Our sacred tongue is German."

This was not the direction Ben wished their discussion to take, and he purposely slowed the car. There were other more intriguing subjects, at least for him, but their time together was running out. If he was going to make the link to a future meeting he *must* pay attention and talk about the things of interest to Annie.

He recalled Zeke mentioning High German during one of their initial conversations. "Say, Annie, how well do you know Zeke Hochstetler?"

"He's my best friend's husband. I've known him since Essie, I mean Esther, first met him," Annie said. "He's a hardworkin' farmer—raises pigs."

"He's a curious fellow, but I like him. A man of few words, though. He drops by the harness shop quite often."

"Nice of you to spend time with him."

*As if no one else wants to?* Ben considered.

Annie offered no more about Zeke. And Ben guessed he shouldn't ask why Esther and her children were staying at the Rancks', suspecting a good enough reason.

Glancing at Annie, he gripped the steering wheel. But Annie held his gaze now, too, and it was all he could do not to simply stare back at the most engaging girl he'd ever known. Pretty and innocent all rolled into one unique package.

The silence was thick.

At last, he said, "What do you know about the covered bridges in the area?" He knew he should've been more specific.

"Which ones?" she asked.

"The long red one, over on Belmont Road."

"Well, I know plenty. What do you want to know?"

Here they were already traveling the road leading to Annie's father's house. Should he pull over? If she protested, then he would continue on. But if she said nothing, he would buy himself extra minutes.

Tremendously aware of her presence, he raised his hand from the gearshift and let it come to rest at two o'clock on the steering wheel, turning off the road slowly. When the car rolled to a stop and she did not speak up, he believed he had not offended her.

"Did something, well, out of the ordinary occur there?" he asked.

"I didn't know for certain just what all the upheaval in the community was 'bout that bridge—not when I was little, I mean."

"Do you mean something bad happened?"

She nodded slowly.

Had he stumbled onto a painful topic? Had there been an accident here or . . . worse?

"Can you tell me more?" He turned to face her.

She sighed heavily, as if the telling were too difficult. "I best not say more."

"Sure, Annie. I understand," he said. But he didn't.

Then she surprised him and reached for the handle. There were tears on her face as she opened the door and stepped out.

*What have I done?*

Leaping out of the car, he hurried to catch up with her, stumbling through the remnants of snow and slush. "Annie . . . wait!"

She kept walking, fast. Not looking back, she slipped and nearly lost her balance several times.

"Annie . . . I didn't mean to—"

"*Nee*, no, it's not your fault." She stopped to look at him. "I never should've told you a thing. It was ever so wrong of me."

*Exactly what did she say?* He still was perplexed. Reaching out, he touched her black shawl. "I'm sorry, Annie. Whatever I asked about that bridge . . . I would never want to hurt you."

She looked at the ground, eyes downcast. "I don't know why it still pains me so."

*What does?* He refused to ask. His curiosity had done more than enough damage.

"Please, let me take you all the way home. It's too cold for you to walk. Too dangerous." Fact was, it was bitterly cold now and the sun was sinking fast.

He reached out to her yet again, hoping she might understand the gesture as merely an offer of apology.

But she surprised him when she accepted his help, her small mittened hand slipping into his own. "I really shouldn't, but . . ." She stopped midsentence, then began to walk with him toward the car, still clinging to his hand as they picked their way back through the frozen muck.

"Hold tight, Annie," he said. "I won't let you fall."

She gasped lightly, stopped walking, and stared at him. "What?"

Startled, he asked, "What's wrong?"

She looked confused but seemed to shake it off. "Oh, nothing, Ben. Just a trick of my imagination, prob'ly."

He smiled, hoping his fondness for her wasn't too obvious. "It's icy, that's all."

Her eyes were fixed on him again, as if she hadn't heard, as if she were suddenly deaf. A frown shimmered on her brow, and she blinked back tears.

*What's with this girl?*

"Come, let's get you home," he said.

# Chapter 9

Once Ben had gotten her safely back into the car, he drove Annie closer to her house. She thanked him warmly for the ride and waved good-bye before heading up the road toward the turnoff to the driveway. She was glad Ben had agreed to let her out some distance from her house. *No sense worrying Mamm or anyone who might be observing.*

Confusing as it was, she would not erase her memory of having spent this forbidden time with Ben. She refused to berate herself and deliberately kept looking forward as she walked, even when she heard Ben calling to her.

He called again, and lest she be as rude as Lou's Denver friend, she turned around. Ben had gotten out of his car again and was motioning to her. "What is it?" she asked, her heart leaping.

"Annie . . . would it be possible for me to take you to dinner sometime . . . say, this Friday night?"

Oh, she wanted to accept, but first she must calm her breathing. "Well . . . I . . ."

"We could meet at a restaurant if that would suit you better," he offered quickly.

She shook her head, sighing, unable to control how she felt. *Oh, this is just so hard!*

He stood there looking at her, waiting for her answer. "Or I could meet you—anywhere you say."

*No, I shouldn't . . . I can't.*

He stepped toward her, eyes bright with hope.

*I'll regret it if I agree*, she thought, *I just know it*. But she surprised herself and said, "Well, I 'spose just once, maybe."

His handsome face lit up like a streetlight. "Where, Annie?" he asked.

"Up the road a ways, but wait till after dusk," she said. "Is that all right?"

He was nodding his head to beat the band. "That's perfect. I'll see you Friday!" Then, turning, he hurried back to his car.

Annie headed toward her father's house, willing herself to slow her pace. She mustn't slip and fall flat on her face here in the road with Ben watching, no doubt, as he drove past. And she would not second-guess this most peculiar situation to death. Still, it *was* a terribly dangerous place to put herself, seeing him again.

She sighed, wondering what would happen if ever someone were to see her with Ben. She'd had every intention of taking baptismal instruction next May. Now, though, nearly everything was topsy-turvy in her head. Not that she would go back on her word about her art, but Ben Martin certainly had not been a part of the handshake agreement with her father. She'd never considered him at all in the promises she'd made. And yet, how could she possibly prepare for becoming a member of the church now?

*Ach, the wonderful-good feel of my hand in his!*

Hurrying toward the house, she noticed the spot where the scarecrow had been but was no longer. *What the world happened to it?* She scanned the area, knowing for absolute certain it had been standing right there where she was looking . . . at the edge of the garden. Had the wind blown it down? But there had been no fierce gales recently. The thought that someone had come in the night and carried it off, the way some farm tools were known to disappear, bothered her terribly. She could not understand why she felt so traumatized when things seemingly walked off and were never returned. To assume certain things were permanent fixtures—such as the scarecrow she and her younger brothers had constructed last spring—was clearly a mistake. She thought of Zeke, poor man. He must surely be experiencing similar feelings, what with his wife and children gone from the covering of his house. And yet, far as she was concerned, Esther's leaving was his own terrible fault. *Puh!* Zeke was not the kind of man *she* would ever care to marry.

Her thoughts leaped swiftly back to Ben, and she decided then and there he was nothing at all like Zeke Hochstetler. Of course, she would never know that for certain, because she would never let herself fall in love with an Englischer.

Making the turn around the side of the house, she heard one of her brothers calling from the back door. "Hullo, Annie! 'Bout time you got yourself home."

She looked up and there was Yonie, sporting a worldly haircut. *What on earth?* Her favorite brother looked just like the fancy city boys over at the outlet shops. "What's that ya did to yourself?" she said, heading up the steps.

"Got me a haircut, is all." He was grinning.

"What's Daed gonna say?"

"Nothin'."

"You'll catch a tongue-lashing. You'll see." She pushed past him and waited for him to close the storm door on the porch.

"I already talked to Daed. He didn't seem to mind."

"Well, he must be blind, then."

"Not blind neither. And thanks to the grapevine, he knows plenty about the car I bought."

"You did what?" She stared at him. "Well, little brother, what's come over you?"

"I'm havin' me a fine, gut time, that's what. I'll join church whenever I'm good and ready. Not before."

"And you're still seein' Dory Zimmerman," she said, flabbergasted. "Does our father know about *that?*"

"Not unless you broke your promise and told."

She shook her head. His ongoing relationship with the newspaper carrier's daughter wasn't for her to criticize. Still, she was miffed. "I did no such thing, Yonie. You know better than to accuse me thataway."

"Well, good."

She hung her shawl on the wall hook, then bent over to pull off her boots. "Seems to me there's a double standard round here," she muttered softly.

"What's that?"

"Just never you mind." Annie looked carefully at Yonie's hair cropped above his ears and parted on the side. She could not believe Daed had merely disregarded the deed. How could he not care one iota about Yonie looking as if he'd stepped out of a fancy barber shop like the one over in Strasburg, which was probably where he'd gone? And the even bigger issue—Yonie's having a car and brash enough to fess up to the preacher about it!

*Who does Yonie think he is?*

It wasn't what her brother had done that bothered her no end, it was Daed's reaction to it. That is, if Yonie was being straightforward.

She shook her head, truly perplexed.

*How is it I have to give up my drawing and painting, and my brother can own a car and drive it to court his worldly girlfriend? Something's awful wrong with this.*

She felt like blowing her stack and might have if Mamm hadn't called her to come and set the table for supper.

"You seen Yonie's hair?" she whispered to her mother after Yonie left the outer porch.

Mamm glanced at her. "Be careful not to judge, Annie."

"Judge? Well, look at him!"

"Oh, I've looked, believe me."

"And did you say anything to him? Did Daed?"

Her mother shook her head and raised her finger to her lips, intending to shush her. "Don't make a big stink out of this."

*Well, I'll see about that.*

"It's not one bit fair." She pushed the utensils onto the table.

"Sure, it ain't . . . but this is the way your father wants to handle it. So best be keepin' your nose out."

"So I'm guessin' being born a boy has more advantages," she muttered, hoping Mamm hadn't heard her once she'd let the careless words slip. Right this minute it was awful easy to ponder dear Esther's plight . . . her constantly being under the thumb of a hardhearted husband. *Jah, the difference between a man and a woman round here is altogether maddening!*

When she had finished helping in the kitchen, Annie rushed next door to the Dawdi Haus and upstairs to the bedroom she shared with Lou for the time being. She opened the door, cautious as always, since Lou's arrival had brought with it darling Muffin, the ever-smiling Russian Blue cat. "Kitty, kitty," she called, and he leaped off Lou's bed and came running to her.

She reached down to pick him up and carried him to the chair where she sat and petted him, talking softly the way she liked to do. "You sweet little thing. If all the barn kitties could see the special treatment you get just 'cause your fur is such a perty blue-gray, I'm sure they'd all be clawin' their way in here."

Muffin's elfin eyes alternated between half mast and squinted shut as he lay in her lap, his paws tucked under his plump little chest. His purring brought her a welcome sense of calm, even though she was not going to let the sun go down before talking things out with Daed. "Judgin' or not, I have to know what's what!"

Louisa found Courtney at the Gap outlet—one of Courtney's favorite stores—trying on a pair of jeans. Louisa recognized her black spiky-heeled boots visible beneath the dressing room door. "When you're finished, we need to talk," she said.

"Maybe you need to, but I'm done," Courtney answered through the door. "I'm leaving tomorrow night."

"Well, your mission wasn't accomplished, and you can tell Michael I said so."

"Actually," Courtney said, poking her face out, "to put it to you straight, I'm glad for Michael you didn't go through with the wedding."

"Well, that makes two of us," Louisa shot back. "Have a good trip home. And keep my name out of your conversations with your new boyfriend."

"What?"

"You heard me."

"No . . . that's where you're messed up, Louisa. He loves you. I promise you." *Promise all you want.*

"I've gotta get going," said Louisa. "If I don't see you before you leave, have a smooth flight. I know how bumpy things can get near Denver."

"Hey, that's the nicest thing you've said to me the whole visit."

*Yeah, maybe so.* Louisa hesitated, realizing she was probably right. "Well, then, good-bye."

With that Louisa hurried through the store toward the exit. *Now, to call a cab and catch up with my real friend.*

But before Louisa reached the door, a chenille sweater caught her eye. Christmas red. *Do I dare try it on?* Still upset over Courtney, she pulled it off the rack, removed it from the hanger, and went to find a mirror. Before coming to visit Annie, shopping often had a way of numbing life's disappointments for her. Maybe she needed a good dose of splurging right now.

Holding the sweater beneath her chin, she saw how perfect it was with her coloring. *Mother always said I looked splendid in red*, she thought, wondering why that memory had surfaced now.

*Oh, why not. I'll try it on.* But she wouldn't wear a red sweater here. Not after having dressed Plain for this long. She didn't want to offend Annie and her family.

Even so, she was mesmerized by the soft feel, the alluring color. *What would it be like to wear normal, modern clothing again?* she thought while heading to the dressing area. *Would I begin to crave more fancy attire? The finest clothes money can buy?* She sighed, feeling the old pull.

Returning to the back of the store, she saw Courtney standing in front of the three-way mirror, checking out her reflection in a pair of flared jeans and a plum leather jacket, price tags dangling. Courtney looked up and was obviously surprised to see her still there, let alone carrying the red sweater.

"Well, look at you," she scoffed. "Change your mind about being Amish?"

Louisa's cheeks suddenly felt warm.

"I thought you were heading out."

Louisa nodded. "I was."

"Hey, that would look chic over the cape part of your dress," Courtney taunted.

"Wouldn't it?" Louisa held it up for effect, feeling a bit catty herself.

A clerk appeared, looked her over—up and down—and frowned. "May I help you, miss?"

"Jah," Louisa said, then groaned.

Courtney rolled her eyes and wiggled her fingers in a mocking wave. "See you in the next life."

"Whatever that means."

Over her shoulder, Courtney called, "It means, plain Jane, that you're coming back as a full-fledged Englisher next time. I *hope*."

Louisa felt lousy. *This visit was a bomb from the get-go.*

"'Bye," she whispered, watching Courtney hurry back to her dressing booth.

Turning, Louisa spotted a mannequin with a lovely tan moleskin skirt and cream-colored blouse. "Nice," she said, hurrying to inspect it. *My suede boots would look so great with this!*

The same dumbfounded clerk asked if she needed assistance, and Louisa thought again of Courtney, still fuming. "I'll try on this outfit," she said. "Size two, please."

The clerk found the items and led Louisa back to the dressing rooms. Stopping outside the booth where Courtney's bare feet and hot pink toenails were now visible, Louisa paused, gathered her resolve, and said, "Hey, Court, I really want to apologize." She felt weird talking to the door.

The door opened and her friend grimaced.

"Look, I'm sorry," Louisa said. "Okay?"

"What for?" Courtney shrugged coolly. "You're following your heart, right?"

"But I hate this tension between us."

"So return to Denver with me. Make *everyone* happy."

"I can't do that."

Courtney scratched her head dramatically, then looked up. "Michael didn't want me to say anything . . . but since you're so stubborn, I guess I will anyway."

Louisa wasn't sure she wanted to hear about Michael.

Dressed now in her own clothing, Courtney led her to two waiting chairs in the common area and sat down. She patted the other for Louisa, who sat, too, her defenses rising again.

Courtney leaned close, pinning her with an intense gaze. "What if I told you Michael has decided not to partner at your father's law firm?"

Louisa swallowed. "He what?"

"He must love you a lot to give all that up. Don't you think?"

"No way he's walking from the firm."

"Don't be so sure. I think he wants to prove something to you in a big way."

"Then why didn't he want you to tell me?"

Courtney shook her head. "Maybe he wanted to say it himself. Remember, he wanted to fly out here? But you shut him down?"

"Courtney . . ." Louisa frowned. "Michael and I closed the door on our relationship . . . months ago."

Courtney stared at her. "He's a great guy, and putting it bluntly, you're nuts to ignore him."

"Sounds like you've gotten to know him pretty well since I've been here."

"All I'm saying is count your lucky stars that Michael's willing to give the whole thing another chance . . . after you left him, basically, standing at the altar."

"Hey, you know that's not true."

"I don't see you throwing away that kind of love, Louisa."

"Honestly, I doubt Michael and I ever really had the devoted kind of love two people should marry for. The 'in sickness, in health' kind," Louisa said. The image of Sam's gentle eyes crossed her mind before she could blink it away.

"This is the real world, not some fairy-tale romance. No love is perfect, right? But Michael loves you and you love him. Or at least you used to."

"Yeah, I used to do a lot of things, Court."

Now it was Courtney's turn to sigh loudly.

"Listen, I don't want you to leave like this." Louisa reached over and squeezed Courtney's arm. "You have one day left here. Let's make the most of it—do something fun together, just the two of us. I'll take you to this art gallery I know, then out for lunch at a Dutch smorgasbord. Okay with you?"

Courtney's eyes were sad, even defeated, but she smiled gamely. "Sounds good, Ms. Stratford . . . but you're buying."

# Chapter 10

Ben drove back to the harness shop where he found Irvin and another man negotiating a price on a new harness. Resuming his work, Ben checked the measurements for a custom miniature horse harness before cutting the leather.

He had never been awestruck by a girl before, and a Plain one at that. But Annie's personality was unlike any young woman he had dated. She was a peculiar yet appealing mix of beauty, naiveté, and spunk. She knew her mind and was rarely hesitant about speaking it, but only if she felt she was in a comfortable environment. Ben smiled to himself. *She's definitely become more at ease with me.*

Thinking ahead to the best choice of a restaurant for their first real date, he wondered how it would go . . . the two of them out together, and Annie vulnerable to the public eye. Inwardly he cringed at putting her at risk in any way and was contemplating rethinking where he might take her for supper when in walked Zeke Hochstetler.

"Ben, hullo again!"

Ben motioned him over to the large table where he worked. "What can I do for you?"

"Well, I came to ask Irvin if he could spare an hour or so," Zeke said, glancing over at Irvin and the farmer still haggling over cost. "Need some help mendin' a fence, and I mean that literally."

Ben smiled at his quip, though he found it curious that Zeke should drop by twice in one day. "I'd be happy to help with your fence," Ben volunteered. They both looked Irvin's way. "Looks like he might be tied up for a while, but I could get away once I'm done with this piece." Ben patted the dark leather.

"All right, then, I'll wait and take you over . . . then bring ya back."

Ben nodded in agreement.

Meanwhile, Zeke looked over at the wooden horses' heads of all different sizes along the shelf near the wall. He began to pace.

"Make yourself at home," said Ben.

"Don't mind if I do." Zeke wandered over to a chair and sat down. He pulled out a folded paper from inside his black work coat and began to read.

Nearly a half hour later, when Ben had completed his work, he went to speak to Zeke, who was dozing. Ben felt uncomfortable observing the man's chin and bushy beard leaning heavily on his chest. The tired-out farmer probably needed his forty winks more than Ben needed to wake him.

He thought of kind Esther . . . and how her husband was fending for himself these days, and he felt genuinely sorry for Zeke.

Ben and Zeke worked together to right the broken fence. The air was nippier than it had been earlier, even though the sun tried to peek through snow-laden clouds. Still, the exertion of sawing, toting lumber, and hammering kept Ben plenty warm.

When the job was complete and the fence was up and sturdy again, Zeke took him inside for some hot coffee. Dirty dishes were stacked in the kitchen sink, and Zeke apologized for the mess, saying he didn't know of any husband who kept a clean kitchen when the missus was away.

They sat and drank coffee, Zeke at the head of his table and Ben perched on the wooden bench. Zeke offered some sticky buns he'd gotten that morning from a "kindly neighbor," and Ben accepted, all the while thinking how terribly vacant this big old farmhouse seemed.

Later, on the way back to the harness shop, sitting under heavy lap robes, they rode near a cemetery, or as Zeke called it, "the People's burial ground." Ben was more interested in the interior of the fragile-looking coach, the Plexiglas windshield and the ultra-plain dashboard, than in an Amish graveyard.

Zeke held the reins as if it were second nature. He was clearly skilled in anticipating the signals, the slight nudges from man to beast and horse to driver that were their essential tool of connection. "Say now, what would ya think if we stopped off here for a minute?" Zeke asked, staring up at the fenced-in cemetery, set high on the hill.

"What's here?"

"I'd rather not be alone in doin' what I must." His voice had become a whisper, and the pink in his cheeks from the cold seemed to vanish.

Ben assented, though cemeteries made him feel on edge—always had.

Zeke turned toward him, the light slowly coming back into his brown eyes. "Been puttin' this off for too long, I daresay."

The horse slowed and the carriage came to a stop along the roadside. "I'm hardheaded, Ben, among other things," Zeke said. "I berated the brethren for the longest time . . . demanded to see where they buried my poor brother."

Ben wasn't sure he'd heard correctly. "Your *brother* died recently?"

"No . . . no. He was just a boy . . . his bones are buried back behind this here graveyard somewhere. Preacher Jesse and the bishop didn't even bother to give him a tombstone . . . nothin'."

Ben found this startling. "How did he die?"

"Not for certain on that."

"Wait now, you've lost me," Ben blurted. "Why are you only now going to see his grave?"

"You don't know the half . . . and it's too long a story, I fear." Zeke paused and said nothing for the longest time as they sat in the carriage. "I should never have uttered a word, and if you think twice 'bout telling anyone, well, I'll have your hide."

Ben bristled. "Who would I tell? And do you mean to say his death is a secret?"

"Jah, no one knows his remains were ever found. No one but two of the ministers, that is. And they intend to keep a lock on that." Zeke sighed loudly. "Up until last fall, I assumed he had been kidnapped. Then my memory of that night began to fade and nightmares began filling my sleep. I dreamed he fell into the hole I'd dug for his dead puppy dog . . . fell and hit his head. At least I think it was a dream. Then, lo and behold, if his bones weren't found buried in a farmer's field last year, not far from my own house."

Ben was speechless.

"None of this was ever reported . . . the kidnapping nor the death."

"Are you serious?"

"It's our way—*das Alt Gebrauch*—the old way. Jesse Zook wants nothing to do with the outside world. Wants to follow the bishop's orders on that . . . ev'ry jot and tittle." Zeke gave a nervous chuckle, then composed himself. "Only the Good Lord knows why I'm tellin' you."

Quickly, Ben asked, "How long ago was this?"

"My brother was only four, and I had just turned eight." Zeke's hand shook briefly. "Sixteen endless years . . ."

"Sorry, I don't mean to pry."

"No . . . no. Don't apologize." Zeke was seemingly composed and was pointing out the narrow road that led to the hillside cemetery. "It's quite an elevated area, this here graveyard, so I'd suggest ya hold on but good." Zeke reined the horse to the right and onto the path hardly distinguishable due to drifted snow. "We've had some buggies actually tip over on this stretch."

Ben grabbed hold of the seat and held on.

Ben and Zeke stood at the back of the cemetery near the fence, looking down at the snowfields below—the vast white valley dappled with farmhouses, barns, and silos.

*Like a picture on a calendar*, Ben thought, although the sky was a gray-and-white mixture, the sun deeply cloaked.

"I've come here for many a burial," Zeke was saying. "But my brother never got a proper one." He stared at the rows of small grave markers. "'Twas Preacher Zook himself who unearthed the bones he and the bishop buried round here somewhere."

"I don't get it. Why weren't you and your family notified immediately?" Ben felt this was incomprehensible.

"I was told privately . . . then warned to keep mum. See, it's like this: Most of the People thought my brother had been abducted. No one wanted to think he was dead. But I thought it. Something in my gut knew it." He reached into his pocket and pulled out a paisley kerchief and wiped his face. "I want the killer found . . . punished. Whoever it is."

"What's the hold-up?"

Zeke looked around. "I need to find the grave first, but with all this snow . . ." He began muttering nearly incoherently now, and Ben felt sorry for him. "What was it again?" Zeke whispered to himself, shaking his head. "Eight long steps and . . ."

Ben didn't know what to think. The guy had a weird streak Ben hadn't noticed before.

Zeke trudged past a gravestone and headed toward the opening in the cemetery fence. Ben followed him up the slope and into the wooded area. And if he wasn't mistaken, Zeke was counting to himself as he walked.

Soon Zeke called to him from the thicket of trees. "I should've known the snow would be too deep."

Ben appraised the area. "Your brother's buried up *here?*" He glanced back at the actual cemetery.

Zeke nodded and struggled to speak. "S'pose it seemed fitting . . . since he disappeared . . . or died . . . in a grove much like this." His chin trembled. "I threatened Preacher Jesse with goin' to the police months ago. . . ."

Neither spoke for a moment; then Zeke brightened and turned to place a hand on Ben's shoulder. "But you could do it."

Ben frowned. "Do what?"

"Report his death." Zeke's eyes glistened. "I won't rest till I get to the bottom of this. But I'm forbidden, so I'm askin' you to do it for me."

Ben became instantly uneasy. "I agree, the police should be notified, but why would they believe an outsider? They'd want to know where I heard this, and then wouldn't the ministers trace it back to you?"

Zeke shook his head. "Maybe, but it wouldn't matter. The bishop can't control what outsiders do." He clenched his fists and turned his face to the bleak sky. His words were spoken just above a whisper, in a strange and chanting tone. "As the Lord God is my witness, I will see this through."

Ben experienced a strange stirring in his chest, as if Zeke were making a covenant with God himself. Then silently they headed out of the woods to the waiting horse and buggy.

On the ride back, as Ben continued to hedge about getting involved, Zeke's mood turned fiercely dark—alarmingly so. He slapped the reins down on the horse's back sharply and began muttering and cursing under his breath.

Ben could hardly wait for the buggy ride to end.

When they reached the thin road leading to the tack shop, Zeke turned to Ben again. "Is that your answer, then? Or will you reconsider?"

Ben swallowed. "I need time to think."

Zeke nodded, averting his dark and brooding eyes. "Fair enough."

Annie found her father in the barn checking on the livestock, preparing to bed them down for the cold night ahead.

"Daed?" She walked toward him. "I best be gettin' something straight."

"What's that?"

"It's Yonie."

"Ah . . ." Daed frowned and straightened right quick. "You're upset 'bout his bobbed hair, I presume?"

"Well, aren't you?"

"Oh, he'll come around in time."

His response aggravated her.

"So, then, what's not at all good for the goose is just fine for the gander?"

"Aw, Annie . . . Annie."

"No, I'm serious, Daed. This is obvious favoritism, seems to me."

He leaned on his hay fork. "No one's favoring anyone. If ya think your sneaking round doing artwork is even close to what Yonie's done with his haircut, well, you're wrong on that. And I'll be the first one to say it!"

She wouldn't let him wound her. Not the way he'd done in the past with issues of the Ordnung. She could see the bias too clearly. Why couldn't he?

"Listen, Annie. Truth be told, Yonie's bob has nothing to do with our agreement, yours and mine."

She thought of Ben Martin suddenly. His inviting her to dinner, her accepting. It wouldn't matter one bit now if she kept her word on the art and failed in the unspoken rule about courtship with an outsider. She was in no man's land, she knew.

She spoke again, willing away the tightness in her throat. "It doesn't seem fair what you're lettin' Yonie get by with. You even know 'bout his car." She wouldn't break her vow to her brother and tell what she knew of his romantic attachment to worldly Dory, also an Englischer.

"You've said enough, daughter. You best be goin' inside now. Awful cold out."

Cold or not, she refused to return to the house. "I'm headin' for a walk," she declared.

"Oh, Annie. Go inside and warm yourself."

She shook her head. "If Yonie can do whatever he wants, then why can't I go for a walk in the snow and not be reprimanded?"

"Listen here! Yonie's a man . . . that's different."

Annie was aghast and too stunned to talk. But only for a time. The pressure inside her was building and she managed to control her voice. "I'm a woman, ya say? Jah, Daed. Seems there *is* a mighty big difference between what's allowed for any man and what's permitted me."

The thin veil between her and the reality of the world she lived in had been torn, and there was no mistaking what flamed in her father's eyes.

Annie made slow progress over the hardened snow and ice on her treacherous walk. She was on her own, and it felt good, especially while struggling with her father's words, which still darted through her mind like so many hornets on a springtime morning.

"Daed's partial to Yonie . . . to men in general," she spoke into the frigid air. "All the People are." She felt her face tighten with the clenching of her jaw. It was too cold to be out here walking, just as Daed had warned.

*I don't care . . . I need to vent my resentment so I don't burst out with something horrid!* Except she'd already talked disrespectfully to Daed, so it was too late to spare herself from that embarrassment. Now she ought to go and ask forgiveness for questioning the man of God.

*Yet how do I repent of something I'm not sorry for?*

She kept on, careful where she stepped. The snow had melted down to fox-deep in some places where the sun had shone two days ago. Now the cloud-blanketed sun receded quickly, making dusk even grayer than the dreary day had been. Working up a bit of a sweat, she stopped to catch her breath. Not wanting to get overheated and then catch her death of a cold, she pulled her wool work coat tight against herself, looking out over the expanse of farmland across the road. She watched as a cluster of brown mules romped together— *trying to keep warm, just as I am,* she thought. Their winter coats were as dark as the moles that burrowed in the meadow.

She began to walk again, toward the house this time. Thinking of the playful mules, she recalled the night their own mules had broken through a gate and taken off running down the road for a good long ways, gotten sidetracked from their flight, and disappeared into the woodlands high on the slope behind the People's cemetery. She, Yonie, Omar, and Luke had helped Daed by searching till the wee hours, taking two carriages and a pony cart and driving up and down the back roads, calling, looking . . . something akin to the night Isaac had gone missing, at least from what Mamm had told her. In the end, it was Yonie who had discovered the fresh mule dung near the turnoff to the cemetery road. She recalled the animals behaving as if untamed until rebridled, when they miraculously became Daed's own once again.

*Like Yonie will become one day?*

She had to laugh out loud. "Oh, jah. He'll run mighty wild. Maybe he won't ever allow himself to be haltered."

More sober now, Annie shivered in the cold.

*I should talk. Will I?*

# Chapter 11

Snow had been falling all night, and the henhouse roof was beginning to sag. Jesse Zook Jr. and Annie's next oldest brother, Christian, arrived at first light to help their father remove the heavy ice. Sarah Mae, Jesse Jr.'s wife, came along, too, with their preschool-age boys, Little Jesse, Richard, and Davy, in time to help Mamm fry up a whole batch of corn fritters for breakfast.

As always, Annie was overjoyed to see her sister-in-law and wondered why Christian's wife, Martha, hadn't accompanied him, as well. When she asked, her brother said Martha was "under the weather," and Annie suspected she might be expecting their third baby.

"Well, if Abner and Priscilla and their little ones were here, we'd have nearly the whole family," Annie said.

"We'll see everyone at Preachin'," Daed said.

Mamm agreed, waving at Dawdi and Mammi Zook as they made their way into the kitchen from the addition next door. Annie's grandparents sat at their appointed places at the long table, waiting for the hot meal to be served. Promptly, Mammi asked Louisa, "Where's that perty Courtney today?"

"She's getting ready to fly home this evening," Lou replied. "I think she's anxious to get back to Colorado."

"Jah, I s'pose," Annie said.

Sarah Mae carried a heavy platter to the table and set it down. That done, she got her stair-step boys washed up, with a little help from Annie, and then settled them onto the long bench on the window side of the table. "Some of the women are having a kitchen shower for Rudy and Susie Esh," Sarah Mae said softly, mainly to Annie.

It was their custom. After a couple married they spent each weekend at a different relative's home for the months following the wedding, in order to receive their wedding presents. And, in the case of a kitchen shower like the one being planned for Susie Esh, the womenfolk would bring enough canned goods and preserves to stock the young bride's cold cellar. Typically they would have thrown a large grocery shower by now, but with ongoing inclement weather and so many down with winter flu, they must have waited.

"That's real nice of you," Annie said, realizing again how happy she was for her former beau and his wife. "I'll be glad to come, if that's what you're askin'."

"Oh, would ya?" Sarah Mae's eyes lit up.

"Why, sure." Annie nodded. "I'll bring Lou along, too." Here she glanced at Louisa, who'd slipped in next to Annie's grandmother. "Would you want to?"

"Hmm . . . I don't have any canned goods to give," said Lou.

Sarah Mae smiled and tucked a napkin under her youngest boy's chin. "Ach, that's fine. Just come and have some hot cocoa and goodies . . . and wish the bride well."

*Wish her well . . .*

Annie pondered the before and after state of marriage for young women. Some seemed to blossom under the covering of their husbands, while others lost their smiles nearly immediately. *Like Esther did. . . .*

"There'll be good fellowship," Mamm added, which meant she'd overheard the conversation. "Louisa should go along for that reason alone."

"When is it?" asked Annie.

"This Friday afternoon," Sarah Mae said, sitting across the table.

"Friday?" Annie wished she hadn't asked at all, because now Lou was giving her a peculiar look. *I haven't even told Lou about my plans with Ben that night,* she thought. Still, she knew she'd have to fill her in sometime. Yet how would she ever get to Susie Esh's kitchen shower, back home, eat supper, redd up the kitchen, and then out the door in time to meet Ben at dusk?

"Not sure I can make it," Annie blurted, not wanting anyone to see the frustration in her eyes. Because she must not let on she was seeing a fellow outside the Fold. Furthermore, she would not, under any circumstances, let Ben down . . . at least not for someone else's kitchen shower!

Aware of her family's curious glances, Annie could hardly wait to get going to Julia's. Ironing would be piled high, and she was itching to get to work. Since this was Lou's last day with Courtney, maybe today would be a good time to chat with Esther. *I really need to!* Annie thought.

Annie felt glad when Louisa told her after breakfast that she was going to "connect with Courtney once more." Omar had evidently offered to take Lou over to the B&B where Courtney was staying.

"You sure she'll be up yet?" Annie asked, glancing at the clock shelf on the kitchen wall. It was not quite seven-thirty.

"I can only hope." Lou seemed discouraged.

"Well, surely things will go better now that you've settled your conflict." Annie didn't mean any harm, and by the look on Lou's face, she understood.

Lou gave Annie a quick hug. "Thanks for hanging in there."

"That's why we're good friends. We never quit hangin'." Annie laughed softly.

Omar stood at the back door, smiling and waiting. Lou waved. "I plan to take Courtney over to the art gallery."

"Oh, good idea," said Annie. "To show her your work?"

"That and we need some time to relax together. So I might not make it over to Julia's at all today."

"Have fun, and don't worry none," Annie said. "I've got plenty to keep me busy." *And Esther wants to talk privately.*

Lou smiled and headed for the back porch and out the door. Annie strolled to the window and watched her get into the carriage with Omar.

*Don't let Courtney talk you into going home, dear friend. . . .*

Louisa realized, as she rode in the buggy with Annie's younger brother, she was no longer the same person who had first come to Amish country. *Three months has changed me big time*, she thought, judging from her reaction to Courtney's attitude. *Was I ever like that?*

She knew she must have been very similar. Why else would someone like Courtney have appealed to her as a close friend? Truly, she did not have the down-home sort of friendliness exhibited here in the Plain community. Come to think of it, Louisa didn't recall ever connecting with Courtney as a soul mate. Not the way she did with Annie. *A best friend who helped me find myself. . . .*

Suddenly Louisa shivered. She was freezing, even though she'd worn the "worldly" red sweater over her slip and beneath her dress and apron. Like expensive long underwear.

Perhaps Omar had noticed her shiver, because he spoke up for the first time during the ride. "Another cold one, jah?"

She nodded, smiling. All of Annie's younger brothers had kept to themselves somewhat since her arrival.

"Enjoy the Sunday singings, then?" asked Omar.

Taken off guard, she shrugged, not sure how to answer. She couldn't know if Omar had seen her and Sam Glick leaving together following the barn singing and dance. She felt strange being asked about it. "Umm . . . do *you?*"

"Well, to be honest, I've only been goin' for a short time." He slapped the reins and the horse picked up the pace. "Turnin' sixteen is the big thing round here, I guess ya know."

She was waiting for him to say something about the pretty girls lined up on one side of the haymow, or at the long table, when the singing began. But he volunteered nothing.

"I'm still figuring out how the Amish community works," she said.

He chuckled, tilting back his black hat. "Seems to me an outsider might never understand."

"Being born into it is the key," she said softly, more to herself than to Omar.

That really got a laugh from him. "Don't see how anyone could up and join the People without feelin' like they've given up everything important to 'em."

She gleaned that fancy Englishers like her were viewed as putting a higher value on modern conveniences than the tranquility and simplicity Amish life offered.

She pulled the heavy coat she'd borrowed from Annie more tightly around her, wanting to agree with Omar. She wanted to tell him how amazingly hard it would be if she or anyone from the "outside" decided to abandon electricity forever, or the warmth of a car on a horribly cold day like this—the modern world as a whole. But she figured her thoughts were of no consequence to Omar Zook. They did get her thinking about the adoring gleam in Sam's eye, however.

*I must be careful not to hurt him . . . or me.*

The Maple Lane Farm B&B came into view as they made the turn. When she got out of the buggy, she looked up at Omar and said, "It was really nice of you to bring me. Thanks!"

He tipped his hat and beamed his appreciation. "See ya at supper, then?"

"Sure will." Waving, she wondered how it would feel to say her final good-byes to Annie, her family, and Sam . . . when the time came.

*I don't have to contemplate that now,* she told herself, heading up the walkway to the stately inn.

Later that morning at the Rancks', James and Molly helped Annie pick up the downstairs bedrooms. Four-year-old James kept talking about his "new chum, Ben Martin," and Annie wanted to ask the boy why he felt such a connection to the Englischer, but she merely listened.

When all the toys were stored and organized according to piece and color in the toy box made by their father, Annie dusted the furniture, shook out the braided rugs, dry mopped the hardwood floors, and made sure there were no cobwebs under the beds or dressers or dirt above the wide doorframes.

Julia was away from the house, assisting a young mother in childbirth, so Annie had not only her cleaning duties to attend to but babysitting besides. And since Esther's eldest, Laura, was off at the Amish schoolhouse not far from the Ranck home, Esther kept Zach and John busy cutting out snowflake designs at the kitchen table while the baby slept soundly in the borrowed cradle nearby.

Close to eleven o'clock, Annie stopped her cleaning and helped Esther make grilled cheese sandwiches and warmed up homemade beef barley soup from Julia's freezer.

It was after the meal, when the kitchen had been made spotless once again and the children were napping, that Annie sat at the table and talked with Esther as she nursed Essie Ann.

"Where's Louisa today?" Esther asked.

"With her friend Courtney."

Esther stroked her baby's cheek, looking down at the cute bundle. "Are you enjoyin' having Louisa here?"

"Sure. But some days I wonder if she's not awful homesick. Seein' Courtney again has made some things resurface, I'm thinkin'."

"I daresay it's been something of a culture shock for Louisa, jah?"

Annie smiled. "Oh, to say the least. But she's interested in experiencing our ways quite fully. I think she's done a right good job of blending in here."

"For now . . . jah."

"She's also quite curious about why we do what we do," Annie added.

"Well, sometimes I am, too." Esther smiled.

Annie assumed she meant the probationary shun placed on her for disregarding her responsibility to her husband. So far, there had been no indication that Esther could not fellowship with church members in good standing or others not yet baptized. "You doin' all right?" she asked. "What I mean is . . . do you know where you'll live next?"

"You're thinkin' I should go back to Zeke?"

Annie was hesitant to say one way or the other. "Might be wise to let the ministers have their say. . . ."

"Well, word has it I just need to pray more and be more submissive—then Zeke's temper will be quelled. But I know better, Annie." She stopped to lift her infant onto her shoulder.

"So Zeke's been gruff with you for a long time, then?"

"Ever so long."

"And it doesn't matter if you're completely obedient in every way?"

Esther shook her head, eyes tearing. "He has an affliction in his soul, is all I know."

"Isaac's kidnapping?"

"'Tis one heavy burden." Esther patted Essie Ann's tiny hump of a back, then continued. "But the great burden-bearer is the Lord Jesus, and I pray Zeke might see Christ in me. Somehow . . ."

"Well, who can *not* see how sweetly long-suffering you are?" *But she's always been that way,* thought Annie.

"I want to be consistently loving, I do."

"Well, Esther, I know the difference 'tween you and a tetchy woman." Annie thought again of her conversations with both Yonie and Daed. It didn't seem fair that the men in the community could get by with mistreating their wives, as Esther had indicated. The favoritism annoyed her terribly, but she was determined not to bring it up with Esther just now. Maybe never.

Esther settled her baby to her other breast and covered herself with a light blanket. "I found the Lord just in time," she said softly.

"What's that mean?" Annie honestly didn't know.

"God's Word—the Good Book—has become my very food. I was tired, no, actually weary of constantly remembering the sins I committed on a daily basis. Now I am trusting in the Lord's grace to forgive me of all my transgressions. I can rest in His mercy and love."

"*You* feel you need to be forgiven?" Annie was bewildered. "You don't mean not fulfilling your family duties, do ya?"

"I mean just everything. The little fibs I might be tempted to tell now and then, the anger that comes up in my throat and flies out my mouth . . . the animosity I feel building up in me each and ev'ry day . . . toward my husband 'specially."

"Really?"

"Him and others."

Annie couldn't even begin to think who the *others* were, but at this moment she was eager to resume her work for Julia. Truly, she did not want to prolong this conversation.

But Esther needed to talk, apparently, so Annie sat still, feeling ever so awkward.

"Zeke was never treated right as a youngster, you must surely know."

*Maybe that's the reason why he's so snippy with his own children*, Annie wondered.

"He was constantly belittled by his father," Esther said.

"After Isaac disappeared?"

"Jah. Even Zeke's mamma joined in, instilling the notion that the full blame of the kidnapping rested on Zeke's shoulders."

"Why on earth?"

"Because Zeke disobeyed his father and left the house to bury Isaac's puppy that night. He had been told not to go at all. He was bullheaded and took Isaac to witness the dog's burial."

Annie had heard bits and pieces of this account, but she had never observed such pity as was evident in Esther's face. "Do you believe it, too? That Zeke was punished by God for disobeying his father?"

"Oh, it's hard to say. And Zeke never speaks of that night—'cept in his sleep, that is. I know he's obsessed with his loss . . . and the fact that he believes Isaac is somehow watchin' over him, from on high."

"Well, it's not like Isaac's become an angel."

At Annie's mention of *angel*, Esther began to weep. "Zeke's had so many strikes against him, and here we are apart from each other. By my own doing."

"You felt you had a reason to leave—it was for your baby's sake. And now that Essie Ann's here, have you thought of goin' back?"

Esther sighed, brushing tears from her face. "Even if I were to return to Zeke, I wouldn't be allowed to share his bed. I'm a shunned woman, ya know."

"You mean you're going to keep on sayin' the prideful things—about salvation through grace 'n' all—that got all this started?"

"Are you askin' if I'm gonna hush up 'bout being saved in Jesus' name?" Esther stared into the milky blue eyes of her baby. "Well, no. I won't renounce my dear Savior. I wouldn't think of it, Annie."

*She'll accept what she cannot see over what she can . . . over Zeke and the church?*

"I best keep my opinion to myself," Annie whispered.

Esther reached out a hand. "You don't have to be put out."

"I guess I am in some ways . . . you're making a decision I doubt I could ever make. Or stick by."

"To open up your heart to the Lord?"

"If you must put it that way."

Esther did not attempt to persuade her otherwise. "It is a hard path . . . the one the church has set forth. We must come to our own fork in the road, and find God's Son waitin' there."

Annie squeezed her hand and released it. "I can tell you've been livin' here with Julia these days . . . hearing all her blood-of-Jesus talk."

"But I'm ever so happy, strange as that must sound, even with my future hangin' in the balance." Esther straightened and looked at her. "Maybe I'm speakin' out of turn, but I see a sad sort of look in your eyes when you hold Essie Ann near. And I can't help but wonder if you might not be longing to be a mother yourself . . . someday."

Annie quickly changed the subject . . . to the attic, where Irvin and Julia had made a special place for Esther and the children to sleep. She missed it terribly—*my former art studio.* Yet just entertaining the thought of working up there again was not acceptable. No matter, she asked Esther, "How do you like your little bedroom up yonder?"

"Well, it gets a bit chilly at times, but we sleep with lots of quilts and cov-ers . . . and I even put Essie Ann in with me. It's not the best setup, but we're all together and that's what counts."

"Except for Zeke," Annie said.

"Still, I can't just rush back to his arms, Irvin has said. Julia says so, too."

Annie gave her friend a concerned look. "Cousin Irvin's not settin' out to convert your husband, too, I hope."

Esther's smile grew. "Oh, that would be just wonderful-good, I'm thinkin'."

"No . . . no. You'd both be shunned."

Esther nodded. "I'm not taking my heart back."

"Sounds mighty odd . . . like you're in love or something."

"Well, I surely am, Annie. I've fallen in love with my precious Lord Jesus."

*No wonder the brethren slapped the* Bann *on her. . . .*

Annie rose and excused herself. "I'll leave you be for now. Must complete things round here before Julia returns and finds me shirking, ya know."

"I'm glad we could talk frank like this, Annie."

Annie wasn't about to lie. In some ways she was sorry she'd ever sat down and listened to Esther go on so. It made little sense to her . . . and the last thing Annie wanted was to get caught up in Esther's zeal for a personal God and whatnot all.

After the cab dropped them off at the art gallery, Louisa introduced Court-ney to Eileen Sauder, the owner, who had shown such interest in Louisa's work. Then, strolling about the corridor, Louisa pointed out her paintings to Courtney among the various framed oils and watercolors on display. Louisa made every effort to be cheerful and to solidify her apology. Courtney, too, seemed to be on her best behavior.

"Here's one of my first Lancaster paintings," she said, pausing in front of an autumnal landscape. "I'm mesmerized by the barns around here, the rolling countryside."

"Nice," Courtney acknowledged, and they moved to the next painting.

"Now, this is one of Annie's peacocks. Did I tell you I actually help feed these critters each morning? I think God was working overtime when He created this guy. I still don't think I did the colors justice, but isn't he gorgeous?"

Courtney shook her head. "Wow, I'll tell you what's gorgeous—it's your work. Seriously, Louisa, I don't think I've ever seen you paint so well, with such . . . peaceful beauty."

"Thanks. That means a lot."

After they had thanked Eileen, Louisa called a cab on her cell phone. Then they headed back outdoors, bundling their coats around them.

"Your students should see your recent paintings, Louisa," Courtney said. "They're really something. What are you working on now?"

"Oh, I've kinda put my art on the back burner these last few weeks. Out of respect for my hosts—the Zooks. Besides, I've had other things on my mind."

Courtney's red lips parted in astonishment. "I can't believe it. You really *are* different. But I still wish I could talk you into coming home and giving Michael a second chance."

Louisa shook her head. "It's over. I know it; so does he."

"But what about the rest of us?" Courtney softened the question with a smile. "Giving up on us, too?"

Louisa smiled back. "No, Court. Never."

"So you'll stay in touch?"

"Sure, but I have no idea when I'm going home, so don't raise my mom's hopes, okay?"

Courtney nodded, then reached for her and gave her a hug. "If that's what you want."

"Jah, it is."

They both laughed as the summoned cab pulled into the parking lot. "Drive us to Miller's Smorgasbord, please," Louisa said when they were settled in the backseat.

"Excellent choice for a buffet lunch," the cabbie said with a smile. "They have the creamiest cheesecake . . . and don't forget the shoofly pie!"

Louisa couldn't resist. "Wonderful-good cookin', jah?"

"Oh, brother," Courtney said, laughing.

When they parted ways, after a not-so-light meal, Louisa secretly felt glad about not having fallen for Michael's attempt at getting back together. She was rather impressed that he had given up the law partnership—an aspiration that had been the last straw between them.

*But I won't let this news affect me*, she thought, relieved the last day of Courtney's visit had gone so well. She was eager to tell Annie all about it . . . and surprisingly eager to start painting again, as well.

# Chapter 12

Ben accepted payment for the newly oiled harness. He offered to help carry it through the snow to the waiting buggy, but the elderly Amish bishop and his great-grandson—introduced to Ben as a "wonderful-gut checkers player"— would not hear of it.

"*Denki*, Ben," Bishop Stoltzfus called over his shoulder.

Needing some fresh air, Ben walked to the back of the shop and pushed open the narrow door, standing where no one could see him. And where he could look out over the vast expanse of fields inundated with drifted snow. The skeletal figures of winter trees punctuated the horizon.

His gaze settled on a grouping of scrappy trees to the south. *What type of trees are they? I suppose Annie knows.*

How quickly his thoughts turned to her, as if she'd been his friend for years. His best buddy back home, Eric, had complained vociferously when he'd told him of his plan to move away. He hadn't been able to say then why he wanted to live in the middle of Pennsylvania Amish country, because he hadn't known himself. Truth was, he still didn't.

His eyes focused again on the distant grove, recalling someone from his childhood who had the uncanny ability to identify various trees. The astute person spoke of the Creator God—an all-powerful Being responsible for the majestic beauty of the woods and the meticulous design of the trees themselves. The tree expert, obscure in his memory, sometimes still appeared in his dreams.

Ben himself had readily recognized the glossy white bark of the wild river birches planted in various yards around Paradise. He had also spotted the tall-growing native cedars with their deep evergreen lacelike leaves. Yet his was a beginner's knowledge of trees.

Exhaling, Ben watched his breath float aloft in the frosty air. "Who was it?" he whispered, aware of the too-familiar sense of frustration he always felt when struggling to remember such things from childhood.

*I'm not the only one.*

He recalled his strained conversation with Zeke, dogged in his determination to discover the murderer of his brother. Yet as pivotal as that night seemed to him, Zeke was terribly confused about what actually happened.

Ben was incensed to think someone could sneak into this quiet community and steal away a small child. Yet wasn't it nearly equally unjust, in a different sort of way, for the People to keep a lid on things, evidently not wanting to make waves by reporting outsiders' offenses? Doing so left victims of such crimes unable to find solace in justice.

*You could report this*, Zeke had said when moved by Ben's pity, and later Ben had reluctantly agreed to consider it. But now he shook his head, for as much as he wanted to help raise Zeke's banner of justice, what would happen if it were known that *he* had caused the police to invade the People's sanctified privacy? It was bad enough for an Englisher to seek out an Amish girl. But this?

His hands were stiff from the subzero temperatures. "It's Annie who is most at risk by associating with me," he muttered, pushing his hands into his pockets. He remembered the spark of awareness in her expressive blue eyes . . . the way they held his gaze. At the same time an ever-present fear was etched on her face: She was afraid of being found with him.

*I must make her feel comfortable . . . and trust me*, he thought, then sighed. *If that's even possible.*

At once he smelled the familiar scent of pipe tobacco and wondered which of the regular Amish clientele had arrived, although he had not heard the clatter of carriage wheels nor the thud of horse hooves against the packed snow.

He wondered if Zeke had returned for yet another visit. Then again, Zeke was not one for tobacco. But Zeke *had* pulled a cigar out of his coat pocket— "from the preacher," he'd said—when Ben agreed to go tramping around in the woods, looking for an unmarked grave, which they had never found.

Thinking back on yesterday's strange afternoon, Ben realized he could not assent to Zeke's urgent request, not without further advice. And who better to advise him than another Amish person, namely Annie herself? Being the preacher's daughter she would surely know the issues at stake for Zeke—the possible shunning aspect, especially.

Torn between frustration with Zeke's circumstance and anticipation of seeing Annie again, Ben headed back inside to the warmth and leathery tang of the shop to tend to his unseen client.

Esther had never intended to overhear Zeke's discussion with Irvin. She had slipped downstairs, leaving her napping children in the attic room to get a drink of water in the kitchen. She heard Irvin talking in the small sunroom off the kitchen, telling Zeke he had proposed marriage to Julia on the tan loveseat in their living room—"on the same piece of furniture where my father proposed to my mother." He chuckled. "Of course, I reupholstered it since that time."

Zeke's response seemed to indicate he was more interested in the process of upholstery than whatever point Irvin was trying to make, which brought a sinking feeling to Esther. *Is he that closed up to love?*

But she knew from being Zeke's wife what sort of man he was. And she seriously doubted if Irvin, or anyone, could change his way of thinking.

As she sipped the cold water, Irvin began to talk straight. "I'm not interested in wasting your time, Zeke . . . nor mine. To put it bluntly, I believe you have been treating Esther wrongly."

*Wrongly? Had anyone ever dared to be this forthright?*

Esther doubted it. No one had ever successfully dealt with Zeke's belligerent behavior toward her, nor toward the church brethren. She knew from the grapevine that her husband had been in jeopardy of the Bann on several occasions. The fact that he had escaped by the skin of his teeth made her wonder what sort of things he had told the brethren to quash their indignation. Perhaps the ministers had shown leniency out of fear Zeke might eventually report his brother's kidnapping, something he had threatened to do off and on over the years.

"Here, let me read what the Scriptures say about the marriage relationship," Irvin's voice broke the quiet. "'Husbands, love your wives and do not be harsh with them.'"

"But that ain't all it says," Zeke snapped. "The woman's to come under the rule of the man . . . she's to submit in ev'ry way." Zeke paused. "And I wouldn't put a bit of weight on that Bible you're readin'."

There was a slight pause. Then Irvin answered thoughtfully, with slow words, "Well, we can read from the King James if you prefer."

Esther had to smile. Poor Irvin had his work cut out for him.

Irvin had evidently reached for a different Bible, and he began to read yet again. "'Husbands, love your wives, even as Christ also loved the church, and gave himself for it.' This means we are to cherish our wives, tend to them as we care for our own body. Give our love away sacrificially . . . surrender it to the good of our beloved."

Esther was stunned. She'd never heard such things coming from a man. *No wonder Julia wears a constant smile!*

But for Esther to trust that such a verse might find its way into Zeke's stony heart, well, she would not get her hopes up. She had never known anyone to act like the devil, but she felt she'd seen his sneering face—when Zeke's rage overtook him. No, Irvin's attempt to convert Zeke was futile. She felt sure she knew what made her husband tick, and it had nothing at all to do with giving himself up for his bride.

After supper dishes were put away and Annie and Louisa were in their room, with Muffin purring in Lou's arms, Annie brought up her secret date with Ben Martin. "It's this Friday, after nightfall," she said, watching Louisa's expression.

A smile spread quickly across Lou's face. "I knew it. This is so great, Annie."

"Now, don't go jumpin' to conclusions. I'm not going to be his girl or anything."

"Well, are you sure?"

Annie let out a little giggle. "Now, listen. I agreed to go with him just this once."

"But you've spent time alone with him already . . . haven't you?"

Annie couldn't hide the truth. "Actually, we've run into each other quite a few times."

"Oh, so you're a couple now?"

"No."

"But that's what *he* wants," Lou said. Then she told her how Ben had asked about Annie some time back. "I said he should ask you himself."

"Ach, you did?" Annie held a strand of her golden waist-length hair in her hands.

"Sure, it beats wishing and hoping. Why should I try to set up a date with you for him when he can do it himself? It's better this way. You know exactly where he stands."

"I *do* like him, Lou. But he's English." Annie felt her heart do a strange dance at the thought of seeing him again. "What am I goin' to do?"

"Have a fine evening, that's what. Ben seems like a wonderful guy."

"But . . . he's off limits. My father will have my head if I'm found out. I shouldn't have agreed to see Ben again."

"Then why did you?"

"Because I have to know . . ."

"If he's the man for you?"

Annie turned abruptly and looked at her. "I'm not thinkin' of marriage. Honestly, I'm not."

"You wouldn't want to abandon your Amish ways, of course. What's wrong with enjoying his company?"

"The way you enjoy Sam's?"

"Umm . . . we're not talking about *me*," Lou said.

Annie smiled at her friend. "Did Courtney get off all right?"

"You're changing the subject," Lou said.

Laughing softly, Annie nodded. "Jah, I guess I am at that."

# Chapter 13

Annie sat in the barn on Friday morning, thinking ahead to her much-anticipated date with Ben that evening. She heard the sound of the milkers and stared at the far end of the barn. Squinting her eyes, she held up her fingers in midair—her thumb and pointer finger—measuring the distance as an artist might, appraising the shape and size of the milkhouse beyond.

"Caught you!" Louisa said, sneaking up behind her. "What're you doing?"

Annie put her hand down quickly. "What's it look like?"

"Oh, I get it. You're missing something . . . big time."

Annie nodded. "The thought that I *must* draw and paint, well it never, ever leaves me. Not even for a minute." She pined for the feel of a paintbrush in her hand. "Some days I feel like I might just waste away."

"It's gotta be tough." Lou offered to help her lay out quilting squares again, like they had one other time when Annie's need to paint had hit ever so hard. "What about that?"

"Mamm was not so pleased with that crazy quilt pattern I created."

"She said that?"

"Oh jah. She was adamant it was much too worldly."

"I'm really, really sorry, Annie." Lou squatted near, smiling sympathetically. "What *can* you do to feed your artistic side now that it's winter?"

"Well, short of going back on my pledge to Daed, I just don't know."

Lou nodded and followed Annie when it was time to go to the milk house. "When's the next quilting bee? Maybe that might help."

"It's comin' up soon enough. I'll try 'n' think ahead to that," Annie replied, not wanting Lou's pity. Not on this day. "I know. I'll focus on Ben. Maybe that'll get my mind off my art."

"He *is* mighty *perty!*"

"Oh, you!" She chased Lou around the barn till the cows began mooing, which was not such a good thing. Not if Daed was going to have calm and contented cows for the rest of the milking hour.

"What would you do if the sounds of the country weren't humming in your ears every night?" Louisa said to Annie later as they swept the aisles. "I mean that hypothetically, of course. I know you're not going anywhere."

Annie wore a fleeting smile. "You're talking 'bout lying in bed and hearin' the owls hooting and the wind keening?"

"I guess, but sometimes it's more than that," Louisa admitted. "There are times when I think about the countryside being the least noisy place in the world. But how can that be true? I mean, the night sounds fill up my head and even sneak into my sleep, too."

"The restless peacocks?"

Louisa agreed. "And other sounds. Muffin seems to hear them, too—she quivers in her sleep."

"Oh, I'm sure. There's something about animals. They not only hear, but they sense things like a brewing storm or, in the case of your cat, the agitation of the barn cats, especially when the moon is full. Ever notice that?"

"Not so much. I'm not into the phases of the moon. I do love the silvery look of the snow when there's a full moon, though." Louisa suddenly thought of Sam, wondering what sorts of sounds he heard each night as he fell asleep in his father's farmhouse. What smells did he love best?

*Why should I care?* she wondered.

Not allowing herself to linger on Sam, her thoughts flew to Courtney, who she knew would not understand nor care to embrace any connection with the Plain world here. Courtney was content with her flamboyant life.

*So does a person have to be drawn to this? Or does life need to be messed up before you crave serenity?*

At that moment, Louisa realized Annie was braver than she by far. Sam had asked to meet her later tonight, and she'd agreed. Yet she had said nothing at all to Annie. *How long can I keep this quiet?*

She daydreamed, feeling surprisingly mellow at the prospect of seeing Sam again, as she watched Yonie move in and out of the cow stalls, hitching up his work trousers as he went. His scuffed boots were ridged with caked mud, she noticed, with pieces of straw sticking out like a sort of barbed halo.

*He, too, has secrets,* she was willing to venture. One night, while Annie dreamed peacefully upstairs, sleepless Louisa had paced the main house's long front room, which was lined with shelves full of books with strange German titles. It was then she had spied the preacher's son outside, though Yonie had been too busy kissing his modern girlfriend to notice.

The next morning, Esther watched the sun come up, her body signaling it was past time to nurse Essie Ann. Propped up with pillows, she prayed silently in the stillness of dawn, her children sprawled in a row along the width of the bed.

*I feel it in the marrow of my bones, dear Lord. I'll be forced to return home . . . and soon. I ask for the grace to do this thing which I dread.*

She stroked John's head. *Touch my dear, frail child, I pray. Thank you for sparing his life on that most frightening night. Oh, I give you praise, Father.*

Essie Ann stirred in her cradle, making her usual soft sounds upon first awaking. Esther would not wait for her to wail. She slipped out of bed and went to her, longing to preserve the peace of this place, her retreat of safety, likening it to the shelter the Lord God had provided for the psalmist David.

*How much longer will I find refuge here?* She did not wish to be a burden to the Rancks, kind as they were, and would continue to help around the house wherever she could, especially with young James and Molly. But although she was inclined to, she would not allow herself to fret. *I will put my full trust in my Lord. I will not be afraid.*

Even so, she fought the looming sense of urgency that things were about to change for her and her dear, helpless children.

Annie was a bit surprised by Ben's somewhat Plain attire. She half expected he might arrive wearing the shirt and tie associated with church clothes or "dress up," as the Englischers called it. But not Ben. His solid blue shirt was open at the neck beneath his dark coat. In fact, he looked like any one of Irvin's Mennonite friends.

*Does he mean to impress me?*

"How are you, Annie?" he asked, opening the door for her. He'd parked out on the road, about a quarter mile up from their lane. The car was still running, and she marveled at how toasty warm it was inside.

"I'm doin' all right. How 'bout you?"

"Glad to see you again." He grinned irresistibly and closed her door. She found herself smiling as he moved quickly around the front of the car to the driver's side, got in, and snapped his seat belt. That done, he turned to her. "I hope you don't mind . . . I made reservations for us at a restaurant quite a distance from here. I thought it might be best, considering our circumstances," he said.

*He means: since you're not supposed to be out with me!*

"Sure, I think that's nice," she said, surprised once more at how relaxed she felt with him. She was glad, too, for a long ride before yet another meal—even though she was not so keen on riding in a car. Even so she'd waited with great anticipation for this night, and Ben seemed to be as careful as any of the drivers her father occasionally hired for the family.

"Am I going too fast?" Ben asked, seemingly mindful of her hesitancy.

She shook her head. "Usually, when I ride in the vans on the way out to Ohio or whatnot, I sit far in the back. But I'll get used to this, really."

"We'll be traveling more slowly tonight because of the weather."

*Jah, good,* she thought. "It's so cold the snow hardly has a chance to melt."

"And more is coming, according to the forecast." He went on to say he had made a habit of following the weather quite closely, via the Internet.

"Louisa has a portable computer," she volunteered. "Sometime she shows me the news and other things on the screen. That is, when we're at Cousin Julia's, of course. We don't have electric in the house, ya know."

He nodded. "I've wondered. Some of the Amish who come into the tack shop have electricity and others frown on it. Can you explain that?"

Happy to clarify, she outlined the differences between several of the conservative groups in the area to the best of her ability. "And you may not know this, but there is a growing number of folk leaving the Old Order for a group called, not surprisingly, the New Order. They're more open to modern ideas. Over in the area of Gap there are Amish who drive cars and have lights in their houses, yet they dress similar to my family and me."

"Hard to understand why there are so many groups."

"Every Ordnung is different, if only a little, even from one regional district to another, my father says."

They talked about Irvin and Julia and Ben's fondness for them. And again about the blizzard that was supposed to blow in sometime during the weekend.

"In Kentucky we wished we had more snow," Ben said. "But here we complain if we get too much."

"*Mer net zefridde,*" Annie said with a mischievous smile. *We're never satisfied.*

Watching the road carefully, Ben seemed distracted momentarily by a pedestrian, then turned to her, smiling. "You're right, we're not."

She looked at him, somewhat surprised. "You've picked up some Dutch, seems to me."

Ben shrugged casually, and she made herself stop staring. He was a curious man. She was careful to answer his questions—mostly about the "Plain society," as he referred to their community.

At one point she asked him if he'd ever read the book *The Riddle of the Amish Culture*, which was highly regarded as a good resource.

"I'll have to pick it up," he said. "You say your people approve of the book?"

"Well, sure, because it correctly represents the Anabaptist community as a whole. The author has lived and worked among us for a good many years now."

"He's English?"

"Jah, and well respected according to Daed. And my Dawdi Zook knows of him, too, which is sayin' a lot."

Ben continued to inquire about the author, obviously interested that someone who was not Amish could be so welcomed by those who were. Annie's mind flitted to the notion that, just maybe, Ben Martin was hoping to be well received, too.

When they arrived at the restaurant after a drive of some forty minutes, Annie could see from the exterior what a lovely place it was. It wasn't a regular sort of restaurant like some of those up and down Route 30, which catered to tourists with signs advertising home-style cooking.

Inside Ben stepped forward and quietly gave his last name to the hostess, who promptly led them to a table for two near a fireplace.

All during the candlelit meal, she found herself glancing toward the door, wondering if someone familiar might walk through and catch them. Several times, Ben asked if she was feeling ill, and each time she politely smiled and shook her head.

Despite being on edge, her conversation with Ben came rather effortlessly as they discussed their growing-up years. At one point something triggered a distant memory, one she had nearly forgotten. "Mamm and Mammi Zook—that's my grandmother who lives in the Dawdi Haus—were cookin' up popcorn in a skillet. My mother must've forgotten what was inside, so when she lifted the lid the kernels right then began popping out of the pan, flying every which way." She stopped, trying to suppress a nearly uncontrollable giggle but did not succeed.

When she had composed herself a bit, she continued. "I remember watching it pop wildly, some bouncing off the ceiling—that high, honest to goodness—other kernels soaring across the room. It was the funniest thing I think I've ever seen."

Ben grinned, glancing at her across the table. "I can see it, Annie. You describe it so well. How old were you?"

"I'm not sure, but this happened at a quilting bee, during the afternoon break, when the womenfolk stopped to stretch their legs and have their fill of . . . well, popcorn." She sighed. "I hadn't started school yet, so I was young."

"It surprises me you remember that far back."

"Lou says the same thing 'bout me."

He shook his head. "It's really remarkable." He reached for the salt and pepper shakers. "I have to confess I barely remember a thing before age five."

"It might be easier for girls," she said. "Maybe your parents could share a few memories to get you started."

He seemed uncomfortable all of a sudden, so she, too, ceased her talking.

She was thankful she'd taken only a very small portion of mashed potatoes, buttered succotash, and roast beef at home. And for good reason. Not wanting to call attention to herself by simply not eating with the family for supper, she'd sat down with them anyway. Now Annie hoped she would be able to eat enough at *this* meal to please Ben, though it was usually the man who would eat up to impress his girl. But she wouldn't allow herself to think that way—not about Ben.

*Why on earth did I share my recollection of the exploding popcorn?* One thing she had not mentioned about that day, and she didn't feel she ought to, was the fact that Isaac Hochstetler had been the only little boy at the quilting bee. Isaac's mamma had not been any too keen on his gravitating mostly toward Annie in play, although both Annie's mother and her grandmother had found it more humorous than cause for alarm.

"How's your meal?" Ben asked, jolting her back to the present.

Truth was, she had scarcely even touched her baked potato. "It's delicious, really 'tis."

"Are you a light eater?" he asked, surveying her plate.

"Ach, no." Then she realized he should know her little secret. "I best be tellin' ya . . . I couldn't just up and leave the house without eating. Mamm, 'specially, would've seen right through it." *She might have, anyway,* thought Annie.

Ben's eyes twinkled. "I wouldn't want to offend you or your parents." He glanced about him before continuing. "But I am hoping to see you another time."

Annie felt her face flush. *Courting?* "I . . . uh, Ben. I don't think . . . I mean . . . this can't go on."

Ben reached across the table and covered her hand with his. "Annie, please listen. I really want to get to know you."

She knew her face was blushing a beet red; she could feel it all the way down her neck, too. "Honestly, I'm not sure how we can get better acquainted." She wasn't going to explain how she'd promised her father she would be obedient for a change. Not since she was committing the sin of disobedience even now, sitting here with Ben in this pretty dining room with white linen-covered tables. Such a lovely, fancy setting for the Englischers present, which she was clearly not.

His eyes reached her heart. "I'm serious. I want to take you out again."

She lowered her gaze to stare at her plate. *It's not fair to ignore him,* she thought but couldn't help it. She slid her hand from beneath the warmth of his own and picked up her fork. She began to eat again, hoping he might do all the talking now. Forget that she had not responded. She was at a terrible loss, unable to comprehend what she felt when she looked into his handsome face with those ardent brown eyes.

"Annie, I don't mean to pressure you."

She nodded her head, because she didn't know what to say.

They passed the next few minutes in silence, except for the soft music she'd never heard the likes of before, which seemed to come from somewhere high in the ceiling.

In time, their conversation began again, returning to more casual matters, and the earlier tension was forgotten. For this Annie was ever so glad.

# Chapter 14

Annie and Ben were making their way out of the restaurant, following a two-hour dinner, when Annie spied Louisa and Sam Glick walking toward them. Annie sucked in her breath.

*Lou?* Taken aback, Annie's stare met Louisa's, and she knew not what to say. Sam turned immediately red-faced, as though caught doing something terribly wrong.

"Well, funny meeting *you* here," Lou said, stopping to stand just feet from Annie as she rubbed her mittened hands together.

"Jah, 'tis." Annie realized her friend had not wanted her to know her plans. "How'd you two get here?"

"Hired us a driver," Sam spoke up, pulling his black hat off in the night air.

"Hey, if we'd known . . ." Ben's voice trailed away.

"What's that saying about great minds?" Lou said, smiling directly at Annie.

"Well, enjoy your supper" was all Annie could say.

Sam and Lou waved and resumed walking to the entrance, and Ben and Annie proceeded to his car.

*What's Lou doing?* Then, realizing that she herself was in a similar jam, Annie squelched a laugh.

On the ride back, Ben talked of Lou and Sam, suggesting it might be fun to "double up," as he put it.

*Double up?* "I don't think we should be seen together—I mean you and me with Sam and Lou."

Ben chuckled. "Then you'll agree to see *me* again?"

"Did I say that?"

"Terrific. When can I come by for you?"

"Oh, Ben." Annie shook her head in frustration but couldn't conceal the small smile that tugged at the corner of her lips.

*He's too fond of me. . . .*

"We could drive even farther away," Ben persisted. "As far as Ephrata, if you'd feel better about it."

They were nearing her home now and Annie debated. It was a truly bad idea for Ben to creep up the road in his car so close to Daed's farmhouse. Awfully risky, especially with Omar, Luke, and Yonie coming and going. Her father's friends in the ministry also stopped by at odd hours for talks in the barn, where the bishop, preacher, and deacon made many private decisions.

She turned to face him. "Ach, I'd best be gettin' out right here."

He braked ever so slowly, till the tires ground to a halt against the crisp snow. "This far away, Annie? In the dark?"

She pulled on the handle before he could get out and come around to open her door. "I had a wonderful-good time. I truly did."

"Annie, wait . . ."

Quickly she slid from the passenger seat but made the mistake of glancing back, only to catch Ben's look of disappointment.

"When will I see you again?" he asked. "How can I contact you?"

She shook her head sadly. "We can't, Ben. We mustn't. This is good-bye."

Closing the car door firmly, she was determined not to break her father's heart on this matter, despite the strong tug of her own.

Louisa felt as oddly out of place wearing her Amish dress and head covering here in the lovely restaurant as she had at the outlet mall last Monday. Had it not been for Sam, who looked as Plain as she did, she might have considered wearing her pretty red sweater with her black suedelike pants. But she wasn't spending her time tonight with a suave guy like either Michael or Trey, and she really didn't miss wearing her own clothes enough to think twice about it. Only occasionally now did she still have passing twinges, missing some of her favorites back home or her normal hairstyle.

Besides, her fondness for Sam couldn't be linked to her feelings for either her former fiancé or her first boyfriend. For one thing, he had many more good character traits going for him. He also seemed interested in her as a person, and not just in what he could get out of her. *And he's cute, too.*

Despite all that, she was going to be cautious and not get too involved this time. She was too smart for that now; she'd learned some things from her past relationships. So, halfway through their shared dessert of New York cheesecake with chocolate sauce, she panicked inwardly when Sam lassoed her with his eyes and said, "I hope you'll stay on here for the time bein'."

"I have a studio of art students waiting for me." She picked up the wine list absentmindedly, thinking a small amount might relax her. Then realizing what she was doing, pushed it aside. "They're anxious for me to return."

His face brightened. "You paint pictures?"

"Yes."

He leaned in closer. "Will you describe some of them for me?"

Immediately she was on her guard, so as not to implicate Annie. "Let's see. My most recent work focuses on country landscapes . . . things found on Amish farms . . . and other rural places."

"Windmills? Hand-held plows?"

"All that and more." She told him about her peacock painting, where every color had been matched to numerous photos she had taken of Annie's birds. "I followed those creatures around everywhere. Can't believe I did that—I actually started talking to them. But, I guess, according to Annie, she does, too, sometimes."

That brought a shared laugh.

"Ah, those peacocks," he said. "No doubt on that . . . a wonderful-good choice for a painting."

They discussed the birds' exquisite coloring and the fanned-out tails, and Louisa realized here was a person who apparently relished some of the same aspects of nature as she. *Is that to be expected from an Amish guy?* She had no other frame of reference, except for her friendship with Annie.

"I like it here in Paradise," she admitted, "but I'm only visiting."

"Well, word has it you're stayin' on awhile yet," he said, face full of hope.

She shook her head. "I haven't decided how long." She wouldn't lead him to think she was setting up a permanent residence at the Zooks', even though his smile faded rapidly with her words.

The light from the moon cast a shadow on the footboard of Annie's bed. Louisa stared at it for a moment, then rose and tiptoed over to Annie and placed the furry ball in her arms. "Here, you hold him awhile."

"Can't you sleep?" asked Annie.

"Can you?"

"Not yet, anyway." Annie let out a tiny laugh.

Louisa returned to her bed, sitting up. "Do you think we'll get slammed by that blizzard everyone's talking about?"

"The cattle seemed awful restless durin' afternoon milking."

Neither of them was willing to bring up the subject weighing on their minds. Instead, Louisa moved away from the topic of cows and snowstorms and mentioned something she had been thinking but had never voiced. "Have I ever told you this? When you wrote your first letter to me—when I wasn't expecting to get a letter from an Amish girl—I was absolutely ecstatic?"

"I'm sure you told me, jah. But it would be fun to sort through the letters sometime."

"Sure would," Louisa agreed. "What I was getting to is I had felt so lonely, being an only child, up until the point your letter showed up in the mailbox. Of course, the one from your non-Amish neighbor, Jenna Danz, arrived around that same time, too . . . but I think yours actually beat hers."

Annie made soft kitty sounds to Muffin. "I know I was awful happy to hear back from you," Annie replied. "I wasn't sure if I would, ya know."

"I felt so disconnected from my family at that time, even though I knew I was loved. I don't know why I felt so emotionally starved, even as a small girl." She plumped her pillow. "Annie, you were the very friend I needed then . . . and now. The way you expressed yourself in your letters managed to break through my foggy, dysfunctional life."

"You must've been as forlorn as I was, floundering over my inclination toward art."

"Yeah, no kidding."

"Well, like Daed often says: Life isn't supposed to be happy all the time. You know—the rain falls on the just and the unjust."

"Speaking of which, what sort of trouble will Sam Glick be in if word gets out about his dating me?"

"I'd say he's fine for now. Who's gonna spill the beans?"

Louisa was relieved. "The last thing I want is trouble for him. He's just so nice." Louisa almost said "wonderful" but caught herself.

"I daresay you've already begun to fall for him."

Louisa tossed one of her pillows across the room. It landed on Annie's bed, and soon it was thrown back. "Okay, if it's an all-out pillow fight you want . . ."

"No, we best keep quiet. Dawdi and Mammi don't need to be awakened, ya know."

Stifling the temptation, Louisa hugged the pillow. "I need to get something off my chest while I'm thinking of it."

Annie giggled just a little. "Now what?"

"You talk in your sleep, did you know?"

"I don't!"

"Yep . . . and you answer questions when I ask them, too, while you're sleeping."

"Louisa Stratford . . . there oughta be a law against such things. Is there? I mean in the English world?"

Louisa couldn't stop grinning. "No laws prohibiting the questioning of an unconscious person, nope."

Annie was trying to contain her laughter, trying her best not to awaken her elderly relatives. "Okay, one more thing before we call it a night," Louisa said.

"Jah, and we better, 'cause those cows will need milking at four-thirty, no matter."

"Here it is. You're a coffin sleeper, Annie."

"A what?"

"You look totally dead in bed."

"What on earth does *that* mean?" Annie asked, her voice higher pitched than usual.

"Legs straight out . . . your hands on your stomach." Louisa stopped to catch her breath, because she, too, was holding back a wave of hilarity. And not being too successful at it.

"So . . . you gawk at me when I'm unconscious?"

"No," Louisa said. "It's just if I wake up and look over at you, I see your coffin pose."

Annie shook her head, her hand over her mouth.

"If you think that's funny, listen to this," Louisa said. "One of my mother's cousins had an interesting situation happen when her husband died. I don't remember his name, but let's call him Jack, to keep it simple. Anyway, Jack's kids and stepkids were each jockeying for a portion of his ashes. So they were divided up in equal parts, and the undertaker advised them to 'puff out the remains with fireplace ashes,' so there was enough to go around."

"Well, for pity's sake!"

"Yeah, have you ever heard anything so weird?"

"I don't even know anyone who's been cremated. I think it's just awful, don't you?" Annie fell silent. Louisa wondered if she might be ready to go to sleep, but soon she heard Annie moving about in her bed. "I wonder if the Lord God will be able to find all of Jack's ashes on Resurrection Day," Annie said softly.

Louisa had never thought of that. "Do you honestly believe everything in the Bible?"

"Well, lots of folk must. I think my father does."

"Lots of it is suspect, if you really think about it."

"I'm tired," Annie said suddenly.

*She doesn't want to discuss this.*

"Send Muffin back to me," said Louisa.

"He's a coffin sleeper, too—look!" Annie said.

Bounding out of bed, Louisa went to see her cat in the glow of the moon. "Oh, you're right. Wow." Muffin was lying on his back, with his forepaws curled in the air and his hind legs stretched straight out.

"Do you think cats understand English?" asked Annie.

"Of course not." Louisa hopped back into bed. "Good night, Annie."

"Sleep well, Lou."

With that, they settled down, but Louisa couldn't stop thinking about Sam Glick, glad for the silly talk with Annie tonight, hoping to have toned down her own unexpected, even frightening, feelings for this really fantastic guy. *Amish, at that. So now do I have to consider joining church with Annie?*

She knew the answer was a resounding negative. She had actually begun to tire of wearing this long-sleeved cotton nightgown to bed. At first it had been a novelty to hang out with Annie in matching ultramodest floor-length nighties during their talks. But it was enough to mirror Annie's attire and hairstyle all day long. While sleeping, she much preferred to wear her satiny nightgown or her own pj's, but that was food for thought for another night . . . if at all.

*I wonder what married Amishwomen wear to sleep.*

*Here we go again,* thought Ben. *First thing in the morning—last thing at night.*

Annie was even starting to interrupt his nightly dreams. At least he was fairly certain the girl he often dreamed about was Annie, for she was every bit as pretty and as talkative.

The stuff of dreams was evasive, and he couldn't always remember the important details—a frustrating feeling. Yet he was fully persuaded something was lurking there, if not taunting him, on the edges of his consciousness, where he simply could not reach far enough to grasp.

He thought now of the delicate hands of the girl in his dreams, as well as real-life Annie's slight yet beautiful hands. The gentle, relaxed way she folded them in her lap as she rode next to him in the car . . . how her hand brushed her cheek while they were waiting to be served at the restaurant. Distracting things . . .

*She doesn't want to see me again. . . .*

"Annie, Annie," he said, heading to the kitchen for breakfast. "What have you done to me?"

# Chapter 15

The predicted blizzard swept into Paradise with such force even Preacher Zook was taken off guard by it. Prior to this storm, a good number of farmer friends had shared complaints about the inaccuracy of weather reports from Englischers, despite their access to radio and television forecasts based on the latest technology. Jesse much preferred the People's shrewd predictions, which were rooted in their knowledge of the land. A man could tell a lot from his mules, who might lie on exposed terrain in full sun one day and stand the next day with their rumps against the wind, signaling a coming storm.

It had taken Jesse and the boys nearly an hour, well before daybreak, to create a tunnel-like path from the back stoop to the barn door. Now Jesse watched Annie, minus her sidekick, emerge from the kitchen door bundled up like nobody's business. *Barbara's doing,* he thought, knowing his wife's determination to still mother Annie whenever possible. Annie paused as if to investigate the size of the yard drifts, running her gloved hands along the tops of the waist-high piles.

Bands of blustery wind came each time Annie lifted her head while picking her way across the yard. The animals' water tanks needed to be filled no matter the weather, and watching her come plodding out to help with chores amidst the gale of wind and white, Jesse had a sudden warm feeling for her.

*My one and only daughter . . .*

He had never forgotten the day her newborn cries pierced the stillness of the bedroom, the day this sweet infant joined his household. To think now there would be only one set of braids in his house, one small girl with her faceless dolls lined up beneath the bedroom window. That girl had grown into a young woman who possessed something of an artistic gift, as Barbara had pointed out on more than one occasion. Their Annie—with the determination of a man and the openness of the sky.

Quickly, so as not to be caught staring, he darted back into the milk house.

Why had she made such a fuss over who—sons or daughters—was most favored? Women were fine for marrying and birthing babies, but men were elected by the Lord God to lead the community of mortal saints. For Annie to have questioned him at all on this point irked him some, yet he would not allow her to know it.

Truth was, he had managed to shield her from outpourings of disapproval by hiding the magazine featuring her art. Just what would she say to that if she knew?

Regrettably, it would not be long before the People would hear of the contest award. He couldn't keep the magazine from finding its way into the hands of a few good farmers who'd insisted on subscribing to an English periodical. And he couldn't fault them. The *Farm and Home Journal* was a fine one, as he knew from reading its pages any chance he could. It was not his place to order those farmers to cease getting the magazine based on a mere art contest. *Exposing my daughter . . .*

There had been plenty of other times when he'd attempted to protect someone from the potential of pain at their own hand, he recalled. Daniel Hochstetler for one. Zeke's father kept coming to mind, even though Jesse wanted to put the unresolved issues to rest. In all truth, he did not believe the burden of blame for the loss of Isaac lay only on disobedient young Zeke, nor did Jesse view Daniel's carelessness at having caused the puppy's demise as the sole reason for the kidnapping. Daniel had been so distracted during his heated debate with Jesse, he'd accidentally rammed a hayfork into the quivering pet's body. Young Isaac had sobbed his way through supper that crucial night.

No, there had never been any doubt that Daniel's defiance of the Holy One had resulted in the disappearance and eventual death of the man's second son. Why the thing ate away at his thinking Jesse didn't rightly know, but it did, and his pondering was an endless stream of irritation. He'd believed he'd known Daniel through and through, only to realize the man he had embraced as a true friend had been a fraud. Why else would a man of devout upbringing turn his back on the divine appointment?

Sighing loudly, Jesse closed the lid on the cooler where milk was continually stirred by power from their bishop-approved air compressor. Now he could hear Annie's voice, hers and Yonie's, across the way, in the milking area. Their terse greeting reminded him that, of all his sons, Yonie had always been most tender to his sister. Until now.

"Aren't you and Mammi goin' to the work frolic this Thursday?" Annie asked her mother some hours later.

"Mammi's under the weather," Mamm replied. "So not this time."

"Well, she didn't look sick to me," Annie replied, wondering if the blizzard had caused some depression. "What's ailin' her?"

"Lower back pains. She could scarcely get out of bed this morning."

"Will she see the doctor?" Annie asked.

"Oh, you know her. She puts it off as long as she can. Needs to have one foot in the grave, nearly, 'fore she'll go."

*What's really troubling Mammi?* It wasn't like her grandmother to complain one speck. Never, in fact, that Annie recalled.

"Well, tell her I'll take her to the doctor when she's ready . . . once the roads clear some," Annie offered, heading to the Dawdi Haus to read, as she often did on their off Sundays—"no church" days. Sometimes, though, they attended church in neighboring districts, since Daed was a preacher.

"Right nice of you, Annie," Mamm said, eyeing her more closely. "She's growin' older, just as we all are."

Annie couldn't help but think her mother was attempting to send a not-so-subtle message that she wished a replacement beau for Annie might hurry and show up.

To Annie, the best sounds of winter were the stomping of boots in crusty snow and the scrunching of skate blades against hard silvery ice. Once the snowstorm blew itself out, Annie had taken Lou off to tromp through drifted pastureland and then skating on neighbor Lapp's pond during the week.

But today Annie was ready to help lay out an intricate "album patch" quilt with the womenfolk at her brother Abner's house. Her sister-in-law Priscilla, who was fond of researching old quilt patterns, had discovered an old Zook family quilt stuck away in an attic. She declared up and down it had been made in the early 1920s, complete with hundreds, if not a thousand pieces.

Louisa had been talking of Annie pouring her artistic inclination into quilt making, so despite oodles of snow, Annie was excited to take the sleigh out for the first time since the blizzard. "I hope the colors haven't been decided on," Annie told Lou as they strung the reins through the horse's bridle.

Lou laughed. "You think you'll have much say in that, Miss Annie?"

"I can hope. After all, this one's for my cousin Fran, who's gettin' close to marrying age."

"Has anyone decided to make a quilt for *you*?" Lou looked at her with a sly grin.

"Oh, you . . . don't you know better than that?" No one knew of her having seen Ben but Lou, who had been sworn to secrecy, especially because Annie had vowed to herself she would never go down that path again. *Going with the likes of Ben Martin. What was I thinking?*

Yet she felt terribly susceptible to him, wishing to know him better, longing for the things she saw in his face. His eyes seemed to open up vast woodlands to her. No, it was the sky . . . or the sea, or something she knew he possessed. Was it merely his Englishness? She didn't believe so, yet, irrational as it was, she longed to be with him.

Years back, she had also felt stirrings of affection for Rudy Esh, but this was not akin to that. Something far different was drawing her.

Annie knew with conviction where her thinking should be in regard to Ben. As wonderful as she believed him to be, she dared not let her heart beat only for him.

She rehearsed their good-byes that lovely night once again, pushing down the keyed-up feelings she had experienced then. *He wanted the promise of another meeting.*

"I hope this get-together with the women puts some zip back into you," Lou said, changing the topic back to where they'd begun.

"Well, look at you talk. I haven't seen you drawing much anymore, Lou. Why's that?"

"I've put my art on hold for you."

Annie couldn't help but frown. "You mean it?"

"Why not, silly?"

"I can't let you do that."

"Hey, my coming has caused you enough nuisance. So postponing my work is all right with me."

"It's awful nice of you, Lou, but—"

"No 'buts.' That passion can wait."

Annie climbed into the sleigh, amazed. "I don't know what to say."

"Say: 'Sure, that's cool, Lou.'"

Annie laughed. "You're such a *Schpundi*—a nut!"

"Look in the mirror . . . er, I mean . . . oh, you know."

Annie picked up the reins, looking fondly at her friend. "All righty. Let's go and use our artists' eyes to lay out a perty quilt for Fran."

Lou tucked the lap robes around her. "Are purples and yellows allowed in the same quilt?"

"Well, if reds and purples are, why not?"

"I haven't seen yellow or white used in any of the quilts here, though."

"Mammi Zook says those aren't such good choices . . . the other deeper colors run into them when washed.

"Makes sense," Lou said.

They were off to Annie's sister-in-law's place on another gray sort of day. Not a soul could possibly see a shadow on the snow that spread itself out in all directions. She wondered if there would be a moon tonight. Even a hazy one, as she often saw during winter nights, would be nice.

*Will Ben look up at its muted radiance over knoll and woods? And will he think of me?*

When they arrived, Annie noticed a few buggies parked in the side yard. *Highly unusual to cut out and piece a quilt as a group*, she thought, assuming Fran and her mother were simply wanting fellowship at this bleak time of year. *How nice of Priscilla to open her house for this.*

Once inside, Annie took a deep breath and peered down at the choice of colors Fran had already picked for the wedding quilt. Nothing out of the ordinary—plum, reds, blues, and touches of orange. *In keeping with her color scheme, no doubt.*

"What 'bout different combinations?" Annie suggested.

"Fran's favorites are these here," Priscilla replied, her black apron tied loosely to cover her round middle. "Besides, how many colors do ya want?"

*A rainbow full,* she thought. No need to speak her mind, though. Priscilla and the others had no idea Annie longed for things she ought not to.

A little more than a handful of women worked to piece together the blocks, creating the small nine-patch squares—twenty-five larger squares in all—set against an even larger gray background, and a plum-colored border, hemmed in the same dreary hue as the middle block.

She didn't quite know why it plagued her, this urgency to recreate the pattern. Perhaps if Lou hadn't brought up the possibility earlier. That, and if she weren't so headstrong herself. At any rate, Annie resigned herself to Fran and her mother's plan of action. Rightly so.

Her mind wandered back to Mamm's insistence that she and Lou attend without her. "Mammi and I, we'll fill the gas lamps and lanterns while you're gone," her mother had replied, which seemed odd. Mamm wasn't one to miss out on some good fellowship. Annie suspected Mamm of being overly worried, truth be known. Mamm was a brooder . . . and this was another case in point.

At the moment there was abundant chatter around the worktable. One of Fran's aunts mentioned having heard a cousin of hers clear out in Wisconsin had cut her knuckle badly while drying a glass. "It broke apart right in her hands. Ever have that happen?"

Across the table, Fran's mother nodded and made a little grunt.

"Well, anyways, both a nerve and muscle were cut and six stitches were needed," the woman continued.

Several low *oohs* were heard, and the woman next to the first began talking. "An Englischer friend of mine from Shipshewana, some of yous may remember, well, she and her husband stopped in at Wannacup for some hot cocoa last week sometime, and here came—least she said this was true—a Plain fella with two perty girls, one on each arm. And neither one was his sister."

This brought a round of *ahs* and a few curious smiles.

Annie liked the table talk. It was one of the reasons she enjoyed work frolics, although typically they were canning or quilting bees. So many stories to hear. Sometimes, between the work and the talk, she imagined drawing a collage, a wall hanging of sorts portraying all the images of things women shared round the worktable.

"And listen to this," another woman close to Annie said. "One of Zeke's cousins over in Honey Brook heard from Daniel Hochstetlers, who've been living on a farm up near Wingham, Ontario, of all things."

"Oh?" said Fran. "Wonder what took them so far away?"

The woman could only shake her head. "Don't know, really. Only heard that Mary died in her sleep sometime recently."

"Zeke's mother?" said one.

"Ain't it just awful?" said another.

Annie's heart sank. Zeke's—and Isaac's—long-lost parents . . . chastised yet again by the Almighty? "Wonder if Hochstetlers have gone fancy," Annie said.

"Well, seems so."

A weighty pause followed. Then Annie filled the silence with her words. "Could it be the nickname caught up with them?"

"Ichabod," someone whispered.

Lou looked at Annie, frowned, and went back to her slow stitching, making Annie feel awful for speaking her mind yet again.

"Daniel oughta be a lesson to us all," said Fran's mother suddenly. "First Isaac's kidnapping . . . now the man's own wife, dead too soon. What a shame."

"A word to the wise is sufficient," said another.

Annie forced her eyes back on her work. So Zeke's family had been located after all this time . . . if the Amish grapevine was accurate. And his poor mother dead.

She felt she must talk to Esther about this. Wouldn't Zeke be comforted to hear something—*anything*—but also terribly grieved at his mother's passing? Annie wondered what Zeke's reaction would be to such news. To put it mildly, Esther's husband was truly a conundrum, not only to her, but to all the People.

# Chapter 16

Annie had not come to Julia's attic to discuss bygone days, but the past certainly seemed to weigh on Esther's mind today. During the course of their conversation, Annie was surprised to discover she and Zeke had talked only minimally through the years about Isaac's kidnapping.

"Zeke's kept it to himself," Esther had said out of the blue. "Sometimes I wonder just how much he remembers, really."

"I s'pose things would become hazy over time," Annie replied, watching Esther stroke her baby. Essie Ann squeezed her tiny lips into a pucker, then relaxed them again into a faint smile.

"He's had nightmares . . . well, I don't know so much now, since I'm not home with him." Esther avoided Annie's eyes.

Annie had hoped Esther and Zeke might have heard of Mary Hochstetler's death directly from Zeke's father, but since it seemed Esther was in the dark, Annie forged ahead. "I don't like to be a bearer of bad news, but I heard something awful sad at Priscilla's frolic. Mammi Rosa said word came from one of Zeke's cousins . . . 'bout Daniel Hochstetlers."

"Oh? That's odd . . . no one's heard from them for years—not even Zeke's uncle, Preacher Moses. Not since after Zeke and I married, anyway. His folks have never even seen our children." Esther's voice quivered.

"I hate to tell you this, truly I do, Essie."

"Well, what the world." Esther frowned, her eyes searching Annie's. "Did Daniel pass away?"

"Not Zeke's father . . . his mother."

Esther's eyes clouded from blue to somber gray. "Ach, such terrible news." She lifted Essie Ann up close to her heart, holding the wee babe there, whispering something against the infant's peachy head.

"Awful sorry," Annie murmured.

The small room felt dismally devoid of light, as though an invisible hand had blocked off the sun from the dormer windows.

Annie felt she ought not say another word. She held her breath, sad for the anguish on Esther's face.

At last, when Annie felt sure her friend might not speak again . . . that Annie might simply have to say her whispered good-byes and slip out of the makeshift bedroom, right then, Esther raised her head. "This will bring such sorrow to Zeke," she said.

"I'm sure" was all Annie could eke out.

"You see, he was always convinced his mother loved him . . . even though she was forced to take her husband's side all durin' Zeke's growing-up years."

"Take sides on what?"

Esther looked away again. When she spoke, her words were faltering. "Mary Hochstetler . . . believed she must follow her husband's approach to Zeke by not interfering. So, in a way, they both belittled him. Zeke once told me the ridicule was near endless." She sighed. "It's one of the reasons I think I must've married him. I felt sad for the way he was raised . . . with no real sense of parental acceptance. His father clearly hated him."

"Hate's a strong word."

"Even so, Daniel *did* put the blame firmly on Zeke's head."

"For Isaac?"

Esther nodded forlornly. "And hearin' of Mary's death, well, I just don't know what it'll do. . . ."

Annie wished the news might soften Zeke's heart toward his wife, but she wouldn't hold out much hope of that.

"Does your Laura know about her uncle Isaac?" Annie asked.

"She's never to know—Zeke is adamant on that."

"I understand." Annie felt herself frowning hard.

"Well, lookin' at you, I'm not so sure you do."

"No . . . no, I don't mean to complicate things." Annie shook her head, pushing away her own happy memories of the boy.

"What Zeke says goes."

"Jah . . ." Annie wanted to cry. "I want you happy again. Honest."

Neither of them spoke for a time. Then Esther looked right at her, her eyes pained. "Happiness is hard to pin down. My joy comes from the Lord Jesus now. He's my everything. . . ."

Annie nodded sympathetically, feeling awkward at Esther's too-familiar remarks about God. "Would you want me to say something to Daed? Have him break the news of his mother's death to Zeke?"

"Jah, in fact, Julia says your father's takin' Zeke to the mud sale tomorrow. Maybe Preacher Jesse's the best one to tell Zeke. But it's in the dear Lord's hands, that's for sure."

Annie rose and kissed the sleeping baby's forehead, then touched Esther's back lightly. "Take good care, Essie."

"You do the same."

Moving slowly toward the door of her old sanctuary, Annie turned and looked back at her friend with her darling baby. She stood in the doorway a moment longer, her old yearnings building with each breath as she allowed her eyes to take in every inch of her former art studio.

*I miss this place!*

She let her gaze linger in the far corner, and something welled up in her as she spotted her framed painting all wrapped in brown paper, part of her secret still secure.

"'Bye, for now," she said, turning to leave.

Louisa made good use of her time while Annie did her regular Friday work routine at Julia's. Making herself scarce in a private corner of the sunroom area, adjoining the kitchen, she plugged in her laptop and began catching up on email. First her art students with more than a few questions, then other friends who continually bugged her about "coming back to civilization," and one lone message from her mother, who urged her to "come home for Easter, won't you, dear?"

Cringing, she felt as if she could actually hear her mother's voice.

*I still haven't been gone long enough.*

Caught up on her email, she sat and stared out the window at the snow-covered yard and trees, wondering if she dare contact Trey. Her response to his repeated overtures was definitely overdue, so when she checked to see if he was online, she was relieved that he was. "Better this way than by phone," she whispered.

Louisa knew now that continuing their relationship was pointless. Not only had she begun to feel differently about Trey and his interest in her, she was in the process of reformatting her view of the world, her life in particular.

Clicking on his screen name in her IM buddy address book, she got the conversation going.

> Hey!
>
> Hey back!
>
> I've been thinking. . . .
>
> Yikes! That's scary, Louisa.
>
> I'm serious. I can't meet you either here or in London.

She waited a full minute before she saw the indication that he was writing a response. She leaned forward to read it:

> Come on, girl, you know you want to.
>
> I thought I made that clear on the phone last time.
>
> Well, reconsider.
>
> Don't be mad. Just please understand.

She felt stronger than ever. This was the right thing . . . letting him know once and for all.

Trey again:

> You're kidding, right?
>
> No.
>
> I want to see you again. I can change your mind. . . .
>
> No. Gotta go.
>
> Wait . . . got power where you are? I'll call your cell.

She had power all right. She'd recharged again here at Julia's and was using her Palm to connect her laptop to the Internet. But she didn't want to hear Trey's voice. Was this Sam's influence? Had she fallen for him like Annie said? No, she merely looked up to Sam . . . and looked down on her past. There was no questioning her resolve where Trey was concerned. He was not in the landscape of her future.

*Don't call me. 'Bye!* She typed it quickly and signed off.

*All guys aren't like this.* She thought of Sam again, hoping she was right. Yet how could she possibly know? She knew one thing: she was weary of the modern dating scene. The Plain culture had it right. You courted. You married, settled down . . . had a bunch of kids.

*Whoa, Mamma, am I losing it or what?*

The realization that she had just slammed the door on her first romantic interest overwhelmed her. And, of course, there was no going back to Michael. She was guy-less for the first time in years. *At least, not a man out in the real world. . . .*

Suddenly sad, she heard Julia's voice. "Louisa, are you in there?"

"Uh-huh," she managed to say, through her sudden tears.

Julia appeared, looking prim as always, her long-sleeved white blouse open slightly at the neck, and her navy blue corduroy jumper brushing her legs at midcalf. "Aw, Louisa . . . what's-a-matter?"

She couldn't speak now. That always happened if someone paid too much attention when she was losing it.

"Well, bless your heart." Julia tiptoed over and pulled up a chair.

"It's not my heart . . . just my dumb head." Louisa wiped her eyes, glad for zero mascara. She sputtered, "I admit to being foolish—I've made some stupid mistakes. That ever happen to you?" She doubted she was making sense.

"Oh my, yes." Julia seemed to understand.

Louisa looked at her and saw the depth of compassion in her eyes. She felt as if she'd come to a fork in the road, made the turn, and refused to look back.

*Julia's only a year older than me, but much wiser. . . .*

"I wish I'd come to Paradise earlier . . . when I was, oh, sixteen. I might've spared myself many things."

Julia nodded. "Plenty of folk have said the same. There *is* a kind of peace here. Some want to soak it up but return home unchanged. Others attempt to box it up, only to lose it along the way. Others embrace it—not only the peace, but the Peacemaker himself."

"Who?" She knew all too well whom Julia was referring to. She had heard similar statements from her deceased aunt Margaret, who talked about Christ as her "dearest friend."

Julia tilted her head, a glow of a smile on her face. "Well, some call Him the Light of the World, others call Him Redeemer and Friend."

"No more *male* friends would be great," Louisa said. She didn't consider Sam just any male, of course. He was the clichéd special person. One of the most important to her at the present time, aside from Annie.

"You've been hurt," Julia said, extending a hand.

"More than once. . . ." She sighed. "I've been wanting to talk to you about God and . . . just stuff."

"Well, I'm here . . . whenever."

The house seemed unusually quiet for as many young children as were present, though Annie and Esther were no doubt keeping them occupied.

"What about right now?" asked Louisa.

Julia folded her hands. "Sure," she said softly.

"So . . . let's see. How do I start?"

The room was still. "Just speak your heart" came the gentle words.

Even though Louisa had been waiting for this moment, she felt nearly tongue-tied, so many thoughts swirled through her head. "To begin with, what's your take on faith exactly? How does it start . . . and where does it lead?"

Julia straightened in her chair. "I can tell you what I've learned . . . what I know in the deep of my heart. Faith is trusting in a person." Julia stopped a moment. "Take, for instance, when my little girl wants to jump off the back step and into Irvin's arms. She knows instinctively that he will catch her. There is no hesitation in her mind. But she has to make the jump . . . take the first step in making that happen, I suppose you might say."

"So faith depends partly on you . . . not just God?"

"Yes, Louisa. Faith is a divine gift, but it is also based on evidence."

"Found in books like the Bible, right?" Louisa recalled Aunt Margaret's comments on this.

"I'd say the Bible is the best source."

She wished she might have been more exposed to religion while growing up. Margaret's belief system and life was such a shadowy memory. "Do you think there is any correlation between faith and love?"

Julia turned at the sound of her children coming into the room. "Why, sure," she said, pausing to give her attention to Molly, who was pointing to an "owie" on her thumb. She scooped the two-year-old into her arms and carried her back to where she had been sitting. "Simply put, faith is trust in a person, and love is a plan of action. It may be described as a feeling, a commitment . . . a decision. But in the end, it's a person you belong to . . . a person you are devoted to, through thick and thin."

"So love and faith are similar?"

Julia kissed Molly's hand. "The power behind creation is really very personal. You are aware of this, Louisa, being an artist. God's power and His infinite love go hand in hand. We matter to Him. Our lives have meaning. I've chosen to live in recognition of this amazing power . . . this love."

"You make it seem so clear," Louisa said. Just then Esther's two boys burst into the sunroom accompanied by Annie.

Louisa was careful not to signal to Annie that she'd bared a corner of her soul to Julia. But it was past time to open up about Sam Glick with Annie. They'd lost some closeness lately, and Louisa missed it.

"Time to wash hands for lunch," Julia told the children. She turned to Louisa momentarily, offering an encouraging smile as if to say, *we'll continue another time.*

Louisa nodded back, to let Julia know she understood. She watched her carry Molly to the kitchen. Julia's confidence was more than appealing.

*What would it take to live like that?*

It was not easy for Annie to approach her father with the news of Mary Hochstetler's death, not since her derogatory remarks about his treatment of Yonie. But Daed surprised her by verifying that Mary Hochstetler had died of a brain aneurysm, slipping into unconsciousness instantly. "We can be glad she suffered very little, if at all."

"How'd you hear?"

"Your grandmother received word from a grandniece in Canada, is what she said."

*No wonder Mammi wasn't well enough to attend the quilting. She loved Mary Hochstetler so. . . .*

"Mary was on the young side, ain't?"

"Early forties, if I recall. Too young to be dyin', I'd say."

Annie sighed. "I saw Essie—Esther, I mean. She hadn't heard and doubted Zeke had, either."

"Well, I'm sure he knows by now," Daed said.

"One would think so . . . but if he doesn't, will ya break it to him?" She wondered how she would feel if Mamm were to pass on at her present age. She would sorrow for her, no question on that, and she'd feel cheated out of the years ahead. *Just as Zeke will . . . and has.*

Daed's jaw was rigid. "Zeke'll be beside himself. Could push him over the edge."

"I think Esther fears as much."

Daed rubbed his pointer finger under his nose. When he did speak, his words were sharp. "Why on earth can't Esther break this news to Zeke herself?"

Annie wouldn't say. It was perfectly clear why not. Fact was, Esther and the children were out of harm's way at Irvin Ranck's—best not to have Esther interacting with Zeke just yet. The bigger question loomed: Would Mary's death soften or further harden Zeke?

Annie made a stronger determination to protect her dear friend. *If need be . . .*

*Chapter 17*

All Zeke seemed interested in talking about on the way to the mud sale was his growing-up years in Honey Brook. He pointed out the street where he'd once walked to a corner store to run errands for his mother, even asking their driver to take them past the small brick house where he'd lived with his parents till he was courting age. "Till Esther came into the picture."

Zeke said this so halfheartedly, Jesse turned to look at him. *He's not too fond of his wife.*

"I've often wondered why your parents just up and left," Jesse said much later, as they made their way across the grounds at the firehouse.

"Honestly, I think they were opposed to Esther. And Dat wasn't happy I'd taken up with the Paradise church district." Zeke twitched his nose. "I never knew why, not for certain."

Jesse figured as much, although he'd never breathed it to a soul. He wondered how long before Zeke might say something about his mother's death—if he knew at all, which seemed unlikely. He didn't want to spoil the day by telling Zeke too early. *Then again, if I tell him late, the poor man might not sleep tonight.*

So Jesse was torn, not knowing when or how to address the miserable news he held warily in his grasp.

It was after they'd enjoyed some chicken corn soup that Zeke asked Jesse if he thought his father's "rebuff of the lot" had, in some way, caused his brother's death.

*He should know it did,* Jesse thought.

Zeke didn't wait for an answer. "This is selfish, on my part . . . I know. But why did I have to suffer for Dat's choice on the matter?"

"God made the choice, Zeke. You know as much."

Zeke fell silent.

"Isaac's kidnapping and death were never about you goin' against your father's wishes . . . buryin' Isaac's puppy." There. He'd said what he'd been fixing to for the longest time. "Your father was wrong to put the blame on you. *He* caused a tragedy, when all's said and done."

Zeke made a muffled sound, eyes raised to meet Jesse's own. "I believed my father . . . all my life I did."

"Well, quit."

"Hard to do when I hear his shouts in my ears, Preacher."

Jesse had never seen Zeke so open and responsive. He would wait for a better moment to tell of Mary's death.

"Dat never forgave me, ya know."

Jesse nodded. "Would seem that way."

"He took Mamm and moved far away from me . . . from you . . . all the brethren here. As a punishment of sorts." Zeke pushed off his hat and scratched the back of his head. "Uncle Moses always thought Dat and Mamma went to another state. Moses has strange feelings 'bout things sometimes. He never got over Isaac's disappearance, either, seems to me."

"Oh jah." Jesse inhaled, feeling the cold air fill up his lungs. *I can't let him keep rambling on. . . .* "Word has it your father lives in Canada somewhere."

"Dat does?" Zeke turned quickly to look at him. "He's not with Mamma?"

"No. What I mean to say is: There was word about your mother. They were livin' in Ontario when your mother fell ill."

Zeke's eyes were sudden darts of fire. He shook his head, turning red in the face. "She died, didn't she? That's what you're tryin' to tell me."

Jesse placed a firm hand on his shoulder, just as he had on other occasions when the younger man was out of order. But now he offered his sincerest concern. "I wish it were better news, Zeke. Truly, I do." He removed his hand. "Your mother passed away in her sleep, here recently."

Zeke put his head down, nearly between his knees as they sat. What little warmth the winter sun had to offer seemed to disappear, and Jesse was aware of the growing knot in the pit of his own stomach.

Suddenly Zeke rose and faced Jesse, his tall body blocking the sun. "It's not okay what I did that night. Isaac went missin' because of me. You know it, and I know it. Just 'cause you say so, Jesse Zook, doesn't mean anything's different!"

With that Zeke strode stalwartly away.

*What have I done?* Jesse wondered, hands clenched.

Ben had driven himself to the mud sale in Honey Brook, assuming Zeke was put out with him. Zeke hadn't shown up at the tack shop since asking Ben to contact the police, or Ben might have suggested the two of them go together.

*He's still waiting for my answer, most likely.*

Ben recalled Zeke's comment about the chicken corn soup and made a beeline to the concession stand. He shivered, even though he'd earlier donned his long johns and the black scarf his mother had knitted for him last Christmas.

He was rounding the bend of one tent when he spied Zeke walking briskly, his arms stiff as a robot as he rushed past him. "Hey, there, Zeke," he called.

Zeke stopped in his tracks, turned, and scowled. "You do what I asked yet?"

Taken aback, Ben shook his head. "Look, I can't just jump like that."

"Why not? You do what your boss tells ya, don't you? You do what your father says to. . . . You need to do what's right 'bout this. Do it for an innocent boy's sake."

Ben wanted to wait and discuss it with Annie, but Zeke was the one in his face at the moment, and in a big way.

Zeke stepped forward; his breath was foul. "Don't dally, Ben."

"Then don't push me," he muttered, saying it more for his own sake than for Zeke's.

"I didn't take you for a bullheaded sort."

Ben stepped forward. "I said I'll think on it and I will."

"Well, fine. But would ya hurry it up?"

*Next time I see Annie . . . if I do, I'll get some levelheaded advice,* he decided. But he wouldn't tell Zeke yes or no now. He wouldn't let him force him into a decision, dead brother or not.

"I'll be seein' ya," said Zeke with a brusque wave.

*Not anytime soon, I hope,* thought Ben.

For the first time since meeting Zeke, Ben had glimpsed his controlling nature. And he was worried for Esther and the children.

Annie was glad for Louisa's eagerness to chat. They were heading out with the enclosed family carriage to deliver a turkey-and-noodle casserole to a sick neighbor. Lou had jumped at the chance to go along, which made Annie wonder what was on her mind.

The air was biting and snow was flying again. Coarse, short hair from the horse blew in on their lap robes. "I'm glad you're comin' along." Annie glanced at her friend.

"Well, hey, I thought it might be fun to get some fresh and frigid air." Lou looked at her. "Actually, I wanted a chance to level with you."

Annie's face grew serious. "About Sam?"

"How'd you know?"

"Seeing you out together, well, I assume you must like him."

Lou looked out at the snowy landscape. "I think I might be falling for him."

"Well, he's awful nice." Annie didn't know what to say, really. "And not one to court many girls."

"That's scary."

"Well, why?"

"If he hasn't dated much, then he's more prone to being hurt."

Annie let the reins fall across her lap. "Well, you're not plannin' on hurting him, are you?"

"He'll be way too vulnerable."

"What 'bout you?" Annie wanted to be careful what she said next. "You might be heading in the same direction."

Lou nodded. "I'm afraid of that. I mean . . . when he walks toward me, at barn singings, or outside after the common meal . . ." She stopped.

"What?"

"I don't know how to describe it. It's just the most incredible feeling. You surely know what it's like to be in love."

"In love or real *love*? There's a difference."

"Yeah." Lou pulled on the lap robe, bringing it up higher, covering her gloved hands. "I know all about infatuation."

Annie looked at her. Lou's cheeks and nose were red from the cold. Or was it something more? "Well, which is it with Sam? Do you even know?"

"That's what I'm sorting out. Trying to make sense of things."

"You'll know in time, Lou. You will."

"But time's my enemy, don't you see?"

"How so?"

"The longer I stay . . . and the longer I agree to see him, the more hurt he—*we*—could be. Oh, Annie, it's a total dead end."

Annie leaned her shoulder against Lou's. "What was it you said to me, not so long ago?"

"Just enjoy the friendship?" said Lou. "See where it goes?"

"Jah, that's right." No matter how much she wished it were otherwise,

Annie's heart could not be swayed from thinking about Ben. But she hadn't come clean with Lou on that. No, she'd kept it tucked away where only she could ponder it, protect it. Especially because she'd sent Ben on his way for good, and the memory of it tortured her.

"Where does friendship that's bound up with genuine love end and romantic love begin?" Lou asked.

"I'd guess it's a fine thread of a line. But you'll know when you cross it, for sure."

"Meaning what?"

"Well, doesn't deep sharing—talking and whatnot—include physical longing, too? A desire to touch hands, face . . . lip kissing." Suddenly, she felt sorry she'd said anything. Many Amish young people, she knew, saved their kisses for after marriage. There were some groups in Ohio who never even held hands until after the wedding.

"Lip kissing?" Lou laughed softly. "As opposed to what other kind?"

Annie picked up the reins. "Oh, go on. You know."

"Pecks on the cheek?" Lou laughed again.

"Well, Rudy wasn't one to let things get too much out of control. I'm awful glad of that now, 'specially since he and I didn't end up married."

Lou leaned back in the seat. "You're long past Rudy, I think."

"You can say that again, even though we courted ever so long." Truth was, Annie sometimes wondered if Rudy and she would have *ever* married ultimately, even apart from the art issue. "I wasn't meant for him," she admitted.

"Julia says things about love I've never realized," Lou said.

"She's a sensible person, no question on that."

Lou nodded her head, shivering in earnest. "I can see why Esther ran to her for safe haven."

"She's got a way about her . . . draws people," Annie replied. "Makes you feel so comfortable." *The way I felt with Ben. . . .*

Their destination could be seen now, and Annie craned her neck to see the gray curl of smoke from the brick chimney. "Well, here we are. Want to come inside and warm up some?"

"Sure."

"You tether Betsy and I'll get Mamm's basket from the rear of the buggy." She climbed out as Lou hurried to tie up the horse. Annie moved back around the carriage and opened the tied flap to remove the sturdy wicker basket, filled with the hot dish and other goodies.

*Did Ben go to the mud sale today?* she wondered as she made her way toward the house. *Will I ever see him again?*

Zeke wasted no time in hunting down Preacher Jesse for the second time during the mud sale. Running into Ben Martin had stirred him up even more. He didn't know why he was so upset just now. Perhaps it was the news of his mother's death. Missing Esther made him scattered in his thinking lately, too. *Murky-headed.* He wanted her back, no matter what Irvin's plans for discussion were. He was tired of cooking, of washing his own clothes. Tired of the wrinkles in his for-good shirts and trousers. *Tired of sleeping alone, too. . . .*

There was a problem with that, though. Even if he got his way and Esther and the children returned, he would have to leave her be. The probationary shunning meant life without the things he missed most. But no, once he got Esther home again, he'd get her to see the light . . . the recklessness of her ways. You couldn't claim to have salvation and still be saved in the long run. He would make her see what nonsense all that talk was if he had to shake it clean out of her.

He found Jesse standing in a long line, waiting for a cup of coffee or cocoa. Knowing the preacher as Zeke did, it would be coffee. Zeke inched forward when Jesse had his back turned, then stood right by him, to the dismay of several customers behind them. "You won't mind if I butt in right here, will ya, Preacher?"

Jesse grimaced. "S'pose not."

"'Tis a cold one," Zeke ventured.

"Jah," Jesse agreed.

"Good for the soup and coffee business."

Zeke decided he'd best be keeping his tongue still till there was opportunity to talk in private. Jesse was the type to speak little, but folks paid attention when he did.

*Like Mamma . . .*

The thought of his mother lying in a wintry grave put a tense feeling in his chest, and a barricade in his brain. He had purposely refused to acknowledge Jesse's news. Fact was, Mamm was the one good thing in his life, like salve on a wound. But the ability to soothe was not always granted her, thanks to his father. *A tyrant of a man,* Zeke thought. *Like I've become. . . .*

When they had their cups of black coffee in hand and had wandered over to an out-of-the-way place, Zeke said simply, "Esther's been gone long enough. I want her home."

Jesse nodded, as if recalling his comment about speaking to Irvin about this. "I'll go 'n' see what can be done," he offered.

"Time Esther gets away from them Rancks."

"I'm with you on that."

"Well, then, I'll expect my woman back tomorrow."

Jesse shook his head. "Did I say that, Zeke?"

"No, now you listen to me. I'll have Esther home if I have to carry her out of Irvin's house. You hear?"

The preacher lowered his eyes. "If you lay a hand on her, she'll leave you all over again."

"I'll bite my tongue more . . . if need be. But I'm not lettin' her have her say!" And he wouldn't. She had a good many lessons to learn yet, and he was just the one to teach them to her.

"Esther's young yet. She'll come under, in time," Jesse said.

Zeke could only hope. A difficult wife was a detriment to her husband. He'd seen this firsthand as a child, because occasionally his mother had the gall to voice her opinion and was squelched for it. Even punished. Like the time the house was so cold she threw extra logs on the fire to warm the kitchen, and from then on the wood was severely rationed.

Often he wished she might have spoken up even more, attempting to spare him numerous thrashings. *Just as Esther does with our children.*

He was startled by this sudden realization. Yet he felt blinded, unable to escape the towering walls of his anger and condemnation, unable to fathom the freedom he longed for.

*I'll be fine when Esther's home.*

More and more he did not trust himself alone in the house. Visions of the past came to him continually, small pieces of a haunting riddle. A clearer recollection forming with each new day: a deep hole, the shovel, Isaac leaning into the puppy's grave, grieving mighty hard. . . .

There had been a deep black sky the night Zeke defied his father. The night when all of the years to come were forever altered. Only a distant yard light had broken the darkness, he recalled. Not a single streetlight shone the way to either the banks of Pequea Creek nor to farmer Fisher's field. Zeke had used his flashlight, a gift from Uncle Moses on Zeke's eighth birthday, to help him see to dig the hole. Or was it *two* holes? Jah, it was all becoming chillingly plain now.

*Ichabod*, he thought and shuddered.

# Chapter 18

Annie tromped quickly all the way out to the barn, scarcely able to wait till she could return to the cozy kitchen and help Mamm with Sunday breakfast.

*Too cold for people*, she thought.

But it was Ben who was the person most on her mind today. More time than she cared to ponder had passed since her impulsive, though needful, good-bye. She couldn't believe she'd left him sitting there, abruptly getting out of the car as she had. But what other choice had she?

Aside from her friendship with Louisa, she felt as if she were going through the motions of her life—no art and no Ben—whereas before she could skip through even the coldest day.

*Nothing's right with me now.*

While helping to put the milking machines on the cows, she overheard Daed talking to Yonie. "I picked up the wrong bridle rosettes by accident over at the tack shop."

Her pulse sped up. Lest she react too enthusiastically, she held back, ever so glad for Yonie's apparent reluctance to make the exchange for their father.

She muffled her smile with her hand. Then, creeping out from between two cows, she stepped forward. "I have to go that way tomorrow, Daed," she said. "I could return the rosettes if you want."

Her father brightened, shooing Yonie off. "That'd be right fine."

*One for me*, she thought, not sure she ought to be keeping score, so to speak.

❖

Right after the common meal, following Sunday Preaching, Jesse motioned to Barbara, and she hurried to get into the carriage for the ride over to Cousin Irvin's place. The day had brought more snow, but it was tapering off now, and he could see the sky was clearing in the north. "We're due for some sunshine," he said to his wife, who sat to his left in the front seat.

"I should say." She leaned against him briefly.

"Is there enough room in here to transport Esther and the children to Zeke's?"

Barbara nodded. "We'll make do."

She wouldn't question him on this, he knew. Barbara was nothing at all like Esther Hochstetler, who had a mind of her own. *Just as Annie does*, he thought.

Jesse was unwavering in his plan. He would not rehearse it again in his mind, as he had lost a good amount of sleep last night, deliberating over today's visit to the Rancks on behalf of Zeke.

When they pulled into the drive, Barbara asked, "How is it Esther fled here?"

"I daresay Julia's responsible for Esther's temporary shunning . . . if you get my meaning. Too much worldly influence. Besides, Esther might've thought she had nowhere else to go."

"But it's not true." Barbara pushed a stray hair back from her forehead. "I s'pose it's time she got back under the covering of our brethren, jah?"

"Which is precisely why we're here," Jesse said as he tied up the horse.

They made their way toward the side of the house, Jesse steadying Barbara as they stepped carefully on the encrusted snow, icy in places.

"Come in, come in," said Irvin when he saw them at the door.

Soon, Julia was present, and she and Barbara went off together, arm in arm, into the front room.

Irvin and Jesse made the turn from the kitchen into the sunroom. "What brings you here?" asked Irvin. He was never one to mince words, Jesse recalled. If Irvin suspected an agenda, he wasted no time discussing the weather or anything else.

Jesse took the seat his cousin motioned to. "It's time Esther goes home."

Irvin reached up and scratched his blond head. "I wouldn't advise it, and I'll tell you why."

Jesse had no interest in listening to his Mennonite relative expound on matters that pertained to the Amish fold. Still, he sat patiently.

"Zeke's in no way ready to resume his role as the head of his house" came Irvin's definitive words.

"Well, ready or not, I'm taking Esther and the children back today." Jesse rose. "It's out of your hands." He might've added: *You had your opportunity and failed*, but he thought better of it.

Irvin got up quickly. "I say she stays here."

"Say all ya want, Cousin. Truth is, Esther's been gone long enough."

Irvin shook his head. "It's a shame for a man to treat his wife as Zeke has . . . and will again, no doubt."

Jesse wasn't interested in Irvin's opinion. "Esther's goin' home. That's all there is to it."

"Well, why not leave it up to her? See how she feels about returning?"

Jesse was irritated at the suggestion. "She's exerted her will enough already. Esther has no say now. Go and have Julia get her ready."

Irvin pushed his hands into his pockets. "The children are all napping, so there must not be any loud talk."

"So be it," said Jesse, glad for no significant ruffle of wills thus far. Despite Irvin's strong character and opinions, he was not a fighter. Not like Jesse, who still recalled the fuss between himself and Annie . . . over Yonie, of all things.

He assumed with his son well into courting age, Yonie would be settling down with a girl soon enough. He wouldn't want to embarrass himself much longer at singings and whatnot. He'd be letting his hair grow out again like his counterparts—the ones headed for the kneeling vow, that is.

Irvin left the room, heading back to the kitchen to talk quietly with Julia.

*Irvin's young enough to be my son*, thought Jesse, hoping the rest of the afternoon would go off without a hitch. He heard multiple footsteps now, Barbara and Julia both going upstairs to get Esther.

Wandering into the kitchen, he was conscious of the peace of this house. He pulled down a small paper cup from a wall dispenser and drew water from the faucet, contemplating his earlier words. *It's past time for Esther and Zeke to reunite*, he reassured himself.

He went to the front room, and in a few minutes, here came Esther accompanied by Barbara and Julia. "Hullo, Preacher Zook," said Esther, looking as though she'd just awakened. She held in her arms her infant, wrapped in a pink knitted blanket.

"Barbara and I will help get you and the children home," he said.

Esther glanced at Barbara and Julia, a worried look in her eyes. "Laura, Zach, and little John are sound asleep," she replied.

It was Irvin who stepped in. "Why not wait awhile, Jesse?" Then, turning to Julia, he suggested, "How about some coffee, hon?"

Julia nodded and quickly headed to the kitchen, followed by Barbara. Jesse wondered if Esther might go along with the women, too, and for a flicker of a second he saw by the angle of her head and the look in her eyes that she truly preferred to.

Sitting in the rocking chair instead, Esther held her baby close. "I'm not sure Zeke's ready for us, Preacher," she said, looking right at him.

"Oh jah, he is." He wouldn't reveal that Zeke had come and demanded her return yesterday.

"Well, what 'bout you, Irvin?" She turned her head and looked pleadingly. "What do you say?"

Irvin glanced at Jesse and back at Esther. "From my discussions with Zeke, I'd say hold off. He's not made much progress . . . and now, from what you've told us about his mother's death, I just think it's too soon. He's irate and distressed. Unreasonable, too, in some of his remarks."

Esther's eyes registered panic. "I have young children, Preacher. A nursing babe . . . two small boys. And . . . Laura is tenderhearted. It troubles her greatly when there is a noisy dispute in the house, or . . . worse."

*There should be no disputing at all,* he thought. Truth be told, Esther seemed to have had too much say already. And looking at Irvin, Jesse wasn't sure how to proceed without causing a squabble here and now.

"Can't I stay put?" Esther pleaded. "We—all of us—are safe . . . looked after here."

Jesse's heart momentarily went out to her. Was he doing the right thing, passing her off from the Rancks to Zeke's volatility? He looked at the sleeping babe; one small fist had managed to escape the blanket. *Lord God in heaven, am I doing right by this family?*

He felt strongly that Esther needed to be the submissive wife she was meant to be. But he also had a nagging feeling in his gut about sending her back prematurely. It was true; Zeke had seemed truly unstable at the news of his mother's passing, angry at his father and at the world in general.

"Just a few days more?" Esther entreated.

He spied the Holy Bible lying on the lamp table nearby and assumed Julia and Irvin had been filling Esther's head with alien beliefs. Something clicked in him just then. "No, I daresay your time here has come and gone. Have Julia help you gather your things . . . and the children."

He did not want to be on hand to witness the removal of Zeke's little ones from this house, their faces pink and their eyes glazed from a Sunday afternoon's rest disturbed.

Excusing himself, he went outside to wait in the cold, breathing deeply, thinking about the cows waiting to be milked . . . and contemplating Zeke, too. But it was a waste of time to think too hard about Zeke Hochstetler. This would not be much of a reunion for the couple, not with Esther still under the probationary shun.

*It remains to be seen how this will go,* he thought woefully.

He must not back down. Taking Esther home to the People was the right thing to do. If nothing else, it was high time for her to come back to the fold.

Fearful, Esther headed back to the attic room. *This is a horrid thing.*

Even so, she began to awaken Laura, then Zach. Little John was always the hardest to rouse from slumber.

Turning, she saw Julia standing near. Barbara Zook had stayed downstairs, for which Esther was relieved. This way, she and Julia could have their parting words in private.

Julia offered to hold Essie Ann, and Esther continued patting her children to wakefulness.

"You must remember what I'm going to say, Esther," Julia said ever so softly, bending to kiss Essie Ann's tiny forehead.

"I must not hesitate to leave Zeke again . . . if need be. Ain't so?" Esther said.

"Why, yes. No question on that. There is a shelter for women—and children—at the Water Street Mission, but it's all the way in town . . . Lancaster." Julia paused a moment, standing and swaying with the infant as she looked first at Essie Ann, then back to Esther. "That is, if you should feel uncomfortable, for whatever reason, returning here to Irvin and me."

Esther could read between the lines, and she was touched deeply by Julia's thoughtfulness and compassion. "Jah . . . you're most kind."

"And . . . we mustn't forget about the newly opened Green Pastures facility, run by Amish. I'm sure you've heard of it. I doubt, though, they have room for more than a few beds, but I can find out for you . . . just in case."

Esther recalled that following communion last fall, there had been a call for Amish house parents, after the main facility in Mt. Gretna first opened. Members of the Lancaster County Amish community had built the place, and it reflected their simple ways and cultural differences—no TVs or other modern amenities.

*A helpful place for someone troubled like Zeke? Or is Julia afraid I might be the one to crack up?* Esther wondered, feeling the tension in her jaw. *Why don't I just stand up to Preacher Jesse . . . tell him I'm staying on here?*

She wanted to speak up more than anything, but sometimes she felt as if she were losing her ability to think clearly . . . to sort things out. In the past she *had* worried she might not be able to manage her domestic responsibilities alone. Yet while living with the Rancks she had sensed none of that hesitancy, not since opening her heart to the Lord.

*So here I am heading back to a hornets' nest. Is this the Lord's will for me?* She cringed at the thought of Zeke tormenting her with the stipulations of her shunning . . . how it would keep her from the family table and the marital bed unless she renounced her salvation.

*Never,* she thought.

"The Lord Jesus go with you, Esther." Julia watched as Esther lifted John out of the bed and stood him on his feet, the two-year-old whimpering softly, rubbing his sleepy eyes.

"And with you, Julia."

"You know you're always welcome at our church . . . let us know if you would like a ride there, or whatever you need."

"I doubt I'd ever be allowed to go, considering the children."

"Well, if so, Irvin and I are here for you. Please keep in touch."

"Jah, I will." Tears blinded her vision. Then, suddenly, she was leaning on Julia's shoulder.

"Prayer is powerful . . . always remember," Julia whispered. " 'For the eyes of the Lord are over the righteous, and His ears are open unto their prayers.' " Julia kissed her cheek, and then those of the children.

"I best be hurryin'," Esther said, reaching down to lift John before asking Laura to take Zach's hand down the steps.

"Jesse and Barbara will look after you." Julia stopped short of saying more.

For the time being, Esther felt protected. After her arrival home, she could only imagine what she would face.

# Chapter 19

She had not been a spiteful child. Esther knew she had been a joy to her parents' hearts. But now . . . *now* she felt just horrid, wishing Irvin and Julia had spared her from returning to Zeke.

Slowly she made her way inside the house, carrying the baby and holding little John's hand. Laura and Zach followed behind, dawdling, and she knew why. Preacher Jesse and Barbara helped carry the few things they'd taken with them to the Rancks' place and set the overnight bag on the kitchen floor. There was also a suitcase, borrowed from Julia, with the items of clothing Esther had sewn for her children and herself while there. A pillowcase full of toys and books Julia had purchased had been left behind in the Rancks' attic, as well as several crocheted items.

"Hullo, Preacher," she heard Zeke call out to Jesse when he saw him. The two men shook hands good-naturedly, though Zeke's eyes were on her as she sat near the table with Essie Ann in her arms.

The kitchen looked remarkably clean for her having been gone so long. She wondered if perhaps Zeke had asked her mother to come over and scrub things up some.

Barbara pulled out a chair nearby, calling to Zach to come sit on her knee. But Zach and John hurried away, with Laura following them into the next room, and Esther heard the lid on the toy box creak open.

"They seem content to be home," Barbara offered.

*For a time maybe,* thought Esther. *Till their father shouts at their mother or pulls their hair and drags them across the room.* But she dismissed thoughts of their wretched past, trusting for a new beginning. Now that she was a child of the living God, her hope for a more suitable life with Zeke was becoming stronger. Still, she felt weary just entering this house, sitting here, looking around at all she'd left behind to escape Zeke's wrath, if only for a season.

When Preacher and Barbara said their good-byes, Esther tried to be as pleasant as always, but she could feel the tension in her face and neck. Her entire body strained under the awareness of her old surroundings, despite Zeke's grinning his welcome.

"You're home," he said, looking her over but good.

"Jah . . . home" was all she could say.

On Monday, Annie was careful not to jingle-jangle the bell on the door of the tack shop more than necessary, thinking it best not to draw attention to herself, since several men were standing around. But after a quick scan of the shop, she saw that Ben was nowhere in sight.

Quickly she headed for the window, facing out toward snow-covered fields, keenly aware of the smell of leather mixed with oil and a hint of tobacco rising off the farmers' woolen work coats.

*Oh, I must at least catch a glimpse of him.*

She straightened, wondering now if her trip here was to be a waste of time. But, no, she wouldn't think selfishly—she still had an exchange to make for her father.

Slowly she wandered through the shop, stopping to look at the assortment of bins filled with bridle accessories. A variety of horse collar paddings in different colors—she couldn't help noticing the brightness of reds and blues.

*Is Ben at work today?*

She pushed a smile onto her face, staying aloof from the other customers, a large group of them now heading for the door. Was it safe to search the shop for him?

She felt suddenly shy. But Ben Martin was her friend, or had been.

Just when she was about to approach the counter and return the bridle rosettes to someone other than Ben, she heard his voice.

"Annie . . . it's great to see you!"

She turned and there he was, smiling. "I've come to return this." She pushed the paper bag toward him. "Daed picked up someone else's bridle rosettes—he wants the ones with the little peacocks." She couldn't help but smile. "I wonder why."

His eyes shone as he took the bag from her. "I'm glad you're here," he said with a lowered voice. "I've wanted to talk with you about something . . . important. I have a few questions about your Plain customs."

She breathed in the dense aroma of the harness shop. "Ask me now."

"Well, it's rather complicated. It could take more than a few minutes."

His eyes were earnest. He must have legitimate questions.

She frowned, because at second glance he seemed almost tormented.

He leaned near. "It's regarding Zeke Hochstetler."

She had told herself she would never see him again, but Ben's request seemed urgent, and she worried there was possibly more trouble for Esther.

*All right,* she told herself. *This doesn't count.*

"I'll talk with ya, Ben. When?"

"Tonight?"

She nodded. "After supper?"

"What time would that be . . . for you, I mean?"

She stopped to think when she'd be finished eating and with kitchen chores. "About six-thirty or so."

"Sounds fine." He couldn't seem to keep his eyes off her. "Where should we meet?"

"Same place . . . just farther up. Near the big white pine tree on the north side of the road."

He nodded as if he knew which one.

"It's the largest tree round these parts. Some say it's nearly four hundred years old."

"You seem to know trees, Annie."

She shrugged. "A little, maybe. But you should talk to Zeke 'bout foliage and whatnot." She waved to him then and headed toward the door, feeling suddenly tongue-tied.

"Annie . . . didn't you forget something?" He held up the small sack with the wrong bridle rosettes inside.

She felt ever so foolish. *He must surely know how he affects me.*

"Oh, puh! I forgot what I came for."

She walked back to the counter, unable to prevent her smile. *I'll see him tonight!* her heart sang.

*Lou and I are two peas in a pod . . . both attracted to fellas we can't have.* Her throat suddenly felt terribly dry. *Am I a Dummkopp to meet Ben?*

He was pleased Annie had agreed to see him, and marveled at the landmark tree she had chosen for their meeting spot. The towering white pine must have been seventy feet high, its blue-tinted evergreen boughs spreading a good thirty feet. He parked his car beneath it, opening the door and getting out to wait for Annie.

He would have preferred it if she didn't have to walk all this way to the car, and on such a cold day, even though the afternoon had been fairly sunny.

She was right on time, and he could not suppress his excitement at first sight of her as she rounded the bend, wearing snow boots, a long black coat, gray gloves, and a blue-and-gray plaid scarf wrapped around her slender neck. *All we need now is a toboggan*, he thought, wishing they might have some fun together instead of the heavy discussion ahead.

He waved, moving toward her, wanting to help her along, even though the road was now nearly clear of snow.

She greeted him with a smile but did not speak, and for a good portion of the drive she remained silent. He rambled, taking the opportunity to tell about his first-ever mud sale . . . the several household tools and a small phone table he had bid on and won.

Then, when he could think of nothing else to say, he brought up what Zeke had told him about his brother's strange disappearance and death. "The boy's body was dumped in an Amish field nearby," he said slowly. "Zeke told me this."

"Wha-a-t?" she gasped, covering her mouth. "Oh, surely not. When did this happen?"

He looked at her, realizing their conversation would be less askward if he pulled over somewhere—at a fast food place, perhaps . . . anywhere.

As he drove, eyeing the various options for parking the car, he summarized what Zeke had told him about the shocking discovery of a child's body and the hushed-up burial. It seemed to drive Zeke mad.

"I can't believe it. Zeke's brother is actually dead?" Annie whispered, pressing her hand against her chest. "I always worried it was so, but now . . ."

It was all he could do not to reach over and pull her into his arms. She was shaking now, trembling from head to toe.

"This is the most terrible thing," she said. "Knowing Zeke and Esther as I do, it's doubly difficult."

She began to cry, unable to speak.

He turned into the nearest parking spot, leaving the engine running to provide heat. Then, reaching for her hand, he held it firmly in his own, glad she did not pull away. "This information is not to be disclosed, Annie. For some reason it is to be kept secret, known only by your church brethren."

"My father knows of this?" A look of horror crossed her face. "Oh, Ben!" She struggled further, letting go his hand to look for a handkerchief in her coat pocket.

Wiping her eyes, she sighed. "Why wasn't this announced from the housetops? The People would want to know. They would!"

He explained that the only reason he had told her was to solicit her advice. "Since I don't know the inner workings of your community. . . . I don't want to sound selfish, but I don't know what to do about a request Zeke made of me."

"Well, what's that?"

He wanted to hold her hand again but would not use her emotional state as an excuse. "Zeke wants me to go to the police. He's anxious for the murderer to be found . . . and every day that passes makes it harder."

"But if the death happened all those years ago, what's it matter?"

"That may be precisely the thinking behind keeping the death quiet, I don't know." He told her he was in favor of making the call to the police. "But there is the problem of Zeke's being shunned, too, if this gets out . . . and how difficult would the news be for your church folk if it should be known that Zeke was behind my reporting to the local authorities?"

Suddenly he thought of detectives combing the quiet farmland for clues, disturbing the peace. "What should I do, Annie?"

"I'm glad you came to me with this." She turned completely in the passenger's seat, studying his face, her eyes lingering. She had warmed to him; he was sure of it. "You must follow my father's wishes, Ben. Tell Zeke no."

"Can you explain?"

"The will of the Lord God and heavenly Father of us all, is the only explanation I can offer," she began, going on to say it was imperative for the People to revere and obey the church leaders.

"Even when it goes against the legal system?"

"The People aren't obligated to answer to the world. When the brethren deem things ought to be a particular way, then it's best to follow." She shook her head slowly, and there was a catch in her throat. "And Zeke knows better than to pull you in on this."

"Does his temper often get the better of him?"

"Sadly so. I've heard bits and pieces from Esther." Annie looked down at her folded hands.

"Is he abusive? Cruel?"

Annie nodded slowly.

"I assumed it," he said.

"Best be keepin' that quiet, too."

He looked at her fondly. Sad or not, she was absolutely beautiful. He held his breath to keep himself in check.

"I won't contact the police," he heard himself say.

"Denki, Ben. Thank you ever so much." She touched his arm, the slight pressure sending a charge of electricity through it.

"No, it is I who must thank you, Annie." He didn't attempt to explain, but he felt she understood.

He must put his hands on the steering wheel and drive her home now that he had the direction he needed. It was unfathomable why he should be sympathetic to the wishes of these so-called brethren of Annie's. Yet he wanted to do what was best, in the long run, for his troubled friend Zeke.

During the drive back, Annie talked nearly nonstop. By the time he turned onto Frogtown Road, he practically thrilled to hear her words: "This must be our secret, Ben. Ours alone."

He readily gave his promise. He cared about Annie's People, with their confusing yet simple ways. More than anything, he wanted to soak up every aspect of the Plain life, to share in its meanings—riddles or not—and he wanted to spend as much time doing so with Annie as she would allow.

So when it was *she* who asked if they could get together and talk again, he was astounded.

"Of course," he said.

"Wonderful-good." She smiled.

And, as before, when he braked the car, she nearly leaped out, this time coming around to his side even before he could get out. "Could we . . . uh, go skatin' somewhere?" she asked when his window was down.

"Roller or ice?" He laughed.

"On the ice might be best," she said, hands on the base of the window, eyes shining. "I know a place."

"This Wednesday I can get off work a bit early."

"Just whenever you say."

He opened his car door and got out. "I'll look forward to it."

"Well, I best be headin' home now, jah?" she said, lowering her head. "I really should. . . ."

He reached out to clasp her arms, resisting the temptation to draw her near. "Teach me all you know about your life here, Annie. Everything."

She raised her eyes to his. "Well, sure. I believe I can do that."

With that, she turned to go.

He leaned against the car door, his chest pounding as he watched her walk down the left side of the road toward the two golden lights flickering in Preacher Zook's farmhouse.

# Chapter 20

Annie did not ask Lou if she wanted to take a so-called journey down memory lane. She simply started pulling out boxes of Lou's letters from beneath the bed, organized by year and month.

The afternoon weather had turned dismal following the noon meal, looking nearly as miserable as Annie felt inside about Isaac's death. But she must not let on what she knew to Mamm or others. And she could not mope around. It was enough that her father was aware and had not revealed it to the People.

*Whatsoever things are pure . . . lovely . . . of a good report . . . think on these things.* She remembered hearing her older brother Christian's wife, Martha, recite the Scripture. Why Martha had it memorized, Annie didn't know. But there was something about the verse that kept her from forgetting it, too.

Today being Wednesday, she was glad to have her chores caught up, content, as well, to pass the time by reading aloud the letters in the upstairs bedroom. Lou, in turn, laughed or shook her head in astonishment, or asked to see proof of a comment or phrase in her own childish handwriting.

"Here's one that might make us cry," Annie said, lowering her voice, lest she be heard by resting Mammi Zook. It was one of the letters where Lou had shared the pain of being an only child.

*"Sometimes I think of you as more than my pen pal, Annie. I try to imagine that you are here . . . or that I am there with you. Do you think I'm crazy for such imaginings?*

*"Oh, and if you're nodding yes when you read this, then I must also say that having a sister is the best feeling of all.*

*"Have you always felt as lonely as I do? I'm only asking because you some-times write how nice it would be to have at least one sister instead of six brothers.*

*"Well, I don't blame you one bit if you long for a sister. And someday wouldn't it be fun if we could meet? Maybe you could visit me in Colorado. But, just between us, the most exciting thing would be for me to see you there in Amish country. I'm not kidding!"*

Annie looked up from the page, reciting the letter's date. "You were only eleven and a half and already curious about Plain life."

"Hey, I remember writing that." Lou rose to look at the stationery, decorated with Beanie Baby stickers. "Good grief, does anybody write snail mail anymore?"

"Well, I do. And Mamm writes to relatives in other states, too—they pass circle letters around, which is fun. Ever hear of one of those?"

"No, but I like the sound of it. Hey, kind of like what some people do by forwarding emails. I'll have to show you sometime when we're at Julia's."

Annie nodded, but immediately her thoughts were with Esther. "Mamm whispered to me yesterday that evidently Zeke got his wish."

"Esther's home?"

Annie said it was so. "Maybe things will be better now for her and the children."

"I hope you're right," Lou said, "but typically abusive spouses continue to mistreat those they love. Patterns don't stop because of a short separation."

"Well, Daed's goin' to be overseeing Zeke now, as I understand it."

"Not Irvin?"

"Far as I know, Irvin and Julia aren't to be contacted by either Zeke or Esther . . . but, knowin' Esther, she won't be able to cut off that close friendship. They've become 'sisters in the Lord,' as she likes to refer to their newfound kinship." Annie felt a twinge of envy.

Lou walked to the window and looked out. "Julia's an amazingly special person . . . I can see why Esther would want a close connection with her, in or out of the Lord . . . whatever sort of sister she wants."

Annie changed the subject. "So . . . are we done looking through these letters?"

Returning to sit on her bed, Lou said she was. "Let's save some for another gray day."

"Wonderful-good." Annie was careful to tuck the letters back into correct order again. Then she slid the boxes out of sight. "Ever think we were s'posed to be friends?"

"Like, uh, pure out-of-the-sky luck?"

"More like providence, like the way my father looks on most everything."

Lou frowned, looking puzzled. "Which is what?"

"Some call it God's sovereignty . . . or destiny." Annie pondered that for a moment. "Ever think that 'bout Sam, too?" she asked, daring to step on Lou's toes.

"Well, I wouldn't go that far." Lou's wide smile gave her away.

"Just think of it. What if you were s'posed to write me all that time . . . then come here and meet Sam? Like it was planned somehow."

"You really mean it, Annie?"

"Oh, I don't know. I just wondered if maybe you're supposed to be Amish, that's all." She threw a pillow at Lou. "Ever think that?"

"Too funny." Lou held on to the pillow, not tossing it back. She clutched it to her chest, as if it were a shield. "Goodness, why would you say such a silly thing?"

"Just 'cause."

"Spit it out, Annie."

"Well . . . I guess I've gotten so used to your hair lookin' like Mamm's and mine, and the cape dresses and aprons and whatnot." She sighed, not wanting to make too much out of what she felt.

"I sometimes wonder what it would be like to revisit my modern life," Lou said unexpectedly. "My mother would love to see me . . . wants me to come home for Easter. I guess it's safe to tell you that I miss my parents."

Annie felt suddenly hollow. "You'd leave here . . . for good?"

"Not sure."

"Well, I'm sorry I brought this up." The last thing Annie wanted was to think about saying good-bye to Lou.

Barely two full days had passed since Esther's return home and already she was beginning to notice the cracks in Zeke's resolve. At first, he'd gone overboard being kind, even surprisingly helpful with Zach and John, which was heartening to her. But that lasted only from late Sunday afternoon through most of yesterday.

Already today there had been several pointed, even cutting remarks, mostly in regard to her required repentance. "You have no choice but to make a confession and soon," he told her when he'd marched indoors to warm up.

She handed him a mug of black coffee. "How on earth can I?"

"Stubbornness does not become you, woman."

She would not respond and risk starting something that would only escalate, especially not with Essie Ann so small and sleeping in the wooden cradle not too far from the wood stove.

"The brethren expect you to give up this nonsense about salvation within the next few weeks," Zeke said suddenly.

She remained silent, standing next to the sink, her weight pushing against it.

"I'll not have you under the Bann forever, Esther. Ya hear?"

She nodded, not in agreement but in an attempt to go along.

"It's high time you submitted." He was standing next to her now, close enough that she could smell the barn on his clothes and feel his strapping shoulder brushing against her. He squeezed her arm till she could hardly feel her fingers. "Ain't right to keep your husband waiting . . . usin' the shun against me."

She guessed he'd think as much. *But, ach, to say it!* Zeke probably didn't care one iota about shunning stipulations. Most likely he would force her to break the rules in due time . . . once Essie Ann was six weeks old.

*Ten days away . . .*

Their lovemaking—if it could be called that—would then become his secret, for he would not go to the brethren with such a confession. And woe unto her if *she* did.

When Essie Ann began to whimper, Esther was relieved. Zeke let go of her, and she turned quickly away, going to her newborn and plucking her tenderly out of the cradle. Without looking back, she carried her baby upstairs to nurse in the stillness of the bedroom.

Ben got his chance to ask Annie about the local trees during their long drive to the secluded pond. She was a storehouse of information, describing not only numerous leaf shapes but differing bark textures and other identifying details of the trees he pointed out on the way.

When Ben expressed how impressed he was at her knowledge, Annie had smiled self-consciously, as if he truly was making too much of it.

But it was not Annie's familiarity with local flora he wanted to focus on this night. He had made a quick trip to the Goodwill store and purchased a pair of nearly new ice skates, and was amused at Annie's ability to smuggle a pair of her own out to the car in a wicker basket, as if she were feigning a visit to a neighbor.

The hours crept up on them as they skated on the millpond, the surroundings awash in a moon-white sheen. When they held hands, zipping round and round on the ice, he felt frozen in time, though he would never have admitted it to Annie. It was as if what was happening was not real at all, but a lucid dream—a weaving together of two hearts amid the tranquility of twilight. The few other Englishers there scarcely seemed to notice them as they flew across the ice, so their secret was safe.

Annie seemed to be an open book about her life, and he felt almost too comfortable talking with her about his family in Kentucky, as well, wishing he might introduce her to them someday. *Too soon to think this way . . .*

Eagerly she told of her longtime pen-pal friendship with Louisa, formerly one of her "big secrets," which made him wonder what other secrets might be locked away from view.

After their first night of skating he had offered to store her skates in his trunk so she wouldn't have to sneak them in and out of the house again.

They met nearly every other night after that. Annie was apparently delighted to return to the same place repeatedly. There the world seemed to go still for them, like a shelter for their growing friendship. At least while they skated they could talk and laugh and enjoy the feel of the blades gliding on ice, even though Ben was concerned that Annie not get too chilled.

Sometimes they would hurry back to the car to warm up before resuming their dance, the night dissolving into a dazzling memory of hoarfrost and snow-clad trees near the pond—*their pond.*

Within two weeks, their secluded meetings began to run together in his mind. Yet he could not blur the memory of Annie's quaint remarks, her appealing smile . . . the firm touch of her small hand in his.

*Never let go . . .* he thought.

And in spite of the bitter cold they endured night after night, Ben was in no hurry for warmer temperatures, nor for the sweet blossoming of spring.

# Chapter 21

The house felt terribly cold to Esther this Lord's Day. Hurrying to get a hot breakfast on the table, she was aware of Zeke's pushing more logs into the belly of the wood stove. The old stove was their best means of heating the house—especially the downstairs. Their two kerosene heaters often stood in the upstairs hallway, near the children's rooms. Though Zeke was proud they weren't "spoilt with central heating," like their English neighbors, he spoke of the spring thaw often, hoping it was not too far away.

Esther hoped so, too. But there was more on her mind today than the coming of spring. The People were planning to meet following the Preaching service today—to vote on whether or not to shun her.

She was in a quandary, no doubt about that. Here she was, grateful to the Lord for her deliverance from sin and despair, from the legalism that had ensnared and dominated her for a lifetime, yet facing the dreaded shunning.

*Will my own mother turn her back on me? Will Annie and my dearest friends? Will my children, in time?*

Esther would not let fear overtake her. She would move only one small step forward at a time, clasping the hand of divine guidance, the precious Holy Spirit. *My comfort in this dark hour . . .*

The Preaching service went longer than usual and much emphasis was placed on "waywardness leading to pride," which Preachers Hochstetler and Zook adeptly wove into their sermons. Esther observed Preacher Jesse's soberness as he stood before them, beads of perspiration on his face. More than once, he paused to mop his brow, occasionally catching her eye where she sat cradling her baby with the women. All the while, she prayed silently for the Lord's will to be accomplished in her life and the lives of the dear ones here. *Thy will be done on earth, as it is in heaven. . . .*

When time came for the members' meeting, following the closing hymn and dismissal of the non-baptized youth, Esther was asked to leave the room. Annie's father would lead the discussion, after which each member would have his or her say about Esther's unwillingness to atone for her sin of pride and defiance. Very soon, the voting would take place.

*The outcome is clear,* she thought, surprised to hear footsteps in the hallway from the upstairs bedroom where she waited.

When she looked, there was Louisa, Annie's friend, wearing a big smile on her face. "Mind if I keep you company, Esther?"

"Why, no. Come on in."

Louisa made herself right at home, sitting on the edge of the bed. John scampered over to her right quick. "It was kind of funny," she said, looking as Amish as the rest of the women. "I think the ministers forgot I'm not one of them."

"Oh? And where's Annie?"

"She left to help watch some of the younger children during the meeting." Louisa lifted John and placed him on her lap. "Want to ride horsey?" He nodded, giggling, and she jostled him up and down. "The deacon shooed me out when they realized I was still sitting there."

"Well, you might've gotten to voice your say and voted me out of the fellowship," Esther said.

Louisa shook her head. "I doubt that. Whatever you did isn't grounds for being kicked out, is it?"

"According to our Ordnung, a person is not to embrace the assurance of salvation in any way." She wouldn't go into this now, but she did say that she knew she was saved. "It isn't only a feeling—it's the strongest knowing I've ever experienced. The Scriptures say I can claim the promise of eternal life, and this has nothin' at all to do with pride . . . and everything to do with the love shown in the ultimate sacrifice of the Lord Jesus."

"Julia talked of faith and love being interconnected, too," Louisa said suddenly.

"I don't see how you can separate them." She wouldn't have minded talking about the verses in the Psalms she'd read earlier this morning, but Louisa rose just then and seemed to lose interest, setting John down and going to pick up Essie Ann.

Esther put her mind on what King David had written so long ago: seeking with all of your heart and finding the peace of God in troublesome times. *Such as now* . . .

She almost wanted to go downstairs and hurry up the process, the inevitable result of embracing *a perverse doctrine*, as the preachers and deacon had repeatedly said when they had met with her during her stay with the Rancks.

Breathing a sigh and a prayer, she walked across the room to stand at the window while Louisa rocked Essie Ann. She contemplated her situation, married to a man who would always uphold the Ordnung and its requirements. *No doubt I'll not even be allowed to sit at the table with my family.*

Suddenly, she felt the need to look into the sweet face of her baby, soundly asleep. She bent to kiss her soft cheek. "A gift from God, I must say," Esther said softly.

"A pretty one, too," Louisa agreed, smiling. "I'll babysit for you anytime."

"Why, that's awful nice." Seeing Louisa so gentle with a babe in arms, Esther had no doubt Annie's friend would be a good option for helping, if ever necessary. She thought, too, of her widowed mother, ever willing and eager to spend time with the children, and with Esther, too. As for Zeke, Mamma had never been too keen on her son-in-law. It was no wonder.

Turning, Esther went slowly to the window and gazed out over the undisturbed fields of white. Beneath all that snow lay hardened ground and narrow hideaways where small critters hibernated from the harsh weather.

*I, too, burrowed away . . . for a time.*

She recalled having walked over a thin layer of soil peeking out from beneath frozen ground just this morning. And she'd slid, catching herself.

Now the sound of Deacon Byler's calling pulled her out of her reverie. She and Louisa—who was clearly enamored with Essie Ann—and the children all headed slowly down the stairs to the solemn gathering.

Had it not been for Louisa and Annie, as well as Esther's mother, young Laura and the boys might have been exposed to the bishop's straight talk directed toward Esther and in front of the entire membership. As it was, the three women and the children scurried out to the kitchen.

It turned out the fellowship of saints, of which Esther had been a part since her teenage baptism, had chosen to put teeth to her formal Bann and excommunication: They would shun her permanently. "Even unto death, until such a time when you will bow your knee and repent," Bishop Stoltzfus decreed.

When the time came for Esther to stand before the man of God, she scarcely knew where to look. *If Zeke should happen to catch my eye . . .*

Yet she did not accept guilt. For she knew in the deep of her heart she had come to her life's crossroad and had elected that "holy and just path."

*I must cling to this for always.*

Meanwhile, as the bishop announced "the blemished one" would lose her status as a voting member, Esther prayed for the strength, determination, and grace to withstand the years of social avoidance awaiting her.

Zeke was clearly put out, even swearing in Dutch, forced as he was to miss the common meal and the fellowship with the men because of the shun slapped on Esther. Forced to miss much more, too.

"You've shamed me! In front of all the People, yet. You are a disgrace, woman." He shook his head. "Ach, and Deacon's wife brought peach cobbler, too," he bellyached, as though the departure from their usual dessert fare was more important than accompanying his family home. But he was required to take Esther and the children away from the meeting place and the large gathering for the meal, where she would not have been welcome at any table.

There were Scriptures the brethren looked to in the case of *die Meinding—* the shunning. One from Matthew came to mind, that she had heard preached since her baptism: *If (the sinner) refuses to listen even to the church, treat him as you would a pagan. . . .* Verses in First Corinthians also admonished believers to abstain from eating and fellowshipping with idolaters and other sinners. Esther was now considered such an offender.

Shielding her baby from the cold air blowing into the front of their old gray carriage, Esther stared at the frost clinging to every imaginable spot as they rode. Ponds, creeks, hollows in fields and on roads, where former snows had melted and now had turned to pure ice. *Perty,* she thought, attempting to keep her chin up despite the reality of the day.

Once home, Esther quickly set about laying out a lunch of cold cuts and butter bread, along with red beet eggs—all made yesterday. Zeke, meanwhile, brought in the folding table and banged it down on the kitchen floor, then got himself situated at their long table, stonily silent for a time.

At one point Zach asked timidly, "How long is Mamma gonna sit over there?"

Elbows on the table, Zeke glowered. "Forever, by the looks of it. Don't be gawkin' at her. Just eat."

*So this is what it's going to be like*, Esther thought. *An outcast in my own home.*

After the meal, she put the children down for naps. Then, hurrying back to the kitchen, she redd things up and headed upstairs for a bit of a rest herself.

Curling up in bed with her Bible and Essie Ann, she began to will her body to relax. Zeke had taken the team and left the house, though he hadn't said he was going anywhere in particular. *Gone visiting, probably.*

She knew she must not envy Julia's relationship with Irvin, but the memory of hearing him tell his wife fond *good-byes* and *I love yous* prior to his heading off to run errands was altogether unlike her experience. That and their many other thoughtful exchanges—verbal and otherwise—made Esther realize that Irvin and Julia's marriage was a strong and happy one . . . a witness of God's love in a couple's life.

*How can I possibly have that with Zeke . . . now? Won't he always resent me for standing firm for my beliefs?* She assumed he would rail against her for not giving in to the People's expectations, for not honoring the Ordnung, in the long run. In Zeke's eyes she was most disobedient.

*In God's eyes . . . what am I?*

The nagging thought persisted. Closing her eyes, she asked for the Holy Spirit's protective covering over her mind. "And help me to keep my thoughts centered on you, O Lord," she whispered.

In all her days, Annie had never felt so torn. Esther had been shunned till death, or until such time as she should bend her knee in contrition. Mamm had whispered the outcome of the solemn meeting at the common meal, and now Annie felt nearly sick to her stomach. She didn't rightly know or understand Esther's stand now that she believed herself to be "saved." Annie only knew how the People looked on such a thing. Pride was the ultimate and original sin. So to excuse Esther, even in Annie's own mind, was to join her in her haughtiness.

She could only hope she might still see Esther occasionally, although that remained to be seen. Mamm would tell her one way or the other, she knew. Daed, too, would say something if Annie was so bold as to bring it up. Non-baptized folk were not to be privy to what was voted upon.

So Esther would live under Zeke's roof and covering, yet not be allowed to partake of food at the same table. She would also not be permitted to pass money or other objects from her hand to the hand of a church member in good standing. There were other, more personal stipulations regarding marriage that Annie suspected but had never been told directly.

It would be a painful life for dear Esther. No, she mustn't even be thought of as dear any longer. Not while she was in this rebellious state. And Annie knew she must attempt to follow her parents' stance on this delicate issue, hard as that would be.

While Annie was tied up with church, Ben drove over slippery roads to locate the old covered bridge on Belmont Road. He had avoided the area altogether after the creepy sensation he'd first encountered. Now he was determined to conquer the peculiar sense of disquiet by walking through to the north entrance of the old bridge.

His snow boots clunked hollowly on the wooden planks as the boards gave with each step. When a horse and carriage came rattling through—folks from another district—the vibrations shook his entire body, and he was suddenly very aware of his rib cage.

*Shakin' your liver loose*—an unexpected phrase came to mind.

He smiled at the recollection and kept going, staring at the back of the Amish buggy, its orange triangle reflector catching his eye as it moved on, up the steep hill and beyond.

Stopping, he uttered a sound, listening to the echo. "Hello," he said quietly, then slightly louder, "Hello-o-o-o." Then he whistled, paying attention to the muted ricochet.

Going all the way out of the bridge and around the long stone abutment on his left, he turned and headed down toward the creek.

The snow lay in great patches, and he could see where pods from the black locust trees had fallen during the recent storm. He recalled someone once saying that cows liked to chew on ground-up locust pods. Stooping, he picked up several, noticing the reddish brown color, the deep, rippled texture, and the beanlike seeds inside. He counted fourteen.

He slipped two narrow four-inch pods into his pocket, recalling how his mother had often shaken her head, offering a bemused smile as she handed back the peach stones that seemed to wind up in the laundry from time to time. Other pieces of nature had landed in the washer, too, but she hadn't ever complained. It was as if she understood his need to pick up things, investigate, and either discard or keep them in his possession. His dad had not been so keen on his collection of "junk," as he called the array of items. But, for some reason, the peach pits had remained a favorite, just as they had for his best friend, Eric, who had carried one in his pocket for as long as he could remember, too.

Slowly, Ben moved toward the grove of trees. Reveling in the tranquility of the area, he was no longer conscious of alarm, as before. He had a sudden urge to bring Annie here in the spring to stand here with him beneath the flowering branches of these beautiful, tall trees. He was impatient to see if he was right about the blossoms, eager to know if they were white as lilies, as in his dreams.

Esther had been reading a Bible story to the older children near the wood stove while nursing Essie Ann. All the while Zach kept glancing at the ceiling, his eyes bright with the awareness of the ticking sound of sleet on the roof. Soon Laura and John were looking up, as well.

"Does the Lord God make the snow and sleet?" Zach asked when she finished the story.

"Our heavenly Father knows just what we need—rain, sleet, snow—and we can trust Him for everything. Even for the weather." She had been cautiously yet consistently sharing with the children, ever so eager to pass along all she was learning about the standard for holiness and godliness as found in the Holy Scriptures.

"The Lord calmed the wind and the storm," Laura told her little brother. "Remember that story?"

"Jah, yesterday." Zach, soon to be four years old, smiled, not so serious now.

"And God rained down a special kind of food," Laura said, looking quite pleased with her good memory.

"Manna," said Zach, looking equally pleased.

They came and gave her a simultaneous hug. "Ach, I love you so," Esther said, kissing each sweet head.

It was evident that Laura and Zach had noticed a change in her. She was beginning to see a tenderness of spirit in them, too. Julia had counseled that the children would become "hungry for more of the Lord Jesus" as they were presented with the gospel over time. *"Laura, Zach, and little John will know instinctively what motivates your life, Esther. Even if you don't talk of it constantly . . . they'll sense God in you,"* she'd said repeatedly.

*These words, which I command thee this day, shall be in thine heart: And thou shalt teach them diligently unto thy children, and shalt talk of them when thou sittest in thine house, and when thou walkest by the way, and when thou liest down, and when thou risest up.*

"Who a person is—how they conduct their lives—will influence a child for righteousness," Julia had said.

*Who I am is going to have more of an effect on people than what I say. At least till they can understand. If they ever do.* Esther breathed a prayer for strength to carry out her responsibility as a new believer both at home and in the community. And for submitting to her husband, as unto the Lord. She felt a renewed compassion for Zeke, which she believed had been graciously given her from God.

Still, Julia had forgotten to take into account that another spirit was at work in this house. *An opposing one*, Esther thought as she patted Essie Ann, waiting for the wee burps. She pondered Zeke's resistance to her study of the Bible, before she sent Laura and the boys upstairs to get ready for bed.

Sitting quietly in the rocking chair, she stared at the day clock on the wall, wondering where Zeke had taken himself off to on such an inclement night. She cherished the nearness of her infant, realizing how much she missed Julia and Irvin—the helpful comments and their devotional times, their children and hers listening to the stories and the prayers.

*Ach, I daresn't think backwards. . . .*

Any minute now Zeke would return. She must brace herself emotionally and hope she would not be wounded by his piercing words. *Nor his increasingly rough treatment of me.*

Had she not been holding her baby, she might've allowed a bit of pity to seep from her soul. It was best she not give way to tears, although it was difficult to understand how one could be banned from the "fellowship," simply due to embracing the whole truth of the Word of God. She had already tried to argue this with the brethren and with Zeke, to no avail. Now it was time for her to live out her walk with the Lord in a non-condemning manner, hoping to win them by her witness, in word and deed. She must let her light shine before the men who wished to rule her ability to choose Jesus Christ as her Lord and Master.

Sighing, she made her way up the long staircase, weary at the thought of the separateness that awaited her. It was not easy to sleep in the cold and distant bedroom at the end of the hall, as she had been doing since returning. Separated from the darling children who'd shared the Rancks' attic with her, all of them together snug and safe. And separated from Zeke, as she would be each night for the rest of her life, though it was not what she would have chosen, given a say.

# Chapter 22

Ben was surprised when Zeke appeared at the door of his apartment. "Hey," he said. "Come on in."

Zeke stepped inside and Ben asked if he wanted some coffee or something else hot to drink. "Always coffee, jah." Zeke stood in the sitting area and looked first at the couch, then the leather chair.

"Sit wherever," Ben said.

Ambling over to the chair, Zeke sat with a groan, as if older than his years.

Ben was still puzzled as to why Zeke would track him down here at home, but he didn't ask. And when the coffee had finished percolating, he chose one of his largest mugs to fill with the dark brew for Zeke. "Sugar or cream or both?" he asked.

"Always black."

Once Ben was settled on the sofa with his own coffee mug, Zeke began to talk about one injustice after another. He rambled, seemingly upset at "the liberals," and Ben found it curious that Zeke had access to current events.

Ben waited for him to bring up the death of his brother again, as blunt as he'd been at the mud sale, but Zeke didn't go there. What he seemed to be working toward was a different sort of request: a wood-splitting workday. "I'm needin' some help to clear out trees damaged in the snowstorm. You got time?"

Ben smiled, hoping his relief wasn't too evident. "I'll make the time. When?"

"Tomorrow's good—after you're done with work?"

Ben paused, knowing Annie would be waiting for him up the road from her house, as usual. "I could help you for several hours in the morning, *before* I head for work."

Zeke grinned. "Jah, 'tis even better. Come on over for breakfast, then. That'll be your pay."

"Sounds fine. Thanks." *Anything for a home-cooked meal*, he thought.

Zeke sat and talked a bit longer, mostly about his being under the weather due to the recent cold snap. "This winter's been too long. Nearly endless, it seems."

Ben floundered for the right words. "Who knows, maybe you'll feel better when spring comes. . . ."

"I doubt that." Zeke shook his head. "Guess a body oughta get used to losin' a part of himself . . . sooner or later."

Zeke quit talking, and Ben understood he was thinking again of his long-dead brother.

A hunting hound barked at the hint of first light in the eastern sky, and early risers all around Paradise estimated how many bales of hay were left in the barn.

Ben drove to Zeke's place carefully, aware of ice patches on the road. *He said to come for breakfast.* But it certainly seemed like an imposition as Ben made the turn into the narrow driveway leading to the house, dark except for a light in the kitchen.

When no one answered his several knocks, he listened at the door and heard a teakettle squealing and a baby doing the same. Inching the door open, he found the kitchen in disarray. Oatmeal was boiling over from one pot on the stove, and Esther came rushing in with the howling baby in one arm and the smallest boy pulling on the hem of her apron.

"Ach, Ben . . . it's you," she said, handing him Essie Ann, still small at just two months old. "Glad you let yourself in." She leaned down to pick up John, whispered something in his ear, and then set him back down. Hurrying to the stove, she removed the pot of oatmeal. "As you can see, it's been quite a mornin'."

"I don't need to stay if—"

"No . . . no, you're here, so have yourself a nice hot breakfast." She said Zeke had been called to help the neighbor but would be back any minute.

He felt strange alone in the kitchen with Zeke's wife, but the three children lessened his uneasiness.

"Goodness me," Esther said, looking over at him holding the baby. "I daresay you've got a gentle way with little ones."

He, too, had just realized Essie Ann had stopped her wailing. "This happens at home, too, when my sister and family visit. Their baby son, well . . . does he ever have a set of lungs!"

"And you calm him, no matter his temper?" asked Esther.

He nodded. "I'm sure it's just a fluke."

Esther laughed, leaning down to swipe a washcloth across John's face, then using the same cloth on Zach's mouth. "Well, I think it's right fine that a young man should have such a soothing effect on an infant."

He grinned at Essie Ann, who was looking up at him.

"Seems she remembers you," Esther said before walking into the next room and calling up the steps, "Laura, hurry down, now."

He chuckled. "Nobody remembers much about the day of their birth."

Esther returned, fanning her face with her apron, while pointing Zach and John toward the table. "I daresay you should think 'bout having yourself a dozen or so young'uns." She looked over at him again. "Sit anywhere 'cept the head of the table."

"Thanks." He sat to the right of the head, across from the boys, who were eyeing him now.

"That's Mamma's place," Zach said. "Or was."

Ben rose quickly.

"No . . . no. That's quite all right," Esther said, motioning him back down. "I won't be sittin' at all."

A curious look crossed Zach's face, and he turned quickly to look at his mother, who was heading across the kitchen again to call for Laura. "Mamma sits alone ev'ry meal now," Zach whispered.

Ben wondered what that was about.

"Dat never says why," Zach said, clamming up when his mother came back into the room.

"Here, let me put Essie Ann down for a nap," Esther said, taking the baby from him. "She woke up mighty early this mornin'."

"Jah, and she cried a lot in the night, Mamma," Zach volunteered.

"Colicky some," Esther replied.

Little John sat still, just staring at him. Ben tried to engage him by wrinkling his face into comical poses. At last John spoke. "You . . . our cousin?"

Zach laughed. "No, you *Bensel* . . . this is the harness shop man. Mr. Ranck's friend."

411

"I *not* silly. He's Cousin Nate," insisted John, squinting now at Ben.

Esther carried over a large bowl of oatmeal. "This here is Ben Martin, boys. You've met him before."

"Jah, Laura says he's the one with the smoothest peach stone in the whole wide world," Zach said.

Ben was amused.

"Ever see Dat's collection of old peach pits?" Zach asked.

"Boys . . . now, that's enough. Mr. Ben's not interested in suchlike."

But Ben found their chatter refreshing.

Soon Laura joined them at the table, sitting next to John and looking bright-eyed. Her parted blond hair shone beneath her white head covering, exactly like Esther's.

"Where's Dat's bag of peach stones?" Zach asked, leaning forward, directing the question to Laura.

Laura shrugged. "Guess they upped and walked off."

"Well, you've seen 'em. I haven't." Zach resumed his attention to his breakfast plate, going for the jellied toast before the oatmeal.

"Best be askin' Dat." Laura drank nearly half her milk and wiped her mouth on her sleeve. "Where is he, anyway?"

"Bessie next door was fixin' to have her calves," Esther said, coming over to survey the children's plates.

"Aw, I want to go 'n' see." Laura frowned.

"Me too," said Zach.

"Jah, and me do, too," said John, poking his chubby chest.

"Well, now, Dat can take all of you over yonder here 'fore too long." Esther poured more milk for Laura. "Now yous need to stop talkin' Ben's ear off and eat."

"Oh, I'm enjoying this," Ben piped up.

"You come from a big family?" Esther asked somewhat shyly.

"Four younger sisters."

Zach found that funny and made his eyes bug out. "All girls, puh!"

"Aw, Zach," said Esther.

"It's not so bad havin' two of us round here," Laura said, glancing over at Essie Ann in the cradle.

"Well, at least one ain't so lippy just yet," Zach said, smiling at Ben as if they shared a secret, man to man.

"No, but the baby's got a fierce cry," Laura said, "which means she'll be frank enough someday."

"Like Mamma?" Zach said.

Esther laughed out loud, shaking her head, then turned back to the wood stove.

*What a fun-loving bunch*, Ben thought, wondering what was keeping their father.

Ben and the children had finished off most of the oatmeal and jellied toast. Esther, never having sat once, was already frying eggs for the boys and Zeke, offering an egg or two to Ben, as well.

Ben politely declined, not accustomed to eating so heartily at dawn. He was relieved to see Zeke as he entered, and raised his chin in greeting as Zeke came in and sat down.

"Glad you went ahead," Zeke said, explaining how he'd helped his neighbor deliver a calf. "Always fascinating." Zeke looked at Esther just then, and she hurried over with a platter of freshly cooked eggs.

"I s'pose yous offered the blessing?" Zeke said, looking straight at the boys.

"I did this time," Zach said.

"Jah, he led the silent prayer," Esther said, rumpling his hair.

"My good little man," Zeke replied.

Ben accepted another cup of coffee while Zeke downed his meal, but Esther hovered between the stove, the table, and sink, even now that Zeke was here and all of them had been served.

*What's up with that?* Ben wondered. *And why does she sit alone at mealtime?* Everything else about the family had seemed surprisingly normal this morning. And though he knew it was none of his business, he felt glad Esther and the children had reunited with Zeke.

With Annie frequently disappearing to see Ben, Louisa had more time to spend with Sam. Still, she was getting antsy. Here it was already mid-March and she wanted to start making some money again, if not for the sake of paying additional room and board to Barbara Zook, then for her own sense of self-esteem. She wasn't a slacker, and she missed the income from selling her paintings through the local gallery.

She had been eyeing section B—"Local"—of the *Lancaster New Era*, the newspaper at Julia's. The Lancaster Museum of Art, downtown, was of most interest to her. Eileen Sauders, the owner of the art gallery on Route 30, had been talking about an April event—the Spring Art Walk—which was to include some of her own acquisitions in a regional show, sponsored by the museum.

Louisa was also beginning to feel the need to extend herself, to give back something to this community she had come to respect, something even more than attending quilting bees and canning frolics here in Paradise, although that was important, too. She decided to apply for a position teaching art to younger students.

By keeping her days free for delving into the Amish culture she so enjoyed, she could spare a few evenings a week, passing on her love of fine art to children. This would not impinge on her seeing Sam, either. Besides, with the plowing and planting season coming soon, he would become rather scarce, as he had already warned her.

When she really thought about it, she knew she couldn't resist putting down a few roots here. Although it was beyond her ability to imagine how her romance with Sam could possibly move forward, Louisa realized she was trying on the Plain life in her head. Not playacting, as she had been doing all these past months, but seeing how it fit her—for real.

She tried to be attentive at Preaching services, but the sermons were in Dutch. And seemed pointless. She soaked up both Annie's and Sam's perspectives, noting that neither had joined the church as of yet. She even listened more closely when Annie's grandmother, Mammi Zook, talked in the quiet of the evening. She enjoyed the quaint and interesting way Mammi's Dutch and English became mixed together while doing needlepoint and cross-stitch. Mammi seemed almost too eager to have Louisa sit with her in the small front room of the Dawdi Haus.

When a voice mail showed up on her Palm, saying the museum contact person wanted to interview her ASAP, Louisa let out a little whoop of joy. Quickly she thought better of celebrating, since she hadn't told Annie yet, waiting to first see how things went. She'd gone so far as to apply online in order to keep from having to ask to borrow Julia's car. Until now.

Louisa knew she ought to bounce the whole thing off Annie before moving ahead. It wouldn't be fair to reintroduce the world of art, not now when Annie was looking ahead to the beginning of her baptismal instruction classes next month. Annie had managed to stay away from her artistic passion to date—at least Louisa believed she had—and she didn't want to interfere in any way with the plan Annie and her father had worked out. She didn't know exactly how Ben Martin fit into *that* equation, and Annie hadn't said much lately about her love life.

That night, after playing three games of checkers with Mammi Zook, Louisa laid out the whole plan to Annie upstairs.

414

"You mean it, Lou? You're gonna get a job here?" Annie's eyes lit up.

"Don't get the wrong idea," she insisted. "It'll be for only six weeks this summer . . . after I get back from Denver."

Annie frowned. "You're still thinking of going home for Easter?"

"I've already told my parents, so no turning back."

"Well, jah. I can see that." Annie's mood quickly returned to elation, and she asked if Lou had called the museum back.

"I wanted you to know first," Louisa said.

"Even before Sam?"

Louisa smiled. "Anyone ever tell you you're trouble?"

"All the time."

Louisa guessed Ben had been teasing Annie. "So . . . what's new with you and your beau?"

Blushing, Annie replied, "I need to borrow some fancy clothes."

"You what?"

"Just a perty skirt or dress . . . something 'specially modest."

Louisa pounced. "Well, let's get you out on the town, girl. Time for some new threads? I say we go shopping!"

Annie grimaced. "Now listen . . . I'm not askin' for attention. I just need to have something to wear out . . . well, in the modern world every so often."

"In Ben's world, you mean?"

A poignant silence filled the room, and Annie sat there on her bed like a stone statue, unflinching, looking down at her hands.

"Listen, you don't have to tell me anything if you don't want to." There. She'd released her friend to protect her private thoughts and plans. But the silence was telling.

*We've both lost our heads . . . and our hearts.*

Annie's request for a modern outfit came because Ben had purchased tickets to the musical *Behold the Lamb* at the Sight and Sound Millennium Theatre for the Saturday afternoon following Easter. "I haven't decided yet if I'll take down my hair, though. And I don't know 'bout my Kapp, either," Annie said a few days later.

Louisa found it interesting that Annie would even consider going out dressed fancy but still looking very Amish from the neck up. "I think it would be better to wear your cape dress and apron if you aren't going to do something cool and different with your hair."

*Oops, did I say that?*

But either Annie didn't catch on or she chose to ignore it. Her argument for wearing English clothes was that the weather was getting nicer, and she was beginning to feel strange about being seen with a fancy fellow when she looked so Plain herself.

"So . . . maybe Ben's influencing you?"

"Only a little."

"A little? Come on, Annie. Listen to yourself!"

Annie moseyed over to her bureau and opened the middle drawer. "Truth is, I'm crazy 'bout him, Lou."

"I think I know the feeling."

Annie turned. "You?" She broke into a smile. "Does this mean . . . ?"

"I have no idea what it means, but I'm going to find out." Louisa felt half empty without Sam, and when he held her near, she forgot every other guy she'd ever dated.

*What comes over me when I'm with him?*

She had tried on many scenarios in her head, including one in which Sam finally decided to join the Amish church. Would she still want to be with him?

*"You and I . . . we'll know better when you're away for Easter,"* he had said, which made her wonder how that could be. *"Absence makes the heart grow fonder,"* he'd added.

*"Yeah, and sometimes fonder of another."* She hadn't meant to be glib, but she knew this firsthand. One case in point: Trey's leaving for London had made her susceptible to Michael's attention. And the last thing she wanted was to view Sam's affection, in any way, as a replacement for that of her former fiancé.

*"I'll be true to you, Louisa,"* Sam had promised. *"No matter how long you're away."*

His words had thrilled her and made her want to celebrate every moment they had together, yet she feared the very thing that would eventually keep Annie and Ben apart would one day tear Sam from her, too.

*The revered Ordnung.*

Footsteps in the hallway. Esther sensed them first in her subconscious, half bracing even as she dreamed. Dread filled her veins, and her legs tensed.

Now came the slow creak of boards outside her room. Hazily she attempted to open her eyes. Only slightly awake, she was aware of the darkness . . . of the crib in the corner. The unfamiliar movement in the room.

"Esther . . ."

Zeke's voice.

She attempted to make a sound. But her words got lost in the mist of drowsiness, and she wondered if she ought to remain silent. Or was she actually dreaming?

She felt the bed give way beneath his weight. Her husband was not waiting for her answer.

Moving her arm, she pulled the covers up.

"Ach, good . . . you ain't sleepin' this time."

"Well, I was. Truly, I was."

"I've been without you too long." His lips brushed her temple, her hair.

"But . . . the Bann," she said, quickly becoming alert.

"Well, then, God help us both." He stroked her hair, caressed her face.

She felt a distant yearning within, surprised by it . . . and soon with his persistent kisses, she was unable to resist his ever-tightening embrace. *Such tenderness tonight. Does he love me after all?*

Torn between her apprehension and her own latent desire, she said no more. She remembered the Scripture about an unbelieving husband being sanctified through his wife, and the thought gave her a smidgen of hope.

Later, when Zeke had fallen asleep, she slipped her arm from beneath his. Zeke started and gasped in his sleep.

Esther froze.

"I'm sorry . . ." he moaned hoarsely. "So sorry."

Esther's heart began to pound. *Can it be? Is he finally repentant for the way he treats me?*

But before she could open her mouth to respond, Zeke moaned again. "Oh, Isaac, I've wronged you so. I'm ever so sorry. . . ."

# Chapter 23

Julia wouldn't hear of it; she insisted Louisa take her car.

"No need to offer money for gas!" she admonished and said she'd be praying for Louisa, too.

Appreciative of her generosity, but not surprised by it, Louisa took the offered keys and waved good-bye to Annie, as well as to little Molly and James. "I won't be gone long," she told Julia, who smiled and said to take all the time she needed.

*There should be more people like her,* Louisa thought, heading out the side door of the house to the detached garage. She felt strange wearing slacks again—chic black dress pants and a soft pink top—business casual. Her dress boots were easier to get used to again, because she often wore Yonie's or Omar's sloppy ones out in the peacock pen with Annie or when helping with barn chores. She had grown accustomed to seeing her feet in black.

Julia had been nice enough to volunteer one of the children's bedrooms, where Louisa had changed clothes, getting some assistance with her hair from Annie. The middle part hadn't seemed to want to disappear, so Louisa remedied that by brushing all of it over to the side and scrunching it up a bit. She sprayed it lightly, pleased with the flowing, mussed-up look.

Downtown, she parked in the lot adjacent to the museum, glad for her trusty MapQuest directions. The woman she was to meet, a Janet Blake, ushered her into a small yet well-furnished office. Within twenty minutes, Louisa had not only secured the teaching slot for the summer ArtSmart classes for seven- to twelve-year-olds, but she was told she could possibly be filling in for a pregnant teacher, as soon as next week.

"I can't tell you how excited we are to have you on board here, Louisa," the well-coiffed woman said. "We like to employ young people with art degrees. Too many artists hole up in their studios, disinterested in teaching." Janet seemed intrigued when Louisa mentioned her address in Paradise.

"I'm staying with an Amish family," Louisa explained.

"How remarkable. Is this a particular study—the Plain life, perhaps?"

"I'm visiting a friend."

"Well, I've seen some fine work by an Amish artist . . . and not so long ago. Also from the Paradise area, I believe."

That caught Louisa's attention. "Where was that? At a gallery?"

"As a matter of fact, my friend Eileen Sauder owns one on Route 30. She often speaks of a young Amishwoman, about your age, who has brought paintings to be framed . . . and soon are sold. More recently, though, the artist has not been supplying any new work."

Louisa realized Janet was most likely talking about her. "I know that gallery," she admitted.

"Eileen has been getting requests for more paintings. She phoned last week, inquiring if I knew anyone among the Amish community . . . in Paradise, in hopes of locating the artist."

*I need to let Miss Sauder know I'm limiting my output,* thought Louisa, wondering if at some point, once she was well established, she might want to begin accepting work on commission.

She realized her thinking was askew. She was behaving as if she were going to continue to live here.

Janet reminded her to pick up a parking permit before leaving and thanked Louisa once again for applying. "I think you'll enjoy teaching here," she said, pushing back from her desk.

Louisa thanked her for her time. "I hope to see you next week." She smiled and headed out the door, willing herself not to linger at the walls filled with fine art.

Outside, she decided to walk a while, since her interview had been rather short. Taken by the lovely historic buildings along the tree-lined street, she walked up East Marion and turned on North Cherry, wondering what it might be like to lease a small downtown apartment. She breathed in the air, filling her lungs as she wandered the cobblestone streets, enjoying herself immensely. She caught herself doing a double take when glancing down at her clothing.

*How strange I look to myself. . . .*

When she turned onto North Duke Street, she spotted the public library and hurried to cross the busy street. Upon entering the stately old building, she noticed the lofty ceilings and impressive crown molding, thinking again how wonderful it might be to live in such a neighborhood.

Discarding the notion as pure fantasy, she strolled through the rows of bookshelves and located the magazine section. She picked up several of her favorite art-related magazines and scanned through feature articles, deciding she missed this world and should start a subscription promptly. *When I decide how long I'm staying. . . .*

When her cell rang, she checked the ID and grinned. Sam was calling from the barn phone his family shared with a neighbor. "Hey," she answered softly, having received one other call from him at this number. "Can you wait just a minute?"

Not wishing to disturb the other patrons, she promptly made her way to the entrance. "Okay, I can talk now."

"I had to hear your voice, Louisa. My day isn't complete unless I do."

"Oh, you're sweet. Well, guess what I did today?" She didn't wait; she told him of her new teaching job. "I wish you could see the museum where I'll be working. It's just magnificent," she said. "The current art exhibit is so amazing."

"I've wandered around downtown some," he said. "I even took the walking tour with a group of tourists once."

"Really, when was this?"

"After class one day. I was dressed for the occasion, too," he said, chuckling into the phone. "Fancy, ya know."

She smiled. "I've got some mighty fine wheels today."

He admitted having had a car not so long ago, which didn't surprise her.

"You really must have pushed the limits during your teen years."

"More than you know. And I don't mean to say I'm proud of it . . . well, only of my community college degree."

Louisa wondered if he had dated other English girls, perhaps. "I need to return Julia's car," she said, checking her watch. "And change back into my Amish clothes for supper at the Zooks'."

"Dr. Jekyll and Miss Hyde, jah?"

Louisa chuckled.

"When will I see you again?" he asked.

"I think I'd better hang out with Annie this week."

"Oh." He sounded glum. "That's no fun."

"How about sometime over the weekend?"

"Saturday night?" he asked. "Wear your English clothes and we'll go somewhere as fancy folk."

She wondered how she'd pull that off. "I may have to change somewhere, after I meet you." She was thinking of not offending Annie's parents again.

"That's plenty easy. It's done all the time."

These were strange remarks coming from Sam, and she could hardly wait to hear more. When he said, "I'm sendin' a fond good-bye to you," she knew she missed him terribly, too. "Till Saturday, Louisa. Take good care, ya hear?"

"You, too. 'Bye for now."

Julia had emphasized the fact that children will absorb the spirit of God in their parents' lives, but Esther sat quite alone at a folding table in the kitchen, as Zeke and the children ate their supper together. Zeke did not speak either to the children or to her during the meal of veal ring, tomato zucchini casserole, and mashed potatoes. She had labored tirelessly to please him, although she knew how fond Laura and Zach were of the zucchini dish, too.

The past few days, Laura and the boys had witnessed, yet again, the rage simmering within their father. And for all the nights Zeke made his way into Esther's bedroom, he was not at all a placid man by day. Nothing seemed to put a permanent smile on Zeke's face.

*How will our children soak up the love and acceptance of their heavenly Father if they don't see it in Zeke?*

She brooded during the meal, only glancing at her family twice before Zeke called out his desire for pie and more coffee. She leaped up, responding as she knew he wished her to. She was careful not to allow tears in front of the children, although once Laura had caught her off guard as she read her Bible alone.

Laura, more than Zach or John, had been curious upon their return home, asking why she slept alone in the bedroom, "so far away from Dat."

Because she did not wish to expose Laura to a needless fear of the Bann and shunning, she told her daughter, "You'll understand better one day, when you're lots older." She had not said a thing about joining the Amish church or committing one's entire life to a kneeling vow. A first-grader need not know what lay ahead. Esther pondered how she might steer her little ones toward the grace of the Lord Jesus. *Live out the life of faith before them,* Julia had instructed, but Julia's words and the life she lived with her thoughtful Irvin were fast becoming a distant memory.

*I need the fellowship of believers,* thought Esther. But it was foolish to even consider, given she'd heard tell of women losing their children if certain brethren got wind of Sunday school and church attendance at a worldly meetinghouse.

Such things could be grounds for a husband to separate from the wife and take custody of the children.

*Surely Zeke will not go that far.*

Sighing, she wondered what was to become of her darling children over time.

Lest she create a nervous stomach as she ate, she began to count their mutual blessings, one of which was Zeke's growing friendship with Englischer Ben Martin. A most unlikely person, to be sure. Even so, Ben's coming to help Zeke chop and stack wood had been nothing less than an act of kindness— something that had put a short-lived spring in her husband's step. The sound of wood giving way to axes and chain saws had been comforting that morning, as was Ben's holding and effortlessly quieting Essie Ann.

Zeke had long declared that wood cut and stacked and put in the woodshed in late winter would burn far better in late autumn. He was smart that way, and now he had a sidekick of sorts, or so it had seemed from Ben's and Zeke's cheerful banter as they left the house together, axes slung over their shoulders.

Finished with her meal, Esther rose and cleared her table. Zeke excused himself to head outdoors, leaving the children and their places messy, but Esther didn't mind. She often felt something of a reprieve when her husband opened the back door and exited, as if the contentious spirit followed out, right behind him.

Sam leaned forward, close enough to kiss her again. Louisa flinched; they'd kissed enough. "Sam, can we talk for a while?"

She leaned against the door of the car he'd borrowed from a cousin for the evening. "We *need* to talk." She wanted to be near him, sure. Her heart beat crazily when he looked at her that way, his dearest eyes . . . filled with love.

"I wish you'd stay." He reached for her hand. "In Paradise, ya know."

She yearned for his embrace, his amazing kisses, but an inner voice cautioned her.

He sighed, releasing her hand. "I have an idea . . . a place I want to take you very soon. A kind of celebration."

She wished she couldn't guess what was coming, though part of her was eager for it. What girl didn't long to be cherished? Proposed to? But Sam was enmeshed in the Amish world . . . and she was a hindrance to him.

"I want you to understand something." He folded his hands as if in prayer. "I'm in love with you, Louisa."

She held her breath. Oh, the power . . . the impact of such a declaration. Hadn't she wanted to hear this? Hadn't she suspected as much?

His eyes were earnest, as if waiting for an answer in kind.

"Oh, Sam. I love what we have . . . yes. But I'm far from being Plain. Farther, perhaps, than you know." She was thinking of her eagerness to paint and draw again . . . to teach, to earn money . . . and more.

She touched her blouse collar and glanced down at her pretty new skirt.

"This is the real me. *This,*" she said softly.

"Ach, I wouldn't change a thing 'bout you." He said no more. And all during the drive home, she resisted the urge to look at him for fear she might change her mind about what she knew she must do.

"I'm freaked," Louisa told Annie upstairs, in the privacy of their room.

Annie perched on her bed, peaceful as a dove. "Well, I can see that."

Louisa paced the length of the long room as Muffin poked his kitty head out from beneath Louisa's bed and watched.

"Sam wants more than I can give." Louisa groaned. "I should have listened to my head instead of thinking I could just have fun without either of us getting hurt." She stopped pacing. "Now he's in love with me."

"You're just so lovable—could that be it?"

Louisa felt like crying. "Oh, Annie, what'll I do?"

"Tell him the truth."

"Which is . . . ?"

A train whistle sounded in the distance, and Louisa flopped onto the bed. Muffin leaped up and snuggled his head into the crook of her arm.

"Tell Sam how you feel 'bout him." Annie went to her, eyes sympathetic.

Louisa shook her head. "Don't you realize what that means? I'd have to leave my life for good. If I were to follow through . . ."

"Ach, what's so wrong with that?"

"Well, you didn't leave your art for Rudy."

"No," agreed Annie quietly. "Not for Rudy." She reached over Louisa and stroked her cat. "But Sam . . . Sam makes you smile like nobody's business. You should see how your eyes shine like stars when he walks toward you. He's all you've been livin' for here lately. Ain't so?"

"You don't get it." Louisa leaned her head back on a pillow. "I don't *really* belong here. I thought maybe I did, but I don't."

"How can you say that?" Annie blinked her eyes and a frown crossed her brow. "Don't be too hasty to decide. Besides, I like havin' you here. You're my sister."

Lying there, staring at the high ceiling, Louisa wondered how she had ever fallen asleep to the sound of beeping taxis instead of the call of barn swallows. How would she ever find such peace anywhere again? But Sam . . . where did he fit in?

"People do crazy things for love," Annie said softly. "Things even harder than changing a lifestyle, I daresay."

Louisa looked at her and nodded, scarcely able to speak. Could she ever really belong to Sam, give up her art? Live under the Ordnung? But on the other hand, how hard would it be to leave him behind? Give up the chance to journey toward Julia's remarkable faith? And dear Annie—how could she say good-bye to her?

*Funny,* she thought. *A man brought me here . . . and a man's sending me back.*

"Annie," she said suddenly, "I don't know how I'll pull this off, but I think I need to go home."

"Aw . . . Lou."

"No, really. I should have admitted this before. To you . . . and to myself."

"Admitted what?"

Louisa sighed. "Courtney's visit stirred up a bunch of unresolved issues. At first they pushed me toward Sam, but now, well, I just don't know where I should be."

The two dressed for bed, saying no more.

# Chapter 24

Annie searched for her slippers in the darkness. When her feet found them, she pulled on her long bathrobe.

"Lou?" she whispered.

Lighting the lantern, she was suddenly quite aware of her friend's absence. A quick search—beneath the other bed and in the bureau drawers—confirmed that Lou had taken her belongings. Her luggage was gone, too.

Sighing, Annie sat on the edge of the already made bed, where Lou had sat and giggled and cuddled Muffin and said the most hilarious things.

Here, on this bed, Lou had sketched drawings of two-story barns and haughty peacocks. Here Annie had found Lou's art hidden beneath the pillows when first they'd moved to this room.

She smiled wistfully, remembering all the happy days. "A wonderful, sisterly, good time."

Then, just as she rose to make her own bed, she spied Lou's soft tan skirt and creamy blouse hanging on the wooden wall pegs next to the cape dresses and aprons. "Ach, she remembered!" Annie laughed out loud, hastening to the pretty English outfit and pressing it to her face.

She noticed Lou's fashionable tan suede boots on the floor, and a sand-colored silky pair of hosiery rolled up in a small plastic bag. A pretty gold barrette was nestled in a white box atop two envelopes. One marked *To Annie*, the other addressed to Sam Glick.

Sighing, she sat near the lantern's light and opened her letter.

*Dear Annie,*

*It's 2:30 a.m. and I'm writing this downstairs in Mammi Zook's little kitchen by candlelight. Can you believe it, I'm actually up before anyone in this house? Muffin is already snoozing in his carrier, ready to fly (stand-by) with me, and all my stuff is gathered around me. But I couldn't leave without writing to you, my dearest friend.*

*I'm calling a cab as soon as I sign my name here. I'm not sure if there is enough power left, but I think there is. (I figure if my smart phone is dead, then maybe I wasn't supposed to leave. Our talk about providence still sticks in my head, you see.)*

*I really wanted to say good-bye in person, but I knew if I did, you'd talk me out of going. I also wanted to tell your wonderful family thank you, especially your mom, who was like a second mother to me all these months. But I couldn't wait till the dawn, because I would've changed my mind in a heartbeat. And if I'd stayed and gone to Preaching today, well, seeing Sam again would definitely mess with my head. I really can't go there now, Annie. Maybe someday I'll explain, if I can.*

*Thanks for everything. I mean that. I wish I might have stayed here in your paradise longer. Maybe forever.*

> *With love,*
> *Louisa*

Annie couldn't help but lament cell phones and Palms and fancy whatnots, wishing they'd never been invented. She wished Lou were still here, too.

Staring at the letter, Annie noticed the handwriting looked a bit shaky and wondered if Lou might've been crying.

*She loved being here. And she loves Sam. . . .*

While frying eggs, Mamm shook her head, saying she could not fathom why on earth Louisa just upped and left. "Never even said good-bye."

"She wished she could have thanked the whole family, but her leaving had nothing to do with any of us." Annie couldn't say any more lest she start to cry.

"Well, dear, why don't you think of moving back to your old room?" Mamm suggested.

Annie gathered her composure. "S'pose I could, but maybe I'll just stay put for the time being."

When Daed heard the news, the lines around his mouth showed signs of relaxing. *Obvious relief . . . and no wonder.* But Mammi Zook sighed and patted her chest, her eyes moist.

They all sat down together—Annie, her brothers, Mamm, Daed, and Mammi and Dawdi—terribly conscious of the now-vacant spot where Louisa had always sat.

"That Lou was somethin', jah?" Yonie spoke up at last.

"That's the truth," Annie replied.

"I'll miss her, too," Mamm said.

Daed frowned and cut them off by signaling it was time for the blessing.

They bowed their heads in unison. But instead of offering gratitude to the Lord God heavenly Father for the provision of food, Annie skipped over the rote prayer in her head. This day she was most thankful for Lou's visit—the whole of it—and how an English pen pal had radically changed her life for the better.

Preaching service went longer than Annie ever remembered it lasting. During the membership meeting that followed, she sat in the far corner of the kitchen, entertaining Esther's children by tying knots in her linen hankie.

"Where's your friend?" Laura asked, her arms folded across her chest like she was a miniature lady.

"Heading home now, I 'spect." Coming right out with it was far better than fudging. Truth be known, Annie wished Lou hadn't chosen her to deliver the message to Sam. *She might've mailed it to him,* she thought. But if he were observant at all, he would have noticed Lou was missing, for she'd never once skipped a Sunday gathering here.

Annie felt for the sealed envelope deep in her pocket.

"Why'd Louisa leave?" asked Laura.

"Well, she knew she couldn't stay for good."

Laura turned to look out the window. "Too bad, jah?"

Annie nodded.

"I liked her a lot. She was nice to me and my brothers . . . and to Molly and James, too."

Annie nodded. "She sure was."

"Will she come see us again?"

"Anything's possible, I guess."

Laura turned away from the window, a big smile on her wee face. "That's what Mamma says a lot. 'All things are possible.'"

*A wonderful-good thing.*

427

"Believin' is ever so important," Annie said, starting a game of peekaboo with little John.

"Ach, Mamma says that, too."

When the membership meeting was finished, and the food for the common meal was brought up from the cold cellar, Annie took John, Zach, and Laura back to find Esther, who'd gone for a short walk, as she was not welcome at the meeting. On the way Annie spotted Sam, who looked as dejected as Lou had last night.

When Annie caught Sam's attention, she was glad the Hochstetler children were in tow, or she might have been tempted to stand and chat with him a while, to offer a comforting word or two.

Silently she pulled out the envelope and slipped it into his hand.

"From Louisa?" he asked.

She nodded. Taking the envelope, he walked quickly away.

Annie was glad Mamm was so willing to go visiting during the next few weeks. Nearly every day they dropped in on either Sarah Mae, Martha, Priscilla, or other womenfolk.

The house seemed topsy-turvy without Louisa in it, and even Dawdi agreed with Mammi when she said how much she missed Louisa spending time with her in the evenings, doing their needlework by the fire. "She was starting to understand some Dutch, too," Mammi said, shaking her head sadly.

One morning, while enjoying chamomile tea and cinnamon rolls at Martha's, Annie heard the happy news that her sister-in-law was expecting again. "The more babies in the family, the more fun we'll have, ain't?" Annie said, wishing Lou might be on hand to celebrate.

*All the crocheting of booties and blankets ahead!*

When not going visiting, Annie counted hay bales with Yonie. There was also some talk that Daed and Luke were planning to drive fence posts in the southeast pasture. And Omar mentioned some of the loggers were eyeing the woods up yonder.

*Winter's fading,* she thought, wishing Louisa were here to see the pussy willow buds soon to appear.

With the warmer days came the anticipation of Good Friday's fast day. The membership would contemplate the Ordnung prayerfully, and, if all were in one accord, they would rejoice by taking communion as a group, followed by their twice-yearly foot washing. Shortly after that would come the start of baptismal instruction. Annie found herself looking often at the calendar, counting the days till she and the other applicants would meet with the ministers. She knew she had to be certain of her resolve before making the commitment to study, a thought which kept her awake at night.

She and Ben were still seeing each other every week, and as wonderful as it was spending time together, she also worried she was replacing one vice for another—trading her art for her forbidden beau. She knew she must decide to join church. Or, better yet, as Julia often said, seek to know the will and purpose of God.

Truth was, she had a hard time thinking the Lord could be bothered with what she did or didn't do. *With so many folk in the world, with oodles of needs, why on earth would He care one way or the other?*

Esther continued to grasp hold of hope, but what was happening between her and Zeke had nothing to do with goodness or godliness. She made tiny dots on the calendar for each time her husband dishonored her shunning, not for the purpose of reporting him, but for her own sake—if she should become pregnant again. And what a revelation to the brethren that would be!

She'd known of spouses who did not heed the Bann, disobeying the ministers; they soon ended up shunned themselves. Gently she reminded Zeke of this, yet it was impossible to thwart him. A pattern had been set, and she was helpless to stop it. But she would not allow her interrupted sleep or any of his violent outbursts during the day to rob her of the peace she carried silently within. Her greatest joy came both from the Lord and her children, in that order.

The days marched swiftly into April, and Esther realized she had not visited her mother for quite some time. Eager to get out of the house, and missing her talks with Julia, she bundled up the baby and the boys, while Laura was at school, and took the team several miles up the road.

When she arrived at her brother's place and the small Dawdi Haus built for her mother, Esther was met with an unexpected reaction. Mamma scarcely looked at her and would not invite them in, though she eyed Essie Ann, whose bright little eyes blinked up at her grandmother. "Are ya busy, then?" Esther managed to ask, her heart heavy.

"Well, jah . . . I am."

Esther looked down at Zach and John, both shivering a bit. "I s'pose we could come another time."

Her mother stood as rigid and silent as the glass figurines Esther had seen in Julia's curio cabinet. They caught each other's gaze, and slowly but surely Esther came to understand the full meaning of rejection as she waited on the back stoop.

*The shun . . .*

But something powerful, even bold, rose up in her. "The children are awful cold," she whispered, leaning forward. "Mayn't *they* come in?"

Tears sprang into Mamma's eyes, and she opened the door wider. "Hullo, Zach . . . John," she said, not bending down to kiss them. She rather ignored Essie Ann, and for this Esther felt even stronger pangs of sadness.

*This isn't about the children. She must not treat them so!*

As she watched her children standing in Mamma's small front room with their wraps still on, Esther realized suddenly that the social avoidance meant for her would take its toll on her offspring. This made her feel even more isolated in the face of Zeke's mistreatment of her and their little ones.

"Come, play with the blocks," her mother said, placing a large box on the floor near the small cookstove.

The boys hurried to begin their play, coats still buttoned up. Eventually Zach shed his, but it lay on the floor where he left it. Never before would Mamma have allowed that. She would have asked her grandson to hand it up to her, lest she hurt her bad back bending low. And when tiny Essie Ann became fussy, Mamma did not offer to take her and walk about the room, whispering softly in Dutch, as she had done countless times with her other grandchildren.

Esther had heard of staunch folk who insisted on placing the infant of a shunned church member on a table or other surface before the baby could be passed to another's arms, but she had not expected such from her mother.

She was surprised when, after a time, Mamma offered some hot tea. Eager for something warm, Esther asked if she could help. But she was denied that, being told to sit and wait till the teakettle whistled.

"Ach, Mamma, this is silly."

"No . . . no, the wisdom of the ages, Esther," her mother said with a severe look. "Our church leaders are to be honored."

"Above one's own flesh and blood?" Esther asked, though the answer was within her.

"The brethren are ordained of the most high God," Mamma said. "Always remember this, truly."

*Is this what I must endure for all my days?*

❖

430

Leaning forward in the carriage, Jesse made his way to Al Fisher's farm. Al, who had never known of the alarming discovery on his land, needed help seeding his oats crop, and a few of the neighboring men had volunteered to put in a half day over there, after finishing up their own chores.

Barbara had asked, sweetly as always, if Jesse would be home for supper, and he had smiled and said he would. Her chicken and homemade dumplings were the best, by far, of any he had ever eaten. A big incentive . . . that, and her sweet kisses, still offered after all these years.

Jesse let his mind wander to Annie's English friend, who had surprised all of them by disappearing in the night. He realized anew how fond Barbara had been of Louisa, and it annoyed him.

*Long past time for her to head on home,* he decided. *Besides, Annie will soon meet with the brethren about her baptism.*

He would've patted himself on the back if he weren't out here on the road.

"Annie's goin' to make it to her kneelin' vow, sure looks like," he mumbled, enjoying the ride alone while counting his blessings. It seemed like Preacher Moses had known what he was talking about, as always.

*Louisa was a godsend, after all.*

He contemplated Annie's recent attitude, which seemed to have improved some since Louisa's exit back into the modern world. Barbara suggested with a smile that maybe their Annie had herself a new beau. They both had heard the soft thump of footsteps on the stairs after midnight, though Annie had not stayed out till the dawn with this new fellow, like she had with Rudy Esh, which made Jesse wonder. And none of the fathers were whispering that one of their own was seeing the preacher's daughter.

*Whoever it is, he's surely keeping tight-lipped on it.*

He almost chuckled at the enduring spunk of his daughter.

# Chapter 25

Louisa had hardly recognized her mother upon first arriving home. *She's had a face lift or something drastic. Trying to look twenty-one again?*

But Louisa hadn't said a word, trying to ease herself back into the lives of her stiff and cautious parents. They seemed to walk on eggshells with her, too. Neither her dad nor her mother asked even once about her decision to return, which was a relief, because all Louisa could think about was Sam . . . and Annie. *Paradise.*

Settled once again in her apartment, she wished she might have waited at least until the morning—perhaps after breakfast that final Sunday—to announce her leaving. She had wanted to give Barbara Zook a hug, maybe even a little kiss on her rosy cheeks for being a stand-in mom. But she'd observed how physically reserved the Amish women were upon greeting or saying good-bye. They scarcely ever touched, but their generous spirits were like a bighearted embrace.

Easter dinner at her parents' was an all-out gala, festive in every way, with Daddy's favorite traditional roast lamb dinner, all five courses perfectly paired with five wine options. The entire time she sat at the elegant table Louisa thought of Amish country, wondering what foods Annie and her family were enjoying. Had they left a vacant seat for her, where she'd always sat at the long table? What funny antic had Yonie pulled? In her mind she could see Jesse Zook bow his head, offering thanks, which was the farthest thing from anyone's mind here at *this* table.

Relatives from out of state, as well as local friends, came for the afternoon. Mother was literally shimmering in her new orchid cocktail dress . . .

432

and triumphant smile. She had purchased a new set of fine china just for the occasion. All the expensive niceties of her parents' life did not bother Louisa as before, and she recognized what had made the difference.

"People are anxious to see you, dear," Mother had informed Louisa prior to the grand meal, as if to say: You've been out of your mind long enough. . . .

In some ways Louisa realized she *had* lost it, but certainly not mentally. She had lost something of herself, sure . . . but she hadn't lost her way. She had found a new approach to living, coupled with the abandonment of self. Everything within her cried out to utilize what she'd learned here and now, in part through a strange yearning to extend herself to her domineering mother. This awareness alarmed her at first, so strikingly different it was from the old way of managing their relationship, but she no longer minded if her mom called the shots. As long as it didn't step on anyone's toes, who cared? She was suddenly seeing the world through her parents' eyes—the need to hold on to a daughter, their one and only child—whom they loved and had been deprived of having around for nearly five months. They had genuinely missed her.

And Louisa had missed them.

Soon, though, she wanted to begin sending letters to Pennsylvania—a long one to Annie and one to Mammi Zook, maybe with a few Dutch words included just for fun. And, sometime later, when she truly knew how to express what was most important, she would write to Sam again.

Back in the full swing of teaching her art students, she was already planning the next exhibit. It wasn't as if she had given up too much back in Lancaster. She had called Janet Blake on her cell to apologize for any inconveniences her leaving had caused the museum. She had merely traded one locale for another. Paradise for Denver. The People for the modern rat race.

With all of her heart, she hoped Sam—most of all—would forgive her. If only he could know how his love had given her a fresh perspective on nearly everything. She hoped something of her fondness for him had opened a door on his future, as well.

*I won't forget you, Sam,* she often thought while driving to and from her art studio, her heart full with the memory of him.

*I won't. . . .*

The afternoon sun twinkled through new green needles on the tall white pine tree as Annie happily settled herself into Ben's car, more excited than she wished to let on. *A play based on Christ's final days on earth . . . on an enormous stage, and set to music!*

She had already shared her disappointment with Ben over Lou's leaving. So she decided not to mention it again, at least not during *this* special day.

"Your hair's different," Ben said, winking at her. "I like it."

She couldn't help but smile. She had pinned it up just long enough to get out of the house. Then, on the walk to meet Ben she'd removed her bonnet and let her hair down, clipping the side back with Lou's gold barrette. "If you think this is different, wait till you see my English clothes." Her long black coat covered up the skirt and blouse Lou had so kindly left for her.

"I'm sure they're lovely." He looked at her. "Just like you, Annie. You're always my beautiful girl. . . ."

*My girl.*

"Maybe I'd better show you now, so you're not too awful embarrassed . . . later on at the theater, I mean." The car was plenty warm enough. Still she was glad for the blouse's long sleeves, sheer though they were. Her fingers found the top coat button.

She wondered if he would be surprised at the length of this skirt, only two inches below her knees. *Not that an Englischer should mind. . . .*

Slipping her heavy coat off her shoulders a bit, she said, "What do you think?"

The car swerved ever so slightly. "You look . . . very pretty."

She felt she ought to tell him "thank you," but she didn't. She was almost scared he might prefer such fancy clothes to what she usually wore.

"Did you buy this just for tonight?"

She explained that Lou had purchased the clothes when Courtney was visiting but had graciously left them for her.

He reached for her hand and she thrilled to his touch, glancing down at their entwined fingers.

Then, while still holding her hand, he lifted it to his face and kissed it. The sweet sensation lingered all during the ride down Route 30, to the turnoff toward Strasburg. Secretly she was glad she hadn't worn gloves.

The grand well-lit entrance to the Sight and Sound Millennium Theatre appeared on the right, and he released her hand before making the turn. Reaching into his jacket, he pulled out two tickets.

"Julia said it was awful hard to get a reservation," she said, eyeing them.

"The guy at the box office said they're usually sold out weeks, even months ahead. Of course, this presentation only runs another week."

"Oh, I can hardly wait." She felt giddy.

Ben agreed, breaking into a grin. "It's an enormous tourist draw—busloads come from all different states, even from other countries." He pointed toward several large buses in the vast parking lot. "From what I hear, it's one of the biggest local attractions, next to the Amish themselves."

There was an awkward pause.

"Uh . . . I hope that didn't come out wrong," he said.

"'Course not. We both know how interested outsiders are."

They both had a good laugh over his blunder, and he seemed relieved.

He pulled into a parking spot far from the main entrance and turned to face her, his eyes shining. "About what you said earlier. I want you to know I would never, ever be embarrassed of you. Please remember that."

"All right," she replied and was not startled when he leaned forward to kiss her cheek.

Still, she wondered what he would think when he saw her wearing fashionable suede boots and this relatively short skirt. Her thoroughly English appearance would be revealed when she removed her coat in the bright theater lobby.

Slowly, happily, they made their way to the enormous theater, hand in hand.

Ben had trouble keeping his eyes off Annie as they mingled with the intermission crowd in the vast theater lobby. She had seemed struck by the drama and music as well as the colorful costumes. Having observed Annie's nearly childlike wonderment, her face alight, he wanted to open even more experiential doors for her.

When the lights blinked off and on to alert the attendees to find their seats, he reached for her hand. "Ready for the grand finale?"

"This is just so surprisingly real, ain't so? It makes the Bible characters seem like they're livin' right there on the stage . . . the Last Supper, the Lord's death . . . all of it."

*Christ . . . beloved and betrayed.* He couldn't stop thinking about the theme of the play. The music, the words—it was as if he had never heard this ancient story told quite so effectively. He had attended many movies and dinner theaters, but he agreed with Annie that this production was presented on a magnificent scale. He felt he was almost witnessing the show through Annie's eyes, which made it all the more memorable.

Taking their seats again, he wondered how he could ever ask her to leave the Plain community, if that time should ever come. *If* was the operative thought. Such a thing smacked of pure selfishness. He would be upsetting the apple cart in more than one way, and wasn't it presumptuous of him to think he could threaten the stability of Annie's church district? Of course, her father's church wasn't really Annie's yet in the truest sense. Still, he wondered how Annie and he could ever really be together.

He looked at her, smiling as they waited for the next act to begin. He had been more than surprised by her long hair, now parted on the side, a pretty gold barrette securing its shimmering golden thickness. She looked totally different without the white head covering he'd come to expect.

He hadn't asked her to dress differently for tonight. *Did she do this for me? And if so, why?*

She must have wanted to blend in with the thousands of people in the audience, but he'd had no intention of putting such expectations on her. With or without her prayer cap, she was exceptionally lovely.

Too warm for his sports coat, he removed it, placing it behind him on the seat. Settling back, he ran his fingers up and down his suspenders, wondering what Annie would think of these, his most recent purchase. Funny, he'd worn something Plain for the occasion, hoping to please her, and here she was sitting next to him dressed in contemporary clothes.

Annie leaned toward him. "Your suspenders . . . they look like Yonie's," she said softly.

"You like?"

"Every male I know wears them." Her eyes twinkled.

He reached for her hand. "You don't mind, do you?"

She glanced down. "You mean . . . ?"

"No . . . the suspenders."

"'Course not." She smiled. "You do look a bit Amish, though."

He squeezed her hand, eager to watch the second half as the wide stage curtains whisked open.

*How can I continue seeing her and not endanger her good standing in her community?* he wondered as the house lights dimmed. He certainly did not want to appear reckless by anyone who might discover their secret. Yet reckless he was.

# Chapter 26

The sky was still bright as they drove toward Route 340. Ben asked if she wanted to stop for dinner, and Annie liked the idea. Together they decided on the Family Cupboard restaurant and buffet. *Maybe I'll blend in there . . . not be so recognizable in my fancy clothes*, she thought.

She could not stop thinking about the grandeur of the biblical drama and neither, it seemed, could Ben. They talked about the healings and miracles Christ had performed while on earth. And Judas' betrayal of his Master—what had pushed him over the edge, so to speak? Was it truly Satan entering into his thinking, controlling Judas' actions?

By the time they had finished their salads and were ready to go through the buffet line for the main course, Annie had Zeke and Esther on her mind. The children, too. "Have you seen Zeke lately?" she asked.

"He comes around now and then," Ben replied.

She paused, wondering how much to say. "I go 'n' see Essie every chance I can," Annie said, but she then quickly covered her mouth. "Ach, I shouldn't be admitting it . . . well, 'tis all right for you to know, Ben. She's under the shun, ya know. So I must limit my visits. But . . ." Her lower lip trembled. "It's hard to see her treated so."

Ben reached for her hand. "I think she's a wonderful person."

Annie nodded, unable to respond.

"Friendship . . . and family, don't they count for anything?" he said.

Annie forced a smile. "Some folk observe the Bann to the hilt; others just do their best to try 'n' stay involved quietly. I, for one, might not follow the rules so well."

"When it comes to Esther, you mean?"

She nodded. "'Tis a knotty problem for the brethren. For all of us, really."

"Once you told me there were devils and angels in those beards. Did you mean this sort of thing?" he asked quietly.

"Jah. Heart-wrenching, it is." She sighed, but she wouldn't allow the Hochstetlers' issues to spoil the happiness she'd experienced with her dear beau today. And beau he surely was, although they had never discussed the subject, nor the decisions to be made for the future.

For the time being, she was content to secretly meet him. There was no doubt in her mind he was fond of her . . . and she knew precisely how she felt in her heart toward him.

*We mustn't let our feelings rule*, Annie thought.

Even with baptismal classes soon approaching, she dismissed her quandary, having allowed her relationship with Ben to progress this far. *Guess I'm not much for planning ahead*, she thought, justifying wavering between what she *should* do and the joyful time spent with Ben.

Back in the car, she turned the conversation to commonplace things such as spring plowing and planting—how hard at work she and her brothers would be. From time to time Ben glanced at her in the passenger seat. His gaze seemed to question her comments, as if to say, *Do you mean you'll be too busy for me?*

She couldn't be sure on that, of course, and she had no way of knowing what was to become of their rapidly growing closeness, truly.

As they took the long drive home, Annie stared at Ben's car radio. Soon she would hold back no longer and asked if she might press the seek button. Ben smiled and encouraged her to find whatever music she liked. She was surprised to recognize the song on the first station she found.

"I think Julia listens to this station," she said. "But I can't be sure."

"Ask her next time you see her."

She smiled. Ben had no urgency in his approach to life. He seemed to take things as they came, she realized, as they waited for several cars to cross at a stop sign farther up on Harvest Drive.

But as they did, she noticed a horse and buggy on the shoulder of the road, right where they planned to turn. "Ach, lookee there," she said. "It's my father . . . broken down on the road."

"How can you tell?"

"By the horse . . . it's definitely ours."

They shared a knowing and tender look of momentary indecision, although Annie knew immediately, yet painfully, what they surely must do. Ben seemed to have arrived at the same conclusion, for he made the turn and pulled in slowly behind the parked carriage.

Ben told her to stay in the car, and he jumped out to see what he could do to help. Fiddling with her hands, Annie knew too well what would happen if her father needed a ride home. She wished she might slip out and hide in the trunk, along with her ice skates.

"Puh! I'm to be found out," she muttered, her heart racing with worry. She thought of winding up her hair right quick and finding her bonnet, and she was looking for it even as Ben came walking toward the car . . . with Daed.

*Oh, I'm a cooked goose!* She put her head down quickly, hoping he might not recognize her. The way she was dressed—with her hair down—was a true disgrace to God and the People.

"Mighty kind of you," her father was saying to Ben as he got in the seat directly behind her. "I'll give ya money for gas and your time, too. Oh, looks like I'm interrupting somethin'. . . ."

Ben promptly declined any need for payment as her father had offered, and the two of them talked a blue streak, mostly about the Rawlinsville Fire Company mud sale coming up.

*Maybe, just maybe, he won't recognize me,* Annie hoped, holding her breath nearly all the way home.

As they drove along, Daed indicated he was looking into buying another mule since one of his was ailing and old. Evidently Ben was on chummy enough terms to engage Daed in a lighthearted manner, and she was rather surprised at the camaraderie between them.

*How did this happen . . . when?*

For fun, she let her mind wander. What if she and Ben were husband and wife? What a right fine relationship Ben and her father would enjoy, without any of the *Schtreit*—strife—that was common between some fathers and their sons-in-law.

Imagining Ben dressed as an Amish farmer was not at all hard. A light brown beard, with golden strands that matched his hair, and soft to the touch. Jah, he would fit in right quick. Their baby boys would be as handsome and strong as Ben himself, and oh, their little girls. . . .

She was startled from her musing by Ben looking over at her. She had not been fidgeting, she didn't think. But here they were, where Queen Road became Frogtown Road, and Ben's confident glance said volumes: *Trust me, Annie, this will turn out all right.*

She shuddered at the prospects of being found out—face-to-face with her furious preacher-father. She had folded her hands in her lap so tightly her fingers ached.

Not until Daed climbed out of the backseat and closed the car door, waving his thanks to them, did she begin to relax.

Neither she nor Ben said a word as he backed up and turned onto the main road again, creeping forward toward their usual parting place.

When he pulled over and stopped, she let out a loud sigh. "Ach, Ben, I was beside myself."

He grinned. "No, you were right here, Annie." He reached for her hand. "With me."

Then suddenly she realized she could not simply march back into the house anytime soon, not dressed the way she was. She could put her hair into a bun, if need be, and pull on the outer bonnet, too. But going inside on the heels of her father's return home was too risky. He might put two and two together. "Oh, Ben. What a terrible close call!"

They began to laugh—nearly giggles from her—and he nuzzled her cheek. "What a wonderful-good day, Annie," he said.

"I can hardly believe my father didn't know it was me right here in the front seat."

"Saved by your new look . . . and Lou's clothes," Ben said, obviously relieved.

She was pleasingly aware of him. His eyes, his dear, dear face . . . his mouth. He reached for her hand, eyes searching hers.

*No, no . . . say something—anything!*

Oh, how she wanted to feel snug in his strong arms tonight, but the lovely thrill might lead them to hug and kiss. Rudy's affectionate courting had taught her that. Yet they had remained pure, which was her truest hope now, too. Besides, one lingering kiss, coupled with all the wonderful things she knew and loved about Ben, and she might not be able to put the nix on their relationship as she must. She might end up going away with this handsome man, leaving the People, and breaking her parents' hearts.

*No, impossible*, she thought, leaning away from him, against the door. *I could never do that.*

"I guess you're stuck with me for a while—at least long enough for your father to get some help with his broken-down buggy and turn in for the night," Ben said. "Unless you want to try to slip into the house in a few minutes."

He had a good point. "No, for the sake of not getting caught, I best wait a bit."

"Well, what would you like to do?" he asked.

"Let's go walkin' somewhere."

"We could drive over to Park City Center . . . have ice cream, ride the carousel. How's that sound?"

"I like your idea, Ben."

"I like *you*, Annie." The echo of his words and the emotion behind them was quickly imprinted on her heart.

# Chapter 27

$A$nnie was almost grateful for the unexpected turn of events, happening upon Daed as she and Ben had earlier, because Ben treated her to a most exciting evening. She noticed only a handful of Mennonite women the entire time they walked the corridors of the pretty mall.

Later, when it was time to return home, Ben waited till there was not a single light flickering from her father's house before turning off the car's headlights and creeping halfway up the drive. Then he caught her off guard and gently reached for her hand.

After his tender good-bye kiss, she pulled her hairpins out of her pocket and began to pin up her long locks. "I had such a good time," she said. Quickly she opened the glove compartment and found her black bonnet.

"Ever ride on a carousel before?" he asked.

"Never, but it was wonderful, I must say."

"We can do it again." His eyes were drawing her back to his arms.

"Jah, that'd be right nice sometime," she said, resisting her feelings. "Well, I'd better go in." She offered a smile, then opened the door and stepped out of the car. "Good night, Ben."

Heart pounding now, she hoped against hope her parents were soundly asleep. She made her way around to the back of the house, heading quickly for the kitchen door of the Dawdi Haus. She let herself in and inched her way through the kitchen silently, then to the stairs.

*If I can just make it to my room without anything creaking.* She held her breath and removed Lou's fancy boots. Cautiously she tiptoed up the steps.

442

She might've missed him altogether had she not glanced toward the small sitting area between her room and Dawdi and Mammi's. A rustle in the darkness—not a sound, but a feeling. Someone was definitely sitting near the window.

"Annie . . ."

Her heart caught in her throat. She was less than a yard from her own room. Pulling her long coat closed, she wished to hide the suede boots in her hand . . . her feet and legs nearly bare in Lou's flesh-colored hosiery.

Dare she dart into her room, close the door, simply refuse to talk?

*Daed must not see me this way. . . .*

"Annie," her father said again stiffly. "You will begin your baptismal instruction, as planned." Then a glimmer of light from a match as he lit a lantern.

The single beam revealed her treachery. *If only I'd worn my dark stockings. . . .*

But there was something terribly amiss. Why was he waiting for her?

"Come here to me, daughter."

Now she could see him, sitting tall in the old cane chair, a quilt folded on the slats behind him. He was fully dressed, and, no doubt, put out at having to wait up for so long. An early riser, he preferred to go to bed not long after sundown most evenings.

She made her feet move forward, holding the beautiful boots behind her back, ever so glad for her long coat, though it was not fully buttoned.

"I saw you today . . . with Ben Martin."

"When?" she asked, feeling stupid.

He rose suddenly. "Do not continue your pretense!" His voice boomed over her, filling the room. "And without your Kapp yet . . . your hair down—a disgrace! If it's not one thing with you, it's another."

She froze in place, biting her lip.

"I order you never to see the Englischer again!" With that he picked up the lantern and carried it out of the room. Down the stairs he went, with no effort to restrain his footsteps.

*Never see Ben?*

She breathed in and held it, till her lungs nearly gave out. She remained standing there with locked knees in the blackened room, aware of Mammi Zook's muttering to Dawdi in the next room now, asking him in Dutch, "What the world is goin' on?"

Quickly, lest she encounter yet another fuming relative, she dashed into her room and closed the door.

❖

Too ill and forlorn to attend Preaching service, Annie stayed in bed, covers piled over her head, lifting them every so often to breathe a bit before relishing the darkness beneath yet again.

She did not care to see the light of the day, nor did she wish to eat breakfast with the family. Her barn chores could be done by one of her brothers. Or Daed, for that matter. If he was going to cut her off from Ben, then she would simply lie here till it was time for them to come and bury her. That's how she felt, but she knew, eventually, she would get up, wash, and dress. But not for the Lord's day, and not for any particular reason except to be up and combed and wearing her clothes. Plain once again.

She waited till the house was hushed and drained of people to make a hasty search for any stray brothers. Then she returned to the Dawdi Haus, to Mammi's little gas-run refrigerator. Hungry in spite of her grief, she made two pieces of toast and a cup of hot tea.

Sitting at her grandparents' small table, she realized not a soul had come to either check on or inquire of her. *Well, maybe they had.* Hiding beneath the covers had worked, apparently. Or had Daed already told them what she had done? And now she was alone with the place to herself till midafternoon, when they'd all return for milking.

She recalled Ben's wonderful smile and the adoring way he looked at her, his consideration in helping her into the car and the careful way he drove. She felt so protected with him. She could still feel the press of his lips on hers, the tickle in her stomach even now at the thought of being nestled in his warm embrace. *Is this love . . . when you long to be with someone beyond any good sense?*

"Oh, Ben . . . I already miss you," she whispered into her warm tea.

She finished eating, then cleared off the table. She quickly washed and dried her plate and utensils, few as there were, and put them away for Mammi Zook.

Then she went to her room again, found some stationery, and curled up in bed. "This is for you, Daed," she muttered angrily. "And for all the People."

She began to write her farewell letter.

*Dear Ben,*

*I will make this short, since it is a waste of time and paper to write something that doesn't make sense to me. Yet I should've seen this coming. (How could I have expected anything different?)*

*My father did recognize me with you yesterday and has demanded that I not see you ever again. It pains me so. I never wanted to think this day would come. Truly, I didn't! I wanted only to think of you . . . of us.*

*So long, Ben. It seems impossible to say good-bye. Yet for the sake of my family . . . and my future . . . I know I must.*

*Yours,*
*Annie Zook*

Ben was overjoyed to receive his mom's phone call the following Tuesday, saying she'd located his birth certificate. "Here it is," she said into the phone. "Benjamin David Martin . . ."

"That's great, Mom. Send it by overnight mail."

"Well, it would be nice if you came home," his mother said. "You could pick it up then."

"Sure, I'd love to come home—for a visit. But I'm not sure when that'll be. So just pop it in the mail . . . I still need it to get a Pennsylvania driver's license. Then I can finally open a checking account here, get a bit more established." He didn't know why it pleased him, this phone call from home.

*My birth certificate, at long last . . .*

After he hung up, he wandered outside to pick up his mail. The day was warm, and the faint scent of spring wafted on the breeze.

He did not recognize the handwriting on the single letter mixed in with the usual junk mail. He was tired, having stayed up late both Saturday night, after dropping Annie off, and then again last evening, burning the midnight oil online with his sister, Patrice.

Then he'd stared into the darkness, lying awake and weighing plans, ways to attempt, at least, to make things work with Annie and her family, unable as he was to discard his deep affection for her.

When it came down to reality versus hope, he guessed he was on the losing side. To be audacious enough to think Annie would leave behind all that she knew, and seemingly enjoyed, to be with him? He assumed he was treading on very thin ice.

*But our love . . . it's real. We can make it work.*

He grabbed the remote and switched to Fox News, ready to catch up on the world. He had begun to feel incredibly isolated here. At times he loved the area—particularly when with Annie—yet at others he barely tolerated its smallness.

Reaching for the letter, he tore it open with his finger, not bothering to use the opener in his desk drawer. He saw his name and began to read the first line, only to scan down to see Annie's signature at the bottom.

445

*No!* he groaned inwardly.

He read the entire letter, brief as it was, then pressed it to his forehead. *Impossible to say good-bye.* Yet she had written those very words.

Reading it again, he shook his head. Torn and hurt as she obviously was, he would not fight her decision. He'd caused Annie Zook enough trouble.

Standing, he walked to the window and back, running his hand through his hair. "I'll bow out and give her time—some space—to figure out what she wants."

He could only imagine what was going on at the preacher's house . . . and in dear Annie's heart.

The next day, after locking up the tack shop, Ben drove to Irvin's, hoping to catch him before he left to visit a supplier. But upon arriving, Julia said he'd just missed him and invited him in for coffee. "You look pale, Ben. Are you ill?" she asked, treating him like a big sister might.

He assured her he was fine.

"Well, would you like some chicken soup?" She seemed to think food could fix anything.

"No, I really shouldn't stay." But he was already in the door and moving toward the kitchen in a fog. He sensed Julia's ability to calm his nerves, although he was not the sort of person to tell just anyone his problems.

He sat down at her table, and soon James and Molly came to show him a favorite book. When they scampered back to the living room, he said, "I know this may be sudden . . . well, it is." He paused, gathering his wits. "I don't want to spring this on Irvin, but I do need to return home. Very soon." He stopped again, wishing this weren't so difficult. He would miss his work and the good pay. "I need to give my notice today, Julia."

She tilted her head in the usual way, eyes filled with understanding, giving him the benefit of the doubt. Maybe that was why folk liked to be around her. Julia seemed to know how to let you off the hook and wasn't into the control thing like so many women seemed to be.

"Irvin would want to say good-bye and wish you well," she said. "I know I speak for him on this." She took the portable phone out of its cradle and offered it to Ben. "Would you care to tell him yourself? He has his cell phone with him, I believe."

He accepted the portable phone, though he might have used his own cell. There was no turning back. He would exit Annie's life and spare her any further pain. *The best thing for all concerned.*

Irvin answered his call promptly, and Ben felt as though he were going through the motions. Swimming in a haze of lost causes, lost dreams.

Irvin asked him to stay on at the tack shop for at least two weeks, so he would have time to hire someone to take his place. Ben understood and agreed, not wanting to shirk his duty. He was thankful Irvin had given him the excellent job in the first place, entrusting him with a lot of responsibility.

"All right. I'll stay until you find a replacement," Ben agreed.

When he hung up, he accepted a second cup of coffee, glad for the nice distraction of Julia's children. He enjoyed their playful expressions, their need to push their own interests—books, toys—into his lap or onto the table before him.

Julia cooked supper, seeming to take care not to disturb him. Every now and then she reminded the children that "Ben isn't a playmate." He might have been amused were he not so immobile. He felt unable to push through the blur of where he and Annie had been and where they were now. In a short time, they'd gone from enjoying many hours in each other's company to absolutely zero.

Julia asked if he would like to stay for supper, but he declined gratefully. He must figure out how to get out of his lease, if possible. If not, he'd have to make arrangements to sublet.

He remembered his manners. "Is there anything I can help you with before I go?"

"As a matter of fact, there is." Julia said there were a few things Esther Hochstetler had left in the attic room. "Would you mind bringing them downstairs for me?"

"I'll do you one better," he replied. "I'll haul them over to Zeke and Esther."

"Well, I appreciate that," Julia said, returning to the stove. "And I know Esther will be glad for them."

Upstairs in the small room, he stood in the center of the attic space and struggled with his loss of Annie. *Buck up*, he told himself, realizing he would miss not only her, but also Irvin and Julia and their children . . . not to mention the good men coming and going at the harness shop.

*I made a foolish mistake, falling in love. . . .*

He sat on the only chair in the room, head bowed. After a time, he straightened and noticed a long, rectangular item in the corner, propped up between the wall and the bureau.

Getting up to look, he saw that it was a frame, tightly wrapped in brown packing paper. The name *Zook* was written in the corner with a felt-tip pen. Curiosity tugged at him, and he found himself opening a loose corner. He peered inside, intrigued to see part of a painting. He knew he was snooping, yet he removed the small strip of tape and saved it, then carefully unwrapped the entire large piece.

He stared at the painting inside—a haunting, yet remarkable rendering of the covered bridge on Belmont Road . . . the cluster of trees, and the stream below. "This is the very image. . . ." He could not believe how perfect a likeness the artist had created as he scrutinized the beauty of brush stroke on canvas. *Unbelievable!*

Opening his wallet, he extracted the folded copy he'd carried since Christmas. Smoothing it out, he studied it closely. "They're identical," he murmured.

Wondering who the artist was, he searched for a signature in the bottom right-hand corner. Finding it, his mouth dropped open. He ran his hand through his hair. "Annie Zook . . . you do have your secrets."

*No wonder her eyes saw all things beautiful.*

"She's really good," he said, wondering why Annie had never told him of her talent.

Wanting to stare longer at the superb work, yet knowing Julia might wonder what was keeping him, he began to wrap the paper around the frame again, even placing the tape exactly where it had been before.

Satisfied the painting was positioned just as he'd first found it, he stepped back and shook his head. "No wonder . . ." He turned to look out the window, at the fading sky. "Annie, it was *you*. You brought me here."

# Chapter 28

Soon after morning milking, but before breakfast was served, Esther went to check on Essie Ann, down the hall in her crib, when she thought she heard weeping. But how could that be? Laura was out feeding the pigs just now, while Zach watched over John in the kitchen, the two playing quietly together. Not another soul was in the house, except for her sleeping baby.

Or so she thought.

The nearly eerie sound continued and she felt compelled to go and stand by Zeke's bedroom, the door slightly ajar. Inside, Zeke was muttering and whining to himself like a child fussing over having been harshly disciplined.

*Well, for goodness' sake,* she thought, wondering what was troubling him.

Listening in on the peculiar exchange—in essence, what it was—Esther was stunned. Zeke was saying he most certainly deserved to be shunned now, just as his wife was. "If the men of God knew my sins, they wouldn't think twice on it." Here he stopped, and a kind of sad and despairing wail poured out of him. "I know now what happened. . . ."

She swallowed hard, and it was all she could do to stand still and not let her feet take her right in there, right now, and comfort the poor man.

Zeke continued his odd dialog, switching to take the side of one of the preachers. "What do you have to say for yourself, Ezekiel? You pray more . . . nothin' changes. You can't keep strikin' Esther, frail thing."

Zeke moaned again. "It's rippin' out my insides . . . who I am. Who I've always been . . ." He paused. "Nothin's as it seems. Nothin' at all."

Trembling, she moved closer to the door and peeked through the sliver

449

of an opening. There Zeke sat, on the bed they had always shared before her shunning, rocking back and forth, his big hands covering his face and part of his beard. "With pride comes shame," he said. "Ach, one wretched sin begets another and another. Ain't so, Lord God?"

Esther hadn't the slightest notion what he meant, and she inched back, afraid. She took in a slow, long breath. *O Lord in heaven, help us!*

Zeke had been strangely quiet the past few weeks, so Jesse thought it might do them both good to stand out in the barn and talk, now that spring was in the air.

*Too early for straw hats yet.* However he had seen a horde of bees droning over some dried-out wood at the neighbors' yesterday. Birds, including a few barn swallows, were back in the neighborhood, starting with the first robins two weeks ago, and the finches just today.

But it was the stubborn way the new grass had begun to shove its way up through old thatch that told him warmer weather was near.

He clicked his cheek as Betsy trotted down Belmont Road, heading north. His noontime dinner of fried chicken sat heavy on his stomach as he made his way to Hochstetlers'.

He wondered how Zeke was getting along with his headstrong woman. He figured it wouldn't be much longer and Esther would give in to the demands of the Ordnung. Whatever had gotten into her recently was clearly dangerous.

He turned his thinking now to the task that lay before him, feeling mighty responsible, considering his big push to return Esther to Zeke's precarious nest.

Zeke stared at the neighbors' barn telephone, clutching it till his knuckles turned white. He'd run all the way here, compelled by an urgency that had been mounting all day. Slowly he lifted the receiver to his ear and dialed 9-1-1.

A woman's voice came on the line, and he said right quick, "Send the police to my house at once."

"Please state your name, address, and phone number for verification, sir."

He managed to eke out the requested information, having to peer at the number printed on the telephone.

"What is the nature of your emergency?"

He began to weep. "My brother . . . Isaac Hochstetler is dead. He's . . . dead, and too young to die." He choked back heaving sobs.

The woman attempted to calm him, or at least he thought that was why she spoke in such measured tones. But he was beside himself. "So you best be gettin' the police out here, and quick."

"How did Isaac die?" came the dreaded question.

He stammered a bit, then inhaled sharply, dropping the phone and letting it dangle and sway on its cord. Wiping his face with his paisley blue handkerchief, he stumbled back up the road to his house.

Jesse spotted fresh tire tracks in a stubble-filled cornfield to the east. Curious, he followed the tracks with his eyes, craning his neck as the horse pulled the carriage past. He had occasionally given some thought to the faster, less strenuous work a tractor could offer. Even if he had the funds for that type of equipment, he couldn't justify entertaining such thoughts for longer than a few seconds, if at all. Truly, being a minister stymied much inventive thought.

For a moment he understood something of Annie's inner struggle, her desire to create. Surely that was inventive as well. He was convinced, however, once she gave her lifetime vow of submission to the church and the Lord God— once she settled into marrying, too—she would forget her foolish penchant for drawing and painting. He could not deny his daughter's *great talent*, as Barbara regarded her ability, but he would not go so far as to agree that Annie had a God-given gift.

Looking at the sky as he neared the Hochstetler farm, Jesse was in tune with the change of season. Winter was beginning to shed her long woolens for the fluttery skirts of spring. He'd thrilled to the softness of the soil in Barbara's garden plot, surprisingly ready to be spaded up and set to hand plowing. He'd even seen two earthworms already hard at work aerating the black soil.

"Gee," he commanded the horse. Zeke's black watchdog wagged his tail near the turn into Hochstetlers' driveway.

Right away Jesse spotted the police car parked near the backyard.

*Now what's Zeke gone and done?* He clenched his teeth, and his palms broke out in an unexpected sweat.

Debating whether or not he wanted any part in this—*Should I simply turn around and head home?*—Jesse sat there, his brain suddenly clouded. If the bishop had been the one pulling up to Zeke's place just now, this might be a different story.

What happened next made him flinch. Up ahead, coming out of the barn, was Zeke, flanked by two police officers.

"Ach, no . . ." Jesse whispered, dropping the reins.

His mind flew to Esther. Where was she? Had her husband lost all sense of control and blackened her eye this time? Slammed one of the children against a wall? Worse?

Or had Zeke told them what he knew about Isaac's remains?

Jesse climbed out of the carriage, patted his horse's rump, and walked to where the driveway ended and the sidewalk began.

"All right, then," he heard Zeke say, nodding, as he followed the man and woman in uniform to the waiting car. Zeke made eye contact with Jesse but only for a second. Then he bowed his head.

Jesse shuddered, but he removed his hat and approached the police in spite of himself. "I'm Zeke's minister, Preacher Zook," he said. "What's the trouble here?"

The tall, blond officer might have passed for one of the People, with his scruffy start of a beard. "We're taking him in for questioning," the young man replied, glancing over at Zeke, who was now sitting in the backseat of the patrol car.

Jesse scratched his head. "Well, now, you sure this isn't some mistake?" He tried to catch Zeke's eye again. "We Amish aren't at all interested in getting the outside world mixed in with our own. I'm sure you understand."

The policeman nodded. "I've heard as much." He motioned for Jesse to move away from the car with him. Then, standing near the house, he lowered his voice. "Between you and me, I'm not exactly certain what we've got here . . . but I can guarantee one thing: We'll get to the bottom of it."

"I'd be glad to take him off your hands," Jesse said.

"Meaning what?"

"I'll take him on home with me. Keep him away from the family until he cools off. . . ."

The officer looked at him sharply. "Are you implying the man is violent, sir?"

*Ach, no. Now what have I said?* Jesse hurried to explain. "I'm just tellin' you, I'll be responsible for him. Look after him . . . see what's what." Jesse was much too shaken to convey the sort of confidence the dismal situation required.

"I'm afraid I can't do that. When a man makes a call like Mr. Hochstetler did, my partner and I can't ignore it. He'll most likely be detained a few hours, if he cooperates fully."

Jesse frowned, wondering what Zeke had told them. Jesse knew he best be making another attempt to keep the pot from boiling over. Nothing good could come of hauling Zeke off to the English world. "I'm willin' to come along to town, for that matter, if it would help," he said, not sure what good that would do. But it sounded accommodating, and he was all for that.

"We can handle this." The policeman stepped back. "Now if you'll excuse me . . ."

*No, no . . . stop him.*

Helpless to do more, Jesse watched as the car pulled forward, turned around, and headed toward the road.

*What a pity I didn't arrive sooner.*

Suddenly it struck him—Esther might need him.

He hurried around the house and stood at the back door, leaned his forehead against it, aware of his pounding heart. He called out to Esther, "Anybody home?"

"Ach, Preacher Jesse," she said when she came to the door, babe in arms. She lowered her voice to a whisper. "They've taken my husband away."

He followed her into the kitchen, where she laid Essie Ann in her cradle and hurried Zach and John into the front room. "Don't forget your toys," she said softly, although there was an obvious unraveling to her voice. It was clear her emotions were ragged.

"Are you all right, Esther?" He saw no marks on her face, nothing to indicate a scuffle.

"This ain't what you think, Preacher. Zeke took himself down the road to the neighbors and called the police. Oh, I just don't understand."

"What did he tell them?" He led her to the table to sit.

She sighed and rested her head between her hands. After a time, she looked up. "I heard only bits and pieces." She fumbled for a handkerchief in her dress sleeve. "Something about knowing where someone's bones are buried. I thought he said Isaac's. . . ."

Jesse groaned and stared at the tablecloth. The checked pattern made him dizzy—nauseated.

"What'll happen to him?" she whispered, eyes dull.

*Once the world comes rushing in . . .*

He'd heard of Plain communities wracked by such things as crime and police involvement. The Mount Hope, Ohio, shootings during the harvest some years back was one case in point.

Quickly now Jesse regained his sense of duty. "I don't know a lot about the English world, Esther, and neither do you. We'll have to do the best we can, that's all." *We'll have to keep our noses clean, too,* he thought, not wanting to be mixed up with whatever things Zeke might say under interrogation.

*Zeke knows I buried those bones!*

"I'm awfully scared, Preacher. Honest, I am."

Looking at Esther's sorrowful face, he realized, quite unexpectedly, that he was breaking the rules of her shunning.

"I'll see if Barbara might come stay the night," he offered. This poor woman shouldn't be alone after such a day—shunned or not. He could not allow more pain to fill her eyes. "I'll go 'n' fetch her straightaway and return shortly."

"Kind of you" was all Esther said, wringing her hands.

He walked to the back door, and when he turned briefly, he saw that she was still seated like a stone, her eyes fixed in a vacant stare.

Later that afternoon, Esther searched outside for Laura, who had taken herself off to the outhouse but not returned in a reasonable amount of time, as Zeke always demanded of them.

When Laura was nowhere to be seen, Esther headed quickly to the barn. There, the late afternoon sun shone through slats in the wall, creating ribbons of light on beds of straw. She found Laura sitting on the edge of one of the hay holes, her little legs dangling through. "What's-a-matter that you're up there all by your lonesome?" she called gently.

"Mighty scared, Mamma."

Esther was glad to have found her. Truth was, Esther was terrified, too. Not for the reason Laura was, probably, but she felt ever so helpless, worried what might become of Zeke.

"I want us to stay with Auntie Julia again," Laura said, her voice muffled.

"Aw, honey-love, I'm right here."

"Still, can't we go back?"

*Of course she misses Irvin and Julia,* Esther thought sadly. The Rancks' home represented a deep and settled kind of peace for Laura. *For all of us.* Galatians referred to it as "fruit of the Spirit," and Esther longed for such a life. *With Zeke out of the house, perhaps we'll enjoy a few hours of serenity.* Yet she knew she should not relish the thought of Zeke's absence.

"Mamma?" Laura's small voice brought her back.

"Well, darlin', I don't see us goin' much of anywhere," she replied. "There's oodles to do around the house."

And there were the pigs. Zeke's herd required plenty of work, and between herself and what little help Laura could offer, especially now what she was at school most of the day, Esther felt she might have to hire some help. With what money, she didn't know. Either that or register a plea with Preacher Jesse for some assistance from amongst the menfolk. *This is awful bad timing my being shunned and all. What if Zeke is gone for a long while?*

Even her older brother would be reluctant to assist them, and she would definitely need help with the sows pregnant, or "in pig," as Zeke often said.

She assumed her mother would come to check on them—bad news traveled fast—hopefully offering smiles and hugs, at least for the children.

"I have an idea, dear one," she said. "Why don't we ask the Lord Jesus to take care of Dat?"

"Jah, let's." Laura's hair bun was coming loose as she inched slowly down into the hay hole. "I want to jump," she said.

"Well, I may or may not catch you, depending how you fall," Esther warned her, glad the conversation was changing direction.

"Then I best not try. I wouldn't want to break my leg and be a burden to you." Laura rose quickly and walked to the door leading outside, then came around to return through the lower barn door. "There now. I'm all done bein' gloomy."

"Well, even the dear Lord was *drauerich*—sad." She began to tell Laura the story of Jesus' good friend, Lazarus, who had become sick and died. As they walked to the pigpen, preparing to water and feed the swine, she wished she could hurry through the sorrowful part to the happy ending.

Fact was, Laura would want to know what had happened to her father today. And the schoolyard grapevine might help out with that all too quickly for Esther's liking, although she wouldn't mind knowing something more herself. Whatever came, she'd not soon forget this day and Zeke's absurd muttering in the bedroom. *Oh, Lord Jesus, will you hover ever near?*

*Chapter 29*

The day after Zeke was taken away by the police, Jesse hurried out the back door at Bishop Andy's and climbed into his carriage. Together the ministers, including the bishop, old Preacher Moses, and the neighboring bishops, had gathered to hash over Zeke's latest attention-getting stunt. The People, as a whole, were sure to get beat up in the media, they feared. Bishop Andy did not berate Jesse for being unable to dissuade the police from taking Zeke into custody, but the disappointment was evident in his aging eyes.

The consensus among the brethren was to lay low for the time being in the hope the police would soon realize Zeke was not in his right mind. But if the investigation spread to exhuming Isaac's remains and questioning the People . . . none of them had any idea what would happen then. The police had indicated that Zeke would be held only a few hours and released but he had yet to return. So what could have gone awry? Not even Esther had received word.

*What's Zeke thinking, calling the police?* Jesse wondered.

Back on the road now, the gentle, humdrum sway of the carriage up London Vale Road settled Jesse's frayed nerves, offering a sort of reassurance. A body could rest away the cares of the day, the week, and even longer perched in a horse-drawn carriage, letting the air hit his face. At once he felt sorry for the moderns who rode around in cars, completely enclosed. *'Specially this time of year when the air's fresh as a pasture filled with wild flowers,* he thought. *And Zeke, stuck in a jail, of all things!*

Suddenly he thought of Yonie, riding around in a car like an Englischer.

He'd heard of the vehicle for some time but had never laid eyes on it. He hadn't let on just how upset he was, and he would continue to hold his peace. He wished Yonie would grow up and quit dabbling in the world. *Annie, too.*

For the time being, Jesse would turn a blind eye to Yonie's Rumschpringe and hope Annie was altogether free of her sinning days. *Not even her mother has noticed any new artwork all these months*, he thought, and was glad of it. And word was, Irvin's tack shop employee had given notice—planned to return to Kentucky here before too long. If not for Annie, Jesse would be sorry to see Ben Martin go. *A right fine and helpful fellow.* Still, better that Ben was out of the picture for good.

Jesse reached into his pocket and pulled out a handful of salted peanuts, enjoying the snack as he headed to the smithy's for a visit. On the ride, he thought again of Barbara's remarks this morning. She had come away from spending the night with Esther and the children worried sick. The way Esther had talked, Julia Ranck might just up and fill the void by taking Esther again under her wing.

*Esther's memorizing and poring over Scripture*, Barbara told him.

He cringed, staring at the cows leaning their heads out of the fence by the side of the road.

*You get one fire put out, and there's always another.*

Truth was, he should try and stamp out this salvation message before it spread. And it could. He knew too many bishops who'd lost a good portion of their members to evangelists and Bible thumpers. He mustn't let that happen here.

❖

Annie placed the suitcase on her bed and opened the lid. She couldn't believe what Mamm had whispered to her about Zeke last evening before hurrying to spend the night with Esther. *Zeke in jail?* There had to be some mistake. Still, it felt somehow providential that Esther was alone without her husband just now.

Looking up, Annie saw Mamm standing in the doorway. "I need to leave home," she said with as much determination as she could muster.

"Oh, Annie . . . no." Mamm lowered her head.

"I'm a humiliation to my family."

"Haven't we been through this before?" her mother reminded her. She came in and sat on the spare bed that had been Lou's.

*No*, Annie thought to herself. This time was far different. She was not leaving because of her inability to resist art. She had besmirched herself, abandoning one of their sacred symbols, her head covering, instead of wearing it as the Scriptures instructed. She'd allowed her long hair to go uncovered, revealing it fully to a man who was not her husband.

*And never will be.*

According to her father, there were more transgressions on the record of Annie's life than she cared to consider.

"I've made up my mind, Mamm. I'm goin' to stay with Esther . . . to help with the pig farm and all."

"Are you sure?"

"Esther can use the help, and Daed can't stand the sight of me."

Mamm didn't contradict her. "Does Esther know you're comin'?"

"Well, no . . . but—"

"Ach, you best be thinkin' this through. She's banned from the fellowship, for pity's sake."

"Well, in many ways, so am I." Annie set about packing her dresses, nightclothes, Kapps, and her small box of straight pins, as well as her best stationery and Lou's letters—all of the things she had brought with her when she and Lou moved over to the Dawdi Haus bedroom last year.

"You know Esther can't care for the children and the farm by herself for long," Annie went on, neatly folding her clothes. "You said you might even try 'n' help her some, Mamm."

"That's different, Annie, and you know it. The brethren will disapprove of you livin' there."

"But I'm not yet a baptized church member."

"And far from it, by the looks of it. Oh, Annie . . ." Her mother rose and hurried from the room, wiping tears away with her apron.

Struggling to keep her emotions in check, Annie braced herself, gritting her teeth. Now wasn't the time to let go, nor was it the place. She'd wept away nearly a week of long nights already. When it was time, weary as she was, she would ask Yonie to drive her up to Esther's. And wouldn't Esther be surprised— ever so happy? The thought gave Annie all the more reason to press onward.

She filled one suitcase and began to pack another. Yonie poked his head in the door and, seeing her there, said, "You're doin' the right thing for yourself. I'd be packin' this minute, too, if I had a place to go."

"Well, if you got yourself a job, you sure could." Her throat tightened. "But is that something a *son* should think 'bout doing?" She hoped he caught her meaning about his being favored and all.

"Aw . . . you're a feisty one."

"I best be leavin', to ponder things." Her breath caught in her throat and she feared she might cry.

"I'll walk up the road a ways . . . get my car for you." He twitched his nose. "Where ya headed? Out to Colorado?"

She hadn't considered that. Louisa needed time to sort out her own problems, so there'd be no going west. "If anyone needs to get in touch with me"—*if anyone cares to*, she thought—"I'll be hangin' with Essie."

He smiled. "You got yourself a good dose of Lou while she was here, ain't?"

"This isn't Lou's doing. I had plenty of gumption before she ever arrived."

Omar appeared in the hallway, poked his brother playfully, and offered to carry her suitcases down. Annie let him, thanking him with a sad smile. Yonie carried her bedding, quilt, and pillow down to the front porch.

Annie took another glance around the room she'd so happily shared with Louisa, then headed downstairs, through the connecting door to the main house and up to her former bedroom. She stood in the doorway eyeing her hope chest with its embroidered doilies and tablecloths. *No need to bring that along*, she thought. *Will I ever need it?*

Her gaze fell on the little desk her father had made, and she ran her hand lightly over its smooth maple surface. But when the image of her father's angry face flickered painfully across her mind, she raised her hand. She would leave the desk behind as well.

She thought fleetingly of her easel and art supplies, boxed up at Julia's. Perhaps she would ask Yonie to stop there first, before they headed to Esther's. But no, she'd made a promise to her father, and she intended to keep her word on that matter, if nothing else.

Reluctant to leave, she made her way downstairs, passing by Luke as she did. He only shook his head as if she'd done something too terrible to mention.

She headed for the front porch, where her belongings were gathered, assuming Daed was in the barn. But she had no interest in saying good-bye.

Mamm came right out and kept her company, the two of them taking in the springtime landscape of newly planted fields and grazing land. The birds were extra bold and boisterous today.

"Too bad the scarecrow's gone," Annie said softly.

"Jah, 'tis." Mamm reached over and pressed her hand on Annie's. "I'll miss you somethin' awful, dear."

"We'll see each other. I'm not shunned—or am I?"

"Knowin' your father . . . you'll be as good as."

The words struck a blow. "Why's that?"

"You're the preacher's daughter, Annie. Never forget." Mamm rose and walked the length of the porch, then turned, and came back. "When . . . *if* you ever return, it'll have to be on Daed's terms."

*No fooling.* They both knew where the brethren stood on such things as creating fine art . . . and there was no tolerance for a courtship with an Englischer either.

She sighed, watching Yonie run up the road, heading for the spot where Ben had always parked . . . where he had waited for her with such delight on his face.

"I guess this is so long for now." She looked at Mamm.

"But not forever, I hope," her mother said, coming to stand near. "I'll not be visitin' at Esther's so much, you must understand."

Annie looked up, taking her hand. "But you'll stop by now and then?"

Mamm sighed. "We'll see. . . ." Her mother's hand went still in her own. "Annie, your father showed me a magazine . . . the perty painting you did."

Annie swallowed, dreading the rebuke that was sure to come.

"'Tween you and me . . ." Mamm paused, wiping away tears. "Ach, I best be still."

"That's all right, you say what you want."

"Truth be told . . . I believe you've got yourself a gift from above. I told your father so."

Annie nodded, grateful for her mother's words, meager consolation that they were.

They both fell silent, until Yonie's shimmering silver car pulled into the drive.

"What on earth?" Mamm muttered, appalled, moving toward the porch steps.

But Annie rose, reached for her suitcases, and whispered only, "Good-bye."

Jesse hired a driver, and he and Bishop Andy rode to the Lancaster County Prison, which served as a holding place for those awaiting trial—and their own Zeke Hochstetler.

At first glance, the place was something out of an Englischer's storybook, Jesse thought, surveying the castlelike structure as they made their way beneath the high arched entrance on East King Street.

Bishop Andy, stating firmly he'd come only to offer moral support, sat in the waiting area, outside the visitation room. Both he and Jesse were nervously aware of the camera high on the wall, monitoring their every move. Jesse hoped the Good Lord might overlook it when their faces showed up on a hidden screen somewhere.

Entering the visitation room, Jesse was directed by the guard to a small cubicle. There sat Zeke, behind the glass partition, obviously pleased to see him. Jesse sat down in a folding chair.

"You're the first to come visit me," Zeke acknowledged.

Jesse doubted there would be many more visitors, but he didn't have the heart to say so. He listened while Zeke rambled on about missing Esther, becoming more aware that the thick glass window was not the only barrier between them.

But Jesse hadn't come to discuss Zeke's wife and children, though it was understandable for Zeke to want to. There were niggling questions, one in particular, and knowing they had scant time for a leisurely chat, Jesse directed the conversation to the business at hand. "Zeke, what happened?"

Zeke shook his head, pulling on his beard. His eyes were dark beads.

"I had me a whole group of tests yesterday." Zeke leaned back and laughed—too heartily for Jesse's liking. "I agreed to let them see if I'm of sound mind or not. I figure if I could strike Esther hard when she was only days from birthin' Essie Ann, then I'm a threat to my own family, ain't I?"

The hair on Jesse's neck prickled. Zeke *narrisch*—crazy?

"They ain't keepin' me here against my will, if that's what you're thinking."

Jesse watched the man more closely, hesitant to judge simply with his eyes. Still, he observed the slant of Zeke's head, the clarity of his gaze, the set of his jowl, and the steadiness of his callused hands.

No obvious signs of mental illness that he could tell, but of course he was no match for worldly experts. He did know that Zeke was a man who said things he later regretted. He pressed the boundaries of the Ordnung and looked for ways to be a nuisance. He pushed folk around verbally and was no doubt dreadful to live with.

Zeke's wounds were undeniably etched on his soul. Anybody who knew him readily understood his loss as insufferable, coming at such a tender age. After all, someone had taken away his little brother—killed him—that long ago and shocking night.

Jesse leaned forward. "You must come home to the People . . . we'll help you."

Slowly Zeke's mouth parted and he began to speak. "I finally figured it out, Preacher, after all these years . . . what happened to my brother."

"And what's that?"

"I did it," he said flatly. "I killed Isaac."

Jesse was stunned at the conviction in his voice. "But, Zeke, you were just a boy yourself when Isaac was lost. You aren't thinking clearly."

"That's where you're wrong, Preacher. I'm thinkin' more clearly than I have in sixteen long years."

*O Lord God*, Jesse thought, sickened. *Can it be?*

# Chapter 30

Esther cried. She stood at her back door and wept tears of pure joy, mixed with laughter. Annie thought it a strange yet lovely sort of sound.

Laura came running through the kitchen and out the back door to throw her slender arms around Annie's waist. "Mamma prayed somebody would come . . . and here you are!"

Esther nodded, brushing back her own tears. "I know the Lord answers our prayers, but this is ever so quick." She reached for Annie's hand and gave it a squeeze. "I'm so happy to see you!"

"Oh, me too, Essie! Me too!" She searched her friend's face, her eyes lingering long enough to see that Esther had not yet been scarred by the Bann. "I was hopin' you might take me in." Annie leaned down to pick John up, not ready to tell Esther why she was here. Even so, it was evident Esther sensed something and was gracious enough not to pry.

"Why sure, Annie. Stay as long as you like."

"Denki. This means so much to me," Annie replied.

"You've got yourself a right heavy one there," Esther said, meaning little John.

Annie and John rubbed noses playfully. "I think you've been eating pork chops again, young man." She squeezed his arm muscles.

John grinned, showing some new teeth.

"Oh, goodness, you don't know how *wunderbaar* it's goin' to be having you here, Annie."

"You sure? I don't want to be a burden."

"Not a burden . . . a blessing."

Yonie was already hauling her suitcases out of the backseat. "Just tell me where you want all this."

Zach hopped down the steps, their big black watchdog barking and wagging his tail and trailing behind him. "Follow me . . . I'll show ya," he told Yonie, then turned and marched into the house.

Esther whispered, "Zach thinks he's the man of the house now."

Yonie followed Zach inside, carrying the suitcases and talking Dutch to the boy.

Esther told Annie she'd moved back to Zeke's and her bedroom the night before, when she realized Zeke must not be returning from "you know where" in a few hours, as she'd first believed. "You can take the spare room at the end of the hall. It's nice and quiet."

"I'm grateful," Annie said. "And I'll pull my weight—you'll see."

Esther waved her hand, laughing. "No doubt in my mind."

Annie set John down and watched him toddle across the back porch, then slipped her arm through the crook of Esther's. "I'll do all I can to help you, Essie. For as long as you'll let me."

Esther's face clouded over. "Not sure how long my husband will be gone, Annie. I heard from your father, there's some sort of investigation under way. . . ." Tears threatened again.

"Aw, Essie . . . let's not fret. Surely something good will come of all this. Surely."

Esther shook her head. "I just don't see how."

The baby let out a holler, and Annie offered to go and get her. She hurried up the back steps and into the kitchen, bent down to the small playpen, and lifted Essie Ann up, resting her warm little head next to her cheek. "Your auntie's here," she cooed at her.

"Ach, I like that," Esther said, following Annie inside and mopping her face with a tissue. "We'll be sisters together."

Annie thought of Lou suddenly and caught Esther's look of cheer. "We always were, jah?"

There would be no further talk of jail or investigations or broken hearts. For today, they would dwell on friendship, laughter, and family—extended and otherwise.

Essie Ann was squirming to be fed, so Annie kissed her soft head and gave her to Esther. Looking round the kitchen, she felt right at home, seeing the clock shelf like Mamm's, the corner cupboard with a few German books and the pretty floral china teacups and saucers, and the green-checkered oilcloth on the table.

"Here, let me help," she said, taking a pillow from Yonie when he came back through the kitchen with her bedding and a bulky quilt. Then she followed him and Zach up the stairs.

In the room where she would sleep, Zach leaned against the door, smiling shyly. Annie took in the cheery light in the bedroom, which was larger than Julia's attic studio, to be sure.

*Plenty of space for an easel and palette*, she thought. *Well, maybe someday . . .*

Setting down her things, she went to admire the handmade quilt folded over the footboard. Immediately she recalled the many quilting frolics she'd attended with Louisa, and how she'd taught her friend the art of stitching.

*I wonder how Lou's getting along. . . .* She had received a birthday card from her and would probably get a long letter soon.

Zach still lingered near, eyeing her . . . seeing her in a different light, maybe. She was now his mother's houseguest, not merely a family friend. "This was Mamma's room before . . ." he began, his voice trailing off.

She nodded and gave him what she hoped was an encouraging smile.

*If these walls could talk.* She couldn't imagine what the bishop's shunning decree had meant for Esther and Zeke.

Going to the window, Zach pressed his hands and face against it, staring out. She looked fondly at the back of his little round head.

*I'll be happy again someday*, she thought, trying in vain to push thoughts of Ben from her mind. *Won't I?*

She realized suddenly, with a great sigh, how very small her own concerns were compared to the trauma in Esther's life. Yet as Esther had so confidently stated, the Lord God had chosen to respond to her desperate prayer.

Annie had not heard it expressed in quite that way before, except from Cousin Julia. But she decided, then and there, to do her very best to be just that answer.

# Epilogue

There's something peculiar about time—knowing when an important event is to take place but realizing you aren't present as you had planned to be. Such a thing happened yesterday, and I brooded over it, imagining the brethren talking with the baptismal candidates while I sat in a Mennonite meetinghouse for Sunday school, of all things. It was the strangest gathering I've ever submitted myself to, but I went along for Esther and the children's sake. Whatever puts a smile on Essie's face is well worth any hesitation on my part. I just hope none of the brethren gets wind of it.

Cousins Irvin and Julia drove both their cars, meeting us here at Essie's, where we divided up, since there were too many of us to squeeze into one vehicle. And Julia, "to be extra safe," had infant seats all ready for the baby and little John, so not only did the two youngest ride in style, but we all broke yet another rule—going in a car on the Lord's Day. Seems anymore I'm breaking rules right and left.

I received a letter from Lou today, somberly delivered by Luke at Mamm's request. I'm going to write back tomorrow, letting her know where I'm staying now, so I can receive her correspondence directly. I'll also offer to send back her skirt, blouse, and pretty boots, since I won't be needing them anymore.

Louisa's letter to me was seven pages long—written on both sides of the paper. She clearly pines for Sam, and I'm not at all surprised, because I believe I know something of what she feels . . . as I think much too often of Ben. I suppose if he were to come looking for me now, I might even consider seeing him again. I've already disappointed my parents so much—what would one more thing matter?

Truth is, he's planning to return to Kentucky, according to Julia. So he must be as hurt as I am over my letter, though we had no business seeing each other, really. How could it ever have worked out?

Honestly, I think it was Ben's curiosity with Plain ways that got us together in the first place. But now? I'm ever so sure he'll be more content in his own world, just as I must smile through the storm of my life here.

And a storm it is. Esther's brother and sister-in-law, as well as her mother, came over yesterday afternoon and carried on something fierce about a magazine cover one of the farmers showed them. Pushed it right into poor Essie's face and said she was giving board and room to the Devil. She never took sides, but when they marched out to their buggy, she whispered to me, "Don't think another thing of this, Annie. You do what the Lord's called you to," and that was that.

I have no idea how almighty God calls someone, though it seems to me I was born with this insuppressible passion for art. Does that mean it's a calling, as Essie seems to think? If so, I'd be doing my heavenly Father's bidding, while defying Daed and the church. 'Tis beyond me, really.

I daresay my brother's in a similar pickle. Laura and I were out on the road Saturday, and who but Yonie came driving along, his English girlfriend sitting smack-dab next to him. He slowed the car and waved, smiling like nothing at all was wrong. I guess what Daed knows and doesn't seem to mind for now isn't an issue. As for Dory, his girl, that's another thing yet.

I'm not so sure I ought to feel sorry for Yonie, though, since he sure looks like he's leaning toward jumping the fence. If he doesn't end up English, when his running-around is through, he'll be stuck right back here with a great big hole in his heart. Like mine.

Esther and I saw Susie Esh, Rudy's bride, out hanging up wash this morning. Looked to me like she might be expecting their first wee one, but I didn't stare, just waved, watching her woeful expression as she turned slowly away. She was shunning Esther, no doubt. Or maybe news of my transgression, the painting on the cover of the *Farm and Home Journal*, has found its way to the Esh home, too.

*Can't win for losing*, Mamm sometimes said when the pressure cooker blew its top, or the fence around the peacock pen fell over.

All the same, the sun comes up every morning and sets each and every night. The moon and stars slide across the same sky I see here that Ben will soon see in Kentucky. The hands of time tick ever so slowly.

Essie says not to fret; seasons come and go. And I say right back to her: "Well, then, 'tis a waiting season. . . ."

Yet it's painful to think of never seeing Ben again. When I am alone in my room at day's end, tired after chores, I lie awake and rehearse his features in my mind, counting the weeks till my promise to Daed is done. Oh, how I long to take brush in hand and paint Ben's face, for fear I should forget him in due time.

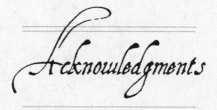

# Acknowledgments

Heartfelt thanks to three storytellers—Aunt Betty, "Auntie" Madge, and Cousin Dave—whose verbal brushstrokes of joy and inspiration are responsible for several anecdotes in this book.

I am grateful for brainstorming fun, which I shared with my husband, Dave, my "big-picture editor," and our bookworm daughter, Julie, who also enthusiastically read the earliest chapters. Also, I offer my deep appreciation to our daughter Janie, our son, Jonathan, and to my parents, Herb and Jane Jones, for endless prayer support and practical encouragement (such as unexpected goodies and brain food).

Although I have mentioned my superb editors numerous times, I cannot repeat too often my gratitude for the insight of Julie Klassen, Carol Johnson, David Horton, and Rochelle Glöege. Also, my thanks to Ann Parrish, who reviewed the manuscript.

A special note of thanks to John and Ada Reba Bachman, remarkably kind to help with ongoing research, and to Rev. James Hagan for expert advice. Much appreciation also goes to my praying partners in various parts of the planet, as well as to regional and cultural assistants and proofreaders who have asked to remain nameless.

Thank you, as well, to my mother's dear cousins for allowing me to refer to and use scene settings from their beautiful colonial inn (Maple Lane Farm B&B) on Paradise Lane in Lancaster County, Pennsylvania.

Thanks, as always, to my devoted readers. In countless ways, these books belong to you . . . and always to God.

# The
# Brethren

# Dedication

To
Roz & Sandra Flower
and
Tom & Elizabeth Quayle
and their darling families . . .
cousins all.

*T*he gravity of the hour fell heavily on the membership that Lord's Day long ago. One by one the men reached for a black songbook in the center of the table, for the drawing of the lot. In keeping with the sacred rite, only one man was to be found among the elect, Jehovah God's choice. The husband of one wife, of good reputation, hospitable, not given to wine, the father of obedient children, with the ability to teach sound doctrine, according to the Scriptures. A God-fearing man whose name, along with six others, had been whispered to the bishop on this most holy day of Communion.

Seven hymnals, each bound by a rubber band, lined the table, and deep within one, a single slip of paper inscribed with the proverb: "The lot is cast into the lap; but the whole disposing thereof is of the Lord." The candidates—selected from the church district by the "voice" of the People—each chose a book, wondering who would be struck by the lot.

The bishop examined each hymnal. Opening the one chosen by the final candidate, he found the lot and uttered the life-altering words: "The Lord God and heavenly Father has chosen our brother Daniel Hochstetler."

# Prologue

If Isaac's mamma were still alive and knew her son's bones were being dredged up, she would surely be weeping now. It was all *I* could do to choke back tears, walking past the People's cemetery this morning. Our sacred knoll was blocked off with yellow police ribbon, and *Englischers* were swarming about like so many ants on a hill.

This must be why Esther hasn't heard a peep from Zeke since he turned himself in a few days ago. Maybe he's not allowed to talk to anyone while he awaits the outcome of what appears to be a mighty serious investigation. But I sure won't be describing the commotion at the graveyard to Essie—I'll spare her that. I just hope the grapevine doesn't spread its tendrils out to little ears, because like their mother, six-year-old Laura and her younger brothers, Zach and John, have been through too much already. It was bad enough when Zeke was causing havoc at home, but this? Seems to me he must've gone completely berserk to say he killed his four-year-old brother all those years ago. And why? It makes not a whit of sense that Zeke and Isaac should be another Cain and Abel, and the brethren must surely think the same.

The People are all a-buzz about Zeke's arrest, but I can't allow myself to stew, 'cause I need all my strength and courage to help dear Essie and her children, who are floundering so. Even though Essie is holding fast to her newfound faith, she also seems to be holding her breath about Zeke. We all are, really, because what one person may be found guilty of affects us all.

I am presently holding my breath, too, counting the days till my six-month promise ends. Then I can pick up where I left off with easel and paintbrush, even though my first responsibility is being a "mother's helper" to my dear friend. So, for now, I keep myself busy redding up for Essie, along with the filthy chore of slopping Zeke's hogs. It's survival of the fittest most days, with the biggest pigs lining up first around the trough, the smallest ones constantly blocked by the fattest ones. A lesson in the demise of the confident, for it is the fattest that get slaughtered first.

In addition to that, I manage to put in two days each week at my Ranck cousins', who have clearly upped their fervor for witnessing since Essie's shunning from the People, and since I left home to stay with her. Irvin and Julia see me as another lost soul ripe for the picking, as does Essie. No doubt about that.

As for Ben Martin, someone came along and snatched up the job at the harness shop, freeing Ben to leave for his home in Kentucky, according to Julia. She says her husband, Irvin, plans to keep in touch with him.

Despite Ben's departure, my life has not returned to normal. Truth be known, thoughts about Ben often keep me awake at night. Daydreams distract me, too. Images I tend to will into existence by my forbidden yearnings, intermixed as they are with my sadness at having sent Ben away. Still, I try to remember what the Good Book says, *Blessed are they that mourn: for they shall be comforted. . . .*

*Who shall lay any thing to the charge of God's elect?*
*It is God that justifieth.*

—ROMANS 8:33

# Chapter 1

A meditative haze parted and soon began to dissipate as a May sunrise spilled onto dogwood blossoms—white, pale, and deep pinks. An early morning rain had dimpled the dirt on the shoulder of Frogtown Road, populated now with pecking wrens and robins.

At the reins in the Hochstetler buggy, Annie Zook breathed in the tranquility, aware of plentiful insects and thick green grass, fresh paint on fences and a new martin birdhouse at Lapps' dairy farm. Clicking her tongue to speed the pace, she leaned forward in the seat, grateful for Zeke's fast horse, as it was a good long walk between Essie's house and *Daed's*.

Only four days had come and gone since she had impulsively packed up her belongings and gone to Esther Hochstetler's, so Annie was surprised to experience a sudden twinge as she made the turn toward her father's house. *Am I homesick already?*

She wondered if Yonie, her nineteen-year-old brother, would be at home when she arrived. *I miss the rascal*, she thought.

Taking in the vibrant springtime colors, she longed more than ever to immerse herself in art once again. *I want to paint my beau.* But Ben was no longer that, and their breakup was all her own doing. Hers . . . and Daed's.

*I never should've written that good-bye letter*, she thought. Yet she had done so to obey her father.

Her separation from Ben was cause for ongoing sorrow. Thankfully, Esther wasn't one to ask questions, even when tears sprang unexpectedly to Annie's eyes. She had come awful close to blurting out her beloved's name upon awakening one morning, only to grit her teeth, forcing down the aching lump in her throat. Speaking his name, even in the private space of her room away from home, would not have hurt a thing. But she never knew what little ones might be roaming the hallway, and she didn't trust herself to even breathe his name lest she be overtaken with grief. Or was it pure foolishness?

There had been plenty of times in the last few days when she had tried to think of some way to return to the lovely, secret world she and Ben had so happily shared—till Daed had caught her riding in Ben's car, wearing her hair down. Exactly which of those transgressions was worse, according to God and the brethren, she didn't know. She had almost asked Cousin Julia for Ben's mailing address on more than one occasion. And even more shameless, she had been tempted to get on a bus, show up at his doorstep, and beg his forgiveness.

*I'd be out of my mind to do such a thing. . . .*

Yet she was beside herself at the thought of living without him.

Annie saw a horse and buggy approaching, coming fast. She strained to see who it might be out so early. When she recognized Jesse Jr.'s wife—her eldest sister-in-law—she wondered how Sarah Mae might act toward her. Still, Annie was eager for any contact with family.

Surprisingly, Sarah Mae offered a warm smile and a wave. "Pull over and stop awhile!" she called out.

Annie was ever so pleased. She leaped from the buggy and tied Zeke's horse to a tree trunk before plump Sarah could even begin to get herself down from her carriage. Annie ran like a girl who had not seen hide nor hair of her kin in the longest time. "Ach, Sarah Mae, 'tis such a nice surprise to see you!"

"And you, too," Sarah Mae said, still holding the reins. "I've been meaning to stop by."

"Over at Essie's, ya mean?"

Sarah Mae was slow to nod. "Well, maybe so . . . but—"

"I know it's terribly awkward," Annie interrupted, "but do come sometime. I know Esther would enjoy the company, just as I would."

Sarah Mae bowed her head for a moment, then raised her pretty blue eyes. "Jesse Jr. could scarcely believe it," she confided, telling how the People had been talking up a storm about Annie's winning the first place award for her covered bridge painting. "Downright surprising, 'tis."

"Jah, I 'spect so." Annie didn't know quite how she felt about this, folks discussing amongst themselves her secret sin. Well, secret till now, anyhow. *Sarah Mae must think I'm brazen . . . and I guess I was.*

Had Jesse and Sarah Mae seen her painting featured on the cover of the *Farm and Home Journal* or merely heard about it through the grapevine? She didn't ask, wouldn't seek out praise or criticism. She had known it was only a matter of time till word got around. So now there were two names floating about—Zeke's *and* Annie's. One a confessed murderer and the other an artist born into the wrong church district—or into the wrong family. . . .

Sarah Mae's expression was questioning, though she spoke not the words Annie might have expected. "I hope you won't be gone from home for too much longer," she said softly.

"Mamm misses me, no doubt." There was that lump in her throat again.

"Not only Mamm . . ." Sarah Mae didn't need to say more.

Annie knew. She, too, disliked the discord between her father and herself. But could she make amends? He was more than put out with her, and no wonder. She had been too hasty in leaving, thinking only of herself. Yet being with Essie and the children was a blessing in disguise, a way to escape her father's rigid expectations.

"I think it best that I stay put for the time bein'," she said, leaning into the carriage. "Especially since Essie needs me."

Sarah Mae sighed heavily, her bosom rising and falling as if she were having difficulty catching her breath. "I'm sure you've heard all 'bout Zeke, then?"

"Some, but Essie doesn't know much yet. What does Daed say?"

Sarah Mae hesitated. "Only that they're holding Zeke until they can figure out if the bones are really Isaac's. Though how on earth they'd do that, I'll never know."

*Little Isaac's dead.* . . . The hard, sad knowledge slapped at Annie's brain every time she heard it.

"Daed's talkin' of sending a letter to Zeke's father . . . to let him know officially of Isaac's death." There was a little catch in Sarah Mae's voice, and she placed her hand over her mouth.

"I feel sorry for Daed," Annie said, "havin' to break such sorrowful news."

Sarah Mae shook her head. "I can't imagine it. But Daed already got his address up in Canada from their cousin Nate, I guess."

Annie shivered. "I daresay Daed should wait till Zeke's father gets over the death of his wife. Seems only right . . ."

"But who's to know if that will ever be."

"I s'pose," Annie said. "Honestly, can a man be expected to suffer his wife's death and his son's all in the space of a few weeks? Ain't like Daed to jump ahead like this."

"Oh, your father's not the one insisting on gettin' in touch with Isaac's father. This comes down from higher up . . . if you understand my meaning."

Annie's gaze caught Sarah Mae's. "This is the bishop's word, then?"

Sarah Mae's hand trembled. "I would not want my husband or any man I know to be in Daniel Hochstetler's shoes. But the brethren know best."

"I 'spect you're right."

"No, Annie, you *know* I'm right."

Annie stepped back, her anger rising suddenly at the mention of the brethren. "Actually, I *don't* know and that's the honest truth. Some days I can't decide whether to cling to what I was always taught or to reach for something altogether new." She paused, recalling recent talks with Esther. "Something that makes wonderful-good sense but stirs up ever so much trouble. Ever think thataway?"

A slow frown passed over Sarah Mae's face. "Can't say I ever have, nee—no."

Annie felt an urgent need to step back, and she did just that, waving good-bye.

"Aw, don't go away mad."

"Oh, I'm long past that," Annie said over her shoulder, returning to Essie's horse and buggy . . . sorry she'd ever opened her mouth.

When Annie arrived at her parents' house she knew, even before detecting the pleading look in her mother's eyes, that she was upset. Mamm had pressed her hand against her cheek upon first seeing Annie at the back door, although Annie hadn't bothered to knock. She'd gone right in, like she always had when living here.

The two of them sat at the table, drinking freshly squeezed orange juice. Mamm's soft blue eyes were somber, even intense. "Ach, Annie, 'tis gut seein' you again."

"Oh, you, too, Mamm." Annie mentioned having seen Sarah Mae out on the road on her way over.

"Jah, she stopped by on her way to market," Mamm replied, staring at Annie still.

"Seems she's mighty worried 'bout Zeke. Which is why I'm here. I just felt I might burst if I didn't talk to you."

"Such a shame for all the People," Mamm said. "Right startling, too, I daresay."

"Yet how can such a thing be true?" Annie paused, wishing now she could right her own wrongs—leaving home so impulsively for one.

"Just why would Zeke lie 'bout something so awful?" Mamm said. "It makes not a bit of sense that he would tell such a story—one that's near impossible to believe. Unless he's . . . not quite right . . . in his mind."

"Even so, if he says he killed Isaac, then who are we to say he didn't?"

Mamm nodded slowly. "Jah, 'tis best not to judge."

Annie turned in her chair, wishing to lessen the distress in her mother's gaze. "For the longest time, I assumed Isaac was alive somewhere. Didn't you?" She looked at Mamm, whose eyes were now downcast.

"It's the most difficult thing, to think of your child as gone forever." Mamm blinked back tears. "In a way Mary Hochstetler's recent passing was a godsend. She went to her grave unaware of the fact of Isaac's death, though thinking him kidnapped must've eaten her up inside."

"And she must have supposed, even known deep within, that her little Isaac had passed over, jah?" Seeing such grief imprinted on dear Mamm's face, Annie swallowed back her own tears, not wanting to add to her mother's sorrow.

"It is one thing, though, to lose a child that way . . . and quite another to lose one to her own stubborn will." The words cut Annie to the quick.

"Oh, Mamm. I never left here out of spite. Surely you know that."

Her mother's reply was slow and soft. "Even so . . ."

Annie rose and went to stand at the window overlooking the backyard and the two-story barn's lower entrance. "I 'spect you want me to talk to Daed 'bout it?"

"Well, *shouldn't* you?"

Something winged up within, like a bird about to soar. *I have no desire to say one word to him.* "I've done too much damage already."

"You're his daughter, for goodness' sake! Why not speak kindly to him . . . see what can be done?"

Annie turned slowly. "I don't know if I can."

"Oh, Annie. . . . We miss you something awful."

Annie shook her head. "I can't talk 'bout this now, Mamm." With that, she hurried out the back door, hoping to find Yonie, the one brother who had always understood her.

# Chapter 2

In his parents' home in Kentucky, Ben Martin awoke early with an unnamed dread. In spite of it, he was determined to make a fresh start. Since returning home, he had not been able to shake his frustration at the way things had ended with Annie. He missed seeing her, talking to her, and spending time with her. He thought of her nearly constantly.

He also thought of her bridge painting, the one he'd stumbled upon in the Rancks' attic prior to his leaving. As close as they had been, why had Annie kept her artistry a secret from him?

Getting out of bed, he reached for his robe and stepped to the window, staring out. Since discovering Annie's painting, he often found himself imagining her at work . . . how she might look as she pressed colored pencils or brush to paper or canvas. Did she stand at her easel or sit on a stool? Where did she work—at home or some secret location? And when would she ever have the time? Considering the great planning that would have gone into the painting of the covered bridge, he was baffled. With all the clamps put on Amish women, he was surprised such self-expression was permitted—or was it? Had she attempted to keep her work hidden from view, just as she had hidden *him* away, slipping out of her father's house and going to their private rendezvous place?

He recalled her eagerness whenever she walked out to meet him at his car. His heart had always pounded at the sight of her, as well. Smiling at the fond memory, he pictured a studio, unknown to her father and the People, where Annie happily hummed while drawing and painting. A cottage in the woods, perhaps? Julia's attic, where he'd seen the marvelous painting? And did she whisper to herself in Pennsylvania Dutch as she worked? There was much he wished to know about Annie—even more so now that he was here and she, there.

He stared down at the street, glad for the stillness before the neighborhood grew noisy. There was no question in his mind that Paradise, Pennsylvania, was as peaceful as any place he had ever been. One of his dreams from the previous night floated into his conscious memory: he had dreamed he was again walking through the covered bridge over Pequea Creek. How long would it be until his subconscious comprehended he was no longer in Pennsylvania?

Ben shuffled to the bathroom. Picking up his electric shaver, he wondered, *How would I look with a full beard?* He stared at his reflection, noticing the unusual dullness of his eyes. Absentmindedly he began to shave, pondering the fact that he'd never known how to go about courting Annie Zook. At first, he figured he'd just wing it, hoping all would go well. And it certainly had, but only for a time.

Then, right when things between them had begun to pick up speed and he was beginning to think she might be falling for him, she'd cut him loose. Even now his curiosity over what might have happened if her father had not caught them together was driving him a little crazy.

*If we hadn't taken the long way back that evening . . . if we hadn't run into Preacher Zook, I might still be seeing her.* But her father had laid down the law and she had chosen to obey him, denying her own heart.

Ben wondered how he ever could have convinced Annie to leave her world for his. In short, that was the kicker. Nothing he imagined, either in the hush of midnight or in the reality of early waking hours, would ever change the cruel fact that they simply were not meant to be together. After all, it had been a no-no from the very beginning for Annie to acknowledge his attention, let alone his affection. Why couldn't he just accept that Paradise was not his home and never would be?

Later, after his two youngest sisters, Sherri and Diana, had rushed off to school in Dad's old beater, Ben washed breakfast dishes and contemplated his plan of action. It was time to get on with real life and stop fantasizing about what might have been. He had always wanted to extend himself to people in need, and he liked the idea of doing something useful with his hands. So building houses in a Third World country seemed like a good way to go. If nothing else, it would distract him and help get the preacher's daughter out of his system.

He plodded across his mom's kitchen to the coffee maker, poured another cup, then settled at the table while his mother dried the dishes. "I've been thinking about making a big change in my life," he said.

"Getting married?" She turned from the sink to wink at him.

"No, the Peace Corps."

Her grin faded but he rushed on. "I started researching this possibility more than a year ago. I think now might be a good time to apply." *Since I can't have Annie.*

Mom froze in place at the sink, dish towel in hand. "Oh, Ben," she said, shaking her head. "Please . . . you can't mean it."

"I'm entirely serious. I meet all the requirements. They prefer people who speak more than one language, but . . ."

"Well, you *did*," Mom murmured, almost to herself. "Not that it would help you any."

"What?" he asked, not understanding.

"Benjamin . . ." she said, as if she had only enough breath to form a single word.

She walked to the table and stood behind a chair across from him, no doubt formulating her next attempt to talk him out of it. "This doesn't make sense. First you rush off to Pennsylvania for no apparent reason, and now you're home for only a few days and you want to volunteer overseas?" She stared down at her hands, fingers tense as she gripped the back of the chair. "Ben, please forget this idea."

"Mom . . ."

"I can't think of you leaving again. I can't—"

"Mom, relax. It won't be forever." But even as he spoke, he was aware of the quiver of her lip, the pallor of her face. *Why such a dramatic reaction?*

With a loud sigh, she pulled out the chair and sat down. "I know your father will be glad when he hears what I'm going to tell you. You see, it's been a long time coming. Perhaps even too long."

He hoped whatever she was about to say was not as alarming as her somber face seemed to forecast.

"Oh, honey, I don't know how to start. . . . This is so difficult." She blinked fast, as if she might cry.

"Mom? What is it?"

488

She inhaled deeply. "Ben, hear me out. Please . . . try to understand."

He nodded and reached over to cover her hand with his own. "Did someone die?"

"No . . . son. What I have to tell you has nothing to do with death. On the contrary, it's about life. *Your* life."

# Chapter 3

Determined to find Yonie, Annie first peeked in the barn but saw only Luke, another younger brother, shoveling manure. *My least favorite barn chore of all!*

Going to the buggy shed, she saw Daed checking the steel bands on the buggy wheels. Quickly, so as not to be seen, Annie crept away. She hurried past the woodshed, then out behind the barn toward the manure pit.

Eventually she spied Yonie plowing with their youngest brother, Omar, behind a team of eight mules, preparing to plant sweet corn in this big field. She would happily wait till they paused for a break, whenever that might be. And if Omar went inside to get some of Mamm's sweet lemonade, which he sometimes did, then she and Yonie would talk. Omar was pretty understanding that way, aware of her closeness with Yonie.

She perched herself on an old tree stump at the far edge of the empty field, glad for these warmer days of spring. The distant hill sloped in shadowy patterns beneath midmorning's light, and she gazed in all directions. This was her whole world, as far as her eyes could see, right out to the horizon—with the sky hanging like a sheer veil over it all.

She thought of Ben, wondering what captured his attention when he sat outdoors in Kentucky. What intrigued him about nature? She recalled he had been quite taken with the variety of trees here in Paradise and smiled at the memory. She realized they hadn't spoken much about his home surroundings, although he had mentioned his family—his parents and four sisters—quite often. Annie had written down the girls' names, hiding the paper in her box of letters from Louisa. Evie, Patrice, Sherri, and Diana. Ben had enjoyed speaking of his sisters, but he'd asked many more questions about *her* life.

Her eye caught sunlight bouncing off an airplane high in the sky, brilliant like a beacon. Then, just as quickly, the light disappeared, and she was struck by its fleetingness. "Life passes too quickly," she whispered, thinking now of her friend in faraway Colorado. Annie wished she had access to one of those fancy smart phone gadgets Lou had used so often to keep in touch with her outside world. Annie was not at all bashful about voicing how much she missed Louisa. She'd said so to Essie, and to the Hochstetler children, too. Just now, though, she told it to the bumblebee lazily buzzing nearby. "What I wouldn't give to see Lou again." Truly she had enjoyed the companionship of her fine and fancy friend, the sound of Louisa's voice . . . and their near-nightly talks about Ben and Sam.

*Will she be surprised that Ben and I are no longer together? That I'm staying with Essie?* She could only imagine the shock on Lou's face when she read the letter Annie had recently sent. *Lou will ask how I like "hanging with Essie."* Annie laughed at the thought of one of Lou's favorite expressions.

She looked up and saw Yonie walking toward her. Omar had stayed behind with the team, but he waved to her nonetheless.

"Hullo, Schweschder!" Yonie called, all smiles.

She rose quickly and strode through a furrowed row to meet him.

Yonie stopped and removed his straw hat, then wiped his forehead with the back of his arm. "What brings you home?"

She saw the mischievous twinkle in his grayish-blue eyes. "You mean I can't drop by for a visit?"

"Not according to Daed, no."

Her breath caught in her throat. "You can't mean it."

"He's mighty put out with you, Annie. I 'spect he'd like you to stay far away . . . till you come to your senses."

"Just 'cause Essie's under the shun and I'm stayin' with her?"

His blond hair shone beneath the sun. "Why's that any surprise? You should know how he'd take it—you rushin' off like you did. Choosing Esther, of all people."

She squared her shoulders. "Well, *you* can't say a word 'bout it."

He slapped his hat back onto his head. "I can if I want to."

She eyed him curiously. "You've got yourself a mouth on ya, brother. Next thing, you'll be getting hitched to Dory."

Yonie stepped back. "Just never you mind."

"Ah, so you might be, is that it?"

"What I do ain't for you to say."

She wrinkled her face. "How is it Daed keeps lookin' the other way? Are you ever goin' to quit your running round and join church?"

He chuckled. "Lookee who's talkin'."

She thought defiantly of her boxes of art supplies, the many sketchbooks waiting to be filled. And fill them she would, with pages and pages of drawings. She would begin the minute the day dawned marking the end of her six-month promise. She must answer her heart's cry, and she could scarcely wait.

Yonie looked at her, obviously amused. "So, why'd you come over?"

She smiled. "Guess you must think I'm here to pick on you."

"Well, aren't you?"

She shook her head.

"You miss fussin' with me, is that it?"

"I guess I do."

He laughed heartily. "Dummkopp, why'd you go and leave home only to come back so quick-like?"

"I'm here for a visit, that's all," she said with a sigh.

"'Tween you and me, I say you're better off." He squatted on the ground next to her, his face serious. "Even with Zeke makin' all kinds of trouble . . . even with Esther under the Bann, 'tis best you're over there."

"And why is that?"

He kept silent, as though deliberating whether to say what was on his mind. Then, when she figured he wasn't going to continue, he cocked his head back before saying, "Daed made you break it off with your English beau, ain't that right?"

If she had ever suspected he might blurt this out, she would've prepared herself, would've managed to keep inside the gasp that sucked air straight into her mouth. "Ach, it's true, but you shouldn't be surprised, jah?"

"I feel awful sorry for ya, is all." He looked away quickly.

"Truth be told, I feel sorry for myself. Ben and I never had a chance . . . not like you and Dory."

He nodded sadly. "Well, it ain't so easy courtin' a fancy girl, neither."

"Jah, I s'pose."

"That's all I'd better say."

Her heart went out to her brother, and she felt compelled to change the subject right quick. Mamm's admonition to talk with Daed continued to echo in her head, and although she didn't know what to say, Annie wandered toward the barn.

Jesse Zook pulled the letter from his pocket and slid it into his mailbox, wishing Bishop Andy might've asked Old Preacher Moses to write and send such grim tidings to Ichabod. Although Jesse *did* agree the time had come to get word to the man.

Rubbing his thumb on a coin in his trousers pocket, he turned and strode toward the house. The place had stood there for more than a hundred years, sheltering one family of Zooks after another. Not a single one of them with a rebellious daughter—at least not that he'd ever heard of. And now with Annie staying over at Esther's place, well, he could hardly let his mind think too long on that, not as defiant as Zeke's wife continued to be.

Stopping momentarily, he looked back at the mailbox and noticed he'd forgotten to raise the red metal flag. He quickly walked back to do so, swinging his arms to hasten his pace.

That done, Jesse changed his mind about heading to the house and decided to cross the road to the barn instead. He craned his neck upward. *The sky's mighty big today*, he thought, taking in the heavens above.

He found his thoughts returning to the brief letter he had been asked to pen, hoping his former friend, Daniel Hochstetler, might in some small way be comforted in knowing the remains of his lost son, Isaac, had been found. *A father's in need of such information.*

Heading into the barn, he wondered how Daniel would react to the news. Had he and his now-deceased wife, Mary, made new connections in another Plain community, clear up there in Canada? "Most likely not," he whispered, shaking his head. Truth was, the man was a troublemaker, just as his son Zeke was.

Prior to Daniel's refusal of the divine lot, his ill temper and touchy ways had often stood in the way of the People's unity, which was required in order to perform their sacred rites, the spring and fall communion and foot washing. It had been surprising to Jesse to learn, years later, that *three* undoubtedly disgruntled members had whispered Daniel's name to the bishop on that long ago ordination day to make it possible for the contentious man to be among the nominees. Even their bishop had never understood it.

*To think Zeke wants me to represent him in court.* He thought suddenly of yesterday's visit to the jail, curling his toes in his work boots. *If it should come to that.*

Jesse made his way up the ladder to the haymow and began rummaging around in the corner till he located the old rope swing in its long-standing hiding place. It was the one young Isaac and many other children had enjoyed swinging on for many happy hours . . . even his own daughter had done so. His sons, too. The grove of black locust trees had been something of a play area back then, and he had been the one to hang the swing there, high on the sturdiest branch of the largest tree. Daniel had helped him.

Pulling the swing now from the secure spot, he hoped the confirmed news of Isaac's passing would not bring further animosity toward the man referred to as Ichabod, meaning *the spirit of God hath departed*. The brethren, including himself, had agreed upon the name, and the pronouncement had stuck, even in Daniel's absence.

Jesse breathed in the sweet hay fragrance of the loft and savored the stillness. Silence was his friend, out here alone with the animals and the dwindling hay bales. The quietude had the power to heal him, he knew. He couldn't help but think of Ichabod again, wondering if the man had managed to find the least amount of solace over the years. Did he ever allow the silence of morning to wash over him?

Jesse sat down on an old three-legged stool, one his father had hewn out of leftover wood. He pondered the seeming curse the Lord God had slapped on Ichabod for his refusal of the divine lot. Did such a blight follow a man to his death? Was there no way out?

He wasn't about to delve into Scripture the way his cousin Irvin Ranck delighted in doing. *Even boasts about it.* And Irvin's wife, Julia, had gone and spread her opinions to Esther, causing confusion amongst the People, he knew. To think his own Annie was living with a shunned woman. Unthinkable! *And what of my embarrassment over Annie's art boldly printed on a magazine?*

There were shuffling sounds, and he turned to see his daughter standing not but a few feet from him. "Annie," he said.

Face solemn, she stared at the long rope in his hands, the wooden seat hanging limply near the floor. "Where'd that come from?"

He looked at her, this young woman who continued to defy him.

"It's our swing—mine and Isaac's—isn't it?" she asked.

He nodded. "I've kept it, safe . . . all these years." He wouldn't admit to wanting to give it to Zeke years ago. He was too struck by the pout of her lip, the distrust on her face.

She moved near and touched the swing with tears in her eyes. She whispered hoarsely, "Why, Daed?"

Stunned by his daughter's reaction, he handed the whole thing over to her. "Here, keep it. It's yours now." With that, he left her standing there, clutching the rope to her chest with trembling hands.

# Chapter 4

As she watched her students at their easels, Louisa Stratford understood again why she had not been able to deny her love for teaching for very long. Four students, including Cybil Peters, a girl with exceptional talent, worked to the strains of Secret Garden's *White Stones*, one of Louisa's favorite CDs for creating an atmosphere of repose. To her musical taste, there was something inspirational about the ethereal blend of violin, oboe, and guitar.

Louisa demonstrated light values, linear perspective, and vanishing points at her own canvas, where she was creating a pastoral scene complete with mules grazing in the foreground and a windmill in the distance.

"Remember," she said, "in one-point perspective, the height as well as the width of the object is parallel to the painting's level surface."

She moved to Cybil's painting of two white swans, pointing out the imaginary extension lines and vanishing points.

Roman, the only male student, asked for assistance with his painting of a tall southwestern-style vase with sunlight pouring down on it from an open window.

"How's the shading?" he asked.

She kept her voice low, so as not to disrupt the concentration of the others, but someone opened the studio door and walked in before she could respond. She wasn't sure at what point she became consciously aware of him, but when she turned to look, she was surprised to see Michael Berkeley, her former fiancé, standing there.

He looked more handsome than she remembered, maybe because an easy smile lit his face in place of the disdain he'd worn during their dismal farewell. He was also more casually dressed, in khakis and a blue oxford shirt. This was new, as Michael was typically "money walking," in fine tailored suits over crisp white shirts and designer ties. She couldn't quite resist the urge to glance at the clock. Wasn't this considered business hours? Had he taken the day off? Or had he really given up the partnership at her father's prestigious law firm, as Courtney had suggested?

Louisa braced herself for his direct approach, remembering all Courtney had said about how Michael wanted her back, wanted a second chance, wanted . . . her. But although his smile was warm and friendly, he didn't walk over. Instead, he paused at Cybil's easel, greeting her and nodding his head appreciatively as she explained the piece she was working on. He laughed at something the young woman said, and Louisa remembered that Michael had met quite a few of her students during the years they had dated.

Trying to concentrate on Roman's question, Louisa offered a suggestion but knew she was only half focused on her work. What was Michael doing here? After a few more minutes, he wrapped up his conversation with Cybil and casually made his way over to where Louisa stood.

"Hi, Louisa."

"Michael."

His eyes met hers, and then he looked away. "I'll bet it feels good to get back here."

She shrugged, her defenses rising.

But before she could reply he continued, "In this studio, I mean. You always were a fantastic instructor."

She smiled briefly at the compliment but felt instantly skeptical of his sincerity and motives.

"Your students missed you," he said.

"And I missed them."

"Though I'm sure you're fond of your friends in Pennsylvania, too."

She shrugged. She wouldn't admit to missing Pennsylvania. She wasn't interested in opening the door to friendship—at least not to the kind of intimacy they had once shared.

Michael said, "Courtney mentioned you created quite a new life for yourself there."

"Did she?"

"I was surprised to hear you'd come back."

It was on the tip of Louisa's tongue to say flippantly, *Really? Even though you sent her to haul me home?* But she resisted. He was being very polite, and she had her students to think of.

"I missed my parents." She swallowed hard. What exactly had Courtney told him? Would he ask her about Sam?

But he only said, "It's really great to see you again, Louisa."

She couldn't say the same. In all truth, she wasn't sure how she felt about seeing Michael again. So instead she asked, "How do you like the way I set up my studio?"

He looked around. "You rearranged everything."

"Yes. Someone once told me—I forget who—that if you don't get to travel as much as you'd like to, move the furniture around a lot." She laughed softly, and Michael joined in. His laughter put her at ease, and she suddenly felt as if they were long-time friends, picking up where they'd left off months before.

Michael straightened. "Well, I'm on my lunch break. I'd better head back."

"It's only ten o'clock. . . ."

He shrugged easily. "My only free hour. I'll be tied up with client meetings the rest of the day. You remember how much I *love* meetings."

She laughed again. She wanted to ask about the firm, but she hesitated. Had Courtney already confessed to him that she'd let the cat out of the bag about his job change? She didn't want to reveal that Courtney had betrayed his confidence, so she simply nodded. She was curious, though. She was surprised, in fact, given this opportunity, that he didn't tell her about leaving the firm himself. Surprised, too, that he made no reference to their past, nor to the possibility of seeing her again.

Instead he looked around the room once more. "Well. I just thought I'd stop by . . . and welcome you home." He met her eyes again. "Take care, Louisa."

She nodded. "'Bye."

With one last grin, he turned and left the room, with only a brief wave in response to Cybil's farewell.

Louisa was stumped at Michael's appearance and his even faster exit. Had Courtney exaggerated his determination to resume their relationship? If not, then why hadn't he asked her out? She strolled over to help the next student, feeling relieved that Michael hadn't pursued her, yet there was another emotion present, as well. Was it some misguided sense of wounded vanity . . . or was she truly disappointed?

❖

Esther's body trembled and she felt her legs might not hold her as she crept away from the window to the chair. Sighing, willing back tears, she slowed her breathing. *I can do this. . . . I must be all that my children need . . . with your help, Lord Jesus.*

Esther refused to look out the window yet again, to stare at the spot where the police car had come rushing into the drive a week before. They had asked for Zeke and she had quickly led them to the barn. There, she and the police had slid open the big door and found Zeke pacing, the same way she'd seen him do in their bedroom. Before she'd scurried back to the house to look after the children—and to escape the nightmarish scene—she'd heard him mutter something about knowing where Isaac's bones were buried.

*Will my life ever be right again?* She knew she must pull herself together before Essie Ann awakened, which would be soon. Laura would be home from school any minute, too. "What's he done, dear Lord in heaven? What has my Zeke gone and done?"

Leaning her head back, she thought of all the years, the tears, the ongoing conflict in this house. She breathed in the present peace of the room, attempting to count her blessings. *Oh, I must think on the good things. The great goodness of my Lord and Savior. Place your hand of compassion and mercy on my family,* she prayed. *Especially on Zeke.*

She thought of Annie, who had readily taken on the role of guardian—more like a she-wolf than a young woman, railing under her breath that morning about Zeke's abusive streak. *"Maybe he'll try slapping around one person too many down at the jail,"* Annie had said, as if she wished it so.

Esther wrapped her arms around her middle as uncontrollable tears sprang to her eyes. Was this how it felt to mingle the light with the darkness? She wondered about that particular Scripture. Zeke had repeatedly taunted her, demanding that she abandon her "ridiculous" beliefs and come back to the Amish church. *"You'll be happier back here. Return to my side."*

But how could she ever go back? Tears clouded her vision; maybe they were tears of relief. She didn't rightly know, because she felt awful sad, too. And each day that passed, she felt trapped in one horrid pressure cooker, as if she might blow up if she didn't cry. So she let the dam break, sobbing into her hands.

❖

As Louisa's first class of students was leaving, her mother stopped by the studio unannounced, as she often did lately. Louisa was eager to show what she was working on and the many photos of Amish farms she had taken over the months in Paradise. What she didn't tell her mom was that she'd just missed Michael—the son-in-law of her dreams—by about fifteen minutes, a thought that made Louisa bite back a smile.

"Here are some of Annie's peacocks." She pointed out one in the photo with a prominent fanned-out tail. "I did a painting of this one. I need to contact the gallery owner in case more of my work has sold."

Mother nodded. "I'd like to hear more about your Amish friend Annie."

She smiled, remembering her friend's contagious laughter, the way Annie's eyes lit up, especially when whispering about Ben Martin, whom she was no longer dating, according to Annie's last letter. What a shocker that was.

"I'm not sure where to begin." She thought of asking why her mom hadn't shown much interest before this, but she had no intention of spoiling this pleasant moment. "When Annie and I first began exchanging letters, she would draw little flowers and animals on each letter to me. It's funny, because she insists now that I was the first to notice her talent."

Mother listened as Louisa recalled that Annie had never drawn stick figures like some kids did. Her sketches, usually in the margins of the letters she wrote, most often depicted the birds, newborn animals, or flowers of spring, Annie's favorite season.

*Springtime in Paradise.* . . . Louisa shrugged off the memory, willing it away. *This* was home now. Here, where her true roots were deep, where she had chafed under the ongoing prospect of becoming materialistic, like her parents. She had run from here for dear life and now, surprisingly, was back and making a bumbling attempt to reconnect.

*How can I possibly fit in here? I know too much about life. And about love.* . . .

Sighing, she heard her mother making superficial comments about Pennsylvania Amish traditions, admitting she had "conducted some research" while Louisa was there. Mother sat stiffly on one of the stools, appearing out of place. "You rarely showed me any of Annie's letters when you were growing up. I know I should have asked about her long before this. I *was* always curious, though. I never knew why you felt so close to her."

This surprised Louisa, but how could she explain that hers and Annie's correspondence had been a special world of their own making? "Annie was someone who understood me right off the bat. Funny, isn't it? A Plain girl with no sense of social decorum . . . who seemed to just *get* me. Even from our earliest pen pal days."

"But you left her world behind," her mother stated. "You came back to your real home."

Louisa cringed. She hated hearing that, but she looked into her mother's face and saw the absence of barbed insinuation. No, Mother wasn't being the prickly pear she could certainly be. Not today, not here in Louisa's small, cheerful studio.

"I came back for lots of reasons," she said. "If anything, I think I found my way—my good senses, you might say. I found everything I've ever longed for in Amish country. Especially peace."

"Since I have no idea what that means, I'll just say how nice it is that you found yourself with your Amish friend, though that *is* hard for me to understand. All your education, your wonderful upbringing . . . doesn't that amount to anything?"

*My upbringing wasn't so great.*

"Your father and I—"

"Please, let's not bring Dad into this." She felt beyond weary at the thought of her father's financial aspirations for her future. *What's done is done, as Annie's Mamm says.* She excused herself and rose quickly.

"Louisa, what is it?"

She fully understood where her mother was coming from, so she tried again. "Have you ever had your senses thoroughly awakened? Have you ever experienced the incredible feeling of community—neighbor caring for neighbor?" She sighed, fighting back the frustration. "And that's only part of what I experienced so fully with the Amish, Mother."

"But Amish people are behind the times. Certainly you know that."

The pronouncement stung. "We'll talk later." Louisa rose and went to get her purse.

Her mother rushed toward her, desperation on her face. "I want to hear more, Louisa. Believe me."

She turned around, forcing a smile. "I can't now, Mother. Really . . ." She headed for the studio door, determined not to lash out in anger.

"Wait. Before I forget, Courtney called. She wants to see you but says you aren't returning her calls."

"I'll catch up with her."

Mother frowned, touching Louisa's sleeve. "Well, please, give her a call soon."

Exhaling, Louisa lifted her chin. "I'm not opposed to seeing Courtney, and if you must know, she is one of the main reasons I came home when I did."

"Really? I had no idea."

Louisa opened the studio door. "I'm sorry, but I need to get going." She hurried out of the strip mall and to her waiting car. A half hour remained before her next students would arrive, and Louisa was in need of some coffee and some air.

# Chapter 5

Preacher Jesse watched his daughter prance shamelessly up the back steps and into the house, carrying the rope swing he'd just given her. *She struts about like a peacock.* "And does as she pleases," he added aloud, spitting out the words. Such a time he'd had lately, folk fussing from all directions, since near everyone in Paradise, or so it seemed, had now heard of Annie's painting on that there magazine cover. "Downright bigheaded she is," he muttered to himself, lifting the harness over Betsy's small ears. "Comin' back here to my house . . . ach, without so much as an apology yet."

He was still mumbling and fretting when a police car turned into the lane. He'd heard from the smithy and others that oodles of Englischers were in the neighborhood, going from farm to farm, asking questions.

His neck hairs prickled as the police officer opened the door and climbed out of his vehicle. "Not on this property," Jesse whispered to himself, making a beeline toward the officer. *I don't want Barbara to have an encounter with him.*

"What can I do for you?" he called, recognizing the tall blond man as the same one he'd spoken to the day Zeke had been taken away.

"I believe you're the preacher I met last week. Preacher Zook, isn't it?" The man smiled. "Lots of folk with that name around here." He pulled out his ID and showed it quickly. "I'm Officer Kipling . . . and thanks for your time today, sir."

Jesse was once again intrigued by the gold badge on the navy blue uniform shirt and could scarcely stop staring at it. "What brings ya over here?"

"I'd like to ask you and your wife a few questions regarding Ezekiel Hochstetler."

"Well, now, things will work better if you put your questions to me and leave my good wife out of it."

The policeman frowned, blinked his eyes, then continued, "How many children eighteen or older live in your house, Mr. Zook?"

*This man must be deaf!* "As I said, no need to be talkin' to anyone but me, Mr. Kipling."

The younger man seemed taken aback, but he pulled out a small pad and pen from his shirt pocket. "Thanks for your cooperation, Mr. Zook. I appreciate it."

Jesse squared his shoulders, inwardly preparing for what lay ahead. "Glad to be of help."

Annie and her mother peered out the kitchen window. "Ach, what's this?" Annie whispered, her heart in her throat. She'd heard more than she cared to from Essie about *her* frightening day with the police, though on that day, Zeke had been the one to call them. Not a soul had invited this intrusion today, as far as Annie knew.

"Oh, what do you think they want?" Mamm said softly. "I've never seen the likes of this."

She wouldn't frighten Mamm unduly by describing the alarming scene at the cemetery. "Come, let's head over to the Dawdi Haus and stay put with Dawdi and Mammi Zook lest they become frightened, too."

"Jah, gut."

They headed to the front room and opened the connecting door. Annie wondered, all the while, if Essie might be sending a prayer toward heaven were she here witnessing all this.

*Thank goodness she's not!* Annie thought. Esther had been through enough trauma for a lifetime.

"What're ya doin' with that swing I saw ya bring in?" Dawdi Zook asked, lifting his chin toward the adjoining door.

"It's the one Isaac and I used to play on at the locust grove," Annie explained. "I want to have it put up again. It's been down too long."

Mammi smiled, as did Mamm. "You and Isaac were quite the youngsters," Mammi said.

To this, Dawdi agreed with a nod. "Never saw anything like it the way the two of yous took to each other. You'd-a thought you were twins or some such thing."

Annie hadn't heard that before. "Isaac's surely in heaven, jah? Little ones go there, even before judgment day?"

"That's up to the Good Lord," Dawdi was quick to say.

Annie sighed. *Everything's up to Him*, she thought.

The birds suddenly quieted when the police car pulled into the lane. Esther ran from the barn into the house, closing the back door securely behind her.

In the kitchen, she found Laura standing on a chair at the sink, wiping the counter clean. "Bless your heart." Esther hurried to her daughter's side. "You're the best little helper, ain't?"

Laura nodded. When her lower lip trembled, Esther gathered her near.

"I miss Dat." Laura buried her face in Esther's neck.

"Well, sure you do."

"When will we see him again?"

"Soon . . . soon," Esther said, shushing her. She had no knowledge of when Zeke might return, but she had every hope that it would be right quick. " 'God is our refuge and strength, a very present help in trouble,' " she said, quoting the Psalms. She must not let fear overtake her—must keep her heart wide open to the Lord Jesus. She knew all too well the lack of joy that came from shielding her heart.

When loud knocking shook the front door, she breathed in sharply. She wondered what might happen if she simply ignored it. Most of all, she must not let on her worry, not in front of the children.

"Why is someone at the *front* door, Mamma?" Laura asked, her eyes wide.

"I'll go 'n' see. You stay here with your brothers and baby sister." She kissed the top of Laura's head and turned to go, heading through the small sitting room between the kitchen and the long front room. Her heart pounded so hard she could scarcely breathe.

Timidly she opened the door. There stood two police officers, a man and a woman, both dressed in navy suits with trousers, and bright gold badges on their shirts. *Like the policemen who came for Zeke.*

"Mrs. Hochstetler?" the woman said. "Mrs. *Esther* Hochstetler?"

She wondered how on earth they knew her name. "Jah."

Both of them held out thin wallets with their pictures in leather frames. "Officers Keller and Landis," said the dark-eyed woman with long black eyelashes, which were surely painted on. "May we come in and ask you some questions?"

Esther faltered, hand on her throat. *What would Zeke say to do?* Her husband was not here, and neither was Annie. It was just the children and herself, so she must decide how to answer on her own. "What's this about?" she asked softly.

"This shouldn't take much time, if you cooperate with us," the woman named Officer Keller said. "Your husband is Ezekiel Hochstetler, is he not?"

"Jah, goes by Zeke . . ."

"We've been assigned to ask those in the neighborhood to attest to his character," Officer Landis continued.

"Well, I've known him a gut long time." Esther assumed they knew as much, but she felt terribly uneasy and hesitated to let them in.

"We'll be brief," said Officer Keller, smiling through pink lips. "You just tell us what you know. It's as easy as that."

Esther's palms were sweating and she felt queasy. Her experience with Englischers was ever so limited.

Officer Keller frowned and pushed back her hair. "There's nothing to be afraid of, Mrs. Hochstetler. This won't take but a minute."

*One minute?* She was feeling ever so put upon. Was she required under God to speak with them?

"What you know may help your husband," Officer Landis said.

"If that's so, then I . . . s'pose." She opened the door a bit wider.

"Thank you," the two said in unison and stepped into the house.

Esther offered them a place on the settee in the front room, then excused herself to hurry to the kitchen. "Laura, dear, are you all right? Mamma's goin' to be busy for a short while. Keep your eye on your sister and brothers, won't you?"

Her daughter's eyes glistened as her focus darted toward the front room and back. "Oh, Mamma, what's goin' to happen? Why are those Englischers here?"

She realized that Laura was worried the police people might be here to take all of them away, just as they had Zeke—even she herself wasn't so sure they wouldn't. "You call if you need me, ya hear?" she told Laura.

"I will, Mamma."

*Poor thing. First her father's gone, and now this.* Esther couldn't help but pray as she headed back to the waiting officers. *I trust you for wisdom, O dear Lord.*

Zeke Hochstetler recalled holding his drinking glass up to the gas lamp at home some weeks back to peer through it curiously. Esther had muttered something about it looking as if he were searching for some answer in the glass, and he'd mocked her but good. What was it about that woman, thinking she could flap her lip whenever she dared? He could hold a glass up to the light and stare through it if he wanted to.

Frustrated, he stopped his mental rambling. He was torn in two. One part liked telling Esther what to cook him for supper or demanding how many logs to throw into the belly of the stove to warm the house. The other part of him knew he'd been terribly harsh, even brutal, with her. Sure, he could make her do his bidding—during the daylight hours, and after dark, too. Wasn't he the head of his household under God? Yet requiring his family to be at his beck and call, allowing no lip from any of them, had gotten him hardly any respect.

Stiffly he paced in this strange English place, though it was no longer as foreign to him as the day he'd arrived. *The police detectives must be done digging up Isaac's bones,* he thought, recalling how he'd given them directions to the burial spot. He was surprised the brethren had not reprimanded him for doing so.

Continuing to pace back and forth in his cell—his cage—he suddenly wondered what it would be like to wear the heavy fur coat of a lion or a tiger— the nap and wool of a powerful animal's skin connected to his own body. Yet he grew weaker with each step. *What'll they do to me when they see I was telling the truth all along?*

He'd had the oddest feeling not a soul believed what he'd said about killing Isaac. At least one of the detectives had looked askance at him. Only when he'd insisted he could direct them to the bones—the proof they needed—did he get their attention at last.

*Isaac . . . my brother! You didn't deserve to die. Still, I spared you a life of dread. I kept you from becoming a man. I cut you off before you could become like our father . . . and like me.*

He sighed heavily, feebly stroking his beard. He let his thoughts slip away further, back through the blurry curtain of years.

They'd gone north on Belmont Road, he and little Isaac, both disobedient as all get out that night. No, it had been *he* and not his innocent brother who had ignored their stern father. *"Tomorrow's plenty soon,"* Dat had said. *"Put the dead pup out behind the barn till morning, and then we'll bury it."*

Nonetheless, Zeke had crossed his father, driven by the desire to do things his own way, just as his father's cruel and defiant nature ruled him.

Zeke couldn't help but notice the light at the Progressive Shoe Store as they made their way along the deserted road. Like a distant star the yard light beaconed to them, its message pulsating through the blackness: *Turn back, return home. Beware!*

The small wooden coffin became heavy after all that walking, but never once did Zeke ask Isaac to carry his own dead puppy dog. It was Isaac who'd suggested the grove near Pequea Creek for the grave—a place where they often played while Dat and Mamma visited nearby neighbors—where the now stabbed-to-death puppy had romped and yipped at their heels and splashed in the creek. It had been Zeke's idea to count the steps to the tree and then turn toward the creek. Eight steps and four, for the years of their lives . . . his own and Isaac's.

There was such unspeakable sorrow between them. The silence was thick, except for Isaac's constant sniffling and weeping, which became annoying. Isaac had loved this puppy more than any boy ought to love a pet.

And when the time came, Ezekiel began to dig the hole with the big, hard shovel.

*Angry, vicious strokes . . .*

# Chapter 6

Ben leaned hard on the kitchen table and buried his face in his hands.

*Adopted?*

Completely stunned by the news, he shook his head. "I wasn't born to you and Dad?"

Mom sighed, her face clouded with sudden grief. "We should have told you long ago. Your father wanted to, but the longer it went, the more reluctant I became." She stopped to brush away tears. "I'm so very sorry."

He stared across the table at the woman whom he had always believed to be his mother. "How could you keep this from me?"

Her chin quivered. "It was my idea to spare you further hurt, though I wanted so much to tell you right after your adoption was finalized."

"You don't struggle over whether to tell a baby these things. How old was I, anyway?" He felt overwhelmed with the knowledge of this betrayal.

"You were only four when all the legal work was finished. Well, we assumed you were still that age, although in the end we had to decide on a birth date for you." She stopped to catch her breath. "And every year that slipped by, your father and I worried we should be telling you the truth."

He glared at her. "Why didn't you?"

"We should have. I see that now all the more . . . how restless you are, as if you're searching for something. First going off to work in Amish country and now wanting to go overseas . . ." She covered her eyes with her hands, whimpering. "I'm sorry, Ben. I'm just so sorry."

He rose. "I don't get it. What possible reason could you have for keeping this from me? And what does my move to Lancaster County have to do with anything?" He didn't wait for her answer, though. He felt as if his chest might cave in and suffocate him. Rushing through the living room, he made his way toward the front door, where he yanked his jacket off the coat tree and left the house.

Annie was becoming anxious now, still staring out at her father and the policeman from the kitchen window in the Dawdi Haus. "How much longer will he stay?" she asked.

Mammi Zook came and led her away. "Ach, not to worry, dear one. The Lord God has us all safe in the palm of His hand."

"Honest, Mammi?"

"Oh, jah. I'm ever so sure." Her grandmother's eyes glistened, but not from tears. She'd always had shining eyes. "We'll have us some chamomile tea with honey, Miss Annie," Mammi said, readying the teapot and setting a cup at the place next to hers at the table.

Annie forced a smile and sat beside her father's mother. Dawdi had gone upstairs to rest, and Mamm had returned to the main house to prepare lunch. Annie wasn't so much thankful to have a cup of Mammi's well-brewed tea as she was having this opportunity to simply spend time with her diminutive Mammi Zook. Living with Essie was all right, but Annie missed her family and knew there was little she could really do to help her friend, flustered as she was about her husband. No one seemed to know much about Zeke's crime. Now, it seemed, Daed was getting things straight from the horse's mouth.

She resisted the urge to turn and peer out the window again, trying to be calm about the unexpected police visit. "S'pose they have a job to do," she said softly.

"Jah, according to their ways," Mammi remarked. "We know not the way of the fancy. We live in the world but are not of it."

Annie had heard that said enough times, but as Mammi spoke, it reminded her of the great big world out there, far from Lancaster County. Far away, where Ben Martin lived, on the other side of that seeming vastness that separated them so.

"How does the Lord God keep track of everyone?" Annie had asked the same thing of Julia on occasion. More recently, she'd put the same question to Essie. "Does He look down from on high? Does He care what's happenin' with each of us?"

"Oh, I don't know *how*, but He cares, all right. I know this in my knower," Mammi said, pointing to her head. "I believe it in here, too." She patted her heart, sighing. "Your fancy friend, Louisa, used to ask me things like this, too, Annie."

"She did?"

"Oh my, quite often. A nice girl, Lou was. Too bad she upped and ran off so awful quick."

"She had her reasons."

Mammi nodded her head, the strings on her *Kapp* falling forward. "I thought she might've found herself true love here."

Annie scarcely knew what to say. She wasn't going to admit it by revealing Lou's secret meetings with Sam Glick.

Mammi had a peculiar look in her eye as she poured the hot tea. "I have the feelin' Lou might be a good one for getting her pies in early enough to head outside to watch the robins skitter about the birdbath of a mornin'."

Annie laughed. *Mammi must think Lou would make a good Plain woman.* She blew on her tea gently before taking a sip. The taste was so appealing, it made her feel nearly homesick. Yet she was right here, sitting and enjoying such good fellowship this minute. "I honestly don't expect to ever see Louisa Stratford again," she declared.

Drawing a breath, Mammi blinked her eyes several times before saying, "Ah, well, I s'pose we'll just have to wait 'n' see on that, won't we?"

Annie couldn't begin to imagine it. Truth be known, Lou was not exactly a predictable person. She was a woman of many interests, and Annie was just as sure as could be that Lou had returned to the life she'd missed.

Jesse strolled along with Officer Kipling out to his car. His head was pounding at the thought of what the policeman had said to him a few minutes before—that the authorities felt sure they had something big to go on with Zeke, what with him leading them to Isaac's bones and all. Jesse had been mighty careful what he said. He certainly didn't want it known that he'd been the one who had originally found and buried Isaac's remains.

"When all's said and done, how can you punish Zeke for a crime he committed as a child?" Jesse asked, still baffled at the possibility that Zeke had actually killed Isaac as a boy.

"First things first," the man said. Jesse had found out quickly that the officer was not one for offering simple, straightforward answers. "Forensics will determine what it can regarding the remains—the gender and age of the bones."

*They have to be Isaac's . . . no doubt on that,* Jesse thought. But he didn't say as much. The brethren had long ago decided not to divulge the news of the boy's disappearance, and they still wanted to keep their hands clean of any connection. God's ways were misunderstood by outsiders, for sure and for certain—God's ways and the Old Ways.

Jesse was still mighty surprised that Zeke had not implicated either the bishop or himself, as he was so sure he would. Because, after all, it was not Zeke who had discovered and then buried those bones.

And it was right then that Jesse stopped in his tracks. *Was it a crime not to report a missing child? If Isaac was ever truly that . . .*

When the policeman finally left, Annie returned to the field to talk with Yonie, who had just finished plowing that section of land. "You've still got yourself a car, ain't?" she asked as they walked toward the house together.

He looked at her. "Why do you ask?"

"I want you to take me over to the Pequea Creek covered bridge sometime soon. How 'bout tomorrow?" She explained that she wanted him to put the old rope swing back up on the tree, where it belonged.

"What the world for?" he asked, eyes wide.

"Don't ask questions. Just help me get it up there again."

He argued with her a bit more but finally agreed to take along a ladder—tied to the top of his car—because she warned there was no other way to reach the branch due to the thorns. "If I'm to put the swing up, I'll have to smuggle the ladder out of the barn."

"Do whatever you have to. Stop by for me tomorrow, maybe?"

Surprisingly, he agreed. "That might just work." He said he'd heard Daed talking about possibly meeting with the brethren at noon tomorrow. "Jah, that's fine. Be ready, though, so I don't have to wait."

She scrunched up her face. "I'll be ready." Then to herself she added, *Been ready for years.*

"Your bishop, Andrew Stoltzfus, has granted us permission to ask you a few questions," dark-haired Officer Landis said to Esther, folding his hands as he leaned forward on Esther's settee. He glanced at the policewoman next to him. "And Officer Keller, here, will get things started."

The woman had a peculiar habit of squinting her eyes and fixing her gaze on something far away. Just what, Esther didn't rightly know, but it was clear the woman was not at all comfortable with the task at hand. "Is your full name Esther Hochstetler?" she asked.

She nodded.

"How long have you lived here in Paradise?"

"My whole life."

"And how long is that?"

"I am twenty-three years old, as of last September."

"How long have you known your husband, Ezekiel Hochstetler?"

"Since my first singing, seven years ago."

"How long have you known his family?"

"Never much knew them."

The policewoman stared down at her notebook, pen poised on the page. "How many years?"

"Same as I've known Zeke . . . seven."

"How many children do you have?"

"Four."

"Please give their names and ages."

Esther felt her hands go clammy. "Is this ever so necessary?"

The woman offered a quick smile. "It is public record, of course. We just need you to verify."

She breathed in slowly. "Laura, our eldest, is six. Zach is three, John is two, and the baby, Essie Ann, is fifteen weeks old."

The woman flipped her notebook page and scribbled something at the top. Then, looking up again, she continued. "Have you ever known your husband, Ezekiel Hochstetler, to threaten anyone with bodily harm with the intent to murder?"

"No."

"Has your husband, in the past or presently, ever abused you or any of your children?"

She paused. She didn't know quite what that meant. "I'm not sure."

"Has your husband ever punished you or your children unduly?" The police-woman's chest rose and fell, and Esther could see that she seemed to struggle.

*Is this a trick?* She began to whisper a prayer in her first language. "O Lord God be ever near. . . ."

"Esther, please answer the question to the best of your ability."

She wanted to help and not hinder her Zeke, so she considered what she best be saying.

"Explain what you mean by punish?" She managed to eke out the question to the strangers as they looked at her as if *she* had done something wrong. These Englischers had nerve to come here. Then she remembered they'd said Bishop

Andy was all for the questioning. What on earth did that mean? Did he know the sort of things being asked of her this day? And wasn't her own experience as Zeke's wife . . . wasn't that how most women were treated by their husbands? *But Annie says Preacher Jesse is gentle and kind to his wife*, she recalled.

"Has your husband ever physically abused you or your children?" the police-woman repeated.

*Sure he has . . . when any of us disobey*, Esther thought.

"I'd rather not say," she said so softly she scarcely heard herself.

Officer Keller gave a fleeting look to her partner. The man frowned briefly then glanced about the room, as if looking for clues. What did he hope to see—holes in the wall? Broken dishes?

"I really need to get back to my little ones," Esther said, getting up from her chair.

Surprisingly, the officers rose when she did and followed her to the door. She could scarcely breathe as they said their good-byes and left the sanctity of her house. "O my Lord and Savior," she prayed, folding her trembling hands tightly to her breast.

Ben drove to one of his favorite hiking trails, ten miles from the house. His chest ached every time he recalled his mother's shocking revelation.

*Adopted?* The startling knowledge was like a ton of bricks smashing into his psyche.

"Twenty-one and just now finding out?" He parked his car, got out, and slammed the door.

He hurried toward the trailhead, moving swiftly up the dirt path. He was aware of boulders on one side and a shallow ravine on the other. Farther up he noticed some deer—a doe and two young fawns—looking at him momentarily before scampering into a grove of white oaks.

"If I'm not really Ben Martin, who am I?" He asked it of the trees, the sky, and a blue jay nearby as he made his way up the gradual incline.

He had the urge to shout but suppressed his emotions. It was bad enough that his father was scarcely ever at home and his two best buddies were away at out-of-state colleges. The idea of joining the Peace Corps appealed to him even more. For a flicker of a second, he'd actually thought his mother crazy, but knowing her as he did, that notion quickly melted into disbelief. Now, though, he carried anger and a real sense of betrayal with him as he made furious strides up the trail.

He considered his family . . . all the framed pictures of his sisters, parents, cousins, aunts, uncles, and grandparents on both sides. The extended family he'd always known. Not a single person with his blood in their veins? No one he resembled? Why hadn't this fact hit him before?

"They are not my real family . . . not related to me at all," he spit out. "My sisters aren't my sisters." He could not begin to fathom it and suddenly felt more alone than ever before in his life. Lonely and lost, he realized anew how very much he missed Annie.

# Chapter 7

Louisa was already awake the following morning when she heard banging coming from the other side of the wall, from the apartment next door. It sounded like pots and pans tumbling out of a cupboard. At first she wondered if she had been dreaming, but how could that be when she had been looking at the clock off and on for the past full hour? Annie's mother had been such a quiet cook, even graceful at times, adeptly juggling baking many loaves of bread each morning and pies, too, along with many other homemade goodies.

The thought of Annie's mom creating her homespun culinary delights pulled Louisa quickly back to Paradise. But it was not the Zooks' house nor their kitchen that held her captive. She couldn't get Sam Glick out of her mind, in spite of Michael's visit to the studio yesterday. There was something unique about Sam, something she hadn't encountered in any other man. She was still trying to decipher the quality . . . and decide whether she could walk away from it for good.

*Fer gut.*

She smiled. Quaint Dutch words and phrases kept popping into her mind, nudging her back to Amish country, where, she was afraid to openly acknowledge, so much of her heart still resided.

She wondered how Sam was doing. Had he managed to move on without her? Her departure had been too swift even for courtesy's sake, although she had taken a few minutes to write him a good-bye letter. Too often, even now, she had the urge to write him again or to call him at his barn phone . . . just to hear his voice.

Getting out of bed, she hurried to the shower, attempting to push away thoughts of her mad dash from Pennsylvania. It seemed mad dashes were getting to be almost a habit for her. Last year, she had been rather insane to take off so impulsively from Colorado, leaving her parents holding the financial "bag" for Michael's and her planned lavish wedding. And part of her had been equally crazy to leave Sam behind, no doubt wondering what kind of flighty girl she really was, and maybe even thinking *good riddance.*

Reaching for her towel, Louisa determined that today she must discard all thoughts of Sam and set him free in her own mind. "Once and for all," she whispered to her cat, Muffin. "*This* is where I belong, ain't so?" She groaned as yet another Amish saying rolled from her tongue.

Over the noon hour, following the main meal, Jesse huddled with Bishop Andy and Moses in the bishop's barn. "This thing with Zeke could get out of control in a big hurry," Jesse began. "There's no tellin' what could happen."

Andy nodded, slow and long, pulling on his beard. His face looked mighty pale. "I daresay we keep our peace and stay out of the public eye as much as possible."

Old Moses shook his head, eyes solemn, head bowed. He drew in a deep breath; then his eyes rose and met Jesse's, holding his gaze for a time. "Here's what I think, and Bishop, you tell me if I'm wrong on this." Moses leaned forward, as if to be heard better, though it was he who suffered the hearing loss. "The Lord God knows what's what, and none of us is guilty of any wrongdoing here."

Jesse thought on that. "Well, in your thinkin', did we do wrong not to report Isaac's disappearance back when?" He looked right at Bishop Andy.

The bishop was slow to respond. When he did so, there was fire in his eyes and his voice was high-pitched in agitation. "Jesse Zook, you as a minister of almighty God know better than to question the appointed shepherd over this flock . . . of which you have been entrusted with the care, as well."

Jesse groped for the right words and wished he'd kept his mouth shut, even though he felt this was something the three of them must discuss. They did not have their ducks in a row, so to speak, and they were all vulnerable to attack from the outside world. And, what with Zeke wanting representation from Jesse . . . well, he wished they'd been honest from the outset. "I know it was your word we followed, back in the beginning," he admitted, knowing that the rule of thumb was clearly on the side of trusting what the man of God decreed. In this case, it had been Bishop Andy's words that had guided all of them, all these years.

"If we'd been forthright with the police," Old Moses spoke up, "we'd have had an even bigger mess on our hands, I daresay."

The bishop turned suddenly. "We daresn't question the Almighty."

Jesse was reminded once again what his father and father's father had always believed, what the ministry, the brethren, said was always right. "There is little room for budging on this," he stated, hoping to drive home the point that they, each of them, were in a real pickle with Zeke in jail saying who knew what. "We must help the police if need be, but only as much as necessary."

"Jah, we hold steady . . . stay the course," Andy said. "No reason to doubt when God has spoken through His servant."

Jesse had always believed that the bishop was to be honored and obeyed. There had never been any question on that till now. Now he struggled, day in and day out, and not one thing Andy or Old Moses said today, tomorrow, or next week could convince him otherwise. Honesty was always the best way, his father had taught him. Honesty must prevail under the Lord God. Sadly, in this case, covering up the truth had led them down a path of thorns, and Zeke's telling the police where to find Isaac's bones might be only the beginning.

*Days of sorrow*, he thought, greatly fearing what was bound to come. Bishop's decree or no.

Annie was ever so glad Yonie kept his word and came for her at Esther's, although his car looked awful funny with the ladder tied to the top. She called her farewells to Esther and the children and went out to her brother's car with the swing in her arms.

During the ride over to Belmont Road, she was restless and excited both, until she spied a cash box on the floor of the car. "What on earth is that for?"

Yonie's ears blushed red. "Don't be askin'," he said. "I forgot it was even there."

"You're driving the People around for pay, aren't you? Takin' them to work, to the doctor, and whatnot all?"

He nodded sheepishly. "Got the idea here lately, and honestly it's helpin' me pay off my car loan."

"Well, isn't that a fine howdy-do?" She was truly shocked.

"When Daed got wind of it, he told me never to bring my car onto his property till I got my wits 'bout me again."

"And just when do you expect *that* to ever happen?"

He shrugged, pulling out a cell phone from his pants pocket. "See this? I'm a taxi service amongst my own folk. They call me, day or night, and I drive to their houses and take them wherever they want to go."

She held her breath. "I hope you're kidding."

"Nope. I'm tellin' you the for-sure truth."

Sighing, she looked out the window, watching the fields blur as she stared, not sure why tears threatened to fall. "I guess you're not planning to join church anytime soon."

"You guessed right."

She couldn't say anything to him, really. Her own procrastination had been and continued to be a thorn in their father's flesh—for both their parents, truth be known, and for the brethren as a whole. This she knew, though she simply couldn't change anything about that now. *Maybe never.*

When they arrived at the familiar covered bridge, Yonie untied the ladder and hoisted it over his shoulder, and Annie led the way down the bank, toward the grove of trees. In a matter of minutes, Yonie had the ladder in place and the rope swing swaying from his efforts.

Annie stared at it, taking in the beauty of springtime in every direction— the flowering trees, the verdant slope, and the gurgling creek below. For a moment, she was a little girl again, and she and Isaac were swinging together, their laughter on the breeze.

"Hullo? Annie! Quit your daydreamin' and steady the ladder." Yonie's voice jerked her back to reality, and she was sad to return.

The next day, Louisa was pleased when her father called the studio in the midafternoon. "Your mother baked a lemon sponge pie," he said with a chuckle. "Imagine that."

"What's the occasion?"

"I've offered to grill salmon in hopes you'd join us for dinner this evening."

She smiled. Her father was like a puppy dog when he was desperate. "Sure. When's dinner?"

"Come over when you're finished at the studio."

"Okay. I'll bring a salad."

"Sounds great. Your mother will be happy about this," Dad added. "Good-bye, Louisa."

"See you tonight," she said. "And thanks!"

She clicked off her Palm and began the cleanup between classes. When that was done, she hurried to her own easel, anxious to get in some work on her painting of an old barn. *Jesse Zook's barn*, she thought, wishing she'd taken even more pictures of it than she had in her possession.

She often thought of simply going back to visit Annie, over a long weekend perhaps, if for no other reason than to surprise her. Annie occupied such a huge portion of her thoughts. Their letter-writing days had already resumed, yet she still longed to call Annie, to hear her voice. But she knew the nearest phone was the neighbor's barn phone up the road from Esther's. There was always the option of simply writing to Annie and alerting her to what day and time she might call. Of course, Annie wouldn't want to break the *Ordnung*—as decreed by the bishop—and use the telephone for personal communication. Though what was one more broken rule?

And Sam? No point in stirring up anything she couldn't follow through with, even though she missed him terribly. He was somewhat more progressive, as some Amish referred to themselves, so it wasn't out of the question that she might contact him by phone.

*Someday.*

*There's not a lot of wisdom in growing older*, Louisa decided as she sat on a fine upholstered chair at her mother's lovely long table in their spacious, candlelit dining room. Wisdom came in appreciating the true but simple things in life. Things more important than the topics her parents seemed to delight in discussing this evening, like bridge partners and golf scores.

"Did you watch that special on the Triple Crown last night?" her father asked.

"No. I . . . um, got rid of my TV."

He furrowed his brow. "Why would you do that?"

She shrugged. "Never watch it. Mm . . . this salmon is so delicious." Her mouth watered as she cut the tender salmon fillet with the side of her sterling silver fork. Her father had outdone himself with the basil butter. Her tossed salad and the steamed veggies were delicious, and Mother's lemon pie rivaled Barbara Zook's.

Louisa refused to let the aroma of great cooking send her thoughts whirling back to Annie and her people this time. No, this was home, and here she was destined to stay. She had grown up in this luxurious place nestled in Castle Pines, just south of Denver. Sure, it was her parents' exquisite abode now, but it was hers, too. She was, after all, her parents' daughter, Louisa Victoria Stratford. A modern high-tech girl with a yearning for the simple life. And no longer did she wonder how she could possibly fit into this world with its opulence and elitist mentality; she knew how—by being her new self. She would dress the part when necessary, but she would live with an eye for the significant. She would live, if not a less complicated life, then a tranquil one filled with true purpose. For she had tasted and embraced a peaceful, meaningful life, and it had changed her from the inside out.

Following dessert, Dad asked her to join him in his private study. The secluded room was lined with custom cherry wood built-ins on nearly every wall. Louisa sat in her father's favorite wingback chair, a maroon, hunter green, and tan plaid. It was the only piece, along with a coordinating area rug, that had been chosen by her mother for the decor of Dad's home office.

Louisa settled into the comfortable chair, propping her feet up on the matching ottoman. She enjoyed the fire in the gas fireplace and was amused by her father's ritual of selecting a cigar from his cigar box, lighting up, then leaning back in his leather desk chair, his eyes closing for a moment, his chiseled face breaking into a familiar smile. "Well, daughter dear, not only did I miss out on a son-in-law, but I lost a promising young law partner, also," he remarked. Then for effect, or so Louisa thought, he blew the smoke into defined grayish-white rings.

By his tone, she knew he was not angry, only interested in talking about her plans for the future. No doubt he hoped she might say she was resuming her engagement with Michael. "Oh, Daddy, surely you know Michael and I will never be more than friends now."

His smile turned solemn. "Is there no hope for the dashing Mr. Berkeley?"

"I don't see how." *After Sam, I can't begin to imagine it. . . .*

He puffed on his cigar. "It's difficult to understand what went wrong between the two of you."

"I'd rather not go into it."

"You're upset," he said, narrowing his gaze.

She wouldn't reveal the reasons—too late for that. "The Amish have an apropos saying: 'What's done is done.'"

He nodded. "Fair enough." He studied her, then studied his cigar. "You might not know it, but Michael left my firm to become a public defender in a low-rent district." He scratched his head, grimacing. "I tried to talk him out of it, but he was so eloquent. And adamant."

"Really?" she said. "Then a partnership with Michael is evidently not in the cards for either of us."

"He's already getting established in his new area of interest." Dad shook his head again. "Any idea why he would make such a monumental career change?" The twinkle in his eye suggested she ought to know the answer, or *was* the answer.

*Trying to get my attention, maybe? That's presumptuous.*

Reaching for the cigar box, she opened the lid and selected a cigar. "Don't worry, I have no intention of smoking this." She took a long whiff, sliding it beneath her nose, breathing in the rich scent. "Honestly, I don't know what I want where men are concerned. I wish Michael hadn't been so impulsive, leaving you in the lurch, Daddy."

He raised his eyebrows. "Look who's talking."

Mother was calling from the hallway, carrying coffee on one of her sterling silver trays, Louisa assumed. She rose to her feet, thinking, *Saved by café au lait.*

Later that evening, Louisa and Courtney sat on Louisa's funky black-speckled sofa, flipping through fashion and entertainment magazines. After quoting an article about a celebrity wedding, Courtney declared she was absolutely sure Michael was going to call Louisa for a lunch date. "I'd bet money on it."

"Better watch your gambling habit," Louisa joked, but she couldn't disagree more. "You didn't see him playing it cool at my art studio."

"Oh, I've got it all figured out, girl." Courtney's pretty green eyes shone with knowing.

Louisa laughed and reached for her can of pop.

Courtney was insistent, turning a page and swishing her thick shoulder-length brown hair away from her face. "You'll see I'm right."

Wanting to change the subject, Louisa asked, "Ever hear of this?" She looked down at the magazine she'd been reading. "This says that washing your hair with very hot water gets the blood circulating."

"So?"

"It's supposed to really get the creative juices flowing."

Courtney leaned back, pulled her hair in a bunch, then let it go free. "And why does someone as wildly creative as you are need a crutch?"

"I think we all need a boost on low days."

"You have down days? No way."

"You haven't been around when I'm staring at the foreground of a canvas, trying to pull my thoughts into one cohesive idea." Louisa shook her head. "It's not the easiest thing in the world to create day in, day out."

"Okay, so you boil your head," Courtney said. "How's that supposed to help?"

"It gets the blood flowing to the brain."

Courtney hooted. "And this is a *good* thing?"

"Wunderbaar-gut, as the Amish say." Louisa reached down for Muffin, lugging him up onto her lap. "I'll have to tell Annie about it, won't I, boy?"

Courtney's expression became serious. "You ever going to get all that Plain nonsense out of your system?"

"Maybe. Haven't decided yet."

"Well, whatever you do, make sure you say yes when Michael calls."

"We're back to this?"

"Full circle, baby. That's why I'm here, you know. I'm your guardian angel, English style."

To that, Louisa laughed. "You're a dreamer."

"What, and you aren't?"

Louisa stroked her pretty kitty, whispering in his ear, "Tell Court to go soak her head."

# Chapter 8

At breakfast on Friday, Annie helped little John by cutting his sausage into small bites. Then she poured some more fresh milk for Zach. Both boys were exceptionally quiet this morning, and she wondered if they'd heard something of their father's plight.

Esther talked about having seen Julia again. "Your cousin's inviting us to attend prayer meeting sometime."

The brethren weren't so much opposed to prayer gatherings as they were to Bible studies, Annie knew. She had never understood why the Amish ministers were outspokenly opposed to the study of Scripture. "I could baby-sit while you go," Annie said.

Essie looked at her. "You're not much interested, then?"

"Oh, I don't know, really."

"I do wish you'd go with me." There was pleading in Essie's voice. "I wish . . ." She stopped abruptly.

"You wish I'd accept your faith?" Annie finished for her.

Essie smiled, nodding her head. "You know me well, and jah, I surely do."

"Ach, I'm already beginning to feel a bit cut off from the People," Annie confessed. She lowered her voice so as not to involve the children, "Livin' here . . . since you're under the shun and all."

"I wondered if that was goin' to be a struggle."

Annie reached over and clasped her friend's hand. "You know I'd do most anything for ya, don't you, Essie?"

Essie smiled. "It must be hard, you stayin' here . . . being the preacher's daughter, too. That can't help things. Folk expect more from you."

Annie couldn't disagree with that. "I see changes in you, Essie. When you speak of you-know-who, well, I don't notice as much bitterness anymore." She was careful not to spell it out too directly in case Laura and Zach should understand she was speaking of their Dat.

"God is giving me the ability to endure this hard trial day by day." Essie paused to drink her coffee, then slowly she began again. "Without His love, I could not be so calm . . . or forgiving."

Annie shook her head. "You mean you honestly forgive him?"

"Yes. Forgiveness is proof of love."

Annie was stunned. Zeke had treated Essie and the children horribly and now claimed to be a murderer. Could Essie simply overlook that? "Well, your God must be different than mine." *At least, the Jehovah God I grew up knowing.*

"He's filled me up with His loving-kindness," Essie said. "And that's all I can tell you."

Never before had she seen the likes of Essie's attitude. She supposed that if Zeke ever got out of jail, his wife would take him back with open arms. The thought made her worry all the more.

"Oh, you would not believe the changes happening in the Amish world," Louisa told Michael by cell phone. She was driving to the studio, having left the house a bit early, as she wanted to work on her own project before her students arrived. Michael had caught her as she was making the turn into the little strip mall where her studio was located. Now she sat in her car, wondering why he had really contacted her again. Was Courtney right, after all?

"I read somewhere that Amish women are using cell phones, recharging them at their craft shops in town." Michael laughed softly. "Is that true?"

"Yes. Some of the less traditional bishops are allowing them, but only for work-related business." Saying this, she almost felt as if she were betraying a confidence. "They aren't to use their phones for personal reasons." Even so, she had heard some of the women talking fast in Dutch and laughing on occasion. Of course, she hadn't ever questioned Annie on the subject, though she'd wondered. "Why do you ask?" Louisa was curious as to why he would bring this up.

"Ever since you moved to Pennsylvania, I've been noticing articles coming out about the Amish in Lancaster County and in Holmes County, Ohio."

"I'm impressed! One's the original Anabaptist settlement and the other is the largest community of Amish in the entire world." She smiled to herself and added in her best announcer voice, "For two tall lattes, can you tell me which is which?"

Michael paused. "Uh . . . no."

"Wrong answer. Pennsylvania's Plain community came first, in the early 1700s."

He chuckled, then asked, "Why Pennsylvania?"

*Is he really interested?* she wondered. Still, she answered seriously, "William Penn offered land to people who wanted sanctuary from persecution, such as Quakers, Amish, and Mennonites. Some of the original Amish communities migrated to Ohio many years later from one of the original Pennsylvania settlements in Somerset County. I've read up a lot on Annie's people, as you can tell." She waited for his response and was somewhat surprised when he said he'd like to continue their discussion over lunch.

So this was where he had been leading her. "I'm busy with students all day today," she said, which was true.

"I can wait till you're free," he said quickly. "You pick the day."

She flinched. "Michael . . . we really don't want to do this, do we?"

"Do what? Have a harmless lunch for old time's sake?"

*Harmless, my eye.*

"C'mon, Louisa, what can it hurt?"

She didn't know how to answer. His changing career paths did have her curious, though. It was hard to believe he had walked away from the lucrative position offered him by her father.

"We can put a cap on it, if that would make you feel better," he offered.

"Like what?"

"A one-hour lunch. No longer. How's that?"

She paused, then agreed. "All right. I'll meet you for lunch next week. How's Wednesday?"

She felt his exuberance through the phone. "Wednesday it is."

But after his call, she realized he hadn't specified the place. *Which will give him another excuse to phone again,* she thought.

Walking up the sidewalk to her studio, she was reminded once again how shrewd her former fiancé had often been. *Why am I agreeing to see him, anyway?*

Annie quickly finished up mending some odds and ends of clothing for Essie before midmorning. After folding and putting away the children's items, she had a hankering to write to Lou. She had begun to miss her desk back home, wishing at times like this she'd had Yonie haul it over here. Instead she made do with a book in her lap and her stationery placed on top, as she had before.

Happily, she began to write to her beloved fancy pen pal.

*Dear Lou,*

*I hope you don't mind me using the nickname Yonie and I picked for you. It might seem peculiar seeing Lou written at the top of my letter now that you're back teaching your art students again, back in your modern world. Tell me if it bothers you, all right? Also, tell me if you'd rather I didn't bring up your connection to Sam, which must cause you many different feelings nowadays. (If you're anything like me, you're terribly lonesome for him, just as I am for Ben, though no one knows it but you.)*

*Well, enough about that. You haven't said much about Michael in your letters, so I guess I'm wondering how he fits into your life now that you're a fancy girl again, if he does at all. Oh, this is so hard trying to share with you on paper, when we became so close face to face!*

*I miss our talks and all the laughter. It seems like months since you were here. How's Muffin? Is he settled back into his cozy place in your apartment? I wonder if he misses being here.*

Annie paused, looking out the window. "I'm rambling," she whispered. Never before had she experienced difficulty in expressing herself while writing a letter. Never to Louisa, anyway.

She tried to picture the pretty apartment where Lou lived and the studio where she instructed her eager students.

Sighing, Annie resumed her writing.

*I've begun marking off the days on the calendar, and I'm sure you can guess why. On July 17 my promise to Daed will be up, and I have plans to start painting again. Are you surprised? I'm sure my father would be . . . and furious with me besides. There are rumors that the preacher's daughter is caus-ing a stir amongst the People, what with my art published on that magazine cover AND my staying here with shunned Esther. And now the preacher's son is driving a car, too! Add to this Zeke saying he killed his brother, and all of Paradise seems to be in an uproar.*

*I went to see Mamm a few days ago and it felt odd to be a visitor in my old home. I haven't gone to Preaching since moving here to Essie's, but if I were to go, I can only imagine the stern looks on the faces of the brethren and others. Truth be known, I almost prefer avoiding the stress and simply going with Essie and the children to Julia's church.*

*There's more to that. You see, I've been listening right quiet-like when Essie talks about her "Lord Jesus." I'm not saying that I agree with anything thus far, but something is happening inside of me. My heart—Essie calls it my spirit—is growing ever so soft to all her spiritual talk. And I've found myself whispering prayers at night instead of thinking the rote ones in my head.*

*I'm anxious to know what you think. Tell me if it's the strangest thing you've heard from me yet. All right?*

*I look forward to getting your next letter. And I send you a dear hug over the miles.*

*Love from your Amish friend,*
*Annie Zook*

She placed a stamp on the addressed envelope before hurrying downstairs to help Esther with the noon meal preparations, dicing cooked potatoes for a big batch of potato salad she and Essie planned to take to the family of a sick neighbor that afternoon. "I can only imagine how this gesture of kindness will be received," Annie said.

To this, Essie nodded. "We can keep giving even if the gift is refused."

"You just amaze me," Annie said, chopping away.

"Ain't me." Essie's eyes glistened. "It's God's spirit in me."

Annie was beginning to believe her, for there seemed no way Essie's devotion to helpfulness—despite continual rejection—could be from anything other than a heavenly source.

# Chapter 9

Zeke peered through the glass separating him from his visitor at the county prison. He leaned back in his chair and looked across at Jesse Zook, wearing his for-good clothes. "Hullo, Preacher. What's the weather like out today?"

"Mighty nice, I daresay." Jesse paused, a brief smile appearing. "A gut day to be in the clear, Ezekiel."

"What's that ya say?"

"You're free to leave here. The court is releasing you to my custody."

*I'm in the clear?* "How can that be?"

The preacher began to explain what the police had told him—how the initial report on the bones had come back from forensics. "They aren't at all what we thought. It's downright surprising, but the bones are the remains of a six-year-old *girl*! They matched right up with a cold case, connecting a confessed serial killer to the dead girl."

Zeke felt dizzy-headed. Was he dreaming? How could it be . . . Isaac's bones were someone else's?

*Mighty strange if true*, he thought, looking at his arm where they'd taken blood samples. They had taken snippets of hair, too. Gotten permission from the judge, he'd been told, although he hadn't been needed at the courthouse on that particular day. Something called a search warrant had been granted, ordered by the court and coordinated by the police.

"So, you've helped solve a long-ago crime," Jesse told him.

Zeke stared at his feet. They felt awful cold, right through his shoes—through his socks, too. So were his hands, now that he thought on it. In all truth, he had been shivering endlessly for the past few days.

He knew he ought to raise his head and pay attention, so at last he did. "I'm all befuddled." Zeke knocked on his chest with his fist.

"You'll be returning to the People today. I'm here to take you back."

Zeke shook his head. "There's no place for me now. . . . I tell you, everywhere I look, I see blackness, Preacher."

"You aren't to blame for any killing, Zeke. Don't you see, this is not your doing?"

"The voice says so. You just don't know."

Jesse frowned. "What's that you say?"

"In my brain. I hear it, Preacher. Each and every day . . . an accusing voice."

"This will all pass in due time—once you understand you're free. You had nothing to do with your brother's death. That is, if he's even dead. We don't know one way or the other."

"No . . . no, I *am* at fault."

"You're lying to yourself, Zeke. Listen . . . you did not kill your brother as you supposed. The bones are not Isaac's."

Saying he'd meet him out front, Jessie excused himself, but Zeke continued to sit there until the guard came to remove his handcuffs. *I'm goin' home.* And with the realization, he shuddered.

Annie was walking back to Essie's after delivering the potato salad to the neighbor when she saw Yonie driving his car, with Daed and Zeke riding in the back seat, of all things! She stopped walking and watched as her brother made the turn into her family's driveway. *Well, what the world?*

Then she understood. "Zeke is out of jail!" She ran toward the house, not thinking what she was doing. Even so, she couldn't understand why Daed was bringing Zeke back here of all places . . . and why Daed had allowed Yonie to drive them. *Ach, nothin' round here makes sense anymore.*

By the time she reached the yard, the three of them were making their way inside through the back door. Pausing to catch her breath, her brain began to spin through the possibilities. *Did Daed help Zeke out of his pickle? What could've happened?*

Last she'd heard, Zeke had admitted to killing Isaac, which had never made sense to her. But someone's bones were part of all this. What of those?

Annie slowly walked toward the back door and slipped inside. Not wanting to eavesdrop because that sin was equal to most any other in the Good Book, according to her father, anyway, she made some noise in the outer porch, taking time to remove her sweater. Even with that amount of rustling, the men continued to talk in the kitchen, seemingly unaware of her. Since she couldn't be seen, she wondered what to do next. Cough? Shut the door again? Or were they so caught up in whatever they were doing they truly did not care if they were overheard?

What came out of Daed's mouth just then shocked her no end. "You must cease your talk of being guilty, Zeke. Those bones aren't Isaac's. You are mighty troubled, is all. I'll look after you here . . . till you're better able to return to your family."

Annie was glad no mention had been made of her staying with Essie. She was ever so sure Zeke wouldn't take too kindly to that.

Zeke was saying something now, although she couldn't quite make it out. Something to do with wanting Yonie to drive him somewhere.

*No, no . . . not home to Essie!*

Annie cringed as she listened, hoping Daed would put the nix on that.

"Listen to me," Daed said. "It's high time you got some rest and had a nice hot meal. You'll stay upstairs in the Dawdi Haus for a few days. We'll see how you're doin' after that."

Zeke replied, "I wish I could see my wife . . . even just a glimpse of her."

Annie cringed, felt the roots of her hair tingle on her scalp. *Ach, say no, Daed! Essie isn't ready to handle Zeke yet.*

"We'll see what the brethren have to say on that," Daed told him.

"Jah. Always what the brethren want, ain't?" Zeke's speech sounded slurred, like he'd been drinking alcohol, though Annie couldn't imagine how that could be. His words were biting, too. Wasn't this man grateful to be out where the sun could shine on his ruddy face, send a ray of hope to his hardened heart? She couldn't understand why Zeke had always been something of an oozing wound. He'd taken the loss of Isaac much too far, and now he was "mighty troubled," according to Daed. What did it mean for her father to bring him home here to dear Mamm . . . and Dawdi and Mammi Zook, too? Where was the wisdom in this?

Feeling horrid about listening in and not wishing to hear more, she reached for her sweater and let herself silently out the door.

*I must hurry and tell Esther! Oh, poor, dear Essie.*

Everything would have been going according to plan by now. Ben would have applied to the Peace Corps and been making plans to leave home for overseas somewhere. *Anywhere I can make a difference.*

Instead he kept busy around the house for a few days, helping Mom with spring cleaning—sweeping out the rain gutters, hauling large boxes of sorted clothing and other odds and ends downtown to the Goodwill, flipping mattresses, moving furniture, and taking down window drapes to be professionally cleaned. He did all this to pull his own weight, not wanting to leech off his parents while home. Well, while *here*.

Curious as he was, Mom had asked him to wait until Dad returned from a business trip before they delved further into his past. Ben had sensed there was more to the adoption story. Much more.

The evening Dad returned, following supper, Ben sat brooding while Dad reclined in his favorite chair rustling with the paper. Ben reached over to the stack of books and magazines on the end table and idly pulled a few onto his lap. The top one, he noticed, was a Bible. He opened a sports magazine instead. Mom wandered over to sit with him on the sofa. "You're a lost soul these days." She touched his shoulder. "Is it so difficult to discover I'm not your first mother?"

He felt his pulse pound. It was not so much *that* as it was the secret withheld. His life. His right to know. "I'm reading," he mumbled.

She eyed his magazine, then Dad. "I think you'd rather talk, son."

He winced, not even attempting to keep the scowl from his face. This woman had been a party to deceit, as he saw it. He said nothing for a time, trying to find some memory from his distant childhood, wondering why it was easy to remember things that had happened when he was a few years older, like moving out of his childhood bedroom to make room for one of his sisters. But why couldn't he remember anything from his earlier years—not even an important event like a birthday?

Suddenly a strange memory scurried across his mind before disappearing again. This woman, his mom, handing him some new bright white shoes. He remembered looking at them in surprise, the shoes seeming so strange, so oddly foreign to him. Why had he thought of that now? Why could he not recall the day of his adoption? Why could he not make heads or tails of any of this alarming news?

Mom spoke up, interrupting his thoughts. "We'll tell you everything we know, Ben, though it isn't much. I'm sorry we didn't tell you sooner."

"We both are, son," Dad said, getting up and coming over to sit near Ben.

"Why was it necessary to keep my adoption from me?" He clenched his fists, looking at both parents.

Dad leaned forward, staring at his hands. "One thing led to another, Ben. That's the only way to describe what happened."

Mom shook her head and looked like she was trying not to cry. "Your father's right. Nothing about your entrance into our lives was the way we'd planned."

*"Planned"* . . . *not "hoped,"* but he decided the latter was precisely what she'd meant. They had most likely hoped for something, someone far different. Had they simply settled for him?

Dad inhaled slowly. "We were foster parents," he said with some degree of pride. "Had just become eligible to care for children."

Ben listened, furious with them, yet he yearned to know everything they knew and more. He longed to know why his mother—his first mother or real mother or whatever it was you called the woman who birthed you—hadn't kept him.

"I see it in your eyes, Ben. You despise the truth, but you do want to know," Mom added.

He bit his lip. Why was this difficult? Why was he struggling so?

"We can't let you simply imagine the rest," Mom said.

He had to hear the story—how it happened that he'd come to be adopted by the Martins. "All right, tell me. Tell me everything."

"You officially became Benjamin David Martin," his dad started, "six months to the day after your arrival on a stranger's front porch in downtown Marion, Kentucky."

Listening, Ben guarded his soul.

According to the Department of Social Services report, the wide-eyed boy was approximately four years old on the day he was discovered lost. He was too traumatized to speak, and for months they understood him to be mute, but not deaf. When he did finally talk, after the adoption was final—and after months of therapy—his language was considered a folk rendering of the Pennsylvania German dialect, or so said the linguist who had been hired to translate the boy's terror-filled babbling. This meant he was from Pennsylvania or any of the other numerous states where the Pennsylvania Amish had migrated to find fertile land.

When asked his name, the boy answered in halting English only after much coaxing. "I . . . Zach," he whispered. Short for Zachary, the linguist concluded.

Vague on his hometown and his parents' names, the boy eventually hinted at having been taken against his will by a big *Mann* who frightened him. The boy knew little more, or at least was too disturbed to say.

The Martins received Zachary into their home while officials searched for his family. But his description had never shown up on any missing persons report.

"So we kept you and cared for you," Mom explained, "and your dad and I loved you so much we secretly hoped you might become our son. Then in a surprisingly short time, you were eligible to be adopted."

Ben considered these puzzle pieces of his life, so foreign to him. How did they fit together with what he *thought* he knew? "I didn't know where I lived?" he asked.

"No," his father spoke up. "And even after extensive searching by the authorities, we never found out where you were from."

"My parents never reported me missing?" *How bizarre is that?*

"We always wondered about that, as well. Made no sense . . . you were the most darling boy." Mom looked at him fondly. "We thought perhaps you'd been orphaned. We had so little to go on. You wore ordinary clothes—though they were very big on you, I remember. You had no identifying marks, no medical bracelet, no backpack of belongings that might have indicated your origins."

Ben fiddled with the magazine in his lap, growing more and more frustrated.

"You carried nothing, Ben, except for an old peach stone in your pocket. You clung to it as if it were a prized treasure," Dad said.

Staring at them now, Ben suddenly felt strangely disconnected from these people. Had he always been so completely unaware they were not related to him, or had he known on some subconscious level? "You still have no idea who my parents were?"

"Sadly, no."

He was beginning to think he must have been dropped off by the side of the road . . . dumped like some unwanted stray.

He leaned forward, staring at the floor. He recalled a nagging memory from the past—a mischievous cousin's visit, and Sherri and Patrice jumping all over the joke about him being adopted.

Aware of the silence, he asked, "Did my sisters ever suspect I wasn't their biological brother?"

"Not that I know of," Mom offered.

"Why did you change my name from Zach to Ben?"

Mom sighed. "I suppose that was selfishness on our part. Your Dad had always hoped . . . always planned . . . to name his son after *his* father, Benjamin David. When we adopted you, we had all but given up hope of having a son of our own. But you became our son. Our only son. You have to understand that we loved you as our own from the beginning, Ben. Still do. We became so attached to you, loved you so much, that we, or at least I, feared someone might try to take you away from us. You may think that paranoid, but I've talked to enough adoptive parents to know it's a common fear. We wanted to give you a new identity as our son and, yes, to protect you."

"Protect yourselves, you mean," he whispered. He was moved by her words but fought the compassion that swelled within him, burying it under his pain, his feeling of betrayal.

"I don't know how we kept it quiet for so long," Mom went on. "Your dad's work associates knew, as did a few of my girlfriends. It was an enormous risk we took . . . and now I see it was so unnecessary."

"A little late for that." Wanting suddenly to be alone, Ben rose and hurried from the room, the books and magazine still in his hand. He tromped downstairs to his bedroom off the family room, where they'd moved him on his twelfth birthday, when he was old enough to want his own space. *A boy needs his privacy,* the man of the house had said. And they had all agreed their only son should move downstairs to the basement. *More up than down,* Mom had said. Funny he should remember that. In effect, she'd wanted him to know he was gaining ground, getting a much larger room—his own bath, things like that. But with more space came more responsibility, he had been told.

Ben paced a while, did fifty fast sit-ups, then lay on his bed, staring at the window. Another memory fluttered through his brain, so short and insignificant he scarcely believed it was a memory at all. Green shades on windows in a long front room of a farmhouse. *Was it Zeke and Esther's house?*

Restless, he picked up the Bible he'd inadvertently brought downstairs with him. He thumbed through it and his eyes fell on a Scripture he'd heard somewhere before. *"And we know that all things work together for good to them that love God, to them who are the called according to his purpose."*

"All things?" he muttered, reading the verse again. "How can that possibly be?"

Feeling the need to get out of the house, he grabbed his keys and headed back upstairs and out to his car. In some illogical way, driving over the winding country roads seemed to be a good idea right now. He was eager for the serene sight of thriving stands of trees and horses grazing on lush grassland.

*"All the beautiful, simple things,"* Annie had often said with a big smile on her sweet face. How he missed her!

What if he simply wrote her a short letter? Would that be so bad?

*No,* he reminded himself, *I don't want to cause her any more trouble.*

Yet at this moment she seemed more closely related to him than anyone on the face of the earth.

# Chapter 10

With the news of Zeke's release, Annie's emotions were a jumbled mire of relief, then worry, and back again. When she arrived at Hochstetlers', Annie sat Essie down and told her in hushed tones everything she'd overheard about Zeke. "Your husband's free. . . . The bones weren't Isaac's after all."

Esther looked both numb and sad.

"I thought you'd be happy to hear this," Annie said, intently looking at her. "Zeke's innocent."

Tears welled up and Essie turned away.

"What is it?"

Essie shook her head. "I can't believe this. He's out of jail, ya say? Comin' home?"

"Well, no, not just yet he's not."

"Why not?"

"He needs some lookin' after, according to Daed." She explained that her father was handling things. That in due time, Zeke would return home again.

"So then, something's still the matter?"

"Zeke's a little mixed up, I guess. Still thinks he's guilty. Might be best for my Daed to oversee him for a time, especially with young children in the house here . . . and the baby."

Essie burst out sobbing again. "And . . . ach, Annie, another . . . on the way, too."

Shocked that Essie should cry over such a thing, Annie didn't know what to say.

"You daresn't breathe a word . . . 'cause you don't know what the Bann requires of marrieds, Annie." A frown on her face, Essie glanced toward the doorway. "And I'm not goin' to say fully." Essie nodded her head, hands shaking as she fumbled in her pocket for a hankie. "Zeke's sin will be found out, is all. He'll be shunned, too."

Annie didn't comprehend at first, but slowly she began to put it together, feeling terribly embarrassed as the light dawned. "I'm awful sorry for you both. Not 'cause of a new life coming, not that at all." She patted Essie's arm softly. "Are you sure you're expecting another wee one?"

"Jah. Now I am."

Annie kissed Esther's cheek and wiped away her tears. "Well, this is a good time to be puttin' your newfound faith to work, ain't so, dear one?"

That brought the sweetest smile to Essie's face, and Annie took heart, hoping she hadn't spoken out of turn.

At noon the day after his release, Zeke sat stiffly in the small front room of the Zooks' Dawdi Haus. Preacher Jesse's parents had vacated the room a quarter hour before, making their way feebly over to the main house. Zeke had watched them without offering to assist, not because he didn't want to but because he felt too weak to move. By now they were surely preparing to sit down for dinner. Zeke, however, had no desire to eat, having refused all offers of food and drink since coming here. He was not at all inclined to change his mind on that point.

Talking to himself about having to stay here at the preacher's place, he was somewhat irked when he looked up and saw Jesse standing in the doorway with Irvin Ranck right behind him. "Look's like you've got yourself some company," Jesse said. "Since you ain't hungry, maybe some talk will give you an appetite."

Nodding awkwardly to Zeke, Irvin looked sober-faced at first. "Hello again, Zeke. I drove right here when Jesse told me of your release. Certainly hope you don't mind me barging in."

"Not to worry," Jesse offered, slipping back through the connecting door and leaving the two men alone.

"Take a load off, Irvin." Zeke motioned toward the vacant chair. "I know you've got something to say, jah?" Zeke hung his head, then jerked up. "I'm out of jail, but what good's it doin' me?"

Irvin sat across from him, unbuttoning his windbreaker. "I'd say, time to rejoice."

"No joy in it for me."

Irvin leaned forward, face beaming. "Well, there can be."

Zeke breathed in mighty deep. "I guess then you've never had to put up with such a heavy cloud. Guilt, I tell ya. Thick enough to slice through. Nee—no, solid enough to chop through with a hatchet."

"You're not a murderer, Zeke."

He shook his head. "But I was responsible for Isaac. I know it."

"But you didn't kill him, don't you see?"

"Oh, sure I did. In every way important, I did."

"Look, Zeke . . . you're not thinking clearly."

He huffed at that. What gave this man, this outsider, really, the right to come over here and talk like this?

Irvin wrinkled his brow. "You got your life back. A second chance, so to speak."

That caught Zeke's attention. But even so, he didn't see how this changed anything. He was still as guilty as before this recent news that the bones were those of a missing little girl. Just because the bones weren't Isaac's didn't mean he hadn't caused his brother's death. Why was this so hard for everyone to accept?

Irvin pulled out a small New Testament from his shirt pocket. "This may sound peculiar to you, but I want you to imagine the Lord Jesus nailed to a crossbeam. For you He died, Zeke. For the blame of sin you feel so strongly."

Zeke sighed, pulling on his beard. *Same old salvation talk.* He was starting to feel nauseated. From not eating, he guessed.

Irvin kept yapping. "No matter what you've done . . . or think you've done, God's Son can and will forgive you."

Zeke wanted to stop up his ears. Feeling strangely dizzy, he closed his eyes, then blinked them open, only to find Irvin still sitting there, his hair parted on the side, combed like it always was, eyes bright, face clean-shaven.

"We can trust the Savior even when we can't trust ourselves."

Zeke ran his hands through his hair, wishing he could sort out all the chaos—the unrelenting noise—in his head. His leg twitched and he felt pressure behind his eyes. "You're goin' to get me shunned if you keep talkin' this way." He glanced toward the preacher's side of the house. "Himmel, you sound like my Esther, you know that?"

Irvin nodded, smiling. "Better to be shunned on earth than for God to turn His back on you on that day of days."

Irvin's words jolted Zeke.

"Miracles still happen," Irvin continued.

"Maybe for other folk . . . not for me."

"God's love outshines all, even when we think we're unworthy."

Zeke sneered. "The Lord God has left me. Ain't that easy to see?"

Just then, Preacher Zook's dismayed face appeared in the doorway. He had heard, probably, Irvin's salvation talk and wanted to put the nix on it. "Why don't you join us for a nice hot meal?" Jesse was including both men in his invitation.

"I'll accept if Zeke here will." Irvin rose and waited.

But Zeke stayed put. He could feel his neck muscles tense. "Count me out," he uttered.

❖

Ben stared out the window, watching a bird preen on the sill. *Love conceals itself deep in the gaps of longing, between finding and losing . . . and finding again.* He didn't know where he'd heard this, or if perhaps he had read it somewhere. Either way, it was true of him. "All too true," he whispered, glad for the privacy of the empty family room.

Torn between loneliness and concern for Annie's family situation, Ben decided to take a risk. *At the very least, she and I can be friends*, he told himself. *And I could use a friend.*

Writing the date, *Saturday, May 6*, he began to put his thoughts on paper.

*Dear Annie,*

*I wish we could have said a proper good-bye before I left so suddenly. I've wanted to let you know that I'm back in Kentucky again and doing well. It's good to be home.*

He lifted his pen and shook his head. What he'd written so far wasn't even remotely indicative of his true feelings, but he didn't wish to worry her.

*My sisters were glad to see me again, but you know how it is with siblings. I still wish I might have had the opportunity to introduce you to my family.*

*I just wanted to say again that I enjoyed getting to know you. I won't forget you, Annie, nor can I simply dismiss my time in Amish country, short as it was. I hope you'll be very happy—whatever you decide to do.*

He cringed. Is this what he really wanted to say? No. He wanted to tell her how disconnected he felt. How much he missed their conversations. How much he missed *her*.

But what good could possibly come of it? He took a deep breath and finished his letter.

> *I'd love to hear from you, just to be assured that things are all right. But please don't feel any pressure, as I understand your situation. (I'm sending this in care of Irvin Ranck in hopes that it might find its way to you.) The last thing I want to do is to trouble either you or your family, as I have in the past.*
>
> *Your friend,*
> *Ben Martin*

Rereading his letter, Ben was tempted to crumple it up and throw it away. *How can I be so selfish? Surely she's glad to be rid of me.*

In the end, desperation won out and he mailed it.

Late in the afternoon, Annie had just returned from her usual Tuesday cleaning job at the Rancks' when Julia Ranck came driving up the lane. *Maybe I left something there,* Annie thought.

All aglow, her cousin came rushing into the house through the back door. Dressed in one of her floral-print dresses, Julia called to her, standing in the middle of the kitchen, smiling to beat the band. "Annie . . . Annie!"

"I'm right here, for goodness' sake." Annie set the baby down in her playpen and hurried to greet her. "Did I forget something?"

Julia held out an envelope. "It arrived in the mail right after you left."

Annie's heart leaped at the sight of Ben Martin's name on the return address. *Why's he writing to me? Oh, I hope he's all right.* She studied his firm hand and saw her name written beneath Irvin's, where Ben had sent this in order to avoid her father's scrutiny, she guessed.

"For goodness' sake," Annie whispered, moving toward the sitting room, away from the kitchen. "Do you mind?" She wished to read the letter in private, so she slipped away, leaving Julia alone with the baby in the kitchen. She knew Essie was upstairs getting the boys up from their naps, and Laura was playing outside.

Annie sat near the window for the best natural light and held the envelope next to her heart. "Dare I read it?" she whispered into the quietude. "Dare I not?" She opened the envelope, unable to draw a full breath, she was so elated.

When she'd finished reading Ben's words, she couldn't stop smiling. *I won't forget you, Annie. . . .*

She folded the letter feeling giddy, and then at once she felt sad, too, missing him.

With a sigh, she slipped the letter into her dress pocket. Her first free minute she would write a reply, as there was nothing and no one to hold her back now that she was not living at home.

"Oh, Ben, I have so much to tell you," she whispered, brushing a tear away. To think he'd contacted her again. He surely knew how fond she was of him . . . how she'd dreaded sending him away.

She inhaled deeply, straightened her apron, and headed back to the kitchen and Cousin Julia.

# *Chapter 11*

Wednesday at noon, Louisa met Michael in the lobby of Maggiano's Little Italy on the Sixteenth Street Mall in downtown Denver. When he had called back to suggest this restaurant, she hadn't been surprised. It was one of her favorites.

"Hey," he said, smiling when he saw her. She noticed his eagerness and returned the smile.

They were shown to their reserved table, with a red-and-white-checkered tablecloth, surrounded by Old World ambiance—fake bread in baskets and bottles of wine on the wall. After they were seated, Michael asked how her day was going.

"Really well. How about yours?" she said, turning the question back on him.

"Interesting. I'm in the middle of helping with legwork on a much-publicized murder trial. It's time-consuming but challenging."

"Sounds like it," she said. "Are you enjoying your new line of work?"

"Yes, very much. Though it's a whole different world than all those prenups and divorces I used to handle."

"I don't know . . . divorce and murder both sound pretty violent to me."
He chuckled.

Then she asked more seriously, "Have you been successful in dodging the media?"

"So far." He handed her one of the menus. "And since I really can't talk about the case . . . let's see what you'd like to eat."

She opened the menu and scanned the choices. "I don't see any apple butter on here," she joked. "Or shoofly pie."

He glanced over his menu at her. "I've heard of that pie. Sickeningly rich, right?"

"The mother of all rich desserts. The best is the wet bottom kind, unique to Lancaster County."

He closed his menu. "Louisa, look, I'm not here to discuss Amish desserts, as I'm sure you know."

"Neither am I." She looked over at him. "So why *are* we here, Michael?"

He was staring at her. "I'd like to see if there's anything left of us," he said, his voice noticeably ringing with expectation. "Is that so surprising?" He continued talking, rehashing their past—all the things that had led Louisa to cancel their wedding last fall—then voicing his frustration and anguish at her sudden leaving.

She let him talk, listening and wanting very much not to hurt him further. Even so, she was hesitant to let him think this luncheon date heralded the continuation of their former relationship. Although the way she felt when he smiled at her almost made her wish he'd never revealed her father's matchmaking scheme.

"You must try 'n' eat," Barbara Zook coaxed him.

Zeke shook his head in short jerks. He had been sitting in the same chair all day—for more than a full day, he realized. He'd sat here to sleep, to read, to stare, and now he was sitting here telling the preacher's wife to leave him be, in so many words.

"You'll feel better if you have something, Zeke," she said, standing in the doorway that led to the large front room of the main house.

She smiled. "You're welcome to have your pick of pies. I've got apple, and there's chocolate silk. Oh, and a few slices of banana cream from yesterday. Which would you like?"

He knew she was hoping he'd bite. And the banana cream did sound mighty tasty, but it reminded him of Esther, and that put him right back under the mist in his mind. The haze of tormented thoughts and his grief over the news of his mother's death—all of it—overwhelmed him. Even though he saw that Barbara's mouth was still moving, he heard not a word.

Some time later, Preacher Jesse came over to see him, bringing a tall glass of water. "Here, best be drinkin' this. . . . Small swallows to start." He was telling Zeke what to do, and Zeke didn't like it—not one bit. "You'll dry out on us and we can't have that."

"Might land me in a hospital somewhere," Zeke whispered.

"Which might not be such a bad idea, really."

Zeke didn't know what Jesse meant. "What's that ya say?"

"Been over to see the folk at Philhaven, in Mount Gretna, today. They've got a room waitin' for you if you'd like to go and get to feeling some better."

*They can't get me to eat here, that's why.*

"I'm fine here. Don't need no doctor." He'd heard all about that place for mental folk. There'd been a call for Amish house parents some time back, if he remembered correctly.

"Come on, Zeke. What do you say?" asked Jesse.

Zeke bowed his head, the lump in his throat threatening to turn into a tear in his eye. "I'm not myself. Ain't been for quite a while." A sudden fire ignited in him. "But I have no interest in goin' anywhere 'cept home. So leave me be!"

Jesse sat across from him. "You're to be in my custody, Zeke. Don't think it was easy getting the police to do it that way. They wanted to release you to an English institution first, but I spoke up. It's 'cause of me you're not there already. They believe you to be a detriment to your family . . . from your own mouth. Remember what you told them that day the police came and picked you up?"

Zeke wished he had earplugs or something to push into his ears. He sure didn't want to be reminded of what he'd said or what he didn't say . . . or what he should've said. Truth was, he was here now, in this chair, and he didn't much feel like budging.

Jesse reached over and put a hand on his shoulder. "I'll see to gettin' you there, if you'd like to get better."

"If you need to be getting back to your routine here . . . you and your missus, then just say so." He knew he was glaring, because he felt the burning behind his eyes.

"You're no bother a'tall," he heard Jesse say, but he saw the frustration in the way the preacher's eyes squinted, his mouth all pinched up.

*I'm in the way.* He recalled having the same feeling as a boy, of being rejected by those who supposedly loved him most. His father, for one. "I know when my welcome's wore out." Reluctantly he rose. He refused to be underfoot the way he surely was here.

Passing through the kitchen, Zeke tuned out the chatter from both Jesse's wife and his elderly mamma, then scuffed his way outside toward Yonie's car.

The entire ride was a blur in his brain, and when they arrived in Mount Gretna at the sprawling place called Philhaven, he was startled by Jesse's strong hand helping him from the car and up the walkway.

"You'll have plenty of folk visitin' you while you're here," Jesse told him, guiding him toward the entrance.

"Esther too?"

"Jah, soon, Zeke. Soon."

He didn't know whether to believe the man of God or not, though he wished he could. The flat tone of Jesse's voice made him wonder if he would ever lay eyes on his sweet wife again. "They won't hurt me, will they, Preacher?" He shuddered.

"Ach, no. They're here to help. You'll see that soon enough. You'll meet with doctors twice a day."

"Not sure if I ever remember bein' well. It's been a long, long time, if at all." It felt good to admit this, though the confession was all wrapped up in the fires of guilt that burned in his soul night and day.

When Zeke asked more about where he'd be sleeping, Jesse kindly explained. "You'll have your own bed, that's certain. You'll feel right at home here. The whole place is Plain just like you're used to—no carpet on the floors, no TVs, computers, or radios. You'll like the peace of this place, Zeke. I promise you that."

He didn't reply, allowing Jesse to lead him to the door of the complex, trying hard to push away the notion that he was being led like a lamb to the slaughter.

"I'll stop by your house tomorrow and pick up several changes of clothes for you," Jesse said as they made their way inside.

"So you'll visit again?"

Jesse nodded, removing his hat. "You can count on that, Zeke. Jah, I'll see you tomorrow."

And if he wasn't mistaken, Zeke thought he heard a catch in the preacher's throat and wondered why.

# Chapter 12

On the Lord's Day, Annie went with Essie and the children to the Rancks' church yet again. But after they'd all come home and eaten together, she'd felt the need to get outside and drive the horse and buggy.

Allowing Zeke's horse to plod along at his own pace, Annie pondered some of the things the minister had said from his fine wooden pulpit. She wondered if she dared crack open a Bible and begin reading the Gospel of John, which the Mennonite pastor had preached on today.

But then, in the midst of all her brooding, she spied Sam Glick walking toward her along the road. "Hullo!" she called to him, pulling on the reins.

"Annie . . . it's good to see ya." He nodded cheerfully, but his eyes turned sad when he asked about Louisa. "Is she doin' all right, do you know?"

Annie climbed out of her buggy to talk, keeping the reins in her hand. She told him Lou was living back in her own apartment and had started to teach art again.

Sam quickly changed the subject to Zeke. "I hear he's at Philhaven now."

Annie didn't let on she'd seen him with her father and brother on the day they'd brought Zeke home. "Jah. I hope he'll be all right, in time."

Sam pursed his lips, frowning. "Do you think it's true, then? That he might be a bit mental like they're sayin'?"

Annie figured Zeke must be awful bad off, otherwise her father would have kept him at home and looked after him there. "Well, I guess you'd *have* to be to think you'd killed your brother when you were only eight, jah?"

Sam nodded. "Seems like a long time ago to be just now comin' forth with something like that. Never made much sense to me when I heard it."

"Sixteen years of despair, thinking you're the one responsible for your little brother's death. I'd say a body could get awful hazy in the head thinking that way, don't you?"

"And now, what with the bones not bein' Isaac's, it seems like maybe there might be some hope in all this." Sam leaned down and picked up a twig off the ground, snapped it, and tossed the pieces toward the roadside ditch.

"Hope that Isaac could still be alive?"

Sam shrugged. "Wouldn't surprise me. Would it you?"

"Hard to believe, but I guess maybe it could be true—Isaac out there somewhere in the modern world, livin' with Englischers." She wasn't about to admit she'd fostered that hope for years. It was one of the reasons she'd painted the locust grove by the covered bridge.

Sam talked of the weather and then, surprisingly enough, he asked Annie what she thought of his writing a long letter to Louisa.

"Why are you askin'? I say write it and send it off. Let Louisa know how you feel."

He grinned at that. "Jah, I've thought as much, but . . ."

Annie took note of his hedging. "You oughtn't be worried that she won't write back. Are you?"

He shook his head. "There are worse things."

*Jah, that's the truth.*

"So what're you waitin' for? Write your letter and see what she says."

"Ain't what you may think, Annie. I'm not writin' to tell Louisa that I love her."

The sun felt unexpectedly too warm now. "You don't care for her after all?"

Sam pushed his hands into his trouser pockets. "That's just it," he said softly. "I do love her. And I'd do most anything to make her understand how much."

Eager to know what on earth was holding him back, she said equally quietly, "You want me to pave the way for your letter, is that it?"

He came to life. "No, no . . . don't you dare, Annie!"

"Well, what, then?" She studied his face, which was now as bright as a ripe red McIntosh apple, unsure what he meant to say.

"I'm makin' ready to do something big. And if you say a word of this to anyone, I'll . . . You just better keep mum!"

She laughed. "Oh, I'm shakin', Sam . . . look at me."

"Don't, Annie. I'm serious. I'm on the fence, ready to jump."

"Ach, I should've known." She sighed, pondering his statement. "Every fall, when baptism rolls around and you don't join church, I wonder why not."

"That's what I'm putting in my letter to Louisa. I want her to hear it from me first. Maybe she can give me some pointers about the English world."

"Oh, Sam, are you sure about this?"

"For sure and for certain."

This was good news for Louisa . . . and bad for the community. Annie could only imagine how hurt Sam's family would be, not to mention the brethren. Yet another strapping young man lost to the People.

A letter with the name Samuel R. Glick in the corner of the envelope was waiting for Louisa in her mailbox when she arrived home on Wednesday afternoon, along with several pieces of junk mail and a colorful postcard of London's National Gallery in Trafalgar Square. *Louisa, please reconsider?—Trey* was scrawled across the back in a slant. More pressure, and she had no interest in this lame attempt by her former boyfriend. Her reaction had nothing to do with her lunch with Michael. There was simply no future for her and Trey. As for Michael, she really didn't know how things might go between them. He had taken her out for one nice meal and offered sensible, serious reasons why she should think about dating him again. And she had been tempted. But opening Sam's letter now, thoughts of Michael flew from her mind.

*Hello, Louisa!*

*I've waited longer than I wanted to, really, to sit down and write. You see, I'm making every attempt to go fancy, as we Amish say. It is a tedious process, but one that has been a long time coming. You may have guessed as much, but even I didn't know how much I wanted to start a new life on the other side of the fence till a few weeks ago.*

*I wanted you to be one of the first to know, not that I'm presuming it will have any bearing on our friendship.*

*There are a good many things I've learned already since coming out from under the authority and covering of my father. I am living with a former Amish couple who are in the business of helping folk like me make a new start. I will pay them room and board for the time being, with the understanding that I'll establish myself in a house of my own (I just may build one) in the next year or so.*

*So, odd as it may seem, I'm working at a home improvement store. Thanks to my college degree, I am already in training for assistant manager. Imagine that! Honestly, what I'm learning ferhoodles me at times, trying to understand how these English think. (Don't take that wrong! I didn't seem to have much trouble understanding you, now, did I?!)*

*I've purchased a cell phone. If you wouldn't mind, I would enjoy calling you sometime . . . to see how you're getting along there.*

*Always your friend,*
*Sam*

"Wow." Louisa set the letter on the coffee table, imagining the stir Sam's leaving the Amish would cause.

Looking at the letter again, she noted the way he'd signed off. Hadn't he vowed to love her always before she had so impulsively flown home? His words had burned in her memory for days, even weeks, afterward. So why the platonic-sounding sign-off? And why did it bother her?

Louisa sighed. What did she want? Was it Trey? Definitely not. Was it to renew her relationship with Michael, her former fiancé? She considered Sam Glick's confidence in pulling away from his staunch roots for a completely new life in the so-called modern world. That took real courage, and even though she was completely stunned at the timing of it, she wanted to let him know how pleased she was—without leading him on, of course. The fact was, Sam was comfortable with himself, and his leaving the Amish life behind was one more indication of that. But did that make him the man for her?

The more she contemplated her trio of male admirers, the more she realized there had been a reason for her meeting Sam when she did. "Annie would say to get myself back there before he gets away," she told her unconscious pet, watching as Muffin napped near the window. "What does his leaving mean for me? Or should I even be thinking that way?"

Louisa leaned her head back, reliving her arrival in Paradise, Pennsylvania, with Muffin in his pet carrier. She smiled, remembering how wound up she'd felt, yet anxious to meet Annie and her family and friends.

*One of the best things I've ever done for myself.*

# Chapter 13

*Sometimes feelings must be expressed,* Annie thought. That was certainly true today. She hurried to gather her pale yellow stationery and best pen, then made a conscious effort to slow down as she shaped the words. *Don't hurry. This is too important.*

Stopping, she collected her thoughts. *If I were ever to see Ben again, what would I say? That I often dream I am forever trying to find my way back to him . . . always lost?*

She began to pour out her loneliness, even heartsickness, during the days without him, going so far as to admit second-guessing her resolve to obey her father's command. She wrote of living with Esther now, of feeling torn between staying with an outcast woman and returning home even while she embraced the unparalleled freedom and complete responsibility for making her own decisions.

Then, stopping the flow of too-honest expression, she looked down at the things she'd written, reading them carefully. Her letter seemed more like a personal journal entry than the kind of sentiments she ought to be sharing with an Englischer like Ben.

*I shouldn't send this. It's too forward.*

She decided it might be best to wait a while before responding to Ben's letter. Folding the stationery, she placed it in her drawer.

And wait she did. For several days, she tried to distract herself, keeping busy and trying to enjoy spring's blossoming blizzard of color. But the brilliant shades of loveliness all around only reminded her of her other love—and made her want to paint all the more. She wondered how she would explain her snug

549

little art studio to innocent young Laura, Zach, and John once she got things unboxed and set up at Essie's. Oh, how she itched for the day her promise to her father concluded. *The end to the absence of my art, my life.*

Daily, and at night as she lay awake waiting for sleep, she contemplated the intense heart tug toward her great passion. She even considered having Cousin Julia take her to the gallery where Louisa had found such success in placing her paintings, to see what might be possible for *her* work. With Julia, she would not have to put any effort into explaining, for her cousin fully understood and appreciated her talent. After all, it was partly due to Julia's submitting the painting of the covered bridge and the locust grove—with the wonderful-good swing at the center—that she was in the pickle she was in now. Of course, being caught with her hair down—Ben at her side—had been the last straw.

*Nearly shunned, I am. Just like Essie.*

She contemplated their similar situations: Essie's heart captivated by something—*someone*, as she put it—forbidden by the Amish church. Annie's affection directed toward her art, also prohibited. "We're related in our sin," she said right out into the air, feeling frustrated and terribly bold.

A full week after she'd received Ben's letter, Annie was still undecided about sending hers to him. Pausing as she dusted the woodwork in her bedroom, she stared at the dresser drawer where she'd hidden the letter.

*Dare I mail it?*

Instead, she rose and left the room, heading downstairs to help with the children while Essie prepared supper. But when she found Essie peeling potatoes, she noticed streaks on her pretty face. "Ach, you've been crying," she whispered, leaning her head against Essie's.

Nodding, her friend placed a hand over her eyes momentarily. "Happy tears, I should say."

"Oh?"

Essie eyed the children and motioned for Annie to follow her into the sitting room. "I received a letter from Zeke. He says he's had several visitors and is getting some good help for his . . . uh, problems."

Annie had heard from Julia that Zeke was settled in and growing accustomed to his new home away from home.

"His handwriting . . ." Essie said softly. "Ach, I can actually read his writing. Oh, Annie, could this place—this Philhaven—be the thing that brings Zeke back to his senses? Might we be reunited?" Then, as suddenly as her optimism had emerged, her countenance shifted and the confident smile faded. "Ach, no. I'm shunned. And nothing's ever going to change that."

Annie's heart sank, but there were no hopeful words in either her heart or her mouth. The way she saw it, there would be no happy ending for the couple. Not as long as Essie held on to her assurance of salvation.

With that, Annie traipsed upstairs, retrieved her letter to Ben, stamped it, and slipped it into the outside mailbox.

One morning, nearly two weeks after he'd sent off his letter to Annie, Ben's mother called up the stairwell.

"Mail call!"

Eagerly, Ben opened the envelope she handed him, barely able to contain his excitement and surprise. *Annie actually wrote back!*

As he pored over the letter, he lost himself in her world again. He felt a lump in his throat as he read her admission of how much she missed him. He read and reread her letter, comforted by the unexpected honesty of her words. *This is just what I needed.*

But then he began to read between the lines. Annie was as good as shunned. She'd changed her mind about baptismal instruction, and she seemed rather angry with her father.

*My fault.* He folded the letter and placed it back in the envelope. Sitting at his desk, he pulled out a piece of paper and began composing a reply.

*Dear Annie,*

*So good to hear from you. Thank you for your wonderfully honest letter—and for trusting me with your feelings.*

*I was sorry to hear about the problems between you and your father. I can't help wondering if I'm partially to blame.*

Ben stopped writing. This wasn't good enough. He needed to talk to her in person, find some way to correct the problems he and he alone had instigated.

*Who am I kidding?* he thought, chuckling at his own rationalization. *I can't stay away from this girl.*

Against his better judgment, he picked up his phone and called Irvin Ranck, guessing his former boss would be at work this time of day. After offering a greeting, he said, "I'd like to come back and talk with you, face to face . . .

even though it may seem as though I just left. There are some . . . family issues I want to discuss with you. If it's all right."

"Why, sure, Ben. I'd be glad to visit with you," Irvin said. "And you should plan on staying with us."

"I wouldn't want you or Julia to go to any trouble."

"No trouble, Ben. I know Julia will be happy to have you."

"I can easily sleep in your attic room," he offered, recalling Annie's framed painting stored up there.

"Well, that's fine, if you wish."

Ben wanted to make things easy for the Rancks, and he didn't want to cause extra work for Julia or anyone. He was thinking now of Annie, as well, knowing she cleaned for the Rancks and helped with their children.

"When will you plan to arrive?" Irvin asked.

"Is tomorrow too soon?"

"Not at all."

"Then I'll probably drive straight through—takes about twelve hours if I don't stop much. If I get away early, as I hope to do, I should be there before dark." He despised motels, so he could avoid staying in one if he stepped on it.

"In time for supper?"

"I doubt it, but I'll let you know when I'm on the road."

"Sounds good, Ben. We'll look forward to seeing you."

They said good-bye and hung up.

Wanting to let his mom know about his sudden plans, Ben went in search of her. He found her outside working in her patio garden.

"I'm going back to Pennsylvania," he said. "Tomorrow."

She turned. "Why?"

"I still have so many questions. And after what you told me about my first language, Lancaster might be the place to get some answers."

Mom squeezed his arm. "I think I understand, honey." She attempted a brave smile. "This wouldn't have anything to do with that letter I gave you . . . the one with a girl's return address on it?"

He smiled back. "Well, maybe just a *little*."

While packing for his trip, Ben wondered if Annie had any idea he might show up. He could even visit her, now that she was staying at Esther's. But Irvin and Julia's home was close to Jesse Zook's, and the preacher would no doubt hear of his return. Ben wondered how to connect with Annie without creating even more problems for her.

❖

Annie rinsed out a washcloth in warm water and some liquid soap, hand-ing it first to five-year-old James, then to Molly, almost three, waiting as they washed up before sitting at the table for lunch.

Minutes later, when Annie was helping carry the platter of roast beef sand-wiches to the table, Julia whispered to her, "Ben Martin's arriving tomorrow night for a visit. I thought you might like to know."

Astonished, Annie almost said, *Are you sure?* But she knew better than to question her dear cousin and friend. "Why's he comin' back, I wonder."

Julia seemed unable to conceal her cheery smile. "Must be a good reason, I would think."

Annie couldn't believe her ears. *Ben's going to be here . . . in this house?* She cringed, recalling her too-forward response to his kind letter. Is that why he was coming?

"He just called Irvin at work. Wants to talk about 'family issues,' he said."

"Family? Whose?"

"His own, I suppose. But to tell you the truth, I'm not sure." Julia turned her attention to putting the finishing touches on their lunch, ceasing her talk of the unexpected visitor arriving tomorrow!

Annie could scarcely eat, let alone concentrate on her chores at hand. What was so urgent to bring Ben all the way back from Kentucky?

After the children were tucked in for afternoon naps, while Julia went out to run a few errands, Annie carried the dry mop and other cleaning items upstairs to her former art studio.

Upon opening the small door, an onslaught of memories invaded her thoughts; she missed this cozy, inspiring place where she'd spent many happy hours drawing and, ultimately, painting.

But her feelings were mixed, because Esther and the children had also occupied this room not so long ago. *And now Ben will stay here, too.*

It wasn't that the room had to belong only to her, for that was impossible. This was not her house. It was the home of her father's cousins and she had been merely blessed to have the room offered her. *Blessed?* She pondered that, realizing yet again how influenced she was becoming by living at Esther's. Truly she was more than curious about Essie's devout faith.

Sighing, she set about working from the top down, the way all the women-folk had been taught as young girls to clean house, beginning by wiping down the window frames, then cleaning and shining windowpanes. Next were the sills below and going over the walls with a damp rag. She dusted the bureau and carefully went over the legs and spindles of a lonely chair, getting in all the crevices, before washing down the woodwork. At last she dry mopped the floor.

When those tasks were completed, she put clean sheets on the guest bed brought up originally for Esther's use. It felt an oddly intimate gesture, making the bed where Ben would sleep. Smoothing the top sheet, she remembered the warm feel of her hand in his.

Looking around, she believed the room to be ready. She knew it was a downright silly thing to stay up here for as long as she could, feigning to clean, when she was all finished. Pining for the past, for what was, had nothing to offer her, yet she was somehow tied to this place, this room. And to think of Ben staying here, where she'd painted and allowed her heart to open wide to her love of art . . . well, it seemed peculiar.

*Ben's coming to talk about family, Julia says. What could that possibly mean? Isn't he coming to see me?*

She was afraid she might wear out the floor where Ben was concerned, pacing the small room as she was. It wasn't at all like her. Stopping, Annie sat on the chair, wondering why it was so hard to say good-bye to a place, let alone a person.

Sighing, she thought back to the first time she had ever met Ben—over yonder in the harness shop. As she did, she happened to notice her large framed painting, wedged in between the bureau and the wall. She knew another box of her paintings lay hidden in the storage cabinet, as well.

She rose and went to pick up the painting, noticing the slightest tear in the brown paper, something she'd not seen before. Quickly she dismissed it as the result of its being propped up here in this room, where young children had stayed and played and slept with their distraught mamma.

Pressing on the tape that held the wrapping together, she ran her fingers across the top of the frame, feeling the sturdiness through the paper, vacillating over whether to open it up and see it again for herself.

The painting . . . no, it was the setting that held a curious appeal for her. But with the startling news of the day—Ben's return—she felt strangely hesitant. A perplexing sense of having shared a tragic event fell over her just then, as if she had been in a buggy accident and managed to survive. She became a survivor of sorts whenever she looked at her own painting, though she had no idea why she felt that way now. So many long years had passed since they had lost Isaac.

Annie set the painting down lightly without opening the packaging.

She began to pace again, unable to bring herself to head downstairs, feeling stuck here.

*Being up here has stirred me up but good.*

She stopped long enough to stand in one of the dormer windows overlooking the vast fields and grazing land below. Her mind was a jumble of emotions. *Why do I still feel so close to Isaac—closer than a friend, or even a sister?* She supposed it was some form of "Absence makes the heart grow fonder." Surely she and Isaac wouldn't still be as close had he grown up in Paradise like any other boy from their church district.

*And now another boy has been taken from me.* She was thinking of Ben, and her father's hard stance—his insistence that she break it off. He had every right as a minister ordained of the Lord God to do so, yet he had not demanded the same of Yonie.

She felt angry, nail-spitting mad, for having sent Ben away. Reliving her father's waiting for her in the darkness on the night she'd tiptoed back into the Dawdi Haus—hoping to hurry to her bedroom unnoticed—it was all she could do to keep from clumping her feet across the floor now, but she forced herself to be sensible. She turned to pick up the chair and carried it back to the window. Sitting there quietly, she let the sun shine on her face and shoulders.

Terribly weary, she recalled having gotten up late last night, in the wee hours, and feeling as if she hadn't fallen asleep at all, even though she knew she had. At some point she had wandered downstairs to look for some of her own newly baked cookies. She'd taken only one and poured a small glass of milk before padding back up to her room in her bare feet, mindful of the sleeping children. She had stared out the window then, too, wondering how you went about talking to almighty God the way Essie did, so personally and so effortlessly. She longed to do so herself, but did you have to break the Ordnung before you could pray that way?

She guessed so, but she didn't rightly know. She was afraid to ponder it too much now, lest she think herself right into Essie's way of believing . . . and that was not what she was being paid to do at the moment.

Rising and returning the chair to its original spot, she allowed herself one more fond look around the room. *I hope you enjoy your time here, Ben. . . .*

# Chapter 14

Sitting near her wide studio window, Louisa drank her coffee, intermittently looking at her nails. *How did I ever manage without a professional manicure all those months?* She laughed softly and reached for her purse, pulling out a fingernail clipper. She knew precisely how: she had filed her nails herself. No biggee. *Mother must have thought I'd lost it for sure.*

She trimmed off a piece of unruly cuticle skin, then dropped the clippers into the small zippered pocket of her purse. She turned her attention back to the window, looking at the colorful flowers in the window box outside. The owner of the building had pushed red, yellow, and white silk flowers into the hardened earth along the walks, as well as the window boxes. An illusion of springtime. This being Colorado, the month of May often came with heavy snows and blowing winds. The "Albuquerque low" could easily close down the treacherous Monument Hill to the south and the I-25 corridor as a whole. As a result it was generally pointless to set out geraniums or other flowering plants until after the Memorial Day weekend in this unpredictable region. Still, the silk flowers were lively and pleasant if you didn't stop to look too closely—much like her own life had been, she realized, before her sojourn in Paradise.

Thinking about the short growing season here, she let her mind wander to Lancaster County, to the Zooks' farm there. She recalled the outhouse, the Saturday night baths, and washing her face each morning using the basin and pitcher Annie brought to the bedroom where she had first stayed. Later she and Annie had moved over to the cozy bedroom in the Dawdi Haus.

"Dawdi Haus." She spoke the Pennsylvania Dutch words that described the addition built onto the main house, remembering how Mammi Zook had taught her to pronounce the vowels. Now, without thinking, she began to put her hair up "by heart," as Annie often said, without the aid of a mirror, holding the thick bun she'd made of her own tresses, missing the community created by the Amish women in particular and the Plain life in general. *Have I learned enough about peace?* she wondered. *Did I stay in Paradise long enough?*

The sudden loud chirp of her phone startled her out of her musing, and she quickly let her hair fall, reaching to answer her cell. Checking the screen, she grimaced but answered, "Hey," knowing it was Michael Berkeley.

"Louisa . . . hi. I was hoping I'd catch you before you left your studio."

"Yep, I'm still here."

"I'm dying for an espresso. How does Starbucks sound? I could meet you there, or pick you up. Whatever you say."

She found this bordering on funny. "Well, you'll never guess what I'm sipping at the moment—coffee with just the right amount of chocolate. So you'll have to count me out." She paused. "But thanks."

"We could do pie instead." He was coaxing.

"Thanks anyway, Michael," she said, hard as it was to be semi-rude.

"All right. How about I come over and . . . we could talk?"

"What about?"

"Stuff . . . you know. Your day. Mine."

This wasn't the sophisticated and cool attorney she'd known. He was dying here and she was making him grovel. "Maybe some other time."

"Sure. See ya." He hung up.

She clicked off the power, not wanting to endure a repeat performance. Most girls would be thrilled to spend time with a guy like Michael. She'd seen the way other women eyed him, discreetly, of course, back when the two of them were dating. Michael was the most handsome guy she knew.

"Let's see . . . he's also bright, articulate, and rich, and he knows how to woo a lady." She sighed, reaching for her coffee mug and breathing in the delicious aroma before taking another sip. *So what's wrong with me? Why aren't I ready to take up where we left off?*

Finishing her coffee, she could hardly wait to get back to her apartment to change into her powder-pink sweats and cushy socks. She wanted to curl up with Muffin and peruse her new issue of *The Artist's Magazine*, but first she had to clean up her studio. As she picked up the last of the brushes to wash, she fondly recalled how hard she and Annie had worked to clean up after themselves in the little attic studio at Julia's, especially without sink or access to water.

But that was the way of creativity; if there wasn't a mess to show for hours of inspiration, there probably wasn't much art to show for it, either.

Louisa went to the sink and rinsed out the brushes and her coffee mug, letting the water run longer than necessary. Staring into the sink, she decided to make a phone call. She felt nearly compelled to talk to Annie's Mennonite cousin Julia Ranck, having thought so often of their talks together.

*If Julia lived nearby, I'd be hanging with her a lot these days.*

Louisa turned her phone back on and called Julia. She was delighted to hear Julia's voice and such a cheerful greeting.

"It's wonderful to hear from you!" Julia said. "I was just sitting here enjoying a cup of tea."

Glad to have this opportunity to reconnect, Louisa asked if it was a good time to chat.

"Why, sure. What's on your mind?"

She couldn't just dive in and say she wanted to hear more about Julia's God, could she? She meandered a bit, groping for the right words, and as was typical of Julia, she eased things along until Louisa found herself close to tears, hungering for all this woman had to say about the Lord.

Later, after thanking Julia for her time, she hung up, then set to work scouring the paint from the sink. The smell of the nonabrasive cleanser made her nauseated, reminding her of car trips her family had taken when she was a young girl. Her mother would take along plastic bags in case of carsickness. Louisa hummed, thinking, *I'm redding up but good*, and laughed softly.

Washing her hands, she eyed the CD player and realized that the music had stopped. She dried her hands, and as she went to select a new CD, the door squeaked opened across the room.

Glancing over her shoulder, she was surprised to see Michael, sporting a vase of red roses. "Yikes," she muttered, wondering why he had decided to show up when she'd tried to put him off.

Michael looked at the flowers. "Something wrong with the color?"

"It's not that. . . ."

"You sounded down on the phone."

*Maybe because I am.* Remembering her manners, she took the vase from him and carried it to the sink. She filled it with warm water and set the bouquet on the counter, near her easel. "They're really beautiful," she said, turning to smile at Michael. "Thanks."

He shrugged, and it was apparent he wasn't sure what to say next.

"It's weird," she said idly. "I was just thinking back to my childhood, when Daddy took us for long drives in the mountains—up to Aspen for the summer music festival or to Breckenridge to ski, and I'd always get carsick."

He was polite, listening, making eye contact, even though he'd heard this tidbit back when they were dating. She had even taken several evenings to introduce him to her family via a bunch of scrapbooks.

She glimpsed the roses again. Fact was, Michael knew too much about her. More than any man she'd ever dated. More, at least, about the specific little things that unfold over time when two people are planning a life together, though not as much about the dreams of her heart as Sam. *And he knows nothing about my craving for spiritual things.*

"I'd like to take you out for dinner." He moved toward her. "Next weekend?" *I shouldn't.*

His eyes shone with sincerity.

She hadn't forgotten their good times. But she found it impossible to overlook how they had gotten together in the first place. *Maybe someday I'll be able to forgive his part in Daddy's scheme. And maybe by then I won't still be hung up on Sam.*

Yet all that was in the past, wasn't it? His recent persistence had nothing to do with a corporate merger. Even so, was it fair to allow him to think he had a second chance with her now? She had no clue how to forge ahead with a friendship, let alone a bona fide relationship that could possibly lead them back to the wedding altar. *Full circle . . .*

"I want to get to know you again," Michael said.

She almost ached to look at him, seeing a hint of the pain he must have endured when she'd abandoned him.

"How's next Friday night?" he asked. "Or is Saturday better?"

*Oh, what to do?* Her feelings kept vacillating back and forth. She turned away, staring at the roses. The Amish didn't do the cut flower thing. Thoughts of Sam poked at her. She still needed to answer his letter, but what would she say? Was Sam the reason she hesitated?

"We need some time together," Michael said, trying again.

*He deserves another chance . . . on his own terms, without Daddy's interference,* Louisa thought. *Doesn't he?*

Sighing, she moved back to face him. "Sure, Friday's fine. Thanks."

His eyes gleamed. "Perfect. I'll pick you up at your place."

"I have a class . . . so why don't I meet you?"

He mentioned Ruth's Chris Steak House down on Market Street.

She knew the place well—one of their former haunts. Very uptown: white table linens, attentive wait staff. "Sounds lovely." She wanted to mean it but felt stuck in limbo. She thanked him again for the roses and the dinner invitation, and watched him head for the door, an obvious spring in his step.

*I must be out of my mind.*

# Chapter 15

Essie shuddered, a bundle of emotions—fear, hope, dread—as she approached the front desk at Philhaven. She breathed a shaky sigh, sending up a pleading prayer for something good to come of this visit.

Zeke greeted her with a big smile and gave her a peck on the cheek. He suggested they sit on the porch and she agreed, relieved not to be meeting him behind closed doors this first time. He led the way and she was comforted to see several staff people about the place. They offered kind smiles, and Essie felt reassured. Zeke could not hurt her here.

She settled into a chair on the veranda, overlooking a cheerful flower garden already blooming with daylilies, lavender, and annuals. Zeke sat a few feet from her, seemingly enjoying the sunshine, as he talked about his doctors and of attending his small-group session.

Small talk was something Zeke had never cared to do—except for his occasional comments about the weather. He inquired about the children, and it was pleasing to know that Laura, Zach, John, and the baby were keenly on his mind. Esther was quite happy to tell him how their Essie Ann was growing so fast, in a real growth spurt lately. And she described how Laura kept busy helping with weeding the flower beds and planting the family vegetable garden out back.

When their back and forth chatter slowed some, she spoke up. "I've come to tell you some important news." She was glad they were alone.

"What's that?"

"Ain't such good news, really." She quickly amended that. "Well, I mean, it *is* but also a bit . . . troubling where you're concerned."

He shook his head, appearing to become quarrelsome. "So, spit it out."

She kept her voice low and leaned near. "I'm with child again."

He moaned and shook all over, as if he had an uncontrollable chill. "I hope you're joking."

"No." She sat still, her hands folded in her lap. "I'm ever so sure now."

He cursed under his breath. "The brethren will have my hide."

Essie felt more sympathy for her husband than she would have thought possible. *Poor man.*

"I'll catch it but good," Zeke said. "I'll be under the shun as soon as you start showin'." He rose and went to stand at the edge of the porch. Hands deep in his pants pockets, he stared out at the grounds, muttering to himself. "This compounds my problems, jah?"

A trace of the old bitterness rose up within her. *He should've thought of this earlier.*

Silently asking God to help her show Christ's mercy, she said, "I'm afraid so. But we'll get through this somehow, you and me."

When he didn't respond for several minutes but only stood there morosely, Essie rose to her feet. "Well, I'd best be goin', then."

Zeke spun around. "No, now, you just wait! You mustn't be tellin' anyone this, hear?" His eyes squinted fire.

"I already have." She moved away from him, heading for the porch stairs.

"I'm not done with you, Esther! Come right back here."

She couldn't bear to be treated like this. "It's time I returned to the children. Annie's home alone with them."

He squared his shoulders. "You must've told *her*, then. Right?"

She nodded. "That I did."

He kicked the chair, his arms flailing.

"Good-bye, Zeke." She left the porch quickly, feeling sad over his response to a new little life but pleased that she'd not allowed him to crush her spirit this time.

Jesse washed his hands at the kitchen sink, watching as Barbara peeled potatoes—creating long brown spirals with her paring knife. *What a terrific cook.* He dried his hands and inched over to kiss the back of her neck, then went to sit at the head of the table, knowing full well supper was more than an hour away.

He'd brought in the mail a little bit ago, glad for Luke's and Yonie's willingness to finish planting the sweet corn. Weary from the day, he found a letter from Daniel Hochstetler addressed to him.

Grimacing, he opened it and silently began to read.

*Hello, Jesse Zook, and greetings from Ontario, Canada!*

*I received your letter and have been thinking what to write back. First, let me say it was a big shock to hear of your discovery. Yet, I was somehow comforted to know Isaac has been found after so many years.*

*With Mary's recent passing, I had been considering making a trip down there to Lancaster County sometime. Then when you wrote of Isaac's remains, I felt nearly compelled to return. I'd like to see his grave.*

*For all the harsh words between us, Preacher, I would hope you and I might be able to talk some whenever I can come. Meanwhile I have a great yearning to see Zeke again and to lay eyes on his children—my only grandchildren.*

*I remain your old friend,*
*Daniel Hochstetler*

Jesse was downright surprised at Daniel's response to his letter and his interest in returning to visit. And to think the bones weren't Isaac's after all and there was no grave for the man to see. He'd best be writing back to tell him so. Jesse sighed. Just now he would not say anything to Barbara, but he did need to get word to Esther that her father-in-law might be coming unannounced.

*Ach, and what of Annie?* No, it would not do for Ichabod to stay in their midst. Not with Zeke away and the preacher's daughter and one shunned woman running the house over yonder. But there was more to it. The brethren would have a problem with Ichabod's arrival without a confession first.

"Anything interesting in the mail?" Barbara asked.

"Nothin' to speak of." He didn't want to worry her, especially if he could put a stop to Ichabod's plans to return.

Stuffing the letter back into its envelope, he thought of something else that had been flitting around in his mind for weeks now. Esther was no longer attending Preaching service and was taking her children to hear who knows what at the Rancks' meetinghouse of a Sunday morning—Annie was likely going with her. So he'd pay them a visit soon and kill two birds with one stone.

He had an hour till supper. Enough time to write back to Ichabod, informing him of the mistake; that there was no reason for him to come after all. He just hoped his second letter would arrive in time.

Fatigued from driving for more than eight hours straight, Ben began to read billboards to pass the time. One popped out at him: the Hopalong Cassidy Museum. *William Boyd was a native of Cambridge, Ohio,* the large sign with bright lights touted. Ben was glad for any interesting sight, even though he was almost too tired to keep going. He had promised Irvin he would make it there in a single day, though not in time for supper, and he'd called to say as much around three-thirty, to give Julia plenty of notice.

Another billboard caught his eye: the Pennyroyal Opera House, featuring bluegrass music. Intrigued, and noting his gas supply was dwindling quickly, he took the exit ramp, hoping to find a gas station.

But he got distracted listening to a radio talk show and found himself on a back road, entering a small town. Up ahead, he saw a closed general store and a barn-style building bearing the marquee of the Pennyroyal Opera House.

Flickers of a memory, or was it something else, burst into his head. Why did the opera house seem vaguely familiar? Had he driven this way on his first trip to Pennsylvania? No, he'd taken a different route. Besides, the memory felt more distant. Had he and his family visited here once? But who comes to such a location on vacation?

He was really tired—this was exhaustion talking. And this was nuts, pushing it so hard. For what purpose? Just to avoid a hotel and arrive before Irvin and Julia retired for the night?

Reaching the end of the "blink and miss" town, he made a U-turn. Heading back, he noticed the sign: Fairview, Ohio. The town, he noted, had not a single gas station.

*Just great.*

He switched off the radio . . . and experienced another vision. A memory? Someone quite large had sat up in the driver's seat while he sat in the back. Someone with a smashed nose and an obscured face.

No . . . no, he must be remembering something he'd seen on TV or a movie when he was a kid. Sure, that's all it was.

But the memory kept coming at him. He was smaller . . . much smaller, sitting in the back seat. He remembered the pinching squeeze of being buckled in much too tightly. All he could see was the back of the large man sitting up front, behind the steering wheel. Not his father—a stranger.

Ben shook his head; his mind was playing tricks. He needed more caffeine . . . something to eat.

Getting back on the highway, he took another exit and found a small gas station. As he pulled in to refuel, he had another burst of sickening memory: he recalled crying out at such a gas station—similar to this one. He had shouted loudly that night, at the top of his voice, as if his very life depended on the volume of it . . . but there had been no tears. No, little brothers did not cry.

They held it in, he had been told. They were brave . . . very brave. They sat quietly in the back while the big man got out of the car and purchased gas and some candy and hot coffee. That's what they did.

And if they weren't quiet or obedient, they were pushed into the trunk and there they stayed for hours and hours, till they were so cold they couldn't get warm, even though they shivered and shook and their little teeth rattled in their heads. And even though they dreamed they could kick and bite and run fast and get away, they could not. At least not at that moment.

And this little brother was left in that trunk long enough to think he would surely never get out again . . . until he believed that if ever he was found, people would look sadly at him all coiled up in a frozen ball and say, *Der Biebche is am Schtarewe*—the little boy is dying.

Ben shivered and shook his head again. *I've been driving too long*, he thought. *I'm imagining things.*

On Sunday, Annie fretted while redding up the kitchen after the noon meal for Esther, who was busy nursing Essie Ann upstairs.

Even though Annie was not thinking of breaking her six-month promise to Daed, she had begun to envision all the wonderful things about Ben in anticipation of the time she could draw them in a collage. She already could visualize how she wanted to set up the composition on the canvas and felt sure it would not be long after the sketching phase that she could bring it to life with the vibrancy of paint. Sometimes she even crept away to the barnyard and pushed a stick around, sketching out her layout on the ground. Surely that was not prohibited.

*Oh, I can scarcely wait for that day.*

To think of Ben staying over at Cousin Julia's right then seemed terribly strange . . . even awkward. *Will he come see me?*

Finishing up, she checked the time. *Plenty of time before I have to feed the hogs again and help Essie with supper.* She had a sudden eagerness to take a long walk, so she scribbled a note to Esther.

*I'll be back soon,* she wrote, leaving it propped on the table against the paper napkin holder.

Delighted to be in the locust grove along Pequea Creek, Annie sat on the old rope swing, at first testing it with her weight. *Seems nice and straight . . .* She leaned back, stretching her legs forward, allowing the swing to lift her higher and higher, shooting toward the milky blue sky, her dress tucked in carefully on either side. The generous length of the rope made it possible to experience a real thrill like when she was little, she realized, smiling. Whyever had Daed taken it down in the first place? Had he wanted to discourage children from playing at the site of a presumed kidnapping? Or had he not liked seeing the swing . . . and the memories it stirred? Annie continued to lean back and push forward, overjoyed to be here despite the past, reveling in the sunshine and this pretty, peaceful spot.

*Before I sent Ben away, I was ever so happy.*

She leaned into the sway of the swing—hers and Isaac's—thinking back to the many hours spent here, seeing who could swing the highest. And there was the risky jumping, too—jumping off and landing on two feet without falling forward. All childish games, but tantalizingly fun.

*All this was a part of me before I started my art. Still, my love for it must have been there all along,* she thought, having always been intensely aware of the Lord God's colorful palette of nature. She looked at the sky, pondering, as she often did, what heaven was like. Was Isaac there? What was he doing now?

Rising, she turned to look around, wondering exactly where it was that Isaac and Zeke had made a grave for Isaac's special pet.

Wandering down to the creek, she stared at the rushing water, watching it sweep leaves and other pieces of God's creation into a fluid yet textured portrait until she was drawn back to the swing. She sat and pushed herself back with her bare feet, glad for the smile of springtime on the lovely grass, the flowering blossoms in the trees overhead. This place was so private, yet resplendent with color and aroma. "Surely a glimpse into what heaven must be like," she told herself. After all, the heavenly Father was the supreme creator-artist. She closed her eyes, eager for the little tickle of excitement as she swayed back and forth, a welcome sensation she had often felt when she was a little girl sitting right here, swinging double with Isaac.

# *Chapter 16*

Julia Ranck was setting the table for lunch when Ben wandered into the kitchen, young James hanging on to his knee as Ben pretended to limp and stumble. Looking at James roughhousing with their guest, Julia frowned and motioned to him, and her son quickly let go, then headed for the sink, where he put out his hands to be washed.

"I hope you like egg salad sandwiches," Julia said, glancing Ben's way with a smile, drying her son's hands with a dish towel.

"Sounds good."

Irvin appeared from the small sunroom off the kitchen, carrying his Bible. "Well, there he is! How was your night after so many hours on the road?"

Ben laughed self-consciously, having slept through not only breakfast but church, as well. "Sorry I slept so late."

"Not a problem."

The sound of squealing erupted from across the room. Little Molly came charging toward him, running right into his arms. "Mr. Ben's back!"

He leaned down and picked her up, swinging her high, then low again. This brought more giggles from the blond, blue-eyed cutie, and she begged for more. "Do it again! Do it again!"

"Now, Molly, let's settle down to eat," Irvin said, and she obediently, but not so happily, headed toward Julia to have her hands washed before joining her brother at the table.

After Irvin offered the blessing, the children became quiet. The adults discussed the weather, and then Ben inquired about Zeke, thinking he'd make additional small talk, taking the attention off any second-guessing the Rancks might be doing about the reason for his return visit. But he was stunned to hear that Zeke was being treated for depression and a mental disorder.

"There's a fine new center not far from here," Julia spoke up, and Irvin described the facility created specifically for Amish and Mennonite patients, to make them feel comfortable in a Plain environment, similar to their own homes.

Ben felt a twinge of sadness for the man who'd sought him out so faithfully while he had lived and worked here briefly—and for Zeke's family.

"And Annie Zook . . . I'm sure you know she's staying with Esther, for the time being," volunteered Julia, not making eye contact as she poured milk for Molly.

"I'd heard that, uh . . . from Annie. She wrote me."

"Ah, how nice," Julia said, now smiling.

"Was this Annie's choice to go to Esther's?" Ben asked.

Julia shrugged. "I think so. I don't know all the ins and outs of it, really. But Annie's all right. We see her several times a week."

Irvin seemed to agree. "She's figuring some things out, is all. I wouldn't be surprised if she's back home soon, when things blow over."

Ben wondered what things but assumed it had a lot to do with him and with her father's discovery of their dating.

"So, Ben," Julia began, giving him a knowing look. "What *really* brings you back so soon?"

Irvin chuckled. "Julia, he's barely recovered from his trip. Give the man time to catch his breath."

Irvin and Julia traded humorous glances, and Ben felt a subtle twinge of envy, admiring their close relationship.

For a moment, Ben considered telling them about his adoption bombshell but decided to wait. It hadn't occurred to him until now that he preferred to tell Annie his strange news first.

After the meal, he returned to the attic room to make his bed and put his few items of clothing away in the empty bureau drawers, as Julia had kindly instructed.

When he came back down, Julia mentioned that Irvin was taking a Sunday afternoon nap.

"Poor man's all tired out," she explained. "He helped a neighbor chop several cords of wood yesterday."

Ben was sorry he hadn't been there to help. He imagined Irvin walking through the woods, ax in hand, looking up, going from tree to tree, deciding which one to topple, which would make the best firewood. For a passing moment, flickers of just such an outing filled his recollection. Funny, he was pretty sure he had never done such a thing since, growing up, he and his family had lived in town. Still, the memory lingered. Was this something he'd done as a very young boy, before he'd been found in Kentucky?

Feeling the need for some fresh air, Ben could scarcely wait to drive the back roads with every window down, breathing in the rich scents, taking in the splendor of trees lining the road or the varieties of fruit trees filling the orchards. Most of all, he wanted to revisit the old covered bridge on Belmont Road.

Soon he was driving down the road, questions concerning his adoption plaguing him. There was no way of knowing his real birth date, nor his full name, beyond Zachary. He was like a dinghy drifting on foggy seas. And yet for some reason, he felt at home in Lancaster County. Being here was like a sigh of relief, and he was glad he'd made the journey back so quickly.

Spying the bridge up ahead, he pulled off to the side of the road and parked the car, more perplexed as he stared at the quaint yet picturesque site. What was it about this place that kept drawing him? And why had Annie Zook painted such a scene and had the painting so beautifully framed, only to hide it away from the eyes of the People? Did it have some special meaning to her? He knew he could not leave Paradise again without asking.

He thought of the swing in Annie's painting and the spotlight on what had appeared to be a peach stone. Why had she chosen to highlight it, as if that specific detail was in some way important?

Walking through the bridge now, Ben was not afraid. He experienced a nearly compelling sense of hope, though he had no idea why.

He turned to the left and strolled down the grassy slope, looking ahead toward the trees. He noticed a young woman—an Amish girl—sitting on a swing.

He looked again. He hadn't remembered seeing the long rope swing the other times he'd been here.

Ben stopped in his tracks.

*Annie? Or is my mind playing tricks on me again?*

Slowing his pace, he remembered the fear he had experienced the first time he'd come here. Only this time he was nervous for a different reason.

*Is it really Annie?*

Now that he was this close to the girl, he was tentative, not wanting to alarm her. So he made some noise, crunching some dry twigs under his feet, and saw that hers were bare. Naturally they were. This was the third week of

May, and he'd learned quickly that Amish women and girls shed winter's shoes and ran barefooted, ready to embrace the warmth of the sun and earth, as soon as the first bumblebees were spotted.

Unexpectedly, she looked his way and frowned curiously. "Ben?"

A flood of emotions filled him at the sound of his name. "Hello, Annie."

She rose somewhat unsteadily from the swing. "It's *awful* good to see you again."

He could hardly believe she was standing there before him. "I didn't expect to find you here."

An awkward moment passed as neither seemed sure what to say and they just stood there smiling at each other. Ben didn't say he'd missed her, but he certainly had, and seeing her now brought it right home to him.

"I'm back . . . because I can't seem to stay away." He chuckled, offering a nervous smile.

"What could be so important that you traveled all this way?" She quickly told him that Julia had let her know he was coming, and how surprised she was. "My cousins seemed very pleased that you were going to stay with them."

Suddenly feeling comfortable with her, he reached for her hand. "It's so great to see you, Annie."

She grinned. "Did you get my letter?" she asked, then added, "I almost didn't send it, because it was . . . um . . . too honest."

He was surprised at her candor. "Too honest? I didn't think so."

She looked down, cheeks pink. "I was afraid you might think I was too bold."

Ben shook his head. He had other concerns burning in his brain, but in her presence they seemed to slip away. He squeezed her hand before releasing it. Then he pulled out the carefully folded magazine cover from his pocket and showed it to her. "This is your work, isn't it? Your painting that won first place?"

She nodded, looking self-conscious.

"I recognized this spot as soon as I saw it."

She looked wistfully about her. "I guess I just love this place. My brothers and I used to come here to play when I was small. I used to swing on this very swing with my best friend in the world."

"Essie?" he asked.

She shook her head. "A little boy named Isaac."

Something within Ben whirled at the mention of that name. His mind seemed to cloud over, then clear with recognition. He *knew* that name. Or had Annie mentioned it before?

He forced himself to focus. "I know the last time I asked you about this place, it upset you. You said something bad had happened here, but you didn't tell me what. I need to know."

Annie looked at him for a moment. "This is where Isaac disappeared—kidnapped, most likely," she told him somberly. "Remember what Zeke told you, about the bones he thought were his little brother's? Zeke even thought he killed Isaac himself, but it turns out the remains the police found were those of a young girl. So we still don't know what happened to Isaac."

*Zeke's missing brother was named Isaac?*

Annie gestured toward the folded cover. "Where did you get that?"

"From a friend of mine who works for the magazine. I've carried it with me since last Christmas. . . ."

"Even before you came here?"

He nodded.

"Why on earth?"

"I think it's one of the main reasons I first wanted to travel here to Paradise."

"How so?" she asked, clearly perplexed.

"I didn't understand then, but I think I'm beginning to." He took a deep breath. "Annie, I need to tell you something I've learned . . . about my family."

Her face shone with concerned interest. "Jah? I hope everyone's all right."

"I just found out I'm adopted, Annie. I had no idea all these years, but Mom told me when I was home. It still feels like some weird soap opera—"

"Wait a minute," she stopped him. "You're adopted and your parents never told you?"

"I know. If it didn't hurt so much, it would almost be funny. My whole life seems like a cruel joke."

She stepped back a bit and, finding the swing again, sat down. "Jah, how strange for you, hearing it now. How did they come to adopt you?"

He shrugged. "Apparently I showed up on someone's doorstep one night and they took me to child services. I was traumatized, I guess—didn't speak for months. The authorities tried to figure out where I'd come from, but no one had reported a missing boy who matched my description and I couldn't—or wouldn't—tell them my name or where I was from. The Martins adopted me as soon as I became eligible."

He paused to breathe, to fill his aching lungs with air. He almost felt guilty, telling this innocent girl his unbelievable story. He looked over at her to gauge her reaction. She was staring at him wide-eyed.

"Does this shock you?" he asked.

"No. Go on, Ben. It's all right; you can tell me." She tilted her head, her eyes following his every move.

He knew her well enough to know he could trust her with the full story. "I don't really remember much. My mother said I must have blocked it out. I have no idea when I was born or what my full name was. I don't know anything about my biological parents or if they abandoned me or what. I seem to remember some man taking me away in the night, but I'm not sure how much is real or my imagination playing tricks on me."

Annie frowned. "It doesn't sound like you were an infant. How old do you think you were? Does anyone know?"

"About four or five, I guess. As far as my actual birthday, I think they picked a month and day out of a hat and put that on my birth certificate." He paused. "At least I think that's what my parents said. I still don't remember much . . . just glimpses into the past."

He sat cross-legged in the grass, not far from the swing. "I have to level with you, Annie. I'm very drawn to this place . . . to your people, too. I often feel like a fifth wheel on the outside, in the English world, as you call it. Maybe this is why I never felt like I fit in anywhere. Because in some strange way, in the back of my mind, I knew I belonged somewhere else."

She began to swing a little. "You think someone took you away? Or you got lost somehow? What did your parents tell you about that?"

"They don't know much more than I do. But I do know one thing."

She stopped swinging.

He reached into his pocket. "This." He held up the smooth peach stone. "It was in my pocket the night I was found—the only thing I had in my possession that I recognized as mine."

"Oh, Ben!" Annie clasped her hand over her mouth.

He thought she might cry, she looked that distraught, but then just as quickly, amazement shone in her features.

"What is it?" he asked. "You look as if you've seen a ghost."

She rose swiftly and came to him. "Oh, I believe I have!" She placed her hands on his face, tracing his eyebrows and then his cheekbones. "What were you wearing that night . . . when they found you, I mean? And how was your hair cut? Was it fancy-like?"

"I don't know. My mom said there wasn't anything unusual about how I was dressed, just that my clothes were large on me. Why do you ask?" He reached for her hands to keep them from probing his face any longer, baffled by her affectionate response.

"Ben." She swallowed. "My little friend Isaac carried a peach stone in *his* pocket all the time. He disappeared when he was four years old." Again she reached for his face. "It never occurred to me before but . . . you *look* like Isaac."

Ben shook his head. "Oh, Annie. That sounds crazy—"

"You recognized Pennsylvania Dutch, remember? And I've never seen Zeke seek out anyone's friendship the way he did with you. He avoids everyone. Here—" at this she led him back to the swing—"sit down a bit."

He complied, feeling both silly and intrigued.

"Look around you," Annie said. "Listen to the sounds. Do you remember ever sitting here before?"

He smiled, feeling foolish. "Annie—"

She put her hands on his shoulders. "Ben, close your eyes. Just listen for a moment."

He did as she suggested, soaking up the pleasant song of birds and the rushing creek. And as he was silent, he *did* recall something: as a child, he had stood up on a swing. *Here.* He had looked down at the creek as he did so, seeing the trestle of the bridge just beyond. Other times he had twisted the rope and spun quickly round and round, making his head dizzy, till the swing came to a jerking stop . . . a little girl laughing as he did.

When he opened his eyes and looked at Annie, there were tears spilling down her face.

"I remember you, Isaac," she said softly. "Do you remember me?"

# Chapter 17

Annie wanted to stand on the creek bank and spin around, arms wide with joy. She wanted to shout—to tell all of Paradise that Isaac was found at last. But, noticing Ben's reserve, she kept quiet, content to be near him, to savor this discovery alone. For now.

Heart still pounding, Annie was secretly thrilled she'd walked to Pequea Creek on foot, because when Ben offered to drive her back to Essie's, she was free to accept and ride along.

Together they walked toward the bridge while she kept sneaking glances at him. "I can hardly believe I'm here again with Isaac Hochstetler after all these years."

He looked at her intently. "How can you be so sure, Annie? Maybe there's some other explanation."

"What other explanation?"

He shrugged.

She grabbed his sleeve, and he stopped to look at her. "I knew there was some reason why you always seemed so familiar. Don't you feel it, too?"

Ben nodded. "Memories seem to be getting stronger than when I was here before."

"Like what?"

"For instance, I remember filling my britches pockets with bugs, especially daddy longlegs."

"Ach, you're foolin' me."

He grinned. "Now, why would I do that?"

"You honestly put creepy crawlers in your pockets?"

"Someone once told me that pockets were meant for hiding insects and caterpillars and such."

"Well, *that's* interesting. Do you remember who? Zeke maybe?"

They continued walking through the bridge, and Annie noticed how dismal it suddenly became as they reached the middle section—the light of the sky framed at both ends.

"I don't know," Ben said. "But I suppose if it's true that I *am* Isaac, I guess in time all of it will come back. I sure hope so."

"Me too," she replied. "It must be true," she said, repeating the facts that he was the same age as Isaac would now be, and that he had been found in Kentucky in the autumn of the year of Isaac's disappearance, at about age four. "I daresay the smooth peach stone seals the whole thing."

He handed the pit to her, but his manner seemed less sure. "I always wondered . . . because it seemed to have some connection to something I couldn't remember . . . but I somehow blocked out the trauma of what happened." He paused as if remembering something. "When I drove back here *this* time the strangest memories began to bombard me."

Annie felt the peach pit in her hand, like a pebble from a creek, its jagged surface washed smooth with time. "Did you ever know that Zeke—your brother—collected these, too? After you disappeared he did, that is."

"His daughter Laura told me that." Ben opened the car door for her. "To think that Zeke was so sure Isaac had been killed. And from what you told me—that he'd done it himself. Will he even believe it if his younger brother shows up now, alive after all?"

"You'd think he'd be glad, but as troubled as Zeke is, I really don't know."

He closed the door and Annie settled into the front seat, the peach pit still in her hand. It felt peculiar sitting here in Ben's passenger seat again, though she wouldn't have traded this moment for anything. So much had happened since she'd last ridden in Ben's car only a few weeks ago. Here was Isaac! In the flesh.

Ben. *Her* Ben was Isaac! But now she had a job to do—to convince the People, beginning with her own father, that Isaac was indeed alive and well.

Once Ben was behind the steering wheel, she suggested that he not take her to Essie's as planned. "I suppose we ought to talk to Daed first, him being a preacher and all."

Ben turned toward her, looking hesitant again. "Well . . . okay. But first I'd like to see where Isaac—or . . . I—lived before the disappearance. Does the family still live around here?"

He wasn't convinced yet, she realized. "Not long after you were kidnapped, they moved away to Honey Brook. Then, following that, I'm not sure where, but they ended up in Canada eventually."

"Would you mind showing me the way to Isaac's . . . I mean *my* childhood home?"

"Wonderful-good idea. It might trigger more memories."

"Thanks, Annie," he said, face grim.

*He's terribly nervous*, she realized.

The pink light of late afternoon dazzled her senses, and just then she remembered her note to Esther. "Oh, I can't be gone much longer," she said. "I'm sorry, Ben, but I need to get back to help Essie."

"I understand."

"Maybe we should go and talk to Daed tomorrow instead. All right?"

"That might be a good idea. I need some time to process everything."

She could see how drained he was. "But it shouldn't take long to get to the house where you and Zeke lived with your parents, Daniel and Mary Hochstetler." She didn't mention the name Ichabod. "I know how to get there."

"What do you know about them?" he asked. "How many children did they have?"

"Just you and Zeke that I knew of." She'd never thought of this before. "They may have left the Amish life behind altogether, but I don't know for sure." She handed back the peach stone, wondering if she ought to tell him that his dear mother had passed away not so long ago. She didn't know how much to share, especially since Ben wasn't yet convinced that he was Isaac. But for her, there was no doubt.

Ben was amazed at how straightforward, even courageous, Annie was. She made her way right up to the back door, knocking hard and waiting till the owner of Daniel Hochstetler's former house came and answered. The woman who opened the door was middle-aged and clearly not Plain. Annie explained that her friend, Ben here, was visiting and wanted to see the house where he'd lived as a boy.

The woman looked curiously from Annie to Ben but invited them in anyway, saying they were welcome to look around as long as they didn't mind the mess. The woman herself left, saying she was on her way to the grocery store. "My boys are home, though, so no need to lock up—just let yourselves out when you're done." Ben had no idea where the man of the house was, or if there was one at all.

As he and Annie walked from room to cluttered room, they saw TVs flickering and blaring in nearly every one. Several teenaged boys sprawled on sofas in the living room and barely seemed to notice two strangers giving themselves a tour of their house.

Heading to the relative quiet of the second floor, he and Annie found four bedrooms. Standing in the smallest of the four, Ben had a sense of knowing this might have been his room. Annie seemed to detect his desire to be alone and excused herself quietly, going out into the hall to wait for him.

He walked the length of the floor, staring at the walls. Then, turning, he looked out the only window, wondering if he'd ever stood there, noting the low windowsill, only a few inches off the floor.

Looking into the closet, he imagined the kind of Amish attire he must have worn as a little boy. *Why doesn't anything ring a bell?* He looked at the bed, the way it was centered on the south wall.

"*A body sleeps best with the head of the bed facing north,*" someone had told him. When? Was that his first mother's opinion?

He turned and studied the north wall. *No, this couldn't have been my room,* he decided, going out to the hallway and finding Annie there, hands folded. "It seems only vaguely familiar."

"That's all right—could be the English furniture and such." She smiled encouragingly. "Maybe if you walk around the barn a bit?"

"There's a large pond, too." He'd noticed it when driving up. "I wonder if they stock it with fish."

Annie giggled at the notion.

They headed downstairs and out the back door, thanking no one, because the teenagers were now playing video games.

He and Annie strolled around, glancing in several of the outbuildings, seeing three big dogs running free. "Maybe this isn't the place," he said. "Is that possible?"

She shook her head. "This *is* the house."

He stopped walking and reached for her hand. "Annie, I think I know how much you'd like me to be your long-lost friend. But what if I'm not? What if Isaac isn't alive after all?"

She smiled. "You're Isaac—as sure as I'm Annie Zook, I know you are."

"Well, let's see what your father thinks," he suggested. "I'll go and see him first thing tomorrow."

Annie burst out laughing. "You want to help with milkin'?"

He shook his head, "Ew . . . bad idea."

She stopped and looked at him, wearing the cutest expression. Then she rattled off something in Pennsylvania Dutch. "Do you know what I just said?"

"Maybe. Say it more slowly."

She did. *"Es gebt viele schwatze Kieh, awwer sie gewwe all weissi Millich!"*

He concentrated. An alarm went off in him. "I don't understand all of it, but some."

"Quick, tell me which part."

"Something about black cows and white milk?"

"Jah, that's right." She was laughing softly. "Yet another proof, Ben. Little by little . . ."

He wasn't as sure. It still seemed so *impossible.*

He spied an old climbing tree with a bent hook-shaped branch in the side yard not far from the white picket fence. At that moment, a genuine knowing clicked in him, like a falling into place. He knew without a doubt it had been the perfect spot to sit and play "riding horsey," remembering unmistakably a blustery springtime day when he'd climbed too high onto the unique bough, hoping to hide there so he wouldn't have to go to market with Mamma.

When his mother had demanded he come down right this minute, he'd lied and said he had a fever. So she'd scooted him into the house and stuck a thermometer in his mouth to see for sure. Ornery as he was, he bit down hard on it, breaking the thermometer and swallowing some of the mercury. Running to the kitchen sink, he gagged and spit while his poor mamma fretted something fierce, calling for Dat to come. He remembered the strange thickness in his mouth as it all came back to him—the fact that he'd willfully tried to make himself sick that day.

"Ben, are you all right?" asked Annie.

*Maybe I am Isaac. . . .*

He told her what had just burst across the years to him. "I remember that ancient climbing tree—old even back when I was a boy."

Her big blue eyes lit up. "Oh, this is ever so exciting."

He had the urge to scoop her into his arms but gave her a brief hug instead. "Well, let's see what your father says about this tomorrow."

She nodded in agreement, her face turning crimson from his touch.

They walked hand in hand across the side yard to his waiting car, but before opening the door for Annie, he paused to look again at the lofty tree, the silvery underside of its leaves gleaming suddenly in the breeze. Something told him he'd stood here many times before, or near here—possibly staring out his bedroom window at this tree, longing for the morning so he could climb it again.

"Unbelievable," he whispered. He could not take his eyes off the massive tree, surprisingly aware at this moment who the stranger in his dreams had been all along. *My father knew all about trees. He loved nature and revered the Creator of all things.*

Annie touched his sleeve. "Ben?"

He looked at her and leaned down to kiss her cheek. He opened the car door for her and waited till she was inside to close it firmly. Going to his side of the car, he glanced up at the tree once more. "Dat . . . it was you," he whispered. "Where are you now?"

# Chapter 18

Before dawn, Annie stood by one of the kitchen windows at Essie's, waiting for Ben to arrive. She felt the need to pray, to thank the Good Lord for bringing Isaac home. "I never really believed it possible, but you surely knew . . . all along."

When Ben's car pulled up, the thought crossed her mind that it might not be such a good idea to introduce him as Isaac to her father. For a moment, she contemplated Essie's desire to pray about everything. *Should I be asking the Lord God for His help today, as well?*

Opening and closing the back door quietly so as not to awaken Essie and the children, Annie rushed out to Ben, who met her on the passenger side to open her door. "Good morning, Annie. Did you sleep well?"

"It was a short night, I daresay."

He chuckled and hurried around the front of the car. She was glad for the waning moon. She had not forgotten how handsome Ben was, but seeing him now, hurrying around the car with such eagerness, made her heart flutter.

"Are you sure about going to see your father first thing like this?" he asked, buckling his seat belt.

She nodded, determined to press forward, though as the big farmhouse came into view, she wondered how to go about convincing Daed. She had a terrified twinge in her stomach, but there was no putting off something this important.

"I think it might be best if you stay put for now." She hated sounding bossy, but she needed to break the news to Daed slowly and carefully.

"Take your time, Annie. I'm not going anywhere."

The way he said it delighted her, and she got out of the car and headed straight to the barn, asking the Lord God for wisdom.

Zeke sat on the veranda at Philhaven, watching the moon fade in the coming sunrise. He still felt stunned. *I'll be caught with mud on my face with this new baby coming! One thing after another . . . . all problems of my own making,* he thought.

Yet he knew, if given the chance, he would not have done things any differently back after Esther's shun was announced. A man had certain needs—the Lord God ordained marriage for plenty good reason, for sure and for certain. There was nothing the brethren could say otherwise, and even though he was annoyed no end at Esther's baby news, he couldn't help hoping for another son. Laura and Essie Ann were fine where daughters were concerned, but for his plans to expand his hog operation someday he needed muscle and stamina—in short, another young man in the house. Zach would be a strapping fellow when he grew up, but little John was about as good as a girl, what with his asthma.

Zeke looked sadly at the chair where Esther had sat and kept him company a couple days ago, enjoying their first visit since his being admitted here. At least until he'd spoiled it by losing his temper. Such a good, pretty woman he'd married. He felt a lump come up in his throat. "We've got ourselves another little one on the way," he mumbled. "Where will that get me . . . with everything else I've done wrong?"

He was certain Preacher Jesse would take this up with the bishop right quick, if Annie spilled the beans. Truth was, his time was awful short, and there was nothing to do about it but wait. If he jumped ahead and told on himself, he'd bring on the Bann faster than lightning. "Looks like it can strike twice in the selfsame place," he whispered, pulling hard on his beard, not minding the prickly pain he was causing his face. "It's my own dumb fault."

He moseyed indoors to wash up for breakfast. He would have to walk over to the dining room with the other folk residing here. He missed his own table, sitting at the head at every meal, hearing the smack of his children's lips as they ate, the burps that came, especially from the boys, showing their mamma how wonderful-good her cooking was.

*If I'm to be under the shun, I'll be joining Esther at her separate table soon. At least in public.* For a moment, the thought brought him a measure of satisfaction. For with or without Esther, he was to be alone—at least that's what was expected of him . . . if he were ever to be released from this place and allowed to return to his own home.

At the sink, he let the water flow through his hands, then splashed it on his face, getting his beard a bit wet as he recalled that awful long-ago night again.

*Little brother has borne too much grief for one so young,* he had concluded as he finished the task of burial. A muffled sob and running footsteps caught his attention suddenly, and quickly he straightened, catching his breath as he leaned on the shovel, looking about the grove. Isaac had disappeared!

"I killed Isaac," he muttered into the towel now as he dried his face.

Visions of that night continued to play out, confusing him. Even in his dreams the images appeared and disturbed him. One doctor had suggested Zeke felt too responsible for his brother—the reason for his tremendous, black guilt. Another agreed with the first doctor but implied Zeke was not carrying the blame at all but suffered, possibly, from some form of post-traumatic stress disorder . . . speculating that there was much more to the disappearance than met the eye. *"Perhaps you've buried the truth deep within yourself, for some unknown reason."* They had to dig out the reason, get to the bottom of things, so he could then heal and get home.

Some days he believed he was getting less fuzzy in his thinker; other days he just didn't know. But right this minute, he knew he should have abided by the separation requirements put on Esther and himself by the brethren. He should've waited till she confessed—whenever that time might be—before visiting her down the hall at night.

*Just as I should've obeyed my father the night I took Isaac out to bury the puppy.*

While Ben waited in the car, Annie searched for her father and found him hauling milk. "Oh, there you are."

Lifting the lid on the cooler, her father turned to her, his face solemn.

"I have some wonderful-good news, Daed," she said.

He did not crack a smile. "You must be comin' home where you belong."

"No, Daed. That's not it at all."

"Well, oughta be."

She forced a smile. "I want you to meet someone."

He eyed her suspiciously. "At this time of morning? Can't you see I'm awful busy? Your not bein' here has made a hole in things."

"It's important that you come with me," she urged, looking toward the driveway.

"What's more important than doin' needful chores?" His eyes were unsympathetic.

She bit her lip. He wasn't making it easy for her. Considering everything that had happened between them, how could she possibly break this to him? Gently? Or come right out with it? "Ach, Daed, what would ya say if I told you Isaac Hochstetler is alive?"

His brow furrowed in disbelief. He sucked in some air, staring at the cement floor. Slowly, he lifted his head and met her gaze. "Well, now, I'd say you're as crazy as Zeke, maybe."

"But I'm not."

"Say all you want, but if you think such a thing, then I have to pity you."

"Ach, Daed. Isaac's alive, and I can prove it."

He waved his hand and put his hat back on. "I've got work to do."

"No . . . wait. If you won't come out to the car, I'll bring him in, right here to you."

He stopped dead in his tracks, his back to her. "What on earth are you talking 'bout?"

"Isaac's here . . . sittin' outside in his car. Aren't you the least bit curious?"

Her father turned to face her. "I don't know what you're pullin', but I'm not interested in playing any tomfoolery or whatever this is."

"But, Daed—"

"Go 'bout your business, Annie. And I'll go back to mine."

With a heavy heart, she knew she had been quite mistaken to think her father would listen. Maybe no one would. Maybe the People weren't ready to receive Isaac back.

Perhaps Esther was a better choice. *Jah, that's where we'll head next . . . and eventually out to see Zeke in due time.*

She turned to head back to the driveway, where Ben sat with the car still running, which was rather curious. Had he sensed Daed would not grant him a meeting? Was he prepared for a quick getaway?

Slipping into the front seat again, she said softly, "I guess I wasn't thinkin' clearly. This wasn't a good idea. Too much anger between my father and me." Then she began to cry, trying her best to tell him what her father had said. "I'm awful sorry, Ben." She brushed her tears away. "I thought things would go much better."

He reached for her hand. "I read something in the Bible the day I was so disappointed about the news of my adoption. I don't think I'll ever forget it." He paused. "The verse went something like this: all things work out for good to those who love God."

She perked up her ears, because she'd heard Cousin Julia say the very same thing. "Jah, I like the sound of that. And since we both love the Lord God—don't we?—well, I s'pose we can hope in the verse, too."

Ben shifted the car into gear, and they drove in silence for a while. He seemed almost reflective as he stared straight ahead, as if suddenly sad. "I've been curious about the Amish tradition—why you live the way you do, seemingly locked in time. I guess knowing what I do now, my curiosity makes sense."

"Putting it simply, we do what our forefathers did."

"It's especially appealing in a world where things are constantly changing, you know?"

"Some things change, I s'pose," Annie said. "I hear some Amish read and study the Bible. Esther talks of a group called Beachy Amish and others, including the New Order Amish out in Gap, who memorize the Scriptures, and their bishop is all right with that."

Ben drove all over Paradise, past the Progressive Shoe Store, and then over east to the old mill. There, they got out and walked quite a ways before turning back and then stopping to watch a small waterfall across the road from the mill.

She thought for sure he was stalling, finding more places he wanted to see—such as the one-room schoolhouse, which he thought he remembered Zeke attending—before finally heading over to Esther's. Annie couldn't blame him, because the whole discovery was both peculiar and wonderful. She could hardly wait to share the news.

Finally, Ben asked her if she was ready to head back to Esther's. She was careful not to let her relief show as she nodded her assent.

"If Esther doesn't believe us, what then?" he asked.

"I can't imagine she won't. Everything adds up to you bein' Isaac."

To this, Ben chuckled, giving her a wink. "You're a pretty confident woman, Annie Zook."

Her heart pounded, and she knew she was smiling at him far too much. "I don't know if that's a good thing or not," she joked right back.

He asked about Zeke. "Has Esther seen him lately?"

"Once, so far. The People take turns visiting him, she says. As far as I know, he's doin' all right. Essie prays for him without ceasing, just as the Scripture says to."

Ben seemed to contemplate her remark, studying her now. "Prayer must be a powerful thing. I've wondered about communicating with God my whole life."

"So have I."

He turned the conversation back to Essie. "What does your father say about your staying with her?"

It still hurt to think of her father, especially as resistant as he'd been today. "My parents tend to think I'm taking sides with Essie—that I've abandoned them. There are big expectations on me, of course, which causes another rub. For one thing, I should've joined church by now, you prob'ly know."

He nodded, making the turn into Esther's drive. "Sam Glick hasn't joined yet, either, if I remember right."

"And he won't be," she said. "Oops . . . I don't think I was supposed to say that."

"He's leaving the Amish?"

"Maybe so."

Ben asked about Sam and Louisa. "What's happened with them, do you know?"

"Oh, I honestly think they care for each other, but they're miles apart." She didn't feel like going into any of that, not with her former beau—Isaac himself—sitting right here next to her, for goodness' sake! "Come on," she said as he stopped the car, "let's reintroduce you to your sister-in-law and to all your nieces and nephews. You'll love seein' Essie Ann again—she's so cute and growing ever so fast."

Ben got out and went around to open her door. His manner seemed uncertain again.

"What's the matter, Ben?"

He shrugged. "Maybe we should take this slower. Maybe no one is ready to accept this. I'm barely used to the idea myself."

Disappointment and anxiety flowed through her. "No, Ben. . . . Daed's upset with me, but Essie's goin' to fall right over with this news." Then she remembered what Essie had told her about being in the family way again. "Come to think of it, I best be breakin' it to her slowly. I should do most all the talking, prob'ly."

Ben nodded, his eyes tender. "Are you sure?"

Annie took his arm, and they walked around the house together. "Remember that verse you told me—all things are working for good, jah?" More than anything, she hoped they could trust that Scripture.

# Chapter 19

Louisa stood in the aisle at the art store, searching for the thinnest possible brush to create the fine details on her newest painting. She was working on an oil rendering of the Zooks' hay wagon—one of more than a dozen photos she had taken around the Zooks' farm. To bring the painting to life, she planned to include a litter of black kittens with the mother cat lying near, eyes closed while her young slept beside her.

She thought of her own beautiful Russian Blue cat, with his high cheekbones and angular face, deciding she wanted to paint Muffin and send the finished art to Annie as a belated birthday gift. *I need to get right on it*, she thought, eager to finish her current painting and contact a local gallery in Littleton, hoping for a sale. Her goal was to live within her means, refusing any help from her wealthy parents. The fact that she had done exactly that thus far made her quite proud.

*Not in a wrongful way, as Annie might say.*

There were times when she wished she could expedite a project, like the one that had come together so easily for her years ago: the ocean painting she had done at Great-Aunt Margaret's—near the beach, where the sweeping seascape had readily captured her attention. The setting had soothed her then and it comforted her now as she recalled its serene majesty. *Is it weird to miss a painting?* She often did just that, regretting it had ended up in London with Trey, who'd purchased it from her when they'd first met. *Never to be seen again by me.*

Spotting the perfect brush, she chose two exactly alike and made her way to the cashier's counter. On the way, she was distracted by the aisle where acid-free papers of every imaginable color were on display. One particular hue, a unique shade of green she'd come to know as "Amish green," caught her attention. Picking up the sheet, she held it next to her arm, pretending for a moment it was a sleeve, recalling the months of wearing such colors—deep blue, green, wine, and purple.

She thought back to a particular Monday. Wash day. She had been standing outdoors at the Zooks', helping Annie and her mother hang out dozens of articles of clothing, all lined up according to type and size. She remembered the first time she'd attempted to help, quickly learning the way things were expected to be done. Louisa noticed Annie was careful never to offend her by talking nonstop in Dutch with her mother, the way other women did at quilting bees or cannings. Yet another endearing thing about Annie: she was always conscious of Louisa's feelings, even to the point of not saying a word when Louisa happened to hang up one of the Zook boys' broadfall trousers inside out. Much later in the afternoon, when they were taking down the clothes, Louisa noticed the mistake, but Annie merely shrugged it off as nothing.

There were other appealing things about her pen pal and good friend that Louisa missed. It wasn't that she didn't care for her modern friends—she did and very much. Yet she knew that neither Courtney nor her other friends here could hold a candle to all of Annie's lovely characteristics, many of which were fostered by the Plain community she lived in.

Still, Louisa knew life in Paradise was not perfect. If she'd learned anything from her visit there, it was that even the "simple" life could be complex. No matter where one lived, life was stressful. Even for those who chose a less hectic pace, it was impossible to escape the pitfalls of human emotion and the unavoidable problems that resulted. The Amish seemed to take this in stride and made the best of tough situations with help from their families, their community, and their God.

*But I'm here now, teaching the students I missed, wearing my favorite clothes, and seeing my old fiancé.* Thinking the latter, she felt herself shrug inwardly.

Carefully, almost reverently, she placed the "Amish green" paper back on its matching stack and continued to the front of the store to pay for her new brushes.

Long after her last students of the morning had left the studio, Louisa sat on the stool in front of her easel and added touches of texture and detail to her hay wagon painting.

She wanted the painting to not only depict the setting accurately but to draw the observer into the scene itself. She struggled to emulate something of the Dutch master Rembrandt, who'd had the ability to create a sense of natural movement and a bold contrast between light and dark.

Sliding off her stool, she stepped back and studied the overall composition and feel. There was something she wanted to include and was struggling with its absence. *The exhilaration of walking on Amish soil.*

"Remember what it was like to sit on that hay wagon and be teased by Yonie. . . . *Think!*" she told herself.

Moving in closer, she gave the mother cat plenty of whiskers, being almost too generous with the brushstrokes in her rendering of one of the Zooks' barn cats—coal black with a sheen like none other.

To add interest in the foreground, she included a touch of wild tangled vines, then some dabs of purple blossoms and the enticing red of a cluster of berries.

"*Be* there," she told herself, again thinking back to the Zook farm.

She closed her eyes, but it was not Yonie's face she saw in her fond memory of Lancaster County. Sam's fine eyes and contagious smile were before her now, and she groaned. "When will I ever get over him?" she whispered, moving back to the painting, brush poised in midair. "Have you ruined me so completely, Sam . . . for my old life?"

A few more brushstrokes—a trio of distant birds in flight—and the painting was finished. She took meticulous care in cleaning her brushes. That done, she heard her Palm jingle—she was receiving a text message. When she checked, she saw that it was from Michael. *Wanna meet 4 lunch?*

Suddenly feeling guilty after her lingering thoughts about Sam, she sent a quick reply back to Michael. *Thx, but I have some shopping 2 do.*

Pushing her Palm into her backpack, she hurried to turn off the lights and headed out the door to her car, grocery list in hand, not waiting for a text reply.

She was pushing her keys into the ignition when she realized she had forgotten the reference book on Rembrandt that she'd intended to take home. She returned to the studio and located the treasured book. Rather than simply carry it out to the car, she thumbed through it there in the studio, finding the page she had often turned to and gazing at it once again.

Her heart had always been drawn to this haunting crucifixion scene of Christ. Her focus dropped to the crowd below the cross. The artist had painted himself into this scene, she knew from her studies. Why was that? Had he been as intrigued by this particular death as she was beginning to be?

She thought again of her great-aunt, who had once asked her as they sat sunning themselves on the beach, "What do you think happens after someone dies, Louisa dear?"

For whatever odd reason Aunt Margaret had pierced Louisa's thoughts with that unexpected question so long ago. Thinking on it now, Louisa hoped to talk again with Julia Ranck sometime soon. Louisa was eager for something else, as well. She felt she was ready to tackle a thoughtful response to Sam's letter, although she still wasn't exactly sure what she would say.

Annie found Esther busy in the kitchen, making sandwiches with some enthusiastic help from young Laura. The baby was crying, and Zach and John were pulling pots and pans out of one cupboard when Annie hurried inside through the back door. She'd asked Ben to wait out on the step, where she assumed he was gathering his wits. At any rate, she didn't want to barge in on Essie, not with the kind of information she was so excited to share.

She picked up Essie Ann and carried her upstairs, rocking her for a few minutes, and then when the wee one's eyes drooped shut, Annie placed her carefully in the crib across from the foot of Esther's bed.

*Ach, gut. Now for the boys.*

Whispering to Laura to take her little brothers to the sitting room and play for a bit, Annie stood before Esther, who was slicing the sandwiches in half, all of them piled on a single plate. "We've got us some company for lunch," Annie began, waiting for Esther to look up before adding, "and I have the most wonderful-good news to tell you."

Esther's eyes remained on her task. "Well, what?"

"You may not believe it at first, but it's absolutely true. Wait'll ya hear."

Esther stopped to look at her. "What on earth are ya babbling 'bout, Annie?"

"Zeke's brother, Isaac, isn't dead at all. He's sitting out on the back stoop." She motioned toward the back porch. "What's most amazing is you already know him. It's Ben Martin—remember Zeke's friend from the harness shop?"

Esther frowned. "I don't follow."

"Ben was adopted when he was four, the same age Isaac was when he was taken away. Ben is really Isaac." Annie led her to the back door. "Here, see for yourself."

Ben stood up and entered the porch. "Hello again, Esther."

"Ach, I don't rightly know what Annie's been tellin' me, but won't you come in and have some lunch with us?" she invited, clearly shaken.

He glanced nervously at Annie and then offered to shake hands with Esther, but she had already turned and was heading back into the kitchen. Scurrying about, she set another plate while Annie's heart sank.

"This is just ridiculous," she said softly, standing beside Ben and feeling terribly awkward.

*What if no one believes?*

Hurrying back to her apartment with her budgeted amount of groceries, Louisa stopped to say, "Hey, kitty," to Muffin before beginning the process of putting the food items away. She had become something of an organizational freak since her visit to Amish country, alphabetizing her canned goods, for example. She smiled as she placed her purchases in the small cupboard-style pantry, excited to bake from scratch again, as she had been doing since her return. She'd even taken several batches of cookies and muffins to her neighbors and an elderly couple who lived downstairs.

Finished with the chore, she made a salad and poured some freshly brewed sun tea before settling in at the small kitchen counter to eat. She had another hour before her next student arrived at the studio, and feeling an urge to connect with Annie, she pulled out a sheet of yellow stationery and began to write longhand.

> *Dear Annie,*
>
> *I'll be straight with you. I wish we lived closer, and I wish our worlds could collide more often. How's that for sappy?*
>
> *One thing I've wanted to tell you is that I'm basically at capacity with students and still have enough time for my own works in process. I'm finding it a really good balance.*
>
> *Something else—you may be surprised, but I've started seeing Michael again. It doesn't mean I've fallen in love with him. I'm warmly cordial, I guess you could say. Even though I'm reluctant to get anything serious going again, he's definitely letting me know he cares . . . a lot.*
>
> *Between you and me, though, I see Sam's face everywhere. Well, I should rephrase that—I see aspects of his face nearly everywhere I look. He's smiling back at me with those beautiful green eyes of his in the work my students do— in the landscapes and self-portraits, too. At first, when I arrived back here, I thought I might be in mourning, but that seemed too strange. The phases of grief are many—denial, sadness, anger. . . . But what do I really have to grieve about where Sam's concerned?*
>
> *I'm rambling here. Sorry!*
>
> *Hey, I'm sending you a calling card and detailed instructions. Will you use it and phone me from Julia's or from the neighbors' barn phone? You pick,*

*but I really want to connect with you soon. Oh, while you're at it, please tell Julia I'd like to talk with her again, too. Her amazing faith and my great-aunt Margaret's prayers are definitely catching up with me. So, no, I don't think what you shared in your letter about your heart becoming tender toward God is strange at all. I'm right there with you, Annie!*

*Please write again soon.*

> *Love,*
> *Louisa ("Lou")*

*P.S. Tell Sam hi for me if you see him.*
*P.P.S. No, don't. Forget that, OK?*
*P.P.P.S. Call me!*

Louisa had never been one to slam doors or throw things when upset like some out-of-control women she knew. But she had completely run out of stationery and wanted to write another letter—this one to Sam. Searching through her drawers, Louisa began tossing things over her shoulder, wishing she'd taken the time to organize her computer desk and files the way she had her kitchen.

Feeling nearly overwhelmed and hoping she hadn't waited too long to reply to Sam's thoughtful letter, she snatched some copy paper out of the printer and began to write once again.

*Dear Sam,*

*It was really great to hear from you. I hope you don't think I'm rude for not replying immediately. I've thought so much about you since I left. As for your calling me, I would enjoy that a lot.*

*I guess I wasn't too surprised when you wrote about your plan to leave the Amish. I hope the transition goes smoothly. Congratulations on your promotion at work!*

*As for me, my life has sort of returned to normal, although I've made quite a few changes since my return here. I'm teaching a fine bunch of art students again, which is the thing that gets me going every morning. Ironically, many of my own paintings are of things I miss about Amish life—the life you plan to leave. The grass is always greener, jah?*

*Please feel free to call, if you wish. I think of you often!*

> *Your fancy friend,*
> *Louisa Stratford*

She didn't bother to look over what she'd written. She simply folded the letter and placed it in an envelope, addressing it to his new home among Englishers.

Ben was talking with Laura and her brothers at the kitchen table while Annie helped Essie slice pieces of angel food cake. "Walking in the dark is loads of fun," Ben told the children.

"Ach, can ya see in the dark, like a cat?" asked Laura, giggling.

Ben laughed, having a good time, and Annie was glad of it. During the first few minutes here, she had begun to doubt her resolve, but now that the delicious chicken-salad sandwiches had been devoured and the tension had dissipated, she was hoping to convince Essie that she and Ben hadn't completely lost their minds. In the meantime, Esther had acted as if she hadn't even heard Annie's declaration about Isaac.

*She must think I've gone loony.*

Laura piped up again, asking Ben if he'd ever gone hunting for snipes.

"Not recently." Ben caught Annie's gaze across the table.

"Do you know what they look like?" Laura asked, blue eyes shining.

"I've known some to appear under little girls' pillows."

*Don't scare her,* Annie thought, glancing at Essie, who seemed to be enjoying the entertainment, as well.

"That's mighty funny, Mr. Ben," Zach said, leaning forward, his elbows squarely on the table.

"Snipes don't like it inside the house," Laura declared.

"Jah, they stay up high in the trees," Zach said.

"Now, children, I think Mr. Ben is pulling your legs," Essie said, reaching over to wipe a smudge of food off Zach's face.

"Oh, for sure, Mamma. He's got us by the ankles!" Laura seemed more than happy to keep things going. She cupped her hands around her mouth and whispered to Zach loudly, "Look how one side of his mouth moves up higher when he smiles . . . just like Dat's."

Zach nodded. "Jah, I saw that. Same as cousin Nate, too."

Laura started giggling again. "He's got that smooth peach stone, too, remember?"

Annie jolted mentally. "Essie? May I see you in the sitting room?"

"Why sure," she said rather reluctantly.

While Ben kept the children laughing and talking, Annie told Essie again that her brother-in-law, Isaac, was no longer lost but quite certainly found. "The only thing he had from his Amish life on the night he was found was that worn down peach pit."

Essie looked away. "Oh, Annie, this is so strange for you to think this way. I mean . . . we *all* wish Isaac was still alive, and maybe he still is, but honestly . . . *Ben?*"

Annie rested a hand on Essie's arm. "I know what you're thinking, that this must be love talking and I'm making this up—"

"Well?"

Slowly Annie explained her reasoning—that Isaac and Ben would be the same age, that Ben had unexplainable but vivid memories that only Isaac could have, such as climbing the tree at the old Hochstetler place and swinging in the locust grove—"with me!"

Annie quickly told of all the places they'd stopped to visit that morning at Ben's request. And even though she desperately wanted her dear friend to accept the truth of a long-lost brother-in-law, it was painfully clear Essie thought Annie was quite ferhoodled.

"For one thing, I'd expect him to look more like Zeke. Wouldn't you?" Essie said.

"What about your in-laws—the Hochstetlers. What do you remember 'bout them?"

"Very little, really," Essie admitted. "They were not so keen on Zeke and me marrying, I do recall that. But as for looks, well, it's difficult to say."

"Esther, don't you believe me? Zeke's brother is alive."

"Oh, Annie, maybe he is . . . and maybe he isn't. Just because the bones—"

Annie felt her growing frustration. "Esther, no, listen." She stopped. Esther had turned pale and looked sad, as if she pitied Annie. *I've pushed this too far.*

She took a deep breath. "I'll prove it to you, Essie. Just give me time."

Essie, still white in the face, nodded, forcing a smile, and the two women hugged.

Esther whispered in Annie's ear, "I want to believe you, I do. If Isaac were alive, it would be amazing. But . . . it seems so . . . impossible."

Annie kissed Esther's cheek. "I hope I didn't upset you."

Esther shook her head, but her breathing seemed much too labored.

# Chapter 20

Jesse took his time hitching up his driving horse to the family carriage. With the sun so warm that afternoon, he desired the covering of the gray buggy while making the trip over to Zeke and Esther's. He was mighty weary, what with Annie's strange imaginings, saying she'd discovered that Isaac was alive and all. It wasn't that he hadn't been curious; he was. Maybe too much so. And now that she'd left, he felt a twinge of regret. He hadn't even given the poor girl a chance to explain. Maybe if it had been anyone other than his willful daughter suggesting such a thing . . . Still, he was glad he hadn't succumbed, standing his ground . . . finishing his work instead of falling for Annie's wishful thinking. *Isaac alive? What on earth?* True, the bones weren't Isaac's, but to jump to such conclusion?

He was headed over to Esther's, but not for the purpose of setting his daughter straight. He had other things on his mind—namely Esther's defiance. He'd thought surely by now she would have given up her close association with the Rancks and their church. He also felt responsible to protect Zeke's children—and his own daughter—from the onslaught of conversion tactics used by certain zealous folk. *My own cousins, for pete's sake!*

Something else consumed him—Ichabod's coming. Jesse had written back, but if the man came anyway, Jesse would have to do everything within his power to keep that visit in check. Zeke's father had often caused problems—even more than the thorny issues Zeke posed to the brethren. Who knew where it would end if Daniel actually showed up. Especially if the man had gone fancy, as Jesse feared.

594

*If I'd just put off writing to him in the first place, Daniel Hochstetler would not be making plans to return here.*

Jesse feared Esther was much too trusting and could be a prime target for half-truths. Annie, too, though for different reasons.

A shudder swept through him. Had Daniel already arrived? Was *that* why Annie had seemed so swept away with her strange notion of Isaac's return? Had Ichabod arrived in secret to stir up the brethren? *Has he already hoodwinked my own daughter?*

Aware of a newfound urgency, Jesse encouraged his best driving horse onward, before it was too late.

Esther offered Ben another cup of coffee. "Sure, thanks," he said, hoping to hear more about Zeke's growing-up years, or whatever Esther might be willing to share. After her short conversation with Annie in private, Esther looked visibly shaken and now seemed to be scrutinizing him. He felt terrible for not considering the emotional impact upon this poor woman. *Is it worth it? Am I causing more trouble?*

The three of them sat alone in the kitchen now that the younger children were off to bed for naps and Laura was outside playing with the dog.

"Zeke often talked with disdain about his father," Esther said softly, glancing at Annie. "I do know my husband was fond of his mother, who passed away a short time ago."

Annie spoke up quickly. "I knew 'bout this, Ben, but didn't want to put too much on you at once."

He felt sick at the news. Now he would never know his mother, nor would she know he had safely grown to adulthood. Taking a deep breath, he asked what had caused Mary's death, who'd received word, and where in Canada his birth parents had been living. More questions taxed his mind, but he decided to give Esther a break. *Give her time to think.* He was about to suggest as much when Jesse Zook drove into the lane with his horse and buggy.

Annie noticed right away, too, and rose immediately to go to the back door.

"It's all right, Annie," Esther said, going to her.

Ben could hear the two women talking quietly but made no attempt to listen. He mulled the information he'd gathered in only two short days. He knew it was finally time to discuss all he'd learned with Irvin and Julia. *Tonight at supper*, he decided. He had an urgent desire to call home, too. Perhaps his parents had recalled more information that would corroborate his discoveries.

Annie's father was being shown into the house. Ben stood to shake his hand. "Hello, Preacher," he said, instantly aware of the tension between them.

Jesse scowled and looked about the room as if searching for someone. "I'd heard you left town."

"I did."

"But you're back."

"Yes, sir."

Esther asked Jesse to sit at the head of the table, and he did. She offered him coffee and some pie, as she had Ben.

They all sat down together, except for Esther, who stood as she had once before when Ben had come here for a meal with Zeke. He noticed the preacher send a dark look toward Annie, clearly aggravated to find the two of them in the same room together.

So now not only was Esther pale-faced, a reaction to their previous discussion, but so was Annie. Ben tried to catch her eye to alert her to drop the idea of pushing things with her father, but she didn't look his way and forged ahead. "I know you won't believe this, Daed," she said, "but in all truth, Ben here *is* Isaac, back from the grave."

Jesse gripped his chair.

Ben expelled a long breath.

A long moment passed as Jesse's eyes swept from Annie to him and back. The preacher's brow furrowed with obvious consternation. "Have you lost your mind, daughter?"

Annie shook her head. "Ach, Daed—"

"Now, you listen to me. Claimin' this Englischer is long-lost Isaac—just so you can keep carryin' on with him after I forbade you to do so, is that it? Never would I have believed you would sink to something so low."

Ben shivered. *This isn't going well.*

"Daed, I would never do such a thing," Annie said, pain evident on her face. "It's true, no matter how crazy it sounds."

"How's *that* possible?" Jesse looked squarely at his daughter.

"'Cause it is," she asserted and then began to share all the things they had both learned since their meeting at the covered bridge.

When Annie finished, her father continued to stare at her without speaking, his focus darting back to Ben before slowly returning again to his daughter. His expression had softened some, but he clearly remained skeptical. Ben expected him to argue further, but instead he said, "Well, now. Haven't you forgotten something? If he's Zeke's brother, as you say, why was it Zeke never recognized him earlier?"

He turned to Ben. "Didn't you and Zeke spend some time together? At that mud sale, for one?"

Ben nodded.

"Well?"

The question lingered in the air. Jesse had a point, and Annie had no answer.

"Enough said," Jesse announced. "This is nonsense."

Esther looked more frail than she had before, and she moved toward the counter to get the coffee pot. When she did, Jesse asked if he might speak with her and Annie alone. "Why, sure." Esther looked weakly over her shoulder at Ben and said, "That is, if it's all right with you."

Ben took the polite hint, but Annie looked nervous, even alarmed. Excusing himself, Ben headed out the back way, deciding now was as good a time as any to disappear from view and phone his mom.

Worried that Ben had been offended by Daed's outspokenness, Annie poured cream into her father's coffee, listening as he told of having received word from Zeke's father in Canada.

"He wrote a letter in response to mine," said her father, explaining why he'd written initially. "So I wouldn't be surprised if Ichabod shows up, and soon."

Esther gasped. "He's coming *here?*"

Daed nodded. "He'll be lookin' for a place to stay, I'm sure. But let's keep this mum. Don't need more troubles arising." He inhaled deeply and gave Annie another fierce look. She looked down, having recognized the utter disappointment on her father's face.

Jesse continued, "Your father-in-law ought to stay with me, Esther." He looked at them both. "Given the circumstances."

"'Cause of my shunning?" Esther reached for her coffee cup, hand trembling.

"Ain't any good for two women to share one house, especially when both have such unchecked fancies." He darted another disapproving glance at Annie. "This Isaac twaddle is bad enough, but you both goin' to a church on the outside is creating a stir."

Annie wasn't too surprised, yet she hadn't heard much of anything from the womenfolk. Of course, she'd not been attending their work frolics since coming here to stay.

"The brethren expect you to return to Preaching services, Esther—you, too, Annie. These children are at risk."

"What're you sayin'?" Esther asked, her cheeks much too red.

"I'm speakin' of your souls . . . all of yous. Your children, Esther, are to be raised in the Amish church so that grace and peace may rest on this house. This is your husband's desire, as you surely know." He turned to Annie, "And you, the preacher's daughter, are helping this family right out the door. You should be ashamed of yourself."

He put on his hat. "I expect to see you come to your senses, daughter, and return home so God can finish His work of discipline. As for you, Esther, it's time to repent and put an end to this saving grace malarkey."

With that he headed for the door. Only when her father had left did Annie realize she had clenched her hands into fists so tight her palms were nearly bruised.

Sitting in the car, Ben called his mother on his cell phone. She answered on the second ring.

"Mom? Hi, it's Ben."

"Oh, honey, are you all right?" She sounded jittery. "I've been so worried."

"I'm fine, Mom."

He had debated how much to reveal to her, wanting to spare her feelings, but his own excitement got the best of him. "I think I know who I might have been, before I was found that night. Before you and Dad adopted me."

Silence filled the phone line.

Then the thin question, a single word. "Who?"

Gently he told her everything, filling her in on Annie's and his discovery. "You won't believe this, but I could have a brother and a sister-in-law, and two nieces and two nephews." He told of his first parents, that his Amish mother was deceased but that his father lived somewhere in Ontario, Canada. "I'm putting it all together, Mom. It's not as difficult as I thought it might be. Actually, I never expected to find out all this so quickly, or at all." He paused, sensing her anxiety.

"Oh, Ben, be careful. I would hate for you to get your hopes up."

"I know, but it seems possible at least."

She was silent for a time; then she said, "Don't forget us, Ben. We're your family, too."

"I know that, Mom. I hope you won't take all this wrong, but I needed to return here. I didn't realize why at first. It was as if something was *calling* me back. I needed to know about my past, my first family."

"Well, how long will you stay this time?"

"Haven't decided." From where he was parked, he could see Annie's father leaving the house, his head bowed as he strode toward his horse and buggy. "I'll be in touch, Mom. Tell Dad I called."

"I'll do that. He sends his love."

"Please don't worry about me, okay?"

"You know me too well. It's what I do best."

"Yeah, right." He chuckled. "'Bye!"

"We love you, Ben. . . . Good-bye."

Watching Preacher Jesse rein the horse around to make the wide circular turn at the top of the drive, new images emerged in Ben's mind. Indistinct and hazy ones of going to market and farm sales with a tall man. His father? Sitting on the tall man's knees . . . holding the reins with his small hands. He could almost smell the pipe tobacco now as he briefly closed his eyes.

Moments later, he saw Annie as she stood at the back door, waving, and he felt that familiar longing again, just seeing her. She hugged herself as if chilled, looking suddenly lost.

Getting out of the car, he called, "Take a walk with me," and she seemed relieved to accept.

Walking silently at first, they took the mule road out to the vast pastureland, where trees grew in random groves.

Annie was obviously discouraged; he couldn't recall having ever seen her so dejected.

Their eyes met and in spite of what he'd just told his mother, a renewed sense of doubt filled him. "Maybe we're wrong, Annie. Maybe we *both* have unbridled imaginations, as your father seems to think."

Her eyes filled with tears and she nodded. "I just wanted to believe it so badly."

"I did, too."

To redirect their talk to less volatile subjects, Ben pointed out various trees along the way. Then something popped into his head. "Say, Annie, Esther told me a little, but do you happen to know anything more about Zeke's father?"

"Ichabod?"

"What? Don't you mean Daniel?"

"He was always referred to as Ichabod from around the time of the kidnapping, according to Mamm."

Ben recognized the name from American literature. In high school, *The Legend of Sleepy Hollow*—the tale of the infamous and ridiculous schoolmaster, Ichabod Crane—had been required reading. "Why was Daniel called that?"

"Because he refused the lot for preacher."

Annie clearly felt uncomfortable talking about something that reflected so poorly on Ben's true father. On hers, too, for that matter.

"Honestly, I don't know much about it," she finally said.

Ben didn't push for more details, and Annie quickly changed the subject. "Essie was plenty shook up when my father left. Still, she shooed me outside to find you."

Ben knew Esther had been stunned by the possibility of his being Isaac. Preacher Zook's fiery speech likely hadn't helped matters. "Maybe she can get some rest with us out of the house."

She smiled at him as they walked. In the distance, a farm wagon rolled by, pulled by a single horse. Suddenly he remembered an outing he'd gone on with the man he'd called Dat. There was a lingering embarrassment surrounding this memory that caused a strange pressure in his chest.

Annie held tightly to his hand and they walked in silence, enjoying the fresh air and the sounds of spring. Her nearness, the wide-eyed sweetness of her, brought the memory to him more fully.

He remembered riding beside Dat on the buggy bench on a trip to buy their supply of peaches at an Amish farmhouse, seemingly miles away. When they arrived, he recalled being made over by the very pretty young woman who sold the bushels of peaches. She touched his face and smiled sweetly—even gave him free peaches, saying if he squeezed a peach pit hard enough and long enough it would eventually sprout. He could still hear Dat's hearty laughter ringing in his ears over that one.

When they got back to the buggy, Dat said he had forgotten to pay for the peaches. He went back into the house but stayed longer than a curious boy could possibly sit. He followed Dat inside and peeked around the corner, witnessing a stolen kiss, until his father looked up and saw him standing there. Heart pounding, he had hurried back to the buggy and crawled into the front seat. . . .

"Ben? You all right?" Annie was staring at him. "You're breathin' awful hard."

He couldn't possibly share this confusing vision from the past with her, or anyone.

"Let's keep going." He pointed farther away from the house, wanting to embrace fully every moment they had together, because he had no idea how to continue seeing her, recalling the glare of disapproval on Preacher Jesse's face earlier.

They walked for more than an hour. "Should we be heading back?" he asked after a glance at his watch.

Annie smiled warmly. "I can stay out as long as need be."

*Need be?* He wanted to wrap her in his arms, carry her away to another world. But where . . . how? Could they possibly make this relationship work? He'd come back in part to solve the troubles he'd caused, and here he was, the source of even more troubles than he could have imagined.

Maybe he should have remained at home. What did it matter if he were Isaac? But he realized that he couldn't have stayed away. He had this intense connection to Annie, as if he had been born to know her.

He smiled wistfully. Were they soul mates, destined to be together? And yet they'd failed before. What was different now?

He considered this. For one thing, he sensed a freedom in Annie that had been missing before, and the realization of this suddenly spurred him on, giving him more fuel for hope.

Another hour later, they were met by Esther's daughter Laura running toward them, her bare feet pounding the dirt path that connected the field to the barnyard. "Ach, Annie, I'm ever so glad you're back."

"What's wrong?" Annie leaned over to wipe the streaks of tears from the little girl's face.

"It's Mamma . . . she's *awful* sick. She's holdin' her belly and cryin'."

Annie picked up her skirt and ran toward the house. Ben followed. "Can you take her to a doctor right quick, Ben, if need be?" she called over her shoulder.

"Of course."

In a few minutes, Annie brought Esther out of the house and together they helped her into his car.

*Zeke's wife is ill. . . .* The realization of who he might be to frail Essie Hochstetler struck Ben anew. *My sister-in-law?*

Annie stayed with the children while he drove Esther to the hospital. They rode in silence as she closed her eyes and clutched her abdomen. On occasion she whispered, "Please help, dear Lord."

When they arrived, Ben offered to help Esther inside. Graciously, she accepted his arm as he gingerly assisted her in through the glass doors.

At the desk, a nurse smiled with concern as Esther quickly signed in. An orderly emerged, and Ben helped Esther into a wheelchair.

"You are so kind, Ben," Esther whispered before the orderly wheeled her away to another ward of the hospital. Ben followed.

Sitting down in another waiting room, he happened to glance up at the board. *Obstetrics?*

Then Ben remembered Esther favoring her stomach earlier, while Annie's father was drinking his coffee. *Esther must be expecting again already.* It struck him that Essie Ann, whom he'd held as a newborn—his own flesh-and-blood niece—was only four months old. *Doesn't Zeke have any knowledge of family planning?*

# Chapter 21

Jesse noticed Yonie walking out on Queen Road with a girl who was not at all Amish. Of course, this being a warm, sunny day, a long walk with a pretty girl was in order at Yonie's age—*if* the girl weren't English. Jesse was wound up from his visit with Esther and Annie—and seeing Ben Martin there, too. He was tempted to pull the horse over and confront his son. *Ach, where will it all end?*

Yonie spotted him and waved, but Jesse also noticed the redness creeping up from his neck into his face. "Hullo there, Pop!" Yonie called, sounding a bit too flippant for Jesse's liking. But he knew better than to do anything more than wave back and smile. It wouldn't do to rile up that one—not the way the brethren were all in a tizzy about losing several young men to the world here lately. No, he'd keep his peace, bite his lip, and trust for the best.

But Annie, what another story *she* was. He wished he knew what to do. Sighing, he thought of Ben Martin and wondered why on earth he'd come back, trying to pass himself off as Isaac.

The whole thing was wild horse feathers, and Annie should know it. He divided his frustration between Annie's Ben and Yonie's girlfriend—and if she didn't look like the daughter of one of their neighbors, the Zimmermans! *Yonie and Dory—puh!*

*These young bucks and their girls*, he thought, wishing something could be done to eliminate all the nonsense the running-around years served up. Several fathers had wanted to address this subject in recent months, but Bishop Andy had said repeatedly, "It is our way." And that was that.

Truth be known, in Jesse's mind, the knowledge that he was the Lord God's second choice for preacher was ever before him. And he'd nearly convinced himself that was why he'd failed to rein in Annie . . . and evidently Yonie, too.

Annie was worried sick about Essie—scared she might lose her baby. This, along with Daed's reaction to Ben, continued to plague her. She was sure Ben's presence in the community would drive a greater wedge between herself and Daed. Yet why should she care? Hadn't she already cut herself off by not submitting?

She stewed till she was nearly woozy, wondering if Ben and Essie had arrived safely at the nearby hospital, worried that she may have actually caused Essie's pains somehow. Esther had become entirely too upset at the mention of Isaac, and Annie realized she could have handled things far better. *Was I too pushy?*

Annie second-guessed the whole thing while she walked the length of the upstairs with fussy Essie Ann. Now and then, she looked in on Zach and John, always mindful of John's breathing, making sure he was not close to having another asthma attack. Essie reminded her often that the coming of spring and summer were hard on John. *There's something difficult about the changing of the seasons*, she decided, thinking of Cousin Julia's children, as well. In April, James and Molly had had trouble adjusting to daylight saving time. Annie shook her head, thankful that the People did not switch over from fast time to slow time. No, staying the same was the best way to be.

Essie Ann's head popped up off Annie's shoulder again and she began to cry. "Jah, it's all right, little one. . . . Mamma will be home soon." She hoped that was true, because this one would be needing some nourishment here before long, and there was nothing worse than a hungry nursing baby without its mother.

She stroked Essie Ann's soft head, sliding her hand down to caress the baby's neck, feeling the little wrinkles. "You're all right," she whispered. "Now go back to sleep."

Thinking that rocking might do the trick, she carried her to the big rocker in Essie's bedroom, glancing in Laura's room and seeing that she'd fallen asleep with a book on her chest. "Such dear ones," she whispered, and as she patted the baby, she thought of her father's argument regarding Zeke. Why hadn't Isaac's brother recognized him?

*Because he's not in his right mind*, Annie thought, but then reconsidered. Who says Zeke didn't recognize Ben? Not by name, maybe, but in a different sort of way. After all, hadn't Zeke been drawn to Ben? Sure he was. And Zeke rarely made friends with anyone. Maybe the whole unfathomable incident—his brother returning as an Englischer—had stirred up something awful in Zeke's mind, compounding his problems.

Annie closed her eyes just as Esther often did, addressing the Lord of heaven and earth, less sheepish about it each time she did. "O Lord God, I ask that you hear my prayer. Thank you for bringing Isaac back—to all of us—and may it be possible for the truth of his identity to be received by the very ones who need him most. For this I am most grateful, dear Lord. Amen."

An undeniable sense of peace filled the room, and she basked in it, aware now that the sweet baby in her arms had gone limp with sleep. Not willing to take any chances with Essie Ann's awaking, Annie continued to gently rock, feeling the weight of this little one, thinking of all the good things the Lord Jesus, as Essie called the Son of God, had brought into her life. *All the blessings, jah, that's how Essie says it these days.*

She knew Julia saw things the same way. Blessings were a direct gift from the hand of the Father to His dear children. So if that was true, was Ben Martin—well . . . Isaac—exactly that? A divine blessing?

Smiling, she leaned her head back, resting in the truth, if that's what it was. *All things work together for good,* she thought, recalling Ben's words yet again. Why did that Scripture keep coming to her mind? Annie didn't know, but she knew her heart was more open to the things both Essie and Julia said now than a year ago.

Letting her mind drift to Essie's pregnancy, she remembered her mother having let slip once, to daughter-in-law Sarah Mae, that she heartily believed the Lord God knew she would be a better mother of sons than of daughters. Thus, perhaps, the reason why Barbara Zook had birthed six boys and only one Annie.

*What made me think of that?* she wondered. *Would Essie have many more sons and please her husband in that?*

After a time, she heard Ben's car pull up to the back door, and she rose silently to put Essie Ann in her crib, then hurried downstairs to see how Essie was doing. *Let her be all right, Lord,* she pleaded.

Esther was terrified. She had been bleeding for much too long, with intense pains across her abdomen and down her thighs. Suffering with deep dread and complete exhaustion, she longed to be warm . . . craved solitude. She knew her baby was in danger, and she must remain overnight in a hospital, far from her home and Essie Ann, who was dependent upon her for nourishment. "A *wet*

nurse," she had urged upon Ben, explaining how he must rush home to Annie with this request. *"But keep it quiet as to my whereabouts,"* she'd warned him, lest the news spread and the People guess her condition, though she had not come right out and told Ben what that was. Even now, she wanted desperately to protect her poor husband from a possible excommunication, which the brethren would surely put on him for breaking the rules of her shun.

The nurses were helpful and kind, yet she saw how curiously they looked at her. *Because I'm Plain.* She was different, and that was quite clear here in this fancy place, the blank television hovering nearly over her and all the worldly gadgets around her—an electric bed that moved up and down, of all things!

She set to praying for those who would be assisting her during the night, asking God to protect the young life she had conceived, even against the will of the People.

"Complete bed rest" had been the doctor's strict order. Oh, she'd give anything not to have been present at the house when Annie brought her friend over this day! If only there had not been such a constricting in her heart. She had felt instantly nauseated, then she'd stood all the while, serving coffee, wanting to honor the preacher by not sharing the same table.

But to think that Ben might be Isaac had been ever so startling. And if such news was able to upset her so, threatening the life of her precious little one, then what on earth would it do to Zeke? Surely she must not allow herself to fret this way, but, oh, she could not will herself to relax. Every muscle in her body was tense.

*I must rest in the Lord. . . .*

Earlier, after Ben, Preacher Jesse, and Annie had left the house, Esther had set about treating her symptoms with wild yam root—the most bitter of teas—then black haw root bark, homeopathic remedies she much preferred to drugs and this hospital setting. But her efforts had been in vain, and after a time, she had sent Laura to go and fetch Annie, who insisted she go to the hospital.

She could not let this baby die! *O dear Lord, calm my heart and prepare the way for Zeke, I ask. Help this most peculiar news not to disturb my troubled husband any further. . . .*

A couple hours later, when the telephone rang next to her bed, Esther scarcely knew enough to pick it up. But one of the nurses was on hand and did so for her. "Yes, Esther's right here. I'll let you speak with her."

The nurse covered the phone with her hand and said, "It's someone named Ben, calling about your baby at home."

*Let it be good news.* . . . She took the phone from the nurse. "Hullo?"

"Esther, I'm calling for Annie. She's with your children." Ben went on to say that a neighbor of Julia's had driven to the house to nurse Essie Ann in Esther's absence. "Annie's hoping this is all right with you."

"Oh my, yes." *I can trust Julia.* "It was so kind of you to let me know." She felt truly relieved and ever so strange speaking to Ben as though he were family.

"Annie doesn't want you to worry, Esther. She's comfortable taking care of the children and the house for as long as necessary."

"Jah, I know she'll do just fine."

He said a few more very considerate things to her before saying good-bye.

Though deeply grateful for their help, Esther could not stop the flow of tears, and as she wept, she prayed. *May your will be done, O Lord.*

# Chapter 22

$B$en didn't like to think about Annie all alone at Esther's with four little children, managing supper preparations on her own, though it appeared that young Laura was a willing and eager assistant.

Helping Julia set the table as Irvin arrived home, Ben was impressed by her abilities. His own mom was not so keen on putting on a big spread, or cooking in general, except for holidays or special occasions. Typically, she was much more happy having Dad get takeout. His standing joke was that he was the food-getter.

*Happy is the man who marries a cook,* Ben thought.

Irvin kissed Julia soundly on the lips, then hugged James and Molly when they came running to greet him.

"Hello, Ben! How are things?" Irvin moved to the sink and washed up.

"Interesting," he said, glancing at Julia, who'd already heard the news regarding Esther, though he'd remained mum about his more personal news. "I happened to run into Annie by the old covered bridge yesterday."

Scrubbing his hands, Irvin turned and grinned. "Really now. What a coincidence!"

Ben smiled, too. James and Molly were getting settled into their chairs.

"I'm concerned about Esther. How's she doing?" Julia asked, carrying a platter of roast beef and baby onions to the table. She quickly filled Irvin in on the events of the day.

"When I left the hospital, she seemed to be in less pain and was resting," Ben said. He mentioned having called her later, at Annie's request, regarding the arrangement for Essie Ann.

"I'm glad Esther knows about the wet nurse. She shouldn't be worrying about her little one tonight." Julia paused. "Did the doctor give any indication how long Esther would be in?"

"Overnight is my understanding," Ben replied.

"I'll visit her first thing tomorrow, then," Julia said.

Ben nodded. "I think Annie would appreciate it. She'll be busy with the Hochstetler children."

Julia's eyes twinkled. "Well, why not give her a hand, Ben?"

He smiled at her. "I just might."

After the meal, when Irvin had finished helping in the kitchen and the children were off for their baths, Ben welcomed Irvin's company.

These had been a strange couple of days, and he needed to share his news with someone who might offer further wisdom. Someone whom he particularly respected, like Irvin.

As concisely as possible, Ben filled him in on having been told in Kentucky of his adoption.

Irvin listened quietly, nodding his head, his eyes registering empathy. But when Ben finally shared his newfound suspicion that he and Zeke's missing brother were one and the same, Irvin's eyebrows shot up. He scrutinized Ben for a moment, as if wondering if perhaps the young man were pulling his leg. "My, that's quite a leap." Irvin ran his hand through his hair.

"Isn't it, though?" Ben chuckled. "I still haven't had the time to fully digest it." He showed Irvin the magazine cover he'd carried in his wallet since last Christmas. "One thing is certain: Annie's painting led me to come here last winter. And it was also Annie who put it all together about my family history." He shared openly about the strange visions he had had since learning of his adoption, and of his own gradual realization that he was indeed who Annie had said.

"How does Jesse Zook take to this news, assuming Annie told him?"

Ben inhaled. "He doesn't buy it."

Irvin considered this. "Well, there are ways to *prove* that you're Isaac, you know. If you are, that is."

Ben nodded. He'd already thought of DNA tests, which were the obvious means to him, though they would no doubt sound like English mumbo jumbo to Jesse Zook. Likely the preacher would have to approve Zeke undergoing such a test with him.

"I would be willing, if it comes to that," Ben said. "But I'm not ready to push it yet." He paused, feeling tired. "Going from being the Martins' son to finding out that I might have been born here in Amish country has been a jolt to me, no question."

"So what will you do now?" Irvin asked.

"Take things one day at a time . . . if you don't mind letting me stay on a while. I'll pay you room and board—I sure don't expect a handout."

"Oh, we can work out the details later. Not a problem."

Ben thanked Irvin profusely, then excused himself for bed. He had to tread lightly, he believed, especially where Annie's family was concerned. Claiming his identity outright could blow up in their faces.

Yet there was no evidence of hesitation on Annie's part this time. The idea that something had changed in the way she viewed their relationship was both exciting and mystifying, although Ben wondered how long he could hang around before the Amish brethren ran him off again.

*Time will tell.*

❖

Zeke was having a horrible night. Up and down, from his bed to the window he went, missing Esther, wishing for something to grab ahold of while he slept. *An extra pillow would do.*

He wandered out to the common living area and found a throw pillow on the sofa. Carrying it back to his own bed, he got in and pressed the pillow to his chest, all the while imagining Esther's supple and soft body. *I must get well. Must get out of this place and return home, and soon.* He felt desperately lost without his wife.

He propped his head up on his bed pillow and, still clutching the smaller one to his chest, mulled over his day. A long one to be sure, though not as physically exhausting as getting up with the chickens and plowing or planting for hours on end. Still, it had been stressful, with several sessions today including other troubled folk, some more disturbed than he, going around the circle talking about feelings—supposedly suppressed. His doctor had also talked of upping his anti-depression medication, which Zeke wasn't happy about—not that he had much say around there. *Will I ever be well enough to return to the People . . . to my family?*

By the way Esther had walked out on him when she visited, he wasn't too sure if she'd even have him back. But no, why should he think such a thing? He was in charge—always had been. She had no say, under God . . . nor under her husband.

But she *had* been somewhat lippy, standing up to him toward the end. Her attitude had stung him. He wouldn't allow his woman to have the upper hand next visit.

He gripped the pillow and began weeping silently. "Esther, my Esther, ach, how I miss you," he whispered into the darkness.

Ben lay awake as one childhood recollection after another pervaded his brain, as if the floodgates had fully opened. He squelched a laugh, recalling his rough, dry feet as a boy and his fascination with peeling thin layers of the skin—in strips—off the callouses on his big toes until his toes started to bleed. His father belittled him for it, but his older brother thought the habit quite funny. It was Mamma, though, who lovingly cleaned his wounds of the slivers of wood and dirt that sometimes found their way inside.

He couldn't resist the urge to reach down and touch the pads of his big toes, wondering if they were larger than they should be. He didn't feel anything unusual—no indication he had scarred himself for life. He did have one scar on the ball of his left foot, though he wasn't sure how he'd gotten that.

*Scars . . .* He wondered about his parents' decision to keep his adoption quiet. *How much better would it have been, knowing as a child what I know now?*

There had been plenty of adopted kids in his life while growing up. One girl in particular had parents who had made a scrapbook of the day they'd brought her home to be their own. All he'd ever had was his peach stone, although he didn't even know that was part of his secret past until recently.

Another memory popped into his mind, clearer than the rest. A summer day when his father had spent all afternoon in the barn "a-wrestlin' with the angels," according to Mamma.

"More like he's battling the devil," Zeke had spouted off to Mamma, who'd told Zeke to wash out his mouth with soap. But Zeke had muttered on the way to the sink, "Dat's in trouble with the brethren," insisting in a whisper that he'd seen the bishop and the preachers coming down the road, dressed in black.

Mamma had said, "Hogwash," but Zeke had kept talking about the new minister, Jesse Zook, who'd come "talkin' to Dat a-plenty. Before *and* after he got the preacher's lot."

Mamma had shushed him. And Isaac remembered sitting in the far corner of the kitchen, wondering why their father had skipped Mamma's dinner and would probably be breathing the same air as the mules all night.

Had someone else caught him kissing the peach girl?

611

Slipping out of bed, shaking his head at the memory, Ben found the print of Annie's painting in his wallet, folded so neatly along the same crease, he could see it was in some danger of tearing. Going to the window, he held it up in the moonlight, amazed again that even after all these years the peach stone held some significance to her, as well.

He placed the picture back on the bureau and reluctantly returned to bed, not tired enough to sleep. Tomorrow he would go and check on Annie and the children, and spend the day helping her with farm chores—the pigs, whatever was needed—if she wished. Regardless of his determination to spare her further trouble, he longed to see her again.

No, he *needed* to see her.

Jesse knew he'd be dead tired at the predawn milking, but still he sat in the dark of the kitchen, drinking yet another cup of coffee. He craved time alone and was thankful for Barbara's willingness to retire for the night without him hours ago. Ben's return perplexed him no end. He wracked his brain, going over the events of the day and evaluating his memory of Isaac Hochstetler— what the youngest child of Ichabod had looked like. No unusual features nor distinguishing marks that Jesse recalled. For a moment, he realized how useful even a single photograph of Isaac might be, though, of course, such images were forbidden.

He contemplated again young Isaac's face. Daniel's younger boy was like all the other boys in the community—quick on his feet, mouthy at times, worked hard when told to, and played hard with his puppy dog and older brother. As for looks—the same deep brown eyes as Ben Martin's, that was certain, and light hair . . . much like Annie's.

But did this alone make him Isaac? Jesse didn't accept that for a minute. The fact that Ben looked to be about the right age wasn't especially significant, since any number of young men were just as old. So what was it about Ben that drove Annie to decide he was her long-lost friend? Was it merely a ploy to continue their courting? *Surely that's what we've got here . . . a desperate attempt.*

Exhausted now, he carried the cup over to the sink, left it there without rinsing it, and padded up the stairs.

He found his wife sitting up in bed. "Ach, Jesse . . . Jesse, I had another dream."

He went to her and cradled her in his arms. "What was it, dear?"

"Isaac . . . and he wasn't just back, like he'd never been taken. This time, it was much more than that." She started to weep, and he feared she might awaken their sons.

"Shh, now, talk to me, love. Talk to your ol' Jesse. . . ."

She sighed. Then, after wiping her eyes on the sleeve of her cotton night-gown, she told him. "I dreamt the most peculiar thing . . . that Isaac was our own. Oh, Jesse, our very own boy. We'd lost him, just as Daniel and Mary had, and bore the terrible pain of it all, and then he was found. Found, I tell you." She wept like a broken-hearted little child.

*What on earth?* He held her even closer, stroking her long, long hair, whispering, "All's well, love. Simply trust that all is well."

# Chapter 23

Not because she was terribly interested, but because she wanted to be polite, Louisa went with Courtney to the Park Meadows Mall in search of the "perfect present" for Courtney's sister's birthday. "You know how important turning sweet sixteen is, remember?" Courtney joked as they strolled through the vast food court, complete with river-rock fireplace and wood beams, creating a lodgelike interior.

But at the mention of the milestone birthday, Louisa let her mind drift to the Amish tradition of *Rumschpringe*, the years between turning sixteen and making the lifelong promise to the Amish church and to God.

"What would you think if your sister started running around now that she's sixteen?" Louisa asked.

"Berit already does." Courtney laughed. "We all did, from about twelve or thirteen on. Don't you remember?"

"I didn't get into guys till my last year of high school."

"Oh, that's right. Late bloomer."

Louisa shook her head. "Even so, I was pretty stupid. There's way more to life than all that. I wish I'd known before I gave so much of myself away."

"So you're judging *yourself* now?" Courtney wrinkled her nose and picked up the pace, her attitude changing.

Louisa kicked herself mentally. *Keep your mouth shut, Lou.*

They spent the rest of the afternoon going from store to store, window-shopping mostly. At one point, Courtney stopped to admire a skimpy skirt and halter top on a headless mannequin. "Hey, I could see you in this," she said casually.

"Yeah," Louisa said, sarcastically. "Too much of me."

"Seriously, it's so you."

"No it's not." *Not anymore.*

Courtney was visibly put out by the time they stopped for espresso and chai tea. "Maybe you should just go back, return to the simple hick life you crave so much, Louisa. Ever think of that?"

"All the time."

"So what's keeping you here?"

Louisa tried to laugh it off, but it wasn't funny anymore. Courtney evidently wanted a fight.

"Look," Courtney continued, "if you think everyone's messed up because they don't see things the way you do—the enlightened new you—then why do you bother with us pagans?"

Louisa wanted to set her straight, to tell her she *did* care about her, whether she understood her need for the simple life or not. But before she could say anything, Courtney's eyes began filling with tears and her pouty lower lip started to quiver.

"Hey, Court . . . what's wrong?"

Courtney struggled to compose herself, pulling a tissue from her small handbag. "You'll never believe it."

"Sure I will. Try me."

"The absolute worst possible thing . . ."

"You're not pregnant, are you?" Louisa asked, hoping she was wrong.

Courtney snorted with disdain. "Bingo."

Louisa studied Courtney, wondering if she was trying to put one over on her, but Courtney was definitely not kidding. "Oh, Court . . . does anybody else know?"

"You're the first."

"Who's the father?" Louisa wondered if it was Courtney's housemate, Jared. Courtney shrugged and shook her head. "I'm not exactly sure."

"Oh man . . ."

Louisa's mind jumped ahead. She began to ask, "So what are you planning to do?" but the firm set of Courtney's expression caused her to stop short. She felt sudden concern.

"You're not going to—"

"Abort? Oh, you bet I am."

Louisa grimaced. "Oh, Court . . . wait . . . think about this."

"You think I haven't?"

"Of course . . . I didn't mean that." Louisa realized it was nothing more than common sense that had kept her from being in Courtney's shoes right now. Would she have had a similar attitude had this happened to her? It was possible. At least *before* her talks with Julia and her sojourn in Amish country.

Louisa tried again. "I'm just saying you could marry some guy who likes kids. Or be a single mom like a zillion other women. I'll help you. I'll go to birthing classes with you. Baby-sit. Whatever you need."

Courtney wiped her eyes. "What I really need is for this problem to go away."

Louisa sighed. "It's not just a problem, Court. It's a life."

"Yeah, mine. Listen, I don't know why I told you. I knew you would judge me."

"That's where you're wrong. I'd like to help."

Louisa wanted to say so much more. But she knew it would do no good to charge ahead, not with Courtney being so defensive. She changed her tactic. "I love you, Court, no matter what, okay? But can I tell you how my visit to Annie's started me going in a whole different direction? You remember last fall, when I was getting ready to marry Michael?"

Courtney nodded, wadding up the tissue in her hand.

"There I was . . . by all appearances I had everything—money, education, a handsome fiancé—but inside I was empty. Something was missing."

"Like what?" Courtney asked wryly. "Horses and buggies? Aprons and bad hair?"

Louisa grinned at her friend but shook her head. "No. Truth. Meaning. God. I didn't even know it, but I was on a faith-quest. Sounds pretty wild coming from me, I know, but it's true."

It was obvious by the disbelief on her face that Courtney didn't get it. But Louisa forged ahead. "You know, when I canceled the wedding and left here, it probably seemed that I was running *away* from love. But I was really running toward it. My friend Julia told me faith and love are really similar. You put your trust in the person you marry, giving yourself to them, knowing they will keep their vows. Love for a lifetime, no matter what."

Courtney snorted again. "Tell that to my dad. Divorced—again."

"Well, it's not a perfect analogy, since people aren't perfect. But God is, and I'm beginning to see that I can trust Him." Louisa hoped she was making some sense. She talked about God's Son, too, saying the name that was so often flung from Courtney's own lips, but Louisa spoke it with a reverence that seemed to put a curious light in Courtney's eyes. "All I'm saying is how can you refuse someone who loves you that much?"

Louisa paused, noticing the glints of tears in Courtney's eyes again. Then she added, "How can *anyone* say no to that?"

"So you must believe that this Jesus was divine or whatever?"

Louisa nodded slowly, realizing that she did, indeed, believe this. "Yes . . . I guess I do. But I have a lot more to learn." She wouldn't push. Not Julia, nor anyone else, for that matter, could have pushed *her* before she was ready. She'd had to come to the point where she longed for more than life had dished up. And she had been so ready while sitting in Julia's sunroom, eager for much more than Julia had time to give her that day. But since coming home, she'd started reading the New Testament. *Funny, my parents don't even own one!*

Courtney poked at her purchase absentmindedly, squinting as she tightened the tie strings on the designer shoe bag. "Maybe I'm making a mistake."

Louisa brightened. "Really?"

"Chill out. I'm talking about whether or not to keep these funky shoes for Berit's birthday."

Louisa sighed. Just when she'd thought maybe Courtney was seeing a glimpse of something significant. "Maybe we can talk more later."

"Later? Like when?"

"Whenever you want." She meant it.

They got up and walked out of the mall, their pace snail-like in comparison to the way they'd begun the hunt earlier. Louisa felt tense, wishing she might somehow explain the sort of freedom Courtney really needed without coming across as condescending.

"Hey, later," Courtney called to her as they pushed open the glass doors on the east side of the food court.

"Okay. Call me anytime."

Courtney gave a fakey little smile and hurried off to her red Porsche.

*Great*, Louisa thought, feeling as though she'd failed big time. Clicking her remote, she hurried toward her car. Once inside, she checked her Palm for messages and was not too surprised to see three text messages from Michael. "Uh-oh," she whispered. Backing out of the parking space, she promised herself to be a true friend to him.

She hurried home, looking forward to starting work on her painting of Muffin for Annie, knowing how pleased she would be. As for Sam, she was eager to write him again, although she would be careful not to encourage him too much, even though she really missed him.

❖

The bishop had a big talk on about his youth, telling the brethren gathered in his barn about the gazebo his father had built "with all us boys helpin' out." With so much going on in his family, Jesse found Bishop Andy's rambling discourse annoying, but he tried to appear interested.

Andy continued, "There was the homemade seesaw, ya know. Did any of yous have one in your backyards?"

Deacon Byler nodded, and by the look on his face it was rather apparent he, too, was wondering where on earth all this talk of childhood was leading. Preacher Moses, too. At least they weren't talking about Zeke. Or Ichabod, for that matter, as Jesse had already warned that the wayward one might be coming to town, much to the brethren's dismay. Jesse just wished he knew when.

*The news the bones aren't Isaac's should change his mind,* Jesse thought. *But what if my second letter doesn't reach him in time?*

The notion that Jesse had brought this on himself nagged like so many July mosquitoes. Yet something in him wanted to lay eyes on the man who'd renounced the lot, to see what the years had done to one so proud. And, come to think of it, he was exactly the person to declare Ben Martin an imposter, too.

"So, now we have this here problem with young Yonie Zook," Bishop Andy was saying, having switched the conversation abruptly. This brought Jesse back to attention right quick. "Your boy's got himself a rip-roarin' business, I'm sure you know, driving Amish round town and farther. Just what do you plan to do 'bout it?"

"Let it play itself out, that's what," Jesse replied, anxious to move on to other matters.

"Aw, let the boy have some fun," Moses said. "He'll get it out of his system sooner or later."

"Later ain't so gut, though," the deacon pointed out.

"I daresay he'll get himself so rich he'll decide he wants more than that one car of his." Bishop Andy squared his old, rickety body. "Ain't it what you think, Jesse?"

"Could be." Jesse didn't like the pressure. This was his son they were discussing, after all.

"So . . . while you're thinking on that, here's another predicament . . . in the same family." Here the bishop pushed up his glasses and blinked his eyes through them at Jesse before pulling a rolled-up magazine from his back pocket. "Here's proof we've got us some folk watchin' awful close on your household, Preacher Zook."

Jesse hadn't thought *this* was coming and braced himself for the bishop's remarks about Annie's art plastered on the cover of a worldly magazine.

"Just lookee here . . . the preacher's daughter has herself a talent. Don't that beat all?"

The men leaned in to see. The deacon was first to nod and then backed away, as if to say he'd already heard the murmurings from a bunch of the farmers who'd circulated the thing amongst themselves. But Old Moses kept looking at it, seemingly stunned. "What the world did she paint such a picture for?"

"That's what I kept wondering," Jesse piped up, "when first I saw it."

Bishop pointed to the swing. "Word has it that old swing got itself hung up again somehow, just here lately."

Jesse owned up to having given it to his daughter. "She asked Yonie to help her. It sure seemed mighty important to her to get it right back up there, and on the selfsame big branch—just like in the picture." He looked at the painting as it shook in the bishop's feeble old hands.

"I daresay we've got ourselves a dilemma." Bishop tapped on the magazine with his gnarled hand.

"What's that?" Deacon Byler wanted to know.

Moses tugged hard on his beard. "Jah, what?"

"Truth be told, she's mighty good at it," Bishop Andy said, "and if some-one—well, the right person, or the *wrong* one—happens to see this here work of your daughter's, Jesse, she'll be pulled out of the People quick-like, I fear."

Jesse hadn't thought of that.

"How do you plan to rein her in before such a thing happens?" asked the bishop.

"Well, I've been workin' on that for some time now."

Old Moses harrumphed. "Sure don't seem so, not with her livin' over there with our shunned one, Esther Hochstetler."

Jesse didn't have much to defend himself with, because everything the brethren had said was true. And their eyes—all three sets of them—seemed more like fingers pointing his way. He'd failed the People. No, he'd failed his own kin.

*Yonie and Annie . . . two free spirits, exactly alike.* But by the way the men were looking at him, he knew he best be saying something. Anything would be better than this awkward silence. He cleared his throat, thinking of Ben Martin's return. That would get the attention off his family. "Well, Annie's got herself a fancy friend, if I'm so bold to say. And this here fellow claims to be Isaac Hochstetler." He watched their faces, and Old Moses teetered on his chair.

"Oh, now, that's the next thing to profanity, declaring such a thing," Deacon Byler asserted. "Everybody knows Ichabod's boy is long gone."

Jesse shrugged. "'Course without his bones—"

"As for his claim," Moses interrupted, "is he serious?"

"Seems so."

"Timing's mighty odd," the deacon said. "What with Ichabod a-maybe comin'."

"More upheaval for the People," Bishop agreed, sadly shaking his head.

Jesse wished he'd kept mum.

"Well, if he's my kin, surely I'd know if it's him or not," Moses said. "Why don't you bring the boy over to me tomorrow?"

"I'll see what I can do," Jesse said.

The bishop rolled the magazine back up and asked if they all wanted to go inside and have something to wet their whistles, but Jesse thanked him and said he needed to head off to find Ben.

The others followed Andy into the house while Jesse headed for his horse and carriage, wondering why on earth he'd said anything. Then again, maybe having Zeke's uncle Moses look Ben over good would reveal this Ben to be the charlatan he was and put an end to Annie's foolishness once and for all. If so, maybe finally the preacher's daughter would join church.

# *Chapter 24*

Annie stood in the cellar, holding the baby and watching the old washing machine dance across the floor . . . *chug-a-lug, chugga*. She'd taken the liberty of doing another load of wash, even though it was Tuesday, being extra careful when feeding the wet clothes through the pale rubber rollers at the rinsing stage. She'd heard of women getting their fingers caught in the wringers and for a fleeting moment wondered who would take care of Esther's children if such an awful thing happened.

She had carried Essie Ann's cradle down here, keeping a close watch on her while Laura was upstairs with Zach and John. Annie hoped Esther might return home today. If so, having some of the laundry done would be one less thing for her to think about. Annie knew she ought not hold her breath for Essie to come home for sure today, because she'd seen how terribly pained and pale she had been yesterday, and the memory of it dulled the joy she had experienced while walking in the meadow with Ben.

"My dear Isaac," she whispered, still marveling at the truth but also worried about what would happen next. Would the People accept her beloved as the grown kidnapped boy? Was there any hope that Zeke might recognize him now, troubled as he was? She shook her head in dismay. From what she'd heard, Zeke could barely recognize his own shadow these days.

"'Tis a quandary." The words brought Essie Ann's little head up and she looked at Annie with a sweet, sleepy expression. "You know I'm talking 'bout someone, don't you?" She picked up Essie Ann and kissed her soft forehead. "Your uncle Isaac, that's who."

621

She heard heavy footsteps overhead. Someone was walking across the kitchen. Was it Ben returning already? He'd helped her all morning, bless his heart—slopping hogs and carrying wood for the old stove. He'd even shown an endearingly gentle patience with Zach and John. What's more, he'd offered to hold the baby for a while.

Her heart stirred at the possibility that he'd come back. *I must be in love,* she realized.

Opening the cellar door, she was startled to see her father. "Oh, hullo, Daed. What brings you here?" Annie stepped up into the kitchen.

Her father eyed her with the baby, then looked at Laura playing with the boys on the kitchen floor. "Isn't Esther at home?"

"No. But she will be." She thought she best not say where Essie had gone. She hadn't been instructed not to tell, but even so she didn't want to be the reason Zeke got in trouble.

"Is Ben here?" he asked, then quickly explained, "I stopped at the Rancks', but Julia told me he'd come here to help with chores."

"He did, but he went over to the harness shop. He's got friends—"

"I gathered that," he interrupted.

Laura wandered over, looking up at them. "Mamma's awful sick, did ya hear?"

Annie held her breath. *Don't say more . . . oh, please be still.* She tried to get Laura's attention, wishing she'd return to her brothers. "It's all right, dear one. Mamma will be just fine."

A frown grew on her father's face. "Esther's ill, yet she's gone from the house?"

"Jah" was all she said.

"Annie," her father said. "Time to fess up. What's goin' on here? Where's Esther?"

Laura answered for her. "Mr. Ben took her away . . . in his car."

"Where?" Daed's voice thundered through Annie, though he had not raised his voice.

"To the hospital. She's ever so sick."

Her father's harsh and knowing gaze held her own. Had he guessed their secret?

The baby began to whimper, and Annie moved past her father, asking Laura to come hold her sister a bit. Laura beamed at the chance to help, sitting right down on the table bench and opening her arms for the baby.

"There, now, cradle her gently the way you always do." Annie stayed near, watching, hoping her father might head on over to find Ben.

"I'm doin' all right here . . . really. If it's Ben you're lookin' for, you can catch up with him if you hurry."

But her father was smarter than that. "What're you hidin'?"

She felt her heart pounding through her apron.

"What's-a-matter with Esther?"

Laura piped up. "She's got a pain in her tummy."

Annie patted Laura's knee. "Jah, but I believe she's goin' to be better right quick." She bit her lip, trying to keep her composure.

Jesse leaned on the sink, glancing around the kitchen. "Annie Zook, you are the most difficult child ever."

"I've disappointed you, I know," she admitted.

"First your art . . . now this Ben Martin. And whatever you're not tellin' me about Esther." He shook his head, clearly put out.

"Ben is Isaac—of that I'm sure," she said, hoping to distract him from Essie's possible miscarriage.

"We'll know something today 'bout that rubbish." He turned to go. "If he's Isaac, then so be it." His shoulders drooped as he headed for the door.

Annie trembled. What did Daed mean?

Essie Ann began to cry again, and just then Annie heard a car pull into the drive. "Right on time," she said of the wet nurse, wondering if her father might accuse the Englischer of trespassing or worse.

*Lord in heaven, help us all!*

Jesse was exasperated. First Annie had acted for all the world like there was something to hide, and then a strange English woman came driving in like she was expected somehow, hurrying around the back of the house and going inside without knocking! What was going on at Esther's?

When he arrived at the harness shop, Ben Martin was there as Annie had said, standing around with several Amish farmers and Sam Glick. Jesse watched the two of them talking together like they were old friends. He'd heard Sam had left his father's house and was staying in Gordonville with a former Amish family, looking to ease himself away from the People and into the world with some self-appointed missionaries, as they called themselves. The very notion further darkened his mood.

Jesse didn't go directly over to speak with Ben; he first went about his business, taking care to pick up a custom-made draft bridle prior to seeking out the man his daughter was obviously much too fond of.

"Hullo again, Ben." He nodded to both men. "Sam."

"How're you doin', Preacher?" Sam said, offering a greeting before saying a quick good-bye to Ben and turning toward the door.

Because they were momentarily alone, Jesse decided not to mince words.

"Why did you come back here, Ben? The truth. Did you come to steal my daughter away?"

Ben looked shocked. "No, sir."

"Young man, I don't believe for one minute that you're Isaac Hochstetler. For you to make such a claim only confirms my suspicions about your character. Your return can only muddle my daughter's mind. Do you understand?"

"I do, sir."

"Don't you dare take her away from me. You left once. You can leave again."

"I don't want to cause trouble, but I truly believe—"

"Believe what?"

"That I *might* be Isaac."

Jesse shook his head with disgust. "Are you willing to put your belief to the test?"

Ben nodded.

"Fine, then." Jesse explained what he had in mind. When he was finished, Ben looked startled.

"Moses, you say?"

"That's right. It was his idea to have you visit him. He thinks he can identify you. Seems foolish to me, 'specially since Zeke would know better, but he's not . . . feeling so well these days." Jesse didn't know why he was telling Ben this. Likely Annie had already told him about Zeke's mental state.

"I'm willing to meet with Moses," Ben said, stepping back slightly. "But I want you to know something. I *do* remember growing up here. I remember going to a Christmas play at the one-room school, where my brother, Zeke, played Joseph. I remember you and the other brethren coming often to my father's house, too. Things like that . . . and more."

Jesse flinched. This was quite true. Especially after Daniel shunned the ordinance of preacher, he and the other ministers came in hopes of persuading Daniel to follow through with God's calling. Jesse was suddenly curious about how much of those visits Isaac . . . or *Ben* . . . recalled. But he sure wouldn't stand here in this public place to inquire. "I'll get myself over to the Rancks'. Then maybe you can"—it irked him to suggest it—"drive us over to Zeke's uncle's place."

"Sure. When?"

"Tomorrow, at first light."

Ben agreed, but there was more on Jesse's mind. "Let's get something else straight. Even if you *were* Amish, you're English now. And my daughter *belongs* in the church." Jesse's neck hairs stood on end. "Promise me—no matter what—you won't take her away from her people."

Ben's face fell.

Jesse persisted. "Didn't you say you don't wish to cause trouble?"

The young man nodded.

"Well, then?"

"I have no intention of causing trouble," Ben said at last.

"Good man," Jesse said, somewhat satisfied. He tipped his head in farewell, plopped on his straw hat, and headed quickly for the door.

# Chapter 25

*I should have stayed in Kentucky*, Ben thought, wishing Sam hadn't run off. He could use a friend about now. After the heated conversation with Jesse, Ben's head was reeling. *"Your return can only muddle my daughter's mind."*

Had he made yet another mistake? Caught up in a storm of emotions, longing to see Annie again and yearning to discover the full truth about his previous life, he realized he no longer had a choice. He had to see this thing through. *Am I or am I not Isaac?*

And what about Annie? Didn't she have the right to make her own choices? But no, not in her father's thinking. It was fairly clear she had been ruled with an iron rod, though so far she'd managed to escape it unscathed.

He'd forgotten how lovely she was, in every way. When he was with her, the entire world seemed to dissolve to nothing. Could he simply walk away from her because her father objected to him?

*One thing at a time*, he decided, heading back to his car. Tomorrow's visit with Preacher Moses might put a new spin on the truth for Jesse Zook. Ben was counting on it.

Zeke's head felt tight as he sat thinking about the early afternoon session with one of his several doctors. He couldn't keep track of them all. *Doctors . . . they're helping me, aren't they?* he thought, smiling to himself.

Just then he looked up and saw Irvin Ranck coming in the door. "How'd you make it past the front desk?" he asked, getting up to shake his hand.

"Oh, not to worry. One of my cousins works up there, so she let me in."

Irvin didn't make small talk this time. He simply pulled out his New Testament and began to read aloud. Zeke had no interest in stopping him or putting up a fuss; the sound of the Scripture soothed him, and he found himself rocking a bit to its lyrical rhythm.

Zeke listened quietly when his friend began to speak of God's sovereignty. He wasn't so sure what Irvin was getting at, but he didn't feel resistant today to the man who seemed to live to discuss Scripture.

"God knows the end from the beginning, Zeke. Do you believe that?"

"Why, I'd be a fool not to."

Irvin leaned back in his chair, looking relaxed. "Do you believe God has a plan for each of our lives?"

Well, he didn't know that so much. "Providence is what I believe in. Things happen when God allows 'em, jah."

Irvin nodded. "Mind if I pray for you, Zeke?"

Zeke was startled. "I don't know. . . . What for?"

"I'd like to pray a blessing of healing over you. Is that all right?"

Zeke had never been asked such a thing, and he didn't know why a feisty lump rose in his throat at the idea, but it did. He had to swallow hard, several times, to get his emotions back under control. "Herbs and bed rest are for healin'. And doctors . . ." He grinned. "Doctors are *supposed* to help folk heal. I don't think the Good Lord has much to do with any of that."

Irvin disagreed. "Our heavenly Father created foods and herbs and other good things that aid in our health, just as He gives wisdom to doctors and to the folks who established this place of healing. Wouldn't you agree?"

Zeke was tired and ready to quit pondering the questions and things Irvin seemed bent on saying to him. "Nice of you to visit me," he managed to say, struggling again to compose himself.

Irvin rose and put his hand on Zeke's shoulder. "I'd like to pray for you."

Not sure how to put a stop to it without offending his friend, Zeke relented. The words that came out of Irvin's mouth astonished him.

"Dear heavenly Father, I call upon you in the blessed name of my Lord Jesus to touch my friend Zeke with your healing power. Give him the ability to think and reason clearly, I ask. May he have the desires of his heart . . . to return home to his family, a new man and new creation in you. If it be your will, grant him a fresh start . . . and work a miracle in his life. Amen."

Zeke could not see Irvin for the veil of tears, but he heard him say, "I'll come see you in a few days—and I'll keep praying for you," before he left.

Wanting to shake his hand or give him some indication that he appreciated not only the visit but that mighty fine prayer, Zeke rose and stood at the door, watching Irvin head down the hall.

Annie stood at the window, peering down the empty lane once again. It was coming up close to suppertime and there was still no sign of Essie. Hadn't Ben said she would most likely be at the hospital only one night?

She heated up some of Esther's frozen homemade chicken corn soup for the children—and for herself, too, if she ever settled down enough to want to eat. The woman who'd come to nurse Essie Ann had left enough bottles of mother's milk to tide the baby over for the next couple of feedings. *Des gut*, Annie thought, having felt terribly nervous about being so dependent upon Cousin Julia's neighbor, nice as it was of her to drive over here.

Even though it wasn't appropriate for Ben to be in the house with her with Esther gone, she honestly wished he might return this evening, if only for supper. All day she'd thought of him, wondering how they might convince the brethren of Ben's identity. Truth be told, she was anxious to talk to him about anything, but she didn't expect him and he no doubt felt he was doing her bidding by staying away.

*He's fancy*, she reminded herself, but did it really matter? She hadn't joined church and, at this point, had no plans to—not as eager as she was to resume her art.

*What must the outside world be like?* She wondered how modern folk courted. Did they see each other only on the weekends? Whenever they wished to? Was it wrong in *their* families' eyes to spend time together alone in a house?

She didn't know why she contemplated such things now as she stirred the soup, preparing to fry the cheese sandwiches. Glancing over at the table, she smiled as Laura tried to show Zach how to print his name. John sat in his father's rocking chair, the force of his body keeping the chair going as the baby slept nearby in her cradle. All was well in *this* house.

Within her heart, an idea had sprouted, a way to show Ben her willingness to leave the Amish life for him. A way to prove she was ready to move ahead with their relationship . . . and her art, too.

It might not be best to tell him right out but to show him over the next few days. Hopefully he'd stay around Paradise long enough for the truth of the matter to sink in. She couldn't bear the thought of being without him again. "To think, in discovering who he is, he's found me, too," she whispered.

"What's that you said?" Laura asked, turning to look at Annie.

Quickly she brushed a tear away, hoping the dear girl hadn't seen, though it wouldn't have been the first time Laura had noticed her tears. "Ach, Aunt Annie's talkin' to herself yet again," Annie said, hoping to quell any worry.

Laura was nodding her head. "That's all right—you do that a lot. Though if I had such a good-lookin' beau, I think I'd talk to *him* instead."

Annie wanted to laugh, but she changed the subject to something more appropriate.

"Well, I think it's almost time to eat. Anyone hungry?"

Laura rushed to set the table while Annie quickly grilled the open-faced sandwiches, hoping Essie might sleep in her own bed this night. "Lord, let it be so."

"Now you sound like Mamma," Zach said, still sitting at the table, making backward Z's.

"'Tis a good thing," Laura said, helping wash John's face and hands with a washcloth. "Mamma says we should talk to God all day long."

Annie's heart swelled with love, and she wondered anew how she could walk away from the People she loved so dearly. *Yet if it means a lifetime with Ben . . .*

"Come to the table now," she told the children.

Laura helped John get into his booster chair before sitting down across from Annie. She asked to say the table grace, as had become their new custom, and Annie agreed.

"Where's Mr. Ben eating tonight?" Zach asked afterward.

"I don't know."

"Can he eat with us again?"

"When your mamma's home, maybe," she told him.

Zach grinned, showing his gums. "I hope she gets home right quick. I like him."

*So do I!* Annie hoped her blush wouldn't give her away.

"I like *Mamma*," little John said, his lower lip puckered.

"Aw, I know you miss her." Annie tousled his hair. "She'll be home when she's better." *Dear Lord, please let it be soon.*

"Let's dig in now." She filled each bowl with a generous helping of soup, and as they ate, she tuned her ear to Essie's coming, praying it might be tonight.

# Chapter 26

Esther remembered Julia teaching James and Molly a little song about letting their lights shine for the Lord. *"You in your small corner . . . and I in mine. . . ."*

She didn't know why she thought of this as she lay in her hospital bed. More than anything she wanted to be like a candle in the darkness, yet she viewed her life with Zeke as rather dark and dismal. She longed for her husband to "see the light," to share this freedom from sin and despair she'd experienced since discovering the lover of her soul, as one of the songs sung at Julia's church so aptly expressed.

Her concern for Zeke tugged at her heart as she settled herself in for yet another night away from her little ones and Annie. Oh, she desperately wanted this wee babe, caught between life and death, as much as she had wanted each of her other children. But she knew Zeke would suffer if God saw fit to let this child survive.

*My wounded, defiant husband.*

How could he say he loved her while treating her so? Was his harsh love an extension of his selfishness or another symptom of his disturbed mind?

She would not allow herself to think on how he might be treated by the brethren should their secret be discovered, even at this most precarious moment of her wee one's life. Of course Zeke could be reinstated as a voting church member if he were willing to repent. But their being found out was the sort of thing to set him off again, and she had no desire to cause a wedge between him and the People. He needed time to heal somehow . . . time to become readjusted within the family, too, if and when his release came. *If it be your will, O God.* And surely it was the dear Lord's will to reunite families and to mend broken hearts.

The morning dawned while Jesse finished up the milking with Omar, Luke, and Yonie, the clouds giving way to rain.

"It's makin' down mighty hard," Yonie hollered to Luke at the far end of the barn. "So much for heading over to Gordonville with the hay wagon."

Jesse wondered what his sons had cooked up but didn't ask. Better not to know too much these days, though after talking with the brethren it sure seemed like he ought to be coming down harder on them—especially on Yonie.

Still, sometimes taking a backseat to their bantering was better than saying anything. He carried the fresh milk to the cooler in the milk house.

The minute he was done here and had washed up some, he would head over to Irvin's, then ride with Ben Martin out to Moses' place. He didn't quite know what to make of it, but since talking with Ben, he'd become downright nervous about the meeting. If Annie was right and Ben was Isaac in the flesh, well, then he'd sent Ichabod's son packing back last month. And his headstrong daughter had been seeing the long-lost boy they'd all loved and missed for more than sixteen years. *If* Isaac were truly home.

Regardless of what he'd said to Ben about his being English now, he knew it didn't make sense to run off one of their own. The thought had already given him more than one restless night.

On the other hand, if Annie was off beam and Ben was an imposter, Jesse had already extracted a pledge of sorts that Ben would not take his daughter from the People. Once Old Moses confirmed the truth, Jesse would remind Ben of his promise, and surely if Ben had any trace of integrity left, he'd make for the door. Even if he stayed around, Annie would finally see him for the devious fellow he was, what with all those fake memories he was trotting out at will.

Sighing, Jesse headed for the house to change out of his work clothes, although he was sure to get muddy and wet heading down the road to his cousin's place in the rain. *If I weren't so upset at him, I'd ask Yonie to drive me over to Old Moses' place and be done with it.*

As it was, he'd soon be riding in an Englischer's car, so which was worse?

Scrubbing up in the kitchen sink, he noticed Barbara staring at him. "I'll be eatin' breakfast right quick," he said before she could speak.

"Oh, you off somewhere on this ugly day?" she asked, coming to him.

"Got me someplace to be, jah."

"Well, I hope you don't get indigestion like sometimes."

He sensed there was more than thoughtfulness behind her attention.

He turned toward her. "You all right, love?"

She nodded, but tears welled up in her pretty eyes.

"Aw, what's-a-matter?" He took her in his arms. "It's not one of those bad dreams again, is it?"

She struggled but could not speak.

"It sure must be." He kissed her cheek and held her even nearer, glad his elderly parents hadn't come over yet for breakfast.

When she'd managed to compose herself, she wiped her eyes on her apron hem. "No, not a dream. But livin' life without our girl . . . well, it's worse than any nightmare, I daresay." She began sobbing.

He should've guessed she was missing Annie. Jesse shook his head, feeling awful sorry, too, but not enough to say he'd go and seek her out again. What would his poor wife do if she knew of Annie's hopes for Ben Martin? He didn't have the heart to reveal his latest news—not till Old Moses had a chance to weigh in on the matter.

Even so he kindly waited, hoping he could calm his wife with his arms around her. "I'm no prophet, but things are bound to improve, don't ya think?"

She breathed in, her shoulders rising. "Annie surely knows better, but then, so does Yonie. Word has it he's seeing a worldly girl."

There it was again: the judgment of God in those blue eyes. Not as steely as what he'd seen in the bishop's, but mighty close. Truth was, he had failed as a father on two counts, and two out of seven was a terrible proportion in the Lord God's eyes . . . and those of the People.

"Yonie's in the midst of running round." His words sounded hollow even to himself.

"Been mighty long enough, I'd say."

"Jah, but boys . . . they tend to take longer to get all that rowdiness out."

"I s'pose, but still. Everybody watches the preacher's children," she said, pausing. "What's your excuse for Annie?"

Where his daughter was concerned, he was more wary. She'd demonstrated her will, her ability to flit right over to Esther's as if his opinion didn't matter. "I'll think on it" was all he would say, much to her apparent dismay.

"There's more fuss," she said softly.

He clenched his jaw.

"Word is Esther's in the family way," she whispered.

"How do you know, love?"

"Sarah Mae has a friend who works over at the hospital."

Jesse groaned. "Bad news always travels fast, jah?"

Barbara made no comment. He would be sure to verify it when the time was right. Zeke was in a heap of hurt if true. For now, the crazy man was too ill to be shunned anyway. The brethren would simply wait. They would deal with Zeke's sin in Jehovah's time.

The rain rushing against the windows had lightened to drizzle by the time Jesse and Ben reached Moses' place. Jesse saw the aged man through the rain-streaked windshield, headed for the woodshed. Moses glanced over his stooped shoulder as Ben and Jesse stepped out of the car, and Jesse was sure he'd spotted them. But Moses continued on his way. *That's like him*, thought Jesse, somewhat amused.

Jesse glanced at the dreary sky, wondering if they might not get another downpour.

"This is the old homestead," he told Ben, "where Zeke's grandparents lived and raised a whole houseful of young'uns, including Preacher Moses and Daniel."

Ben took in the house, the big barn, and the surrounding land. "I think I remember this place. . . . Yes, that horse fence. I think I helped whitewash it once."

Jesse grimaced but kept silent. *How long will this charade go on?*

"The corncrib's in the same spot it was when I came here to play when I was young. Zeke and I both did, I *think*. I just don't quite remember being here with my brother."

*Surprised he'd admit that.*

Moses came back out of the woodshed and they wandered over to meet him. When they neared, Moses offered a smile. "Wie geht's?"

"Oh, I'm all right," Jesse replied. "I see you're out workin' early."

Moses nodded, glancing now at Ben. "Is this here the man in question?"

"I'll let him speak for himself."

Ben stuck out his hand. "Ben Martin's my name. Good to meet you."

"Moses Hochstetler." He accepted the handshake and let go, looking Ben over, eyes lingering on his face. "I remember young Isaac well. I also happen to know he cut his left foot badly when he was three. Had to have a whole lot of stitches." The old man stopped and inhaled slowly. "Does that sound familiar to you, Ben?"

Ben wrinkled his brow. "Maybe so."

"Then there oughta be a scar to show for it," said Moses. "Somethin' else,

633

too. Isaac always had a swirl in his hair, at the crown. Like a cow licked him hard one too many times and his hair stayed that-a-way."

Ben grinned. "Oh yeah, I've got that. When I had short hair back in school, my mom always tried to slick it down." He turned around and showed them his head.

"Well, I'll be . . ." Moses muttered.

Then, without being asked, Ben sat on a log and removed his shoe and sock and peered down at the ball of his left foot.

Moses leaned down a bit and, frowning, lowered his spectacles. "Sure looks like a scar there to me."

Jesse squinted at Ben's bare foot. "Where?"

Moses pointed to the faded scar snaking across the ball of Ben's foot. "There it is, for sure and for certain."

"How'd I cut it?" Ben asked, still studying the scar.

Straightening, Moses pulled out his blue paisley kerchief, wiping his eyes for a time before speaking. "On a broken canning jar . . . Isaac."

As Ben slipped his sock and shoe back on, Jesse grabbed Moses' arm. "Surely you must be mistaken?"

Moses shook his head, his voice thick with emotion. "Like Simeon of old, I have seen the hand of the Almighty. This here's a miracle of God, I daresay . . . bringin' our lost son home again." He smiled right at Ben; then, next thing Jesse knew, Moses reached around Ben and gripped his shoulders, shaking all over.

Jesse, stunned at this turn of events, couldn't hold back his laughter. *The joke's on all of us. This old man's too blind and senile to count five fingers much less find a scar!*

Ben stood up and smiled like they'd just given him a new horse and buggy. "Wait until Annie hears this."

Jesse shook his head in disbelief. "Proves nothing."

Moses crept closer to Jesse, his face solemn again. "Since we don't know if or when Ichabod is coming, take him to Zeke for a final say-so. I dare ya to."

"Zeke isn't in any condition to identify an insect, much less his brother."

"Perhaps you underestimate him." Moses turned to Ben. "That just might clinch it. I say it's a good idea."

Ben stood there, looking from one man to the other, like he scarcely knew what to do next.

Jesse crossed his arms. "I don't know how that's possible—not anytime soon."

Moses rubbed his cheek thoughtfully. "Maybe you can get Zeke a pass to attend Preaching service here before too long." He turned to Ben. "You're not leavin' anytime soon, are ya?"

"I don't know what my plans are exactly," Ben confessed. "I'm staying with the Rancks for the time being, but I don't want to mooch off them for long."

"Well, you're always welcome over here," Moses told him. "Any close kin of my brother's is family to me." He slapped a hand on Ben's back and moved toward the house. "Come on in and meet some more of your relatives."

Moses was clearly convinced, but Jesse was mighty annoyed. Someone needed to put a stop to this drivel, and if it had to be Zeke, so be it.

# Chapter 27

Annie tried to hold back her excitement but still let out a little whoop when she saw the hired driver bringing Essie home later that afternoon. "Guess who's here," she told Laura, picking up little John as Laura reached for Zach's hand. All of them went rushing out for the welcome.

A peachy glow had replaced Essie's sallow cheeks, and Annie set John down and watched him run to his mamma. "Ach, we're so glad to see you," Annie said, waiting her turn while the children hugged their mother.

"Oh, it's nice to be home." Essie was looking at the children as if she hadn't seen them in weeks. "Ach, I missed yous!"

Annie kissed Essie on the cheek. "And we all missed you. But come now, let's get you inside."

Essie let Annie help her into the house. "The baby's goin' to be all right," she whispered. "Thank the dear Lord."

"Oh, such wonderful-good news!" Annie suppressed her tears of joy.

"We must keep mum 'bout all this," Essie warned.

Annie was glad she'd tried to keep Essie's condition a secret from Daed yesterday. Still, she worried he might have guessed somehow.

Essie sat down to catch her breath, looking around the kitchen. "Everything is so clean," she said, smiling at Annie. "You must've had some help, jah?"

"Oh, just a little," Annie confessed, assuming Esther suspected Ben must have volunteered to assist with outside chores, freeing Annie up to work indoors.

Essie nodded her head. "And did Laura do her share?" she asked in Laura's hearing.

636

"You can be sure of that. Ain't so, Laura?"

The girl's eyes shone with delight, and she ran to her mother yet again, throwing her arms around her waist. "I helped all I could, Mamma. But Auntie Annie did most of it—and cookin' and taking good care of us."

Essie's grateful expression warmed Annie's heart. "I was glad to do what I could."

"Well, I need to be holdin' my wee babe," said Essie, taking Laura's hand and getting up. "She must be napping?"

Annie said she was upstairs in her crib, and Essie headed through the sitting room to the stairs as Laura said, "You missed Essie Ann a lot, didn't ya, Mamma?"

Their happy voices faded and Annie heard only their feet on the stairs.

Eager to check the mail, Annie went outdoors, hoping for a letter from Lou. But there was nothing from Colorado. Even so there was a fat envelope that no doubt contained several "circle letters"—short journal-like correspondence where several ladies wrote about their activities and sent them around to one another—from Essie's five cousins in Wisconsin. Esther often shared these letters with Annie and Laura, reading them aloud, laughing as she did.

*You heard my prayer for Essie, dear Lord,* Annie said, thankfulness welling up in her. She walked back toward the house, where Zach and John had wandered into the backyard and were throwing a stick to Zeke's big black dog. Annie sat on the stoop to watch them and sighed inwardly. Not till this moment had she realized how much responsibility for Essie's children—and for keeping the house running smoothly in her absence—she had carried while Essie was gone. *Help me always to think first of others,* she prayed.

But she knew she would think of herself in *one* way. The tremendous joy she felt with Ben—the thrill that he was pursuing her again—was becoming habit-forming. And lest she wither on the vine again, as she had after his leaving, she determined to get a driver to take her over to the Englischers' outlet stores. Some new, fancy clothing should be just the thing. Without saying a word, Annie would let Ben know her eagerness to join his world.

After meeting Moses' wife, a handful of great-grandchildren, and an elderly grandmother, Ben wanted to rush off to Esther's and tell Annie the good news. *I am Isaac!* To think Moses had remembered the scar.

Equally amazing, Annie had somehow known all along.

When his cell phone rang, he hoped it was Annie calling him—from Julia's maybe. He was surprised instead to hear Julia herself, letting him know

Esther was on her way home from the hospital. Thanking Julia for the update, he disconnected.

He wished he could phone Annie, but since there was no way to contact her at Esther's, he knew he must put off seeing her for a while. Annie and the children were most likely welcoming Esther home right now, and he didn't want to just show up, possibly intruding on her homecoming.

So he decided to call Sam Glick instead, grateful he'd keyed in Sam's new cell phone number when he last saw him at the harness shop.

Hungry now, he first headed for Route 30, looking for the nearest fast-food stop. Then, while enjoying a juicy cheeseburger, he called Sam and they exchanged small talk.

"More than ever, I'm interested in the Plain life," he told Sam.

"Is it the People or is it something else?" Sam asked, a teasing lilt to his voice.

Ben laughed. "You mean some*one* else?"

"Annie seems to like you well enough."

He wasn't inclined to discuss his affection for Annie by cell with a casual acquaintance—former Amishman or not. He changed the subject. "You'll never guess what I just found out."

"You like the smell of pig manure after all?"

Ben chuckled. "I found out that I am Zeke's younger brother." Ben quickly filled Sam in on the telltale scar identified by Preacher Moses.

"No fooling? You're the kid who disappeared all those years ago?"

"That's what I'm told."

They talked a while longer about the kidnapping, Ben's memories, and the events leading up to his meeting with Moses today.

Then, after a time, Sam brought up Louisa. Ben was surprised, once again, at their similar situations, only reversed. Sam invited him over for supper, and Ben said he'd be all for it. Sharing a meal with Sam would be a distant second to taking Annie out, of course, but he also wanted to be sensitive to her needs and not rush things as he had before. Anyway, spending time with Sam might be a good idea for a while, a way to discover all he'd missed here while growing up in Kentucky. His past was calling him home.

Annie wasted no time getting started on her chores the morning after Essie returned home. She was outside in the pigpen slopping the hogs when Ben sneaked up on her.

"Oh, Ben, you scared me!"

He leaned against the fence and smiled at her. "Hello to you, too, Miss Annie. Don't you smell good this morning."

She'd nearly become used to the hog smell, which was no doubt strong on her choring dress. She wrinkled her nose at him but couldn't help grinning at his teasing.

"You're out of breath, Ben. Where'd you come from?"

"I knew I'd find you out here this time of day, so I parked the car up the road and ran down. I didn't want to upset Essie again."

"That's awful kind, Ben."

"Have you heard?"

"Heard what?"

He was clearly excited. "Oh, it's the best news, Annie." Speaking quickly, he told her how Preacher Moses had identified him by the scar on his foot. "Now I'm sure, Annie. I am Isaac."

She wanted to go to him, let him wrap his arms around her, but she resisted, only smiling her best smile. "Ach, I'm ever so glad," she whispered, refusing her tears.

Ben looked over his shoulder at the house. "I'd better go. But I'll see you again soon."

"Jah," she called after him as she watched him hurry around the barn and out of sight. "But not soon enough," she whispered.

Finishing her chores, she headed inside and helped Essie get breakfast on the table. After the meal, she hurried to the neighbors' barn phone, calling one of the several van drivers. *This is the first day of a whole new life*, she decided. She wanted to see what she was up against as far as styles and prices went so she'd know how much money she would need when she was ready to do her serious shopping. Unfortunately, she had very little money of her own, having given much of her earnings to her parents all those years and now helping Essie with expenses. Annie longed to tell Louisa what she planned, having not shared a peep with anyone, even Esther, for fear she might try to talk her out of it.

When the driver dropped Annie off at the outlet shops, she instructed him to pick her up in an hour, then headed toward one of the stores she'd gone into with Lou and Courtney. There, she spotted several pretty pairs of shoes and made a mental note, dodging the startled looks from one clerk. Then she made her way to the next shop, hoping to see something like the skirt and blouse she'd borrowed from Louisa for her date with Ben to the Sight and Sound Theatre last month. Within minutes she saw three similar outfits, fixing her memory on the location of each item, thinking she might even be able to afford at least the blouse right away. When she asked to look at dresses, the clerk's eyebrows shot straight up.

"We do not sell Amish apparel, miss," she said.

"No, I'm not interested in Plain clothing. I'm lookin' for something right perty, to tell you the truth. Something you would wear to have dinner with your best beau."

The woman's brown eyes brightened and she winked at Annie. "Well, I'm happily married, but I still remember those days. Come right this way."

The clerk led her to a rack near the wall, displaying a whole lineup of dresses in every imaginable style and color.

"Are you looking for a particular size?" she asked.

"I have no idea." Annie didn't want to explain that she and her Mamm had always made her dresses and aprons.

"Is the dress for you or someone else?"

"For me."

The woman scanned her quickly from head to toe and said she was most likely a petite two. Annie suddenly wished she had paid better attention to the size of Lou's skirt and blouse.

There were so many pretty things to look at, and she decided to try on several. She narrowed her search down to two dresses and one lovely skirt and blouse outfit. When she asked if they could set the items of clothing aside, layaway was mentioned, but she hadn't come prepared to pay a sizeable down payment. She left the store empty-handed, wishing she might take out some money from her savings account she and Mamm had set up together years ago, when first she'd started working at Cousin Julia's. But how on earth was she going to convince her mother to go to the bank with her . . . especially if she revealed her plan to slowly buy an entire Englischer's wardrobe?

All was not lost, though. She would find a way to make this very nice surprise happen for Ben, even if it meant borrowing money, although she hated to. Daed's admonition to "owe no man anything" had been drilled into her. Still, seeing Ben's expression when first he saw her in new, fancy clothes would be worth it all. *I can scarcely wait!*

# Chapter 28

When Lou's letter arrived in the mail the next day, Annie discovered an extra thick envelope. Too excited to wait, she opened it and began reading even as she cut across the front lawn. Seeing a plastic card wrapped in paper, with an explanation for how to use it, she stood and leaned against the house. *Lou wants me to call her next time I'm at Julia's!*

She also found it interesting that her friend was again seeing Michael, the man she had nearly married last year. *Is she that lonely?* Annie wondered, not quite sure what to think, especially having seen how happy Lou had been with Sam Glick. She felt disappointed, really. She wanted Sam to win Lou's heart.

"With Sam going fancy, it could actually work," she mused. And now that Ben was back, she, too, hoped to move further and further away from the Plain life. She thought again of her plan to purchase English clothing.

*Won't Lou be surprised!*

Looking at the enclosed phone card, she could scarcely wait to get to Julia's and have her help place the call to Castle Rock, Colorado.

Later that same day, she did just that, with surprisingly little input from her cousin. Lou had given Annie her cell phone number, and the call went through ever so fast.

"Oh, Lou, it's wonderful to hear your voice again!"

"I'm right here in my art studio, between classes. How *are* you, Annie?"

"I'm fine . . . and you'll never believe who's come back to Paradise." Annie was glad to have the portable phone in her hand and made a beeline toward the sunroom lest she be overheard by Julia or one of the children. She was thankful Ben had evidently left the house before she'd arrived.

641

"You'll have to give me a hint," Louisa replied. "Is this someone we both know?"

"Ach, for sure."

Annie felt her heart pound just thinking about what she wanted to say. "It's Ben who's here! Can you believe it?"

Louisa was silent for a time, then she said, "Actually, I can. He came back for you, didn't he?"

"No." She had to set her straight. "He came back because he found out he's adopted. You'll never believe this, but it turns out he's Isaac, our kidnapped boy." Annie let the story unfold the way it had from the very beginning.

When she'd finished explaining, Lou said, "This is a shocker . . . but a terrific one. You must feel stunned."

"Well, I am and I'm not . . . if that makes any sense. I'm just ever so excited."

"Now maybe you won't have to jump through so many hoops to spend time with Ben."

"To be honest, I don't know how it will work for us to court, and he hasn't said a word 'bout it, either." She sighed. "My father is still not convinced he is Isaac. But Ben is. He's remembering more and more about growin' up here, and already word's spreading amongst the People about who he is."

Then Annie told Lou of her plan to buy some modern clothes. "Now all I need to do is find out where to sell my hair."

Lou let out a gasp. "What? You're kidding, I hope."

The idea had popped into Annie's head as she had contemplated the situation the night before. "No. Why? It's not so uncommon. I've read that hair this long can go for a perty penny . . . so I need you to find out where I should go here in Lancaster to sell it."

"Annie, this is silly. Does Ben know? I doubt he would want you to do that."

"Lou, listen. This is my big surprise . . . so he'll know how much I want to become fancy for him."

"It's hard to believe you really want to do this, Annie. Hopefully you won't be sorry," Lou said, as if Annie were making a horrid mistake.

"If I really want to be English, I don't need hair this long, anyway. Really, Louisa, I have plenty to spare."

"Well, if you're sure . . ."

Lou said she would "go online" and find out who was buying human hair for making wigs. "Surely I can locate someone there in Lancaster, or maybe in Harrisburg," Lou said. But then she had another idea. "Why not keep your hair and simply open a credit line for your shopping spree? You know, buy now and pay and pay and pay later? Join the rest of frivolous America?"

Annie knew she was kidding.

"Better yet, borrow the money from me. How much do you need?"

"No, Lou. I know you're on a tight budget," Annie said quickly, "but it's awful nice of you to offer." She asked about Lou's art students.

Lou laughed a little. "Well, I know you're not that interested in my students. . . . It's Michael you're most curious about, right?"

Annie had to laugh, too. "I think we know each other mighty well. So have you been seein' him a lot? Like before?"

"Do you mean are we engaged? No. Will he ask me to marry him again? I don't know."

"Ach, do ya love him, Lou?"

There was an awkward silence, and Annie worried she'd offended her.

"Sorry. I'm pryin' too much."

"No . . . I think it's a reasonable question—one I'm trying to answer for myself." Louisa told her that Michael's potential law partnership with her father was a thing of the past and that because he'd given all that up—"possibly to impress me"—she was struggling with why she shouldn't be interested in him romantically for the long term.

"If you love him, then you'll want to be with him. Be his wife, have his children . . . jah?"

"The operative word is *if*, Annie. I'm still trying to figure out how I feel about him. I don't want to let my emotions sway me." She paused a moment. "You know, it's easy to look across the table at Michael and smile at him, listen to him talk, but I'm afraid he's going to fall in love with me again. I need to be more careful."

Annie wanted to ask about Sam in the worst way, but before she could, Louisa continued, "To be honest with you, Michael doesn't share my openness to faith."

"Does Sam?" Annie asked softly.

"I'm not sure. He's changing so much. It's something I'll need to find out."

They talked then about other things: how it was for Annie staying at Esther's, how fast cute little Essie Ann was growing, and how Annie missed her family at home. Annie also told of Ben's interest in her art. "He wants to see all of my work, not just the bridge painting in the Rancks' attic."

"He's seen the one with the old bridge and the long rope swing?" Lou sounded surprised.

"Not only has he seen it but he's been staring at it, I guess. Says it's the reason he was drawn to Paradise in the first place." She told Lou how he'd been carrying a copy of it in his pocket since last Christmas, when first he stumbled onto it.

"Wow . . . is that interesting or what?"

"He says it's a miracle how it all happened, and I'm starting to think it must be, too."

"Oh, Annie, I have a feeling you and Ben will end up together. I saw it in his eyes that first time he asked me about you!" Lou laughed. "I was actually talking to your future husband that day, telling him to ask you out himself. What a riot!"

Annie couldn't help but smile. "Let's not get ahead of ourselves. There's plenty to work out 'tween us, but he found me for a reason, and now he's found himself, too." Annie felt completely overjoyed, sharing such things with Louisa. "Just think, I was being courted by my dear friend Isaac back before we ever knew it."

"That's the sweetest story, and to think it's true."

*Ever so true.*

Lou encouraged her to use the calling card again. "Anytime at all. If I'm teaching, I can always say so and set up a time later. Okay?"

"Oh, this is so much fun. But I could be in big trouble with the brethren if they knew I was using the phone for social purposes."

"But, hey, which is worse—cutting your hair and buying fancy dresses or calling me every few weeks or so?"

Annie hadn't thought of that. "Ach, I see your point."

"You're going to have to get used to this new life of yours."

Before they hung up, Lou said she'd call back in a few minutes with the location of a place to sell her hair, if Annie was sure about it.

"Oh, would you? I'm leaning that way, really I am."

They were saying good-bye, promising to keep in touch, when Annie added right quick, "I hope you won't marry for anything less than love, Lou. Honest, I do."

"And I wish the same for you. You and Ben . . . stick with love."

After Annie clicked the phone off, she sat there thinking about how satisfying it had been to talk to her pen pal so far away. *Nearly two thousand miles away.*

# Chapter 29

Annie was finishing up her work at Julia's late that afternoon when Molly asked her to read a story. The two of them settled down on the porch swing out front, enjoying the balmy weather and the chirping birds. Annie opened the book to the beginning, reading the title page and the name of the author as she had been taught to do in school years ago.

Molly sat ever so still on her lap, listening as Annie read with expression, even taking care to change her voice to suit the animal characters. The story, which was about a puppy chasing a kitten into a schoolhouse, held Molly's interest and was coming to an end when a car pulled up. Before Annie could say anything, Molly whispered, "Oh, look, it's Uncle Ben!" And with that she hopped off Annie's lap and went running out to meet him, her skirt floating in the breeze.

*Uncle Ben?*

Annie watched as Ben leaned down to lift Molly high, his hearty laughter hovering in the air. She recalled how relaxed Ben had been with Laura, Zach, and John—even the baby—and her mind whirled forward to the possibility of a life with him. What would their children look like were she to marry him? And wouldn't he be a wonderful-good father? *A loving and kind husband, too,* she thought.

"Annie! Glad to see you're still here." Ben hurried toward the porch with giggly Molly in his arms.

Her heart leaped when he came near, and she wondered if Molly might run inside and play, leaving them alone momentarily. Ben must have been thinking along the same lines, for he gave Molly's cheek a squeeze and set her down, shooing her into the house. "I'm glad I caught you, Annie. Have a minute?"

"Why, sure."

He pulled up a chair and scooted it next to hers. "I want to tell you something. I've made arrangements to rent a room for a few months in the same house where Sam's staying."

"You did?" Annie was pleased as pie.

He nodded. "Sam and I are becoming good friends. He's giving me some pointers on starting a small business. Did you know he's got a day job, and his own carpentry and remodeling business on the side?"

Annie found this interesting. "Last I saw Sam, he'd talked of leaving the Amish life . . . before it was known. But I hadn't heard how he was doing on the outside till now."

"He seems to be fine. But he misses Louisa."

"He said that?" She smiled.

"Loud and clear."

"Well, I talked to Lou on the phone today, and 'tween you and me, I think she misses him, too."

"Do you suppose Sam's leaving will make a relationship with Louisa more likely?" Ben asked.

Not wanting to let on what she knew about Michael, Annie was noncommittal. "Hard to say. . . ."

She changed the subject. "Do Irvin and Julia know 'bout your plans to rent elsewhere?"

"I told them I plan to move out in a week or so—make space in the attic for whoever might need a place. You never know about Irvin and Julia . . . who they might want to help next."

Annie agreed, and then Ben began to talk of his work prospects. She said it was too bad he couldn't work over at the harness shop as he had before. In part she was trying to tell him she wished he'd never left. She hoped he was reading between the lines just now.

"I'm sure I'll come up with something," Ben replied.

They sat for a moment without talking; then he reached for her hand. "Will you have dinner with me next week? Celebrate the reunion of Isaac and Annie." He smiled broadly, eyes filled with hope.

"Oh, jah, that would be so nice." She was aware of her beating heart.

"How about Monday, when fewer people are eating out?"

"Monday's fine."

"We could drive farther away, too, if you like."

She knew he was being cautious, as they had been last winter—driving long distances so as not to be seen by anyone who might recognize her. "No, that's not necessary at all. Ever so kind of you, Ben."

Julia peeked her head out the door and invited Annie to stay for supper, all smiles.

Annie rose. "I best be goin' to help Esther. But nice of you to invite me, Julia."

"Hard to believe you're passing up my homemade noodles," Julia teased.

Annie laughed. "I guess I am at that."

Ben offered to drive her, but Annie insisted on walking. "I really want to take you," he said as he stood and grinned at her.

"Your supper will get cold," Annie said, glancing at Julia. "Tell him how much better those buttery noodles are *hot*, Cousin."

Julia wiggled her fingers in a wave. "Take your time getting her home, Ben," she said. "I can always reheat the noodles." She winked, then disappeared into the house.

"Not so subtle, is she?" Ben joked as they made their way down the front steps and toward his car.

Annie squelched a laugh, ever so happy to be escorted home by her handsome beau.

After taking Annie back to Esther's, Ben called Julia on his cell to let her know he would not be back for supper. He needed time alone to consider all the years he'd skipped over while in Kentucky, thinking his sisters and parents were his true family. Of course they were still his family, and he had everything to be grateful for regarding the Martins. They'd taken him in when he had needed a family most, making him their own son. Whatever lay ahead, Ben would never forget that.

In spite of his close connection to his Kentucky family, he hoped he could have a face-to-face meeting with Daniel Hochstetler, his birth father. There had been some talk between Annie and her father that Daniel might be heading this way.

Ben wished it would be sooner rather than later. There was so much rattling around in his head about the four years he'd spent living here as a child—nearly too long ago now to separate imagination from reality. Too, he felt he needed—no, *wanted*—to mourn the loss of his mother, that she hadn't lived to see his return. He had some vivid memories of her but not enough to satisfy him. He wished he could talk with Zeke about her and his childhood, hoping his brother might be able to dredge up more memories.

It annoyed him that no photographs were allowed by the Amish brethren. A picture of his biological parents would be a big help at a time like this. And how cool it would be to carry a picture of Annie in his wallet!

The blinds were wide open in the sitting area off her kitchen as Louisa enjoyed curling up in one of her favorite chairs. She loved how the evening's light filtered into the room, this place that had her personality and likes written all over it. She cuddled Muffin, who yawned and slapped his long tail, blinking his pretty eyes. Her cat felt as soft and warm as a feather bed, Louisa thought, recalling how warm and comforting the one at Annie's house had been. Tonight she was snug and cocooned away, soaking up the cozy feeling and glad to have this time to herself . . . and Muffin. She had often wondered what other single or widowed people did for companionship, having read how important the connection with people or animals was . . . and she was once again delighted to have such an affectionate kitty.

She exhaled slowly, contemplating the few times she had gone out on lunch or dinner dates with Michael since her return from Amish country. He had been attentive, endeavoring to woo her back. And she was becoming vulnerable to him, even though she often thought of Sam.

When the phone rang, she assumed it was Michael but was pleasantly surprised to hear Julia Ranck's voice. "Well, *hey*," Louisa said.

"I've been meaning to call you after our last phone discussion. I thought I'd just pick up the phone right now, if this is a good time."

"It's really a perfect time, yes."

Julia explained that her husband was bathing the children and Ben was gone from the house. "Still out with Annie, I would guess."

But it was clear Julia had not called to talk about Annie and Ben, or her children in the tub. She wanted to continue their conversation about Louisa's "spiritual issues," she said. Louisa was amazed at the timing of the call. She was all set to live life to the fullest—to live for God and others, just as Julia and her husband, Irvin, seemed to thrive on doing.

"I'll tell you honestly," Louisa said, aware once again of her openness with this woman. "I've never been this interested in the so-called God of the universe before."

Esther sat up in bed, cradling her baby near. Annie had been so kind to take good care of her during the past two days since her return from the hospital. Now that she was better, she enjoyed picking up the baby prior to her time to be nursed just to hold her and enjoy the fading sky in the window across her bedroom. The days were growing longer with the coming of summer, and she was especially glad for this tender time between twilight and dusk.

Hearing a creak in the hallway, she turned and saw a glimpse of the white cotton nightgown Annie had recently sewn for herself in the crack where the door stood ajar. "Come in, Annie."

"Hope I didn't wake you," Annie said, silently slipping inside.

"Nee, I'm just thinking 'bout this day and the goodness of the Lord." She kissed her baby's head. "And my sweet one right here."

"You seem back to your old self." Annie sat on the edge of the bed.

"Oh, ever so much better, jah."

They sat quietly, looking at each other for an awkward moment, and it was clear to Esther that Annie had something on her mind. "What're you thinkin' tonight?"

"Truth be known, it's my art. I'm itchin' to start up again. Been waiting till the middle of July, which is comin' fast now." She sighed. "You may think this odd, but I feel only half alive without it."

"And yet you honor your father's request." Esther's heart went out to her.

"If it were up to me alone, I'd follow my heart, probably, and paint every single day."

Essie studied her friend's face, nodding slowly. "It's a wonderful-good calling, Annie. But surely your heart is calling you to more than art, ain't so?"

"Ben, you mean?"

"Could be. But I'm not thinking of him tonight. I've seen you changing, Annie, your heart softening to the Lord."

"Maybe so, but I still love to paint."

Essie wanted to share something she'd discovered from her talks with Julia and others at her new church. "I hope you can understand what I want to tell ya, Annie."

"Jah?"

"Sometimes when we love something, if we're willin' to give it up—'specially to God—it is given back. Ever hear of such a thing?"

Annie shook her head. "No . . ."

"Honestly, I think if we cling too hard, the thing we love can't blossom. But if it's released, sometimes it is returned. If it's s'posed to be, that is."

Annie pulled her robe together tightly, fidgeting, and Esther worried she had offended her precious friend. "Just think on it, all right? Don't fret."

Getting up, Annie nodded. "I'm awful tired. Good night, Essie."

"Sweet dreams, Annie."

After nursing the baby, Esther rose and carried her to the crib. She stood there looking down at her miniature angel swathed in the white of the moon, listening to the slow breathing. Her heart swelled with love for her family, and she thanked the Lord yet again for sparing the life of the next new babe. Then she prayed, "Oh, please touch my Zeke with your loving hand, Father. Prepare his heart for you, and call him to know and love you just as I do. This I pray in Jesus' name. Amen."


Ben sat in the Rancks' attic room and read and recited the Pennsylvania Dutch words from the book Irvin had loaned him. Again and again he practiced, trying for not only the correct pronunciation but the cadence of the words and phrases as he remembered hearing—and speaking—them.

Closing the book, he reached for the Bible he had slipped into his suitcase back home. Turning to the Gospel of John, he read all of chapter fifteen, contemplating the concept of Christ being the true vine, God the gardener, and he himself being a branch. *"If a man remains in me and I in him, he will bear much fruit. . . ."*

He had always wanted to be a "good guy," but he had failed, time and again. He struggled with temptation, like anyone, English or Amish. There seemed no way to be consistently kind, patient, loving, obedient—or good enough—while growing up in his father's house. In *either* of his fathers' houses. He needed to be connected with the "source," the true vine; he needed to be grafted in.

Continuing his reading, Ben realized he had never felt this inclined toward the Scriptures. They were telling him he belonged, that he wasn't alone. He did not have to guess any longer; in the fullest sense, he knew who he was.

Rejuvenated, he determined to read several chapters each day, as he knew Irvin did upon first awaking. He would talk to God, too—the real and personal way he had witnessed Irvin and Julia doing—because he was persuaded his being here, and the realization of his identity, had somehow been orchestrated by an unseen hand. Surely, God had called him not only back here to his Amish roots but into a relationship with Him, as well.

# Chapter 30

Other than the letter, there had been no forewarning of Ichabod's arrival in Paradise. Jesse coughed abruptly at the sight of his old friend standing on the back stoop Monday morning, the screen door rattling with his knocking.

As lanky and dark-headed as Jesse remembered, Ichabod stood with broad shoulders, waiting. Not saying a word, Jesse made his way through the utility room and opened the door.

"Preacher Zook" came the familiar, raspy voice.

Jesse refused to say he had been expecting him or to offer his usual welcome. All the anger and bitter disappointment of the years filled him in that silent moment. As they exchanged glances, Jesse noticed the surprisingly congenial expression on Ichabod's ruddy face and saw neither pride nor resentment registered there.

"I've come to visit my son's grave, if it'd suit you to show me the way. Thought I might ride over to the cemetery with you and the missus . . . or however you'd like to do this."

"Daniel . . ." The name slipped out before Jesse could retrieve it. The brethren had agreed to call him Ichabod for a reason, and nothing had changed, far as Jesse knew. The man was still an exile. Yet he seemed markedly different. Was it the loss of Mary or had the years whittled away the ruthless edges?

Leading the man down the steps and through the wide yard, past the freshly hung wash, Jesse mustered up all the humanity he possessed. As they walked, he told of having plowed up the bones initially mistaken for Isaac's. Jesse revealed, as kindheartedly as possible, all the upsetting circumstances surrounding Zeke's shocking admission of guilt . . . then the sudden dismissal of evidence.

He felt wearied by the telling, but the father who had lost so much deserved some explanation. Daniel received the whole of the news at face value, which stunned Jesse further. This wasn't at all the demeanor he'd expected. "I'm awful sorry to be the one to tell you. I did send a second letter, but you must not have gotten it. Seems you've made the trip here for nothin'."

"No . . . no, I 'spect that isn't so." Ichabod tilted his head, looking hard at Jesse. "What with my dear Mary passed on and all my kin settled round these parts, I might just like to . . . make amends."

Jesse scratched his head. Was he hearing correctly? This was not the man he'd known. That man carried an enduring chip on his wide shoulders, ever seeking out conflict of some kind or another.

Aware of how distant they had become, Jesse asked how long he planned to stay in the area.

"Haven't thought it all through yet, Preacher. But I want to see my son and daughter-in-law . . . and their youngsters. How many grandchildren do I have?"

"At last count, four."

"I'll be moseyin' over there, then."

It was urgent for Jesse to catch him up on Zeke's fragile mental state, to say that his son was not presently living at home.

This news seemed to pain Ichabod, and he shook his head. "So much suffering in this old world, ain't?" He removed his hat and pressed it against his chest. "I have something to tell you, Jesse. Something I've played and replayed in my head. You see, part of why I've come is to repent."

Jesse shifted his weight from one foot to the other, hardly able to think, let alone speak. Who *was* this man?

"The Lord God has dealt bitterly with me." The man bowed his head for a moment before raising it with a sigh. "I kept myself afar off, resisting the Almighty. I let my conceit rule me, livin' for myself and breakin' my Mary's heart. Broke it clear in two . . . and then some." He struggled to speak. "I did the unthinkable."

Jesse was stunned, and when Daniel was finished confessing his sin with another woman, Jesse placed a hand on his old friend's shoulder and said, "So, then, will you be askin' forgiveness of the brethren?"

"First you, Jesse . . . then all the ministers, and finally the membership."

Moved now, Jesse extended the hand of fellowship. "I forgive you, Daniel."

A palpable power gripped the two friends as they shook hands. "I was a sinner, 'cept for the grace of our Lord."

"As we all are."

Jesse led him out to the paddock, where a thin haze hung near the ground as they walked and talked amidst the horses and mules, resuming their friendship. Jesse assured him that he would without question find mercy amongst the People. "'Tis our way."

They talked more of Zeke and Esther and the children, although Jesse said nothing of Esther's shunning nor of Ben's claims, wanting to spare Daniel more grief just now. "I'll see if I can't get Zeke out to the work frolic later today . . . over at the bishop's place."

Daniel brightened. "Oh, that'd be just fine."

Right then and there, under the Lord God's heavenly covering of clouds and sky, Jesse offered to have the man called Ichabod hang his hat at his house, to rest up a bit and share a hot meal before heading out to chop wood with the men.

"Mighty kind of you, Preacher." And Ichabod smiled.

Not accustomed to doing so, Jesse had thrown around the word *preacher* quite a lot in order to get one of Zeke's several doctors to consent to a half-day pass. In the space of a few hours, from the time Ichabod had appeared on his doorstep till now, a whole group of hardworking men had gathered to cut wood at the home of their elderly bishop.

Jesse helped Zeke from the van, then paid their driver. Zeke's face shown with appreciation as the men spotted him and began coming to greet him in clusters of threes and fours. In spite of all Zeke had been through, the men were enthusiastic to see him.

*Thankfully so,* thought Jesse.

Suddenly he noticed Ben over by a pile of uncut wood. "Ach, of all the nerve," Jesse muttered, guessing Moses must have let the cat out of the bag about today's work. He hoped Ben would stay put behind the stand of trees, working a two-man saw with one of Jesse's nephews. No need to spoil such a wonderful-good thing as this, a man and his son reconciled on Amish soil. That is, if it didn't backfire. Jesse prayed it wouldn't.

Still observing Ben in the distance, Jesse let out a sigh. There was no point putting it off. Even if Moses couldn't recognize Ben for the imposter he was, surely Daniel would. Despite the inconvenience of the whole thing, they could kill two birds with one stone—be done with the whole foolishness.

Jesse led Zeke around the side of the house, on the look-out for Daniel, wondering if he'd arrived yet. Meanwhile, Zeke was thirsty; he'd like to get his hands wrapped around the well pump in the backyard.

Jesse walked with him to the well, hoping Daniel hadn't changed his mind about coming.

Zeke finished wetting his whistle at the pump, wiped his face on his shirt-sleeve, and looked up to see Jesse wearing a relieved look on his face. Zeke turned to see what on earth the preacher was staring at over yonder.

Squinting hard, he set his gaze on a man swinging his long arms, coming up the lane with a downright confident stride. The man seemed familiar somehow, and Zeke wondered why. Then he knew. *Am I seeing things?*

The man resembled his own father, or at least what Zeke recalled of the sternest man he'd ever known. Fact was, there was a good measure of recognition in Preacher Jesse's eyes, too.

Zeke let out a low groan. "Is that my ol' Dat—and if so, what's *he* doin' here?"

Jesse quickly explained about the letters he'd sent regarding Isaac's remains. "He didn't get the second letter from me, tellin' him there was no need to come."

Zeke's father walked right up to them, and Zeke felt his intense gaze. No question, his father had recognized him, too, despite the passage of years. Zeke felt fireworks exploding in his chest.

Dat spoke first. "Zeke . . . son, mighty gut seein' ya again."

Zeke stepped back, eyeing his father warily. "Been a lot of years."

"No doubt you're surprised." His father let out a nervous chuckle, extending his hand. "I've come to apologize, Zeke."

He stared at his father, refusing the handshake, and an awkward moment passed.

"Son . . . I—"

"No," Zeke sputtered, coming uncorked. "You just listen to *me*. You've caused nothin' but hardship my whole life long . . . even long after you up and hightailed it out of here." Angry tears spilled down his face. He shook his head again and again, unable to control the resentment, the bottled rage. "Don't ya see? This here's a result of your scorn." Zeke pounded his chest. "*This* . . . me."

His father pursed his lips. "I did you wrong. I know this . . . and have no right to ask you for anything."

Zeke frowned, somewhat taken aback. This wasn't the man he remembered. The father who had raised him would have lashed back with similar fury, raising his voice and hurling insults.

Dat extended his hand again. "I've come to see if you'll receive me into the fellowship here, and perhaps someday . . . as your father."

The older man fell silent, looking at Zeke with surprisingly tender eyes. Preacher Jesse said nothing as Zeke studied his father's face. Those eyes . . . that face that had disapproved of him for countless months and years. All the memories of belittlement.

*How can I forgive him?*

Zeke looked down at his father's outstretched hand, now trembling with the effort, and something within tugged at him. He was still that little boy who'd always longed for his father's love and approval. And now . . . was his father truly offering it?

Zeke sighed and brushed his tears away. Irvin's long talks had taken a foothold in his heart, preparing the soil for such a moment. He wasn't the same man and, apparently, neither was his father.

*It's time*, Zeke realized, as years of resentment suddenly gave way. Forgiveness broke loose within and he did the unthinkable: he reached for his father's hand and gripped it. His entire soul shuddered, and he was instantly caught off guard, pulled forward into his father's embrace.

Zeke could not resist, and he wept.


Moved by what he'd just witnessed, Jesse grunted his exit, leaving Zeke and Daniel alone to work things out between them. Scratching his head, he wondered, *Who would've thought?* Daniel had been the harshest of men. A brutal father . . . absent in the flesh and otherwise, for sure and for certain.

Jesse smiled, almost wishing he might pat himself on the back for the part he'd played in this rather unplanned reunion.

The brethren would begin the process of bringing Daniel back into the fold. Such would take little time, as a sincere repentance on the part of the wayward one was the only requirement. Immediately following Daniel's kneeling repentance, the People would receive him back, no questions asked.

*Our way . . .*

He chuckled, resisting the urge to look over his shoulder once again. But he could hear Daniel and Zeke talking quick-like now, catching up on all the years, no doubt. The sounds of a son granting his father forgiveness.

Hopefully things would be settling down by the time Zeke spotted Ben. Then the man he'd once called Ichabod could finally and fully unmask Ben's foolishness. The event was inevitable. He would merely wait for it to unfold.

*Isaac indeed!* Jesse muttered as he continuing observing from afar. Several men now approached Daniel and Zeke, offering their friendly welcome as father and son began to work side by side.

Later, during a short break from their labors, Zeke looked up and happened to see Ben Martin. "What's he doing back here?" he wondered aloud, awful glad to see him. Zeke turned to his father, who was sipping a cup of water. "I want you to meet an English friend of mine."

Zeke hurried his pace as he made his way down the slope toward Ben, his father following beside him.

"Heard you'd gone home," Zeke said, offering a smile.

Ben seemed startled, his expression a mixture of surprise and shock. "I . . . well . . . I'm back, yes."

Despite Ben's strange reaction, Zeke extended his hand and Ben shook it.

Zeke was about to introduce his father when Ben cleared his throat. "I've been wanting to talk to you, Zeke."

"Well, here I am." Zeke chuckled.

A small smile traced itself on Ben's face. He turned to Zeke's father, and a look of confusion crossed his brow.

Zeke's father squinted his eyes, shielding them against the sun. A look of puzzlement crossed his own features. "Do I know you, young man?"

Ben was silent. For a moment Zeke stood back, curious as the two men awkwardly observed each other.

"Ach, sorry. This here's Ben Martin," he said. "And, Ben, this is Daniel Hochstetler, my father."

Ben reached to accept the older man's handshake. "Good to meet you, sir. Very good . . ."

Shaking hands, the two men seemed tongue-tied, eyes locked upon each other. Zeke noted his father's pale face. "What is it, Dat?"

His father stepped closer to Ben, gripping the younger man's shoulder. "In all my born days . . . If you don't look like . . ."

Dat stopped and shook his head, and Ben gave Zeke a quick, almost guilty glance.

*Look like who?* Zeke wondered, following his father's unrelenting stare at Ben's features.

Dat released his handshake and stepped back to appraise Ben. "All this time, I've wondered what the world my Isaac might look like all grown up. And here you are, the spittin' image of my own imagination."

Zeke shivered. "What're you saying, Dat?" He looked back at Ben, who instead of brushing off the strange comment was nodding gravely.

*What's going on?*

Just then Preacher Jesse walked over, looking at them as if he might object

656

to this strange meeting. But he said not a word when he stood alongside Zeke, his brow furrowed with something akin to fear.

Dat chuckled. "Ben Martin, you say? There's no way you might be mistaken on that?"

Ben returned the smile, but his eyes were serious. "I was mistaken for years, but not anymore."

"What's that you say?" asked Zeke's father.

"I have the memories to prove I'm someone else."

His father crept closer, his face displaying a mixture of disbelief and hope. "Isaac?"

Ben simply nodded.

"I knew it!" Dat exclaimed. He burst out laughing and grabbed Ben by the shoulders.

Zeke's mouth dropped open, unable to fathom what was happening right before his eyes. Was this another mental trick? Or was his father as deluded as *he* had been? It made not a whit of sense. And by the incredulous look on Preacher's white face, it made no sense to him, either.

Preacher Jesse spoke up. "So you actually buy this nonsense?"

Grinning from ear to ear, Dat released Ben and turned to Jesse. "This here is my lost boy, I'm tellin' you."

Jesse's face clouded. "He'd like you to believe that."

Dat's eyebrows rose, apparently taken aback at Jesse's objection. He turned to Ben, scrutinizing him further. "So . . . Preacher Jesse thinks you're an imposter? Is that what I'm hearing?"

"Yes, sir," Ben said. "He does."

"But you have . . . memories?" Dat continued.

Ben nodded.

Dat glanced at Preacher Jesse. "Well, then, let's put this to the test and be done with it."

The preacher seemed to momentarily consider this, then sighed softly. "Fine."

Dat cleared his throat and fixed an intense look on Ben. He took a deep breath, as if regretting the words to come, though he spoke them anyway. "My young Isaac was aware of my terrible secret—the dire sin that kept me from accepting the divine lot." He looked at the preacher. "Jesse Zook knows what I'm talkin' about."

Jesse nodded, but Zeke was confused again. *Isaac knew our father's secret? Who remembers much, if anything, from the tender age of four?* It seemed an impossible test.

Dat chewed his lip but didn't speak, as if trying to bite back the tears filling his eyes.

At last he pulled himself together. "When you were young, you loved to carry around a peach stone. . . ."

Ben brightened as he slipped his hand into his pocket and brought out a peach pit, holding it up. "Like this?"

"Means nothing," Jesse interjected.

Dat raised a hand before continuing more soberly. "And do you remember where you first received a peach?"

Ben's grin faded. He glanced first at Zeke, then at Jesse.

"Speak the truth as you remember it," Dat said gently but with conviction.

Ben looked down at the ground, appearing oddly embarrassed. *Or maybe he doesn't remember,* Zeke thought, as Ben seemed to struggle.

"He doesn't know," Jesse said. "Because he's not—"

"The peach girl," Ben finally replied. "The one you . . . liked."

Zeke expelled a nervous breath, and Preacher Jesse's eyes grew wide in apparent amazement.

Nodding sadly, Dat looked at Jesse and said, "My foolish sin was known only by my young son. Mary, bless her dear heart, forgave me in the end. Took me back even though I didn't deserve such love."

Embracing Ben's shoulders again, Dat held on as if he might disappear. "Can there be any more doubt? This young man, this Ben, is my own Isaac . . . in the flesh!" Suddenly Dat laughed robustly, even hilariously, pulling Ben hard into his arms. "My dear Isaac . . . my son."

For a moment, Zeke simply stood there, stunned. *Isaac . . . alive?* Even Preacher Jesse was speechless, stepping back in disbelief.

Zeke felt himself go rigid at the thought of his brother still alive, barely noticing the small crowd of men now gathering around them. And yet . . . hadn't he, too, on some level, felt drawn to Ben? He had always felt strangely at ease with the younger man. His thoughts flew to his previous conversations with Irvin. *God can work miracles!*

Unable to resist any longer, and in a flood of bewildered relief and thankfulness to his sovereign God, Zeke joined his father and Ben, the three of them spontaneously connecting in a circle of love regained.

# Chapter 31

After hanging out the wash at Essie's, Annie phoned Yonie from the neighbors' and asked him to drive her to town for her hair-cutting appointment. He seemed surprised she'd called him, but she felt it better to use his driving services than to have someone outside the community see her looking all skimpy and nearly weightless, like a frail flower, with hair only to her chin. Well, maybe she would have it cut slightly longer than that so she could still pull it into a ponytail for the hot summer months. Even if she did that, she had a good thirty-five inches or more to sell for a wig, which Lou had said should fetch between two hundred fifty and three hundred dollars. "Virgin hair" like hers that had never been cut or colored was particularly valuable.

*That sort of money will go a long way,* she assumed. At least Annie was determined to make it stretch for those shoes, dresses, and maybe even that skirt and blouse she'd seen at the outlet shops. "Or I could always buy some English clothes patterns and sew some up for myself."

She honestly could not wait to see Ben's reaction to her new modern look. She wanted to please him . . . and to please herself, even though she felt jittery at the thought of losing the long, thick hair she'd had since she was a little girl. Yet she had contemplated this moment long enough. It was time for action and she would grit her teeth, if necessary, to get through it.

While sitting on the front porch waiting for Yonie to arrive, she enjoyed the sunshine and watched Zach teach his little brother to play tug-of-war with an old rope. She was reminded of the long rope swing over at Pequea Creek. "Yonie put the swing up just in time," she whispered to herself, still stunned at how things had fallen into place where Ben was concerned—at least in her mind they had.

Yonie's car pulled into the driveway, and she lifted her skirt a bit to hurry to meet him. "I thought you'd never get here," she said, grinning.

"Me too." He told her he'd had to stop off at Dory's.

She laughed. "Well, you're not runnin' much of a driving business, then. How're you ever going to make a dollar if you're such a slowpoke?"

He bantered back in kind, talking cheerfully with her until he pulled up to the beauty salon. He turned and looked at her, frowning his disapproval. "What're you thinkin' of doing, Annie?"

"Oh, you'll see." With that, she opened the door. "I'll call from here when it's time for you to come get me."

He was plainly concerned. "'Bye for now," she said, her heart pounding as she waved and headed into the shop.

Sam leaned forward at the restaurant where Ben had gone to meet him for lunch. "What do you mean you want to return to the life you missed?"

"I want to give my life back." *To my family who lost me*, Ben mentally added.

"It would be a huge adjustment."

"And I can't imagine it," said Ben. "But I can't let it go all the same."

Sam mentioned the dawn-to-dusk hard work, giving up a car for a horse and buggy, wearing homemade clothing . . . all the things that would be required of Ben should he choose to become Plain. "Unless, of course, you were to join up with the Mennonites. Most of them drive cars." Sam wore a mischievous grin. "I'd say keep that nice car of yours, ain't?"

"Well, I was born into an Amish family. . . ." Ben hadn't said it aloud before, and the declaration sounded foreign to his ears. He wondered what the implications might be for his adoptive family—how they would react and whether it might ultimately hurt them—and himself, as well.

But he was curious to know more. "The language barrier—what about that?"

Sam shook his head. "I think you could learn to speak fluent Dutch pretty quickly, Ben."

"It's funny, I still remember some words and phrases . . . and I understand more than I can speak."

"Not surprising, really," Sam replied. "It *was* your first language."

Ben asked if Sam would be willing to coach him, and Sam chuckled.

"I'll trade you. You teach me how to drive a car, and I'll teach you Dutch."

"Thanks," Ben said, laughing.

Sam leaned forward. "Uh, just a suggestion, Ben. You'll be wantin' to quit saying *thanks* so awful much." Sam explained that the use of *thanks* was looked on as suspect and wasn't part of daily Amish conversation. "You can show your gratitude in other ways. But we say it less . . . and show it more."

Ben smiled. "You just referred to yourself as one of the People."

Sam laughed, nodding his head. "I s'pose once Amish always Amish. I've heard that repeatedly from folk who leave the community. You can't take the Plain out of a person. It's next to impossible."

"So what are you going to do about clothes and cars and such, here on the outside?" Ben asked.

"Oh, I'll look and try to act English, but inside, I'll know. I'll always know who I am." Sam looked solemn. "I daresay, you had better have a good reason to leave your modern life behind. But you, and only you, must count the cost on that."

"I'll miss my car, no question. My cell phone, too." Ben found their talk fascinating, especially since Sam was on the way out. "What about my family back in Kentucky? Would I be allowed to stay in contact with them?"

"I don't see why not."

"Ever think of letting Louisa know you've gone fancy?" Ben asked.

Sam lit up. "Oh, I wrote her, all right. Just heard back from her, too."

The fact that Sam didn't volunteer more about Louisa made him wonder.

Surrounded by bright lights and electric gadgets, Annie stared into the wide mirror, feeling guilty as all get out and tempted to flee. She watched as the stylist divided her long hair into several lengthy ponytails, then lopped them off, one by one. *I can't turn back now. . . .*

She hoped against hope that Ben would appreciate her new look. No, she was holding her breath that he would understand what she was going through to become the modern young woman he could wholeheartedly embrace as his own beloved wife.

After the stylist finished cutting, she used a blow dryer on Annie's now barely shoulder-length hair. *Will Lou be surprised I actually did it?* she wondered.

She knew she would have no time to run to the neighbors' phone later today or to sit down and write to her pen pal. Truth was, she wanted to look extra pretty for her dinner date with Ben tonight. She had even purchased a light pink lip-gloss and a compact of pressed powder to take away the everlasting shine on her nose.

Once her hair was fluffed and swinging free when she moved her head, Annie received payment for her hair and went to sit near the window to wait for Yonie to return for her. The blond woman sitting nearby was thumbing through a magazine, and although Annie couldn't see the cover completely, it looked to be a craft magazine.

Not wanting to be nosy, but unable to quiet her interest, Annie asked about the magazine, and the pretty woman spoke right up, obviously happy to chat with her. The woman said she enjoyed creating art from cloth patches and items like bottle caps, soup cans, and paper clips, all arranged in an imaginative design. "It's something like quilt making. All you need is a mental blueprint," the blonde told her.

Annie couldn't help but contemplate her own art—and life. Did she have a plan? Julia called the Bible such a blueprint, and Annie was sure she ought to be following the Scriptures more closely, too. *Why do I resist it so?*

Yonie was not only unmistakably aghast, but seeing Annie with her hair barely touching her shoulders seemed to unlock something in him.

"Nice," Yonie said simply.

"You think?"

"Well, nice for an Englischer, that's for sure," he said. "Not so much for *you*, Annie."

At least he didn't shame her, as she'd braced herself for, even though he'd been nearly as bold not long ago, getting his own hair cut in a modern style. Of course, it wouldn't take much for him to grow it back into the cropped, nearly bowl-shaped cut, though thus far he'd made no attempt to do so.

On the drive back, after a stop at the outlet stores so Annie could make her purchases, Yonie began to talk of college and how he'd been thinking about going. "To make something of myself, ya know . . . besides bein' a farmer."

"This is the first I've heard of it. I guess you'll have to take a qualifying test, jah?"

"The GED. I've heard enough about how mighty hard it is, so I think I may have to get some tutoring in order to pass."

"You might have to study. Imagine that." She grinned at him.

"Sometime next fall, after the harvest, I'll start lookin' for my own place. I'm a noose round Daed's neck." He fell silent for a time, driving with one hand on the steering wheel, one arm leaning on the open window.

His light hair rippled in the breeze, and Annie tried to envision him dressed like Ben or any of the other fancy men she'd seen, with an open-throated shirt or T-shirt and jeans.

"I suppose you'll be marryin' fancy, too?"

Yonie chuckled. "You and your romantic notions."

"Well, you've been seein' Dory for a good long time."

He gave her a fleeting look. "And you've been seein' an Englischer again, too."

"Jah." She wouldn't hedge on that, at least not with her favorite brother. "I hope we won't lose touch with each other, you and me." She felt a lump in her throat at the thought of his leaving. "Where will you go to college?"

"Maybe where Sam attended, at HACC, on the Old Philadelphia Pike."

Annie didn't dare speak for fear she'd start to cry.

"Nothin' stays the same, Annie. It's a rule of thumb . . . of life."

He could say what he wanted, but she didn't quite agree. After all, there were plenty of things that *did* stay the same. Even though she wasn't exactly a good example, what with her new hairdo and published painting, Annie knew lots of folk who embraced the time-honored life of their ancestors. In some ways, the People as a whole had remained similar for hundreds of years. In other respects, all of them were on a path to change. She thought of the people dearest to her and hoped Mamm would be all right, not despairing over Yonie's startling news—and Annie's own new look.

"Poor Mamm," she sighed.

"Jah, I know what you mean," Yonie agreed, seeming to have something of a lump in *his* throat, too.

Picking up the small hand mirror on her bureau, Annie prepared for her special evening with Ben. She removed her head covering first, realizing anew how terribly difficult it would be to continue putting up her hair into a bun with it cut so short. Somehow she had managed to wrap it up—if only for Essie's sake—upon her arrival home today. She had decided to reveal herself as quite fancy this evening to Esther but wanted to be more discreet about prancing around in front of the children. Prior to going out, she truly needed Essie's reaction to her modern outfit and dressy shoes, not to mention the face powder and pretty pink lip-gloss.

Annie knew she looked completely different even to herself. She'd heard of other Amish girls cutting their hair to make bangs and living to regret it, but not her. She was on the way to jumping the fence, and if she got a good response from Ben, she felt sure she might even beat Yonie over to the outside world. Truth be told, everything she did now was either with her art or Ben in mind, and Annie could hardly wait to have both. No need to chose one over the other as she had with her former beau, Rudy.

*I can have it all.*

Worried and excited about his impending decision, Ben knew he couldn't put off telling his family back home. He and his sisters were exceptionally close, and even after the recent tensions between him and his adoptive parents, he still couldn't exclude them from such a monumental life change. They might try to talk him out of it, but better to hear their objections now and give them time to get used to the idea.

When his mom answered the phone, he asked, "Is Dad around? I've got something important to tell you both."

"Uh-oh. That sounds ominous. Hang on. I'll get Dad on the other phone."

Ben waited until he heard the click of another phone being picked up. "I'm here," his father said.

Filling his lungs with air, Ben said, "I'm thinking of going Plain—returning to the Amish."

No one spoke.

He'd thought at least his mother would protest, but he heard nothing.

"You must be freaked, and who could blame you," Ben said, filling the silence.

Finally his dad spoke up. "After everything you've found out about your first family and all, I guess we shouldn't be so surprised."

"I'm already learning Pennsylvania Dutch. It's coming surprisingly easy."

"That's because it was ingrained in you at a young age," Mom suggested. Her voice began to shake. "I always felt you suffered from being cut off . . . longing for your original family. But we don't want to lose you, Ben."

"You won't, Mom. You couldn't get rid of me if you tried."

"Though I suppose you won't be calling us on your cell phone quite so much, huh?" Dad said, attempting a weak joke.

Ben chuckled. "You're probably right. But there's always snail mail."

"Well, we hear the excitement—the confidence—in your voice, son," Dad offered. "We're behind you, if this is what you want."

*He's too polite to say, "You're out of your mind!"* Ben thought. Still, he was relieved they seemed to be accepting his decision so well.

# Chapter 32

Annie's heart was beating fast as she called to Esther to come upstairs. "What's-a-matter?" Essie asked as she entered the room. Her mouth dropped open. "What the world, Annie Zook!"

"Don't be alarmed . . . it's for Ben. It's a surprise."

"You can say that again." Essie shook her head. "Ben's here early. I saw him pull into the lane just as you called me up here." She eyed Annie yet again. "Goodness me, you're a brave one."

Annie smiled. "Look who's talkin'!"

"You're right perty, Annie."

At that she hugged Essie and hurried down the steps, more than ready to see what Ben had to say about her appearance.

It didn't take long for Annie to find out, because Ben was already standing at the back door, ready to knock, when Annie walked out through the kitchen and met him. "Hullo, Ben!" she said, trying not to grin lest he think she was showing off.

He started talking, saying, "I have the best news—" But he stopped and went momentarily silent, staring at her. "Whoa . . . Annie." His gaze lingered on her short hair.

They stood there awkwardly, Ben obviously stunned by her fancy getup.

"Do you . . . like it?" She touched her hair.

"You're very pretty, no matter how you dress or how long your hair is."

She sensed some hesitancy on his part. "What were you about to say? What's your news?"

He told how his father—Daniel Hochstetler—had come to the work frolic and identified him, and of the wonderful reunion with Zeke, as well.

"I think seeing the three of us together blew your father away . . . though now there's no question in *anyone's* mind that I'm Isaac." He smiled broadly.

"Oh, Ben, I'm so happy for you! For all of you!" She reached for him and he returned her embrace.

Stepping back, he cleared his throat. "Are you ready for a nice dinner?"

She nodded, still not sure if he was as pleased as she'd hoped about her new look.

Annie took in the soft lighting and candles as she and Ben were directed to an intimate table for two at the Olde Greenfield Inn. The 1780s farmhouse was well known for its romantic setting, and Ben had told her on the drive that it was consistently ranked as "Lancaster's Best" in several magazines. As they were seated in the well-appointed dining room, a waiter placed a large white napkin over her lap before doing the same for Ben.

Ben winked at her and continued to look her way while she opened the lovely menu. So many choices, from appetizers to desserts.

Glancing over the top of the menu, she saw him staring at her. "You're making me blush," she whispered.

"Annie, you look so beautiful. You always do."

She felt sure he'd added the latter so as not to indicate she'd looked less than pretty in Amish attire. Not accustomed to being looked at so fondly, nor complimented in this way, she suddenly felt tongue-tied.

Hoping to hide her red face, she attempted to read the menu. She couldn't help but notice another couple across the room. They seemed nearly too affectionate for being in public, and Annie felt distracted by the woman's soft laughter and the man's constant reaching over to touch her hands or face. It was as if they ought to be talking somewhere privately together, not being observed in public.

"Are you all right?" Ben asked.

She focused her attention on her handsome beau. "I'm fine. Such a perty place you picked for us."

"The food is supposed to be superb, too. I guess we'll find out, won't we?"

When he smiled, his eyes shone with unmistakable affection. She had not the slightest inkling why he continued to look at her, unless it *was* her lack of head covering or any Plain apparel. She could easily have passed for an Englischer.

She was glad Ben seemed more pleased with her new look now than he had earlier. She was also relieved he hadn't shown any dismay at her decision to cut her long tresses. Of course, she never would have wanted to confide in him why she had done so, because in less than the space of an hour, she'd spent every last penny of the money she'd earned for her "perfect hair," or so the stylist had called it.

When the waiter returned, Ben politely ordered for her the lamb chops she had chosen and then ordered the prime rib for himself. She paid close attention as Ben spoke, soaking up every nuance of the way she wanted to speak and act. *Like I'm English.*

They soon fell into comfortable conversation. Ben talked of having met with Sam several times, his upcoming move, and of wanting to learn to speak Pennsylvania Dutch.

"I've even begun to memorize some basic Dutch words," he confessed.

What he seemed to imply began to dawn on her. "You're more than captivated by our Plain customs," she said. "Ain't so?"

"I think it's safe to admit it, jah."

She smiled quickly, but his eagerness to use her words, even occasionally, was beginning to worry her. "You're sounding like Lou when she was here, Ben."

Suddenly she wondered what he was really trying to say. She noticed his tan suspenders, but he'd worn them before, back when they'd attended the passion play at the Sight and Sound Theatre. He had often worn more simple clothing. She fingered the tablecloth. "You're more taken with Amish ways than ever."

His smile faded. "I thought you might be pleased."

"It's a bit unsettling."

He nodded. "And you're moving toward the English world." His eyes traced her face, her hair.

"I'm eager to paint again. It won't be long now and I'll be free of my promise to Daed." She pressed onward, finally telling him of the momentous handshake, the six-month vow she'd made to her father after all the years of hiding what was said to be a sin. "In spite of what the brethren say, I want to resume my artwork. I hope to set up a studio at Essie's once I'm free to draw and paint again. That'll be a wonderful-good day. I won't tell you otherwise."

She felt nervous as his countenance dimmed. "What is it, Ben? You look upset." She didn't want to spoil this evening, but his reaction worried her. She struggled, unable to explain the incredible pull toward what she'd missed so long. "I can't turn my back on it forever. It's part of me." She sighed. *Why is this so difficult?*

He fixed his gaze on her. "So . . . you're not planning to join the Amish church, Annie?"

She swallowed. "Maybe not."

"You'll stay on the fence forever?"

"Well, no. I'll be jumpin' it."

He leaned back in his chair, cheerless now. His shoulders seemed to sag, and he looked all in. "There's something I want you to know." He reached for his water glass and held it. "What I have to say may astonish you, Annie."

"What?"

"I want to join church, as you say. Here in Paradise. I want to become Amish."

She was stunned.

"In fact, I've already told my family back home. They had about the same reaction." Ben continued, "I have no right to ask this, but I will anyway, in case there's the slightest chance you haven't made up your mind." He stopped, looking at her intently. "Annie, I know you have an amazing talent, but you're also of the Old Order Amish. This is your background, your family . . . but not only that. It's your life."

She would not cry. "Lou said the same thing last year."

He reached across the table to hold her hand. "I believe Louisa's right. And if there is any chance you might finally become a member of your father's church, I would like to ask you to consider something else." He paused, his face registering some hesitation, but just when she thought he was not going to speak again, his expression exuded great joy. "Annie Zook, will you be my bride? Will you marry me?"

She could not speak for her tears.

"I know you're a gifted artist, Annie. But I also feel drawn to the Plain world, the life I've missed—the life I want to return to. Can you understand?"

She shook her head. *Will we always be heading in opposite directions?*

The tinkle of crystal filled the place as Louisa slowly scanned the leather-bound menu of yet another fine restaurant. Michael was talking of driving to Aspen, spending the weekend—booking separate rooms, he'd said—wanting to get some time alone with her away from the busy city.

She should have seen it coming, and she quickly objected, knowing to agree would send the wrong message.

Later, when they were between courses, enjoying the palate refresher of a rounded dab of mint sherbet, Michael took her totally off guard and pulled out a ring-sized box from his sports coat. "Louisa, I'd like to return something of yours."

She blinked, not sure what he meant.

He flicked the box open, just like in the movies. "Remember this?"

Her lips parted when she saw her extravagant engagement ring—a two-carat diamond in the exquisite setting she had chosen when they'd first looked at rings together. *When we were naively in love.*

"Oh, Michael . . ."

"You can make me the happiest guy on the planet if you'll consent to be my bride."

She could not believe he was ready to ask her again. She also could not believe she wasn't leaning forward, removing the ring, and putting it back where she'd worn it for so long. The sight of the glamorous rock made her think of the ringless weddings in Amish country.

The last thing she wanted to do was hurt Michael's feelings. Surely it had taken plenty of guts to dig out this ring she'd not so graciously returned to him last fall when she'd abandoned her engagement promise.

"I'm asking you to marry me, Louisa. This time, like the last, because I love you . . and for no other reason."

*He does care for me. . . . He really, really does.*

She could not look into his passionate eyes for a single minute longer. She needed air, but now their entrées were coming. She could see the wait staff heading their way, bringing the celebration dinner.

*Oh, what should I say?*

# Chapter 33

Annie's eyes had been pink and teary all day, and even little John seemed to notice. He'd crawled up onto her lap while she sat in Essie's front room, staring sadly out the window.

*Ben's going to make his vow to God and the church . . . if the brethren feel he's ready.*

John nestled himself in the crook of her arm, rubbing his eyes with his fists. "I think someone's ever so sleepy, jah?"

The little boy shook his head quickly. "No . . . no, Auntie Annie."

"Well, when Mamma says so, you must go up for your nap." She kissed the top of his head.

And there she sat, thinking about Ben and the fine meal they'd shared several nights ago. She felt guilty for not giving her answer to such an adoring beau. Yet she had withheld it out of sheer necessity, all the while seeing the hurt of rejection in his eyes . . . something she'd not been present to witness the day he'd received her letter.

Essie called sweetly for John to head upstairs, and Zach came in and stood in the doorway, waiting for his younger brother. "It's that time," Essie said, appearing with her hand on Zach's small shoulder. "If yous promise not to talk the afternoon away up yonder, I'll let you have your naps together."

Annie chuckled at trusting Essie. She knew, and so did Annie, that there was no possible way to get these two settled down if they shared the same bed. Even so, Essie shooed them off, following them on the stairs.

Leaning her head back, Annie thought she ought to be ashamed of herself.

Holding tight to her passion for drawing—her treasured paints and brushes, her precious easel and canvas—while such a wonderful young man as Ben wanted to spend his life with her.

*What's wrong with me?*

In her memory, she flew back to the years Rudy Esh had courted her. He had also declared his love . . . had shown her, too, by putting up with her procrastination. She'd hurt him terribly, but once she had set him free, in a short time, he had found a new love.

Was that to happen again? Would she be so foolish as to give up the chance to belong to Isaac Hochstetler? All the People knew who he was, now that word had spread rapidly of Daniel's verification that Ben was his own. *The man who could always identify trees!* She had to laugh at that.

Essie strolled into the room. "We'll see how long the boys talk, won't we?"

Annie smiled. "Laura's playing in her room?"

"Actually, she's asleep, and so's the baby."

"You should quick take a good rest yourself," Annie suggested.

But Essie sat herself down on the chair near the window and folded her hands, looking so peaceful. "I think you need a listenin' ear, Annie. Am I right?"

Annie sighed. "Jah, ain't that the truth."

"Something awful happened. It's printed on your face."

Annie nodded. "You know how fond I am of Ben."

"I assumed as much."

"It might seem peculiar if I told you I could marry him, but only if he remains English." She explained how Ben planned to join church, while she didn't know how she could stay Amish when her heart was so tuned to painting. Truth be told, she had been longing to share her work with the English world like Louisa had when she had been there.

Essie smiled suddenly. "Well, if you *did* marry Ben, we'd be sisters-in-law—now, what about that?"

"My goodness," Annie said, but she knew that was not a good enough reason to give Ben the answer he desired. "But how can I not follow my heart to the outside?"

"There is such a thing as giving up your will. . . . Remember what we talked about before? About being willing to give up the thing we love?"

Not expecting this, Annie listened, surprised at how strongly Essie felt. "Laying down your desires may be hard, but asking the Lord for His guidance, His will, is a good way to live, I daresay."

Annie pondered that, even long after Essie got up and headed back to the kitchen to check on several baking pies. Annie was sure Cousin Julia would have said something similar were she to ask.

Sighing and wanting to walk after being inside much of the day, Annie headed outdoors, miserable at the thought of living her life without Ben and nearly as sad at the idea of turning her back on art, too.

*No matter what choice I make, I lose dearly.*

Louisa wished she could fly out to be with Annie, who was in a catch-22 over Ben's intention to join her father's church. When Annie had called from Julia's to explain her painful dilemma, Louisa felt terrible and had racked her brain, trying to think of some way to help. But really, what could she do? What could anyone do?

Sighing, she put the finishing touches on her oil painting. She was pleased at her realistic interpretation of Muffin. "Fantabulous," she said, eager for it to dry and be framed. She had not made arrangements to mail the large painting, because now that the final brushstrokes had been made, she wondered if she could even part with it.

But she'd set out to give it to Annie, and that was still her plan. She realized that the painting would make a fine wedding gift, if ever Annie were to bring herself to marry. Louisa hoped so, for Ben's sake—Annie's, too—but knowing her Amish friend, that sort of commitment was rather up in the air for now, much as Annie's reluctance to make the lifelong kneeling vow to the Amish church had nagged her all this time.

"What will it take for Annie to take the plunge?"

She laughed, hugging herself. *What will it take for me?*

Zeke had not ceased talking about his father and his "newfound" brother to anyone who would listen, especially the folks in his therapy group. He knew he was jabbering on and on as he clapped his hands and paced the floor, describing yet again the impromptu family reunion. Ach, such a day it had been! The nurses smiled and listened, no doubt assuming he was obsessing on something new . . . something other than his dead brother.

But he knew he wasn't obsessing. Not, at least, to the degree he had been. After all, hadn't Irvin talked of miracles? And Zeke had witnessed one firsthand that day at the work frolic. "Isaac *is* alive," he said repeatedly. "My brother was never dead."

And when the nurse came in to check his blood pressure and take his temperature several times a day, he would simply shake his head. He was growing weary of being here. "I want to go home, and as soon as possible," he told one of his doctors. That afternoon, he said the same to his group leader, too. He was whole now—no need to be here when his family needed him at home.

More tests were administered under the advisement of the doctors. Zeke was terribly frustrated but kept his story straight—he knew to do that much—when telling about Isaac's return.

After additional tests and many further discussions, it was decided that indeed Zeke was much improved. So much so that when both Irvin and Preacher Jesse showed up together, they agreed to look after Zeke for a few days before allowing him to live at home. Jesse and the doctors believed he might be ready to take this next step toward resuming his life. But he must continue his medication. That was imperative.

The nights were taking their toll on Annie. Each night she was unable to fall asleep for hours and lay awake on her side, staring out the window at the night sky . . . or flat on her back, staring at the dark ceiling. In her dreams, her father's house had vanished and Yonie was nowhere to be seen, nor were Daed and Mamm. Ben, too, was out of reach. Often, she found herself falling, arms flung wide, feeling the air billow out her long Plain skirts before landing hard on her bare feet, the grass poking against the calluses on her toes. Annie dreamed of wandering up and down Pequea Creek, seeing it bone dry and grieving the loss of it. Her heart was always pounding as she awakened. Soon Annie began to dread going to bed, let alone falling asleep.

Tormented, Annie asked to read Essie's Bible. Not knowing where to begin, she opened to the book of Proverbs, reading each pithy verse from the beginning forward.

When she came to chapter twelve, verse fifteen, she read the words aloud: "'The way of a fool is right in his own eyes: but he that hearkeneth unto counsel is wise.'"

*Who wants to be foolish? In the sight of God, is that what I am?*

She didn't wish to follow after her own heart, her own way, as she long had. She knew that much. But she *did* want to paint again, more than nearly anything, though she was losing interest in the hectic worldly ways of the English. If being fancy had anything at all to do with the emptiness, even despair, she'd felt in her dreams, then perhaps she was being foolish as the Scriptures stated. Were the nightmares the Lord God's way of guiding her, as Essie liked to say? Was it the will of the heavenly Father for her to join church and marry Ben Martin?

She contemplated how God achieved His will amongst the People. The most familiar was the drawing of lots, their custom for filling the offices of bishop, preacher, and deacon. The idea struck her that she was on the right track, somehow, in considering this.

She continued her reading and was spurred on when she spotted the verse in chapter sixteen, verse thirty-three—*"The lot is cast into the lap; but the whole disposing thereof is of the Lord."*

"What's that mean—disposing thereof?" she said aloud, wondering whom she might ask.

Marking her place, she headed outdoors to feed the hogs, wishing she were on better terms with her father. It bothered her that they had been barely on speaking terms for all this time. What could she do to bridge that gap?

Thinking about whom to approach regarding the Scripture, she remembered that Ichabod was back in town. He'd refused the lot once, long ago, according to Mamm. *Maybe she would know. Jah, sure she would!* Perhaps later in the day she could get her Mamm alone to ask.

Knowing they would not be invited to any canning frolics this summer, she and Essie put up several dozen jars of strawberry preserves on their own. When they were finished, Annie set out to walk to her father's house. Past the towering white pine tree she walked, where Ben had often parked to meet her last winter. Now the sun was a lone fireball in the sky, and she felt glum. She recalled hearing Cousin Julia describe to her children how to know God's will by listening to His still, small voice—that knowing in one's heart. It had to do with opening doors and walking through them as guided by a divine and loving hand, just as Abram of old had trusted God to lead him when the path ahead had seemed so uncertain.

All that aside, Annie understood in part why the People chose to adhere to the age-old tradition of drawing lots, as illustrated in Scripture. She hadn't known that verses pertaining to the lot were embedded in the Proverbs, as well as the New Testament, where she was most familiar with them. In the Acts of the Apostles, drawing lots was the process by which the Lord God had chosen the successor to Judas.

"What if I were to cast lots between my love for art and my love for Ben?" she whispered as she made her way along the narrow road toward her childhood home. Of course, she realized her passion for color and texture on paper or canvas was a very different kind of love than giving one's life away for another. Truly, she believed that was what marriage with Ben would be—giving up her singleness for the sake of joining her heart with his, birthing their children and establishing their place in the family tree.

She had to smile, thinking there were two branches to Ben's "tree" and wondering how she might ever do a counted cross-stitch sampler for their front room if ever she were to give him a yes to his dear question. *He deserves an answer ever so soon.*

Hurrying along the grassy area beside the road, she saw several buggies coming her way. She considered what it might be like coming here to walk as an Englischer, many years from now. No doubt, she would be wearing her hair this short, though free and swinging against her cheek instead of pulled back into its present low, tight bun. And she would be wearing shoes—possibly some stylish sandals—her toenails painted a pretty, deep pink. Where would her husband and children be? *Who* would they be?

She waved at her older brothers Christian and Abner, and they waved back, their faces turning to flabbergasted frowns. No doubt there were strands of her hair too short to stay in the *schtruppich* bun, but she kept going, mussed up or not, and so did they. "Soon all the People will know." Yet she felt no sadness for what she had done.

When her mother laid eyes on her, there was fire in her eyes. "Oh, my daughter . . . my only girl. What on earth has possessed you to cut your hair?"

Annie knew there was to be no talking about divine lots or God's will today, not the way her mother stared and frowned so awful hard at her now.

Annie couldn't bear to see Mamm so upset. "I was thinkin' of Ben," she admitted.

Her mother's face softened. "Well, I can see you're more than sweet on him. I shouldn't be surprised." She spoke of Isaac's and Annie's childhood days again. Then she said, "It was the dearest thing—'tween you and me—when your father came home with the wonderful-good news. He was nearly speechless, completely overjoyed to know our Isaac is alive and well."

"Daed's overjoyed?"

"Why, sure he is. We all are, for goodness' sake." Mamm studied her for a moment. "It is a sign, I daresay. From almighty God." She told of her dreams, especially the most recent one. "I just hope we can bring him back into community once again."

Annie listened, taking it all in, but she was especially pleased to know how her father had responded to Ben being Isaac. She and Mamm sat and talked for a while longer, then she helped her roll out a few piecrusts, just as they'd always done together.

Later, when the pies were scooted into the oven, Annie left the house to go looking for Yonie. She found Luke first. He looked at her nearly cross-eyed before telling her, "Yonie's in the barn, all dressed up. Ain't that awful silly?"

When she located Yonie, he was pulling hard on his long, colorful necktie, which one of the cows had chomped on and was right this minute chewing.

"Oh, Yonie! For goodness' sake!" She hurried to his side, trying not to laugh, but giggles spilled out of her anyway.

Her brother struggled and at last managed to get the dandy thing yanked away from the cow. "That'll teach me, jah?" he said, not at all happy.

"Were you thinkin' of goin' out dressed like this?" She eyed him suspiciously. "You're not gettin' hitched today, are you?"

He shooed at her, but there was a grin behind his eyes.

"Well?" She stared at him, pointing at the mess he had hanging around his neck. "Best be takin' that off before Dory sees ya like this."

Scowling, he fumbled to unknot the slobbery, torn tie. When he did, he wadded it up and tossed it into a trash barrel over in the corner.

He looked so down and out. "I spent thirty-five dollars on that there tie," he fussed. Then he looked at her. "Your hair's all a rat's nest, in case you didn't know."

They shared a good laugh. "We're both in a bad way, I daresay. That fancy tie nearly got you strangled."

He agreed. "Life's got a stranglehold on me, that's for sure."

Something about the way he said it gave her pause, and her mind went back to her own present dilemma. "What do you know about the casting of lots?" she asked her brother.

"Nothin' much."

"Ach, surely you do."

"Well, I have something of a problem with it."

"How so?"

"It doesn't work unless you fast and pray beforehand, I'm told."

*Just what Julia might say!*

He stared down at his shirt, now wet and dirty from his struggle with the cow. "But don't listen to me, sister. Daed says I'm a Dummkopp. Sure looks like he's right."

She smiled at her favorite brother. "Aw, you're not dumb, Yonie. Just ferhoodled . . . like me."

He nodded, wiping at a streak of dirt on his shirt.

"Well, I best be headin' back," she said. "I needed to see you fighting for your own way I guess—you and the cow." Somehow she leaped ahead in her mind, suddenly grasping the stupidity of demanding one's way at any cost.

She waved to him, eager to get back to Essie . . . and as soon as possible, to Ben.

# Chapter 34

After breakfast the next morning, and following her outdoor chores, Annie ran to the neighbors' barn and used their phone. Ben sounded pleased to hear from her and said he'd be happy to bring her art stored in Julia's attic. Annie scurried back to Essie's.

*Ben's been wanting to see all my work, so today's the day!*

When he arrived, Annie was giddy with joy—and nervous, too. She helped him carry the boxes into the front room and then waved him out into the kitchen to wait, saying, "Give me ten minutes."

He smiled, clearly curious, and left the room.

Gingerly Annie opened the boxes and removed the paintings, propping them one by one against the walls, creating something of a gallery around the room.

Essie peeked in to see what she was doing. "My, oh my, what's all this?" she asked, a smile of wonder on her pretty face.

"Ben's been asking 'bout these," Annie told her. "And I've been puttin' him off." *In more than one way. . . .*

After making over the paintings, saying she'd never seen the likes of so many "perty pictures," Esther offered to keep the children occupied. "You know, so the two of you can have some time to yourselves."

But before calling for Ben, Annie looked around the room alone, whispering a prayer for strength. Slowly, her eyes took in each drawing, each painting, recalling the precious time and joy of creating them in the privacy of Julia's attic.

Finally, Annie ushered Ben back into the front room. He seemed genuinely pleased to study and admire her work, beginning with the very first drawing she'd kept, then moving on to her paintings.

When she'd answered his questions about various ones, the two of them settled down on the settee to talk.

"Annie, I'm so glad you called." Ben reached for her hand, scanning the room, taking in all of her art. "Every piece you've shown me here is excellent—amazing. How can I possibly ask you to walk away from this?"

She fought back tears, wanting so much to see his dear face, his eyes . . . the way he looked at her with such affection. "I couldn't decide this before, but now I can." She sighed, leaning her head on his shoulder. "Oh, Ben, I want to join church. I'm willing to give up my art for you."

"Annie?" He touched her face, his eyes searching hers. "Are you sure?"

She looked at him, so near. "And I want something else." She leaned close to whisper. "Is your proposal of marriage still good?"

"Of course it is."

"Oh, Ben . . . I do love you," she professed, her breath coming quickly. "I want to be your bride."

It was all she could do not to cry as his lips found hers in a tender kiss. "We must go and talk to my father right away." Overwhelmed with a mixture of joy and love, she was anxious to do the will of her heavenly Father . . . obeying this sacred ordinance she had so long put off. "I just hope it's not too late to get into baptismal instruction," she said.

"Well, what're we waiting for? My car's outside!" He took her hand and lifted it to his lips. "Oh, and I'll need some lessons on hitching up a horse, by the way."

She laughed. "This is going to be so much fun," she said, following him through the kitchen and outside.

"An adventure," Ben said.

"That's puttin' it mildly," she said, her heart so full she felt she would surely burst.


Jesse was worried when Ben and Annie came rushing out to the barn, nearly breathless, asking if they might talk with him privately. He feared Annie had come to say she was "jumpin' the fence"—planning to go fancy with her beau.

Annie got things started. "We'd like to ask you a favor, Daed."

Glancing at Annie first, Ben explained, "I don't know if you would consider special treatment, but we'd like to have baptismal instruction to join church this fall. I understand we've missed some weeks."

"You and Annie both, ya say?" The joyful words nearly caught in his throat.

"Yes, sir," Ben said.

If ever there was a blessed day, it was this one. Jesse shook Ben's hand, glad for the strong grip—a sure sign of a good man. "I'll see to it that you get caught up, jah. No question on that."

"Thanks, Preacher," Ben said, looking fondly at Annie.

"Don't thank me. . . ." He paused, gathering his wits. Such a fine surprise this was! "I'll teach you all you need to know for that most holy day myself. And we'll talk with the bishop, if need be, and all the brethren, since you've got yourself a lot of catchin' up to do . . . Isaac." He couldn't help but grin now, looking at this fine young man. A man of the People, for sure and for certain.

He turned to his daughter, this girl who'd given him fits a-plenty. "Annie, I'm mighty pleased at this important step you're makin'. You and Ben both." He assumed the next step forward would be marriage, but he would pretend he didn't suspect as much. Let the young folk have their secret romance, as his parents and grandparents and all the great-grandparents before him had done. It was their way. . . .

Zeke agreed to stay put at Preacher Zook's place, at least for a week or so—sharing a room in the Dawdi Haus with his own father. His head was still swimming with all that had happened since Dat's return and the confirmation that Ben was his brother. *God knew the end from the beginning*, he thought.

Several days after Zeke moved into the Zooks' Dawdi Haus, Irvin offered to drive him home for his first visit, and Preacher Jesse rode along in the back seat.

"Miracles do happen," Zeke said, grinning.

As they drove on Frogtown Road, Zeke kept seeing young Amish boys on in-line skates or scooters, and he began to laugh. Not the cackling, irrational laughter he was known for when folk looked at him half cockeyed. It was a hearty, satisfied, even gleeful laughter, born out of overcoming much sorrow and defeat. For the first time in years, he was experiencing hope.

"The lost is found," Zeke said, sitting up front with Irvin. "And don't mistake my meanin', Preacher." He turned around to glance at Jesse. "You've heard of the ninety and nine . . . the lost sheep. Well, that's me. The Good Lord's reached down from on high and found me, I have to say." He hoped Irvin, of all people, understood.

But Jesse Zook's swift words took some of the joy out of the return home when he stated, "The brethren will be wantin' a word with you, when you're able."

Zeke froze, the mirth of the moment fading.

*I've been found out.*

Once Zeke had greeted Esther and was settled in at the kitchen table, the preacher and Irvin left him to visit with her. He sat drinking his wife's tasty brewed coffee while the children napped upstairs. They were alone together for the time being, as Annie had kindly gone home to spend the afternoon with her Mamm. Even though Zeke was enjoying sharing a room over yonder with Dat, he was mighty glad to spend time with Esther now.

He could see in Esther's eyes that she was struggling to recognize him, here in her kitchen where they'd fought and he'd caused her such heartache again and again. No doubt she was confused as to what had transpired in him, but in all truth, the change had come in stages—through Irvin's talks and prayer, his father asking for forgiveness, and most of all his father recognizing Ben for who he was. *Ben was always my brother, and I never saw it! But the Good Lord opened my blinded eyes . . . in more ways than one.*

He had been fortunate enough to see quite a lot of Ben recently—he and Dat both had. Dat planned to sell his home in Canada and move back to Paradise permanently—a bittersweet prospect considering Zeke's impending shun to come. In time, neither his brother nor Dat would be allowed free association with him. Yet even this could not dishearten Zeke. No matter how anyone looked on it, God had worked a wonder in their lives. And Zeke had no doubt they had not seen the end of God's compassion and power. Zeke, after all, considered himself living proof of that.

"We'll trust God to see us through the storm to come," Zeke told his wife, words that still seemed out of place coming from his lips, though ever so true.

Esther nodded, eyes brimming with tears. "It's wonderful-good the way our Lord works, jah?"

He led her upstairs to their room, mindful of the sleeping baby in the corner. Zeke kissed her yet again, vowing never to lay a hand of rebuke on this lovely woman the Good Lord had given to him. "My wife . . . my bride," he whispered, reaching for her hand and pressing it against his heart. "Will ya ever find it in your heart to forgive me? My awful harsh ways?"

Esther leaned up and kissed his face, touching his soft beard. "Ach, how I love you."

He was moved to tears himself and caressed her face. "Dear lady of mine."

They stood together quietly. Oh, how he loved her . . . too much to fall back into his old ways. Still, he planned to talk and pray with Irvin twice each week to keep himself accountable. *For as long as necessary*, the kind man had suggested.

Esther sighed, tucked in his arms. "I prayed for this day to come, Zeke. I prayed earnestly."

"And God heard, didn't He?"

Zeke stroked her face, then was surprised when she took his hand and led him down the narrow hallway to Annie's room, where they could talk without worrying about waking Essie Ann. They sat on the edge of the bed, and Esther's eyes shone with great compassion.

He'd hated mentioning it, as fondly as she was looking at him just now. "We may end up bein' shunned together, and what would you think of that, Esther?"

She nodded. "I presumed as much. Irvin's church will take us in. I know that for sure. If that's what you want."

He leaned his cheek against her head. Repentance wasn't the issue this time. "I want to tell you something. I've become a follower of the Lord Jesus, just as you are, Essie. Through reading Scripture and my talks with Irvin . . . well, it seems so simple. Life really is quite that—you choose to follow God or you don't."

She listened, eyes blinking as the tears fell.

"No amount of talk from the brethren or anyone else is goin' to change what I know in my heart . . . in my knower. God brought Isaac back to me—to us—for a reason. I never was at fault, the way I made myself out to be all those years. I should've obeyed my father that night, jah, but I didn't cause my brother's disappearance." He stopped to kiss her cheek. "I'm on the path to healing. And I want to show my gratitude by givin' all the rest of my days to God's dear son, Jesus."

"I know exactly how you feel," Esther said.

Zeke's heart was full, and he took Esther's hands in both of his and offered a prayer of thanksgiving before he kissed her a dozen times more.

After visiting with her Mamm and brothers for much of the afternoon, Annie walked upstairs to her old bedroom and sat herself down at her writing desk—a gift from her father when she was a girl. Somehow it seemed right that this was where she would pen this particular letter to Lou, as she had so many others over the years. Finding a few stray sheets of paper and a stubby pencil in the drawer, Annie told her friend the good news.

> *I've decided to remain Amish. Are you surprised? Probably not. You said all along this was where I belonged. And you were right! Come this September, Ben and I will be baptized together.*

*I am also going to get married, and not to just anyone, mind you. (I prom-ised you I'd only marry for love, didn't I?) He's my dearest love, Ben Martin, also known as Isaac Hochstetler by a few old codgers here, stuck in their ways. Ain't that a funny one—a fine beau with two full names?*

*You're more than welcome to attend, Lou, if you can get away, though I'll surely understand if you can't. The wedding will be sometime in November. I'll let you know the date and time when it gets closer, just in case you can come.*

The golden, hot summer months passed quickly, and the soft autumnal glow of harvest and of silo-filling days would soon follow.

Ben worked as hard as any of the men in the church district, if not harder, or so Daed liked to say each night at supper. Annie found this ever so satisfy-ing, glad her decision was settled and secure. There was a wondrous peace and a new fulfillment in walking God's path—the way of the People. More than that, she'd secretly embraced Essie's and Julia's love of the Lord Jesus. Ben had, too. She and her soon-to-be husband had talked at length, agreeing to walk the way of the "silent believers," as many amongst the People fittingly did so as not to lose their family connection nor encounter the shun. It was a choice made not out of cowardice but out of respect.

Annie, of course, was eager to move home to spend her last weeks and months as a single woman with her family. So when Irvin, as well as the breth-ren, agreed that Zeke was ready, he had returned to Essie and the children, and Annie asked for Yonie's help moving her belongings back home. This in spite of his joking that she needed to decide where she wanted to be and stay put for once.

In addition to baptismal classes, Sam and Annie gave Ben a crash course in speaking their language, but every now and then he tripped up and said something funny about a coffin when he meant to say a window shutter, or a skull when he meant a handsaw. Slips like that were amusing and fun for everyone he encountered.

Ben had never been one to exclude his family. He wished he could fly home and see their expressions, because he was fairly sure they'd be thrilled for him—once they recovered from yet another shock. His mother especially would be excited, even though she would no doubt cry if she and Dad were brave enough to come to an Amish wedding.

When the phone rang and rang, he assumed no one was at home. But on the seventh ring, his father finally answered. "Hello, Ben . . . saw your name on the ID. I see you're still using your cell phone. How *are* you?"

"Great, Dad. How're you doing?"

"Oh, just fine." He chuckled. "I've been reading up some on the Amish, trying to picture exactly what you're up to these days."

Ben laughed, too, then asked, "Is Mom around? I've got something important to tell you both."

"Not a problem. I'll switch you onto the speaker phone."

Ben waited until he heard his mom in the background.

"Don't know if you're ready for another surprise, but . . ." He paused, wanting to phrase this just right.

"Go ahead, Ben," his father spoke up. "We're listening."

Taking a deep breath, Ben pressed ahead. "I'm getting married . . . and I'd like you to meet my bride-to-be as soon as possible."

He heard a loud gasp on the other end of the line and assumed it was his mother. "My word, this is good news," she said. "Wait till your sisters hear."

"Why don't you bring her on down?" Dad offered. "We'll make room for her in the guest room. Stay as long as you like."

"Thanks, Dad. You'll all love her," he added.

"We love *you*, Ben, so we know we'll love her, too," Mom said. "She's Amish, I'm guessing?"

"Yes. I've talked a little about her before. She's an Amish preacher's daughter named Annie Zook," he said. "The prettiest, sweetest young woman I've ever known."

"Your sisters will want to show her the town, no doubt," Dad said.

"They might even try to modernize her for you," Mom teased.

"Oh, Annie's been there and back already, trust me." He wouldn't divulge the details of their struggle to come to this point—at least not now. Thankfully, that part of their relationship was past. "I'm getting my girl," he declared. *At last.*

# Chapter 35

A few weeks prior to baptism, Ben happily took Annie home to meet his Kentucky family. They wore their Plain attire, which Ben had been doing for some time. His parents seemed taken aback by this, but his sisters said it was "very cool," with something of a wink and a nod. As he had guessed, his sisters took to Annie like she was their own sibling, welcoming her into their home and their hearts. His parents, too, were quickly won over by her kind, endearing ways.

Even though he'd driven his car, he made a point of telling Annie that this trip was it for him. When they returned to Pennsylvania, he intended to sell the car and purchase a family carriage for his first driving horse. The bishop himself had told Ben that, other than the Lord's Day, he was at liberty to call on a paid driver—as were any of the People—whenever it was unsafe or too far to take the team.

While Ben and Annie were gone, Daniel Hochstetler traveled back to Canada to pack up his life there. He then moved his belongings into Jesse Zook's Dawdi Haus, planning to live there permanently, especially as Daniel was not permitted by the brethren to openly fellowship—or reside—with his shunned son and daughter-in-law. Still, there were rumors he was seeing Zeke and Esther quietly, holding family near while attempting to satisfy the Ordnung. Ben and Annie were in a similar pickle—trying to keep a relationship with Zeke and Essie without violating the rules of the shun. It was a constant juggling of both love and dedication.

❖

The rows of benches set up in the barn were conspicuously empty the morning of baptism as Jesse paced along the center aisle. The People would soon file in, the women siting on the left and the men on the right. The barn would get mighty hot if the weather forecast was correct—downright warm for mid-September—much better than meeting in a too-crowded house on this Lord's Day. *At last my daughter will make her kneeling vow to the Lord God and the People.*

Truly Jesse believed Annie had already begun to walk the straight and narrow, and for that reason he had moved heaven and earth, so to speak, to do all he could for both Annie and Ben. Carefully he'd instructed them in the ways of Jehovah God, though he suspected they were doing quite a lot of digging into the Scriptures on their own. Ben, especially, had asked a good many questions, some out of the ordinary, and Jesse hadn't known all the answers. He had felt ashamed, being the man of God and all. But he did what he could, asking the bishop and Preacher Moses, although Ben's questions stirred things up amongst the brethren more than once during the short weeks of baptismal training.

Sighing now, he hoped for the best for his Annie and her beau. He prayed, too, that the Holy One of Israel might cover them with His loving watch-care over their lives and the lives of their offspring, for surely they would marry first opportunity following baptism. Most of the young people did exactly that after making their lifelong promise to the church and to God.

*Jah, Annie's as good as hitched.*

Annie noticed the man formerly called Ichabod sitting with some of Preacher Moses' married sons and grandsons. She wondered what he must be thinking on the day that his own Isaac was being baptized by the very church that had nominated him for preacher so long ago.

When the time came for Annie to bow her head, she did so along with Ben and the other baptismal candidates, more aware of the sweet smells of the haymow during this hushed time of reverence. She felt warm as she sat quietly, contemplating the vow soon to be made. This day represented all the years of her parents' hopes and dreams for her and her brothers yet to join church. She knew she mustn't open her eyes to glance at the People gathered there, nor look at Ben, even though she wished to. Ben had become more to her in the past months than merely a beau. He was her dearest friend, too, and a student of the Word, as he liked to say. *I'm learning all I can about the God who made me,* he would tell her. And she listened with rapt attention when he shared the many verses that had changed his thinking . . . and his heart.

They'd made a secret pact, vowing to live out their days with their eyes fixed on the Lord Jesus. Ben had led the way to her receiving the Savior; Cousin Julia had planted the seed. And dear Essie had watered. Even Lou had played a part.

Several hymns were sung, signaling her to file up to take her place in the center section with all the others, near the ministers' bench. There they sat, waiting for the bishop, the two preachers, and the deacon to enter the barn.

At one point, Annie caught the reverence and wonder in Ben's eyes as the final stanza was sung in unison. *A day of dedication . . .*

She observed the sincerity on the part of her darling, and her heart rose up with gladness for God's guiding hand on her life. Not only for bringing Isaac home but for bringing her, as well, to this most holy ordinance.

Later, during her father's offering of the second sermon, he made a slight departure, repeating much of what had been said at the time of Daniel's recent kneeling repentance. Annie wondered at first where her father was going with his remarks, but she understood more fully when he admonished them that Isaac of old had been given back to Abraham due to his inherent trust that God would provide a lamb. "Jehovah was and is faithful. At times this is demonstrated by the quiet entreaty of others."

Daed paused, looking now at Ichabod. *"You are no longer in exile,"* he had declared on the day of Daniel's atonement. *"From this day forth you are to be called a brother."*

Annie paid close attention as her father made known to them yet again, "You are one of us . . . Daniel."

On her wedding day in November, Annie was quite frustrated with herself for having impulsively chopped off her long locks. Yes, her hair had grown out a few inches in the months since she'd cut it, but even with Mamm's help, twisting her too-short hair into a bun was nearly an impossible chore. When Mamm was finally securing the last pin, a knock came at the door.

Annie was amazed as well as delighted to see Lou standing in the hallway outside her bedroom. "Ach, Lou, you came! I can hardly believe it!"

"Well, you said I was welcome, didn't you? So here I am."

The two hugged carefully, so as not to muss Annie's freshly ironed blue cape dress and long white apron. Mamm slipped out of the room to give them some time alone.

"Bless your heart," Annie said. "I tried not to get my hopes up, but I'm ever so happy you're here."

"Well, just so you know . . . I'll be sharing the wedding feast with another Englisher." Lou's smile burst across her face.

"And who would that be?"

"Oh, you . . ."

Annie giggled. "Sam?"

Lou nodded. "Don't be too excited. I'm not getting serious with him, if that's what you think. For now anyway, I'm focusing on my relationship with the Lord, thanks to your cousin Julia."

"My cousin's quite a zealous witness, jah?" Annie reached for Lou's hand, whispering, "And I know exactly how you feel—ever so free inside."

Lou's eyes filled with tears.

"Oh, Lou . . ." Annie said, squeezing her dear friend's hand. "We've had quite an interesting journey together, ain't so?"


Annie struggled not to cry but sensed Ben's own emotion as he sat next to her, waiting for their time to stand before the gathering of more than two hundred people who were jam-packed into her father's house.

She looked across the faces to see Mamm's, her eyes shining with truest joy. And there were Luke and Omar, solemn-faced, and Yonie, who'd let his hair grow out again, much to Daed's delight. And Essie and Zeke together at last, Essie great with child, sitting in the back with the Englischers, including the Martin family, Lou and Sam, and cousins Irvin and Julia Ranck. *All the People . . . and then some, here for Ben and me.*

Annie's heart swelled with love for her God and her soon-to-be husband. Paradise had never seemed so sweet on any other day, and Annie counted her blessings, glad she had stayed the course. She looked past this most happy moment toward all the years ahead, Lord willing, and realized that on the final day of her life, she could breathe her last knowing she had chosen wisely and well.

# Epilogue

Prior to my marriage to Ben Martin, I donated my worldly English clothes to a women's shelter and put away my art for good. After our wedding day, I was content to cook and bake and tend to my husband, as well as my flower gardens, which bring me such joy and a few raised eyebrows. Such pleasure I find in mixing colors . . . and that's putting it mildly!

Ben and I have joked between ourselves about which name he should use. But since he is more accustomed to one over the other, and since Benjamin is also a good, solid Amish name, Ben it is.

For the first few weeks and months after our all-day wedding service and feast, we made our traditional visits to relatives and close friends as newlyweds, staying overnight on weekends and returning here to my father's house on Monday mornings in time to help Mamm wash clothes. Sam was so kind to help Ben draw up blueprints for our very own home, which we built on some of Daed's land. With Ben's good Kentucky contacts, he's been helping Irvin with the horse business, as well. So this past year since our wedding day, the Lord has opened plenty of wonderful-good doors of employment for Ben.

When I can, I still write to Lou. Her thoughtful wedding gift—the framed painting of her cat, Muffin—is a reminder of the months she spent here in Paradise. She and Sam still correspond by letter, Lou tells me, and talk quite often by cell phone, too, but there is no word of a pending courtship between them. I can still hope, can't I?

After all, my brother Yonie surprised us all by starting to court Susie Esh's little sister, with some convincing talk of joining church next year. Daed and Mamm are so pleased.

Often Ben and I walk down the road to what we refer to as "our bridge," but it's simply boards and stone, the best part of it being the swiftly moving creek beneath. It keeps us ever mindful of life, how it streams by in an awful rush if one is not careful to stop and listen . . . and honestly see.

Right following our first wedding anniversary, Daed surprised me but good, saying he'd been thinking about something for quite a while, insisting I go with him to visit Bishop Andy. So there I sat sheepishly in the man of God's front room while Daed talked the bishop's ears off, trying to convince him that since it was my painting that drew Isaac back home to the People, I should be permitted to use my artistic talents for the Lord God.

Well, I was beyond speechless. The two of them got up and headed out to the barn, leaving me alone, while the bishop's wife busied herself in the kitchen.

Finally, when I felt my head might burst from holding my breath, hoping against hope—and all this after I'd put my longing for art out of my mind—Daed came back in and told me what they'd decided.

"There are certain conditions," he began, and the thought of limitations had never sounded sweeter to me. On the ride back home, he described them precisely.

I was going to be allowed to express myself artistically, but I could never paint a portrait of a person. Not surprising! But horses grazing, peacocks strutting, and landscapes are all just fine to paint, provided I'm completely caught up on my domestic chores, as related to being a wife . . . and someday a mother. Only in the quiet at the end of the day, when all that needs doin' is done, am I free to draw or paint.

So Ben has helped me set up a little studio in our house, and he is always welcome there, watching me stroke the page with a brush or smudge my finger against the canvas for that "just so" effect. Sometimes he even comes in and leans over to kiss me.

Oh, what I would have missed . . .

It is still a surprise to think of Daed sticking his neck out like that. I often recall Essie's prudent words about letting go of something you love—and what a joy there is in having it returned. In my case, it has come in a fuller measure than I'd ever dreamed possible.

So Ben was right all along; God does work all things together for good to those who love Him. I am so grateful to the Almighty for leading me to make the right choice.

For some it's ever so hard to choose wisely. I know this from experi-ence . . . and to my own shame. The memory of my willful ways, of learning to let go and watching what happens when I do, has been a journey to be reckoned with. I have gained the devotion of a kind and loving man, and the respect of my father and the People. I am happy to say the preacher's daughter is truly home.

# Acknowledgments

Typically novelists do not talk about their characters—at least not while creating them. Now that the story is completely told and you are reading this final book in the Annie's People series, I'd like to say something about its characters, who continue to live on in my mind and heart. Just as Annie and Isaac became aware of their special friendship as young children, I, too, have been blessed with the dearest of lifelong friends, who, in some cases, are also my relatives. I wish to thank each one for this precious gift. Some of these dear ones have also offered countless hours of research and fact checking on my novels, and although they have asked to remain unnamed, I am most grateful.

My editors are my joy and delight. Talk about friends! A tremendous amount of thanks goes to Julie Klassen, David Horton, Carol Johnson, Rochelle Glöege, Ann Parrish, and Jolene Steffer.

Also, my first readers help me keep up this writing pace: Dave, my husband, and Julie, our daughter. Thanks not only for your keen eyes but for the delicious snacks, too!

Kudos to Dana Silva, who offered invaluable help with foster care research, as did Kentucky state adoption specialist Martha Vozos. Blessings and appreciation to Hank and Ruth Hershberger, who carefully explained the process of Amish ordination, and Dawn Beasley, who helped research the setting. Many thanks to Rev. James Hagan, who, as a former policeman, answered forensics questions and contacted the Colorado Bureau of Investigation. Hugs to my teacher-sis, Barbara Birch, who meticulously proofread the final galleys, and to my uncle, Bob Hirschberg, photographer extraordinaire, who helped me "live" in the Maple Lane Farm B&B on Paradise Lane, featured in book two, *The Englisher*.

Heartfelt appreciation to my wonderful parents, Herb and Jane Jones, who faithfully pray as I walk the sometimes thorny path of my stories.

All my love and devotion to the dear Lord Jesus, who guides me in all things, heavenly and otherwise.

**Beverly Lewis**, born in the heart of Pennsylvania Dutch country, is the *New York Times* bestselling author of more than ninety books. Her stories have been published in eleven languages worldwide. A keen interest in her mother's Plain heritage has inspired Beverly to write many Amish-related novels, beginning with *The Shunning*, which has sold more than one million copies and was recently made into an Original Hallmark Channel movie. In 2007 *The Brethren* was honored with a Christy Award.

Beverly has been interviewed by both national and international media, including *Time* magazine, the Associated Press, and the BBC. She lives with her husband, David, in Colorado.

Visit her website at www.beverlylewis.com or www.facebook.com/official beverlylewis for more information.

# More From Bestselling Author
# Beverly Lewis

To find out more about Beverly and her books, visit beverlylewis.com or find her on Facebook!

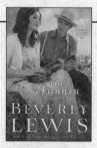

Journey home to Hickory Hollow, the setting where Beverly's celebrated Amish novels began in *The Shunning*! With her trademark style, this series of independent books features unforgettable heroines and the gentle romances her readers have come to love.

HOME TO HICKORY HOLLOW: *The Fiddler, The Bridesmaid, The Guardian, The Secret Keeper, The Last Bride*

Desperate to find her long-lost daughter, Kelly is thrilled when her private investigator finds a child who fits the profile. She arranges a "chance" meeting with the girl's guardian, Jack, and it goes well—so well, in fact, that he asks her out on a date. But when she starts falling for Jack, can Kelly come clean about her motives and risk losing both a daughter *and* a chance at love?

*Child of Mine* (with David Lewis)

# More From Bestselling Author
# Beverly Lewis

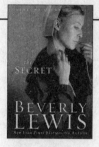

When her mother's secret threatens to destroy their peaceful Amish family, will Grace's search for the truth lead to more heartache or the love she longs for?

SEASONS OF GRACE: *The Secret, The Missing, The Telling*

Their Amish community has been pushed to the breaking point, and Nellie and Caleb find themselves on opposing sides of an impossible divide. Can their love survive when their beliefs threaten to tear them apart?

THE COURTSHIP OF NELLIE FISHER: *The Parting, The Forbidden, The Longing*